INCREDIBLE DOOM

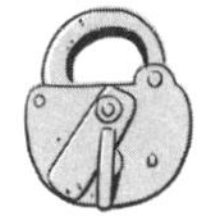

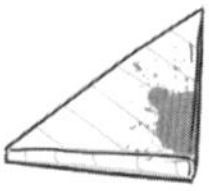

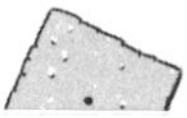

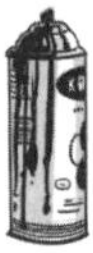

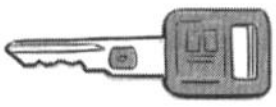

[vol 1]

INCREDIBLE DOOM

[vol 1]

Written and illustrated by

MATTHEW BOGART

Story by

MATTHEW BOGART & JESSE HOLDEN

HARPER alley

An imprint of HarperCollinsPublishers

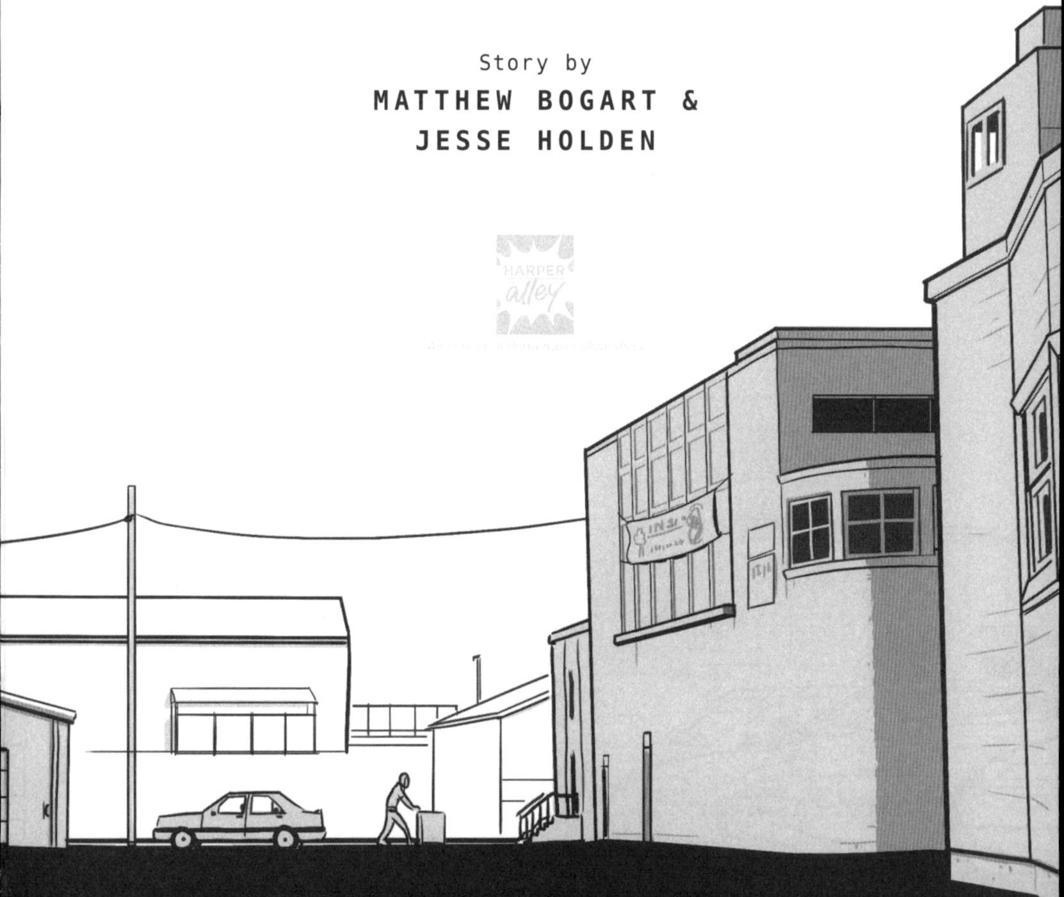

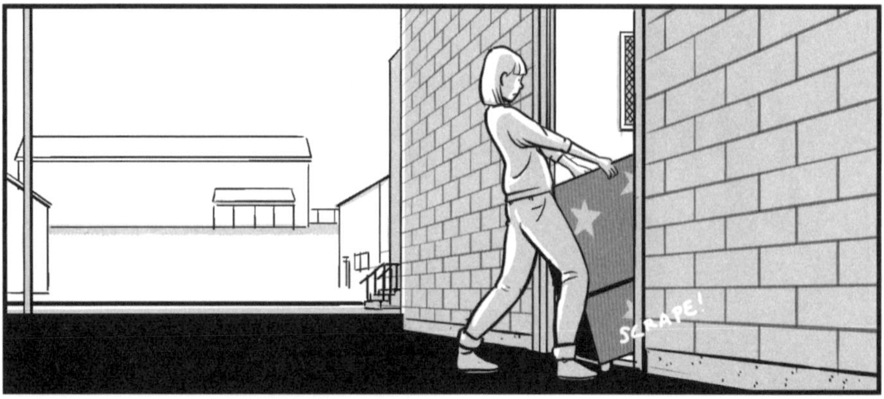
SCRAPE!

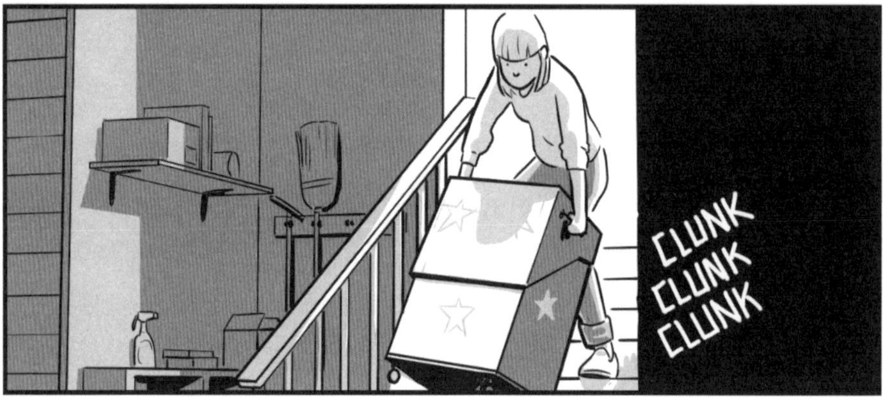
CLUNK
CLUNK
CLUNK

PROLOGUE: 1991

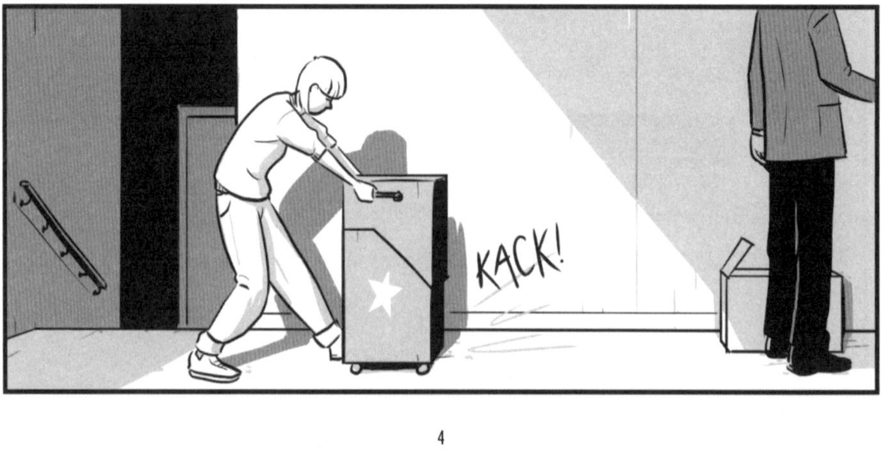
KACK!

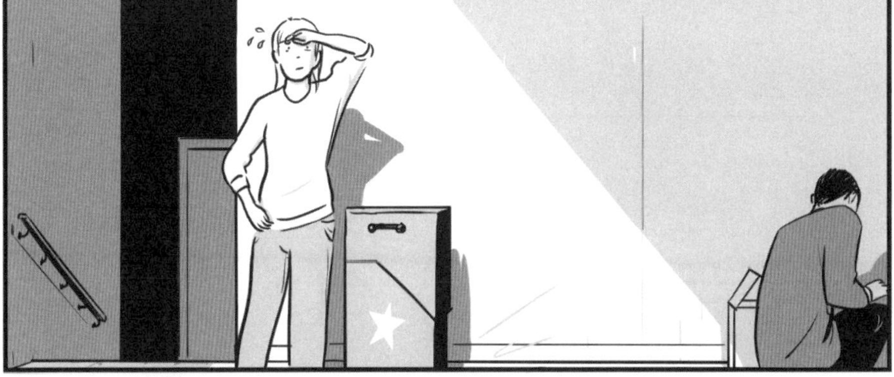

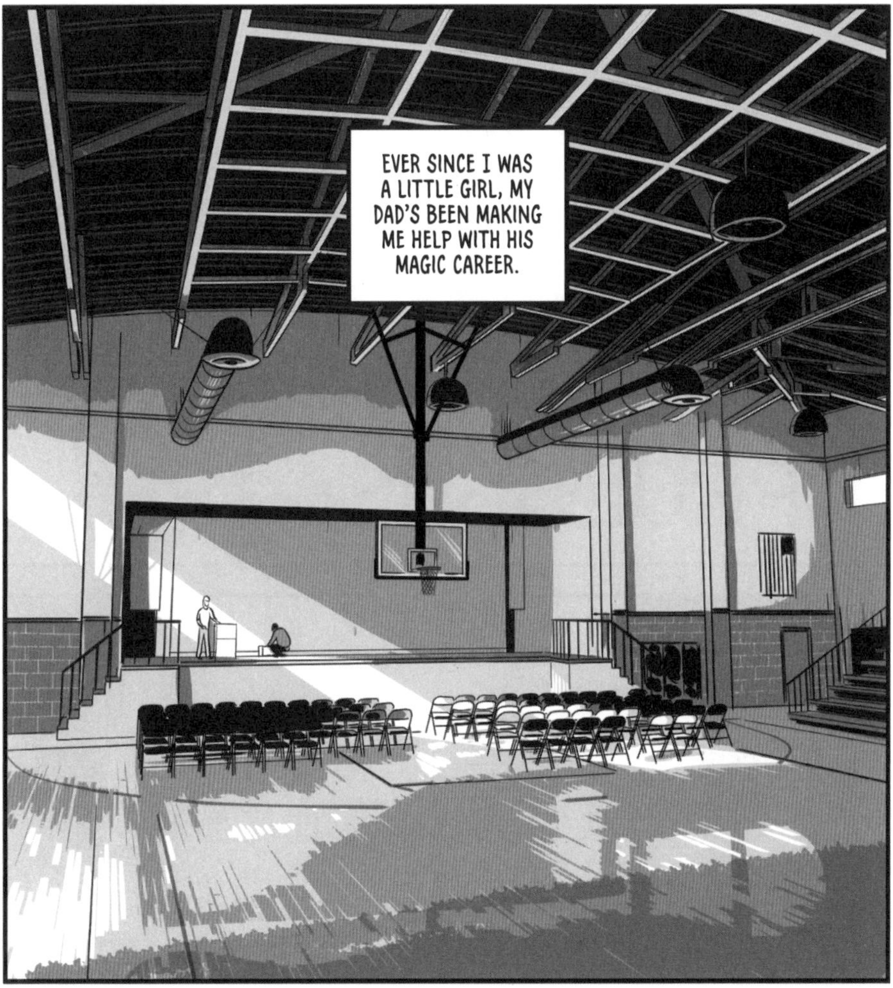
EVER SINCE I WAS A LITTLE GIRL, MY DAD'S BEEN MAKING ME HELP WITH HIS MAGIC CAREER.

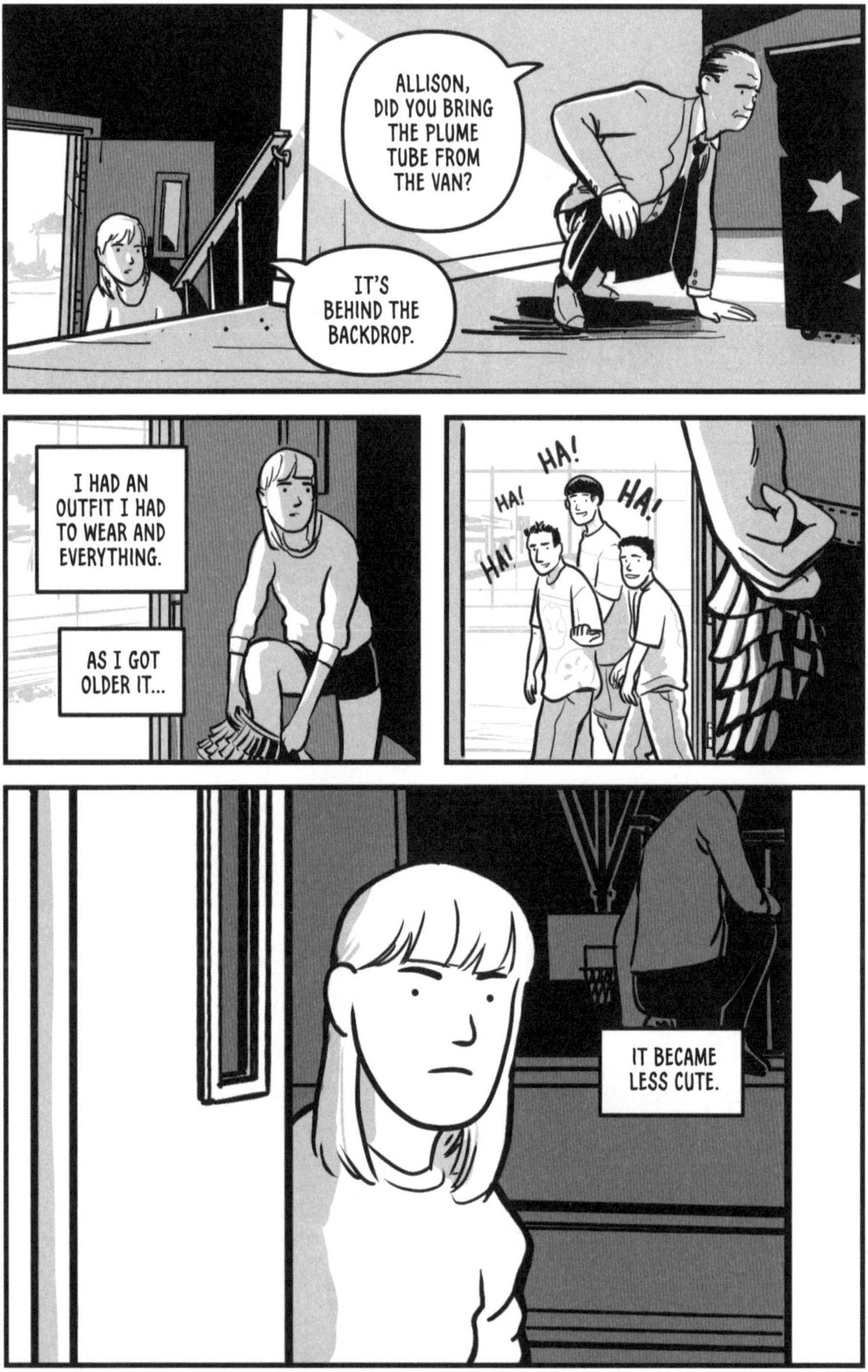
ALLISON, DID YOU BRING THE PLUME TUBE FROM THE VAN?
IT'S BEHIND THE BACKDROP.
I HAD AN OUTFIT I HAD TO WEAR AND EVERYTHING.
AS I GOT OLDER IT...
HA!
HA!
HA!
HA!
IT BECAME LESS CUTE.

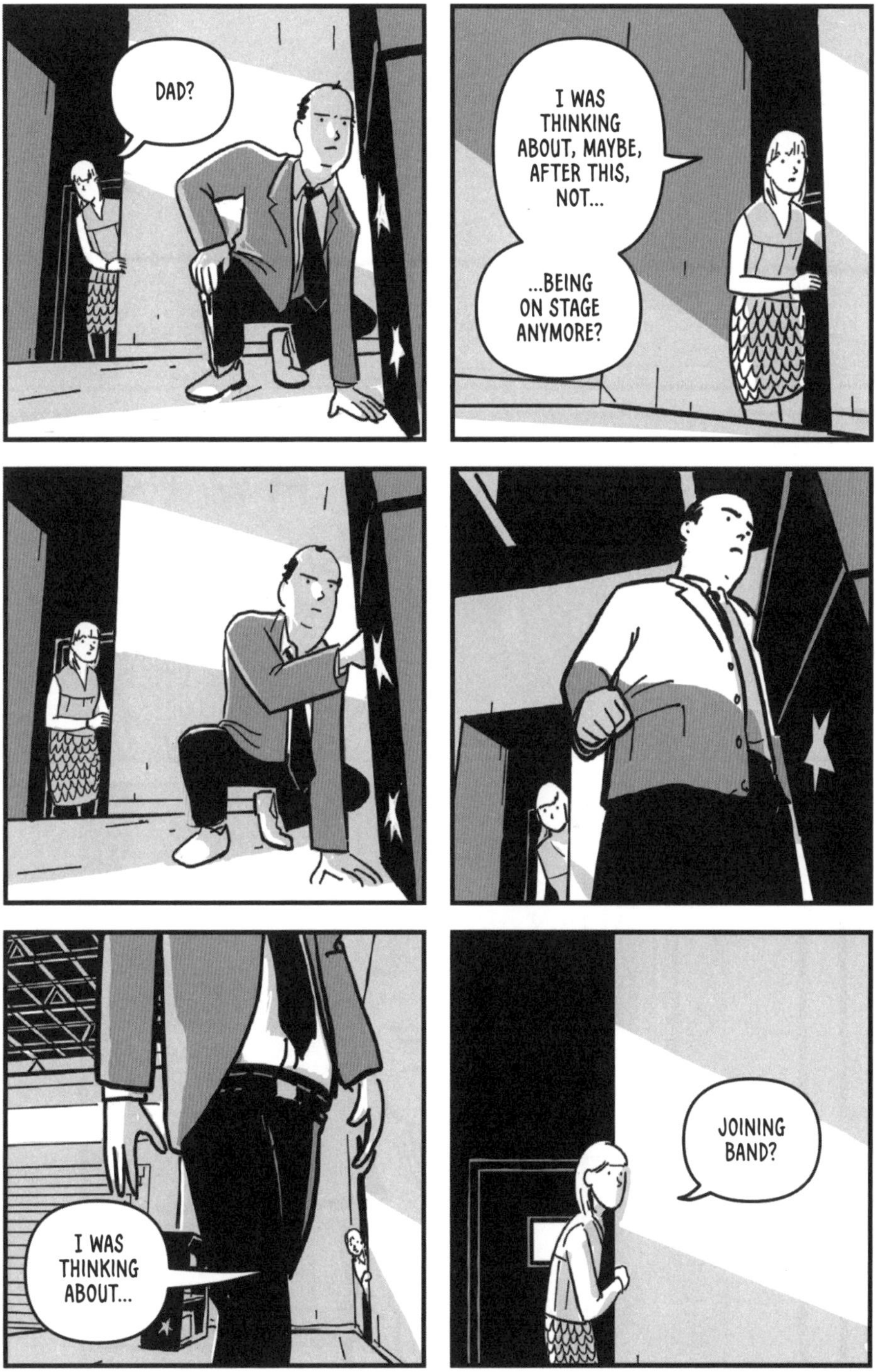
DAD?
I WAS THINKING ABOUT, MAYBE, AFTER THIS, NOT...
...BEING ON STAGE ANYMORE?
I WAS THINKING ABOUT...
JOINING BAND?

WHEN DAD GETS MAD HE'S GOT TWO POSSIBLE REACTIONS. ONE OF THEM IS THAT HE STOPS SPEAKING.

HE DIDN'T SAY A WORD TO ME TILL AFTER THE SHOW HAD STARTED.

I DON'T KNOW WHAT PEOPLE MUST HAVE THOUGHT.

BUT BY THE TIME WE GOT AROUND TO THE EGG-BAG ROUTINE I WAS SO SCARED I WAS SHAKING.

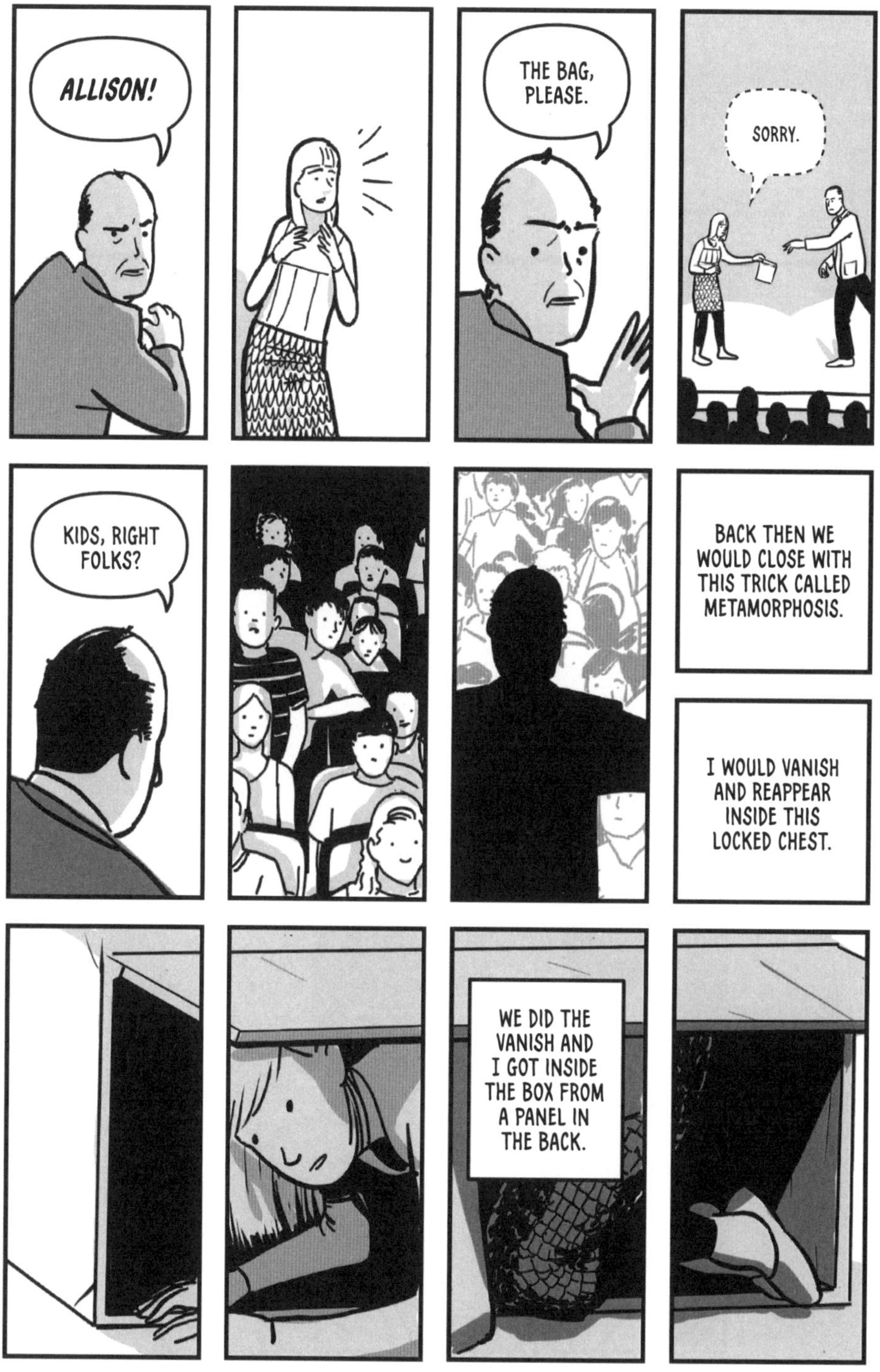
ALLISON!
THE BAG, PLEASE.
SORRY.
KIDS, RIGHT FOLKS?
BACK THEN WE WOULD CLOSE WITH THIS TRICK CALLED METAMORPHOSIS.
I WOULD VANISH AND REAPPEAR INSIDE THIS LOCKED CHEST.
WE DID THE VANISH AND I GOT INSIDE THE BOX FROM A PANEL IN THE BACK.

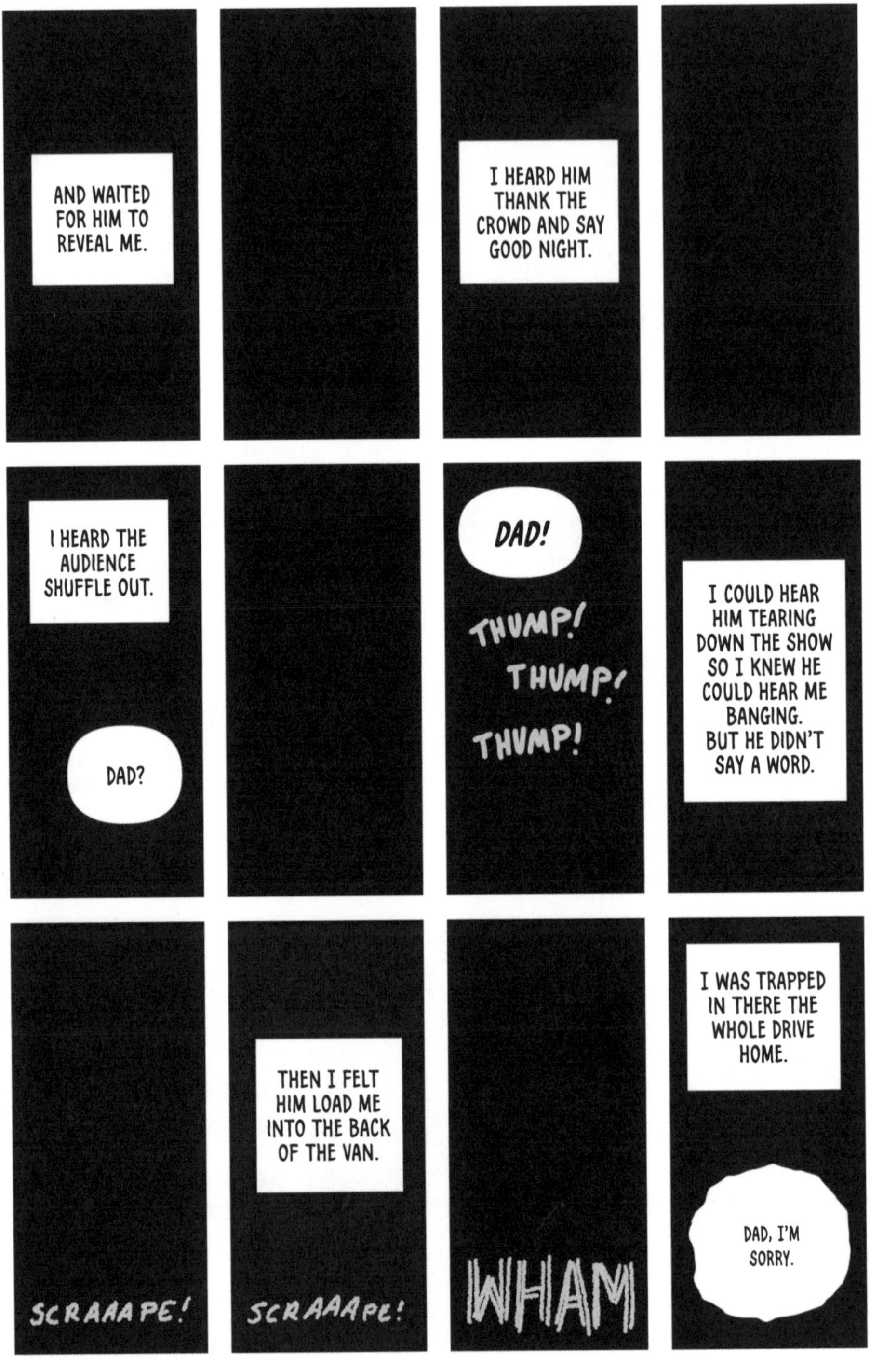
AND WAITED FOR HIM TO REVEAL ME.
I HEARD HIM THANK THE CROWD AND SAY GOOD NIGHT.
I HEARD THE AUDIENCE SHUFFLE OUT.
DAD?
DAD!
THUMP! THUMP! THUMP!
I COULD HEAR HIM TEARING DOWN THE SHOW SO I KNEW HE COULD HEAR ME BANGING. BUT HE DIDN'T SAY A WORD.
SCRAAAPE!
THEN I FELT HIM LOAD ME INTO THE BACK OF THE VAN.
SCRAAAPE!
WHAM
I WAS TRAPPED IN THERE THE WHOLE DRIVE HOME.
DAD, I'M SORRY.

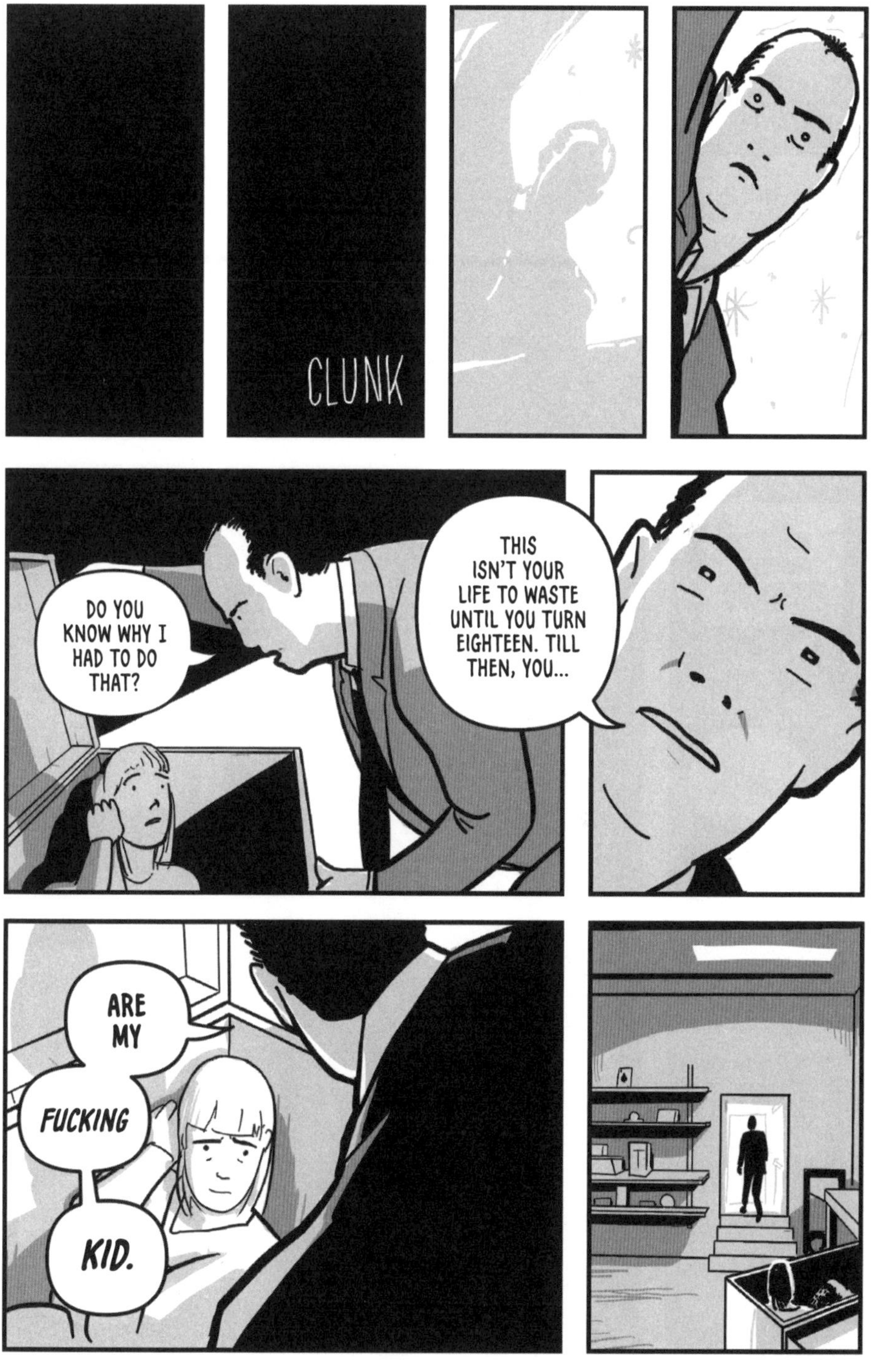
CLUNK
DO YOU KNOW WHY I HAD TO DO THAT?
THIS ISN'T YOUR LIFE TO WASTE UNTIL YOU TURN EIGHTEEN. TILL THEN, YOU...
ARE MY
FUCKING
KID.

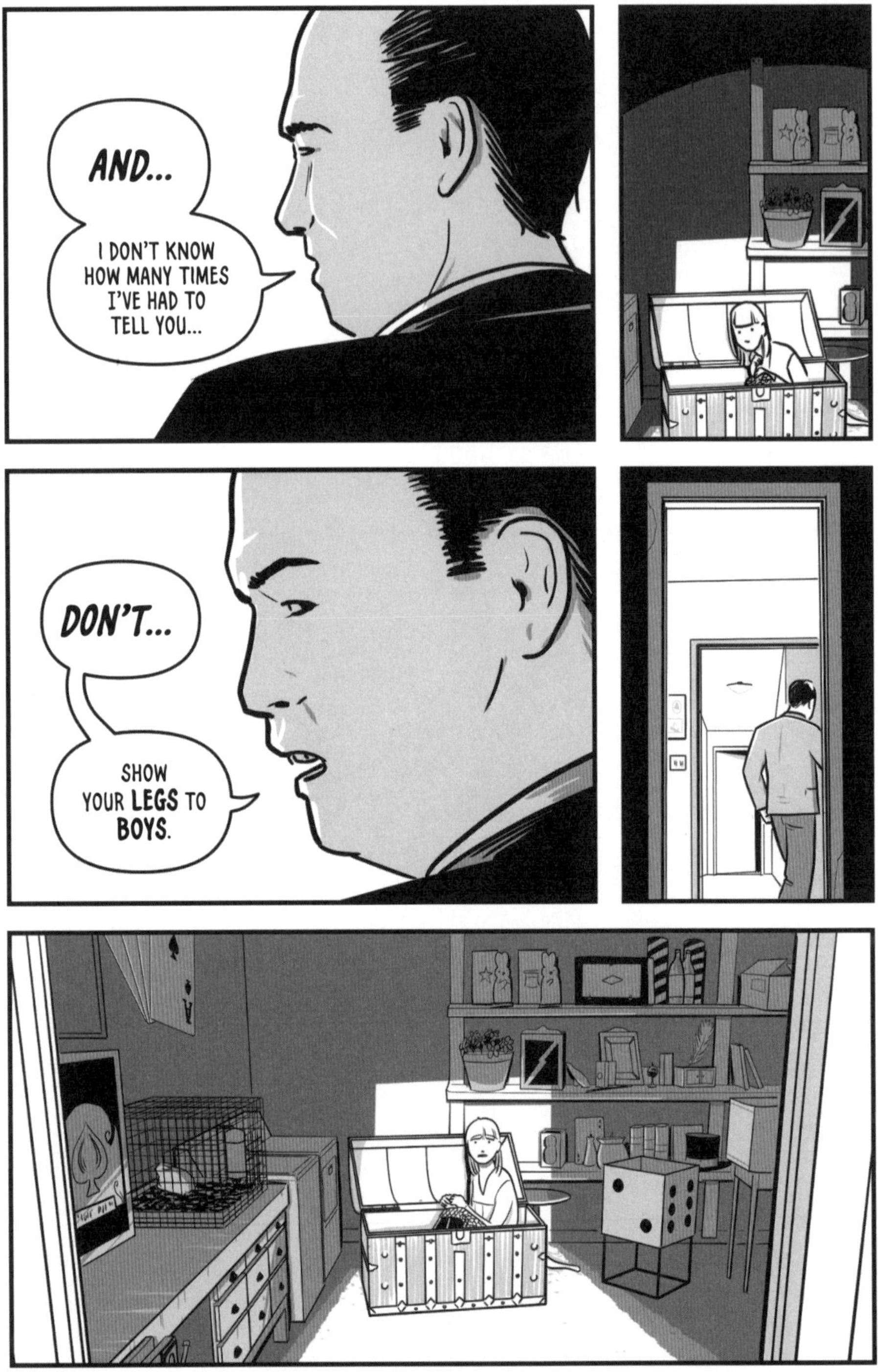
AND...
I DON'T KNOW HOW MANY TIMES I'VE HAD TO TELL YOU...
DON'T...
SHOW YOUR LEGS TO BOYS.

Chapter 1

THE WORLD OF TOMORROW

1994

GU D-- -P+ C+L? U E M+ S-/+ N--- H-- F--(+) !G W++ T R? X?

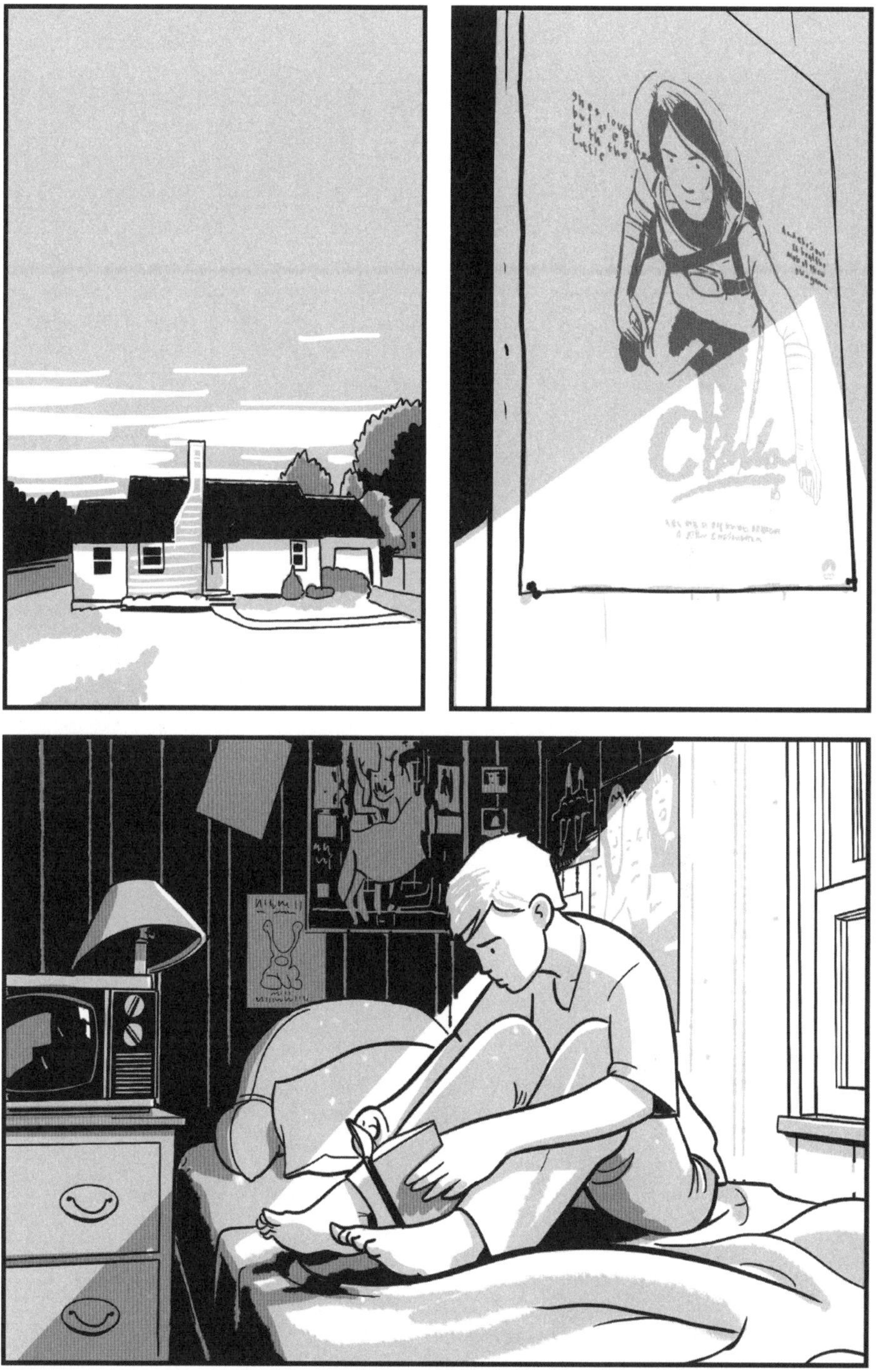

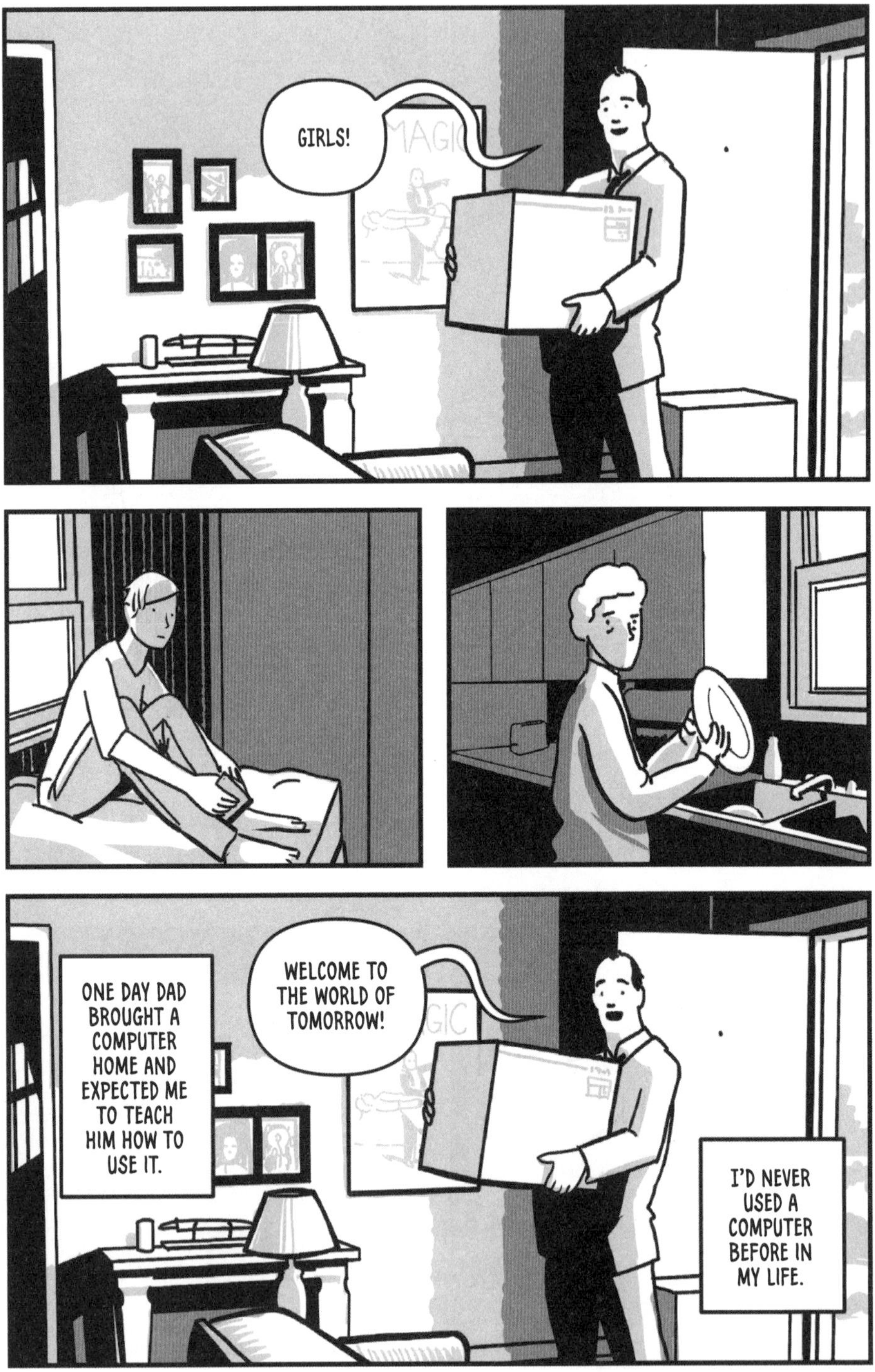
MAGIC
GIRLS!
ONE DAY DAD BROUGHT A COMPUTER HOME AND EXPECTED ME TO TEACH HIM HOW TO USE IT.
WELCOME TO THE WORLD OF TOMORROW!
I'D NEVER USED A COMPUTER BEFORE IN MY LIFE.

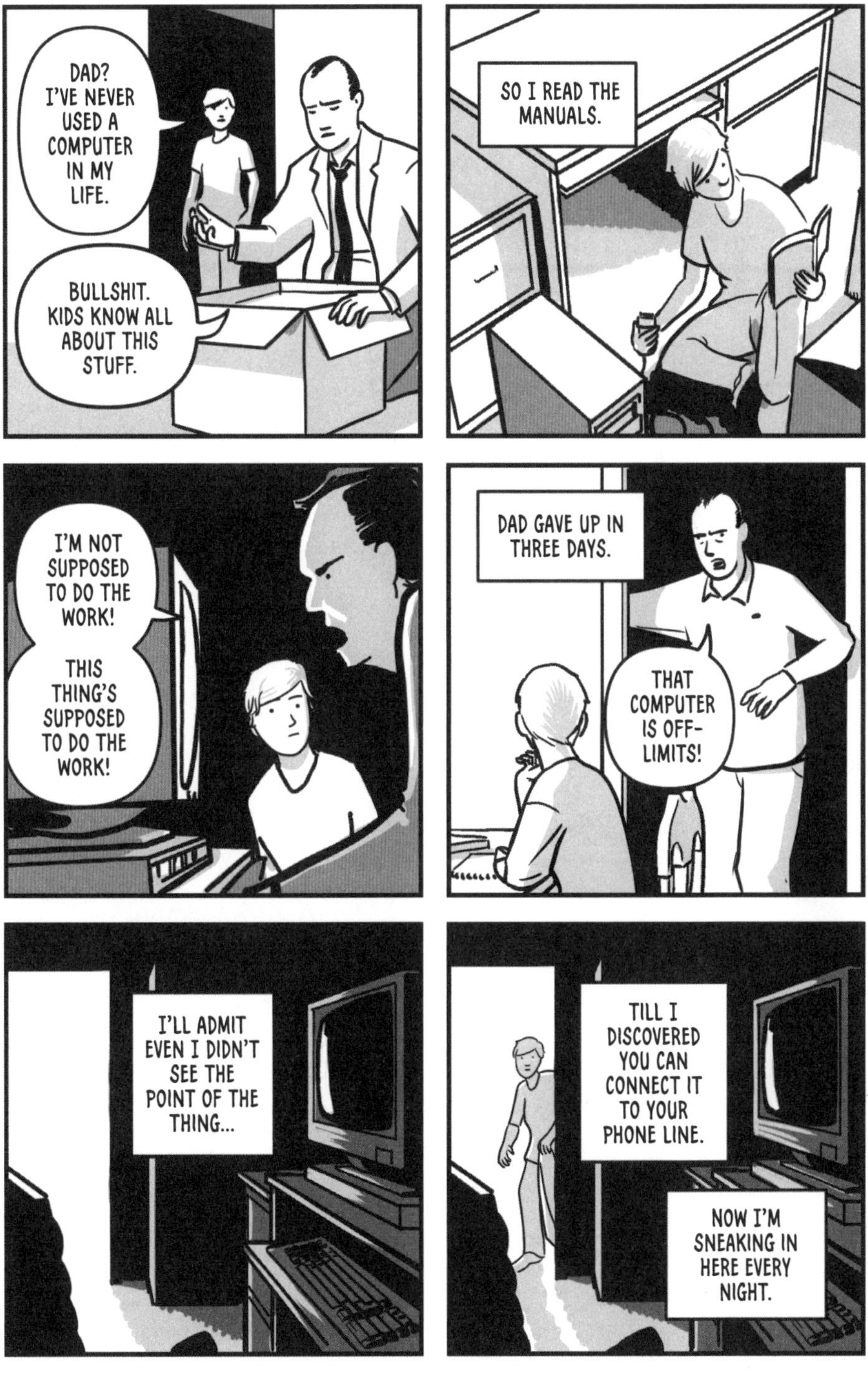
DAD? I'VE NEVER USED A COMPUTER IN MY LIFE.
BULLSHIT. KIDS KNOW ALL ABOUT THIS STUFF.
SO I READ THE MANUALS.
I'M NOT SUPPOSED TO DO THE WORK!
THIS THING'S SUPPOSED TO DO THE WORK!
DAD GAVE UP IN THREE DAYS.
THAT COMPUTER IS OFF-LIMITS!
I'LL ADMIT EVEN I DIDN'T SEE THE POINT OF THE THING...
TILL I DISCOVERED YOU CAN CONNECT IT TO YOUR PHONE LINE.
NOW I'M SNEAKING IN HERE EVERY NIGHT.

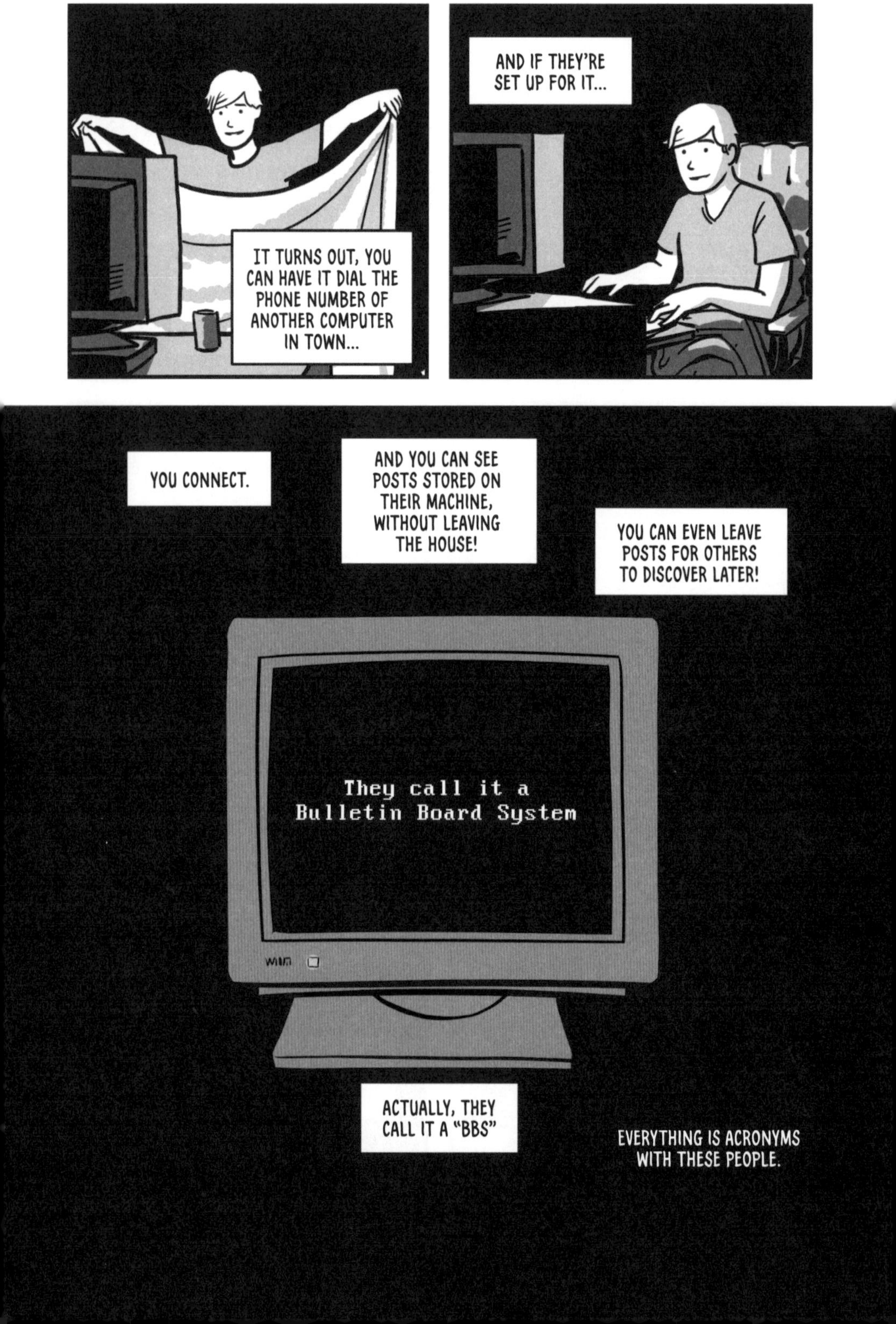
IT TURNS OUT, YOU CAN HAVE IT DIAL THE PHONE NUMBER OF ANOTHER COMPUTER IN TOWN...
AND IF THEY'RE SET UP FOR IT...
YOU CONNECT.
AND YOU CAN SEE POSTS STORED ON THEIR MACHINE, WITHOUT LEAVING THE HOUSE!
YOU CAN EVEN LEAVE POSTS FOR OTHERS TO DISCOVER LATER!
They call it a Bulletin Board System
ACTUALLY, THEY CALL IT A "BBS"
EVERYTHING IS ACRONYMS WITH THESE PEOPLE.

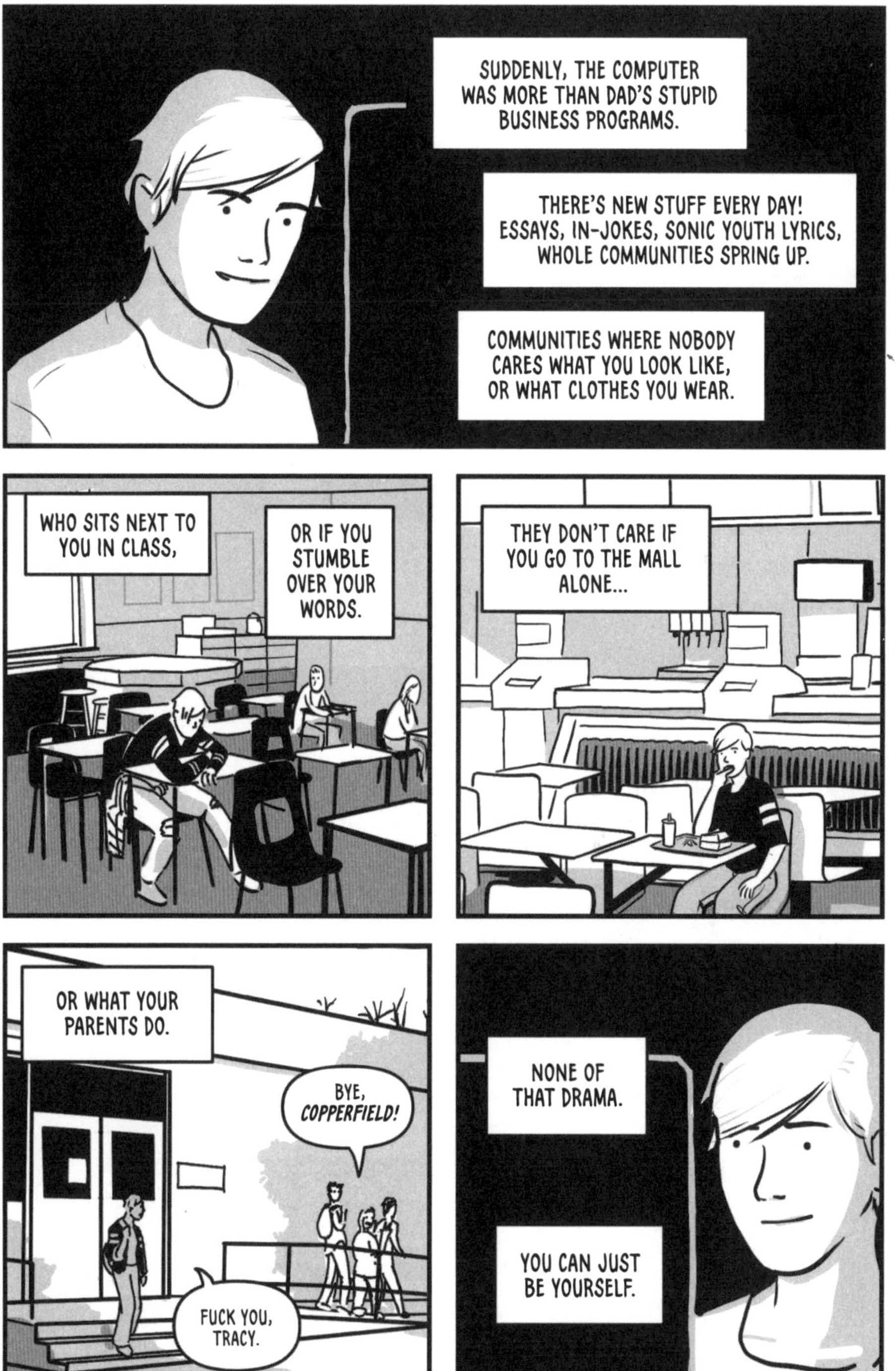
SUDDENLY, THE COMPUTER WAS MORE THAN DAD'S STUPID BUSINESS PROGRAMS.
THERE'S NEW STUFF EVERY DAY! ESSAYS, IN-JOKES, SONIC YOUTH LYRICS, WHOLE COMMUNITIES SPRING UP.
COMMUNITIES WHERE NOBODY CARES WHAT YOU LOOK LIKE, OR WHAT CLOTHES YOU WEAR.
WHO SITS NEXT TO YOU IN CLASS,
OR IF YOU STUMBLE OVER YOUR WORDS.
THEY DON'T CARE IF YOU GO TO THE MALL ALONE...
OR WHAT YOUR PARENTS DO.
BYE, *COPPERFIELD!*
FUCK YOU, TRACY.
NONE OF THAT DRAMA.
YOU CAN JUST BE YOURSELF.

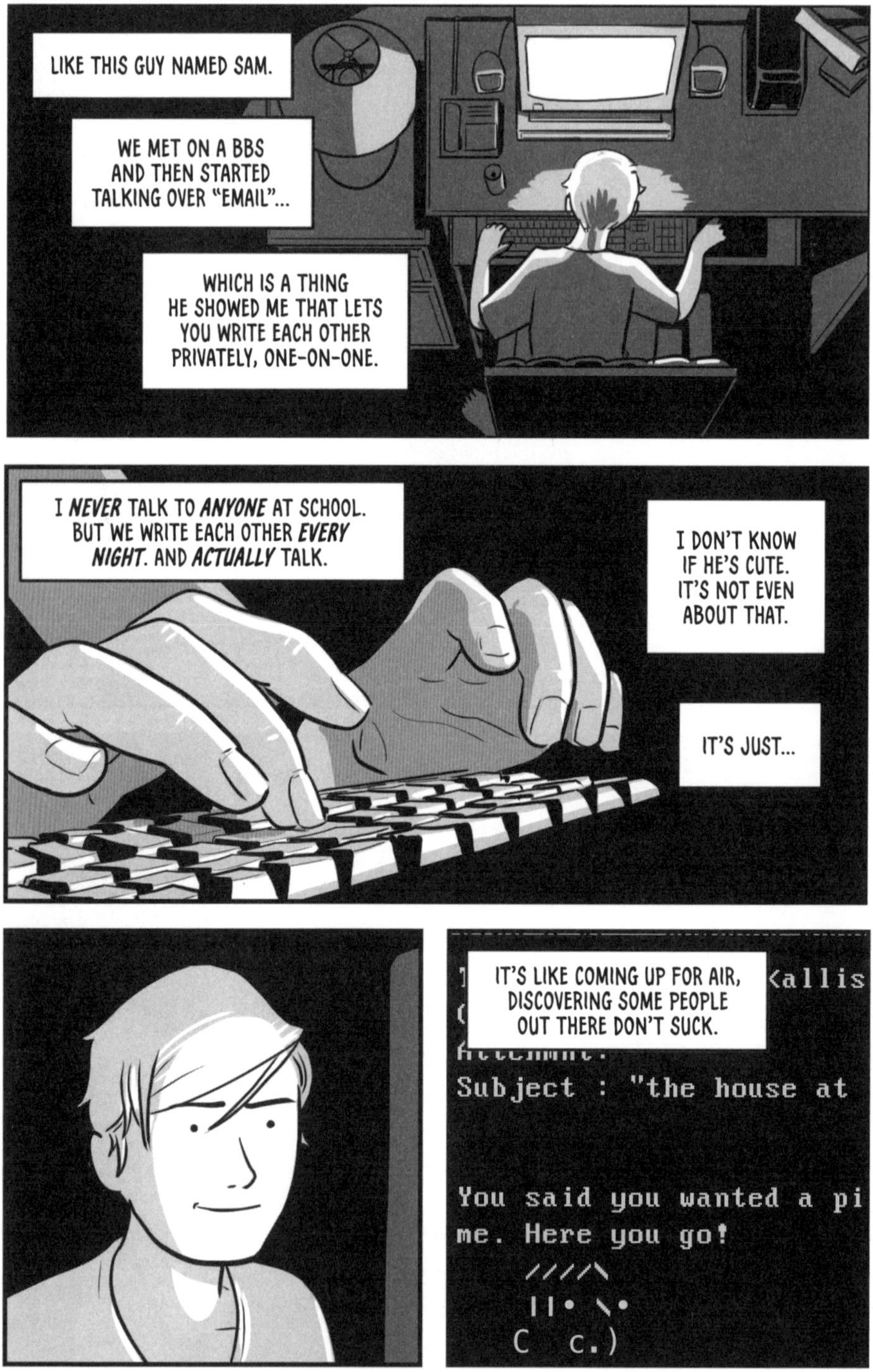
LIKE THIS GUY NAMED SAM.
WE MET ON A BBS AND THEN STARTED TALKING OVER "EMAIL"...
WHICH IS A THING HE SHOWED ME THAT LETS YOU WRITE EACH OTHER PRIVATELY, ONE-ON-ONE.
I *NEVER* TALK TO *ANYONE* AT SCHOOL. BUT WE WRITE EACH OTHER *EVERY NIGHT*. AND *ACTUALLY* TALK.
I DON'T KNOW IF HE'S CUTE. IT'S NOT EVEN ABOUT THAT.
IT'S JUST...
IT'S LIKE COMING UP FOR AIR, DISCOVERING SOME PEOPLE OUT THERE DON'T SUCK.
Kallis
Subject : "the house at
You said you wanted a pi
me. Here you go!

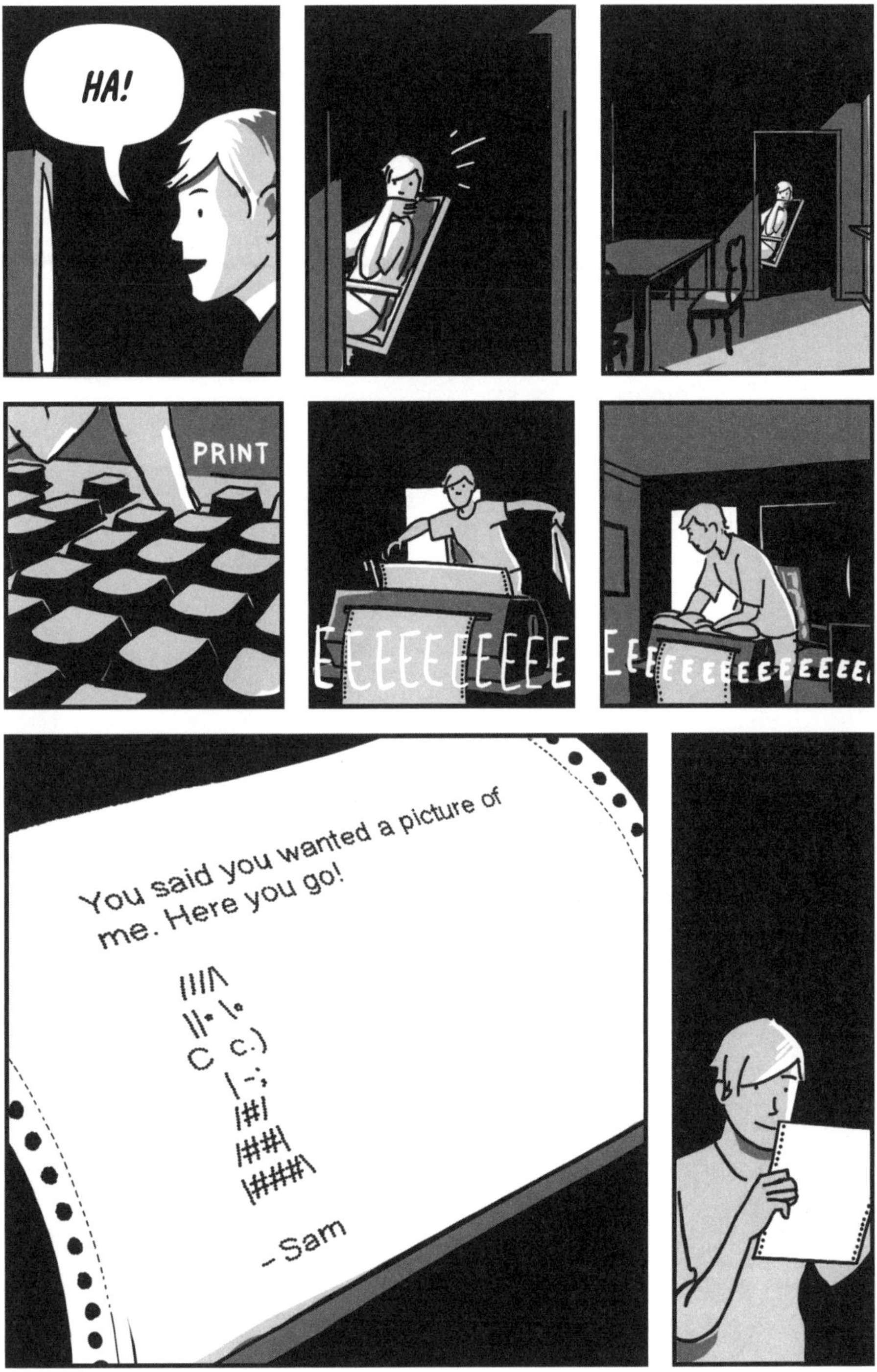

HA!
PRINT
EEEEEEEEEE
EEEEEEEEEEEEEE
You said you wanted a picture of
me. Here you go!
||||\
||• \•
C c.)
\ -;
|#|
|##\
|###\
-Sam

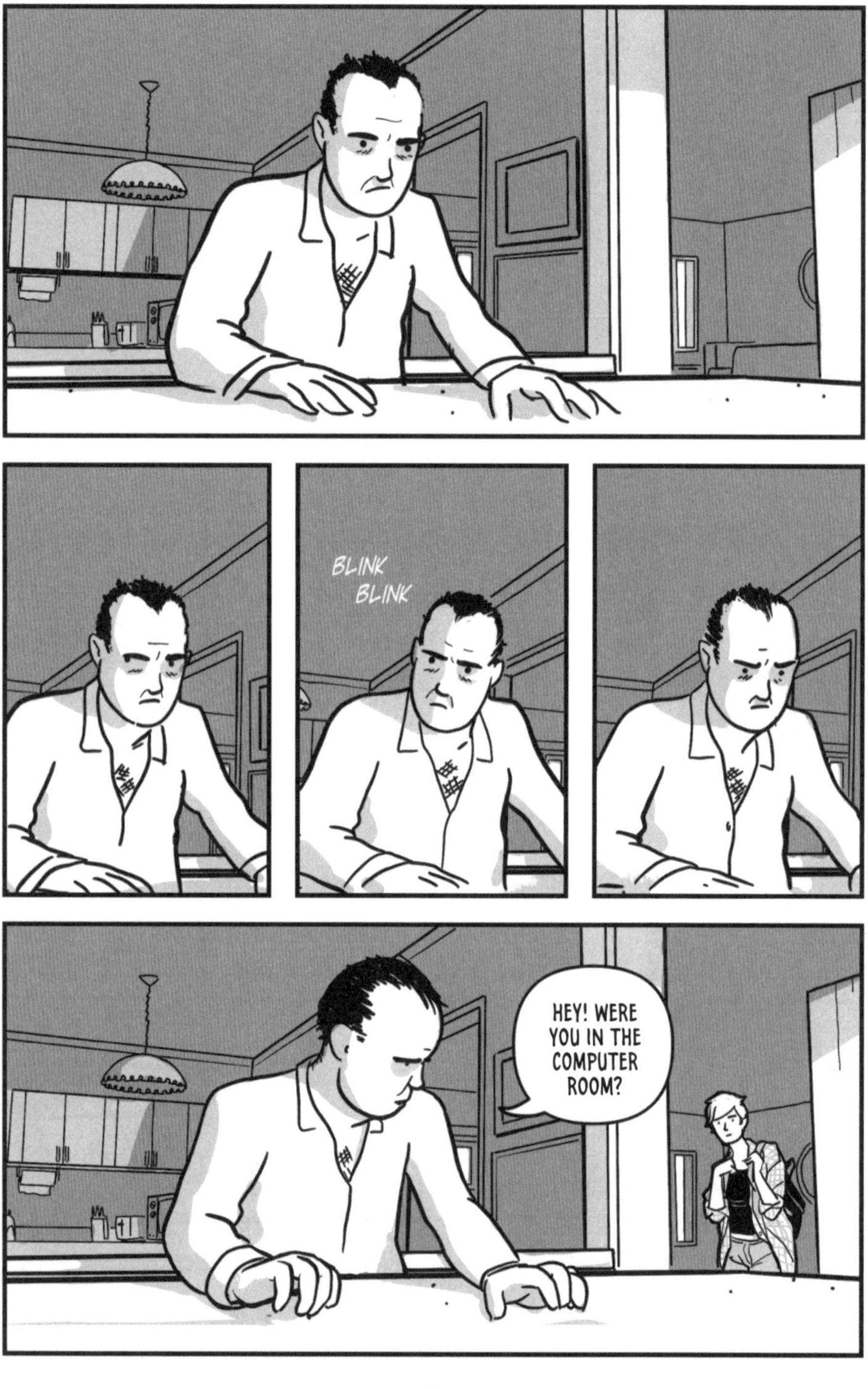
BLINK
BLINK
HEY! WERE YOU IN THE COMPUTER ROOM?

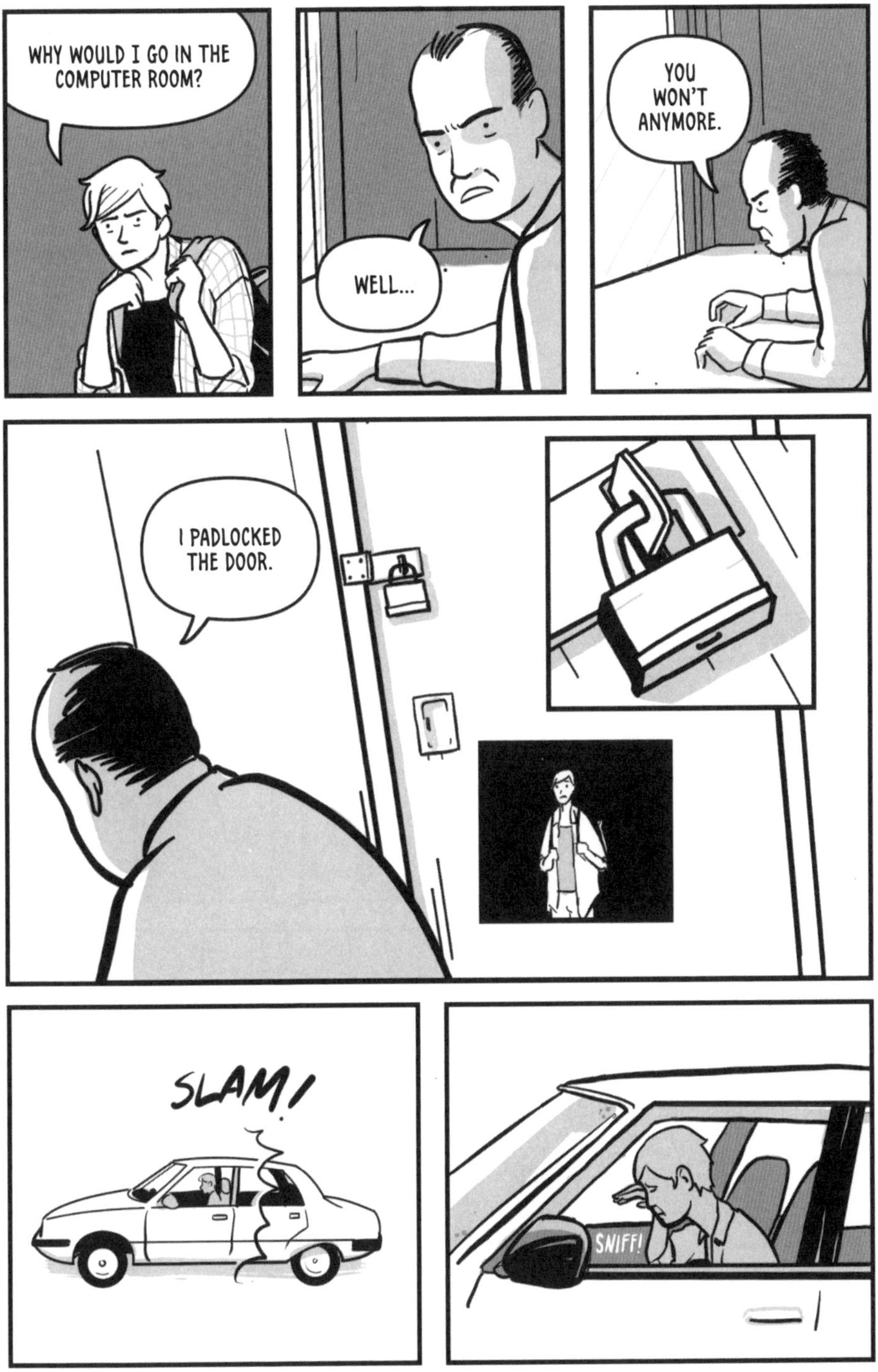
WHY WOULD I GO IN THE COMPUTER ROOM?
WELL...
YOU WON'T ANYMORE.
I PADLOCKED THE DOOR.
SLAM!
SNIFF!

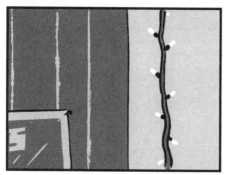

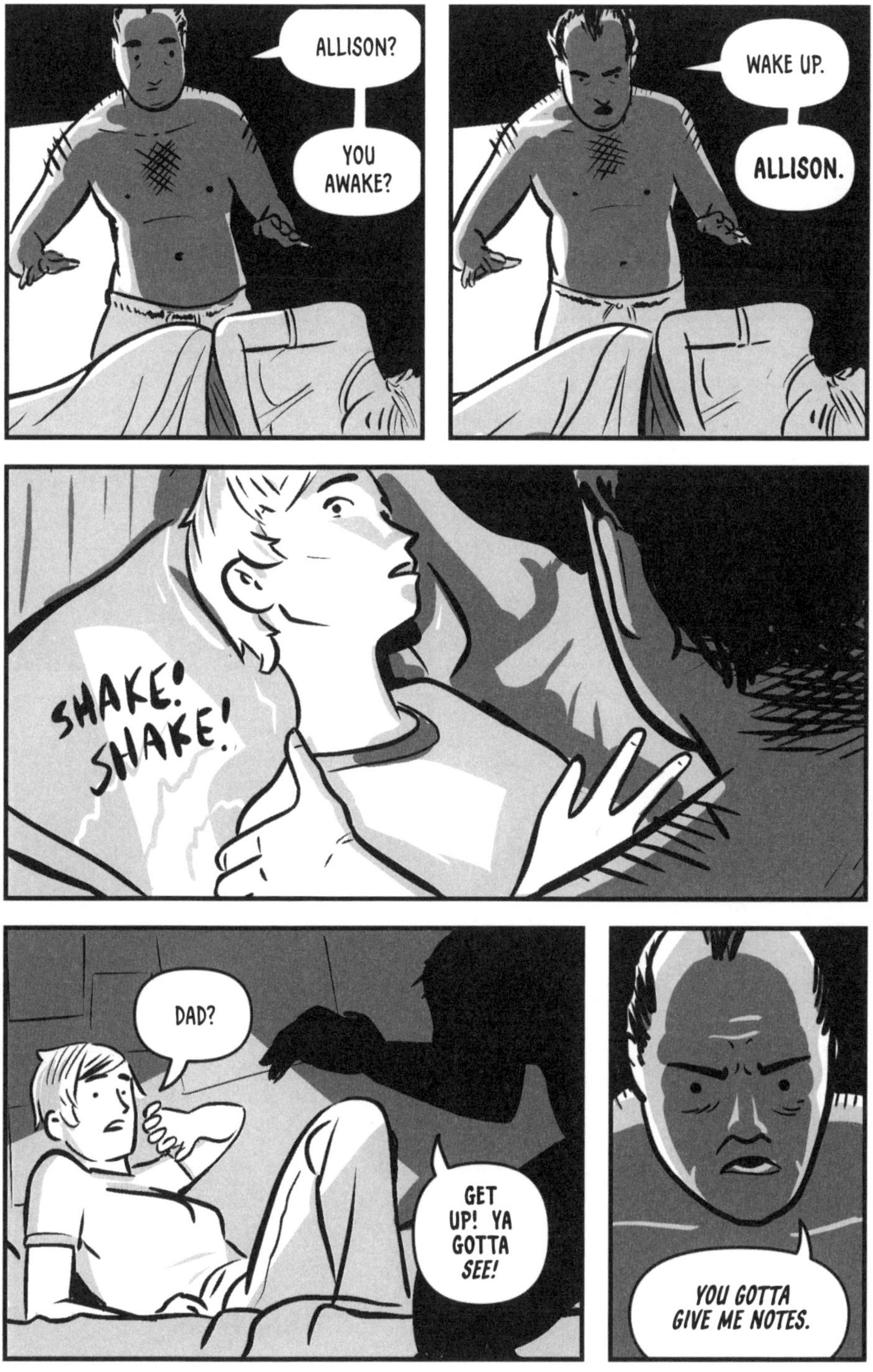
ALLISON?
YOU AWAKE?
WAKE UP.
ALLISON.
SHAKE! SHAKE!
DAD?
GET UP! YA GOTTA *SEE!*
YOU GOTTA GIVE ME NOTES.

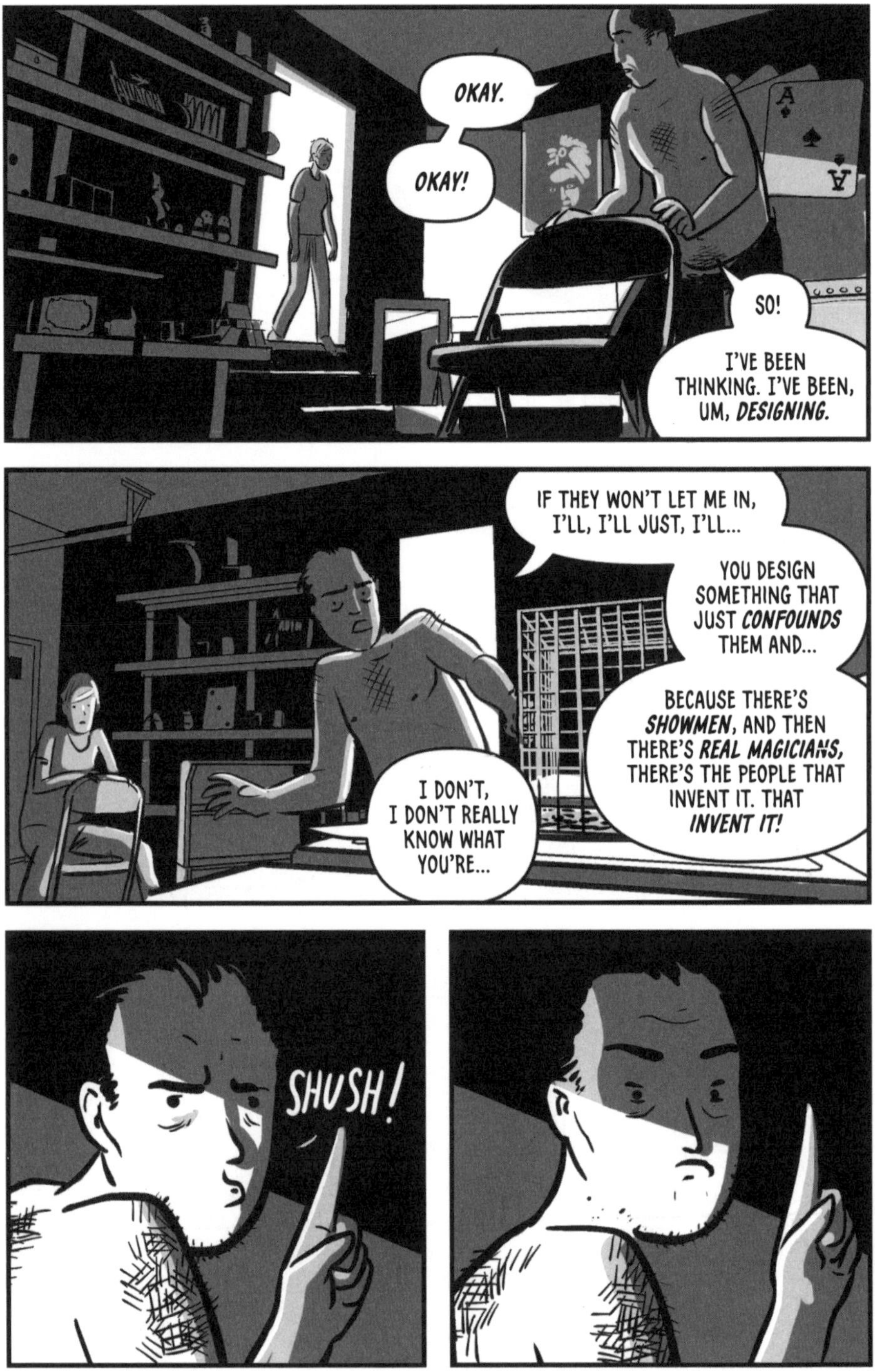
OKAY.
OKAY!
SO!
I'VE BEEN THINKING. I'VE BEEN, UM, DESIGNING.
IF THEY WON'T LET ME IN, I'LL, I'LL JUST, I'LL...
YOU DESIGN SOMETHING THAT JUST CONFOUNDS THEM AND...
BECAUSE THERE'S SHOWMEN, AND THEN THERE'S REAL MAGICIANS, THERE'S THE PEOPLE THAT INVENT IT. THAT INVENT IT!
I DON'T, I DON'T REALLY KNOW WHAT YOU'RE...
SHUSH!

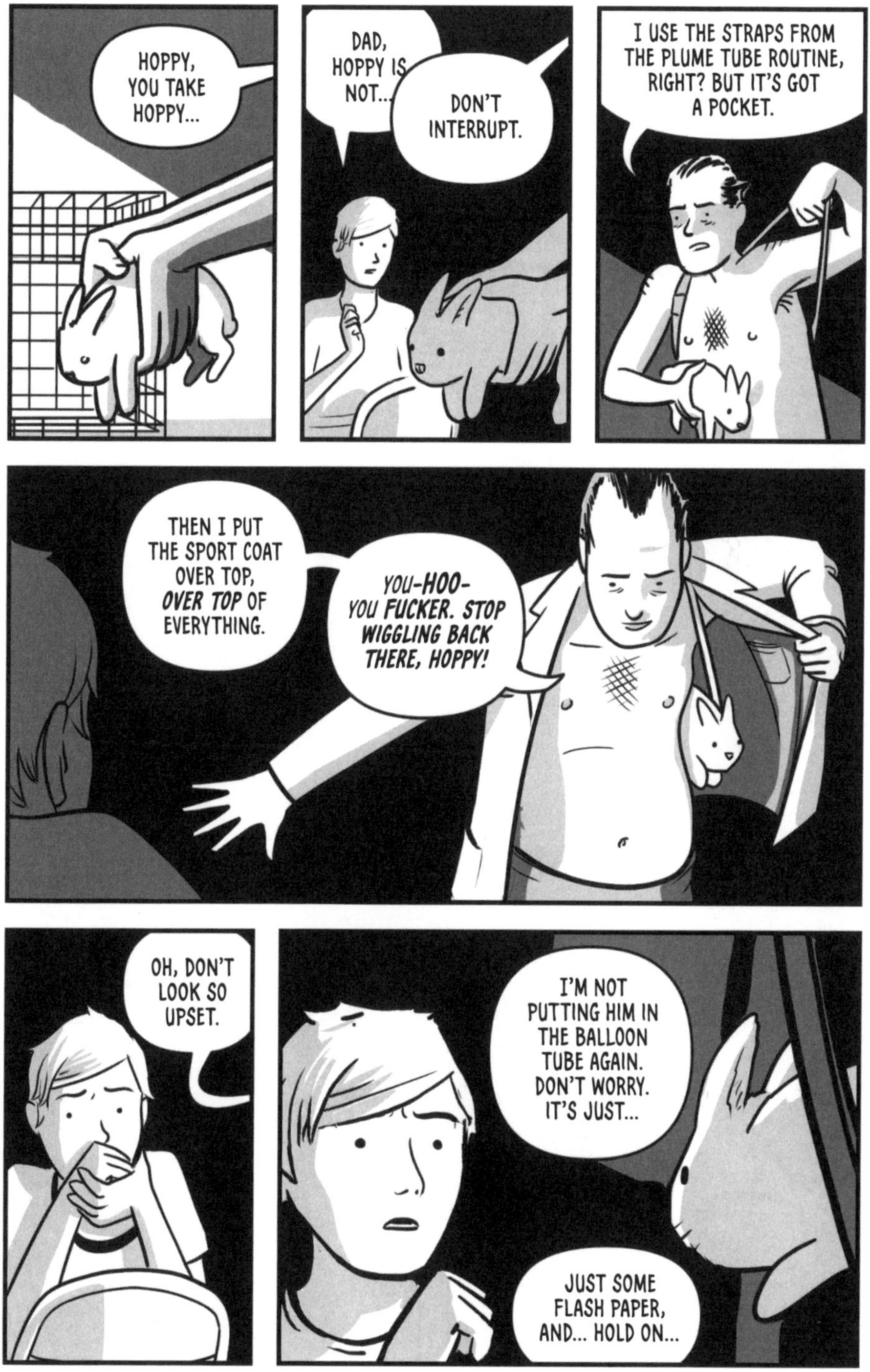
HOPPY, YOU TAKE HOPPY...
DAD, HOPPY IS NOT...
DON'T INTERRUPT.
I USE THE STRAPS FROM THE PLUME TUBE ROUTINE, RIGHT? BUT IT'S GOT A POCKET.
THEN I PUT THE SPORT COAT OVER TOP, *OVER TOP* OF EVERYTHING.
*YOU-**HOO**-YOU **FUCKER.** STOP WIGGLING BACK THERE, HOPPY!*
OH, DON'T LOOK SO UPSET.
I'M NOT PUTTING HIM IN THE BALLOON TUBE AGAIN. DON'T WORRY. IT'S JUST...
JUST SOME FLASH PAPER, AND... HOLD ON...

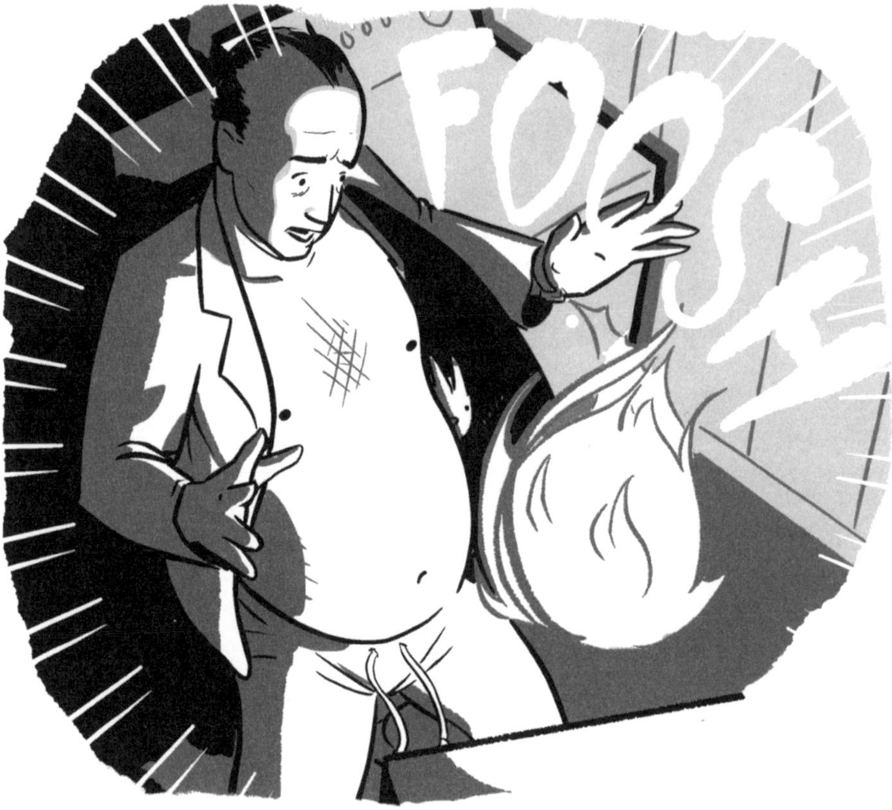
FOOSH

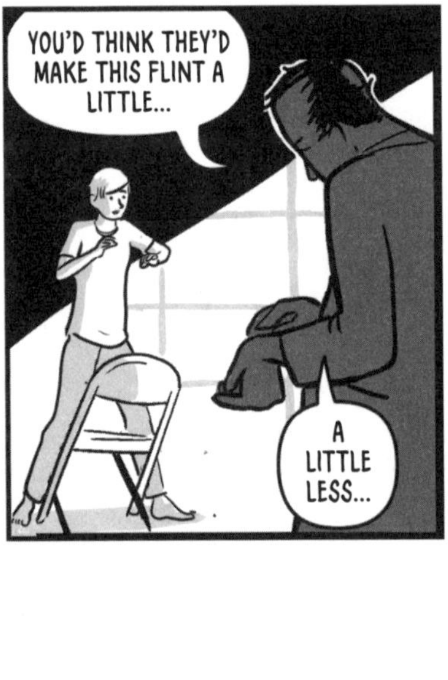
YOU'D THINK THEY'D MAKE THIS FLINT A LITTLE...
A LITTLE LESS...

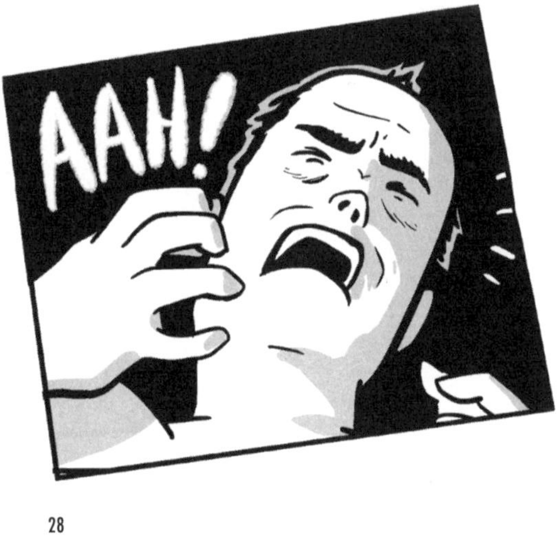
AAH!

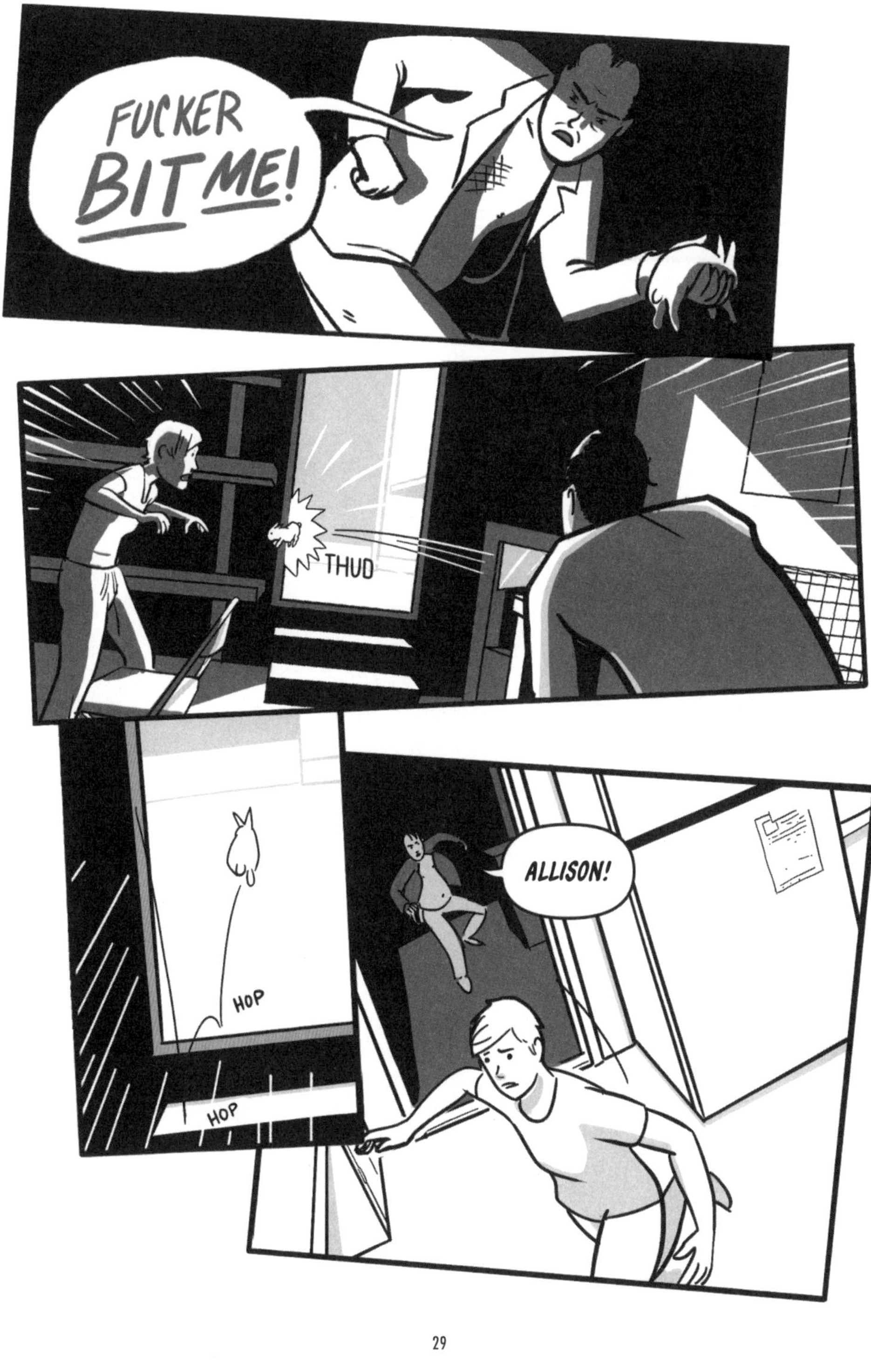
FUCKER BIT ME!
THUD
HOP
HOP
ALLISON!

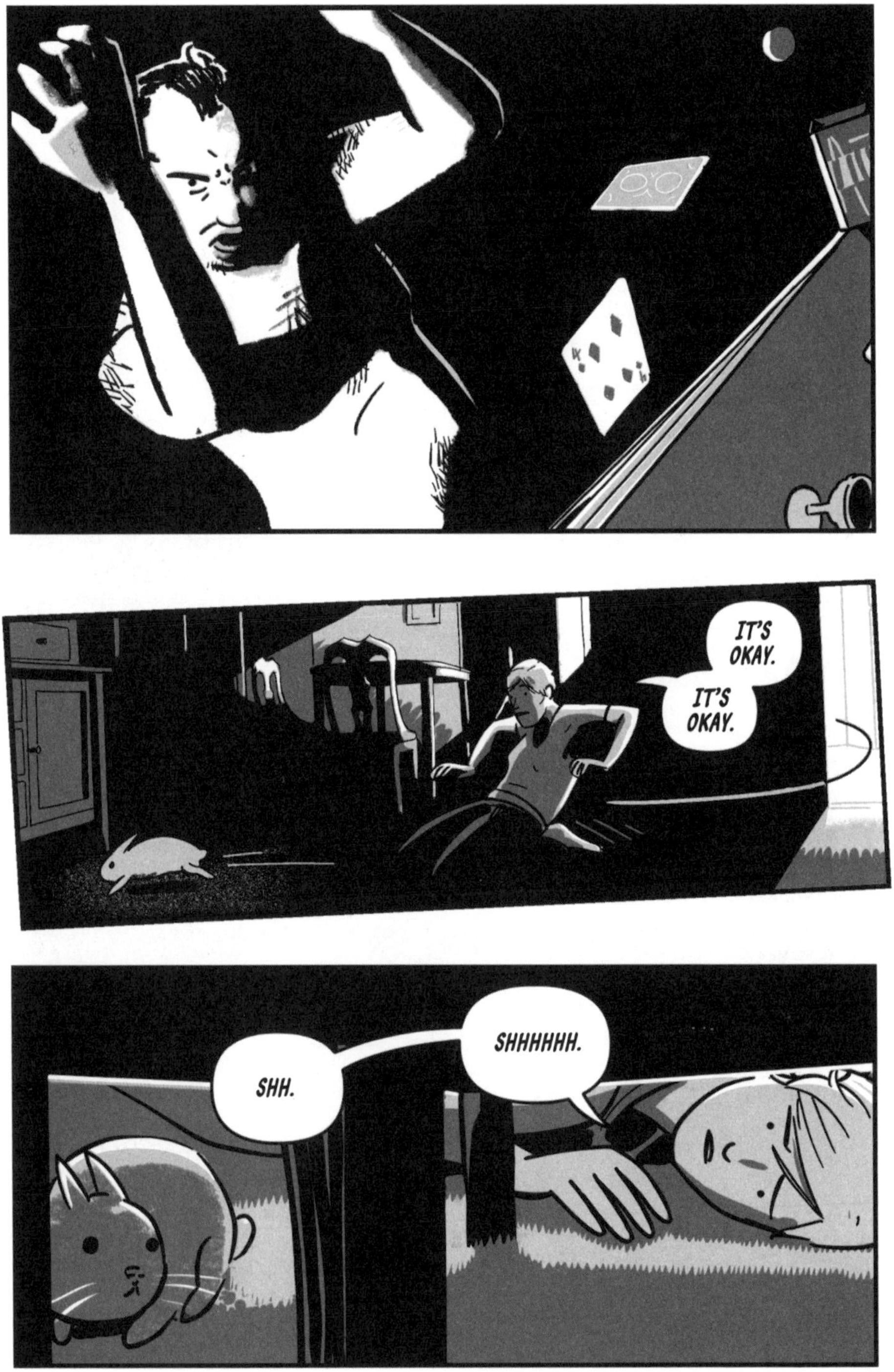
IT'S OKAY.
IT'S OKAY.
SHH.
SHHHHHH.

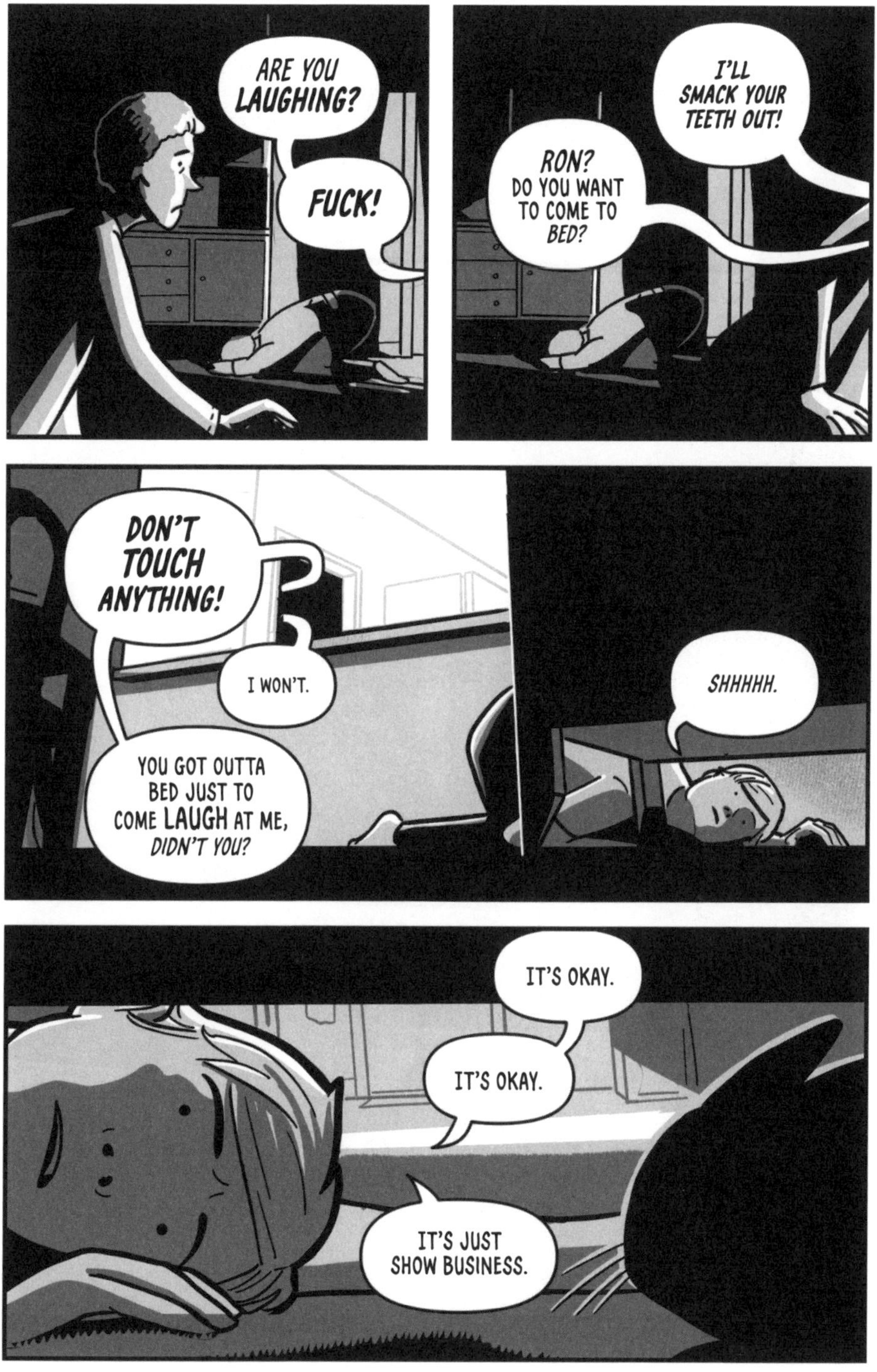
ARE YOU LAUGHING?
FUCK!
RON? DO YOU WANT TO COME TO BED?
I'LL SMACK YOUR TEETH OUT!
DON'T TOUCH ANYTHING!
I WON'T.
YOU GOT OUTTA BED JUST TO COME LAUGH AT ME, DIDN'T YOU?
SHHHHH.
IT'S OKAY.
IT'S OKAY.
IT'S JUST SHOW BUSINESS.

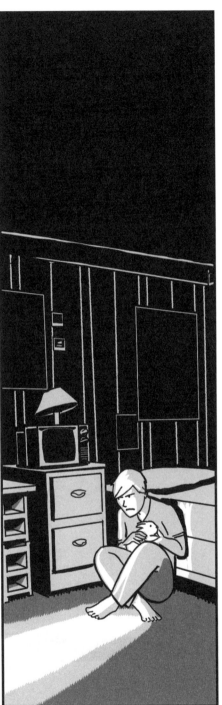

```
starting rpc daemons: portmap rpcd.
starting system logger
starting local daemons: routed sendmail biod.
preserving editor files
clearing /tmp
standard daemons: update cron.
starting network daemons: inetd printer.

Wisconsin UNIX (root console)
4.3+NFS > V.*

login: samir
password: *******
4.3 BSD UNIX #2

-=-=-=-=-=-=-=-=-=-=-=-=-=-=-=-=-=-=-=-=-=-=-=-=-=-=-=-=-=-=-


               4.3+NFS Winsconsin Unix

-=-=-=-=-=-=-=-=-=-=-=-=-=-=-=-=-=-=-=-=-=-=-=-=-=-=-=-=-=-=-


samir# /usr/bin/pine
```

```
PINE 3.06   MAIN MENU                    Folder: INBOX  3 Messages


   ?    HELP              - Get help using Pine

   C    COMPOSE MESSAGE   - Compose and send a message

   I    MESSAGE INDEX     - View messages in current folder

   L    FOLDER LIST       - Select a folder to view

   A    ADDRESS BOOK      - Update address book

   S    SETUP             - Configure Pine Options

   Q    QUIT              - Leave the Pine program



   Copyright 1989-1992.
   PINE is a trademark of the University of Washington.


? Help                    P PrevCmd              R RelNotes
O OTHER CMDS > (Index)    N NextCmd              K KBLock
```

PINE 3.06   COMPOSE MESSAGE REPLY   Folder: INBOX 3 Messages

To   : Allison <allison.r@zephyrtech.net>
Cc   :
Attchmnt:
Subject : "a lot more than just being bored"

----- Message Text -----

Hey Allison

I couldn't sleep. I've gotten used to e-mailing you at 1am.

Ever think about what would have happened if one of us lived in a different town? The billion dollar long distance charges to dial into a BBS in a different area code? We'd never have met.

Thanks for talking about my parents split. I think I'm kind of in the way of them saying what they need to say to each other. I just want them to be done with it. Does that make me a selfish prick?

Aaaaanyway. I got that Daniel Johnston album. I kind of love it? There's a scratch on the CD that makes the line "they were mean to him but he never burned us" repeat and sound like Big Bird when he snores. "They were me-me-me-me-me-me-me-me".

Well, enough about me. What are you doing?
-Sam

^G Get Help ^X Send ^R Read File ^K Cut Text ^O Postpone
^C Cancel ^J Justify ^W Where is ^U UnCut Text ^T To Spell

PINE 3.06   MESSAGE TEXT Folder: INBOX Message 1 of 3 ALL ANS
From: Allison <allison.r@zephyrtech.net>
To: s.omid@campuslink.net
Subject: RE: "a lot more than just being bored"

Sam! You are the farthest from selfish I've ever met!

I missed talking to you too. It's kinda ALL I think about. It's possible I'm a crazy person. You should know that about me.

Hey, there's something we need to talk about as soon as you get this.

Are you up?

Can I have your phone number?

[ALL of message]

H Help   < MsgIndex   P PrevMsg   D Delete   R Reply
O OTHER CMDS   > ViewAttch   N NextMsg   U Undelete   F Forward

Can I have your

phone number?

```
To      : Allison <allison.r@zephyrtech.net>
Cc      :
Attchmnt:
Subject : RE(2): "a lot more than just being bored"

----- Message Text -----

▊
```

```
To      : Allison <allison.r@zephyrtech.net>
Cc      :
Attchmnt:
Subject : RE(2): "a lot more than just being bored"

----- Message Text -----

I don't think I sh▊
```

```
To      : Allison <allison.r@zephyrtech.net>
Cc      :
Attchmnt:
Subject : RE(2): "a lot more than just being bored"

----- Message Text -----

I▊
```

```
To       : Allison <allison.r@zephyrtech.net>
Cc       :
Attchmnt :
Subject  : RE(2): "a lot more than just being bored"
----- Message Text -----

It's 858-5322 but don't call now. It's 1am. My dad's asleep.

-Sam
```

```
From: Allison <allison.r@zephyrtech.net>
To: s.omid@campuslink.net
Subject: RE(3): "a lot more than just being bored"


Better log off. Your phone's about to ring.

- Allison
```

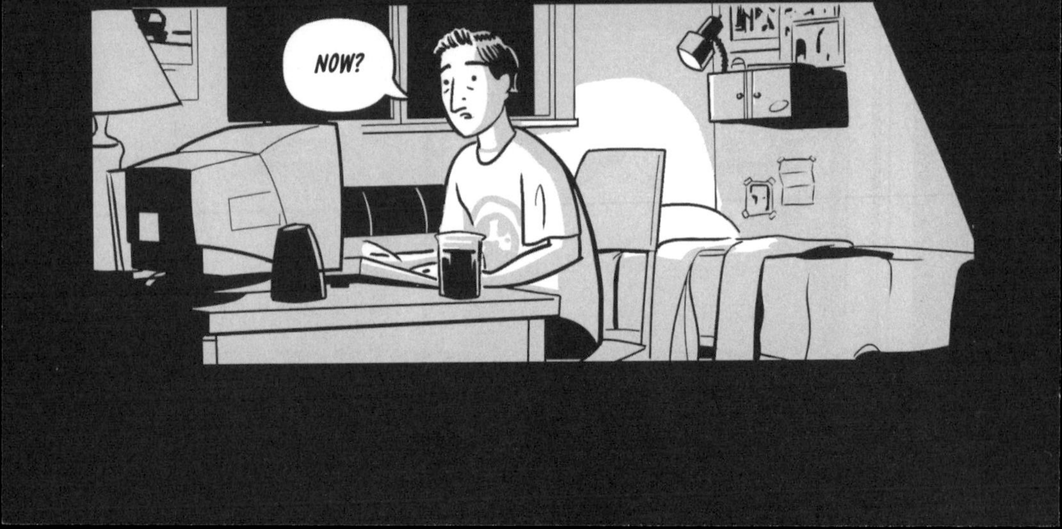
NOW?

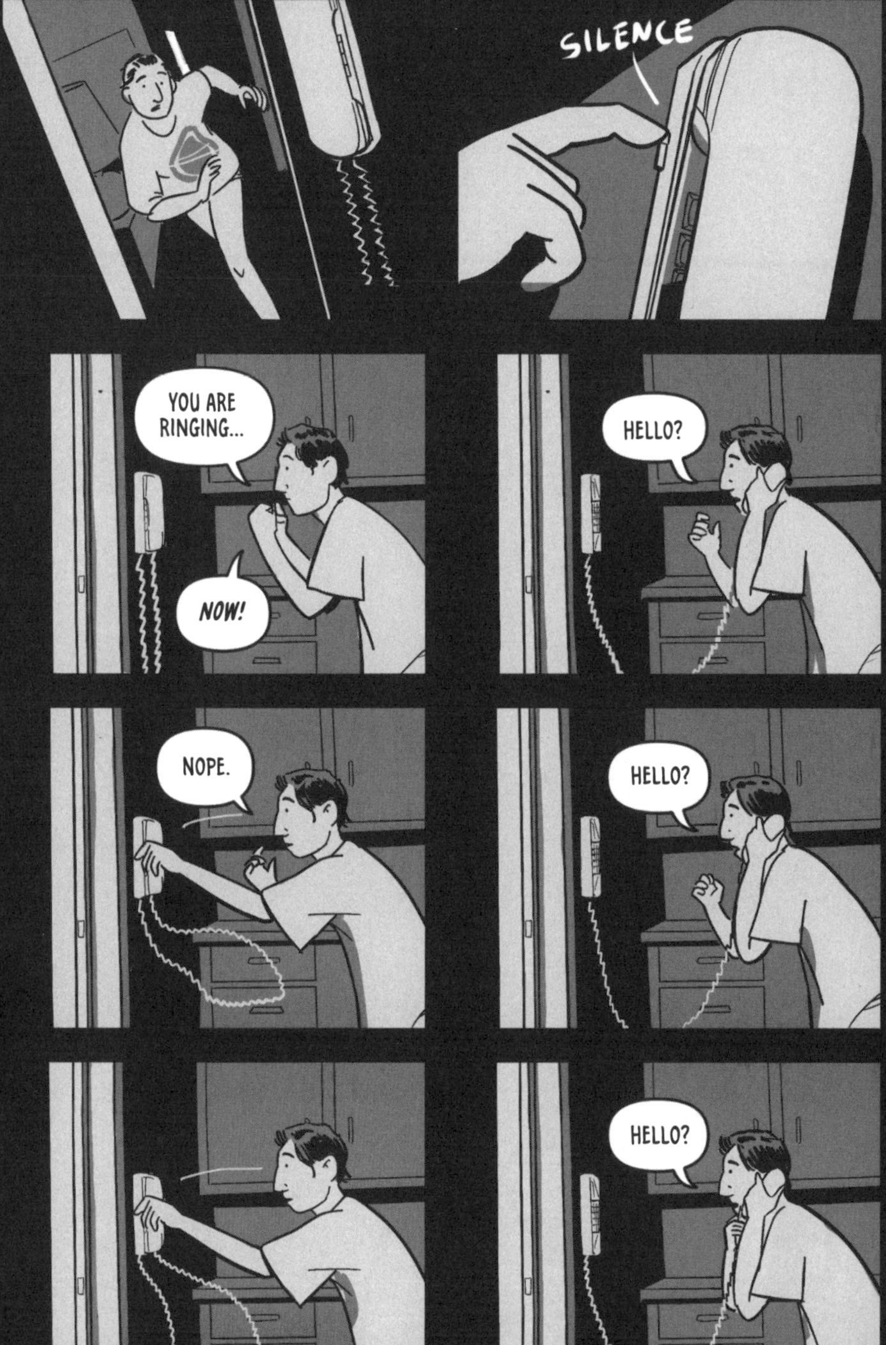
SILENCE
YOU ARE RINGING...
NOW!
HELLO?
NOPE.
HELLO?
HELLO?

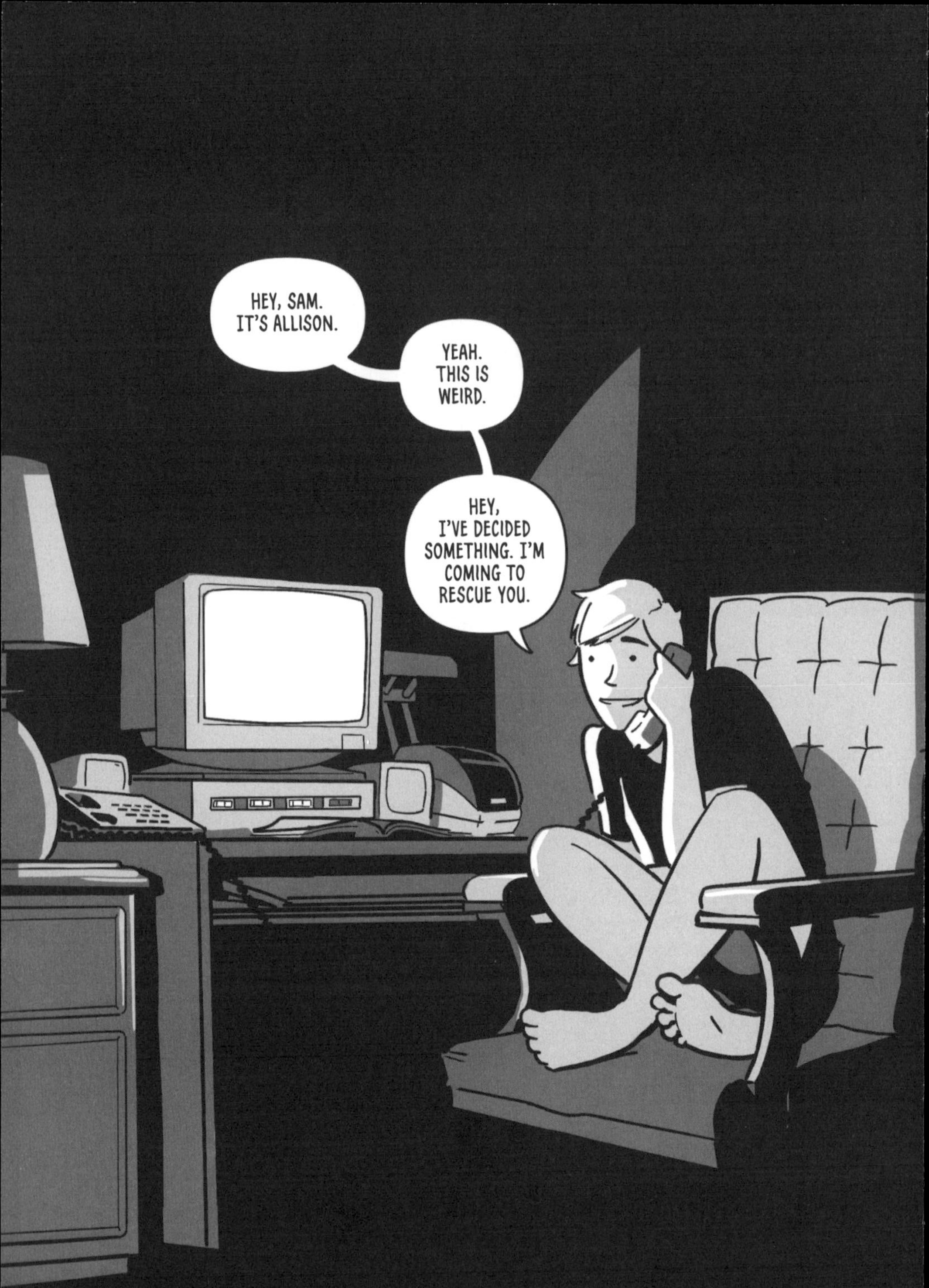
HEY, SAM. IT'S ALLISON.
YEAH. THIS IS WEIRD.
HEY, I'VE DECIDED SOMETHING. I'M COMING TO RESCUE YOU.

Chapter 2

WELCOME TO MALABAR

GAT GCS GM GS d -p+ c+++(++++) l++(+++) u+@ e×
m(+) s+/- n--- h× !f(+) g+ w++ t++(+++) r? y?

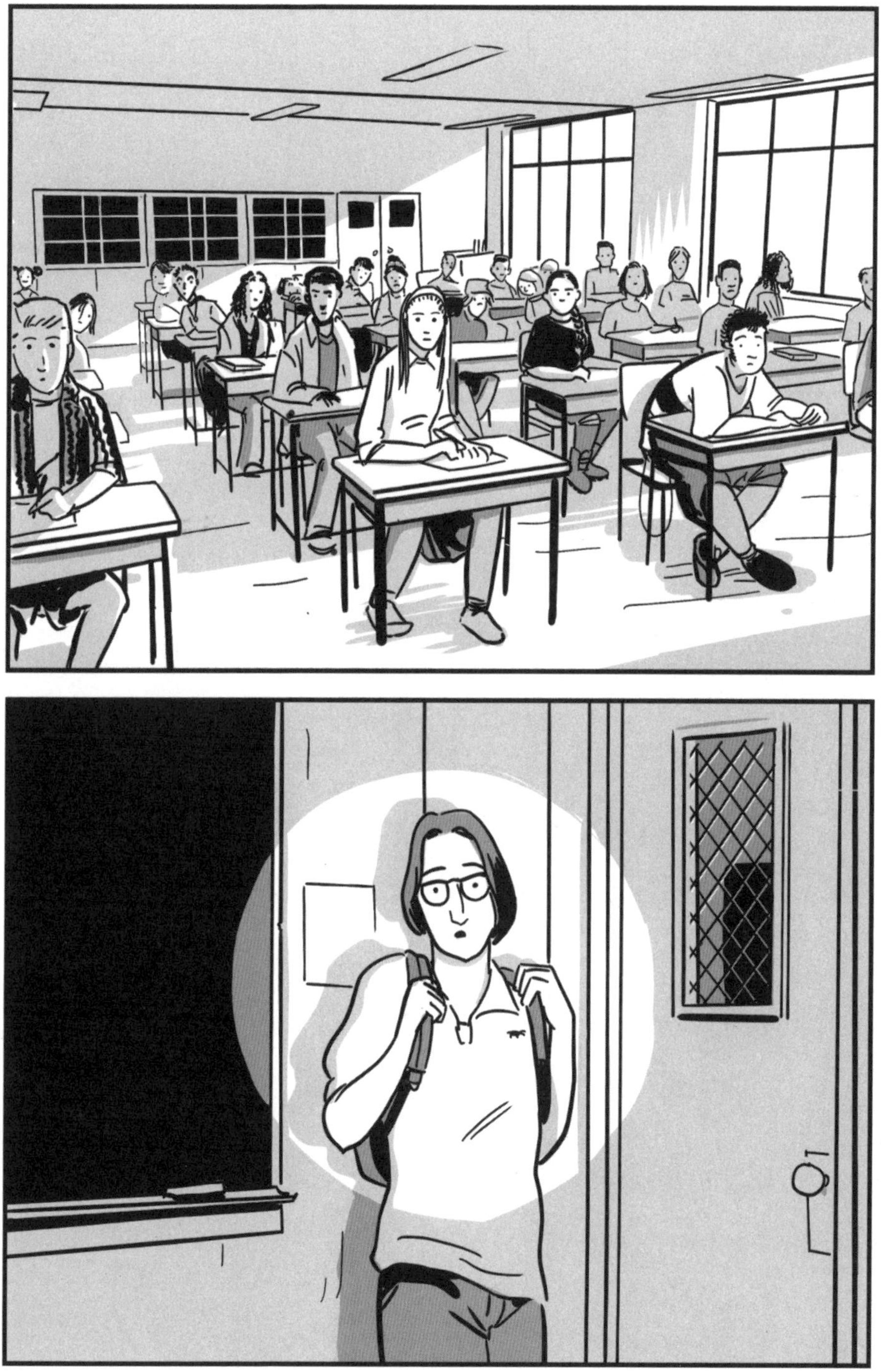

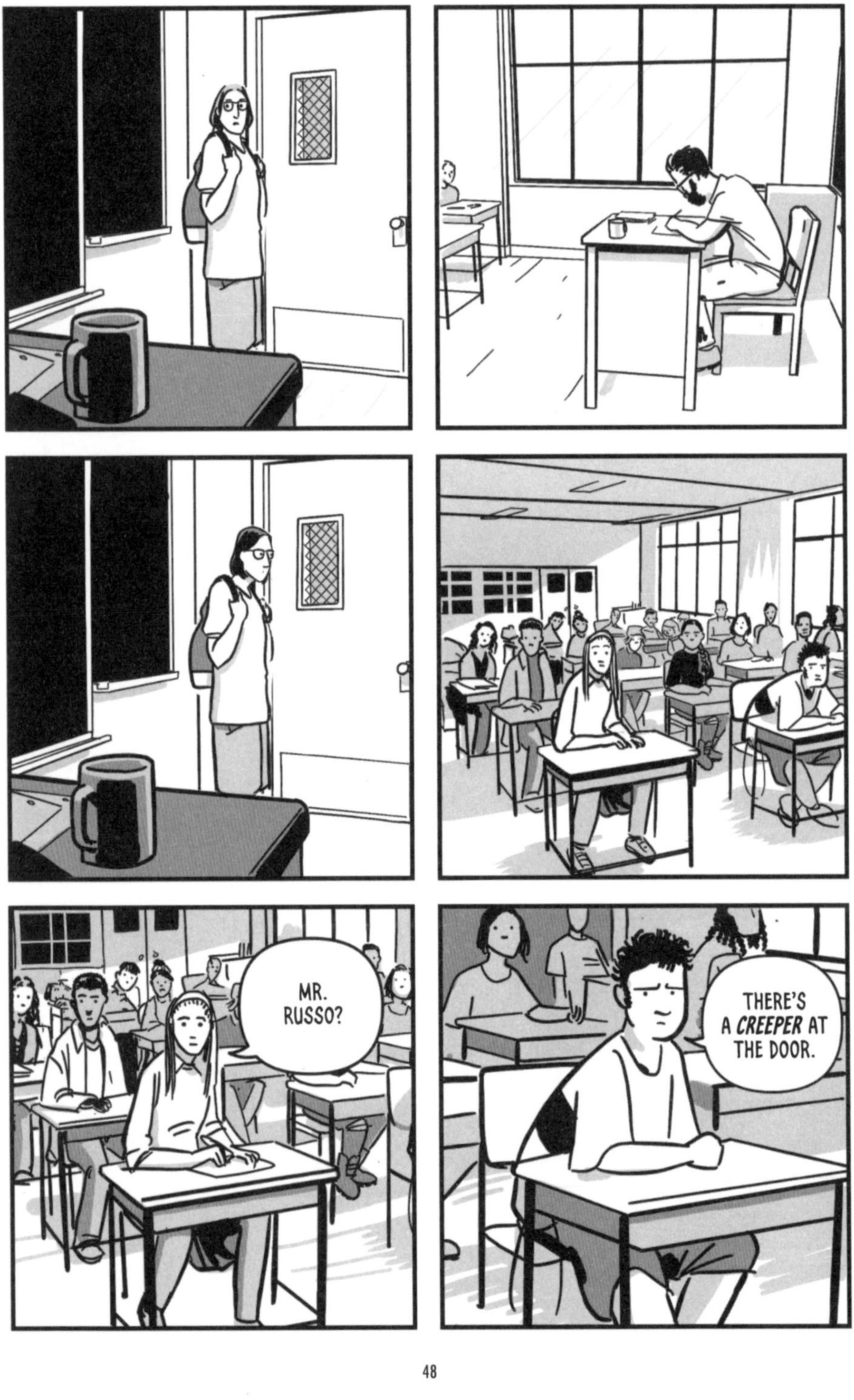
MR. RUSSO?
THERE'S A *CREEPER* AT THE DOOR.

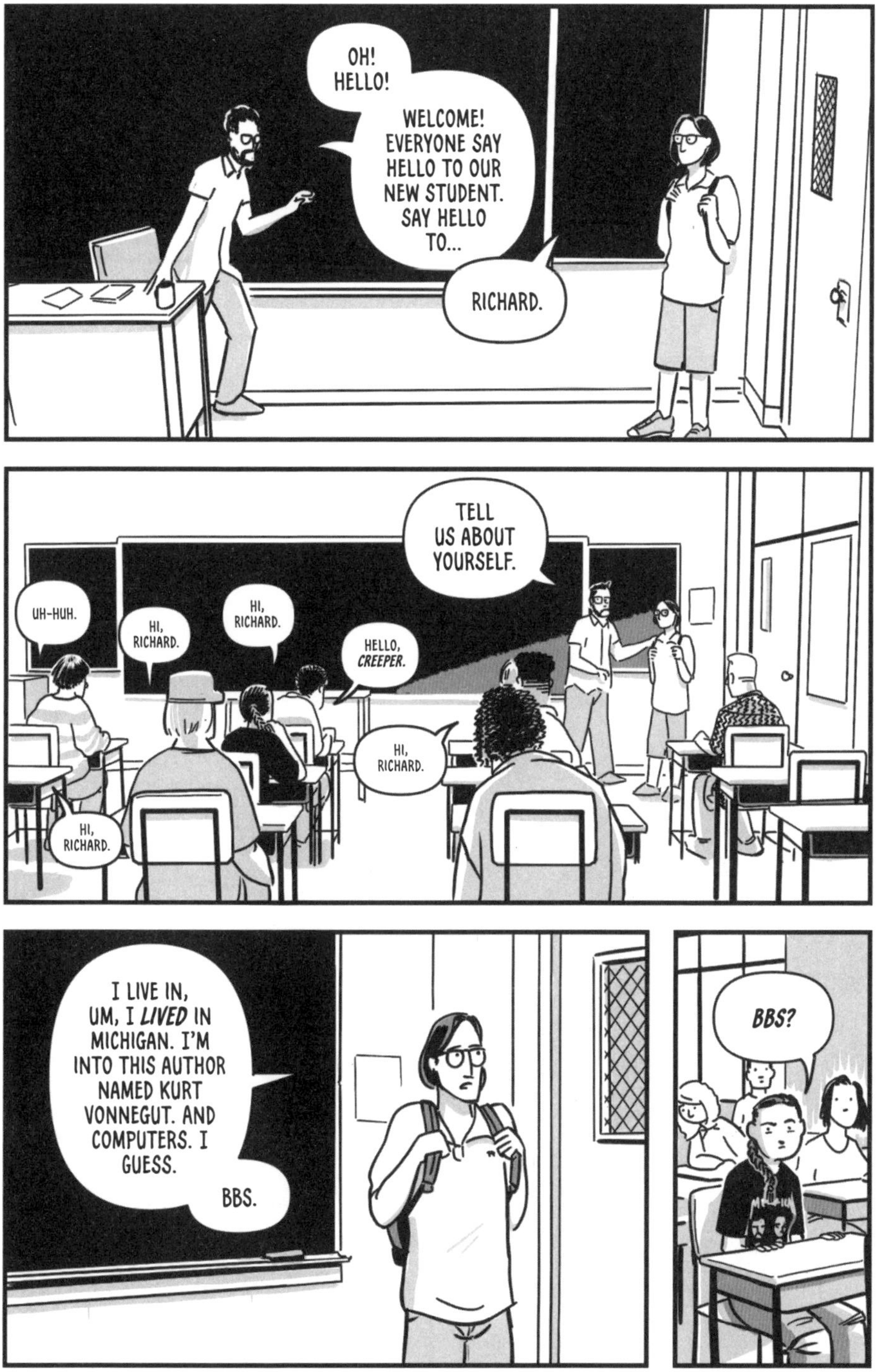
OH! HELLO!
WELCOME! EVERYONE SAY HELLO TO OUR NEW STUDENT. SAY HELLO TO...
RICHARD.
TELL US ABOUT YOURSELF.
UH-HUH.
HI, RICHARD.
HI, RICHARD.
HELLO, *CREEPER.*
HI, RICHARD.
HI, RICHARD.
I LIVE IN, UM, I *LIVED* IN MICHIGAN. I'M INTO THIS AUTHOR NAMED KURT VONNEGUT. AND COMPUTERS. I GUESS.
BBS.
BBS?

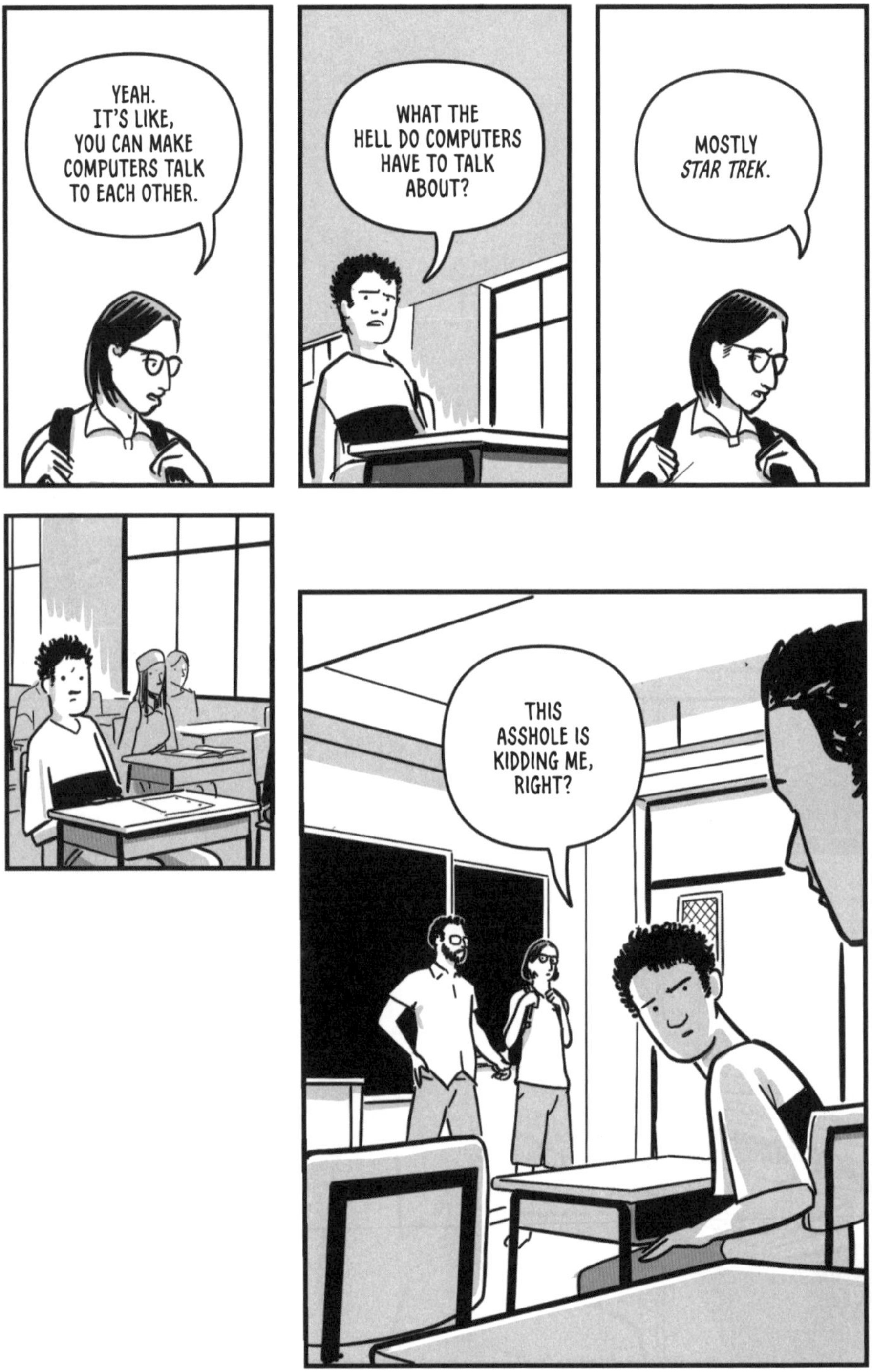
YEAH. IT'S LIKE, YOU CAN MAKE COMPUTERS TALK TO EACH OTHER.
WHAT THE HELL DO COMPUTERS HAVE TO TALK ABOUT?
MOSTLY *STAR TREK*.
THIS ASSHOLE IS KIDDING ME, RIGHT?

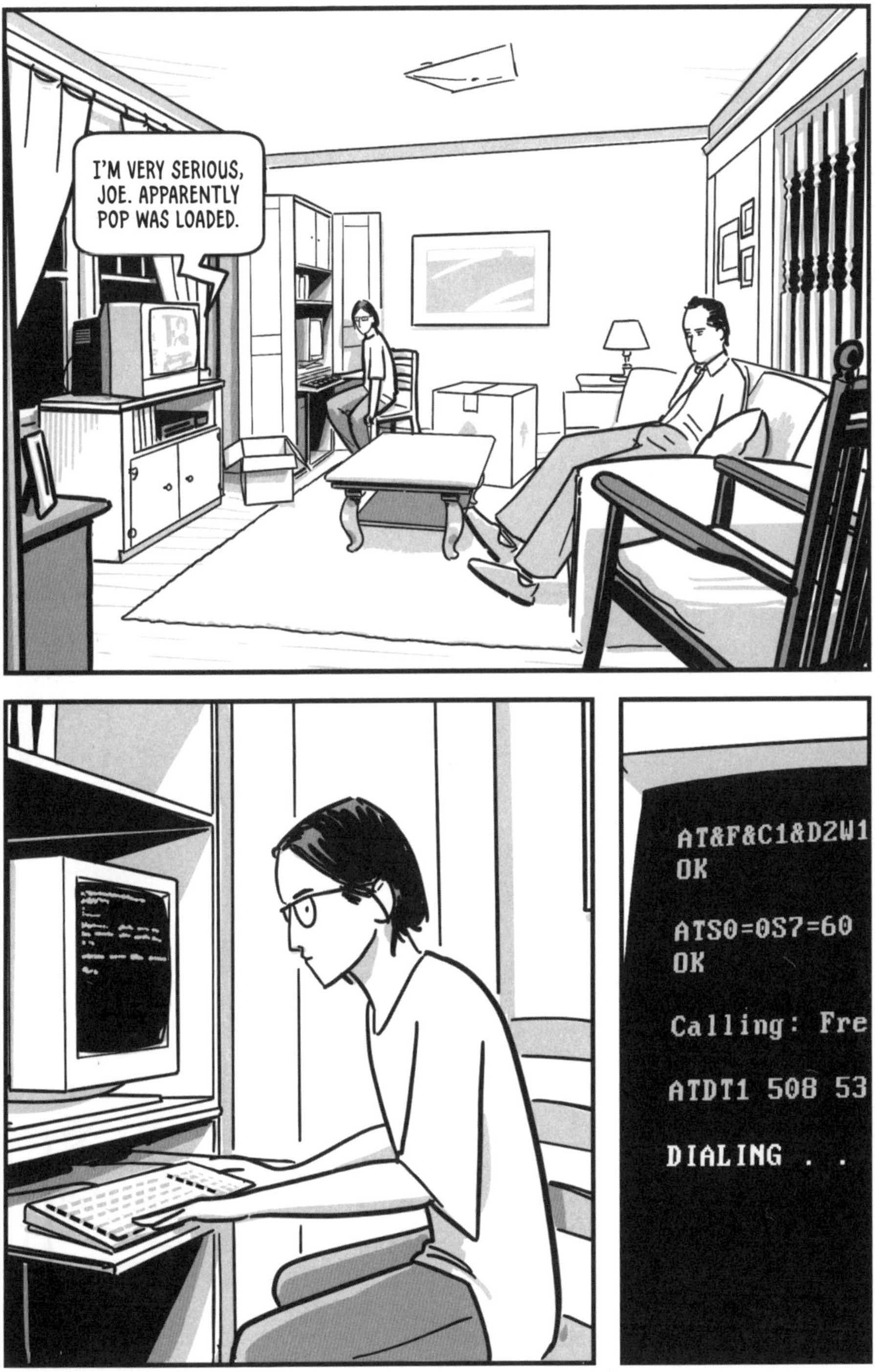
I'M VERY SERIOUS, JOE. APPARENTLY POP WAS LOADED.
AT&F&C1&D2W1
OK
ATS0=0S7=60
OK
Calling: Fre
ATDT1 508 53
DIALING . .

```
DIALING. . . . . . . . . . . .
CONNECT 2400/ARQ/TEL

PCBOARD BBS +v1.2

                _____
=====  /  /___/|  ================
====  /  /__/|/   _____
===  /  /__/|    |  .| .| .)/  \
==  /  /|_|/  \  | \| \|      <
=  /__//  \  \ (_(_|___)____//__<
  |__|/  ./  (_/\_/\_,_____\/

 ,_____,
 | HOOT!    Welcome to FreeBBS! |
 | : Multinode 1200/2400 Baud : |
 | Closed 1-2AM for maintenance |
 ,----|/---------------------,
  {o,o}
  |) )
===\"=\"===========================
Log in with "GUEST" for free access,
"NEW" for new user or Ctrl-D to exit

NAME: radrichard
PASS: ✗✗✗✗✗✗

You've logged.0 of 60 minutes today!
Your session will expire at 10:19:03

MOTD: Don't Panic!! SYSOPS are ditto
and altair

To list available commands, type <?>
```

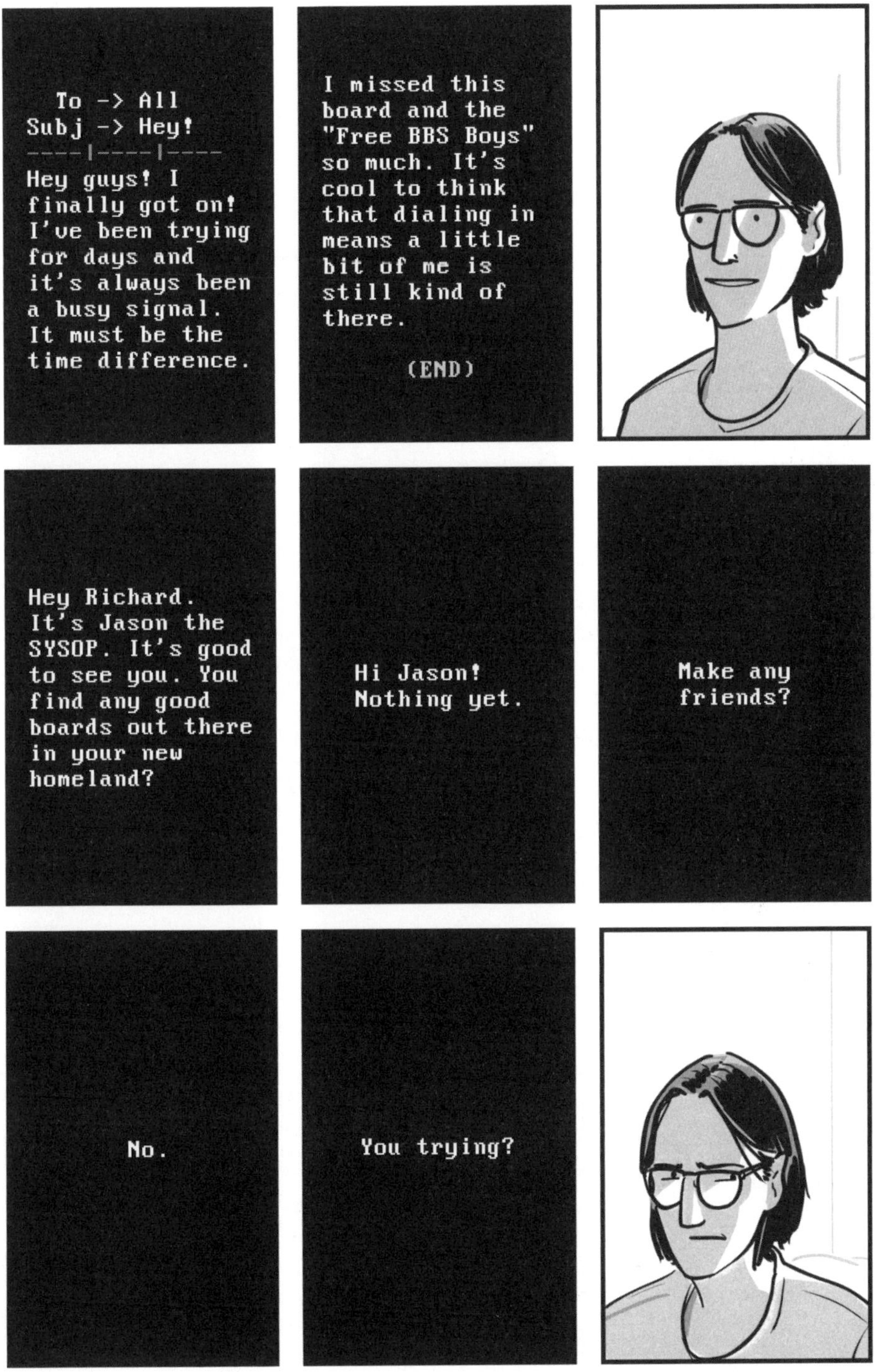
To -> All
Subj -> Hey!
-----|-----|-----
Hey guys! I finally got on! I've been trying for days and it's always been a busy signal. It must be the time difference.
I missed this board and the "Free BBS Boys" so much. It's cool to think that dialing in means a little bit of me is still kind of there.
(END)
Hey Richard. It's Jason the SYSOP. It's good to see you. You find any good boards out there in your new homeland?
Hi Jason! Nothing yet.
Make any friends?
No.
You trying?

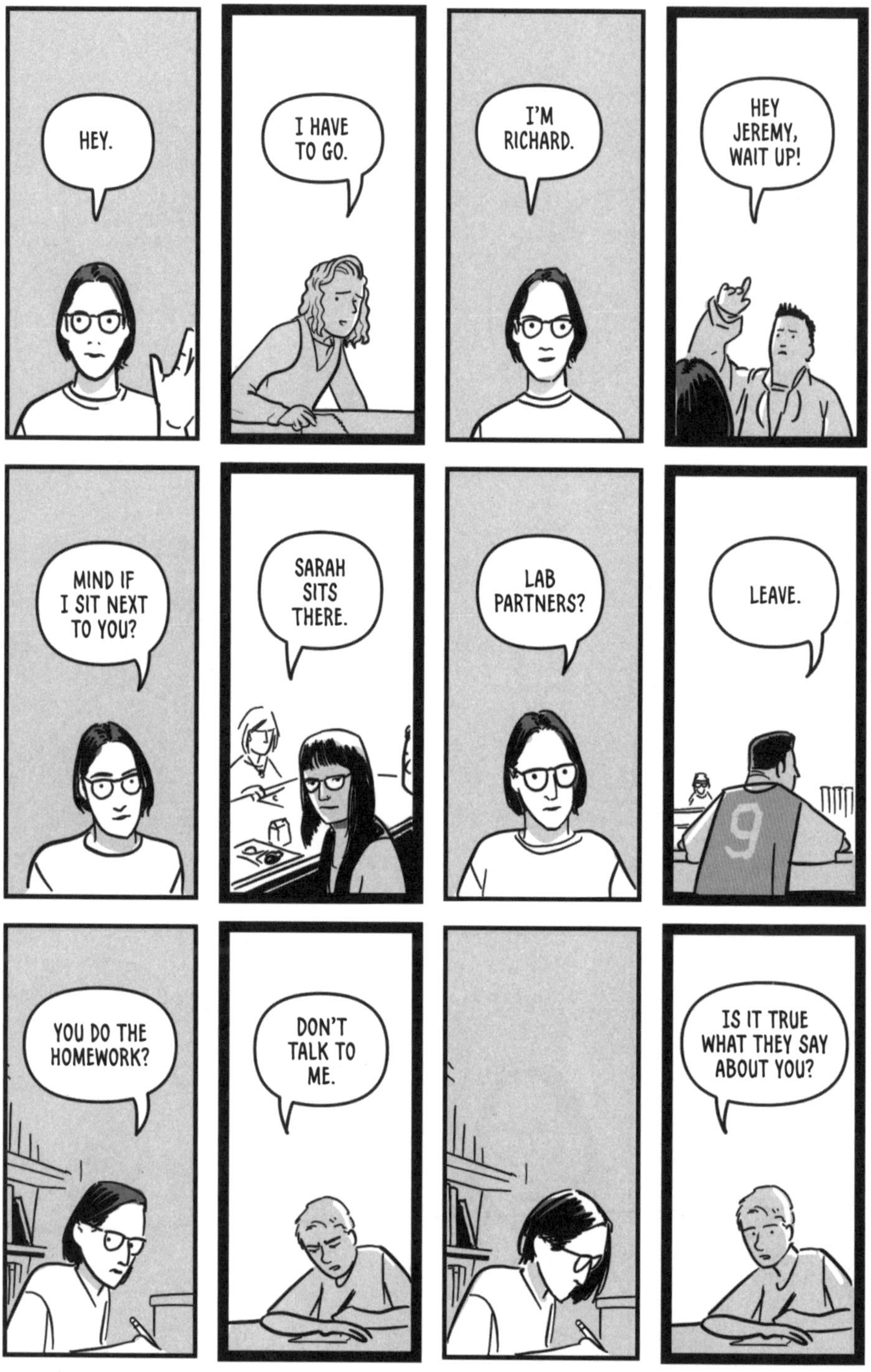
HEY.
I HAVE TO GO.
I'M RICHARD.
HEY JEREMY, WAIT UP!
MIND IF I SIT NEXT TO YOU?
SARAH SITS THERE.
LAB PARTNERS?
LEAVE.
9
YOU DO THE HOMEWORK?
DON'T TALK TO ME.
IS IT TRUE WHAT THEY SAY ABOUT YOU?

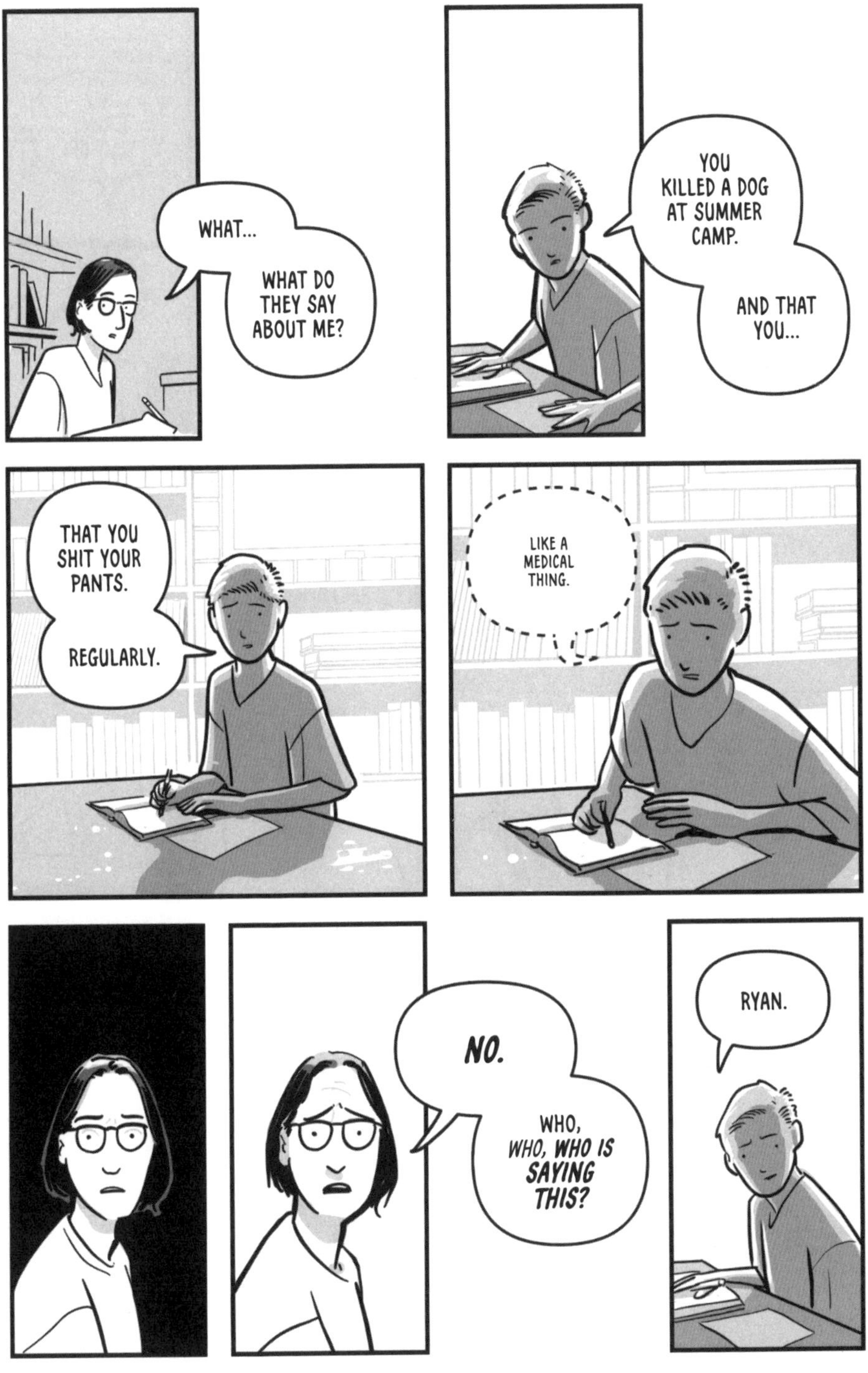
WHAT...
WHAT DO THEY SAY ABOUT ME?
YOU KILLED A DOG AT SUMMER CAMP.
AND THAT YOU...
THAT YOU SHIT YOUR PANTS.
REGULARLY.
LIKE A MEDICAL THING.
NO.
WHO, WHO, WHO IS SAYING THIS?
RYAN.

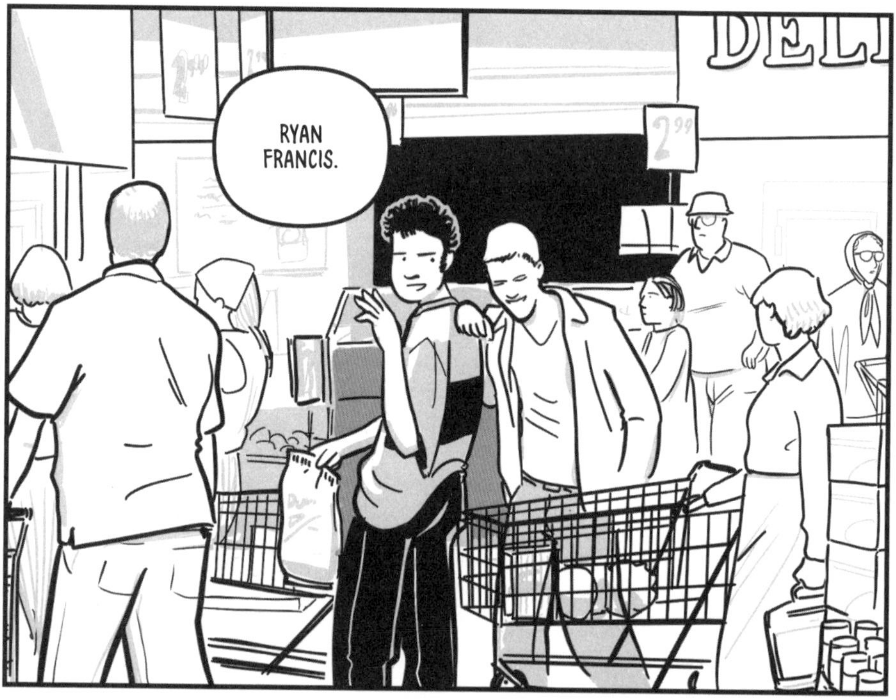
DELI
2.99
RYAN FRANCIS.

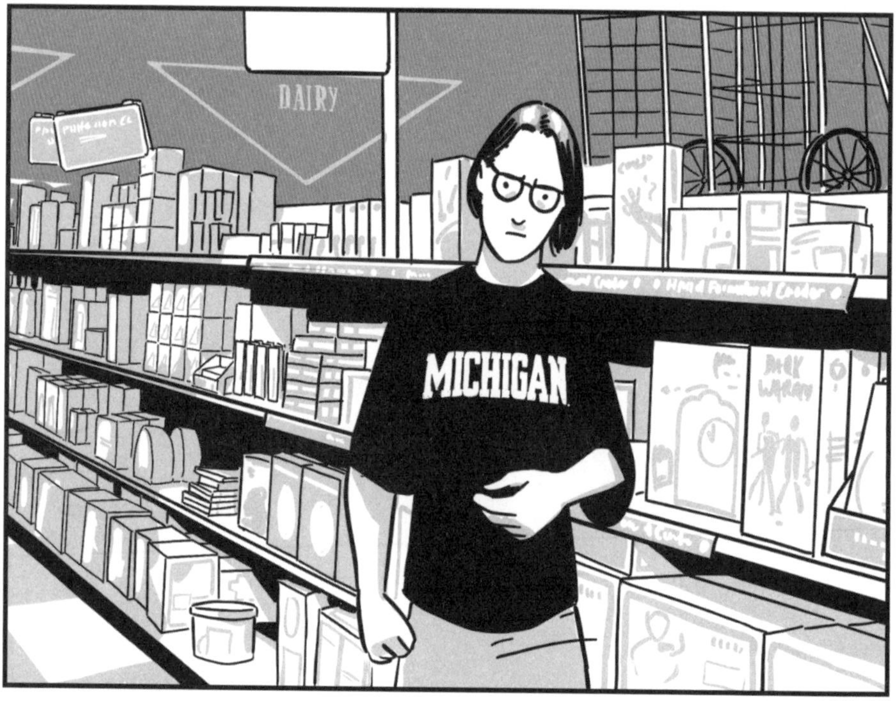
DAIRY
MICHIGAN

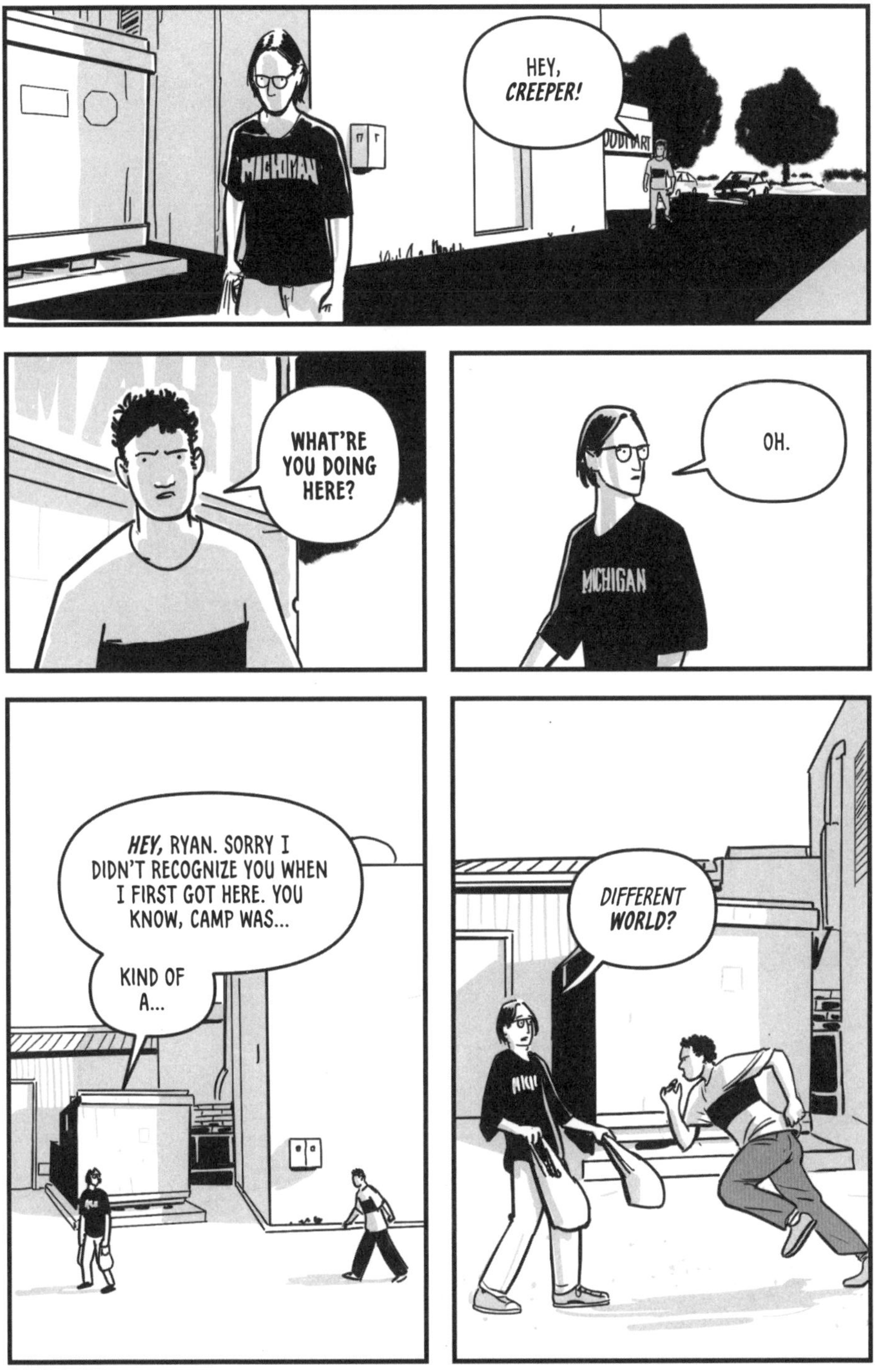
HEY, CREEPER!
WHAT'RE YOU DOING HERE?
OH.
HEY, RYAN. SORRY I DIDN'T RECOGNIZE YOU WHEN I FIRST GOT HERE. YOU KNOW, CAMP WAS...
KIND OF A...
DIFFERENT WORLD?

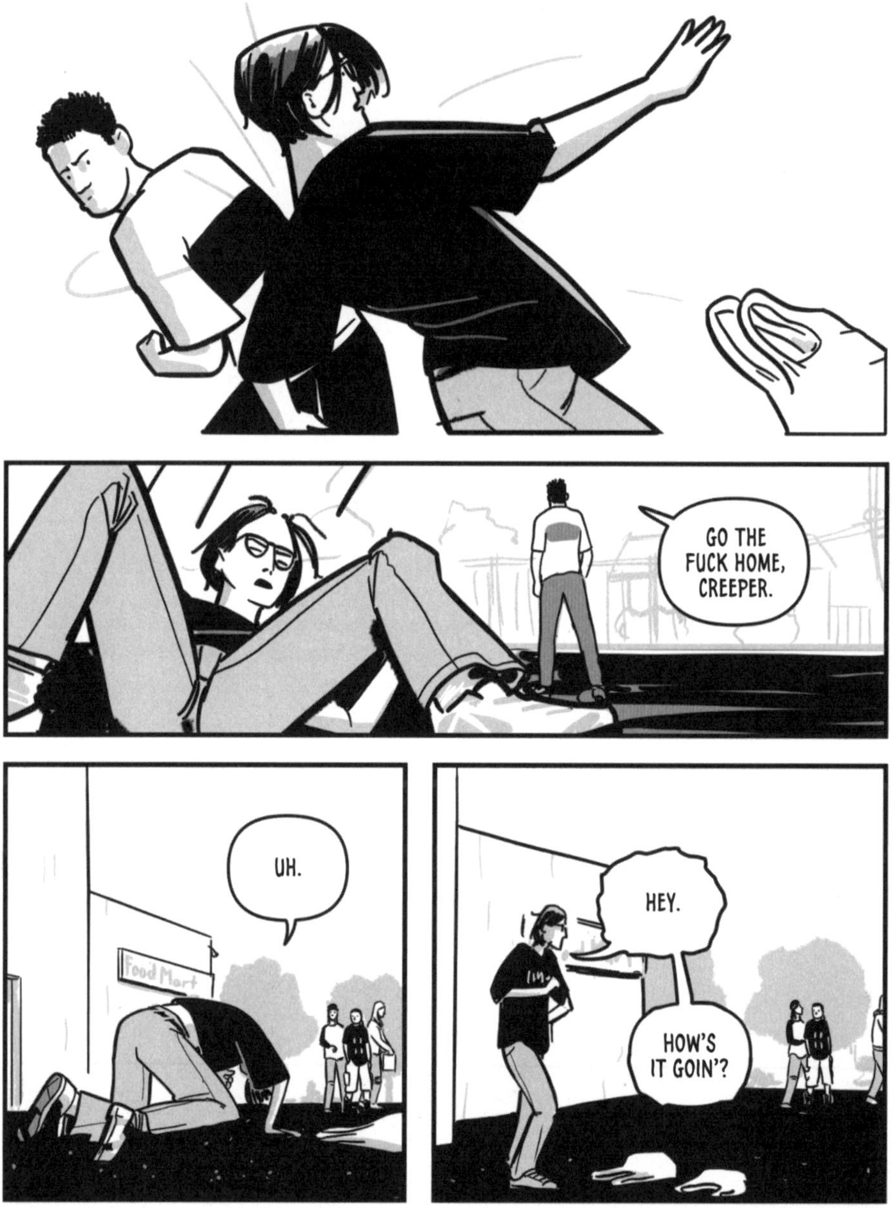
GO THE FUCK HOME, CREEPER.
Food Mart
UH.
HEY.
HOW'S IT GOIN'?

```
   In -> All
Subj -> This Town
----|----|----|----|----|----|----
So...I don't know.
Evidently I'm already screwed in
this new school. I thought I left
the sign that said "Be a dick to
me" in Ann Arbor.

I miss the Denny's on Edgewood Rd.
I miss Larsen Electronics and you
guys.

To heck with these people. I'll
always have this board. Post a
lot about what's going on okay? I'm
just going to live vicariously
through you.

_ _ _ _ _ _ _ _ _ _ _ _ _ _ _ _ _ _ _ _

"It is a hard daydream to let go
of - that one has friends."
- Kurt Vonnegut Jr.
```

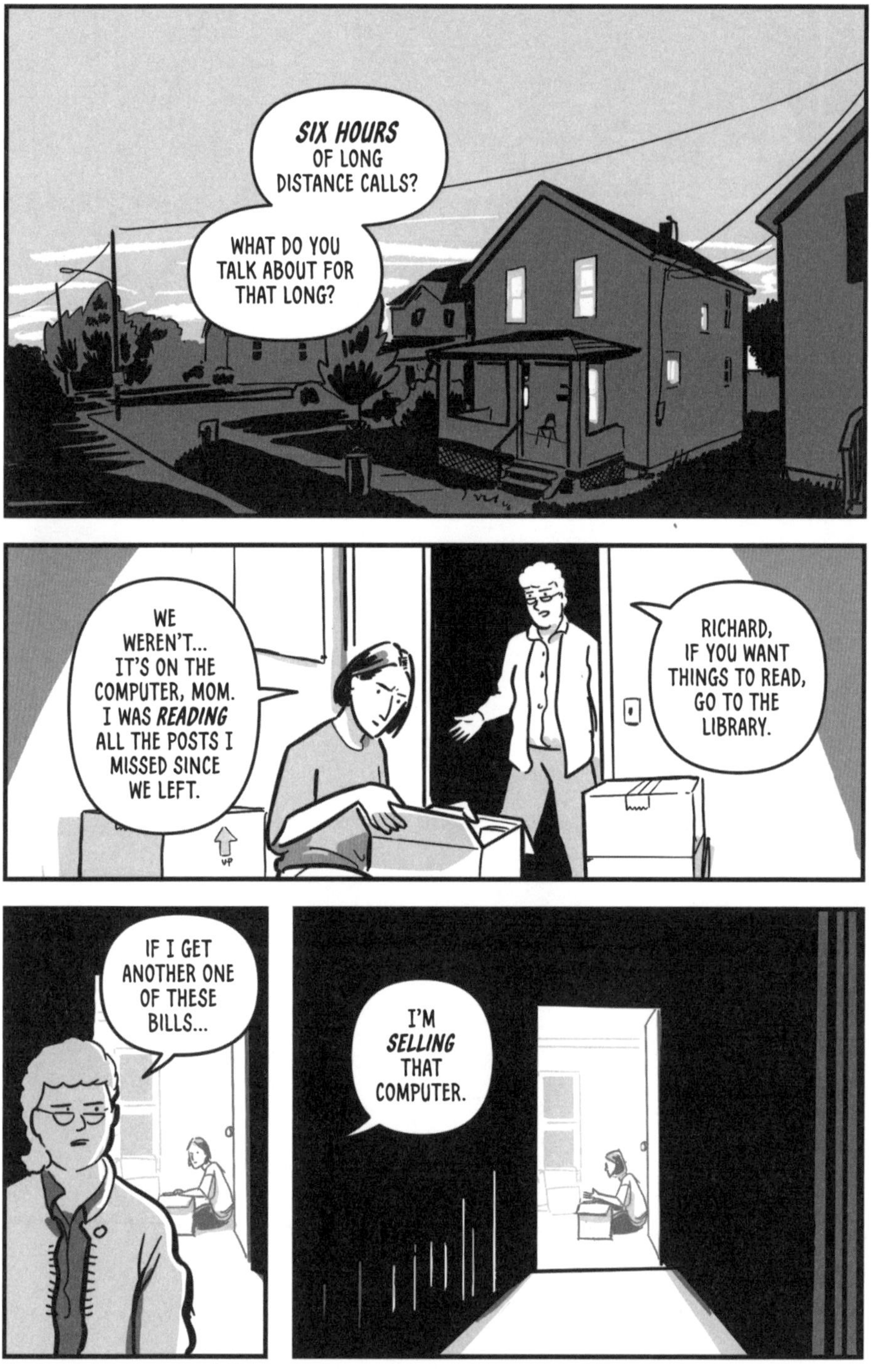
SIX HOURS OF LONG DISTANCE CALLS?
WHAT DO YOU TALK ABOUT FOR THAT LONG?
WE WEREN'T... IT'S ON THE COMPUTER, MOM. I WAS READING ALL THE POSTS I MISSED SINCE WE LEFT.
RICHARD, IF YOU WANT THINGS TO READ, GO TO THE LIBRARY.
UP
IF I GET ANOTHER ONE OF THESE BILLS...
I'M SELLING THAT COMPUTER.

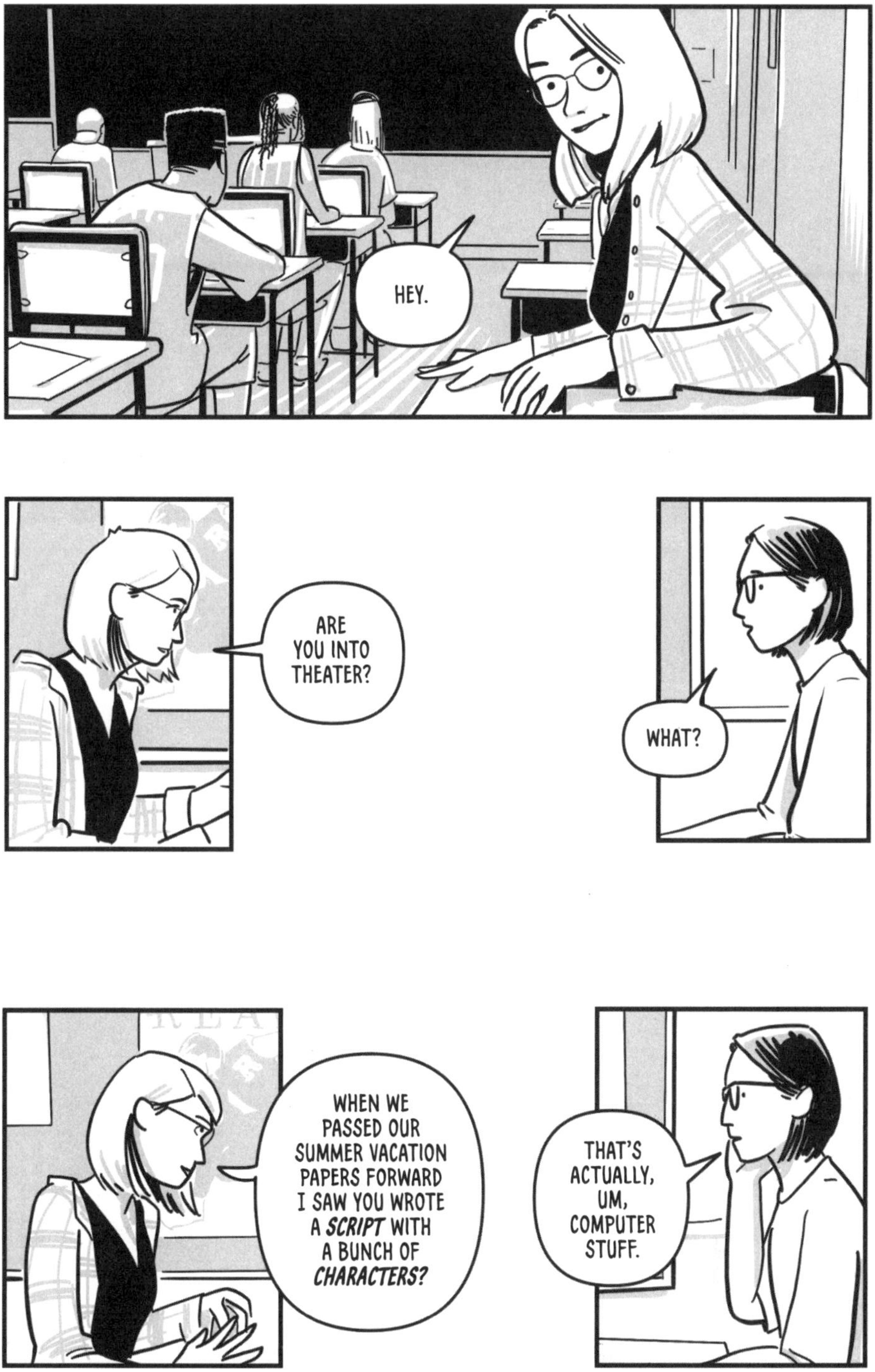
HEY.
ARE YOU INTO THEATER?
WHAT?
WHEN WE PASSED OUR SUMMER VACATION PAPERS FORWARD I SAW YOU WROTE A ***SCRIPT*** WITH A BUNCH OF ***CHARACTERS?***
THAT'S ACTUALLY, UM, COMPUTER STUFF.

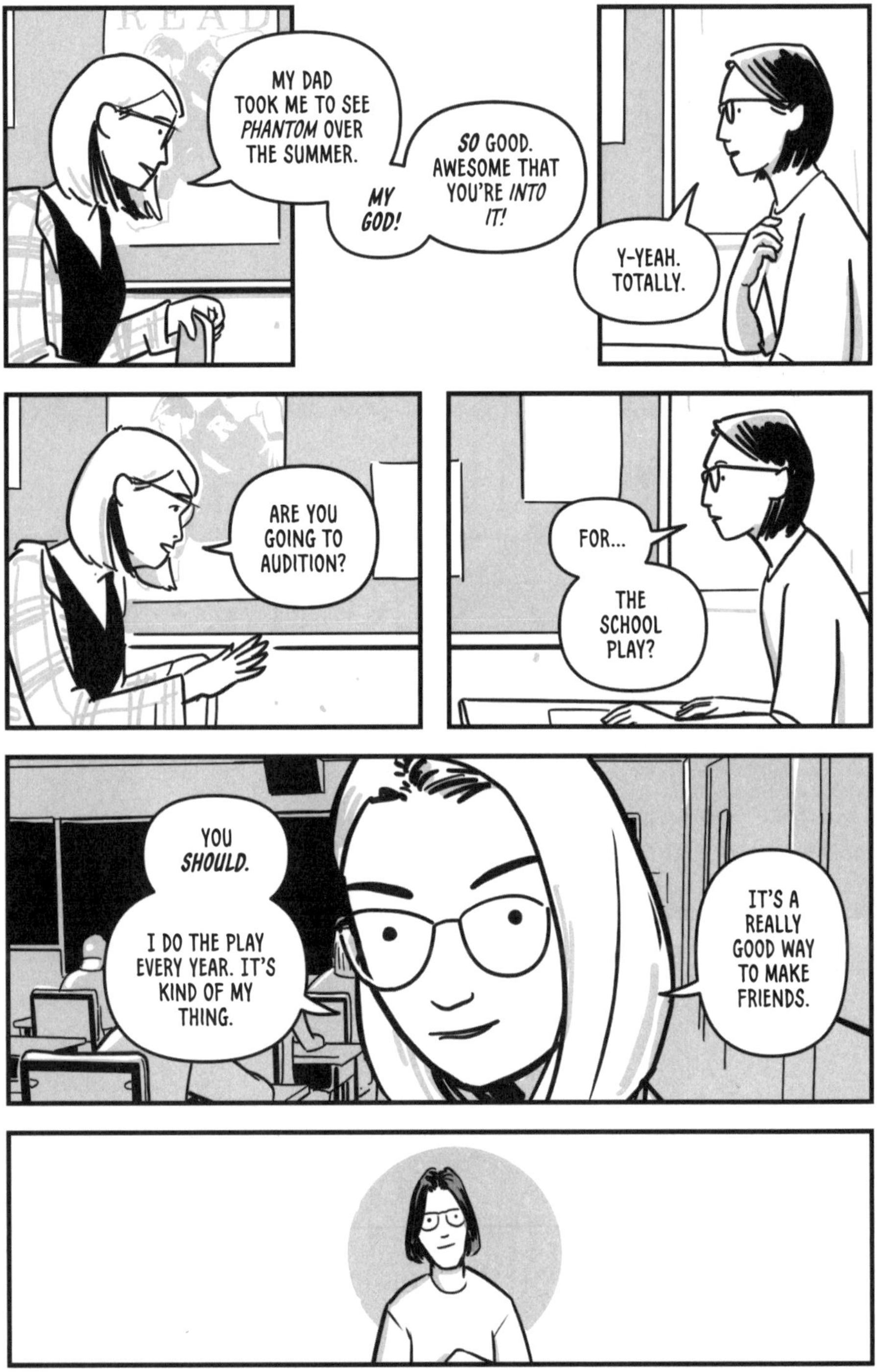
MY DAD TOOK ME TO SEE *PHANTOM* OVER THE SUMMER.
MY GOD!
SO GOOD. AWESOME THAT YOU'RE *INTO* IT!
Y-YEAH. TOTALLY.
ARE YOU GOING TO AUDITION?
FOR...
THE SCHOOL PLAY?
YOU *SHOULD.*
I DO THE PLAY EVERY YEAR. IT'S KIND OF MY THING.
IT'S A REALLY GOOD WAY TO MAKE FRIENDS.

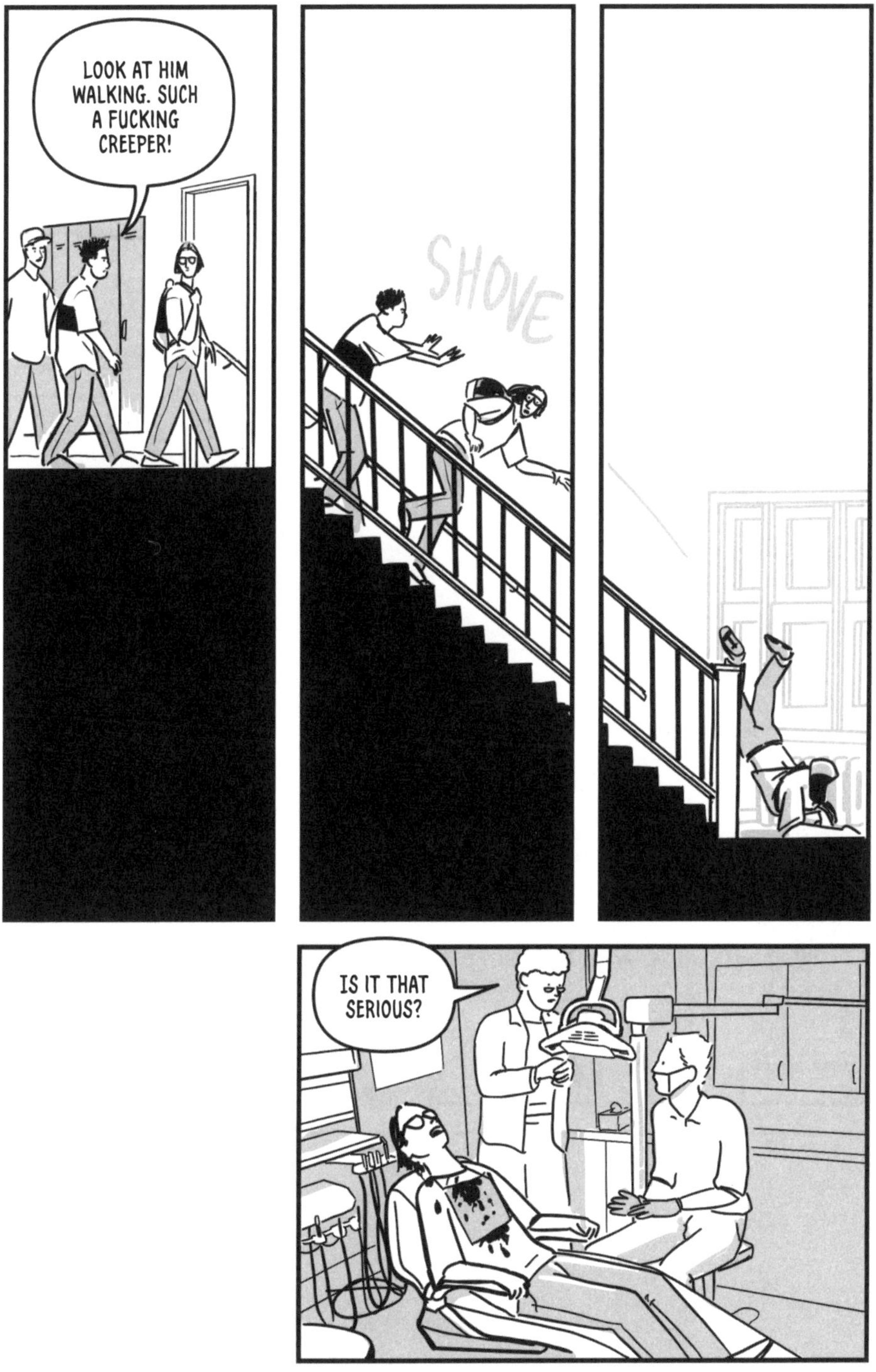
LOOK AT HIM WALKING. SUCH A FUCKING CREEPER!
SHOVE
IS IT THAT SERIOUS?

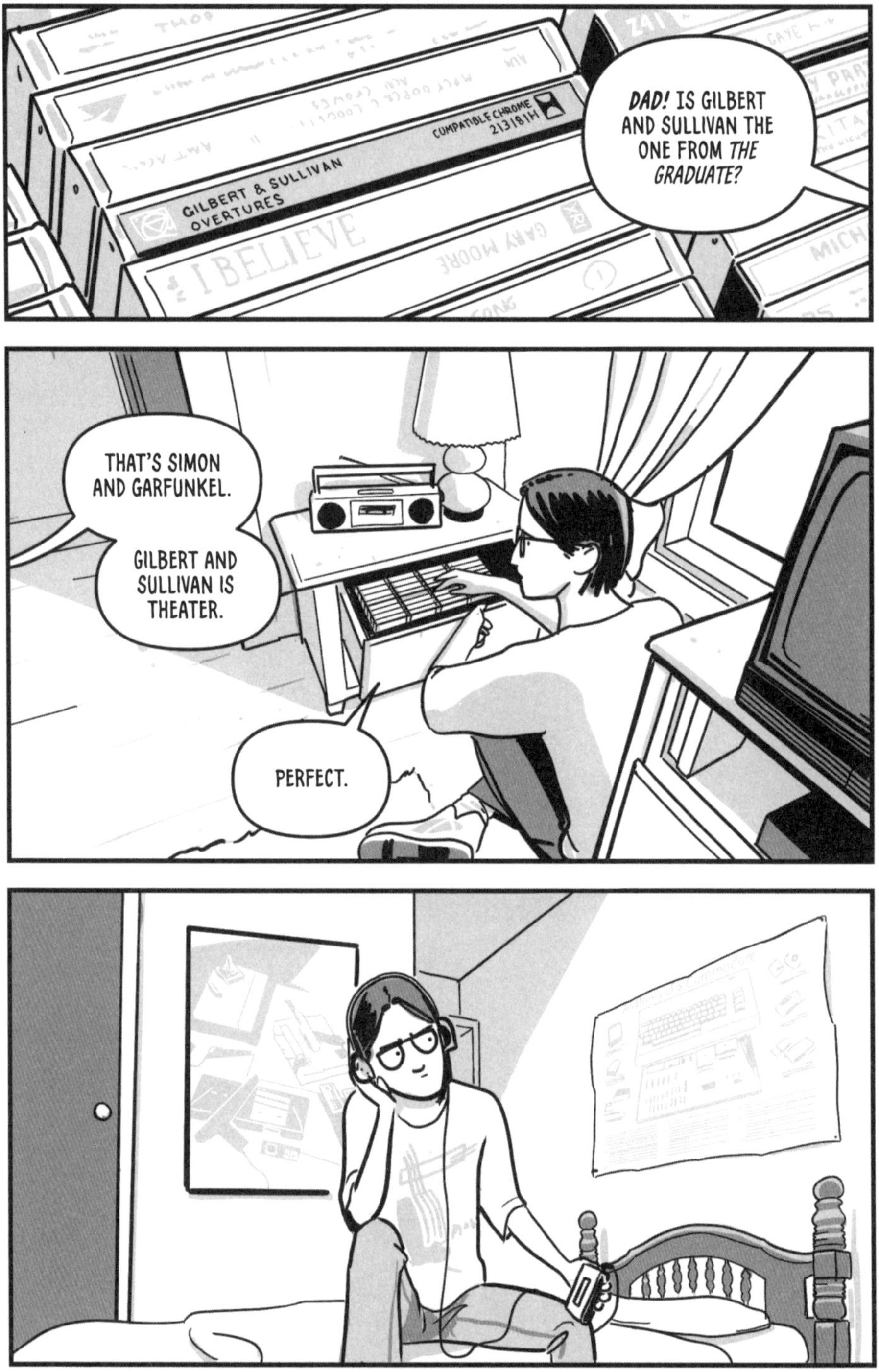

GILBERT & SULLIVAN
OVERTURES
I BELIEVE
GARY MOORE
DAD! IS GILBERT AND SULLIVAN THE ONE FROM *THE GRADUATE?*
THAT'S SIMON AND GARFUNKEL.
GILBERT AND SULLIVAN IS THEATER.
PERFECT.

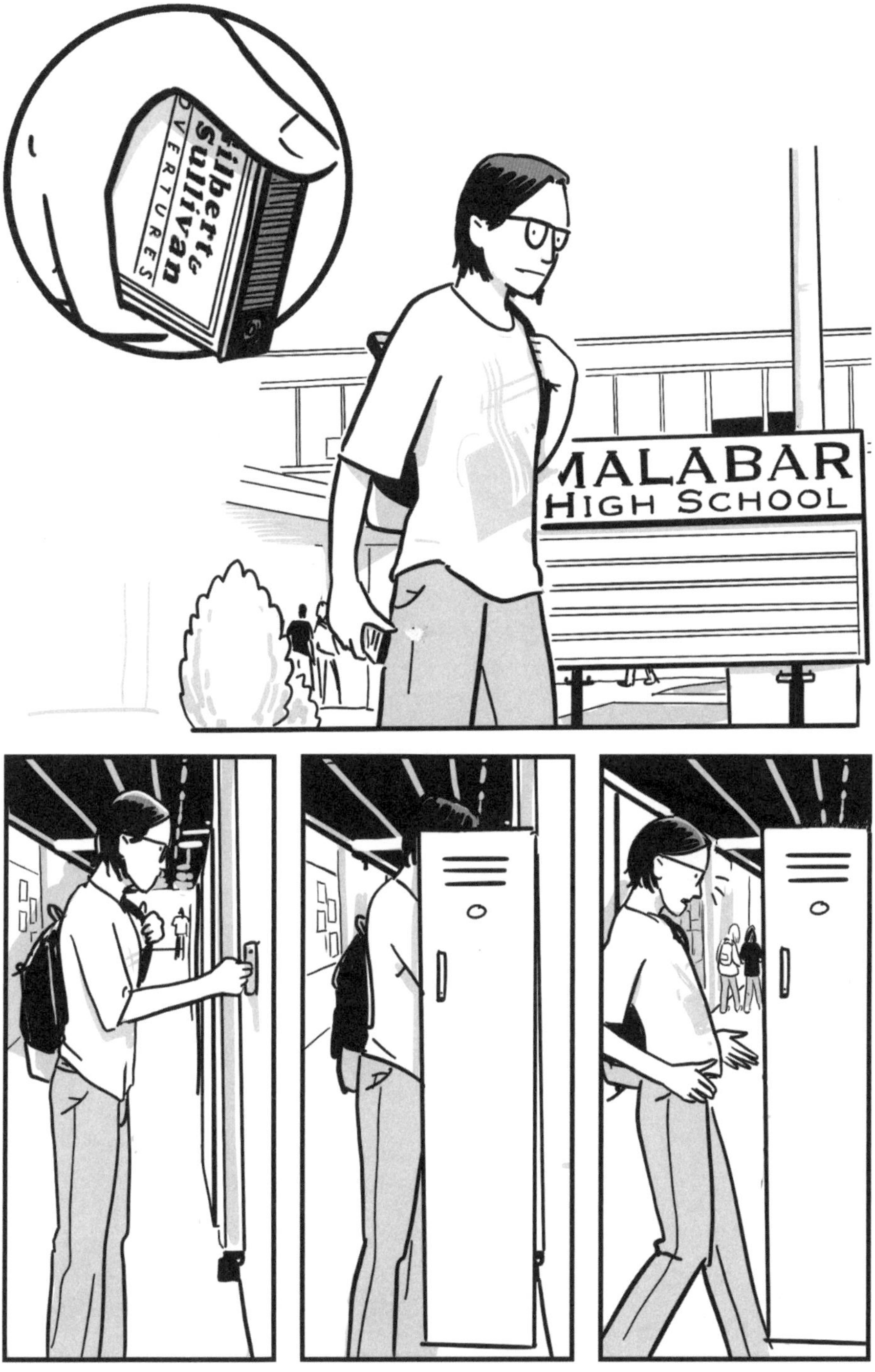
Sullivan
OVERTURES
MALABAR
HIGH SCHOOL

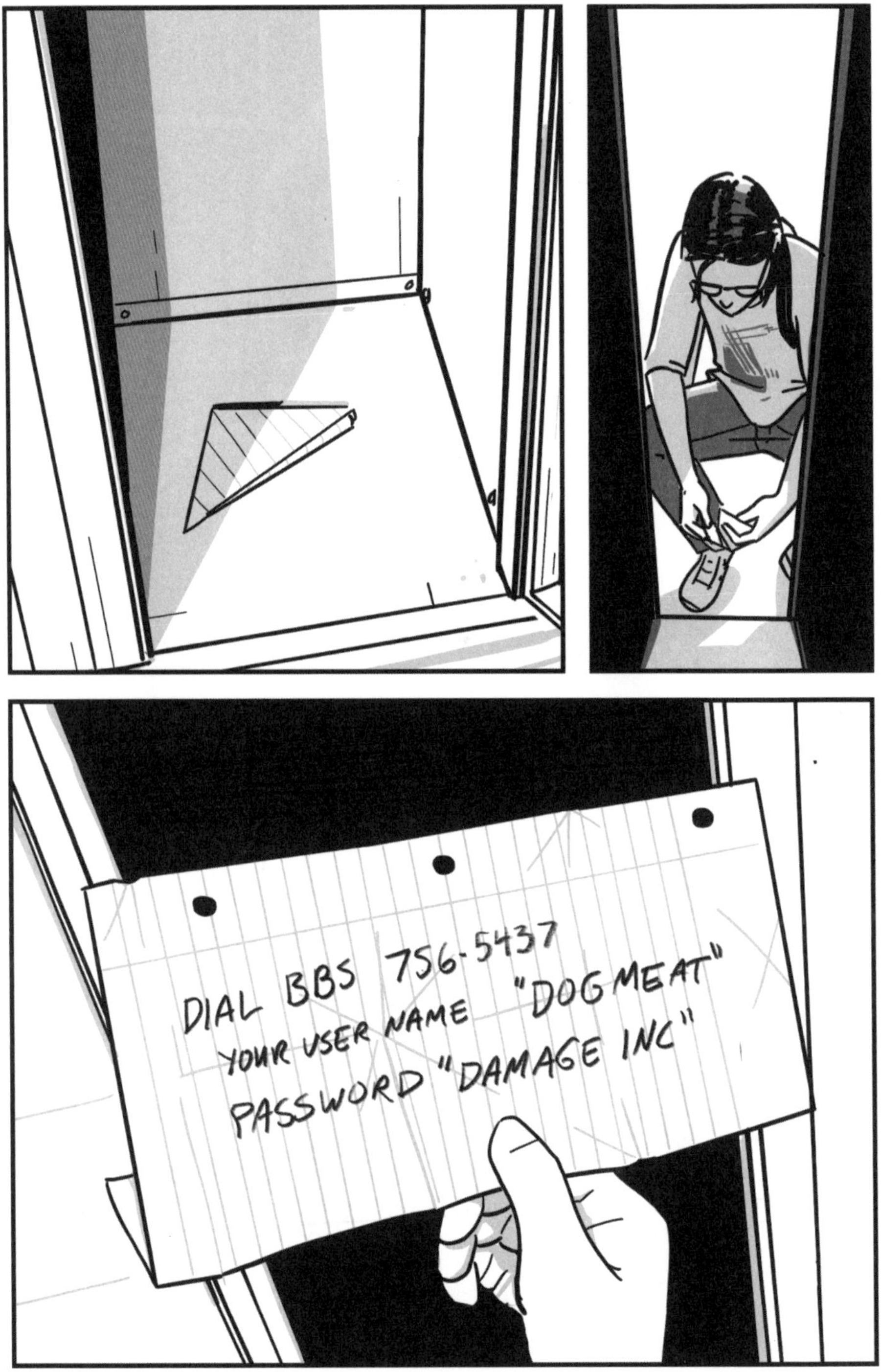
DIAL BBS 756-5437
YOUR USER NAME "DOGMEAT"
PASSWORD "DAMAGE INC"

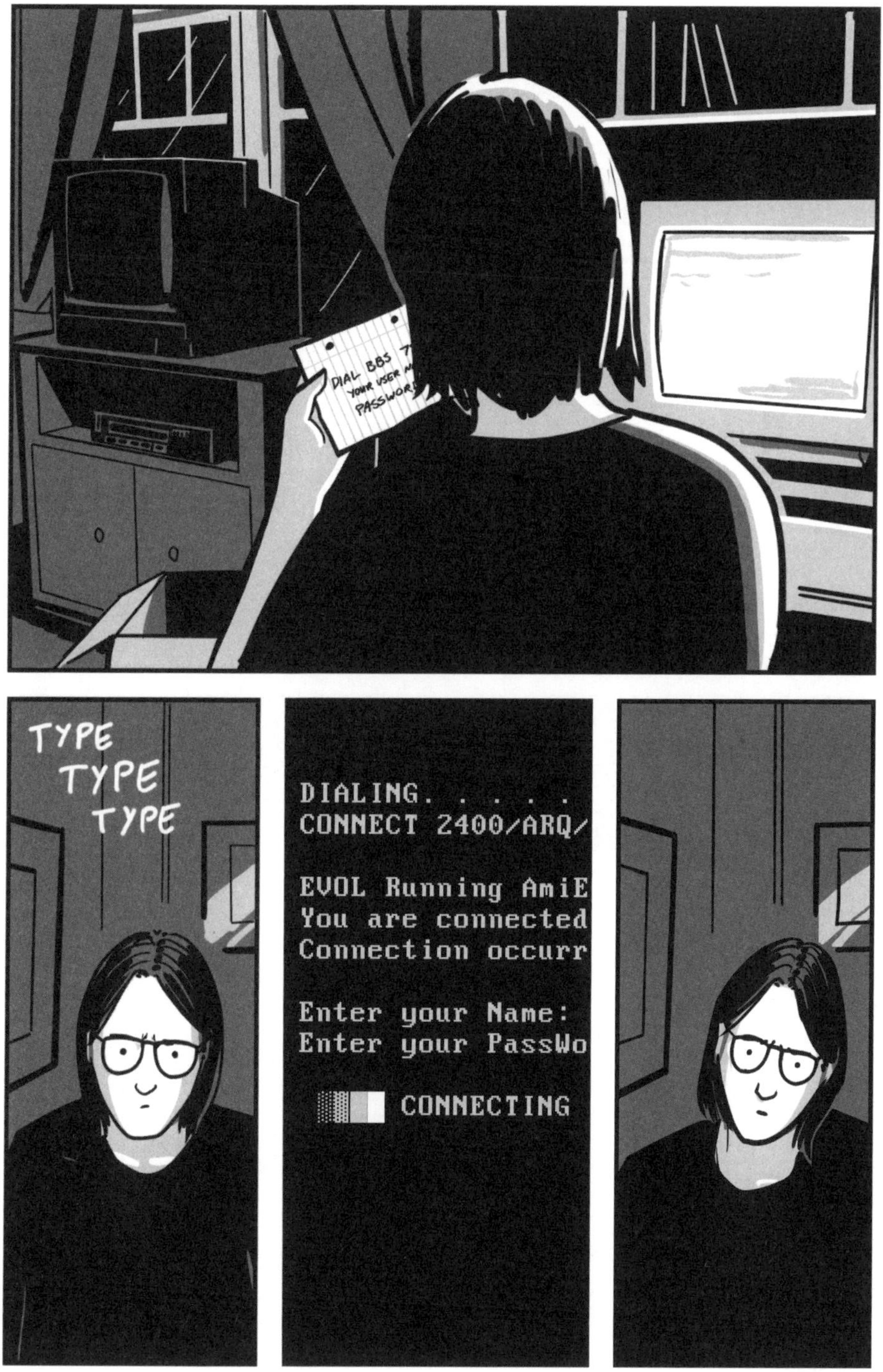
DIAL BBS
YOUR USER
TYPE
TYPE
TYPE
DIALING. . . . .
CONNECT 2400/ARQ/
EVOL Running AmiE
You are connected
Connection occurr
Enter your Name:
Enter your PassWo
CONNECTING

```
DIALING. . . . . . . . . .
CONNECT 2400/ARQ/TEL

EVOL Running AmiExpress 4.12 /X for life
You are connected to Node 2 at 2400 baud
Connection occurred at 11:13:21

Enter your Name: dogmeat
Enter your PassWord: damageinc
```

```
CONNECTING
```

```
CONNECTED TO EVOL BBS
NO GUESTS/NO LAMERS
NO GODS/NO MASTERS                    B B S
```

Welcome "dogmeat"

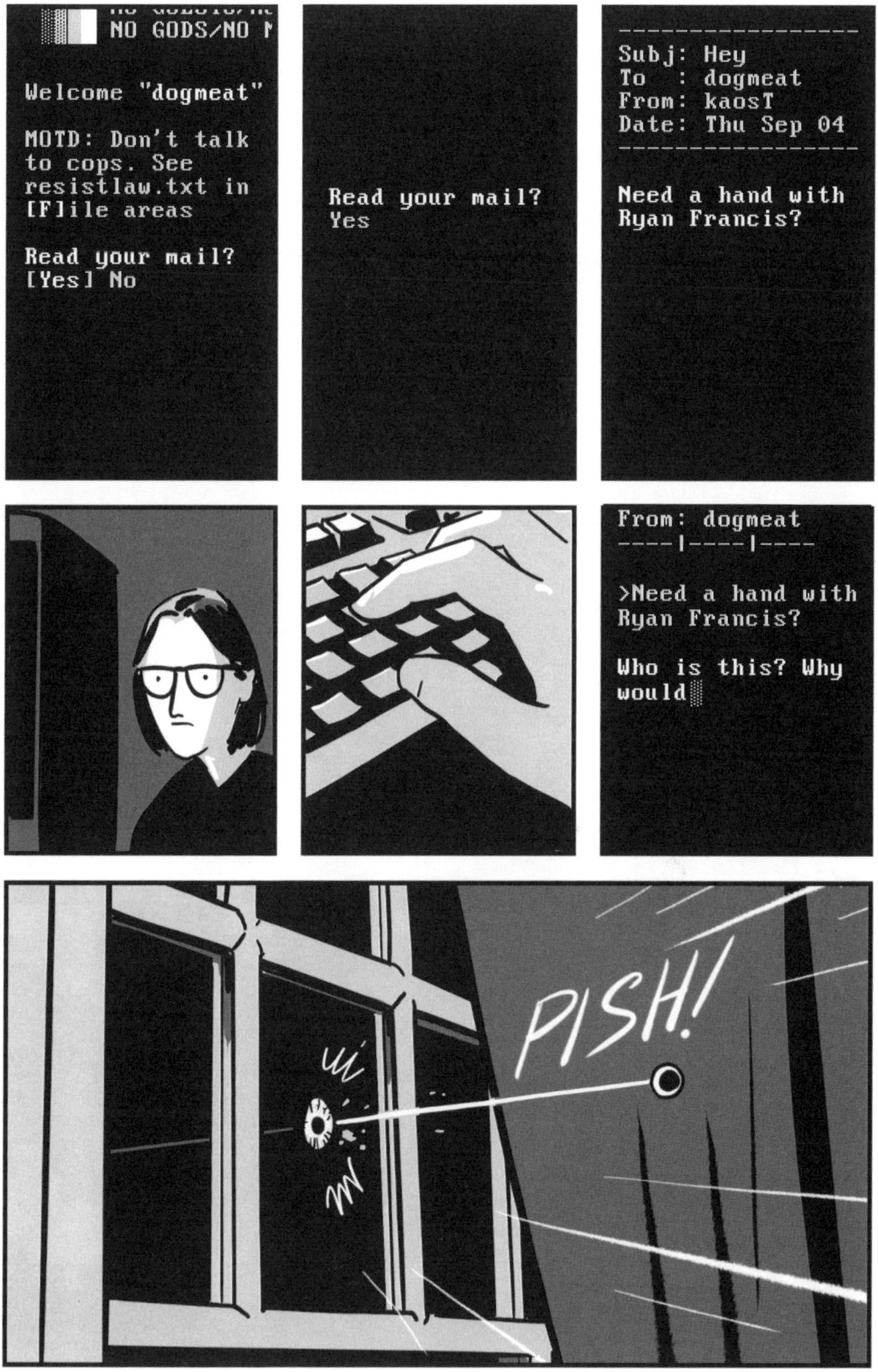
NO GODS/NO
Welcome "dogmeat"
MOTD: Don't talk to cops. See resistlaw.txt in [F]ile areas
Read your mail? [Yes] No
Read your mail? Yes

Subj: Hey
To : dogmeat
From: kaosT
Date: Thu Sep 04

Need a hand with Ryan Francis?
From: dogmeat
>Need a hand with Ryan Francis?
Who is this? Why would
PISH!

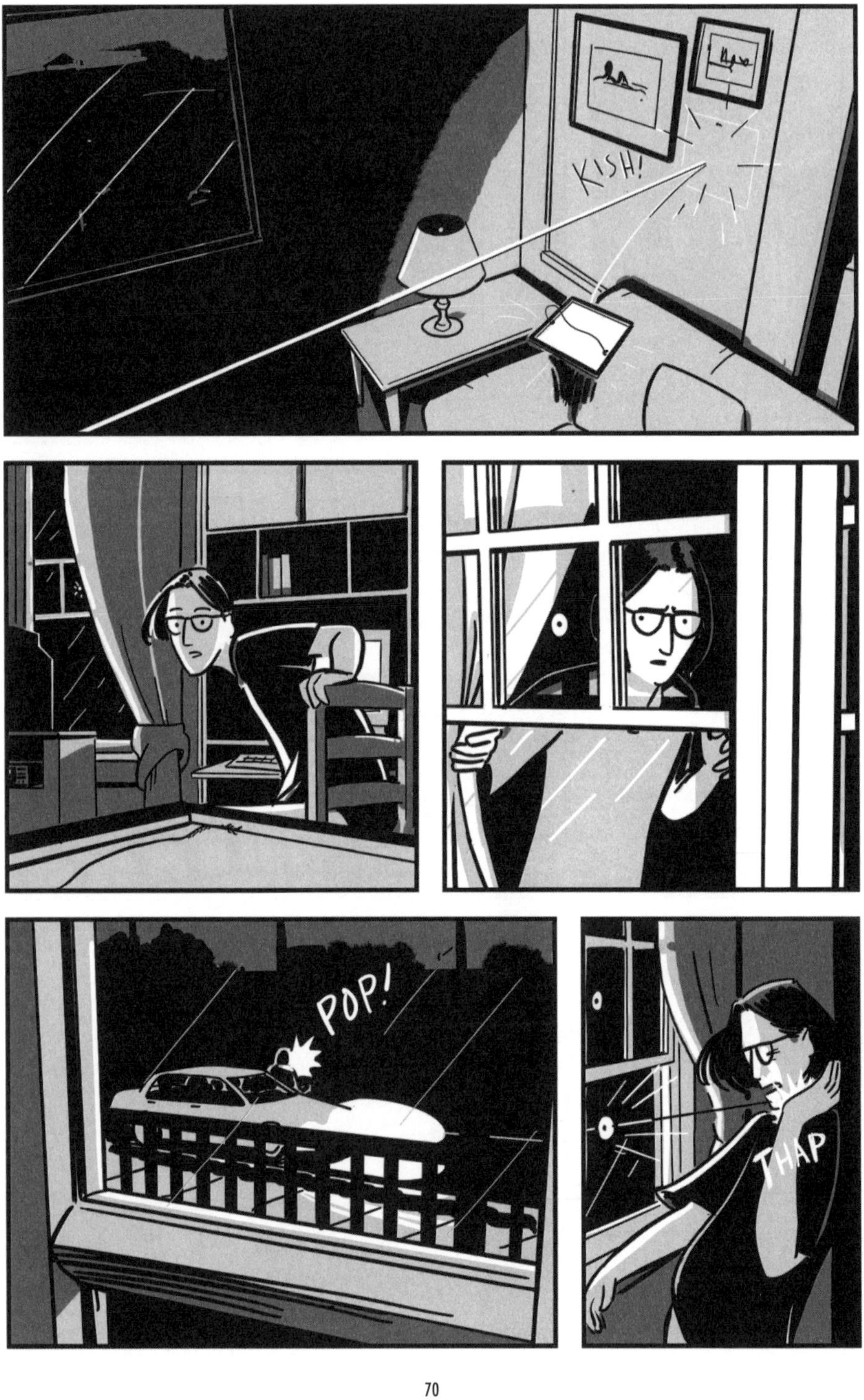
KISH!
POP!
THAP

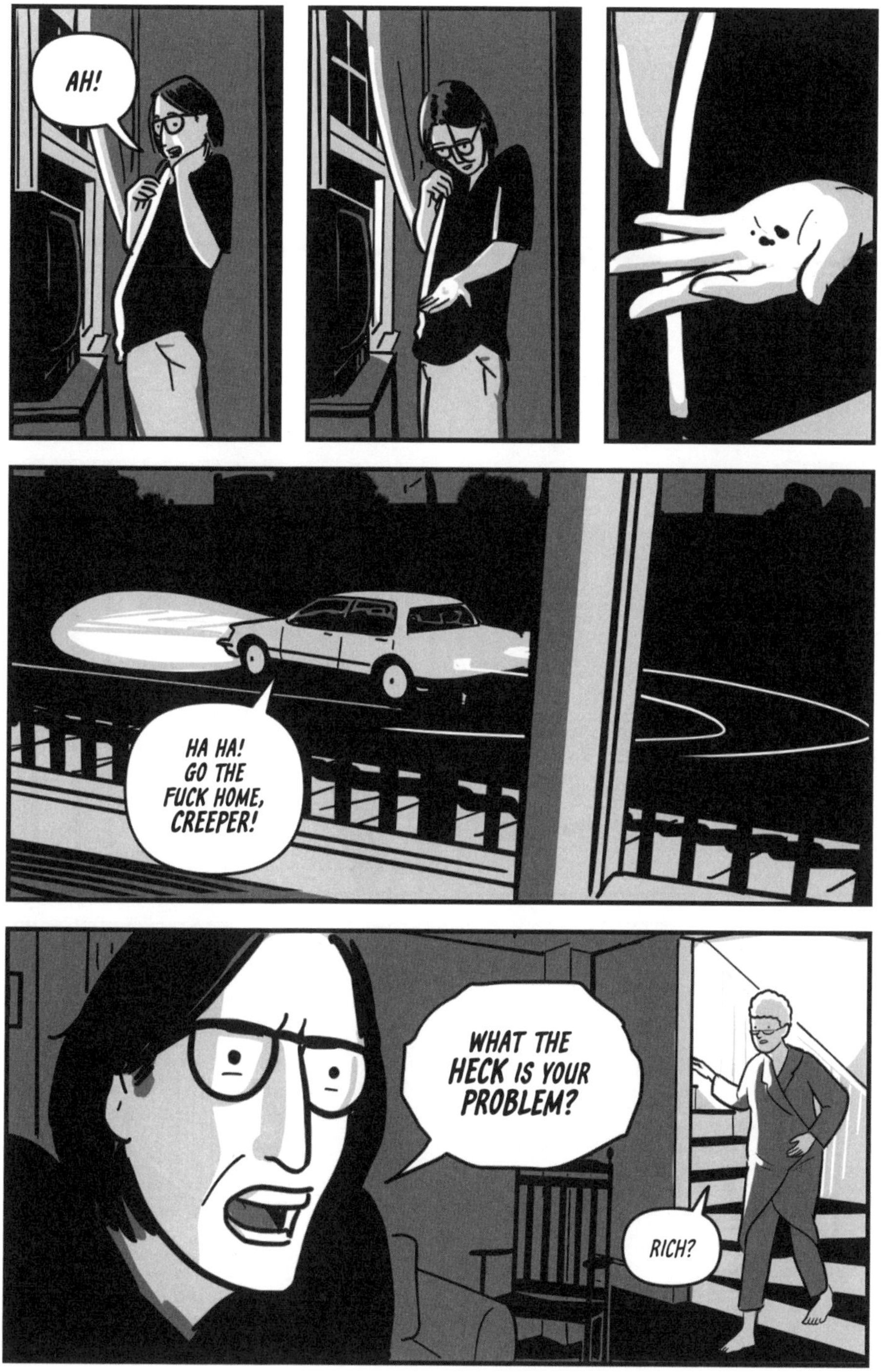
AH!
HA HA! GO THE FUCK HOME, CREEPER!
WHAT THE HECK IS YOUR PROBLEM?
RICH?

```
Subj: Re: Hey
To  : kaosT
From: dogmeat
----I----I----I----I----
>Need a hand with
Ryan Francis?

Whatever you can do.▊
```

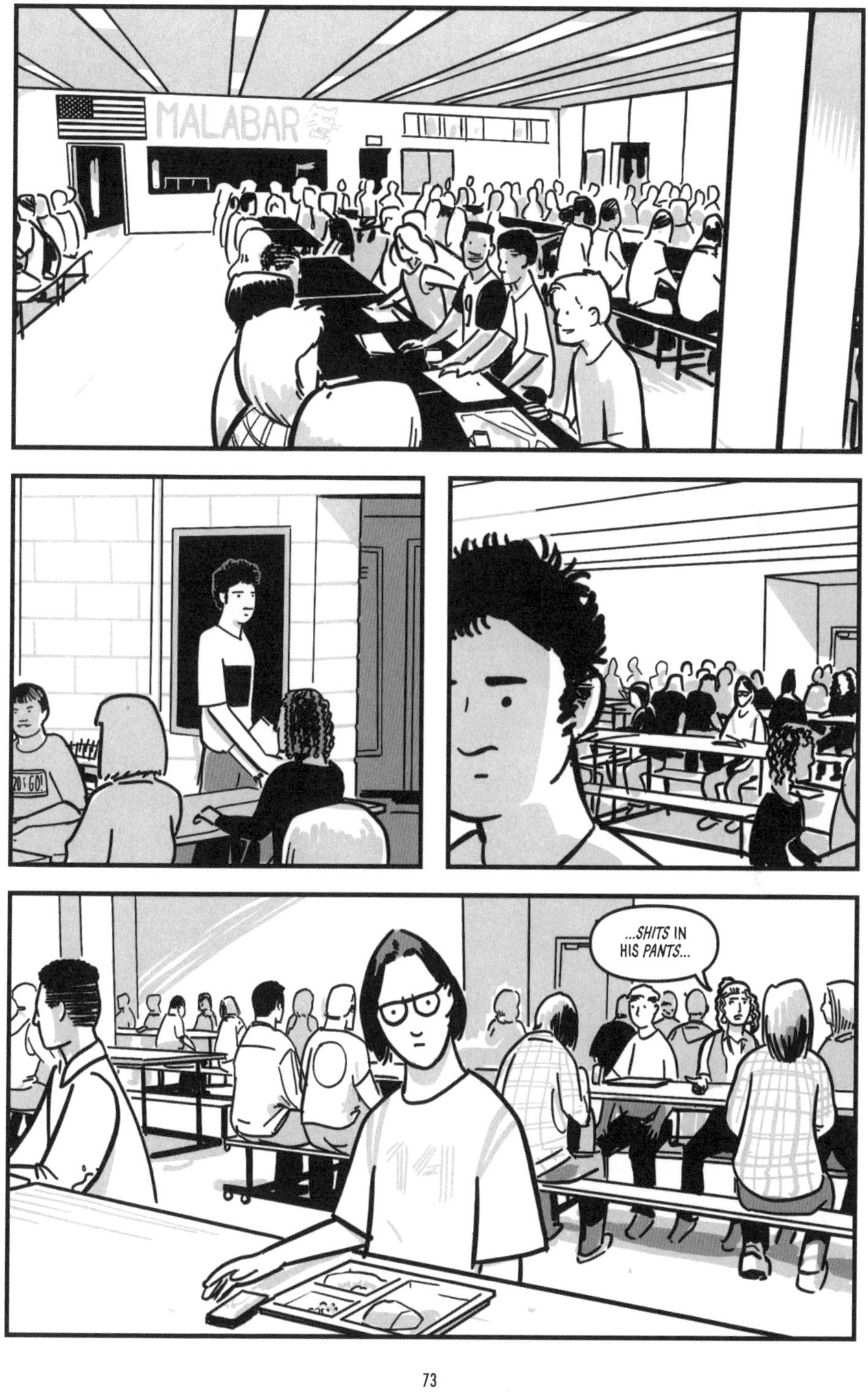
MALABAR
...SHITS IN HIS PANTS...

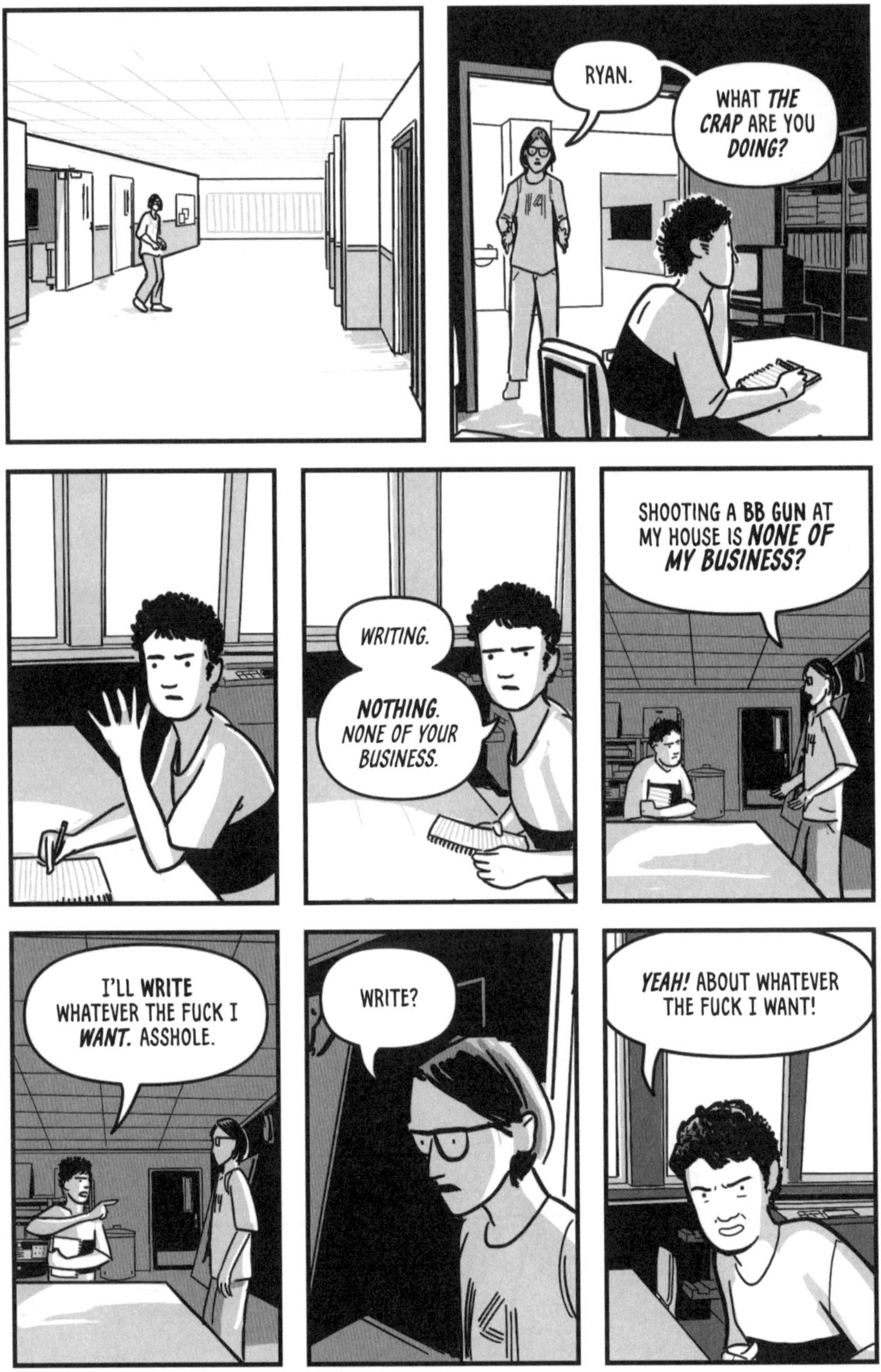
RYAN.
WHAT THE CRAP ARE YOU DOING?
WRITING.
NOTHING. NONE OF YOUR BUSINESS.
SHOOTING A BB GUN AT MY HOUSE IS NONE OF MY BUSINESS?
I'LL WRITE WHATEVER THE FUCK I WANT. ASSHOLE.
WRITE?
YEAH! ABOUT WHATEVER THE FUCK I WANT!

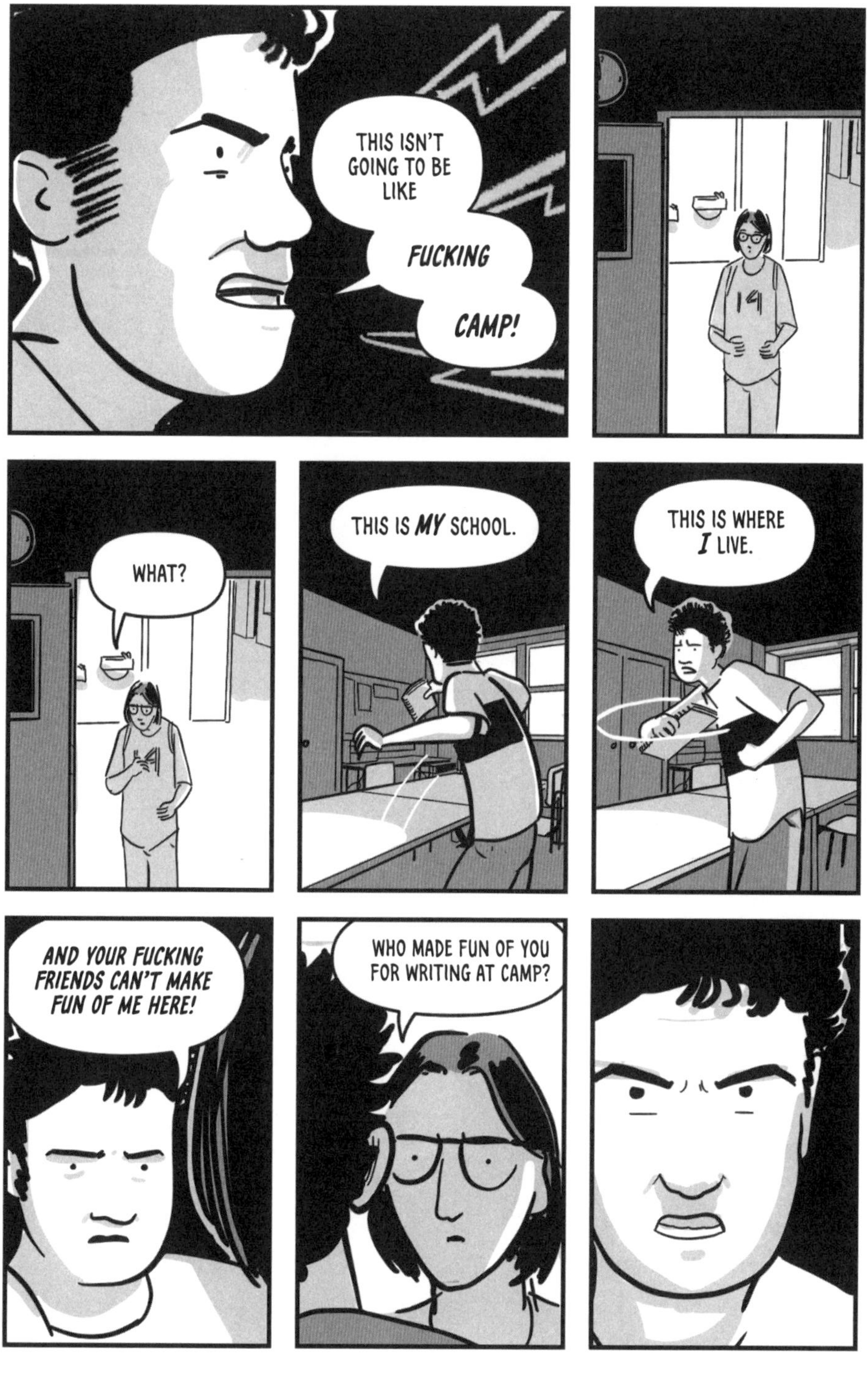
THIS ISN'T GOING TO BE LIKE
FUCKING
CAMP!
WHAT?
THIS IS MY SCHOOL.
THIS IS WHERE I LIVE.
AND YOUR FUCKING FRIENDS CAN'T MAKE FUN OF ME HERE!
WHO MADE FUN OF YOU FOR WRITING AT CAMP?

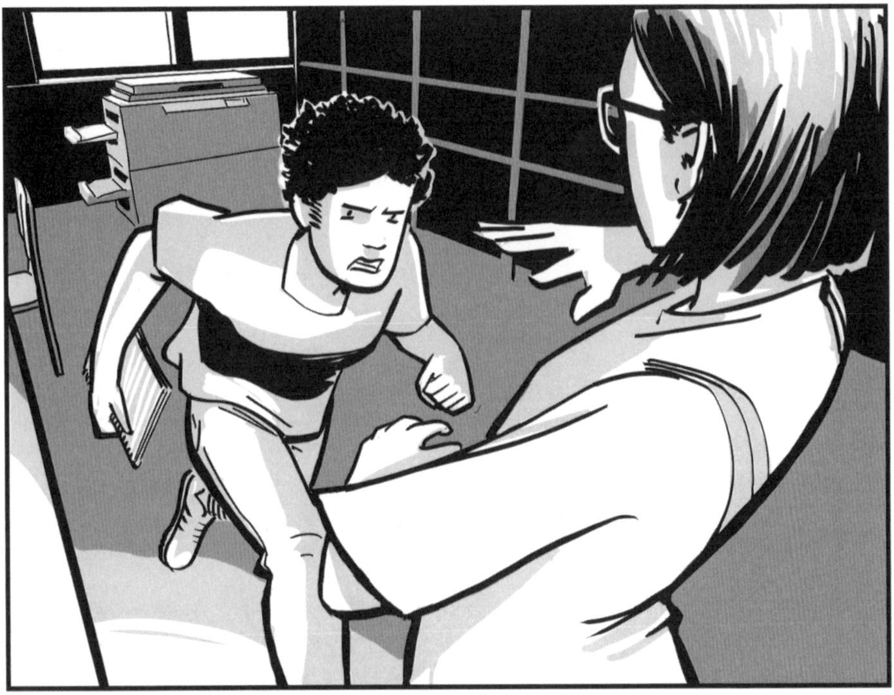

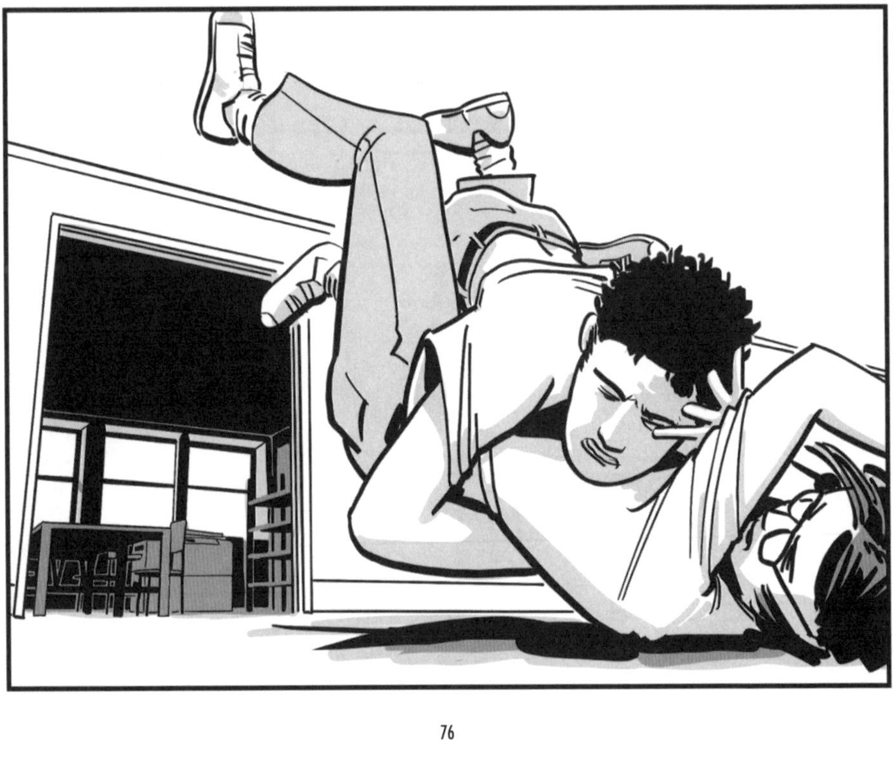

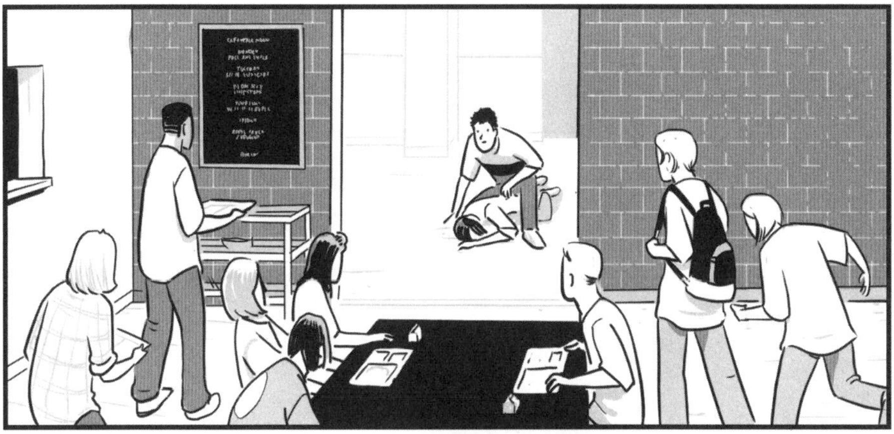

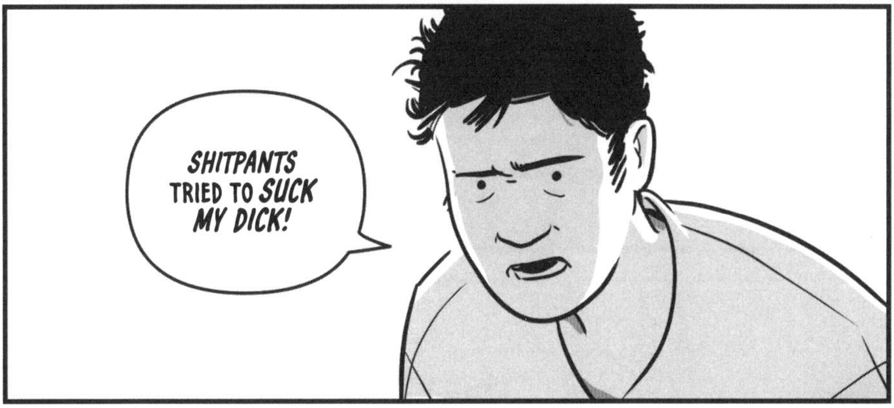
SHITPANTS TRIED TO SUCK MY DICK!

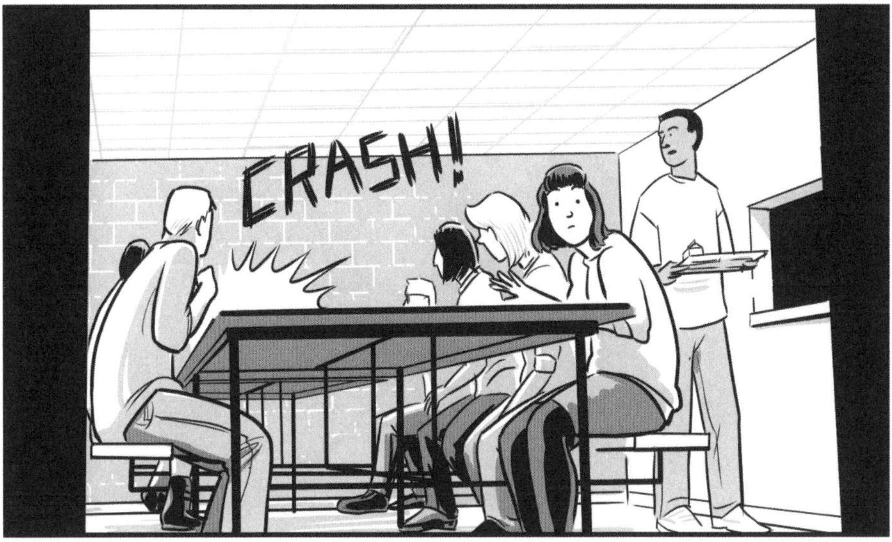
CRASH!

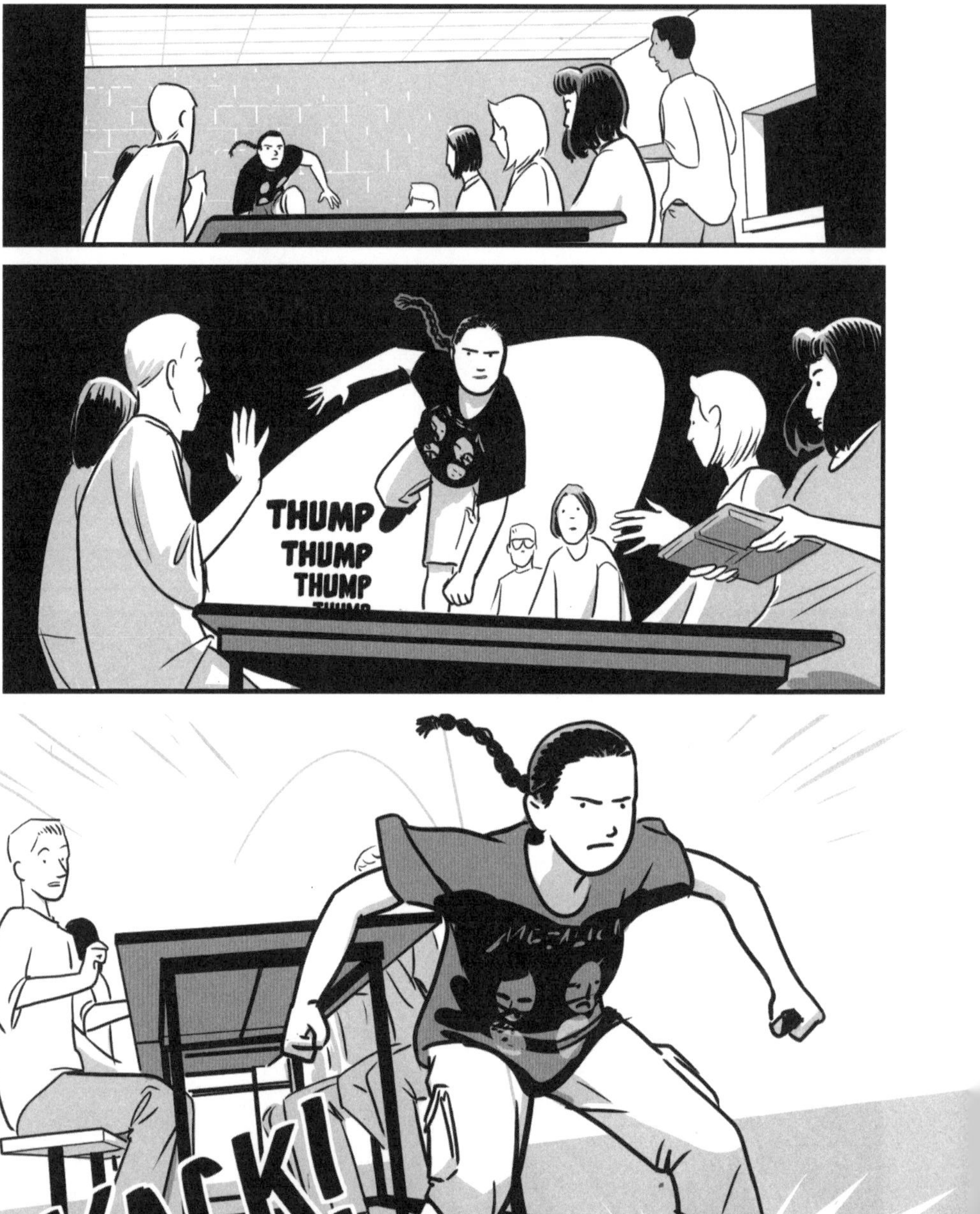
THUMP
THUMP
THUMP
KACK!

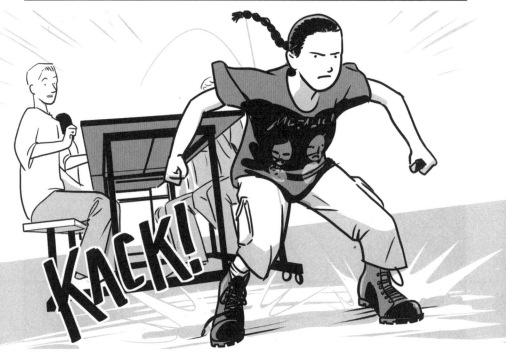

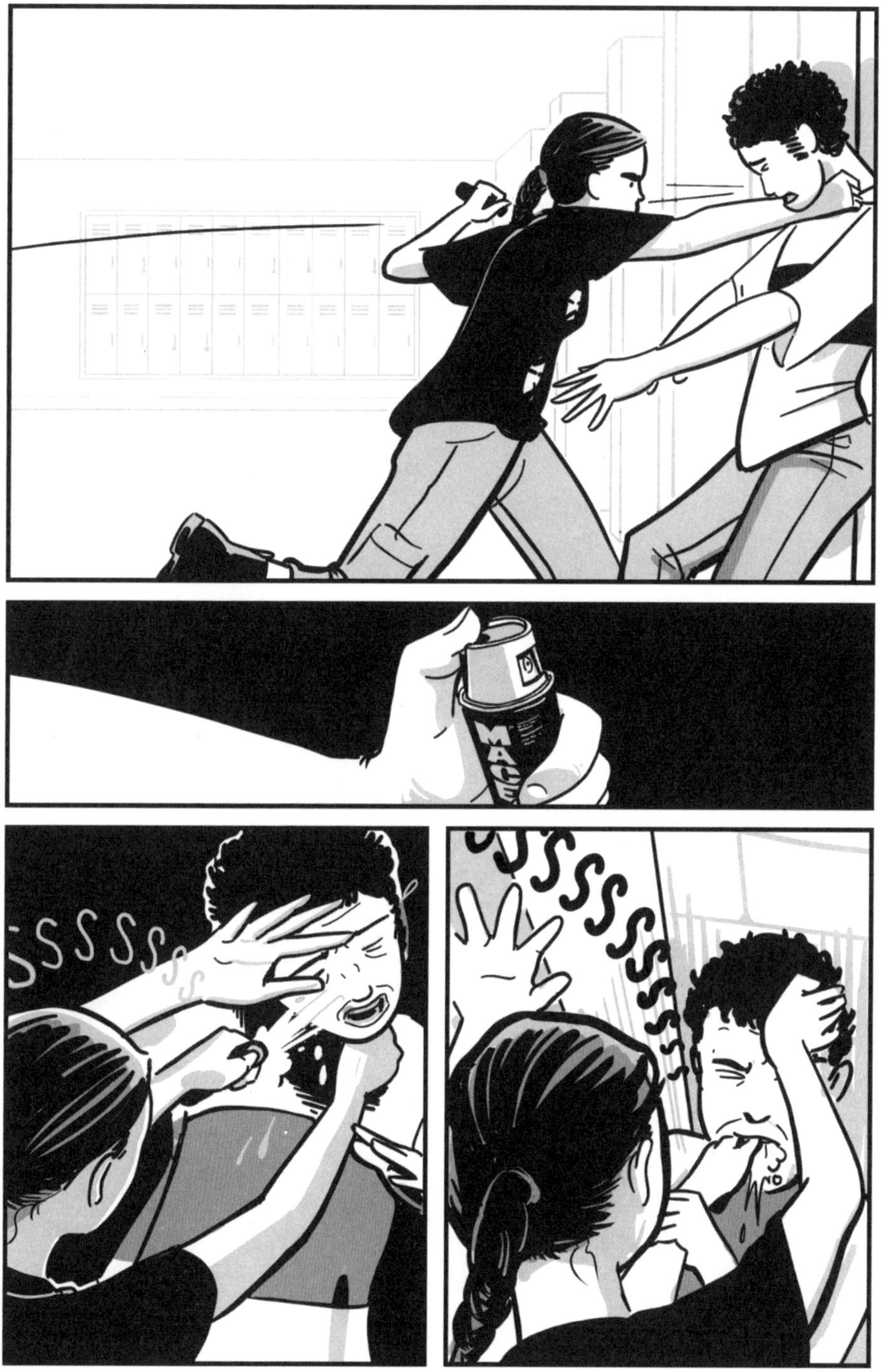
MACE
SSSSSSS
SSSSSSSSS

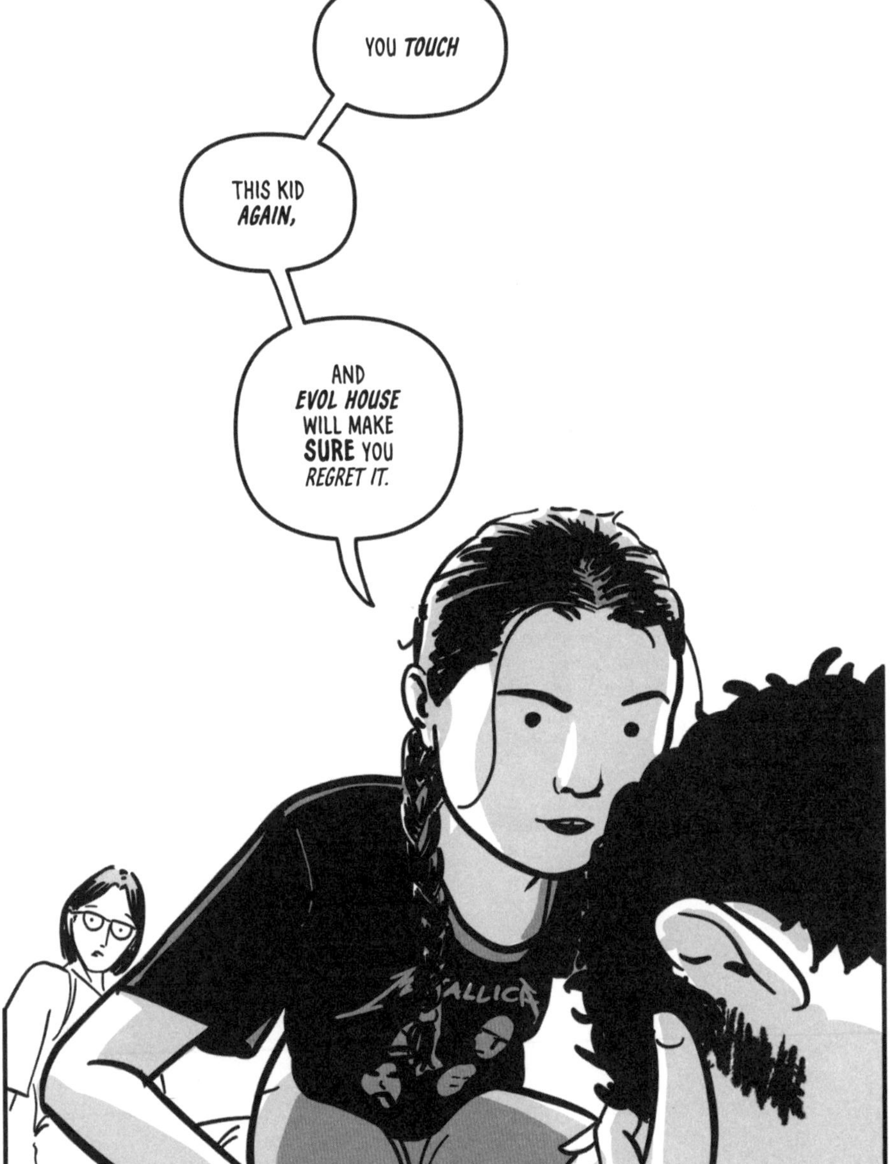
YOU *TOUCH*
THIS KID *AGAIN,*
AND *EVOL HOUSE* WILL MAKE **SURE** YOU *REGRET IT.*
METALLICA

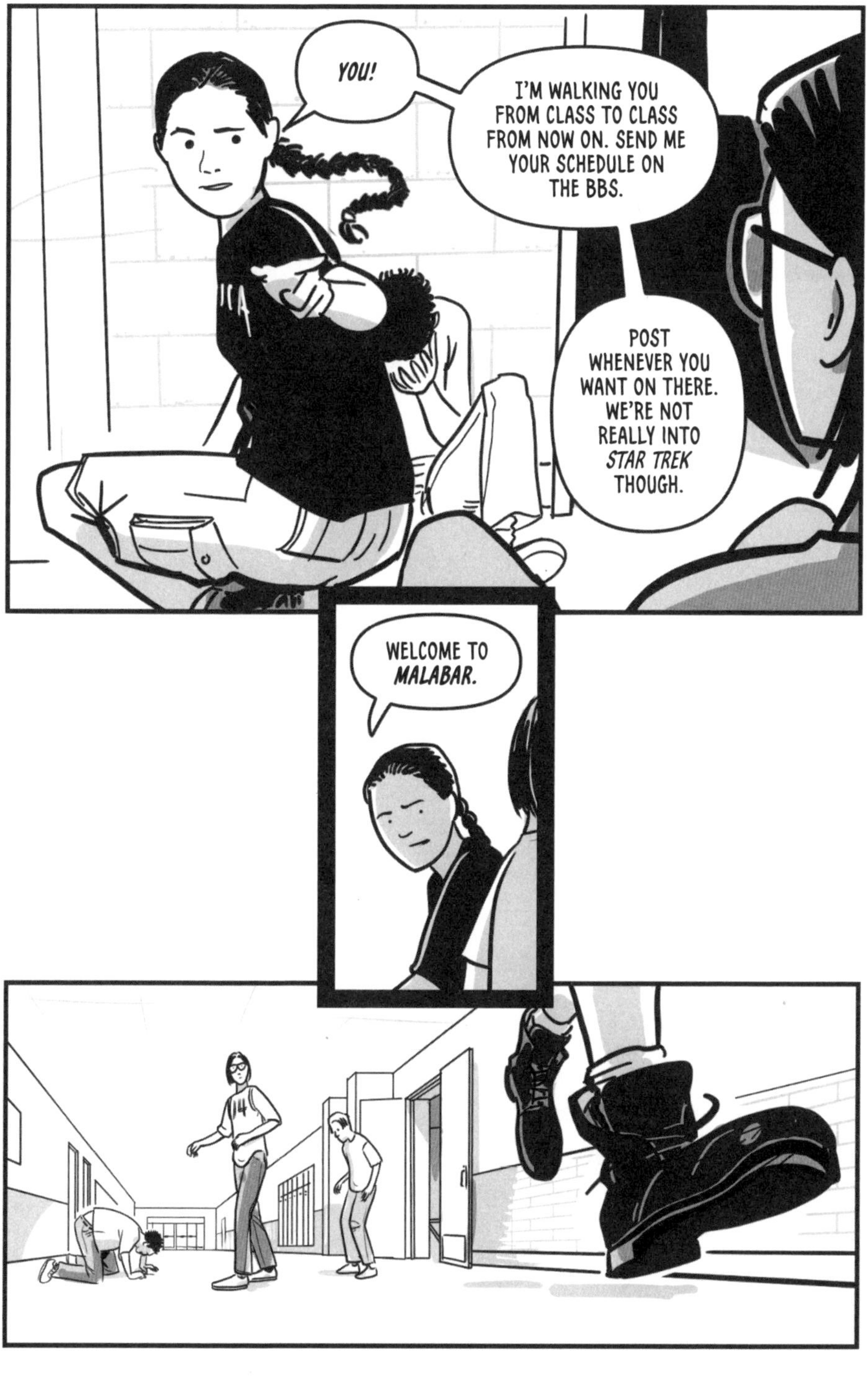
YOU!
I'M WALKING YOU FROM CLASS TO CLASS FROM NOW ON. SEND ME YOUR SCHEDULE ON THE BBS.
POST WHENEVER YOU WANT ON THERE. WE'RE NOT REALLY INTO *STAR TREK* THOUGH.
WELCOME TO *MALABAR.*

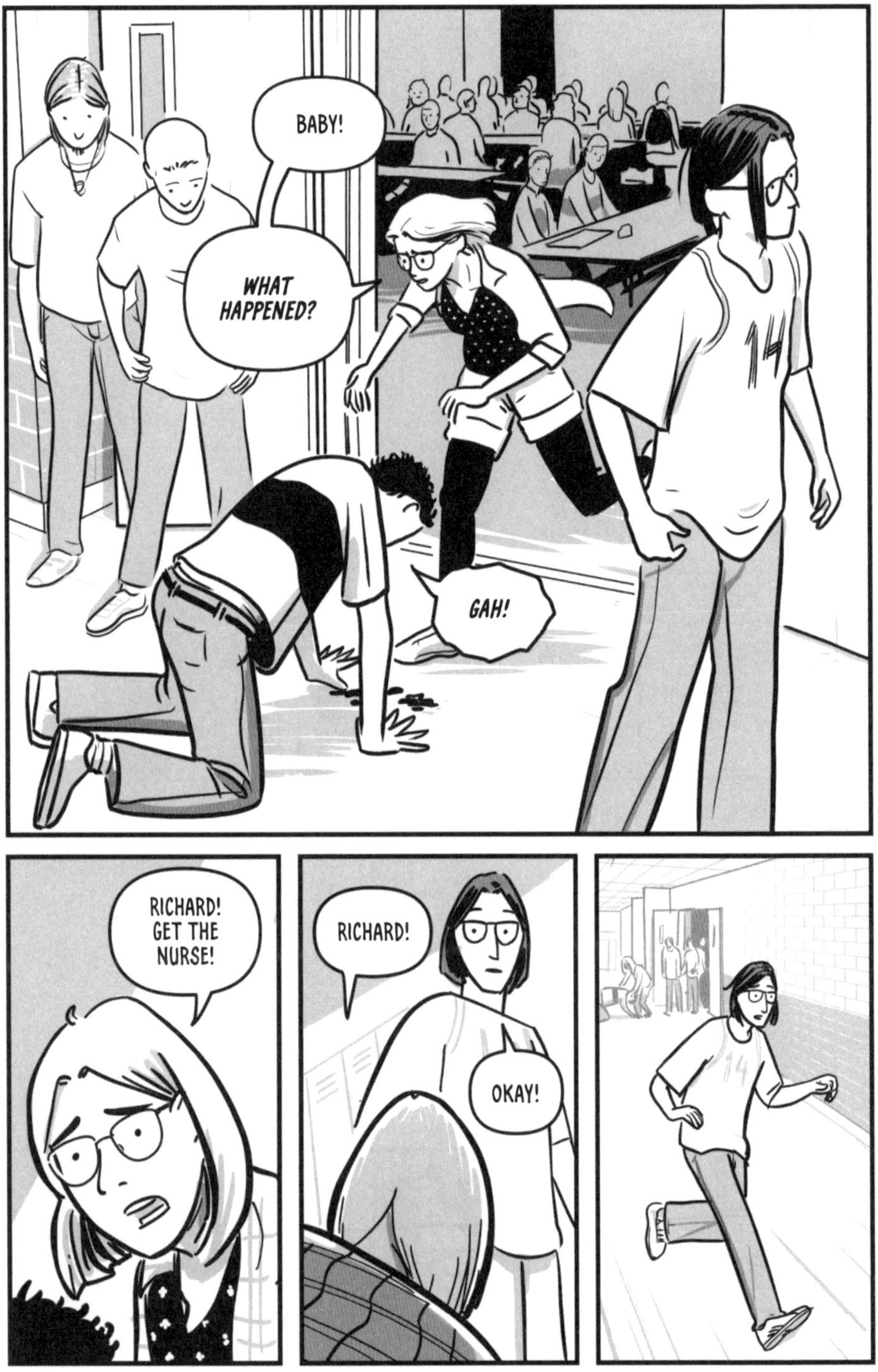
BABY!
WHAT HAPPENED?
GAH!
RICHARD! GET THE NURSE!
RICHARD!
OKAY!

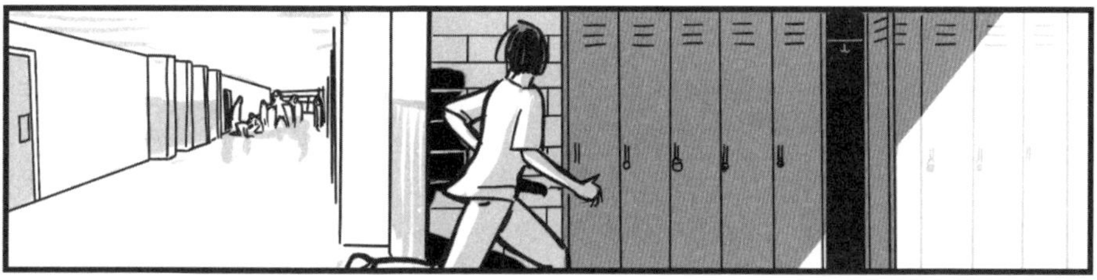

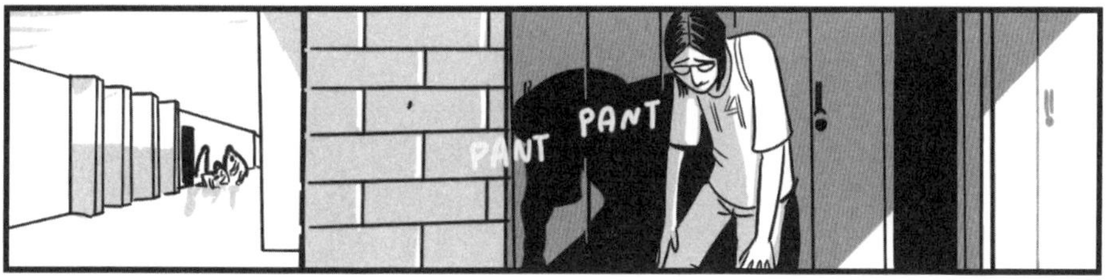
PANT PANT

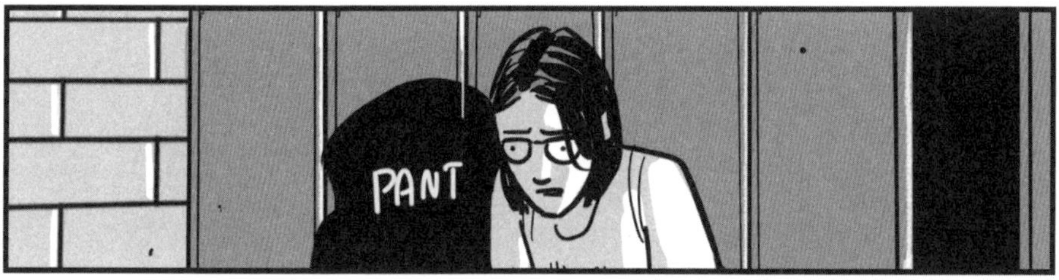
PANT

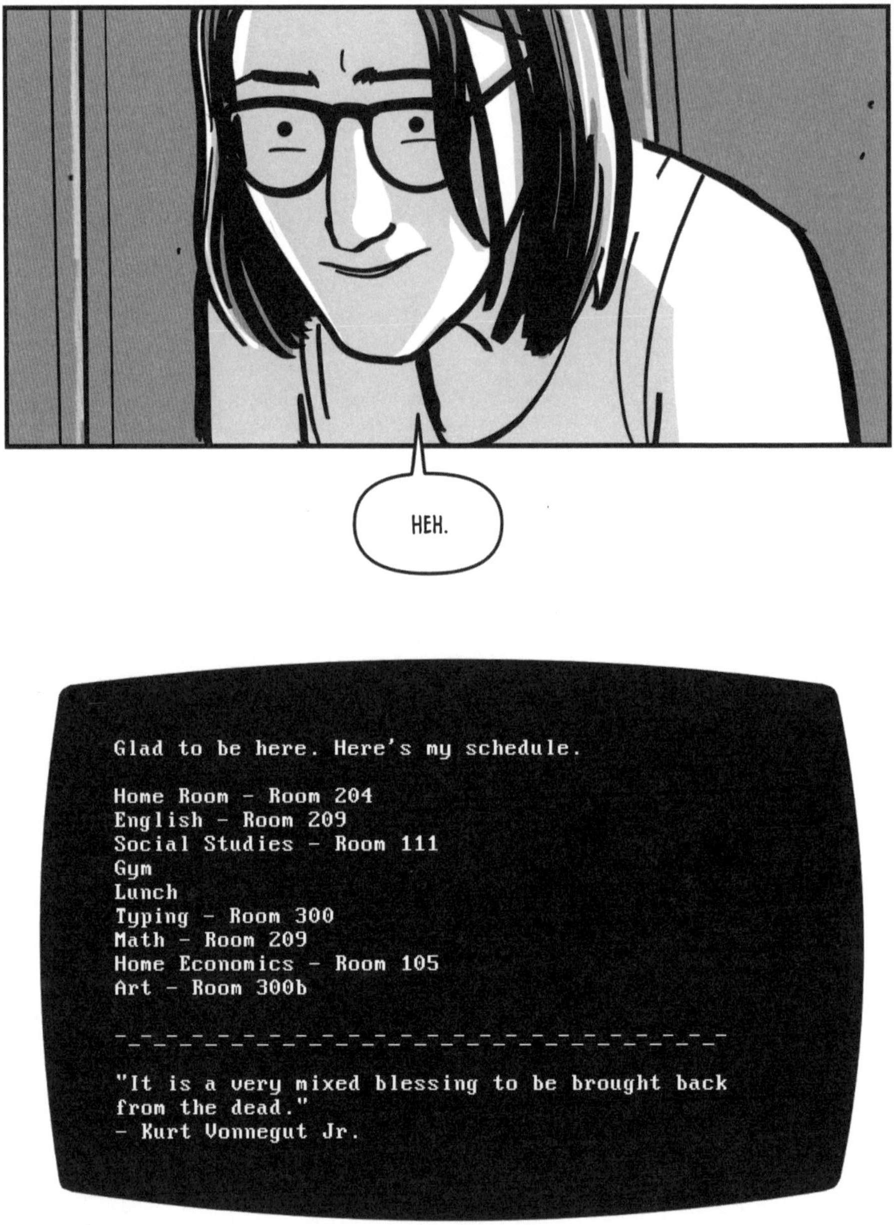
HEH.
Glad to be here. Here's my schedule.
Home Room - Room 204
English - Room 209
Social Studies - Room 111
Gym
Lunch
Typing - Room 300
Math - Room 209
Home Economics - Room 105
Art - Room 300b
"It is a very mixed blessing to be brought back from the dead."
- Kurt Vonnegut Jr.

Chapter 3

EVERYTHING'S FINE

GO d? p c++l u+ e^x m+ s-/- n+ h f^x !g w t+ r? !y

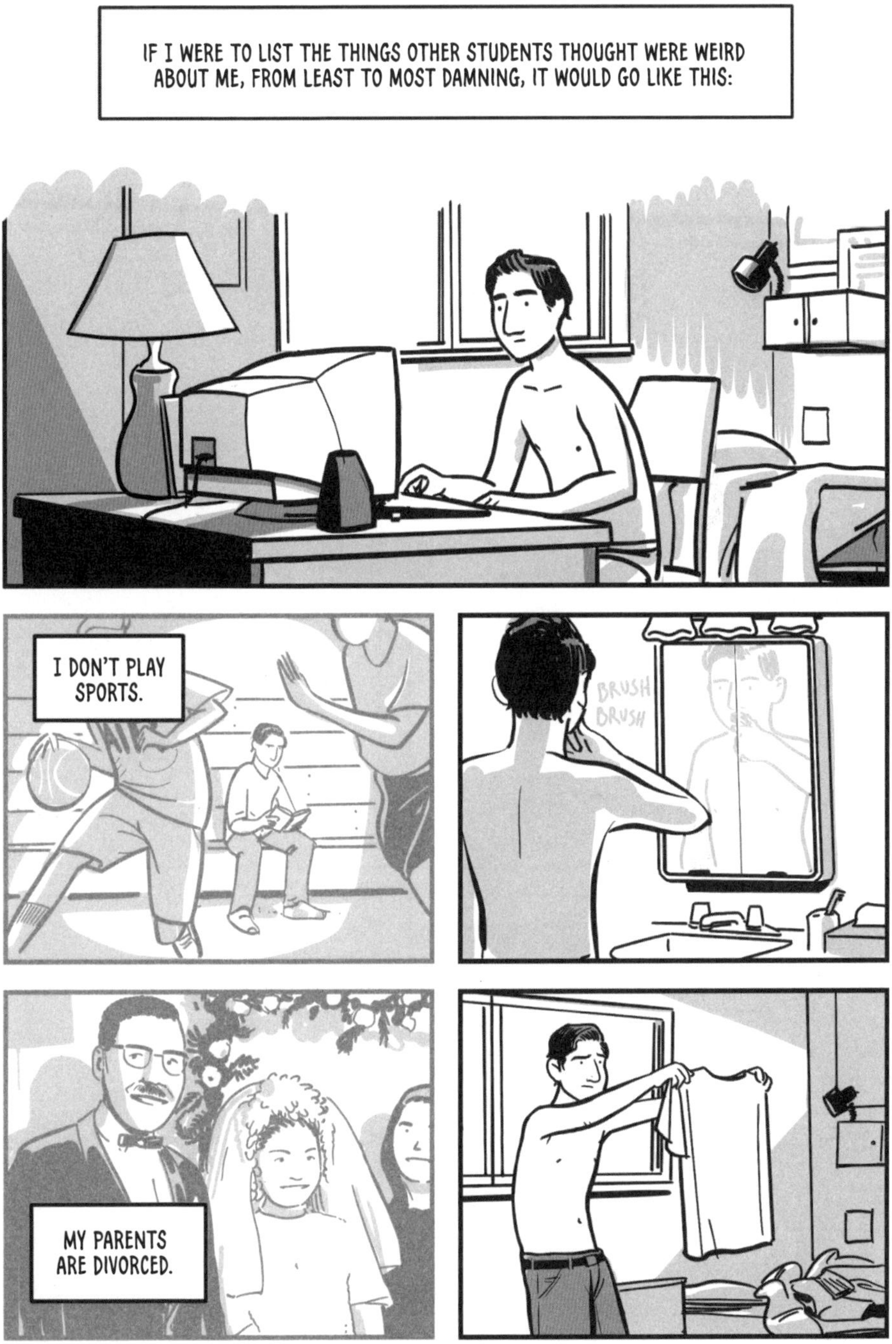
IF I WERE TO LIST THE THINGS OTHER STUDENTS THOUGHT WERE WEIRD ABOUT ME, FROM LEAST TO MOST DAMNING, IT WOULD GO LIKE THIS:
I DON'T PLAY SPORTS.
BRUSH
BRUSH
MY PARENTS ARE DIVORCED.

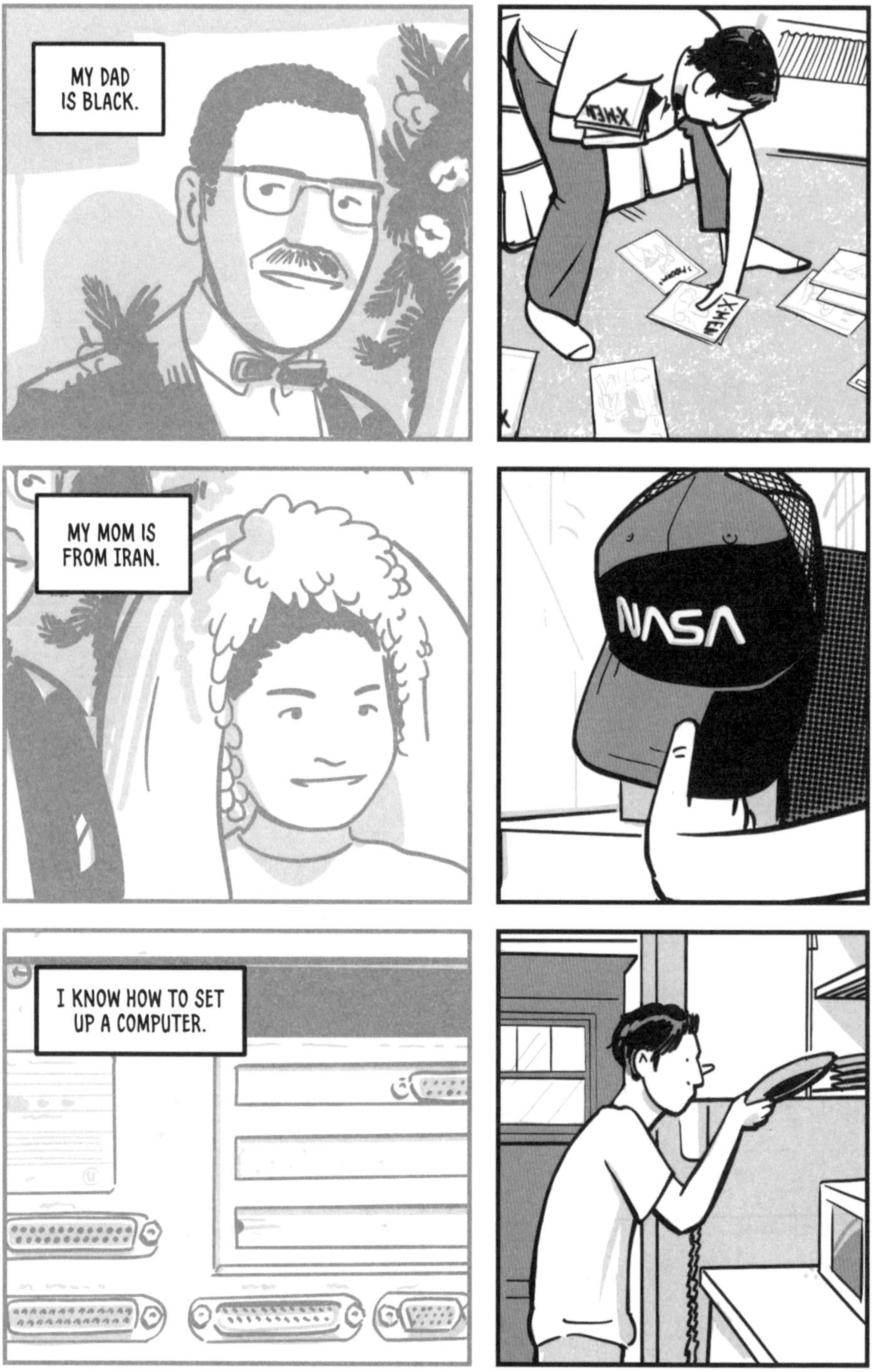
MY DAD IS BLACK.
X-MEN
X-MEN
MY MOM IS FROM IRAN.
NASA
I KNOW HOW TO SET UP A COMPUTER.

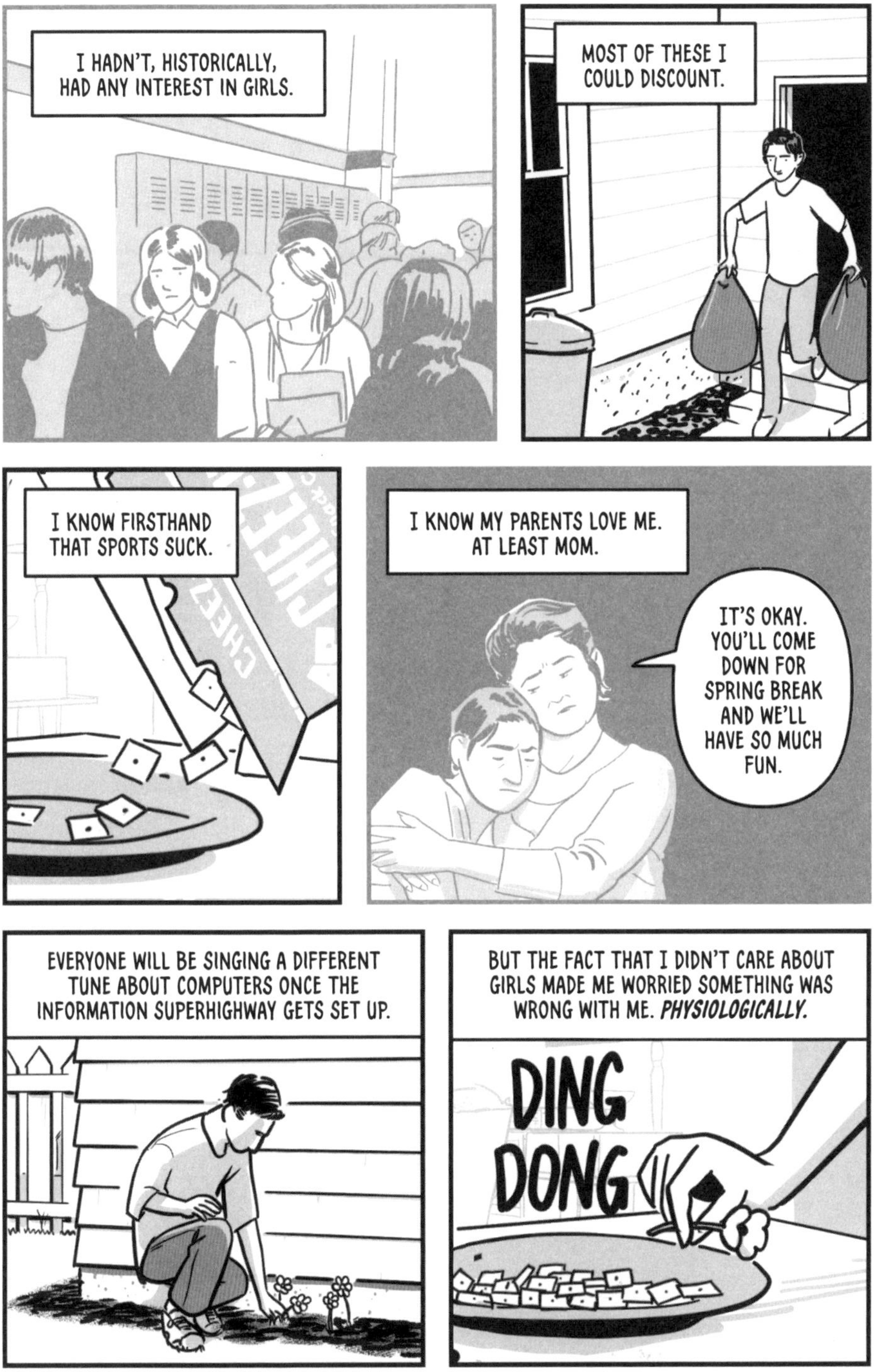
I HADN'T, HISTORICALLY, HAD ANY INTEREST IN GIRLS.
MOST OF THESE I COULD DISCOUNT.
I KNOW FIRSTHAND THAT SPORTS SUCK.
I KNOW MY PARENTS LOVE ME. AT LEAST MOM.
IT'S OKAY. YOU'LL COME DOWN FOR SPRING BREAK AND WE'LL HAVE SO MUCH FUN.
EVERYONE WILL BE SINGING A DIFFERENT TUNE ABOUT COMPUTERS ONCE THE INFORMATION SUPERHIGHWAY GETS SET UP.
BUT THE FACT THAT I DIDN'T CARE ABOUT GIRLS MADE ME WORRIED SOMETHING WAS WRONG WITH ME. *PHYSIOLOGICALLY.*
DING
DONG

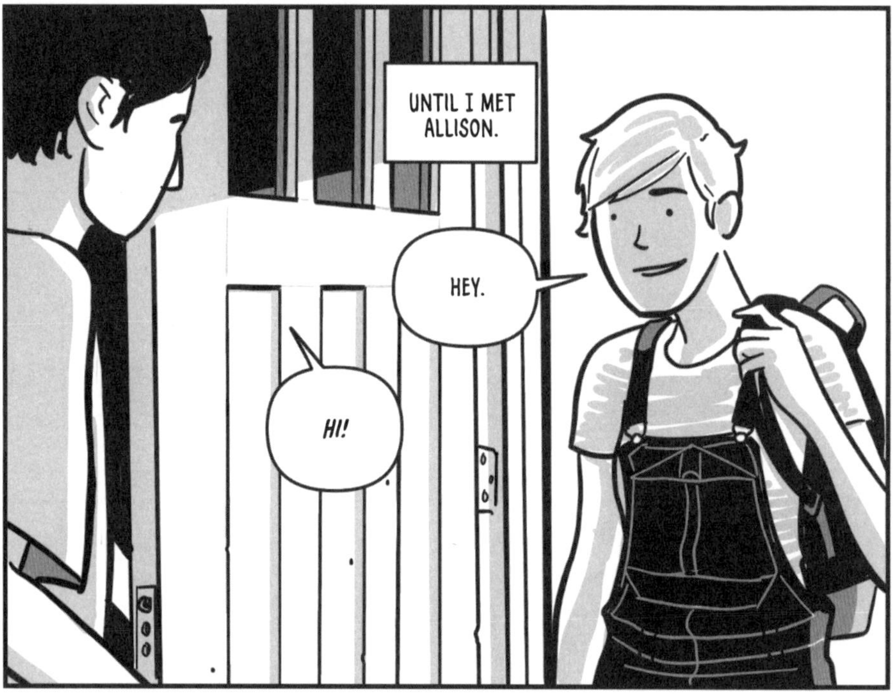
UNTIL I MET ALLISON.
HEY.
HI!

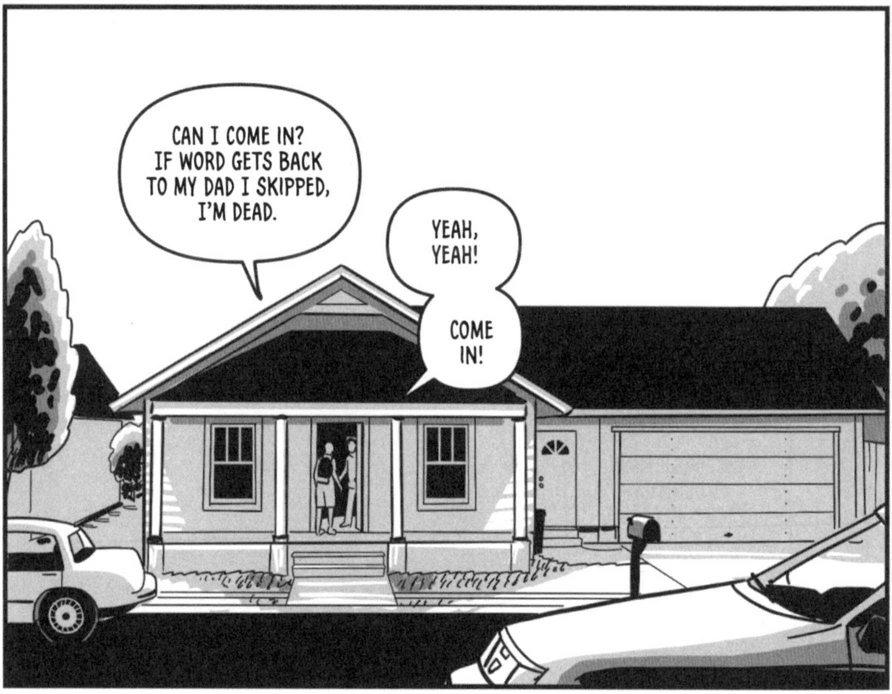
CAN I COME IN? IF WORD GETS BACK TO MY DAD I SKIPPED, I'M DEAD.
YEAH, YEAH!
COME IN!

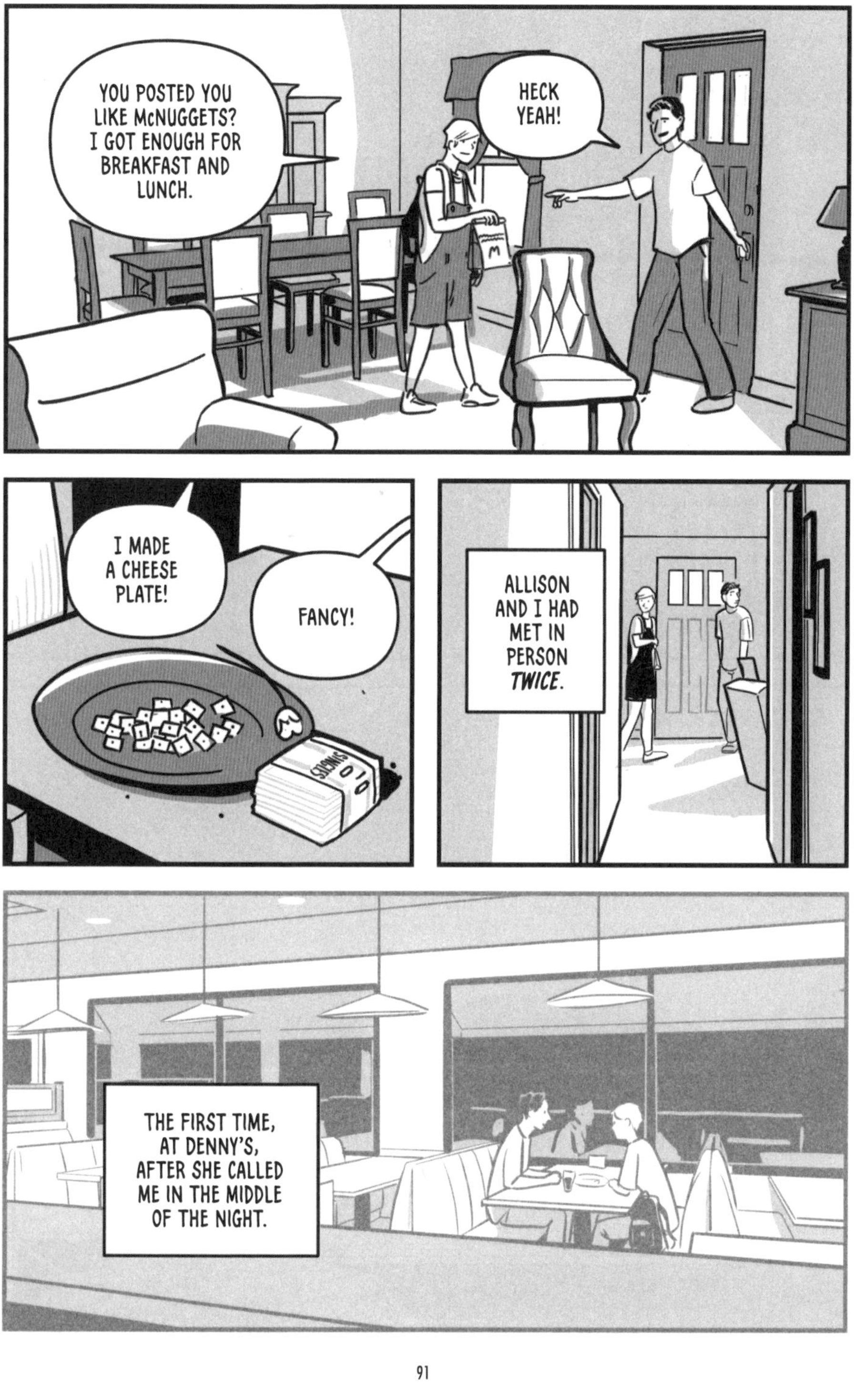
YOU POSTED YOU LIKE McNUGGETS? I GOT ENOUGH FOR BREAKFAST AND LUNCH.
HECK YEAH!
I MADE A CHEESE PLATE!
FANCY!
ALLISON AND I HAD MET IN PERSON *TWICE*.
THE FIRST TIME, AT DENNY'S, AFTER SHE CALLED ME IN THE MIDDLE OF THE NIGHT.

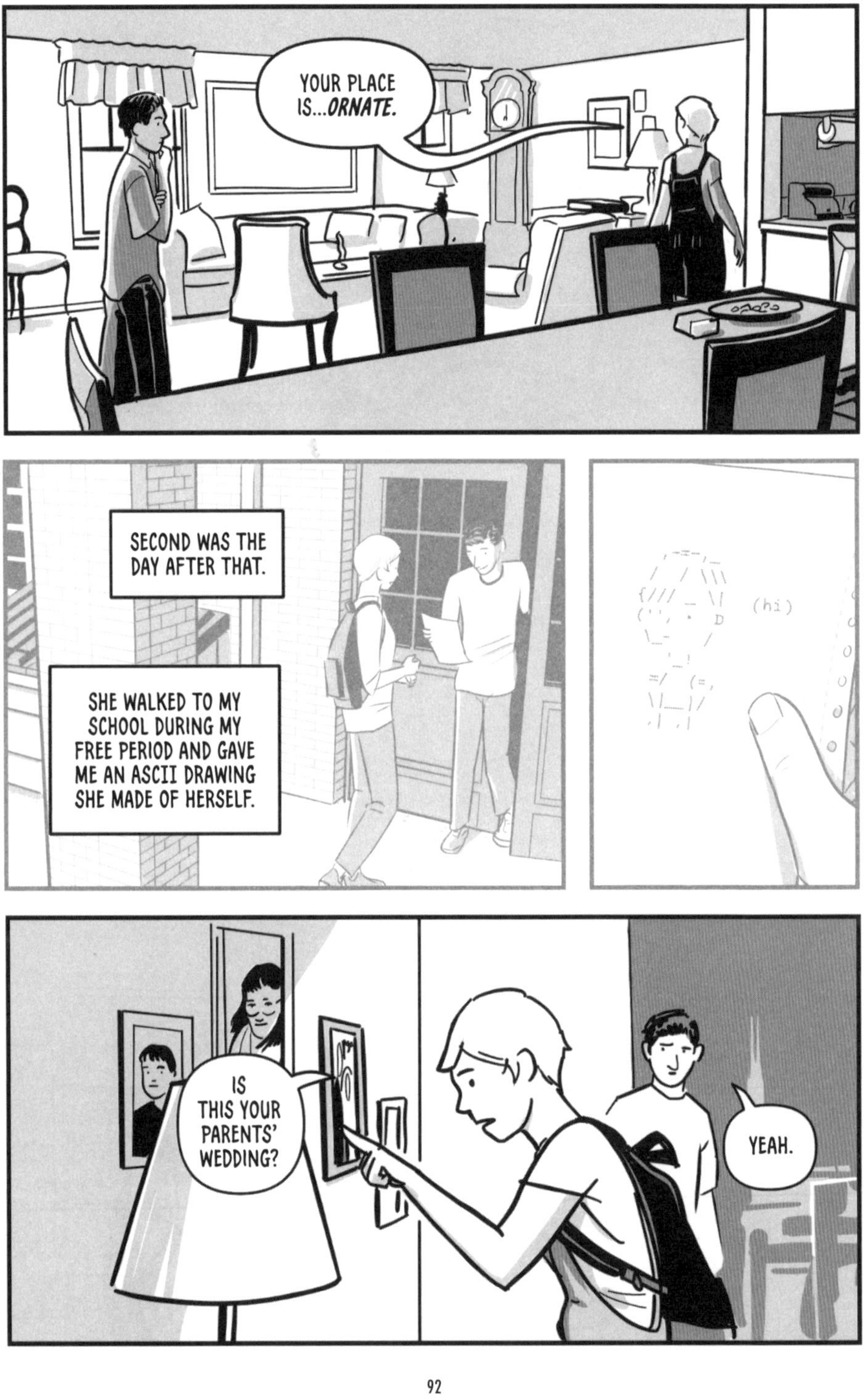
YOUR PLACE IS...*ORNATE.*
SECOND WAS THE DAY AFTER THAT.
SHE WALKED TO MY SCHOOL DURING MY FREE PERIOD AND GAVE ME AN ASCII DRAWING SHE MADE OF HERSELF.
(hi)
IS THIS YOUR PARENTS' WEDDING?
YEAH.

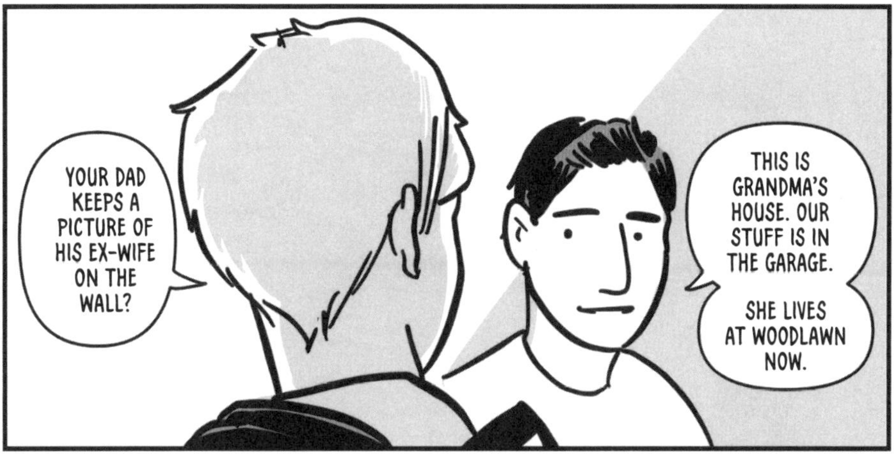
YOUR DAD KEEPS A PICTURE OF HIS EX-WIFE ON THE WALL?
THIS IS GRANDMA'S HOUSE. OUR STUFF IS IN THE GARAGE.
SHE LIVES AT WOODLAWN NOW.

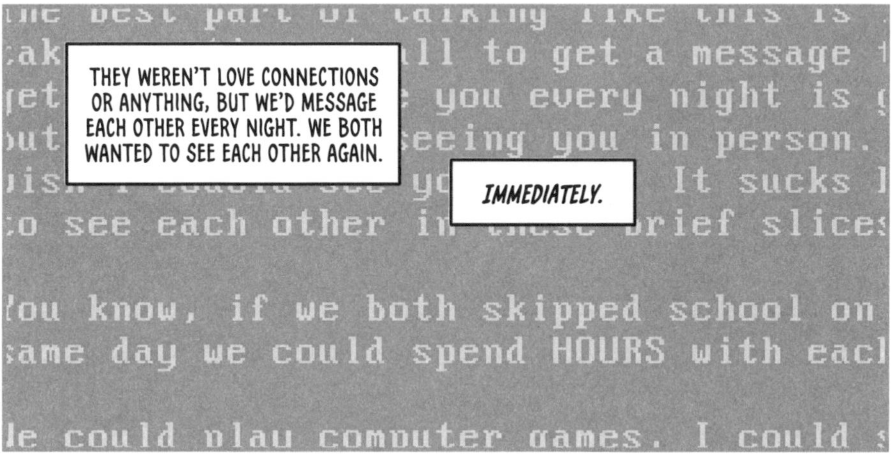
THEY WEREN'T LOVE CONNECTIONS OR ANYTHING, BUT WE'D MESSAGE EACH OTHER EVERY NIGHT. WE BOTH WANTED TO SEE EACH OTHER AGAIN.
IMMEDIATELY.
to get a message
you every night is
seeing you in person.
It sucks
see each other in
brief slice
know, if we both skipped school on
day we could spend HOURS with
could play computer games. I could

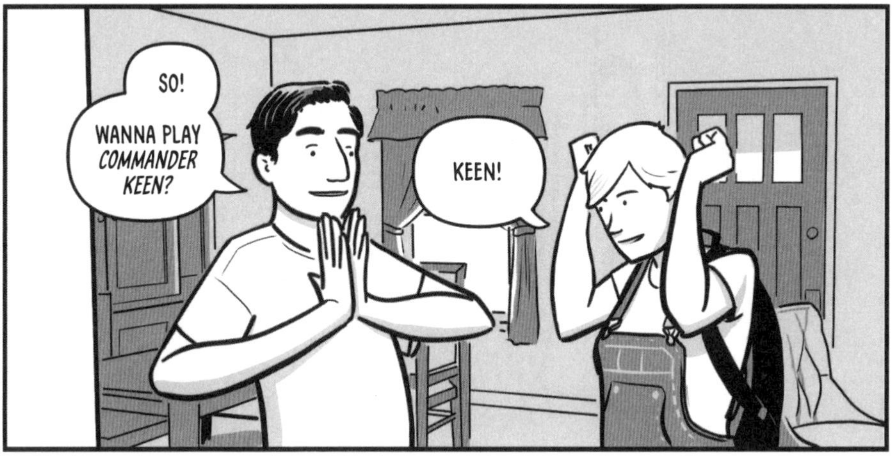
SO!
WANNA PLAY *COMMANDER KEEN?*
KEEN!

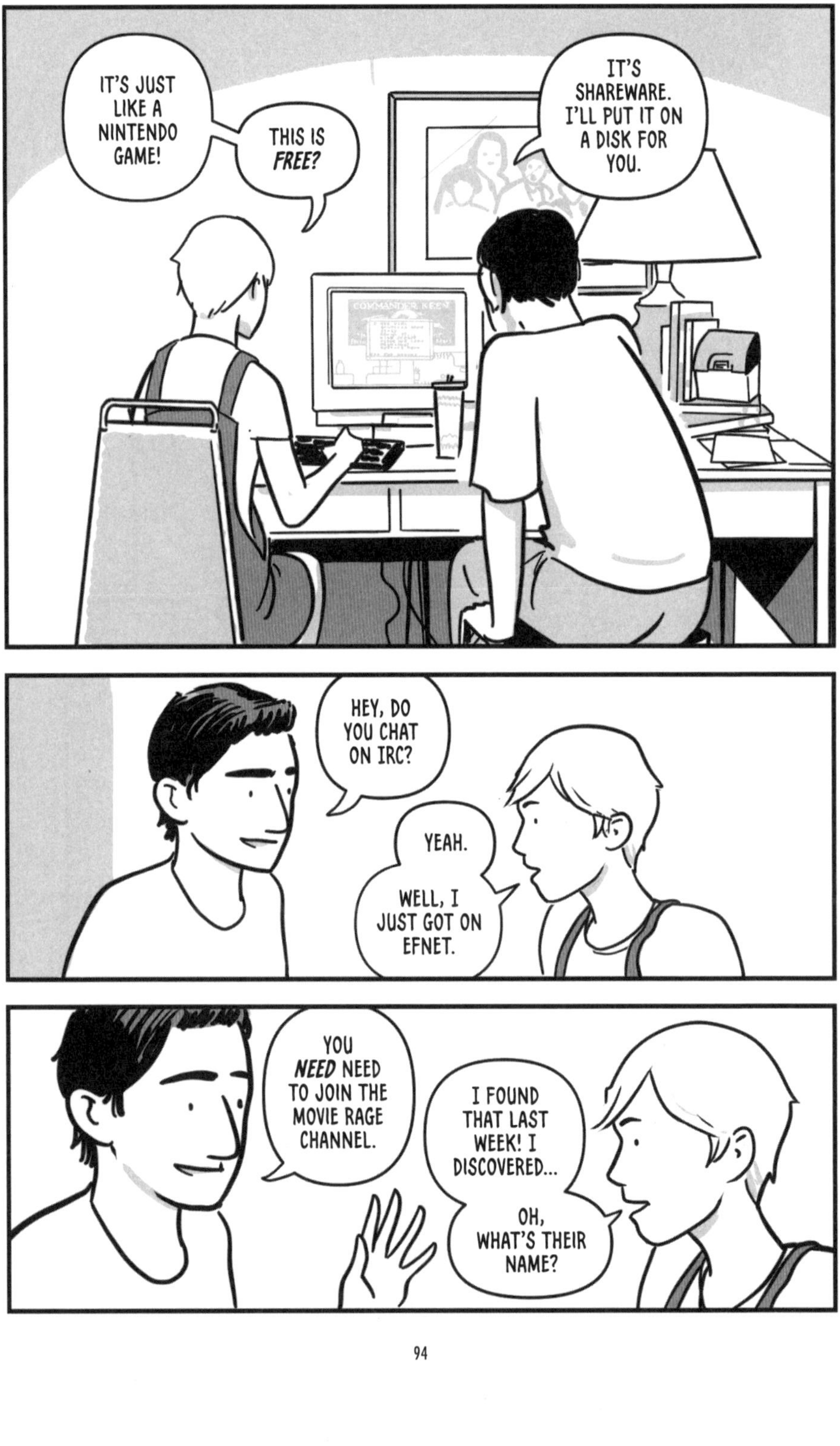
IT'S JUST LIKE A NINTENDO GAME!
THIS IS *FREE?*
IT'S SHAREWARE. I'LL PUT IT ON A DISK FOR YOU.
COMMANDER KEEN
HEY, DO YOU CHAT ON IRC?
YEAH.
WELL, I JUST GOT ON EFNET.
YOU ***NEED*** NEED TO JOIN THE MOVIE RAGE CHANNEL.
I FOUND THAT LAST WEEK! I DISCOVERED...
OH, WHAT'S THEIR NAME?

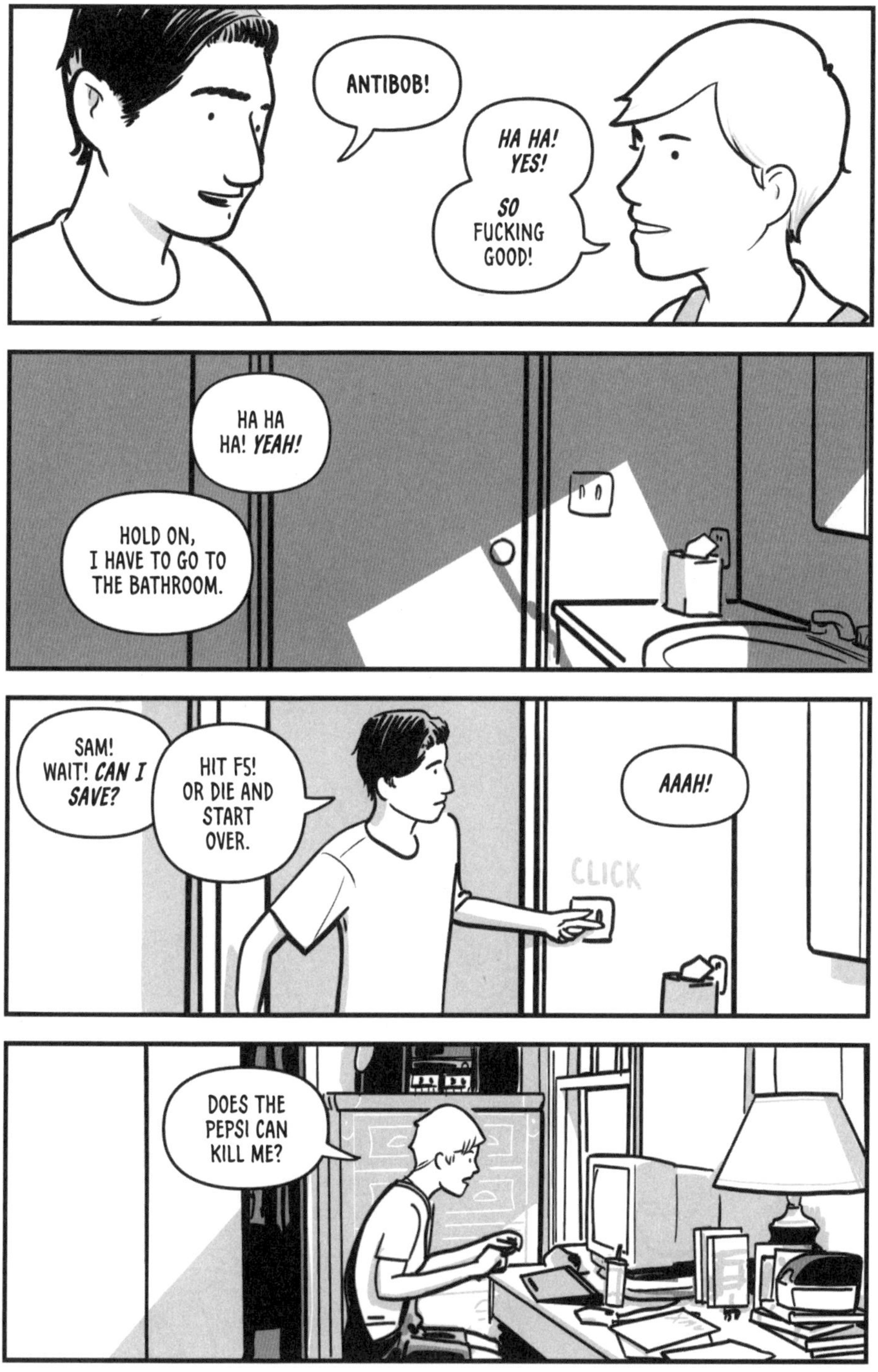
ANTIBOB!
HA HA! YES!
SO FUCKING GOOD!
HA HA HA! YEAH!
HOLD ON, I HAVE TO GO TO THE BATHROOM.
SAM! WAIT! CAN I SAVE?
HIT F5! OR DIE AND START OVER.
AAAH!
CLICK
DOES THE PEPSI CAN KILL ME?

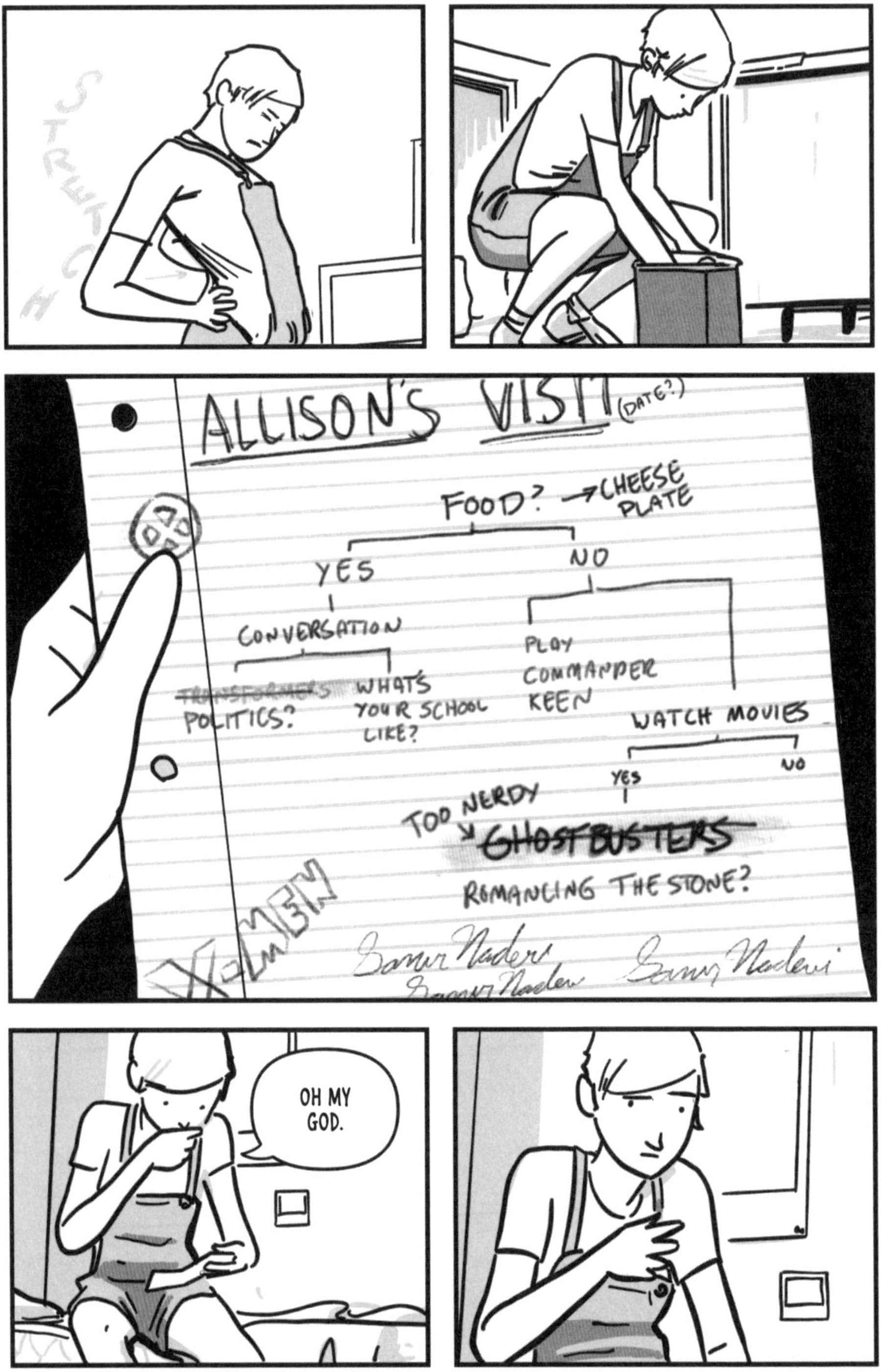
STRETCH
ALLISON'S VISIT (DATE?)
FOOD? → CHEESE PLATE
YES
NO
CONVERSATION
~~TRANSFORMERS~~
POLITICS?
WHAT'S YOUR SCHOOL LIKE?
PLAY COMMANDER KEEN
WATCH MOVIES
YES
NO
TOO NERDY
~~GHOSTBUSTERS~~
ROMANCING THE STONE?
X-MEN
Samir Naderi
Samir Naderi
Samir Naderi
OH MY GOD.

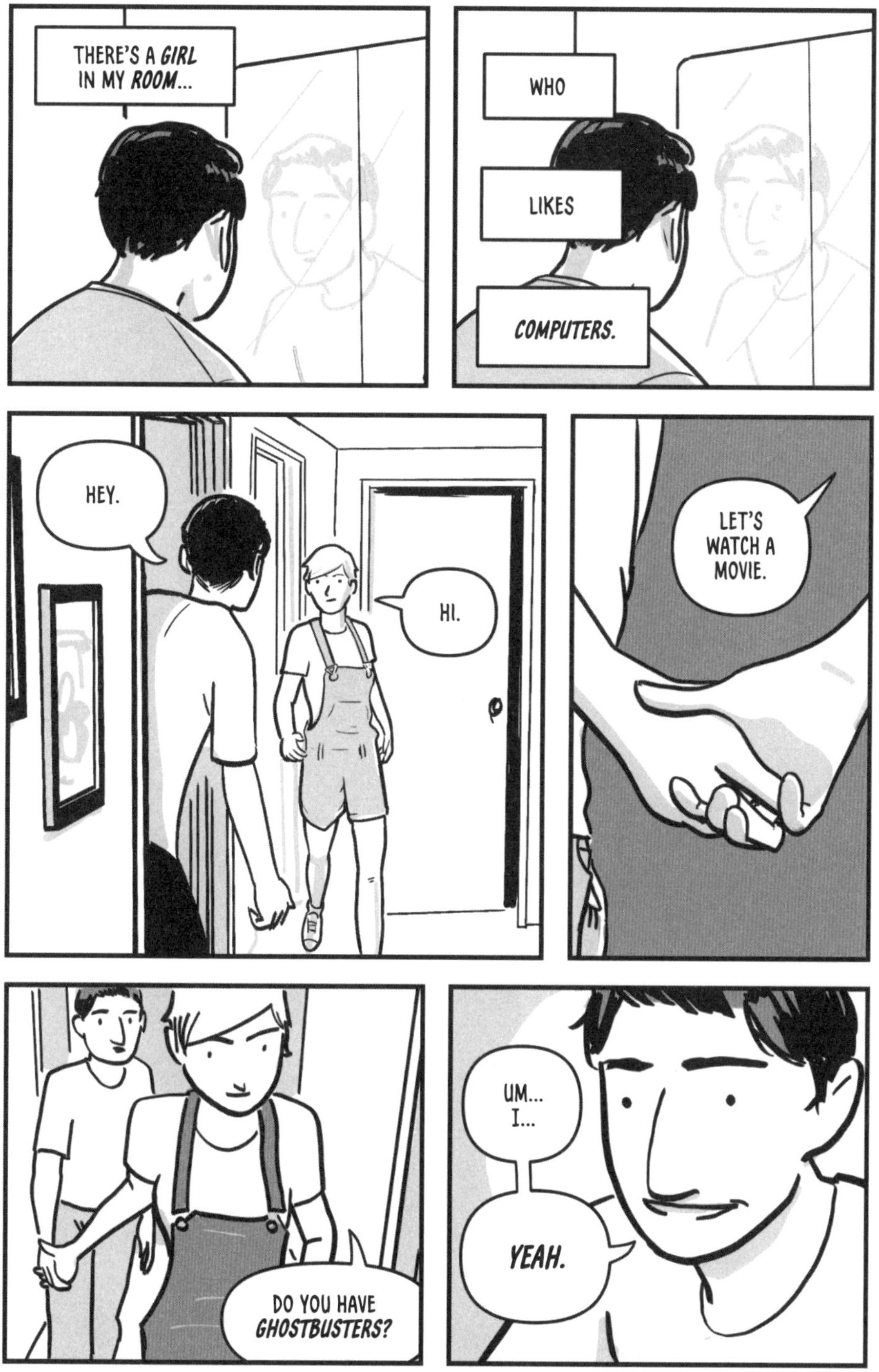
THERE'S A *GIRL* IN MY *ROOM*...
WHO
LIKES
COMPUTERS.
HEY.
HI.
LET'S WATCH A MOVIE.
DO YOU HAVE *GHOSTBUSTERS?*
UM... I...
YEAH.

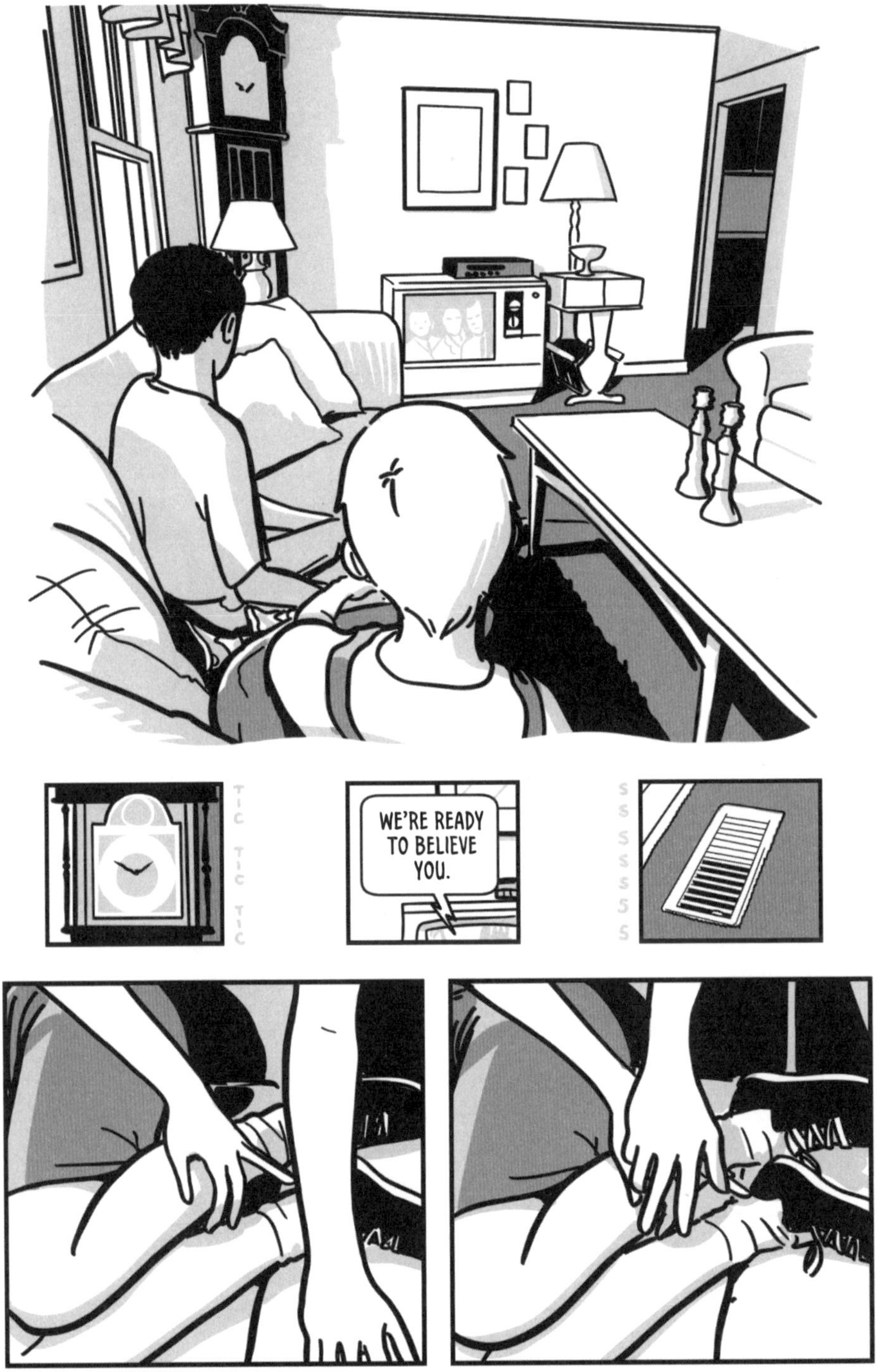
TIC TIC TIC
WE'RE READY TO BELIEVE YOU.
SSSSSSS

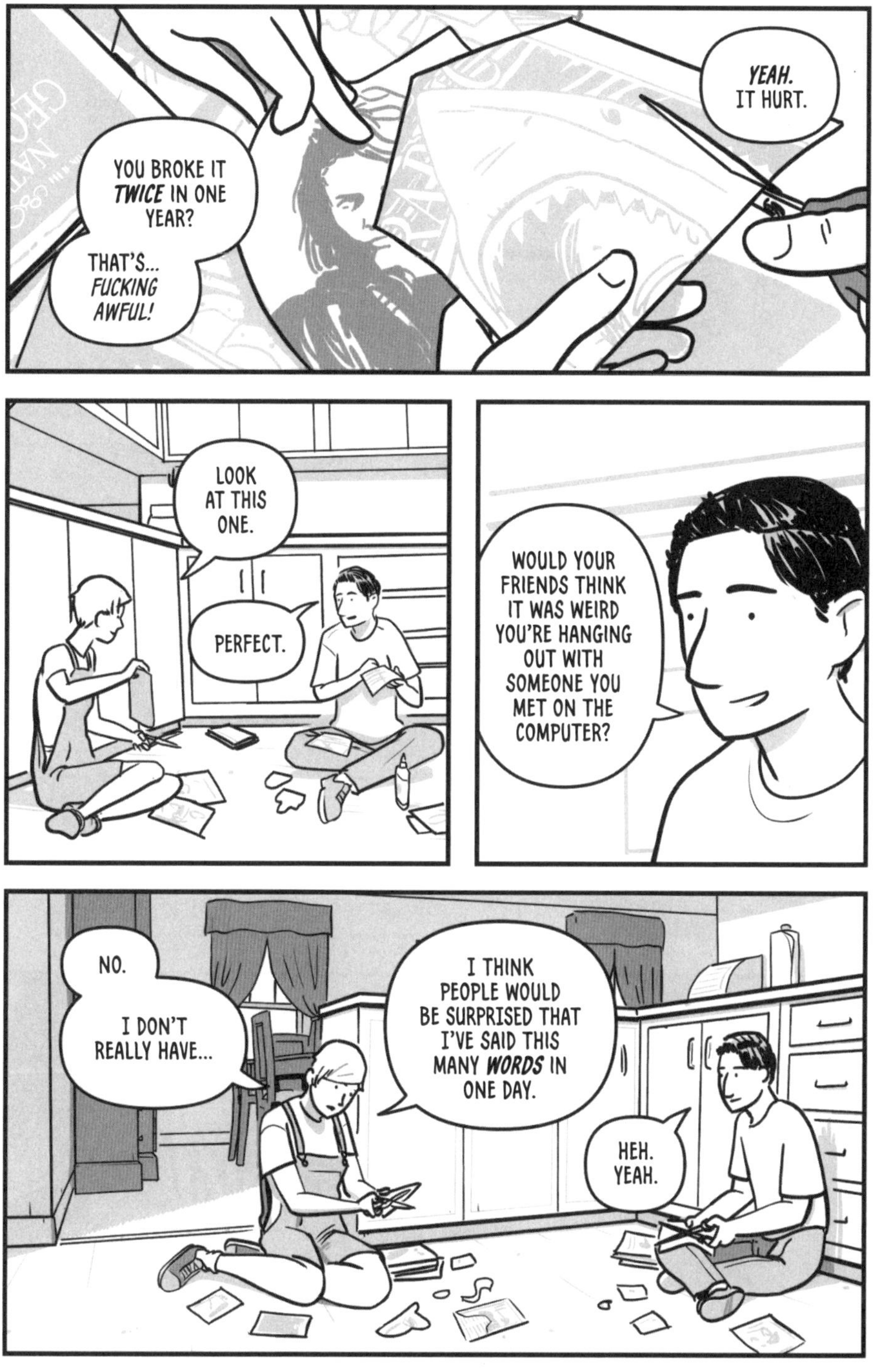
YEAH. IT HURT.
YOU BROKE IT TWICE IN ONE YEAR?
THAT'S... FUCKING AWFUL!
LOOK AT THIS ONE.
PERFECT.
WOULD YOUR FRIENDS THINK IT WAS WEIRD YOU'RE HANGING OUT WITH SOMEONE YOU MET ON THE COMPUTER?
NO.
I DON'T REALLY HAVE...
I THINK PEOPLE WOULD BE SURPRISED THAT I'VE SAID THIS MANY WORDS IN ONE DAY.
HEH. YEAH.

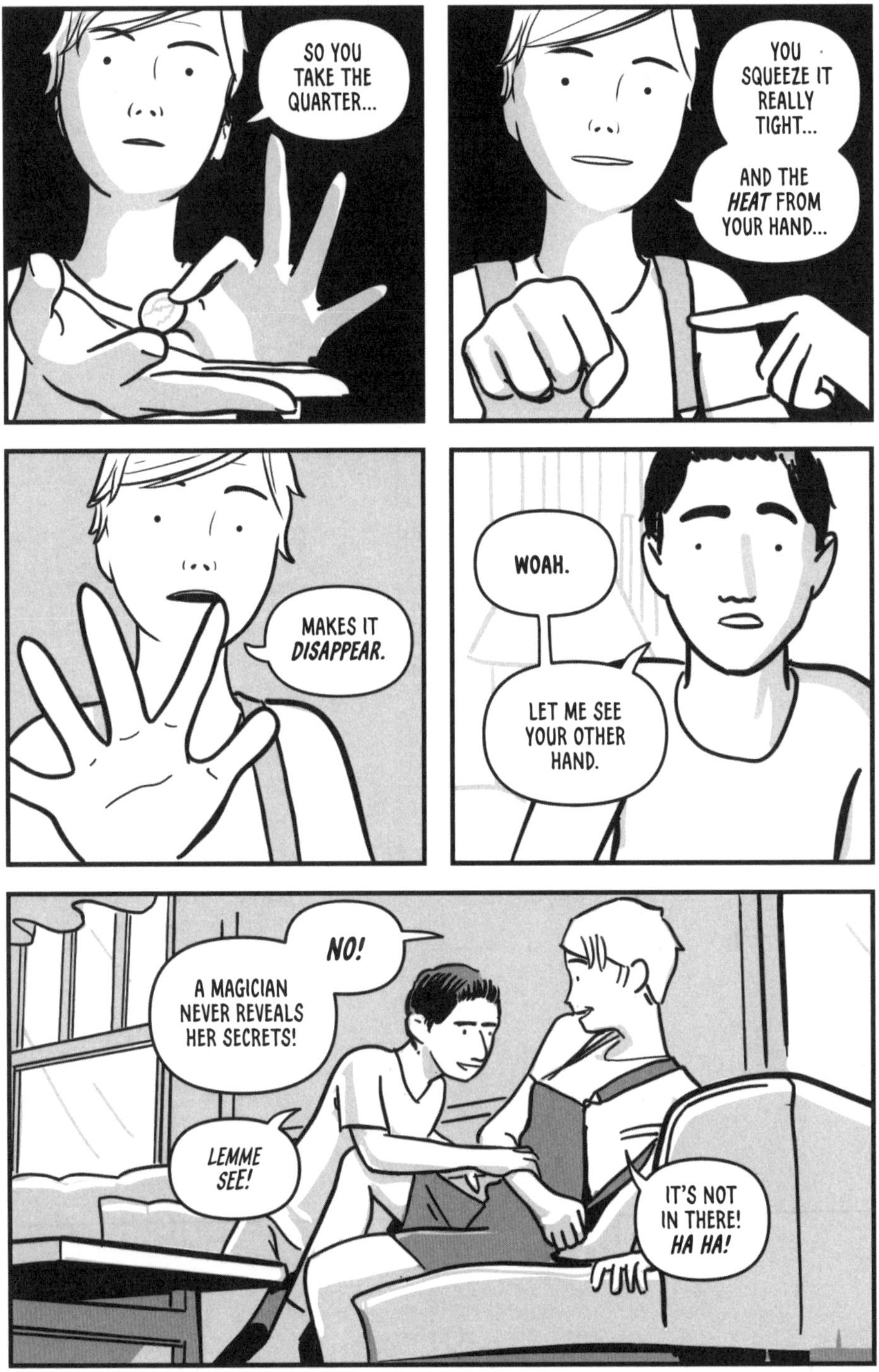
SO YOU TAKE THE QUARTER...
YOU SQUEEZE IT REALLY TIGHT...
AND THE *HEAT* FROM YOUR HAND...
MAKES IT *DISAPPEAR.*
WOAH.
LET ME SEE YOUR OTHER HAND.
NO!
A MAGICIAN NEVER REVEALS HER SECRETS!
LEMME SEE!
IT'S NOT IN THERE! *HA HA!*

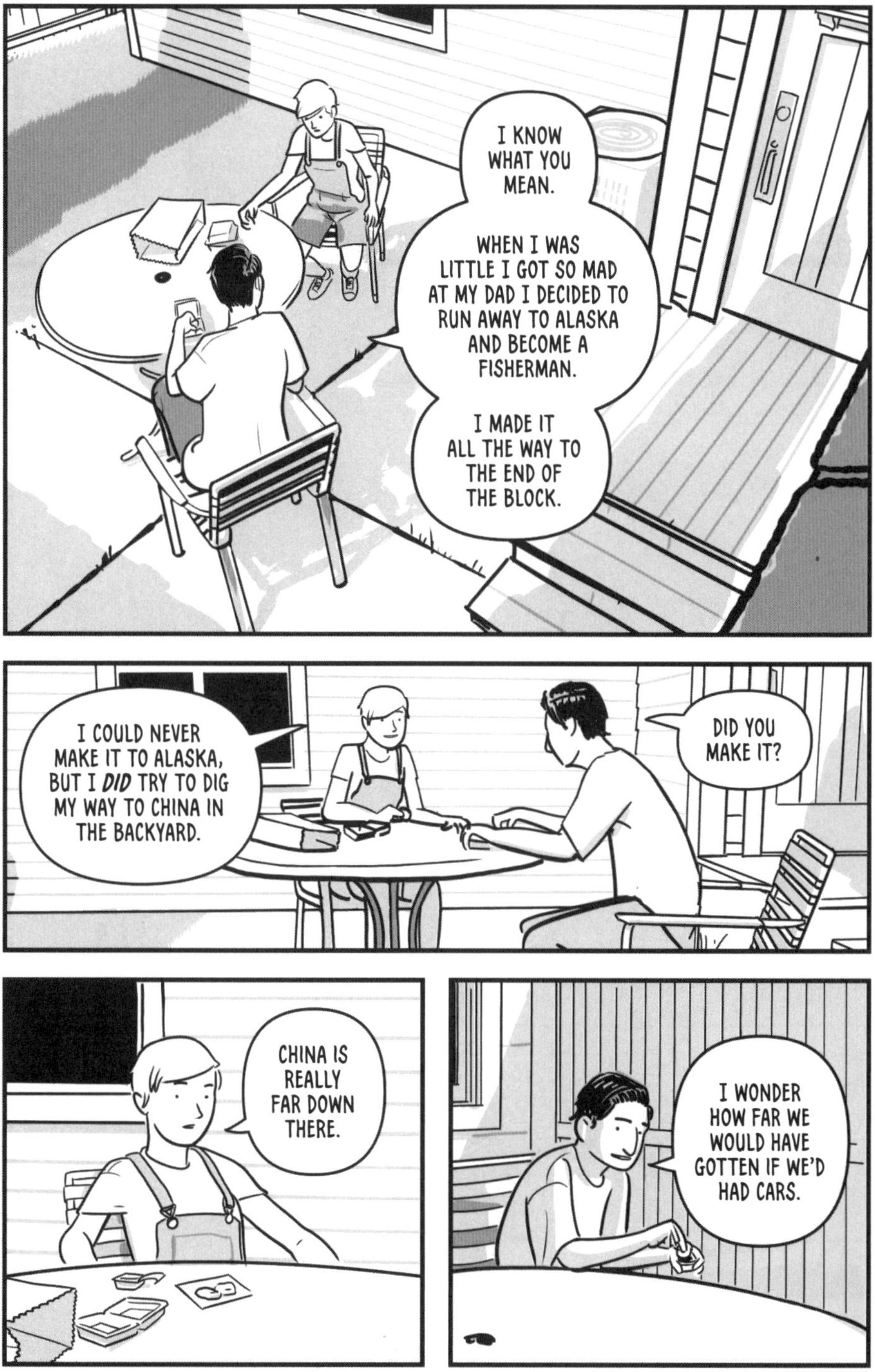
I KNOW WHAT YOU MEAN.
WHEN I WAS LITTLE I GOT SO MAD AT MY DAD I DECIDED TO RUN AWAY TO ALASKA AND BECOME A FISHERMAN.
I MADE IT ALL THE WAY TO THE END OF THE BLOCK.
I COULD NEVER MAKE IT TO ALASKA, BUT I *DID* TRY TO DIG MY WAY TO CHINA IN THE BACKYARD.
DID YOU MAKE IT?
CHINA IS REALLY FAR DOWN THERE.
I WONDER HOW FAR WE WOULD HAVE GOTTEN IF WE'D HAD CARS.

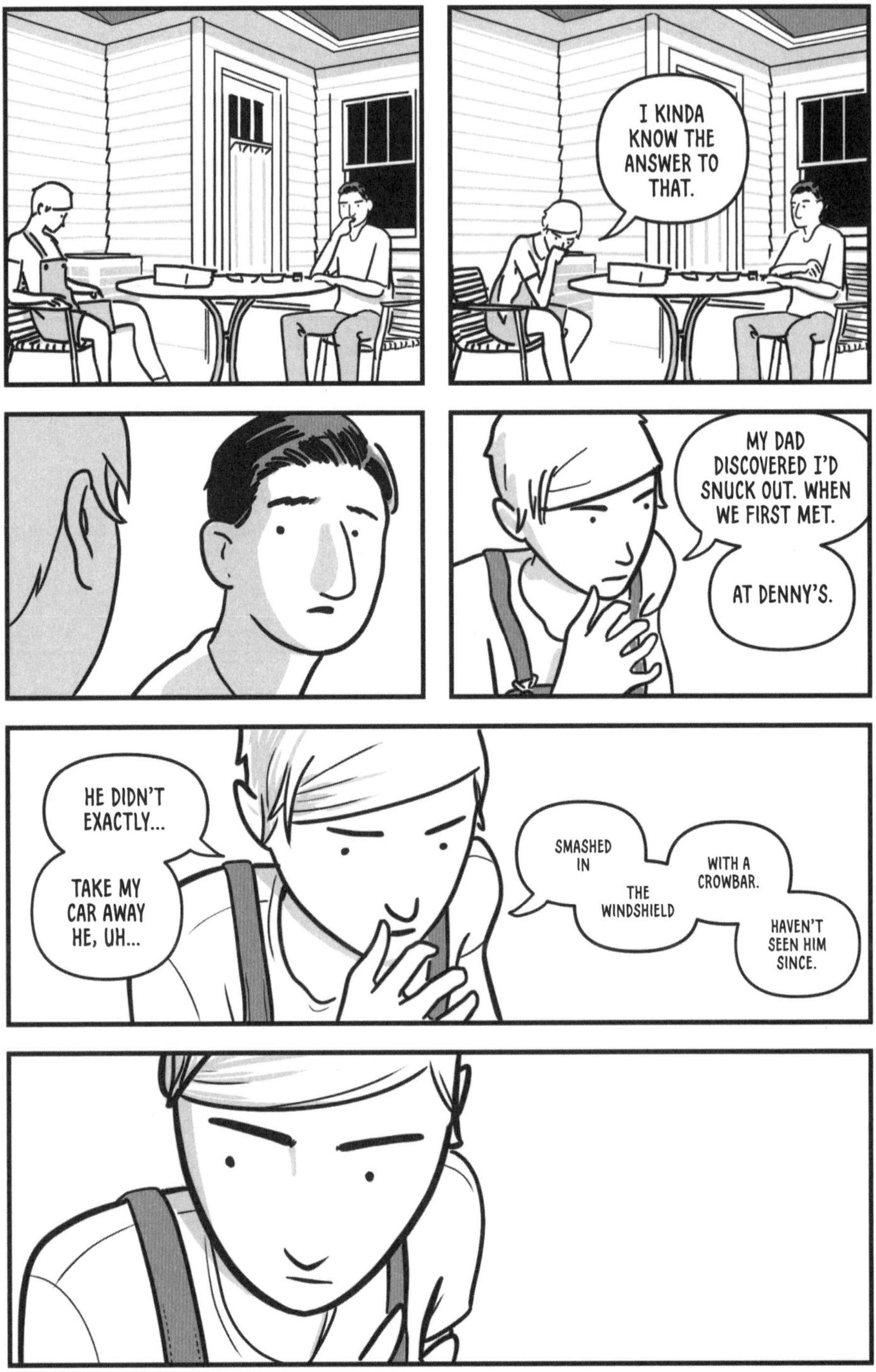
I KINDA KNOW THE ANSWER TO THAT.
MY DAD DISCOVERED I'D SNUCK OUT. WHEN WE FIRST MET.
AT DENNY'S.
HE DIDN'T EXACTLY...
TAKE MY CAR AWAY HE, UH...
SMASHED IN
THE WINDSHIELD
WITH A CROWBAR.
HAVEN'T SEEN HIM SINCE.

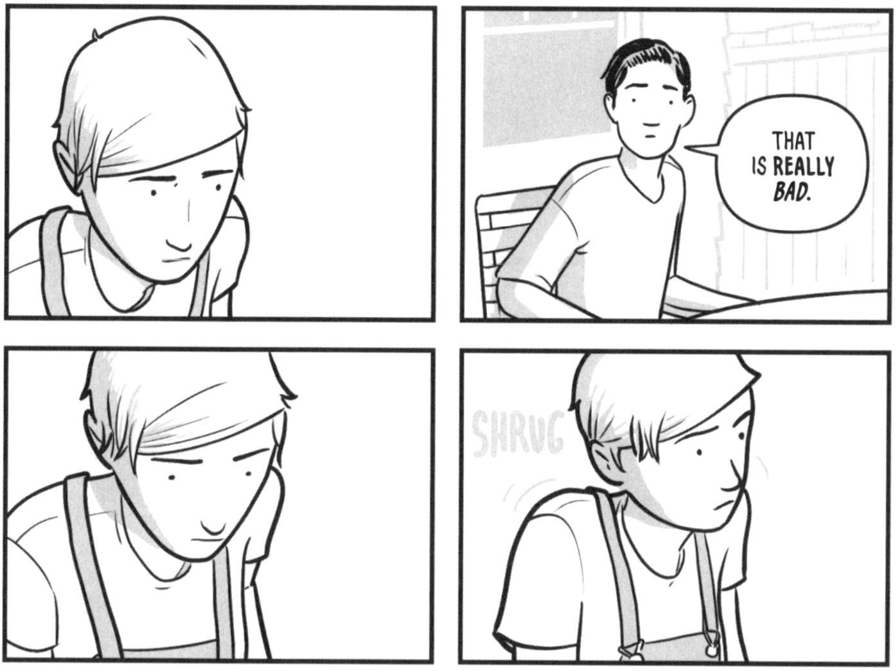
THAT IS REALLY BAD.
SHRUG

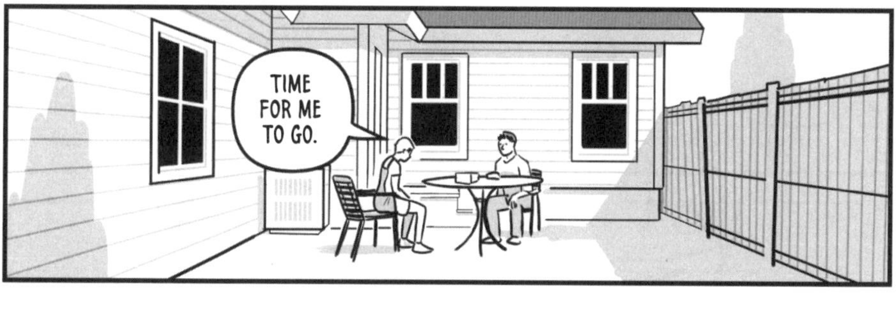
TIME FOR ME TO GO.

DOES SHE WANT ME TO KISS HER?

I DON'T KNOW WHEN THE NEXT TIME...

I DON'T KNOW IF I'LL EVER...

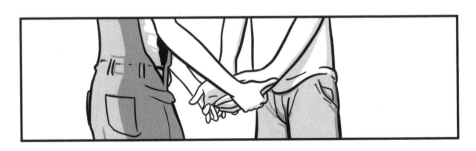

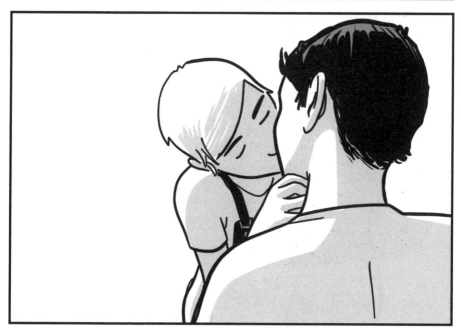

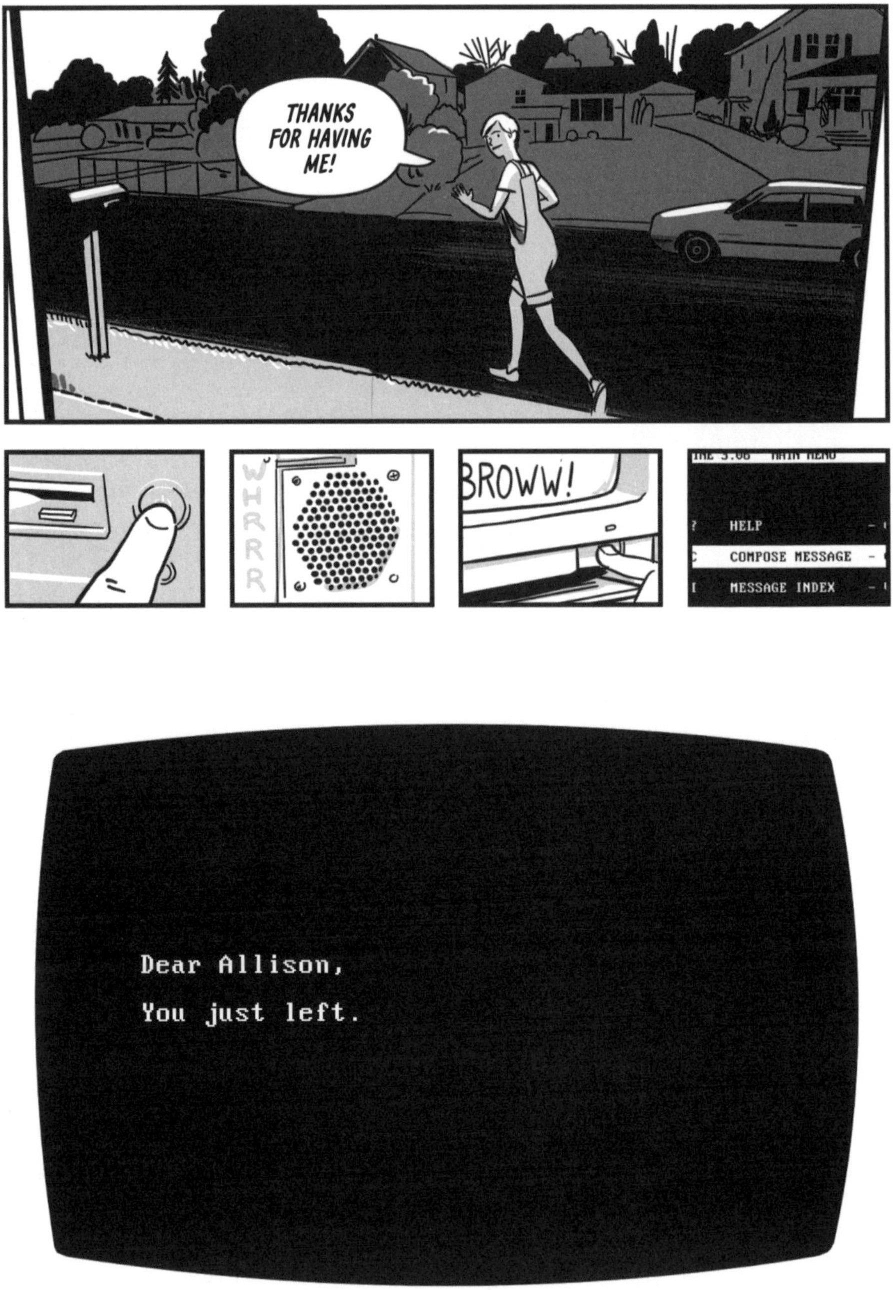
THANKS FOR HAVING ME!
WHRRR
BROWW!
HELP
COMPOSE MESSAGE
MESSAGE INDEX
Dear Allison,
You just left.

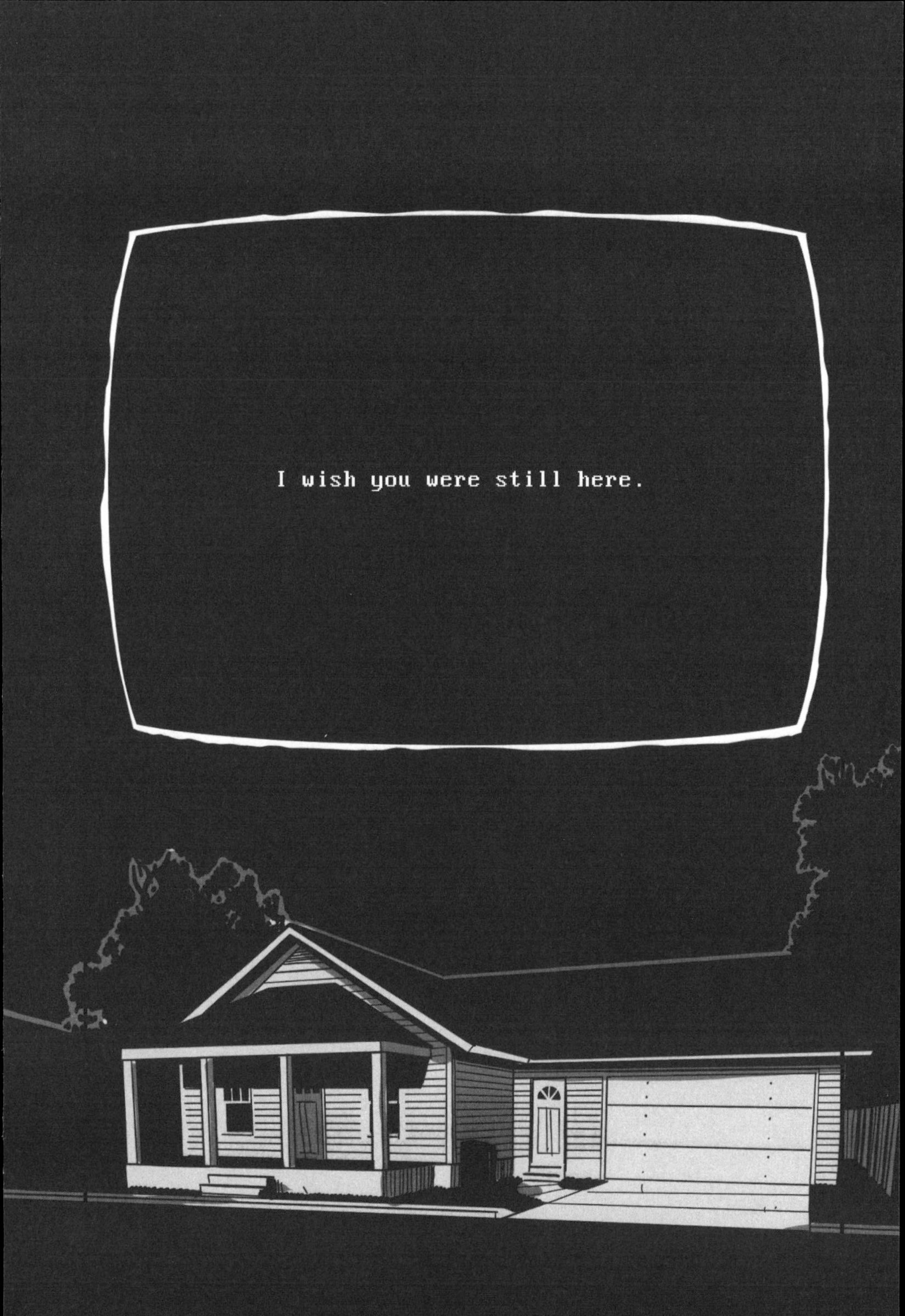
I wish you were still here.

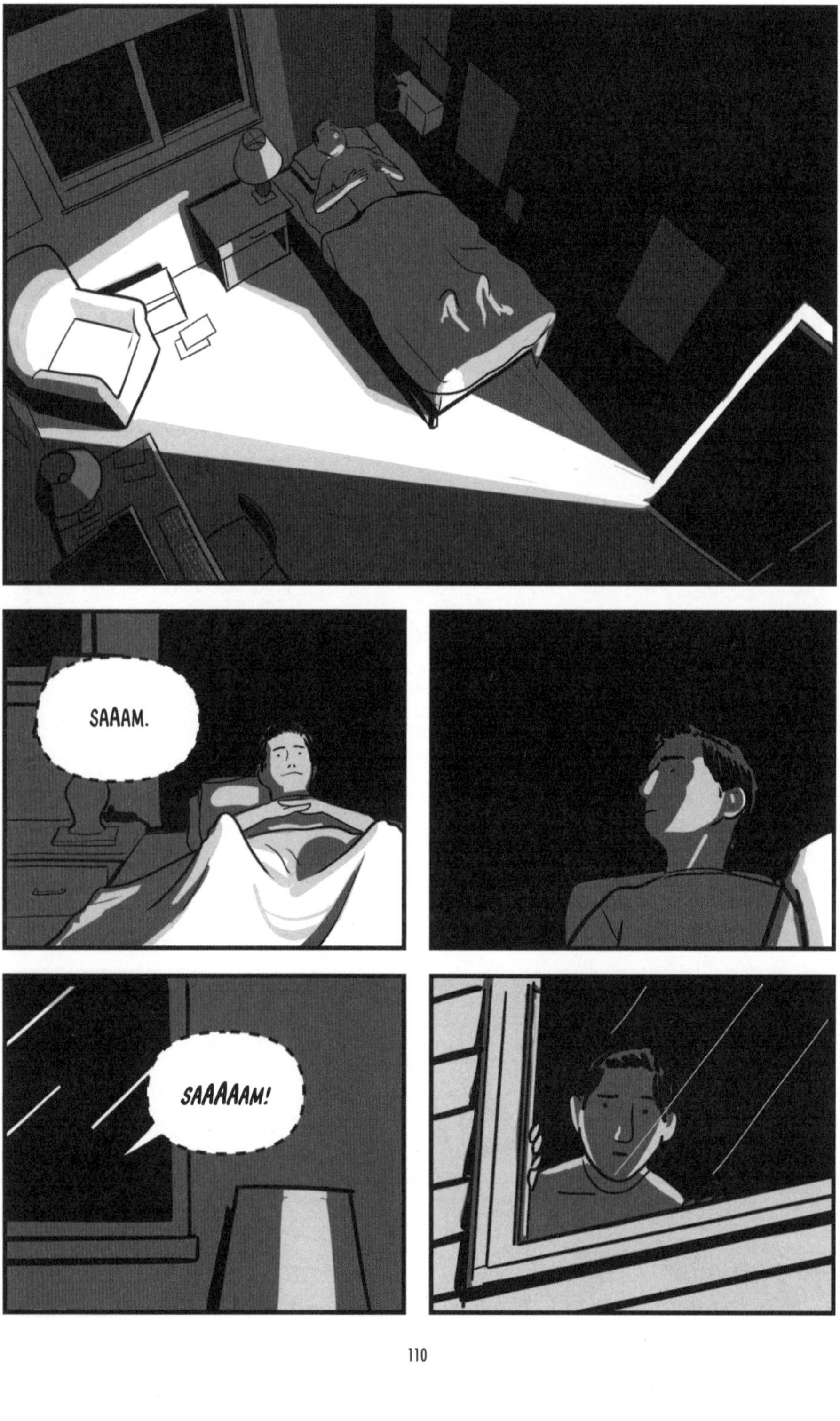
SAAAM.
SAAAAAM!

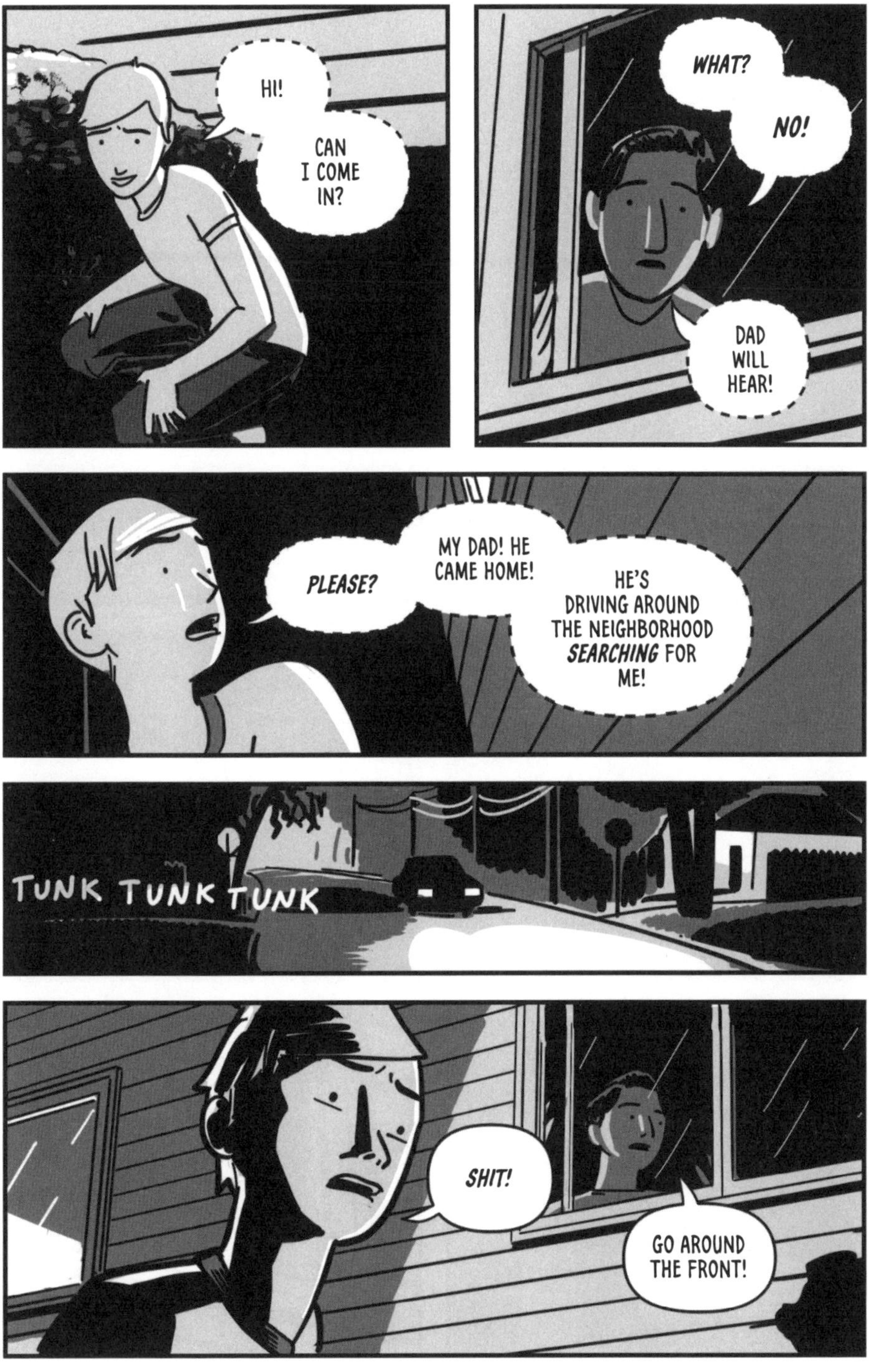
HI!
CAN I COME IN?
WHAT?
NO!
DAD WILL HEAR!
PLEASE?
MY DAD! HE CAME HOME!
HE'S DRIVING AROUND THE NEIGHBORHOOD SEARCHING FOR ME!
TUNK TUNK TUNK
SHIT!
GO AROUND THE FRONT!

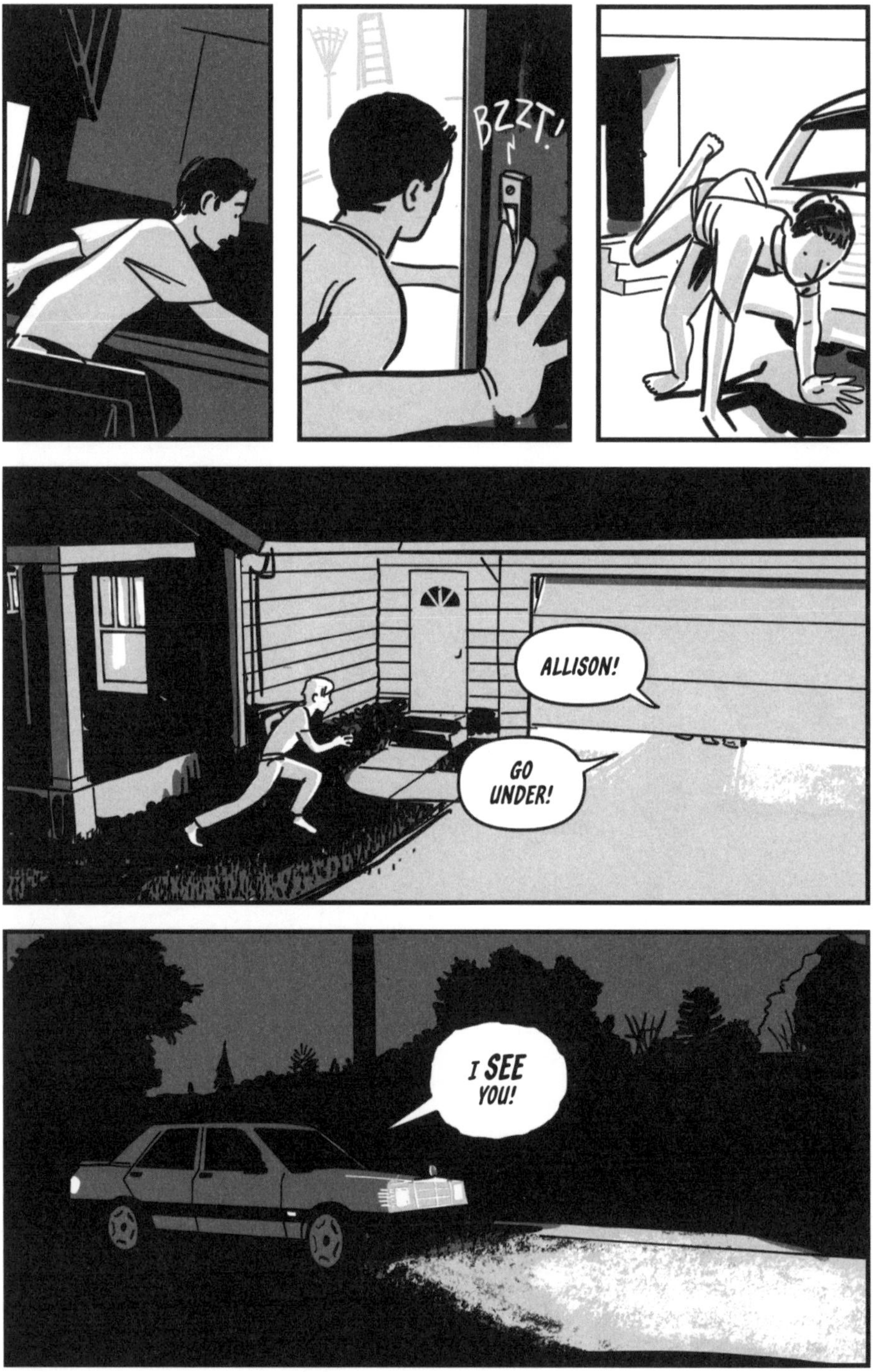
BZZT!
ALLISON!
GO UNDER!
I SEE YOU!

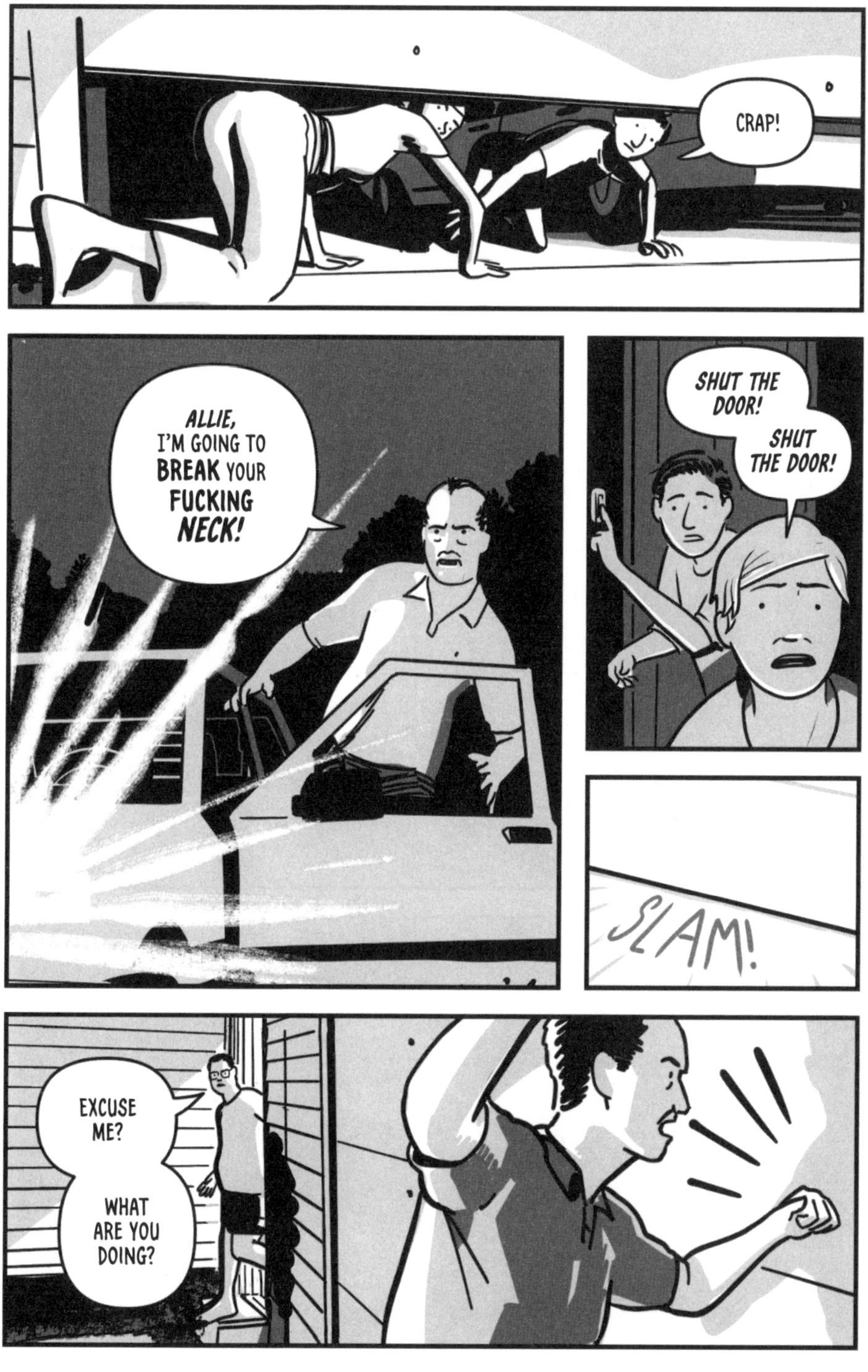

CRAP!
ALLIE, I'M GOING TO BREAK YOUR FUCKING NECK!
SHUT THE DOOR!
SHUT THE DOOR!
SLAM!
EXCUSE ME?
WHAT ARE YOU DOING?

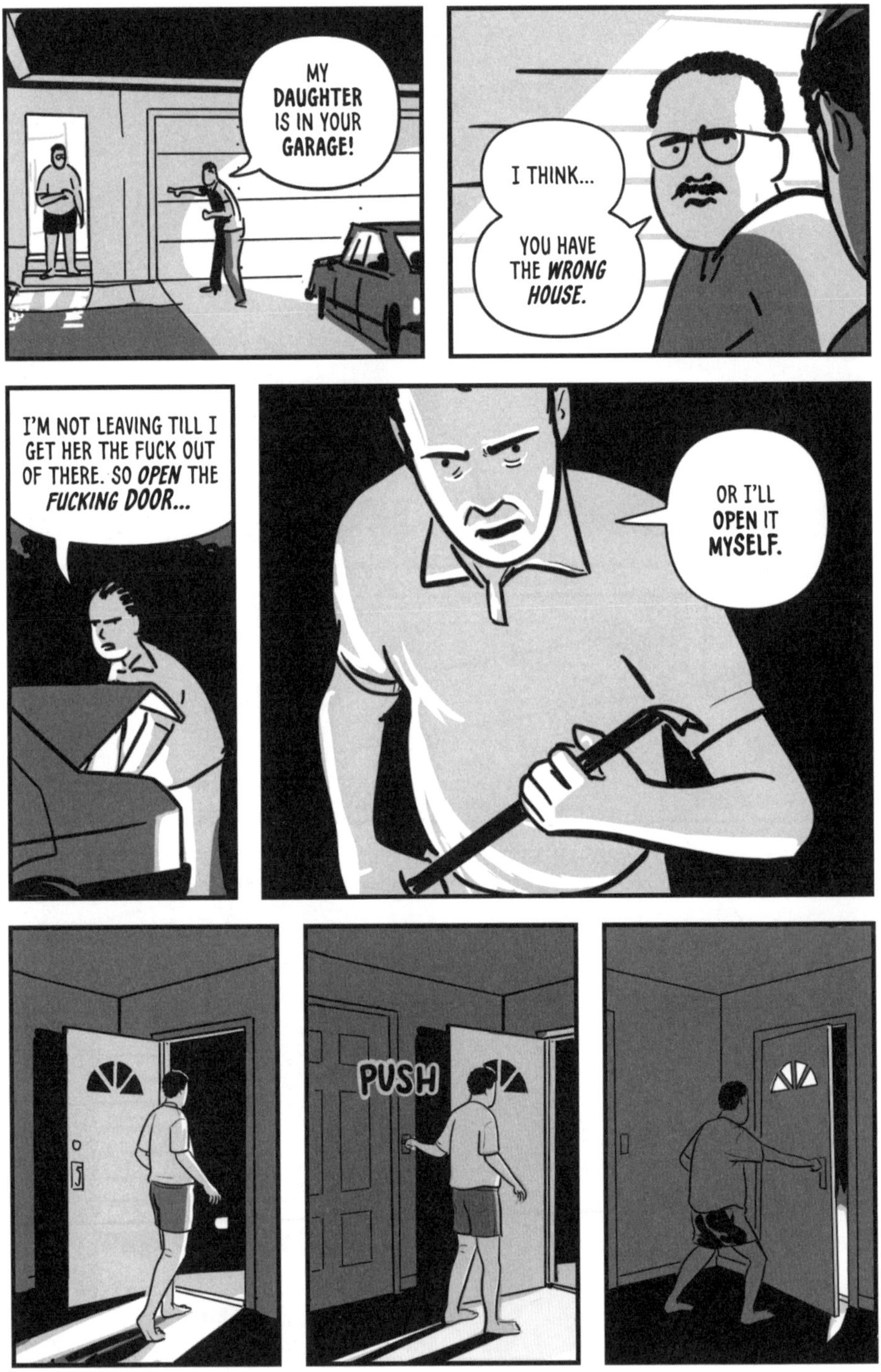
MY DAUGHTER IS IN YOUR GARAGE!
I THINK...
YOU HAVE THE WRONG HOUSE.
I'M NOT LEAVING TILL I GET HER THE FUCK OUT OF THERE. SO OPEN THE FUCKING DOOR...
OR I'LL OPEN IT MYSELF.
PUSH

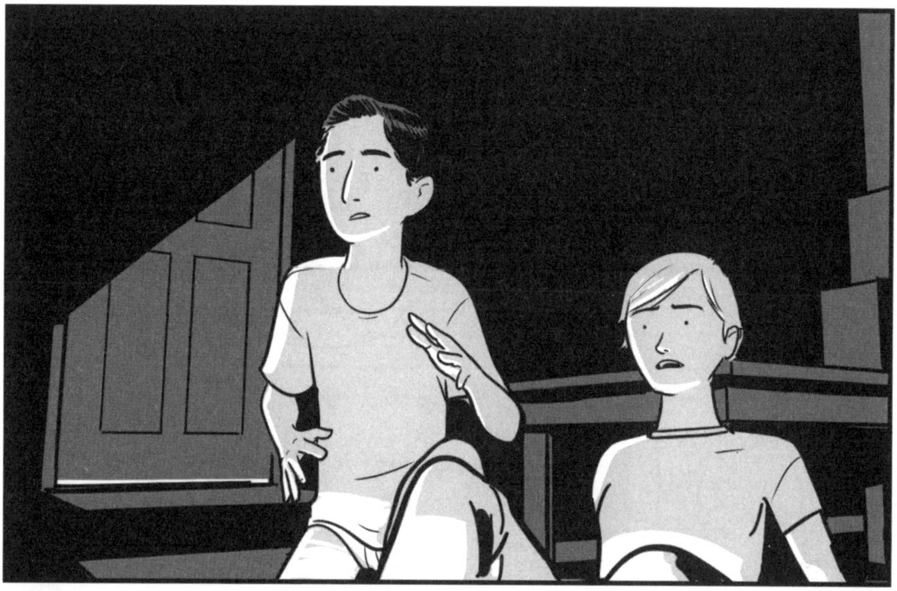

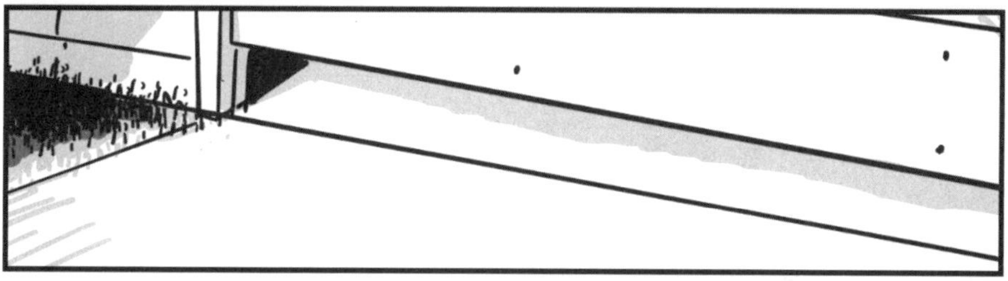

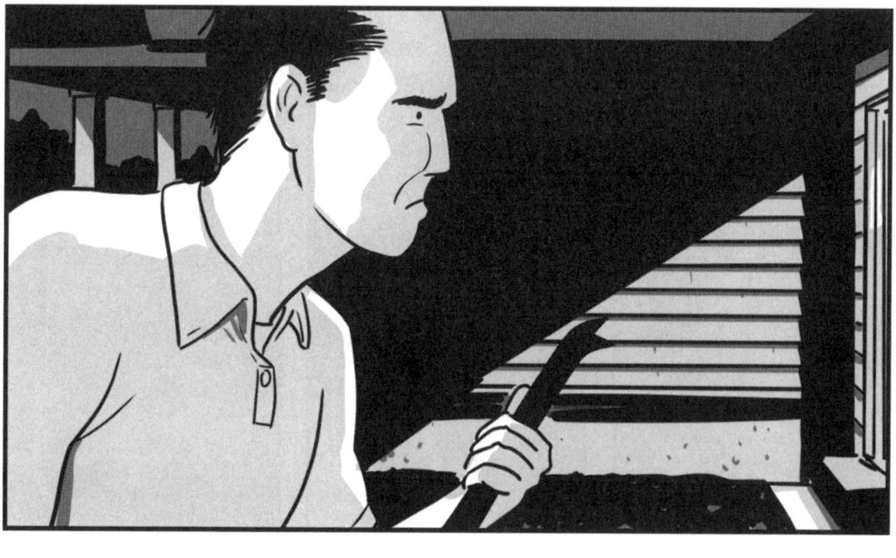

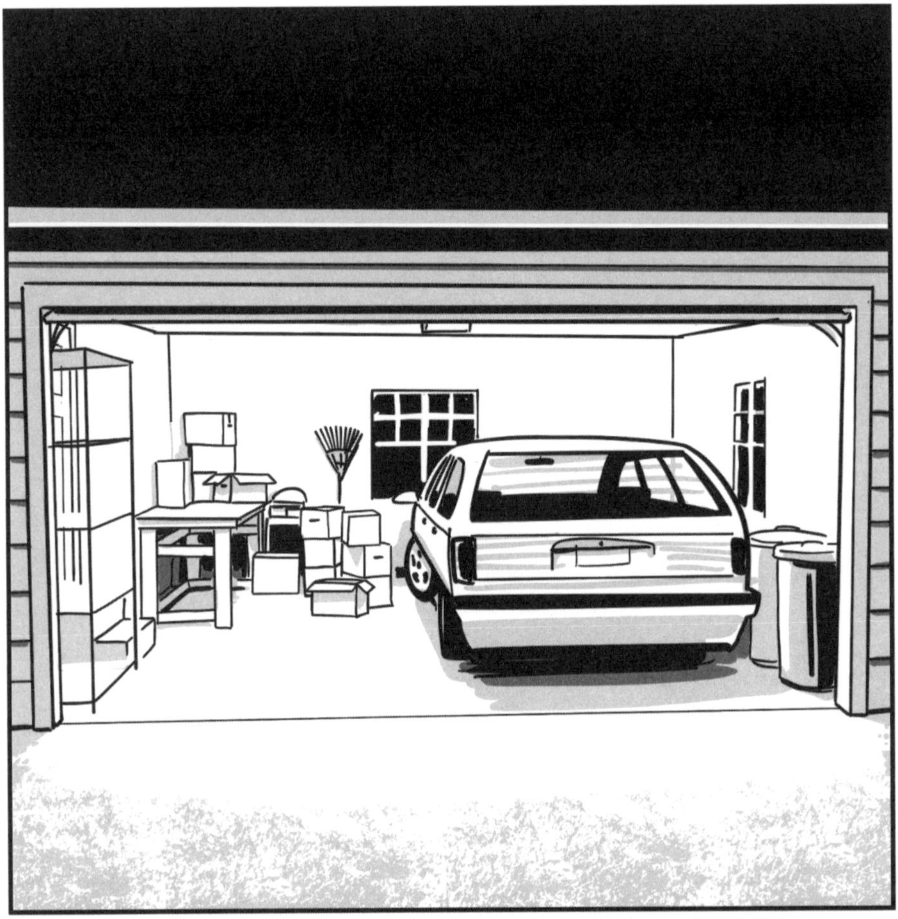

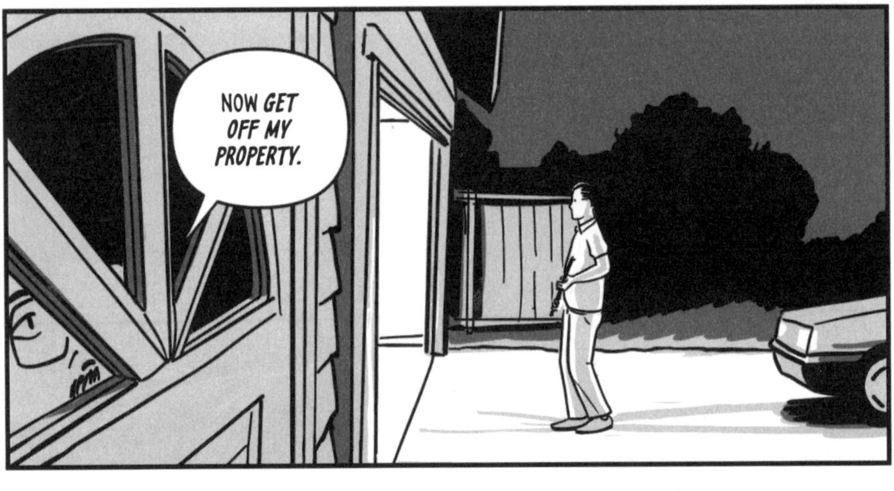
NOW GET OFF MY PROPERTY.

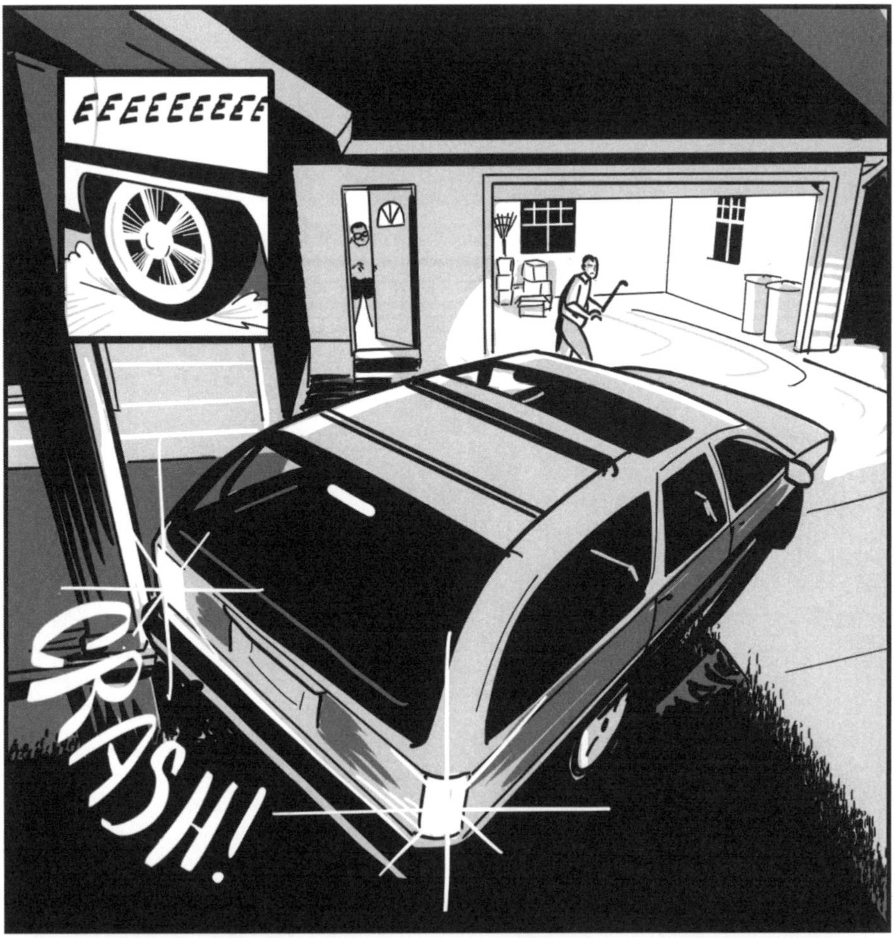
EEEEEEEEE
CRASH!

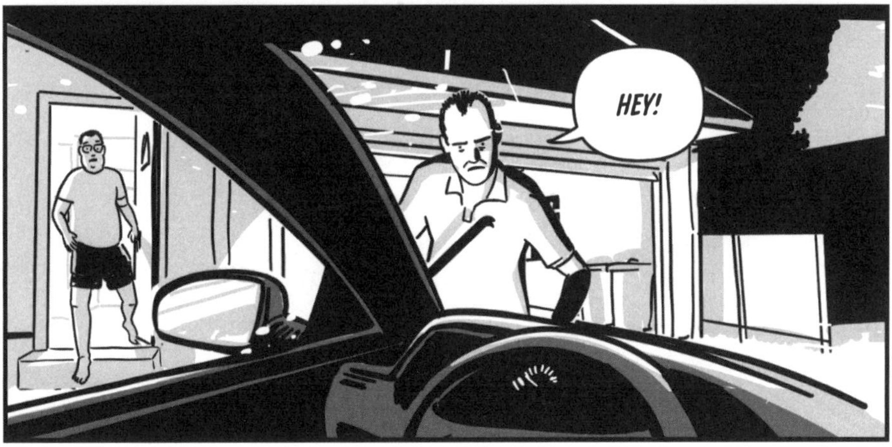
HEY!

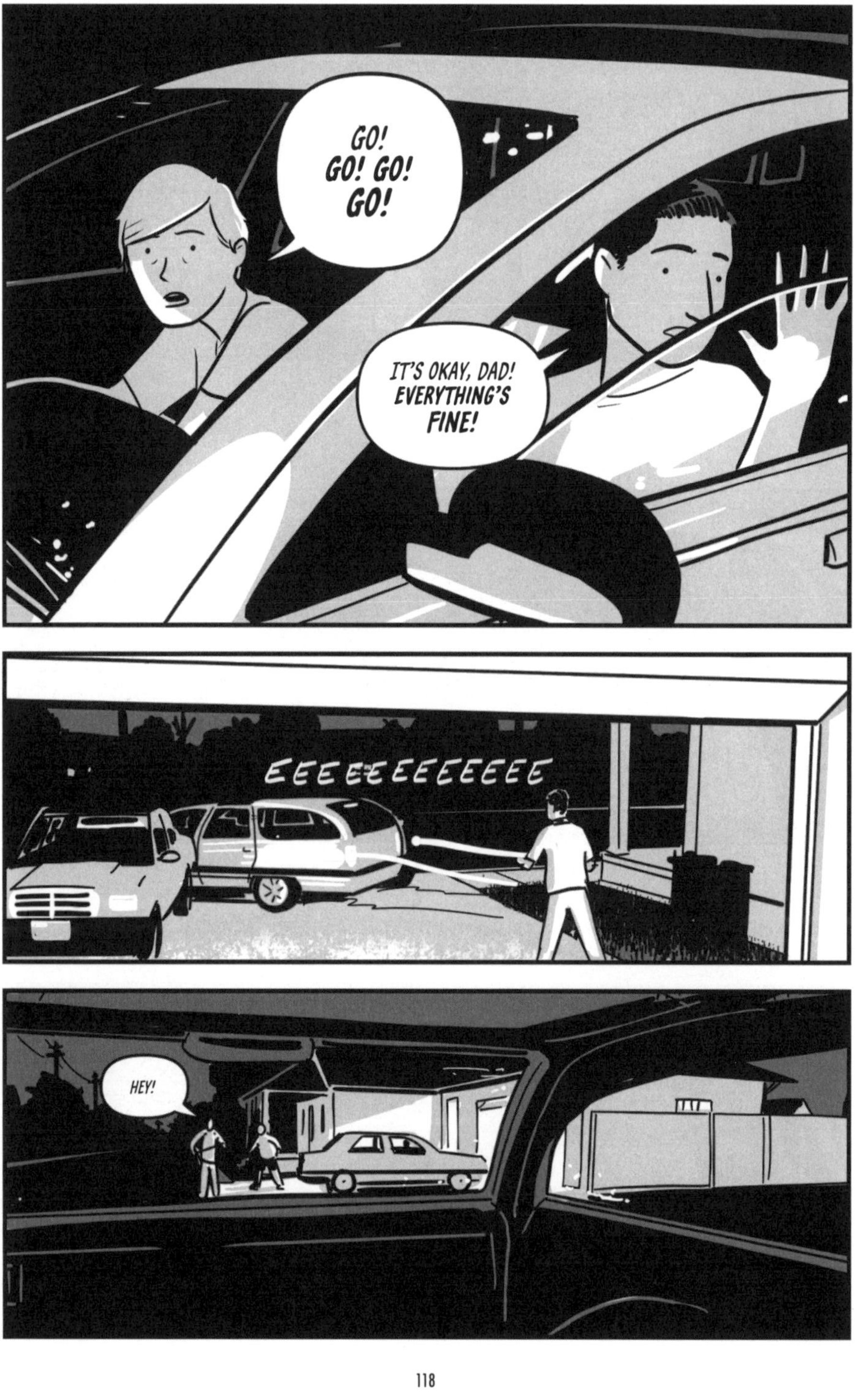
GO! GO! GO! GO!
IT'S OKAY, DAD! EVERYTHING'S FINE!
EEEEEEEEEEEEE
HEY!

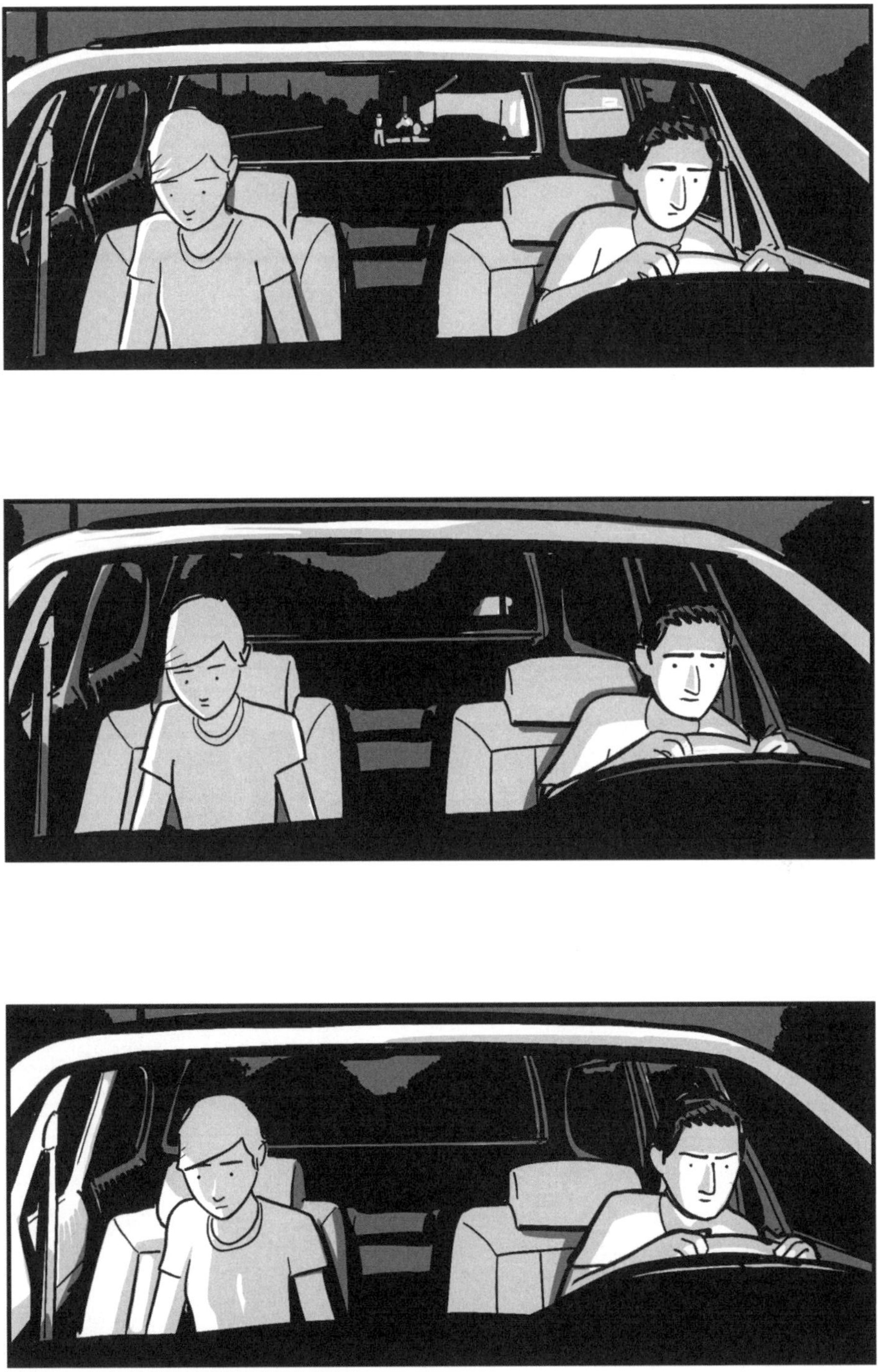

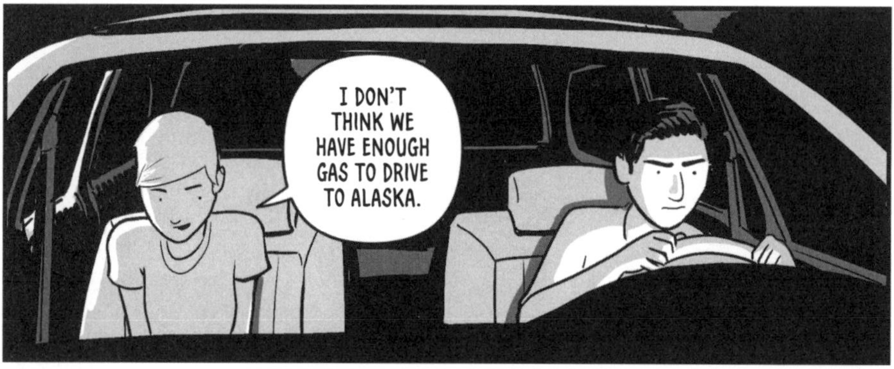
I DON'T THINK WE HAVE ENOUGH GAS TO DRIVE TO ALASKA.

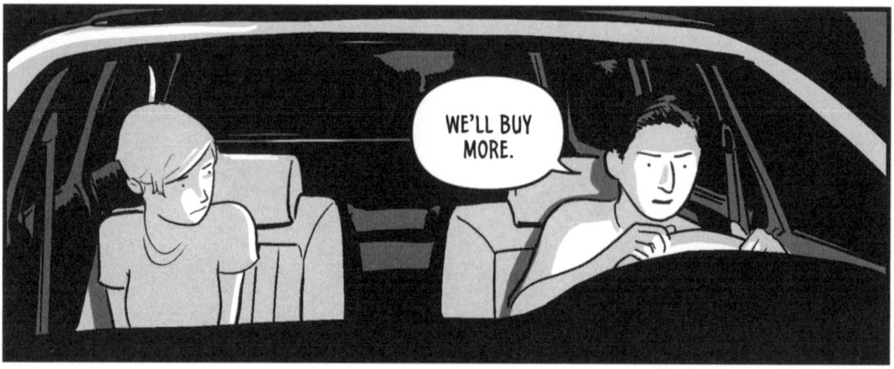
WE'LL BUY MORE.

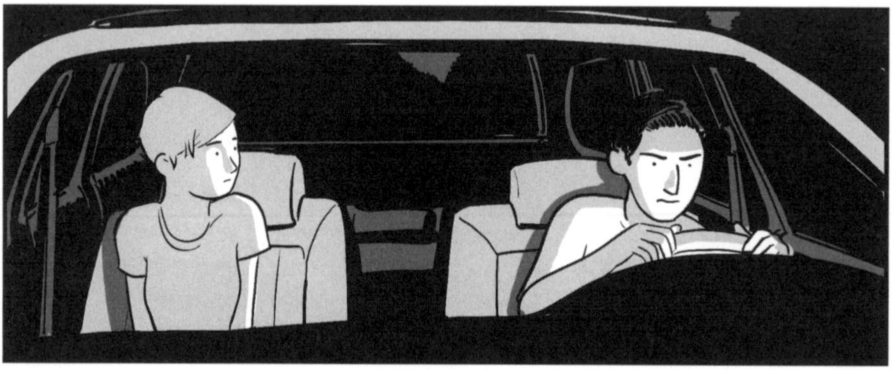

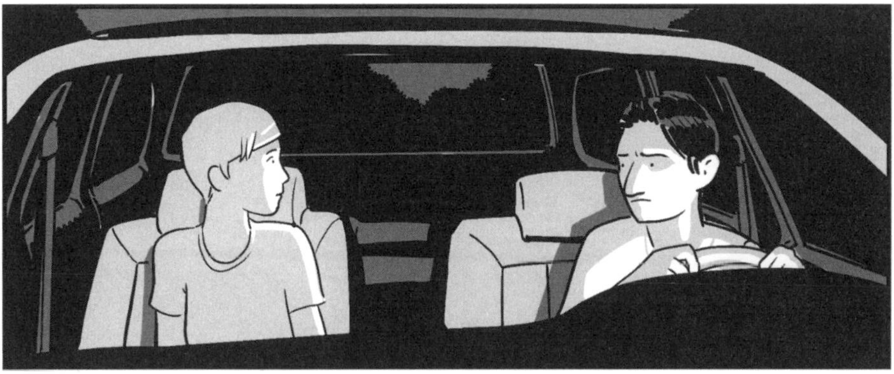

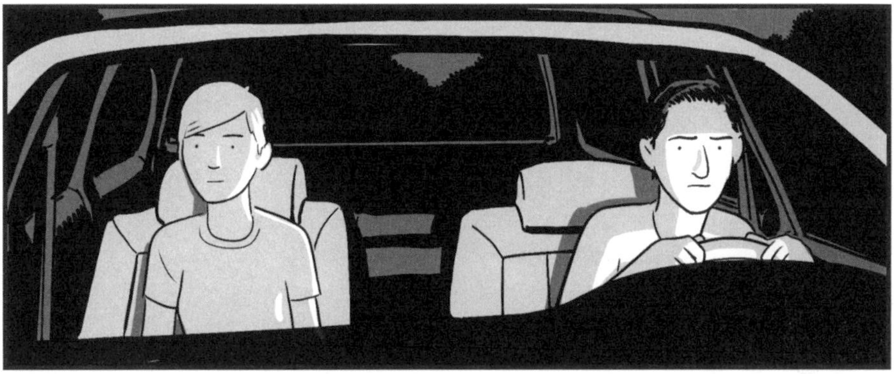

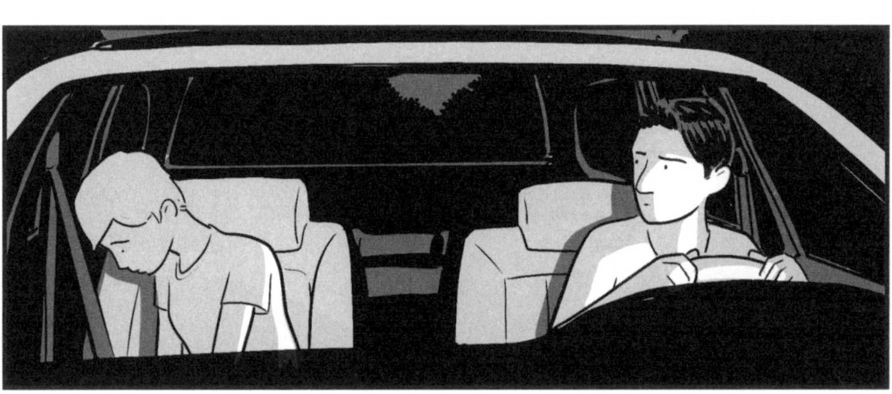

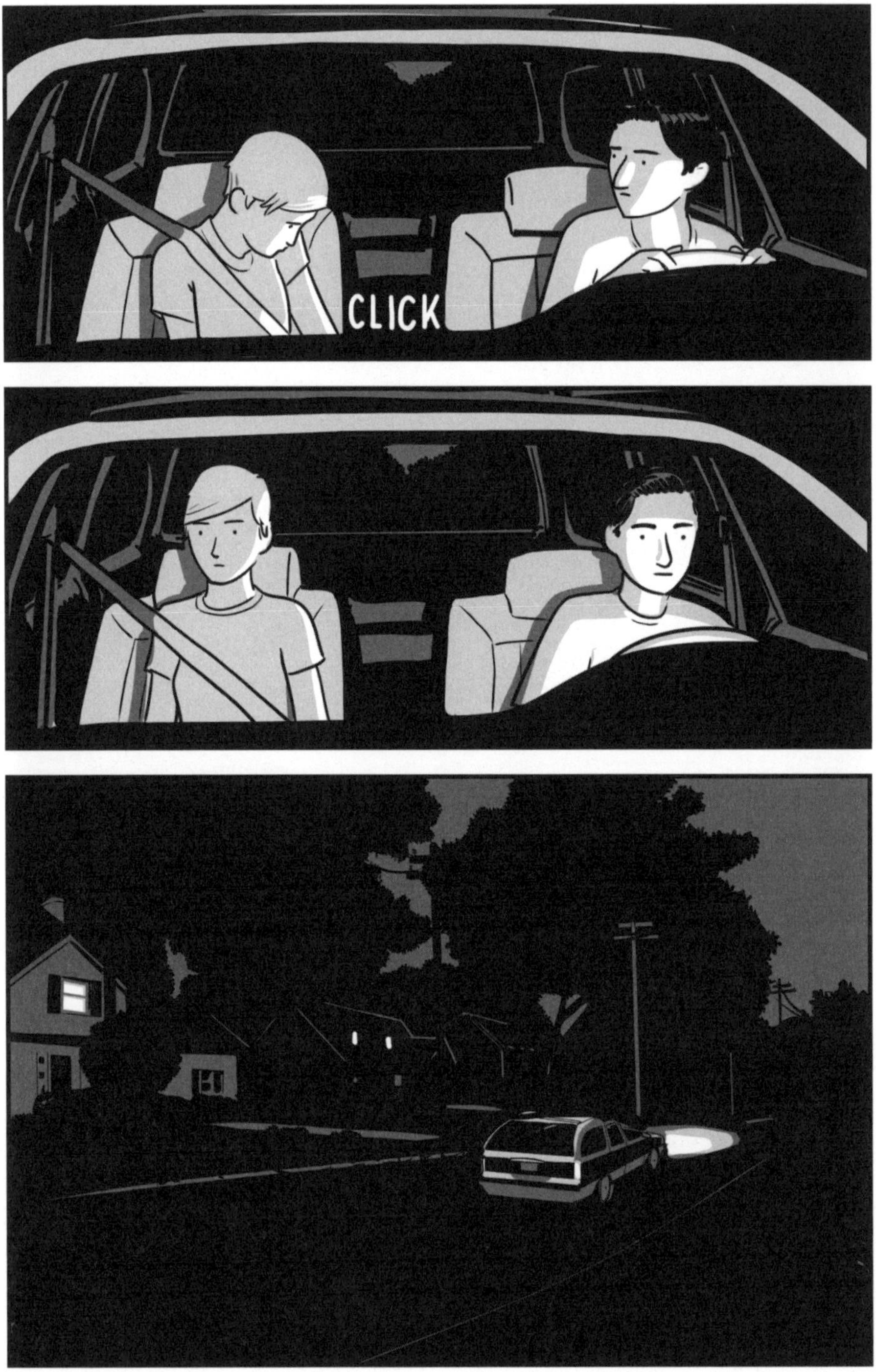
CLICK

Chapter 4

EVOL HOUSE

GAT GCS GM GS d -p+ c+++(++++) l++(+++) u+@ e×
m(+) s+/- n--- h× !f(+) g+ w++ t++(+++) r? y?

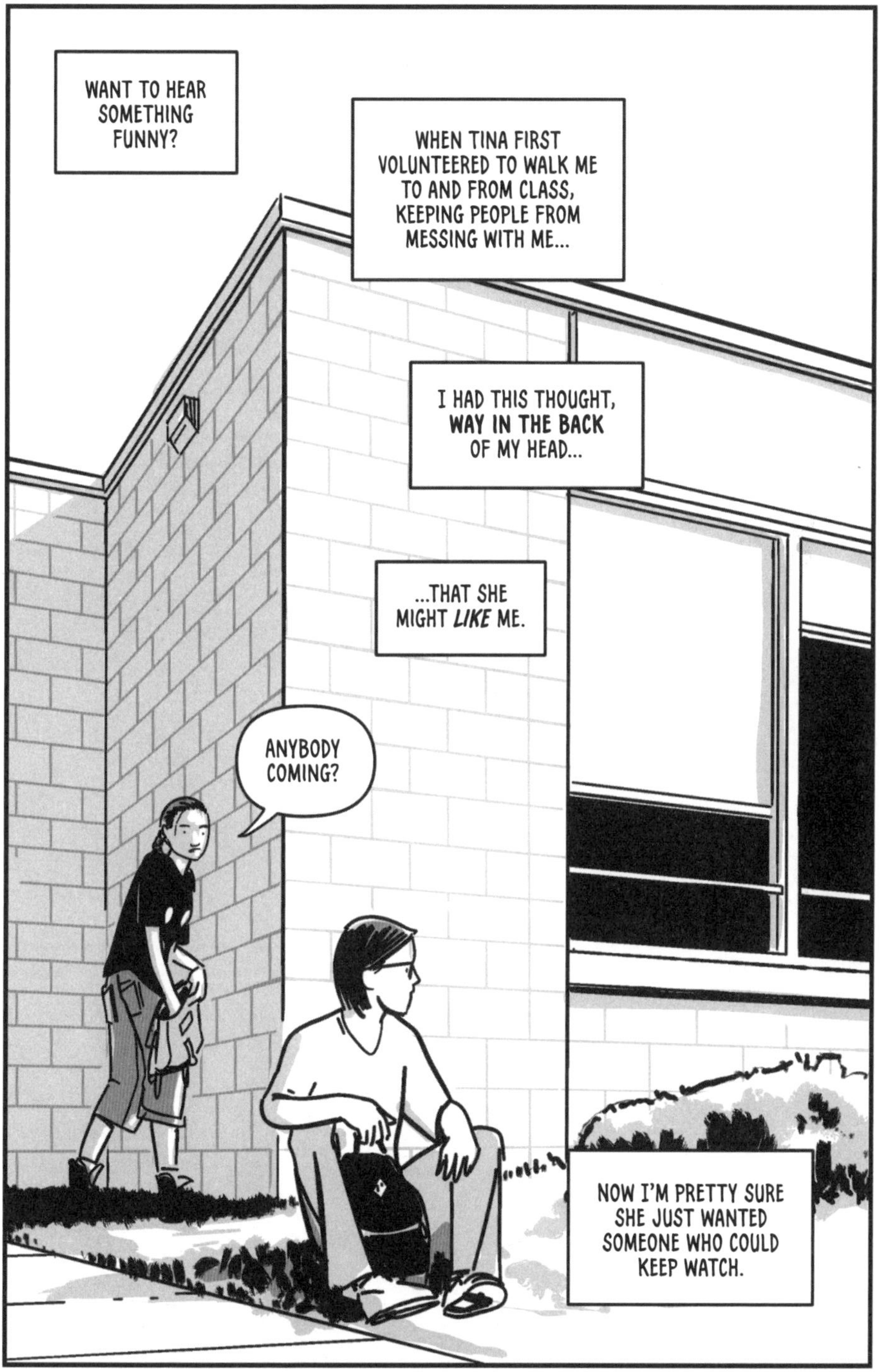
WANT TO HEAR SOMETHING FUNNY?
WHEN TINA FIRST VOLUNTEERED TO WALK ME TO AND FROM CLASS, KEEPING PEOPLE FROM MESSING WITH ME...
I HAD THIS THOUGHT, **WAY IN THE BACK** OF MY HEAD...
...THAT SHE MIGHT *LIKE* ME.
ANYBODY COMING?
NOW I'M PRETTY SURE SHE JUST WANTED SOMEONE WHO COULD KEEP WATCH.

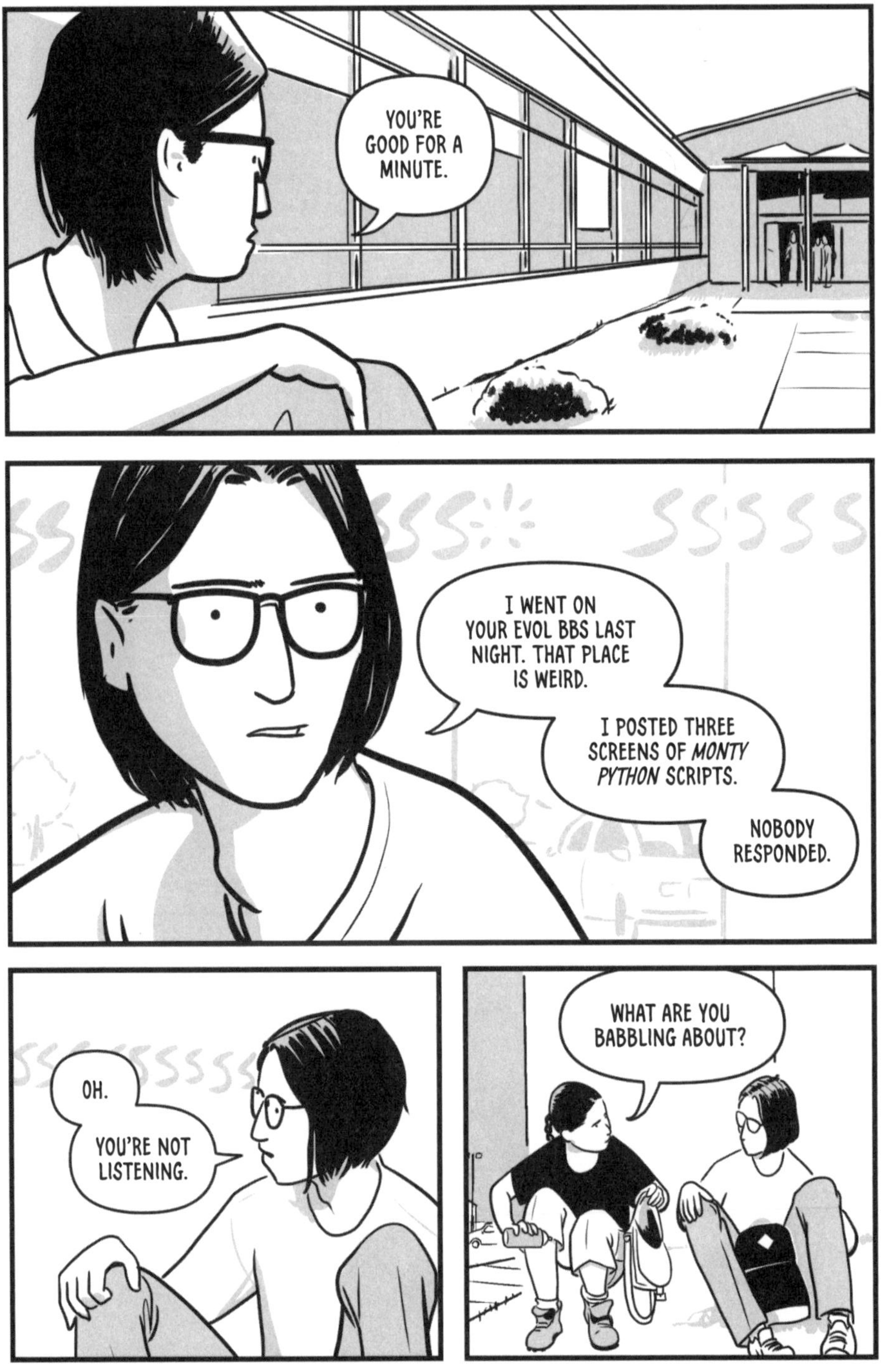
YOU'RE GOOD FOR A MINUTE.
I WENT ON YOUR EVOL BBS LAST NIGHT. THAT PLACE IS WEIRD.
I POSTED THREE SCREENS OF *MONTY PYTHON* SCRIPTS.
NOBODY RESPONDED.
OH.
YOU'RE NOT LISTENING.
WHAT ARE YOU BABBLING ABOUT?

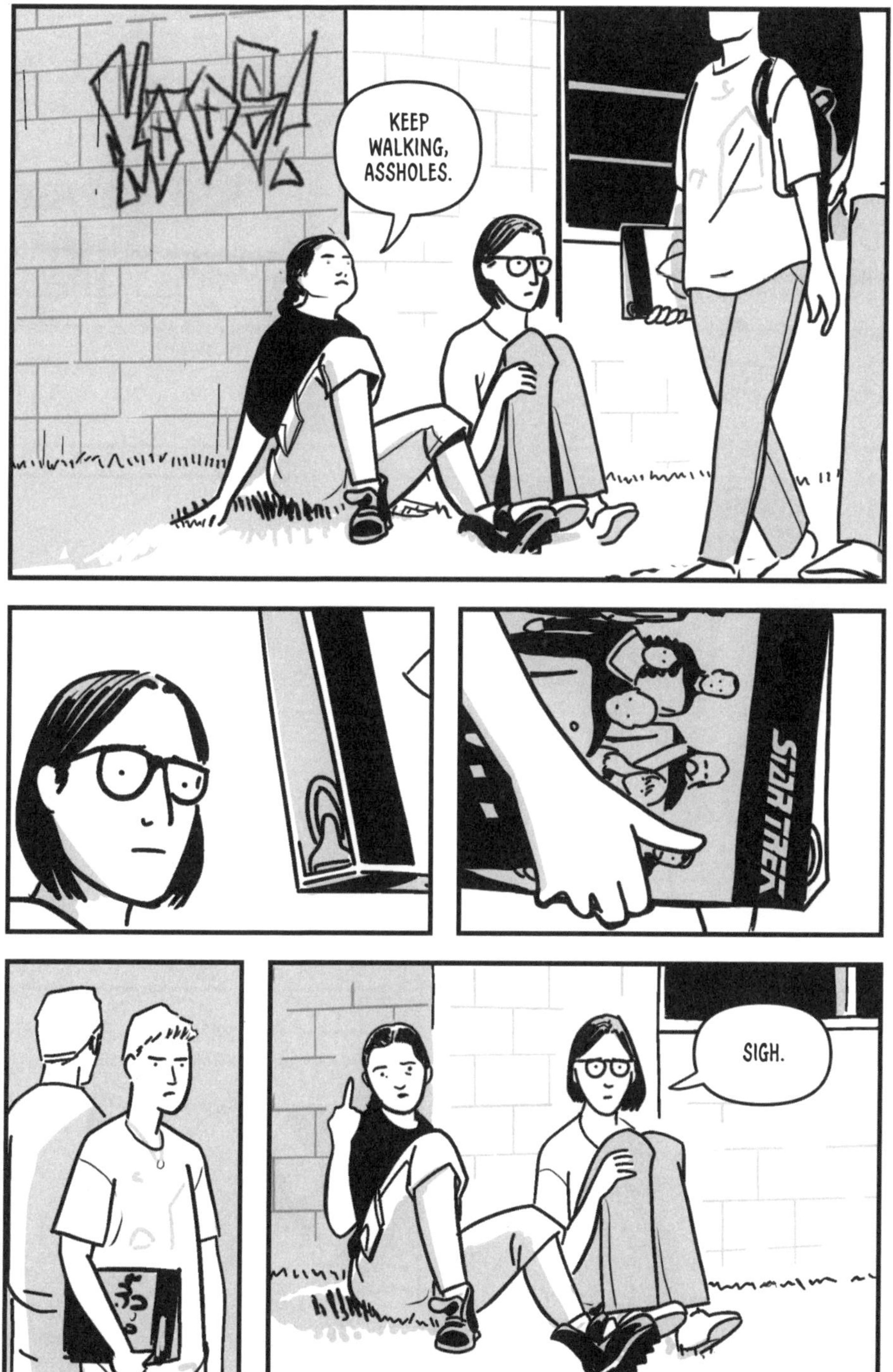
KEEP WALKING, ASSHOLES.
STAR TREK
SIGH.

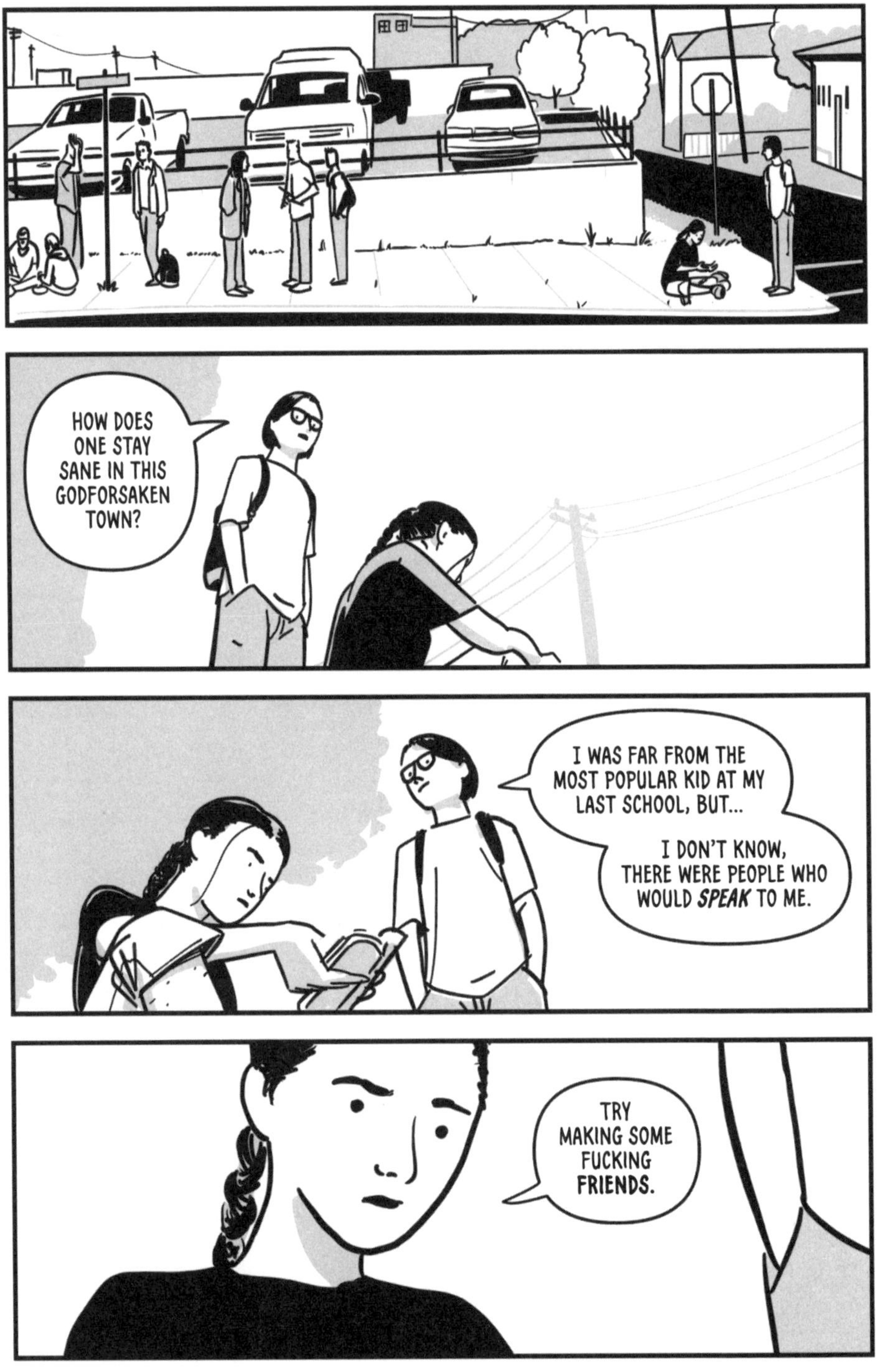
HOW DOES ONE STAY SANE IN THIS GODFORSAKEN TOWN?
I WAS FAR FROM THE MOST POPULAR KID AT MY LAST SCHOOL, BUT...
I DON'T KNOW, THERE WERE PEOPLE WHO WOULD *SPEAK* TO ME.
TRY MAKING SOME FUCKING **FRIENDS.**

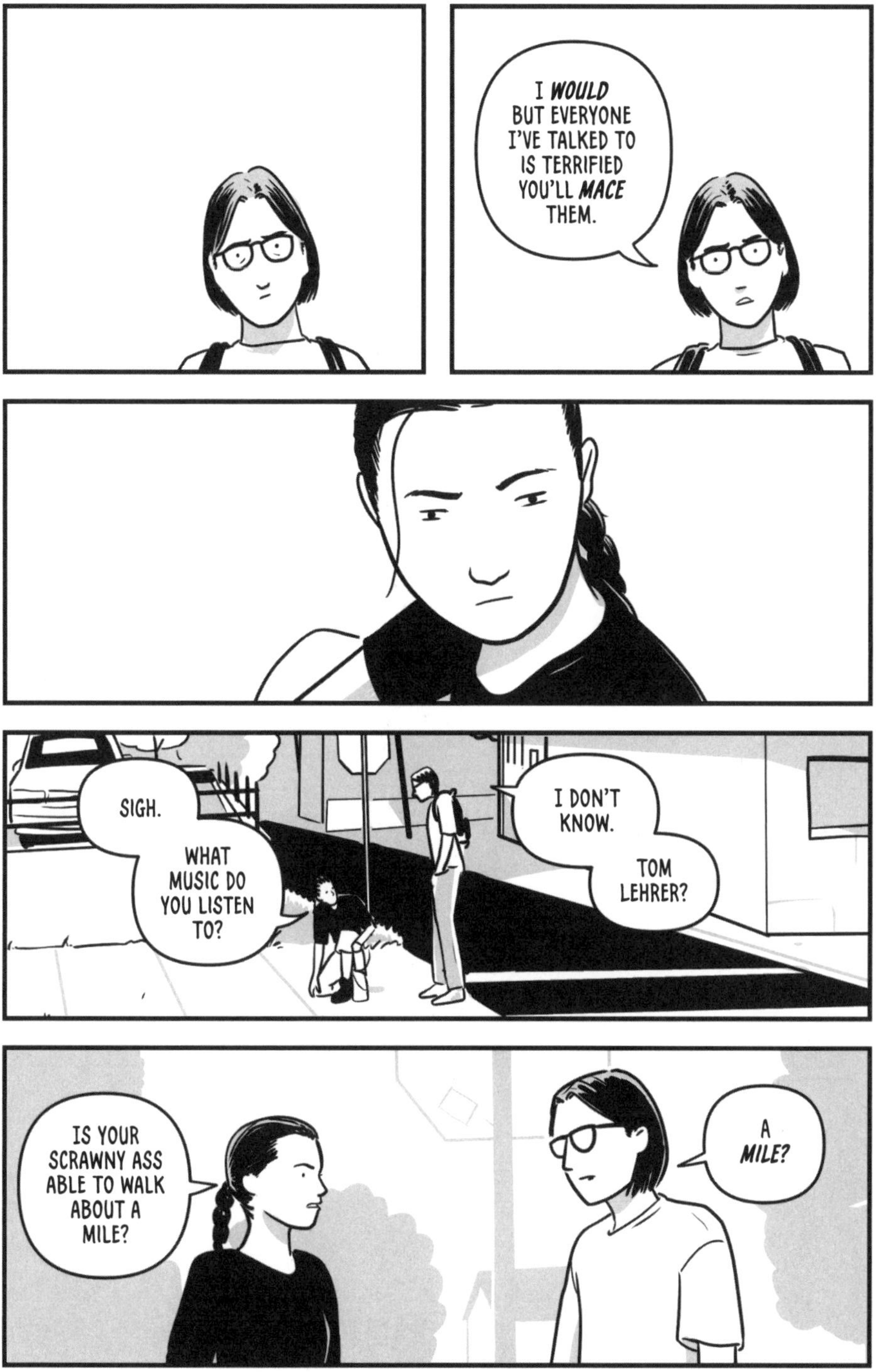
I WOULD BUT EVERYONE I'VE TALKED TO IS TERRIFIED YOU'LL MACE THEM.
SIGH.
WHAT MUSIC DO YOU LISTEN TO?
I DON'T KNOW.
TOM LEHRER?
IS YOUR SCRAWNY ASS ABLE TO WALK ABOUT A MILE?
A MILE?

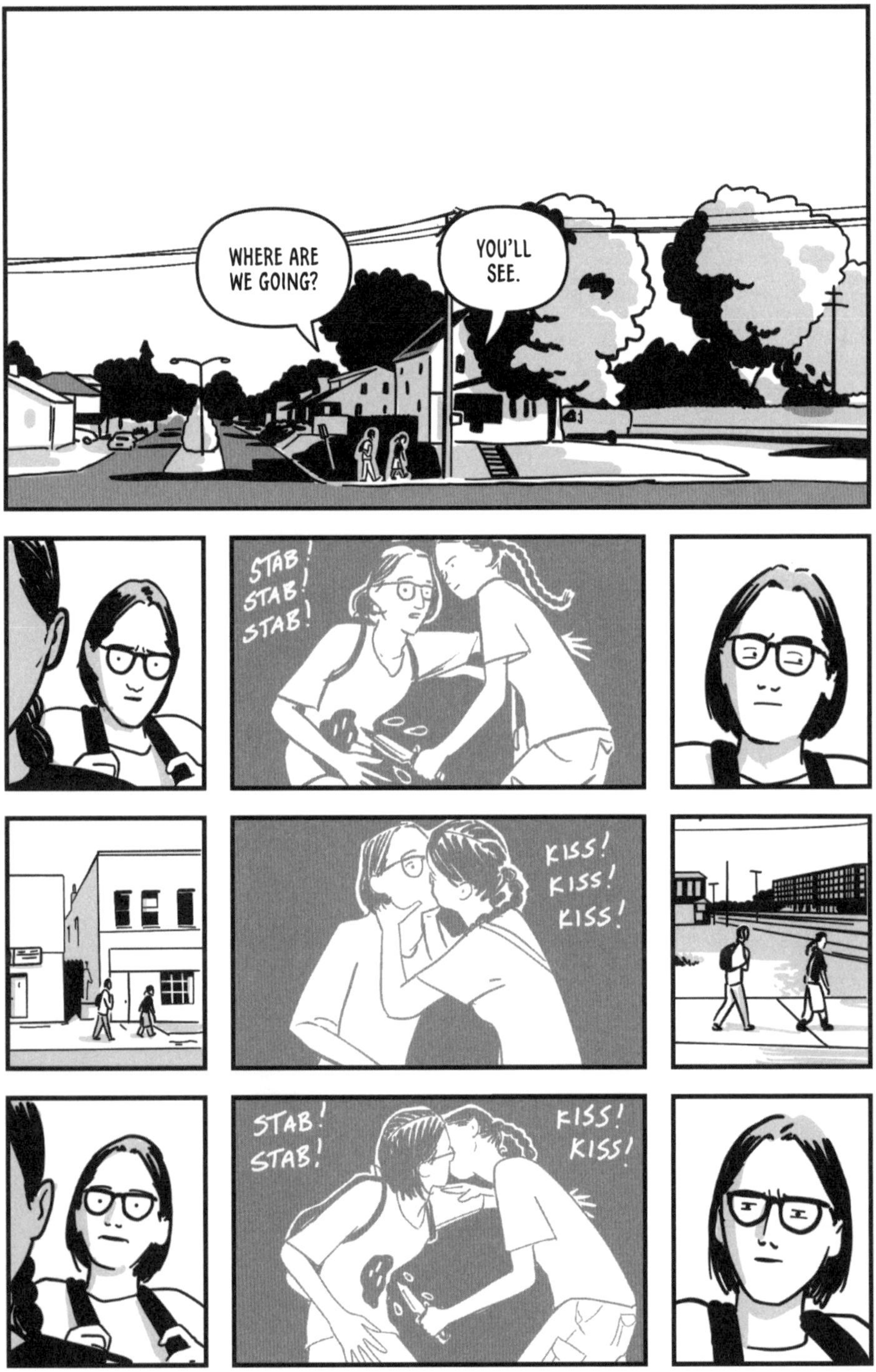
WHERE ARE WE GOING?
YOU'LL SEE.
STAB! STAB! STAB!
KISS! KISS! KISS!
STAB! STAB!
KISS! KISS!

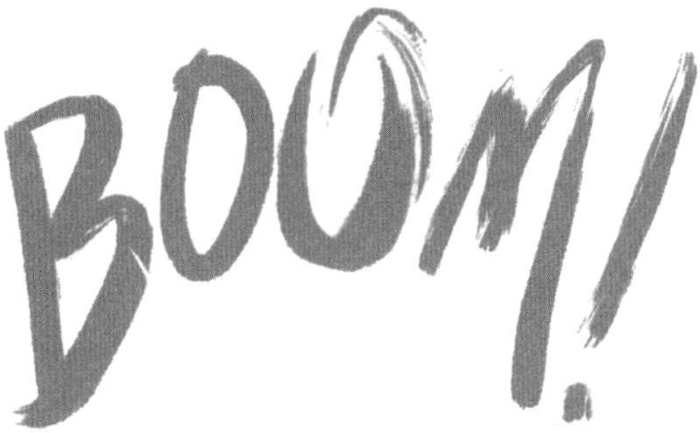
BOOM!

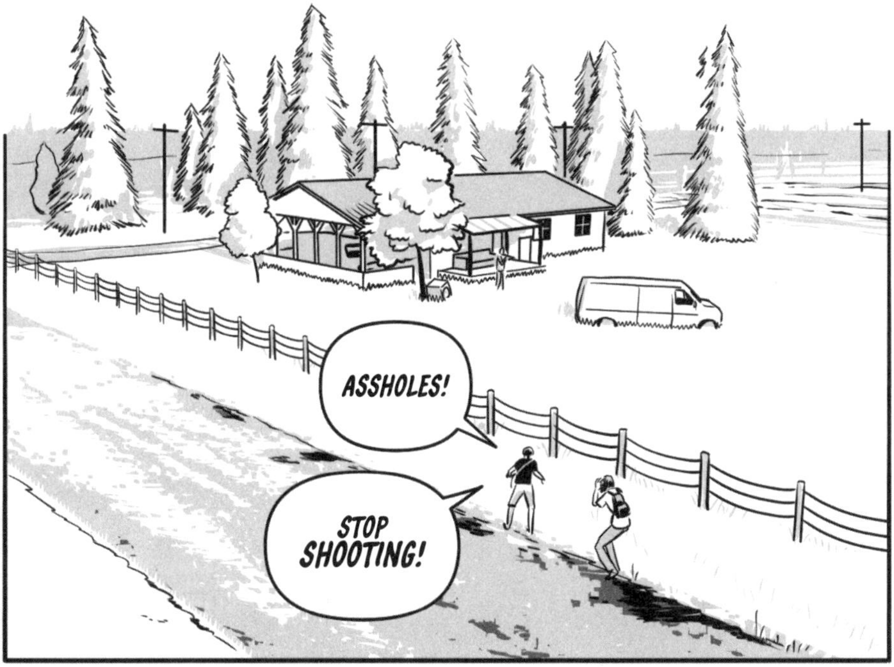
ASSHOLES!
STOP SHOOTING!

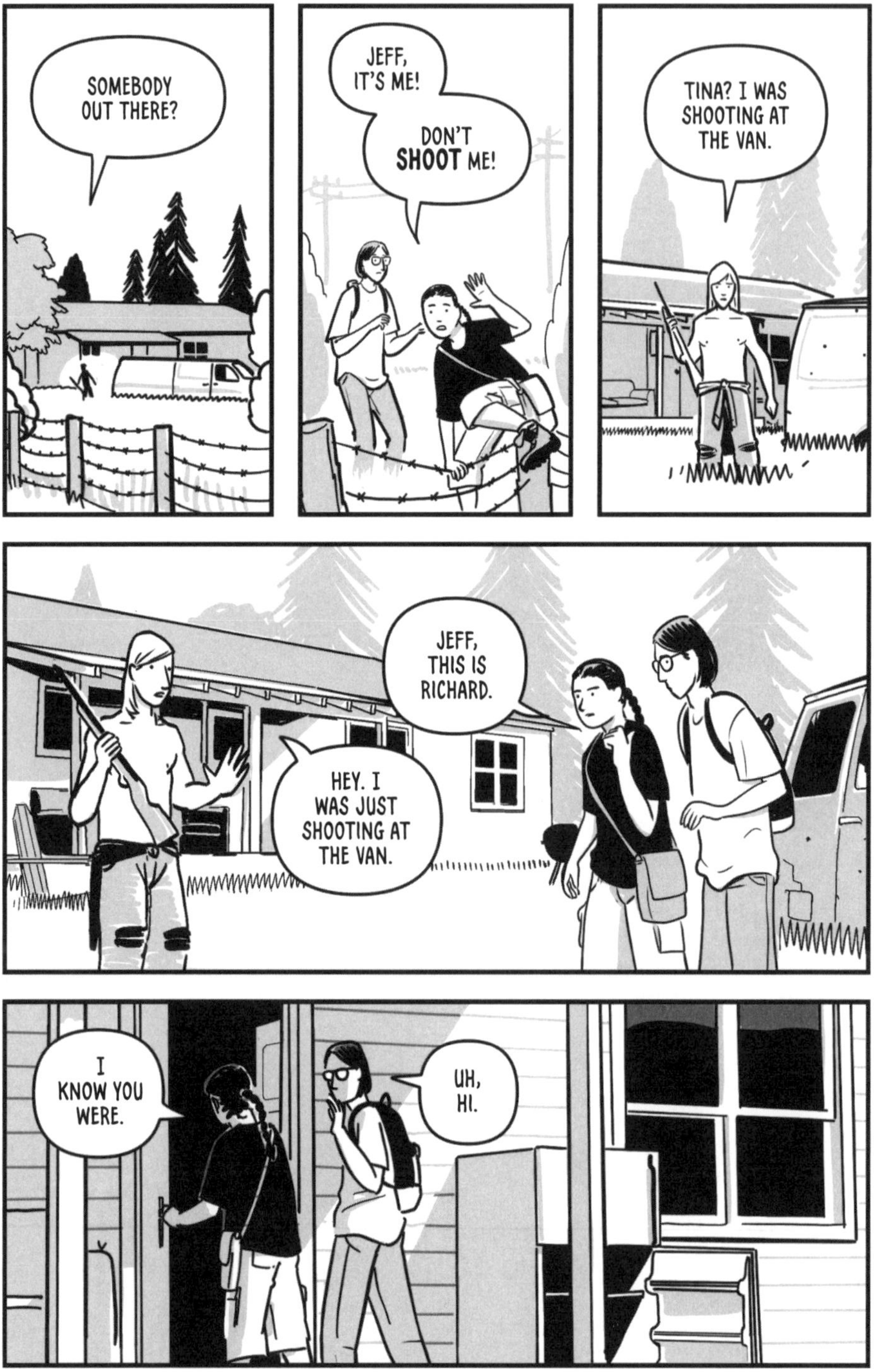
SOMEBODY OUT THERE?
JEFF, IT'S ME!
DON'T SHOOT ME!
TINA? I WAS SHOOTING AT THE VAN.
JEFF, THIS IS RICHARD.
HEY. I WAS JUST SHOOTING AT THE VAN.
I KNOW YOU WERE.
UH, HI.

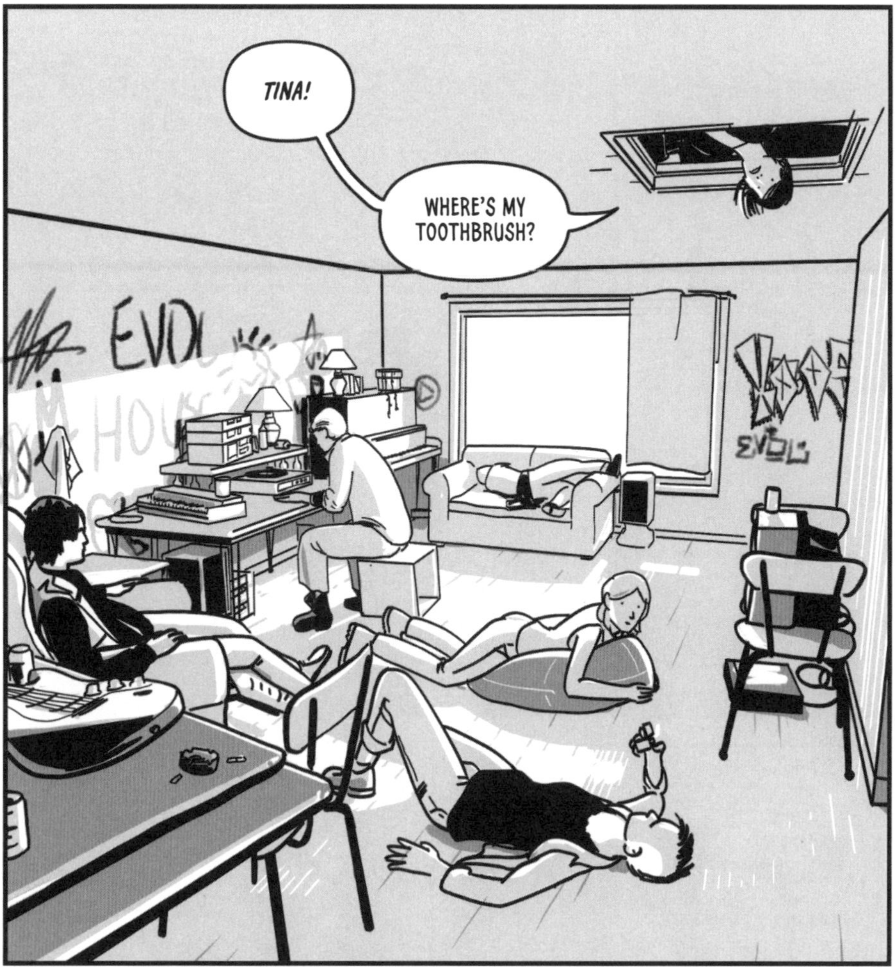
TINA!
WHERE'S MY TOOTHBRUSH?

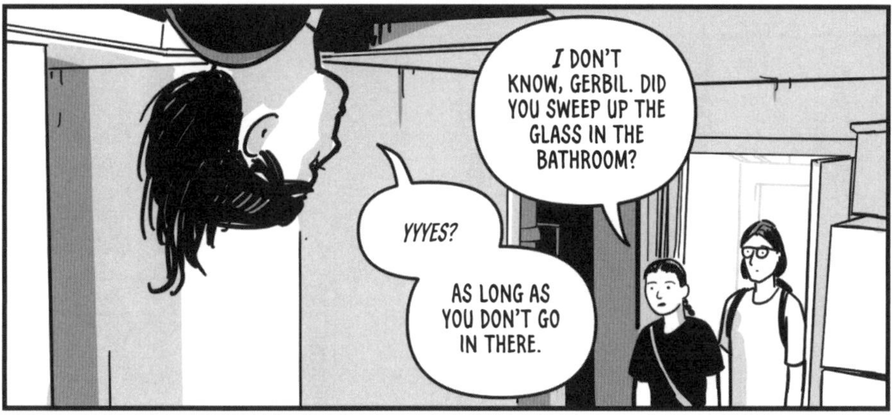
I DON'T KNOW, GERBIL. DID YOU SWEEP UP THE GLASS IN THE BATHROOM?
YYYES?
AS LONG AS YOU DON'T GO IN THERE.

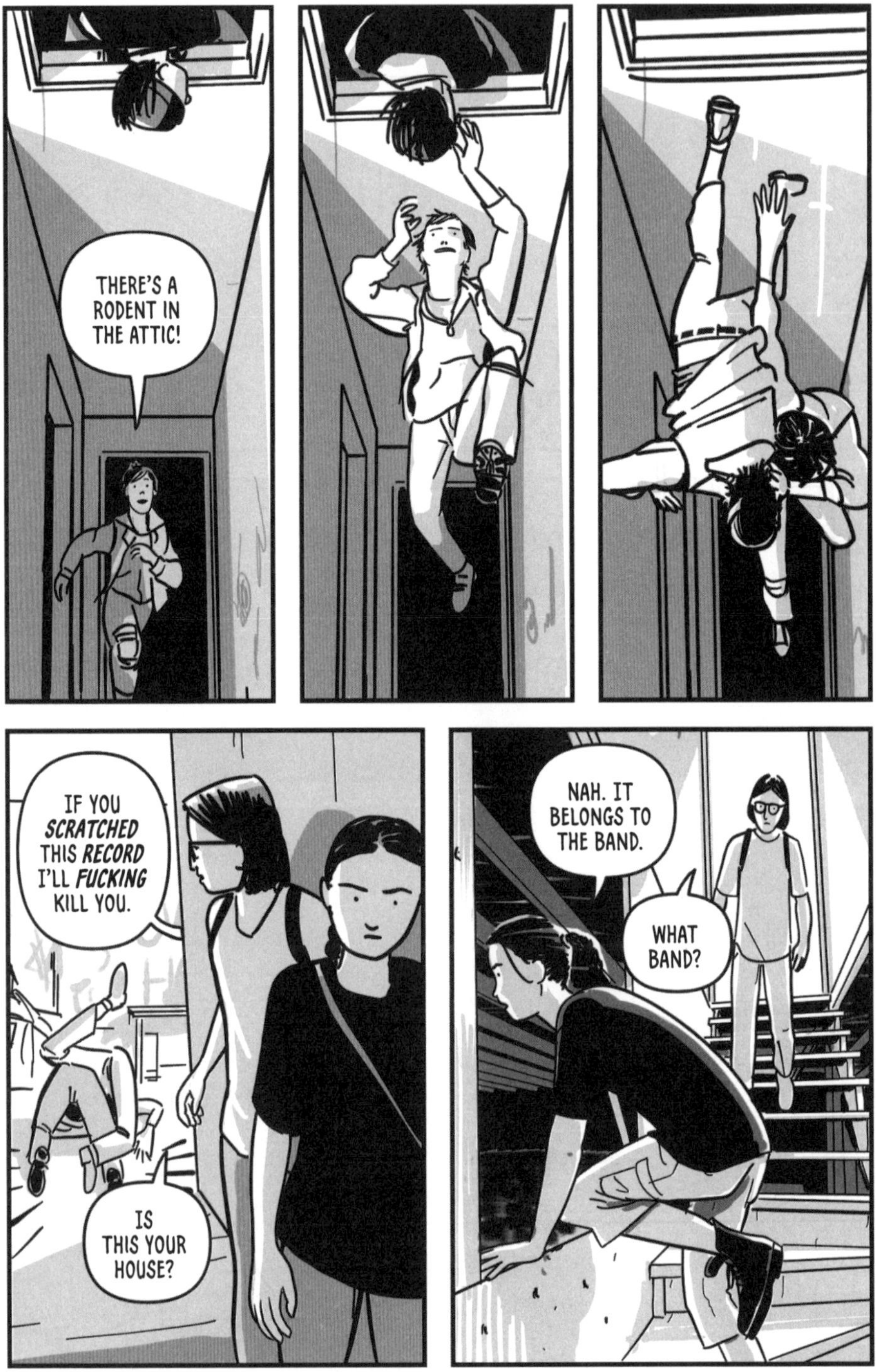

THERE'S A RODENT IN THE ATTIC!
IF YOU *SCRATCHED* THIS *RECORD* I'LL *FUCKING* KILL YOU.
IS THIS YOUR HOUSE?
NAH. IT BELONGS TO THE BAND.
WHAT BAND?

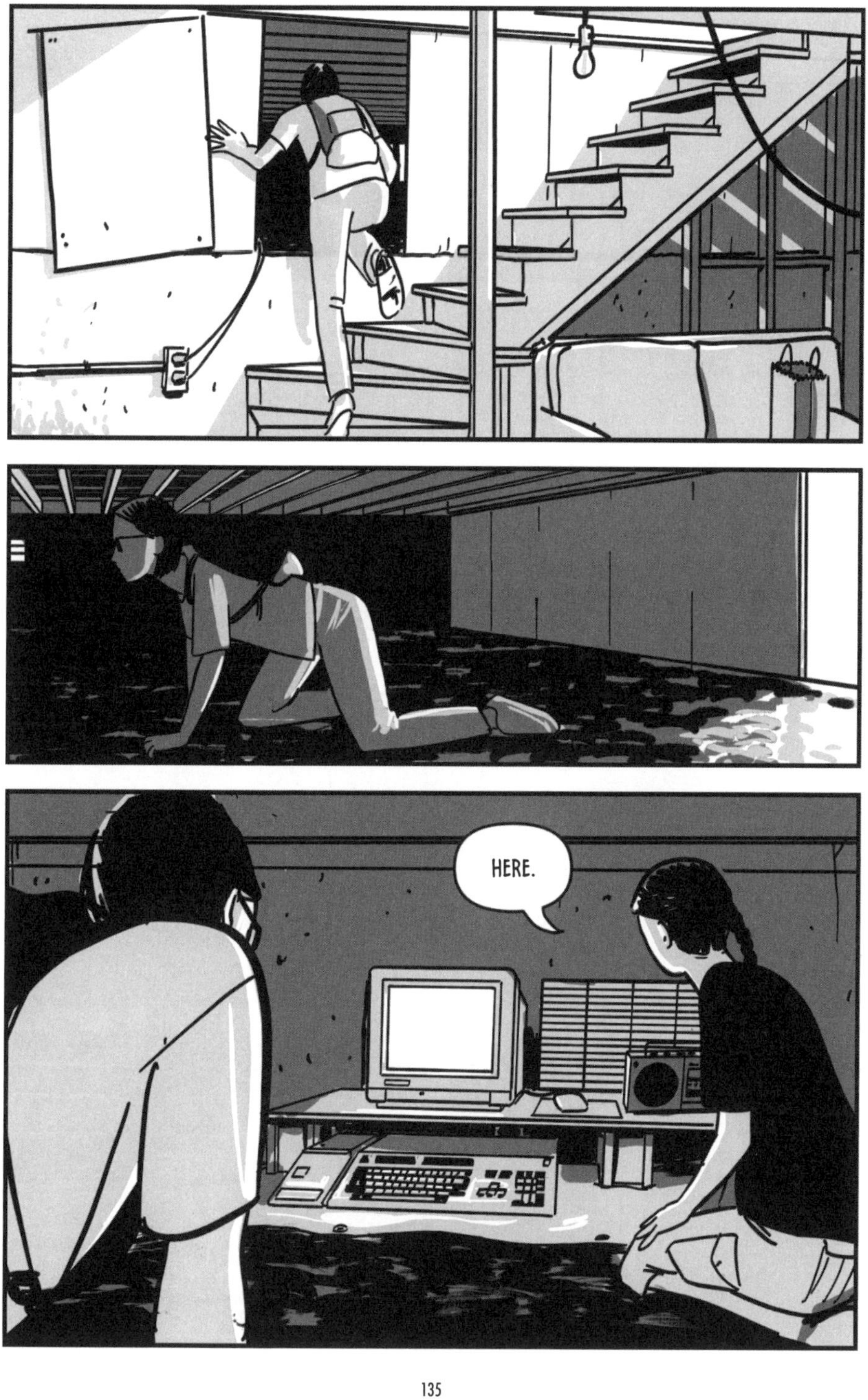
HERE.

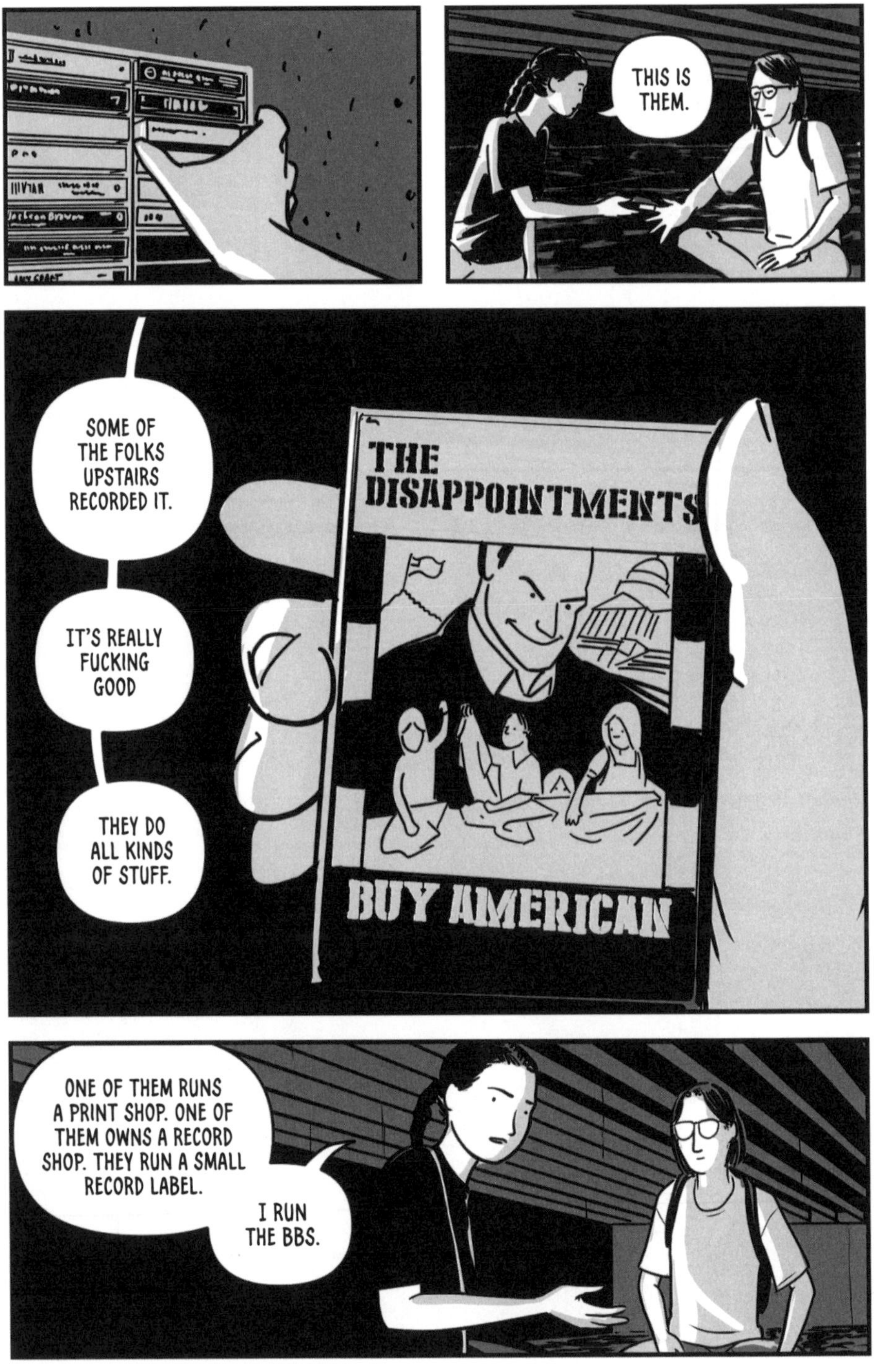
THIS IS THEM.
SOME OF THE FOLKS UPSTAIRS RECORDED IT.
IT'S REALLY FUCKING GOOD
THEY DO ALL KINDS OF STUFF.
THE DISAPPOINTMENTS
BUY AMERICAN
ONE OF THEM RUNS A PRINT SHOP. ONE OF THEM OWNS A RECORD SHOP. THEY RUN A SMALL RECORD LABEL.
I RUN THE BBS.

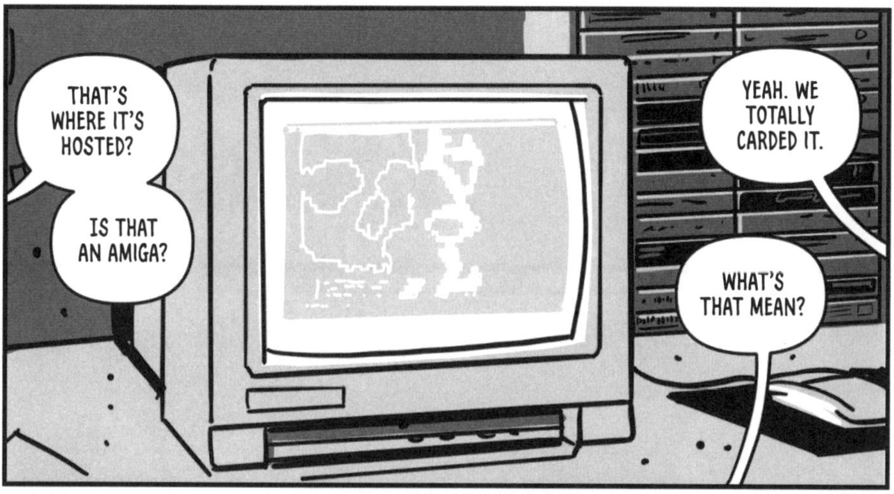
THAT'S WHERE IT'S HOSTED?
IS THAT AN AMIGA?
YEAH. WE TOTALLY CARDED IT.
WHAT'S THAT MEAN?

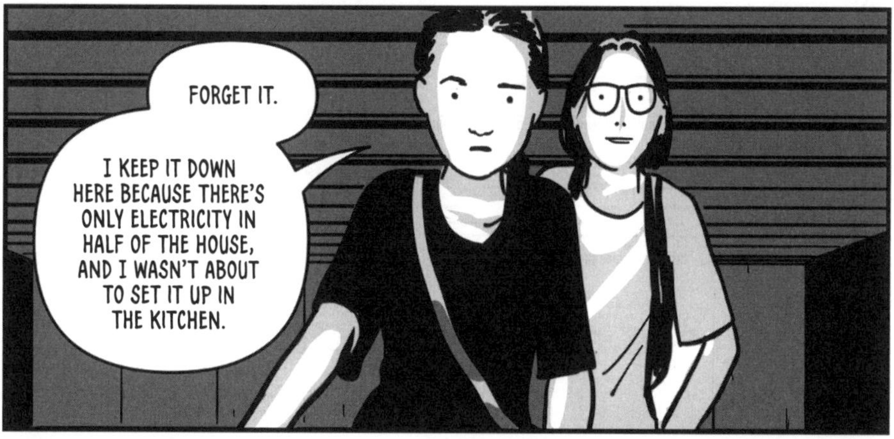
FORGET IT.
I KEEP IT DOWN HERE BECAUSE THERE'S ONLY ELECTRICITY IN HALF OF THE HOUSE, AND I WASN'T ABOUT TO SET IT UP IN THE KITCHEN.

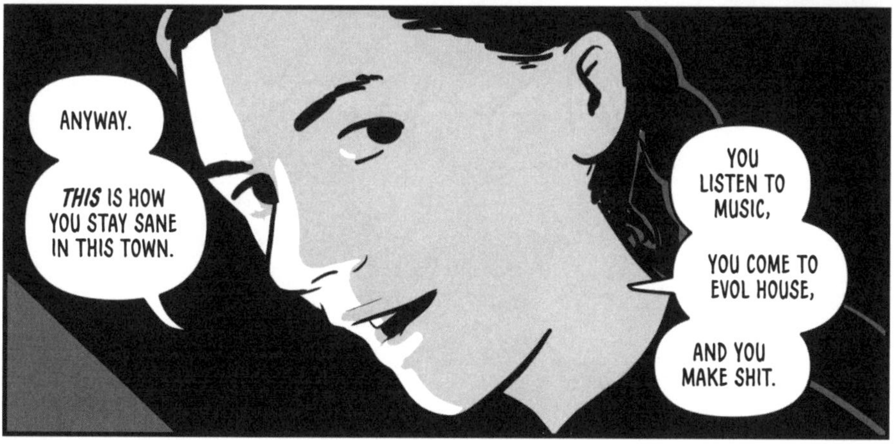
ANYWAY.
THIS IS HOW YOU STAY SANE IN THIS TOWN.
YOU LISTEN TO MUSIC,
YOU COME TO EVOL HOUSE,
AND YOU MAKE SHIT.

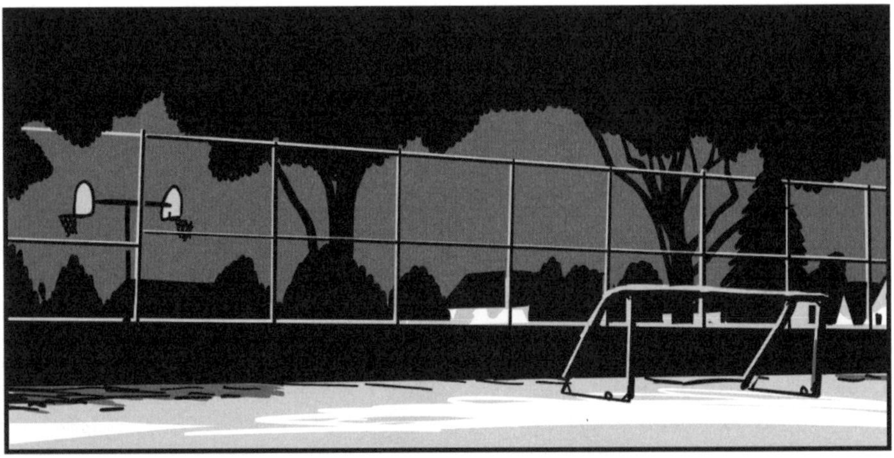

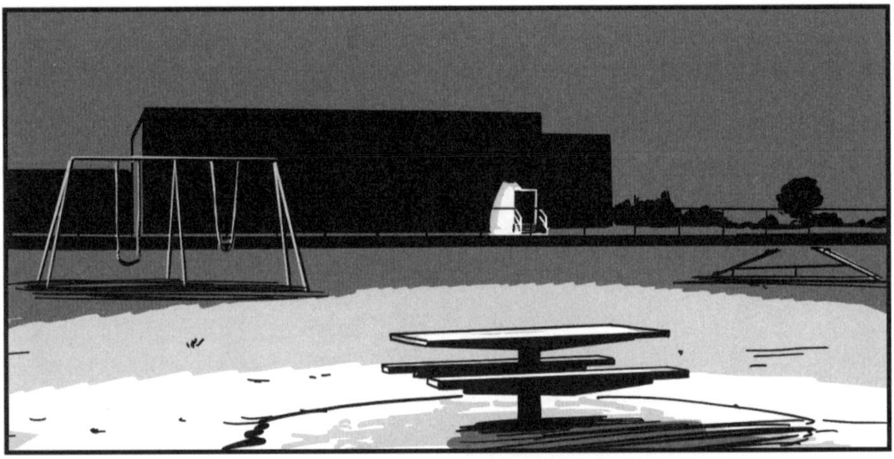

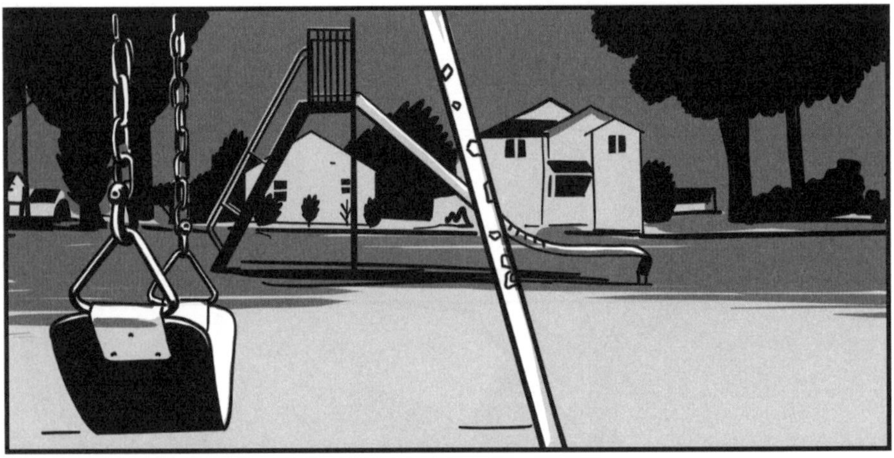

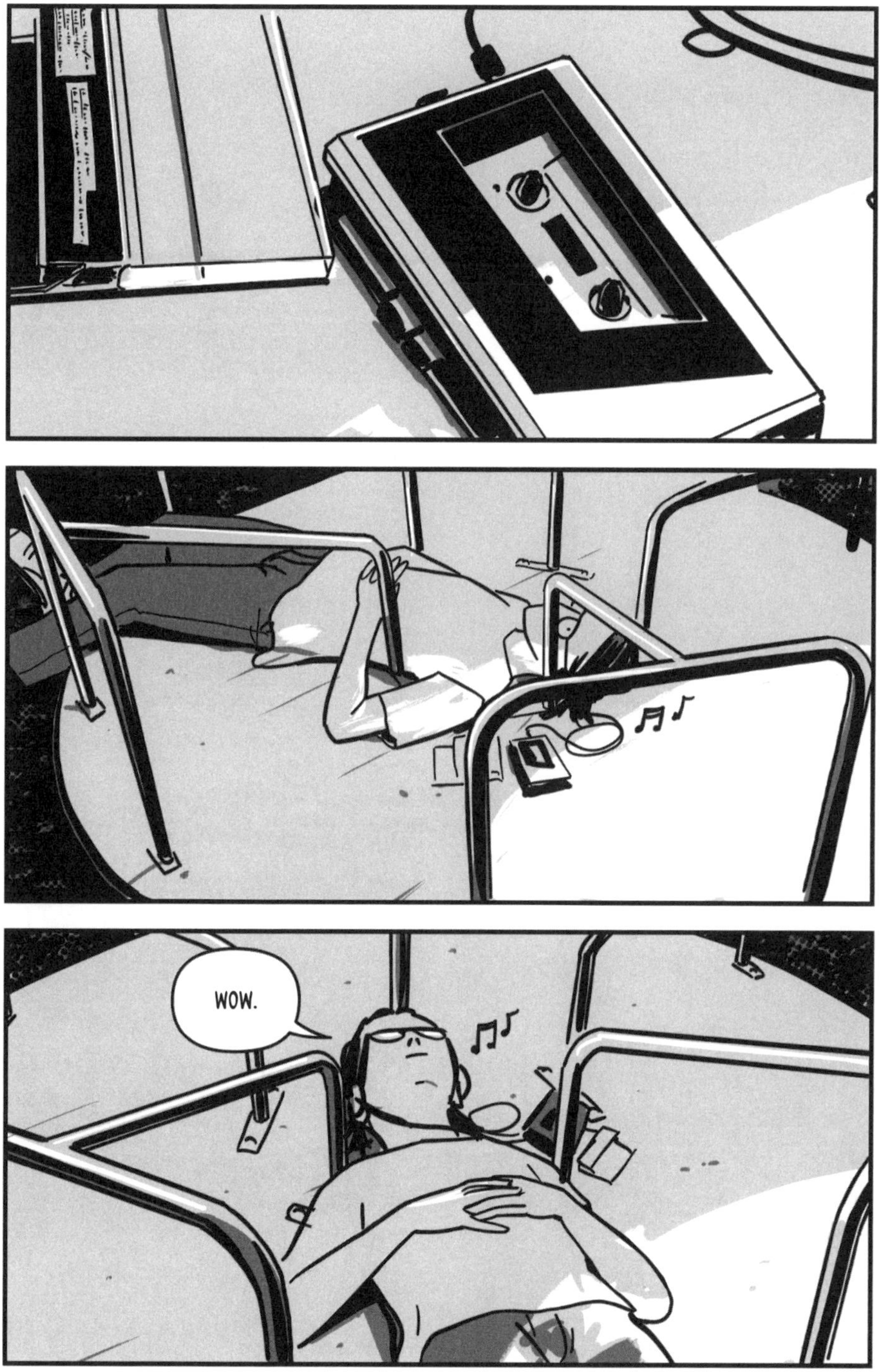
WOW.

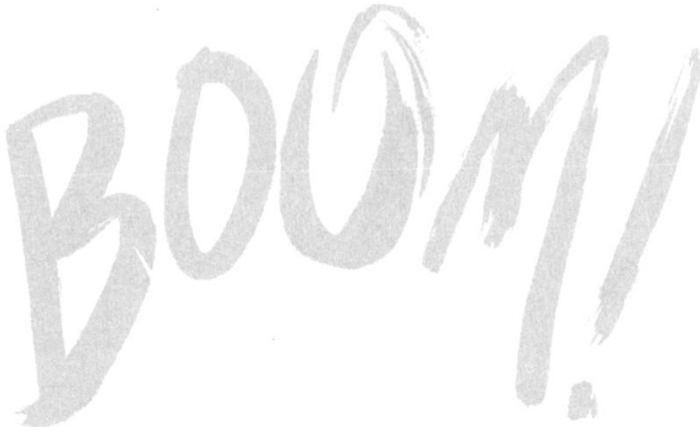
BOOM!

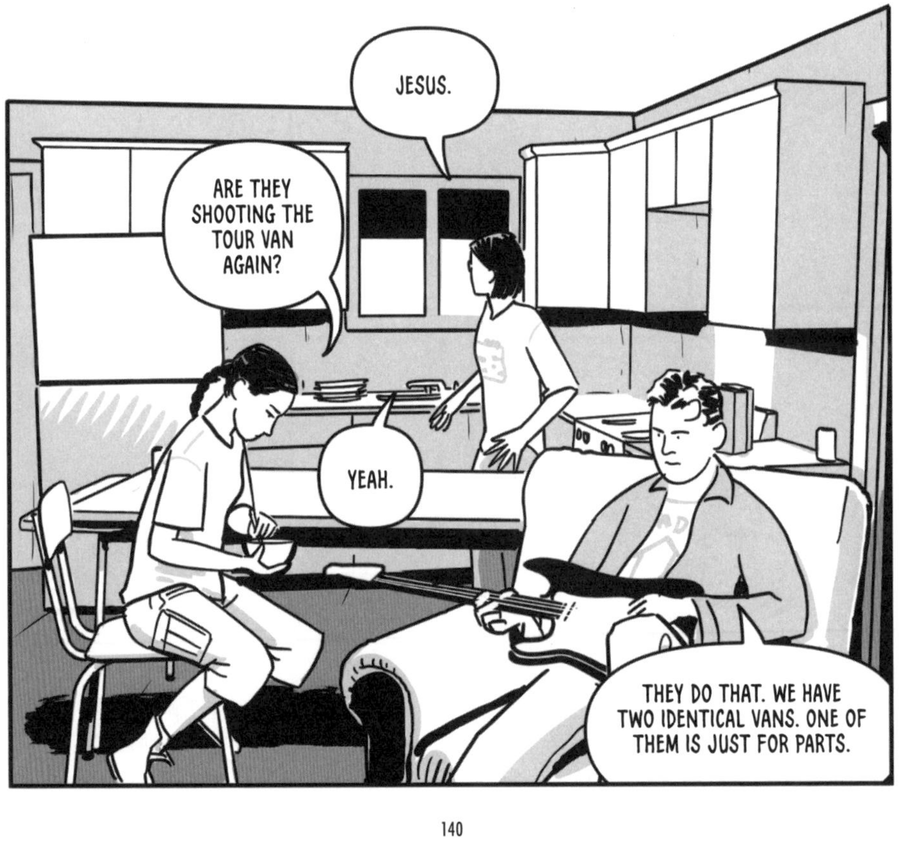
JESUS.
ARE THEY SHOOTING THE TOUR VAN AGAIN?
YEAH.
THEY DO THAT. WE HAVE TWO IDENTICAL VANS. ONE OF THEM IS JUST FOR PARTS.

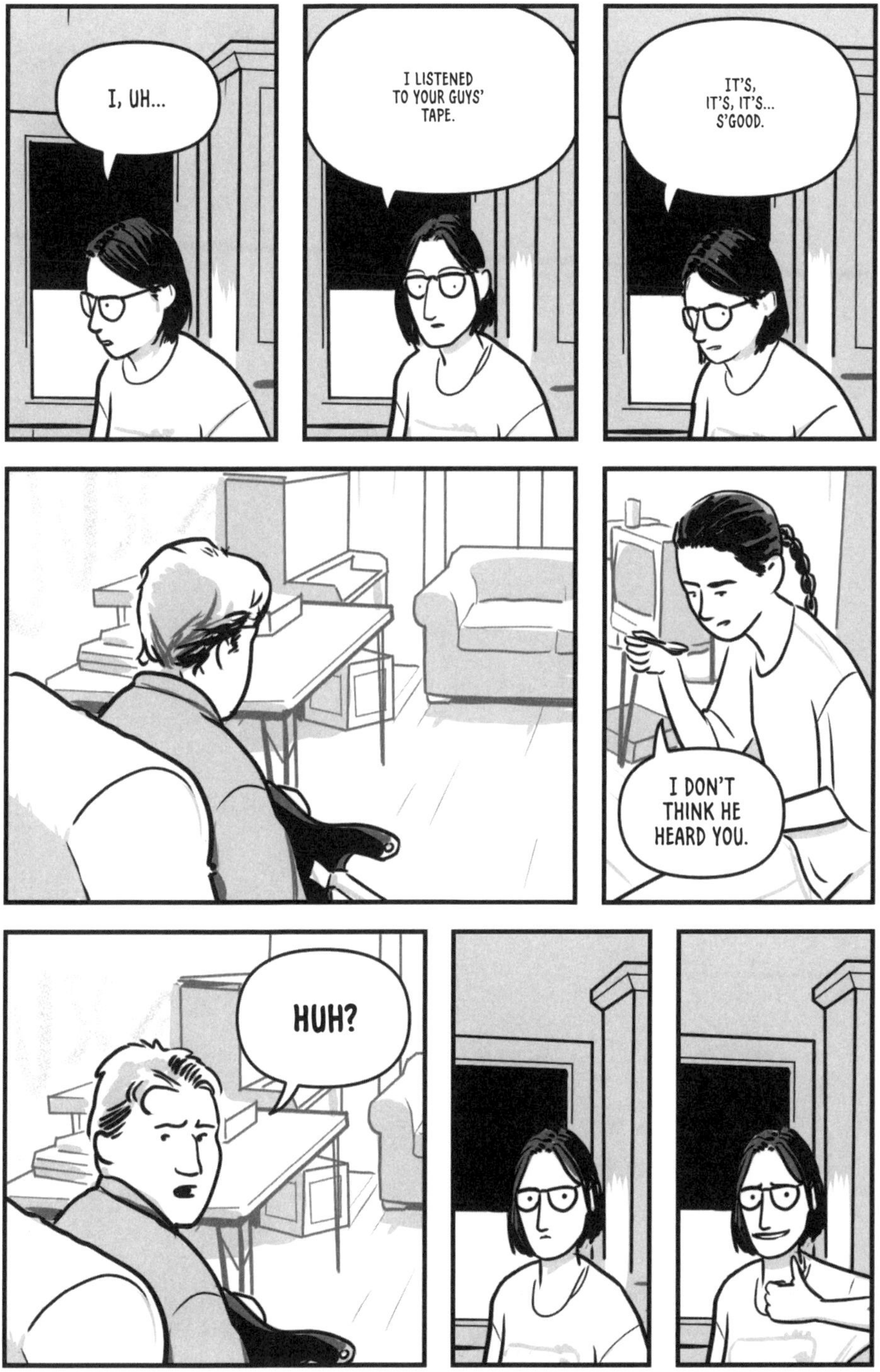
I, UH...
I LISTENED TO YOUR GUYS' TAPE.
IT'S, IT'S, IT'S... S'GOOD.
I DON'T THINK HE HEARD YOU.
HUH?

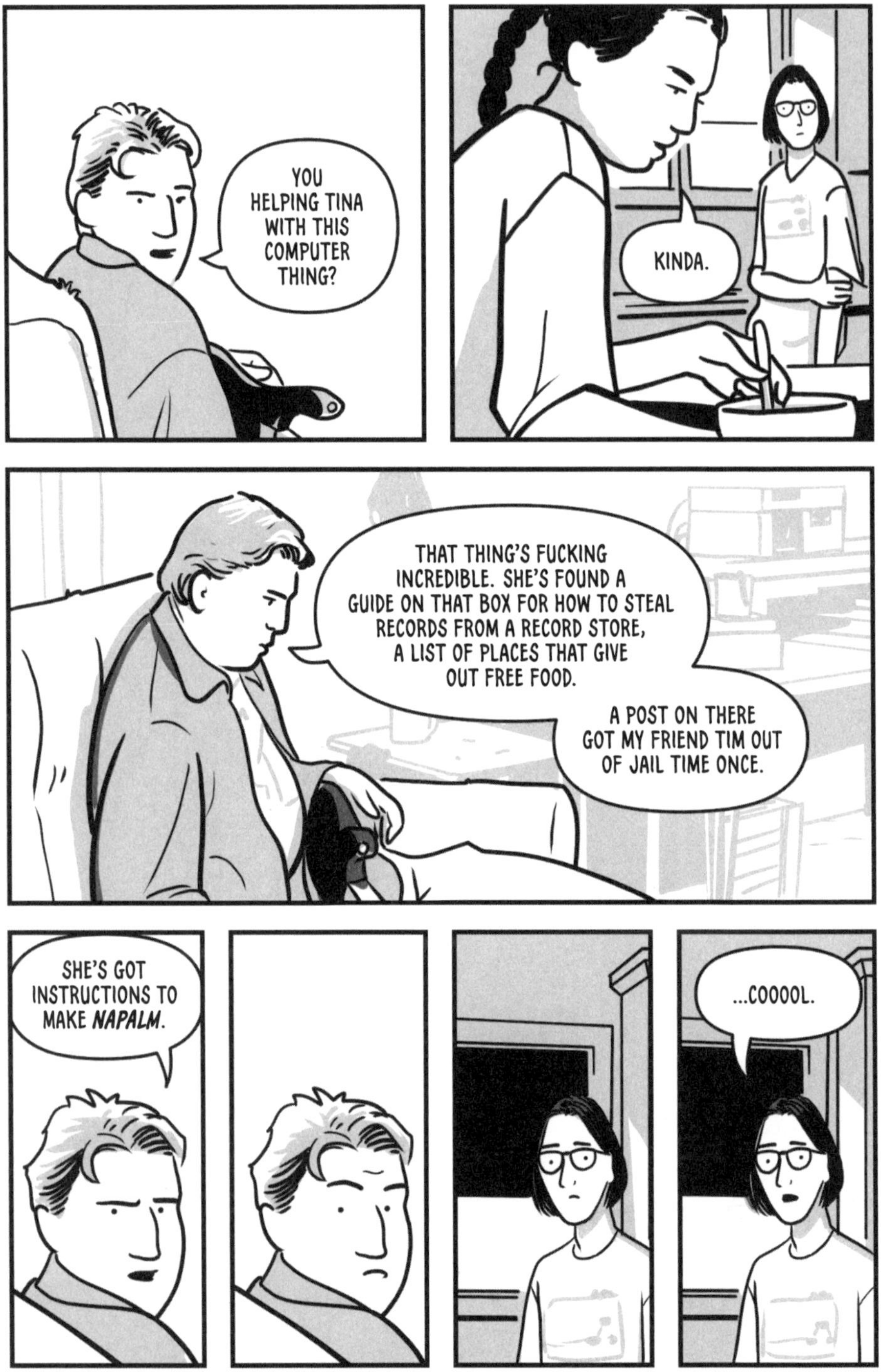
YOU HELPING TINA WITH THIS COMPUTER THING?
KINDA.
THAT THING'S FUCKING INCREDIBLE. SHE'S FOUND A GUIDE ON THAT BOX FOR HOW TO STEAL RECORDS FROM A RECORD STORE, A LIST OF PLACES THAT GIVE OUT FREE FOOD.
A POST ON THERE GOT MY FRIEND TIM OUT OF JAIL TIME ONCE.
SHE'S GOT INSTRUCTIONS TO MAKE *NAPALM*.
...COOOOL.

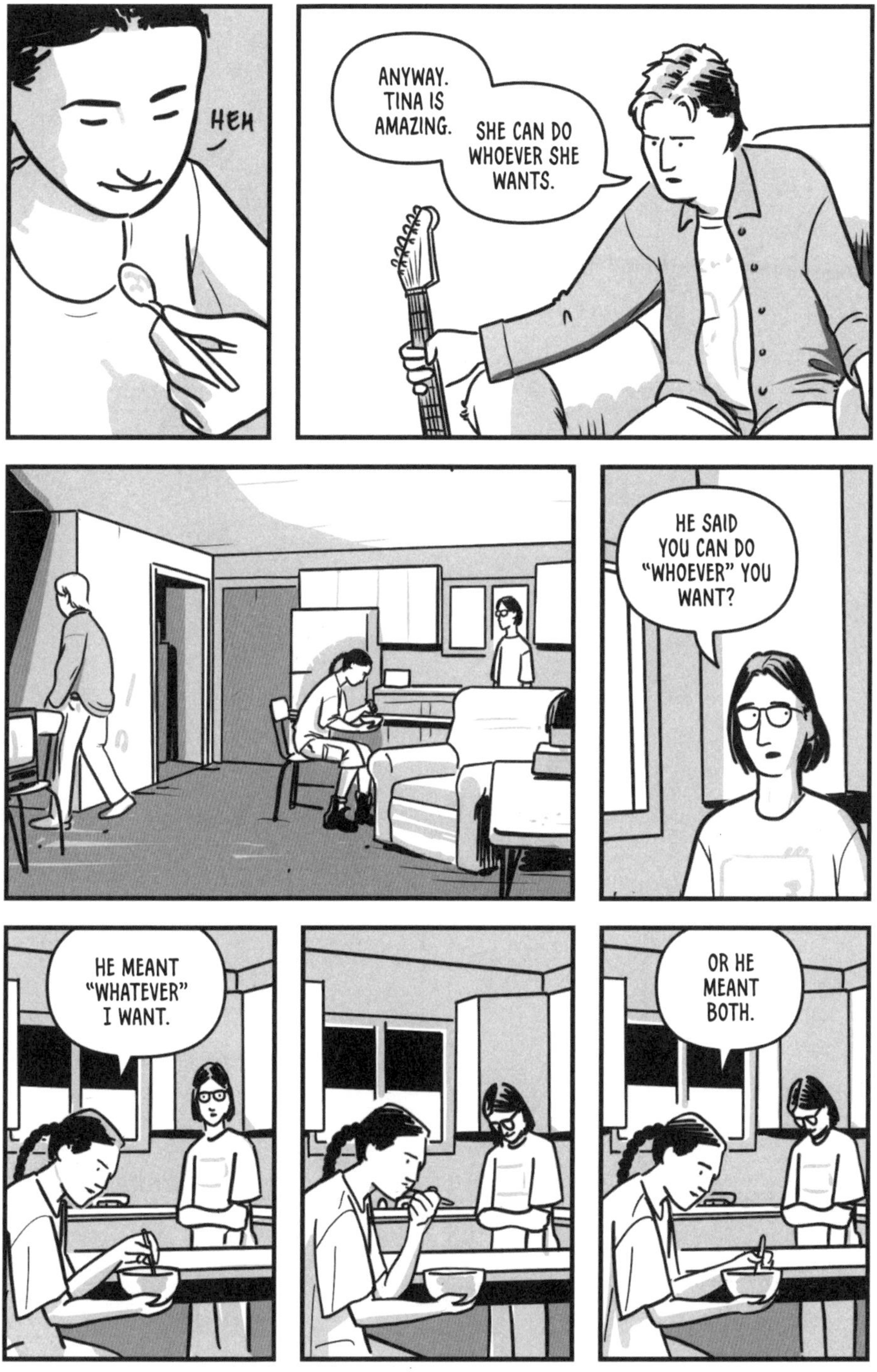
HEH
ANYWAY. TINA IS AMAZING.
SHE CAN DO WHOEVER SHE WANTS.
HE SAID YOU CAN DO "WHOEVER" YOU WANT?
HE MEANT "WHATEVER" I WANT.
OR HE MEANT BOTH.

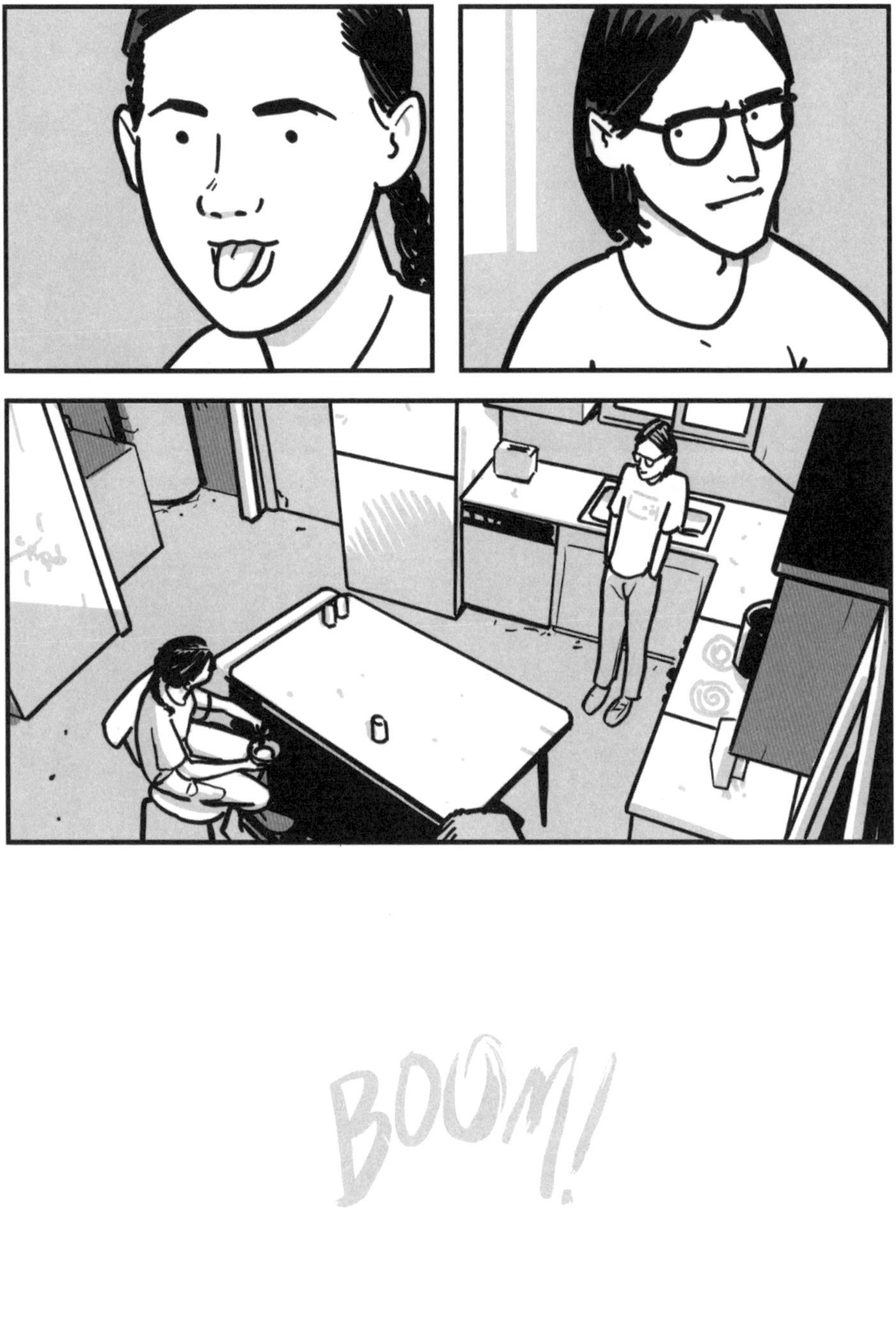
BOOM!

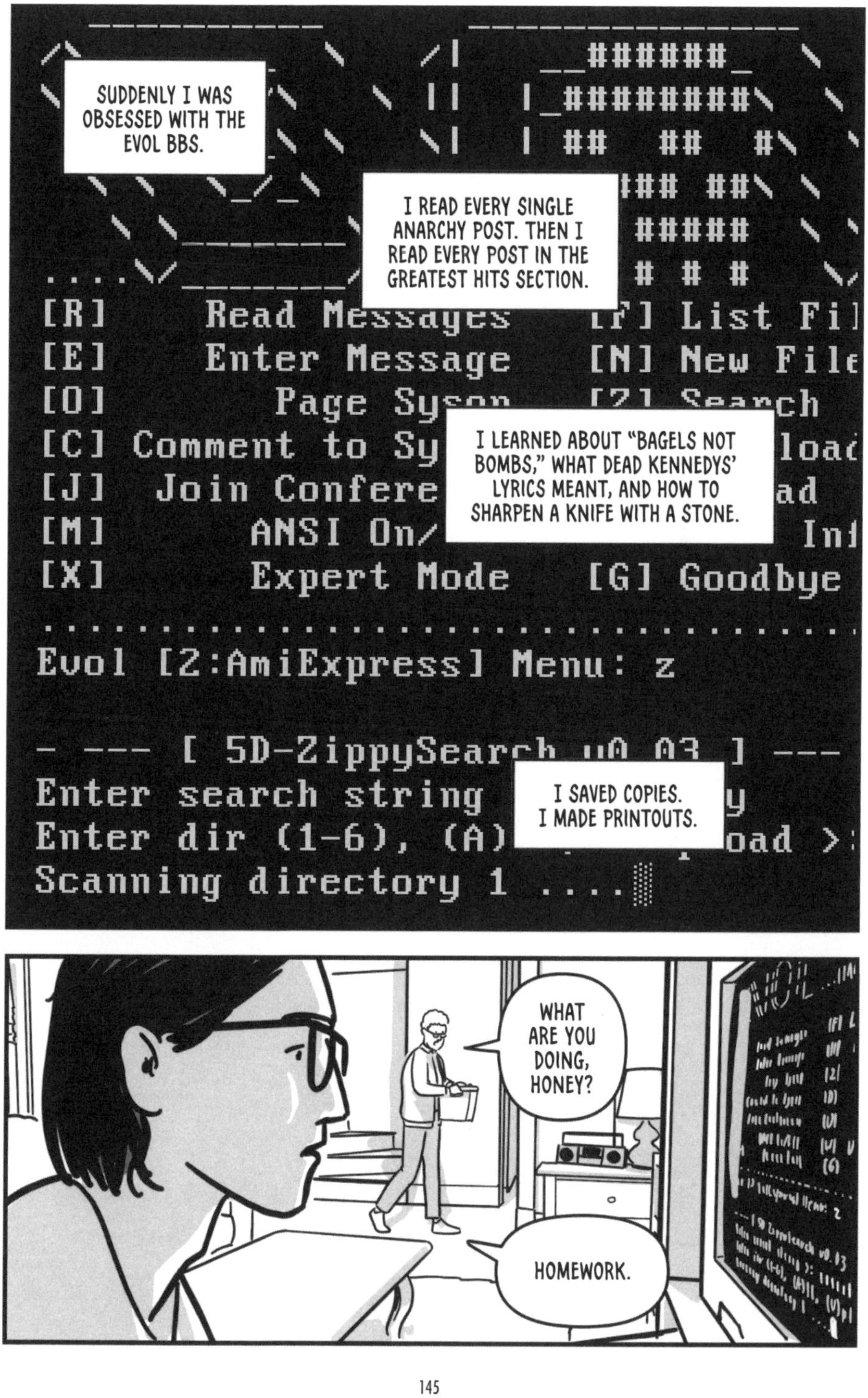
SUDDENLY I WAS OBSESSED WITH THE EVOL BBS.
I READ EVERY SINGLE ANARCHY POST. THEN I READ EVERY POST IN THE GREATEST HITS SECTION.
[E] Enter Message
I LEARNED ABOUT "BAGELS NOT BOMBS," WHAT DEAD KENNEDYS' LYRICS MEANT, AND HOW TO SHARPEN A KNIFE WITH A STONE.
[X] Expert Mode [G] Goodbye
Evol [2:AmiExpress] Menu: z
I SAVED COPIES. I MADE PRINTOUTS.
Scanning directory 1 ....
WHAT ARE YOU DOING, HONEY?
HOMEWORK.

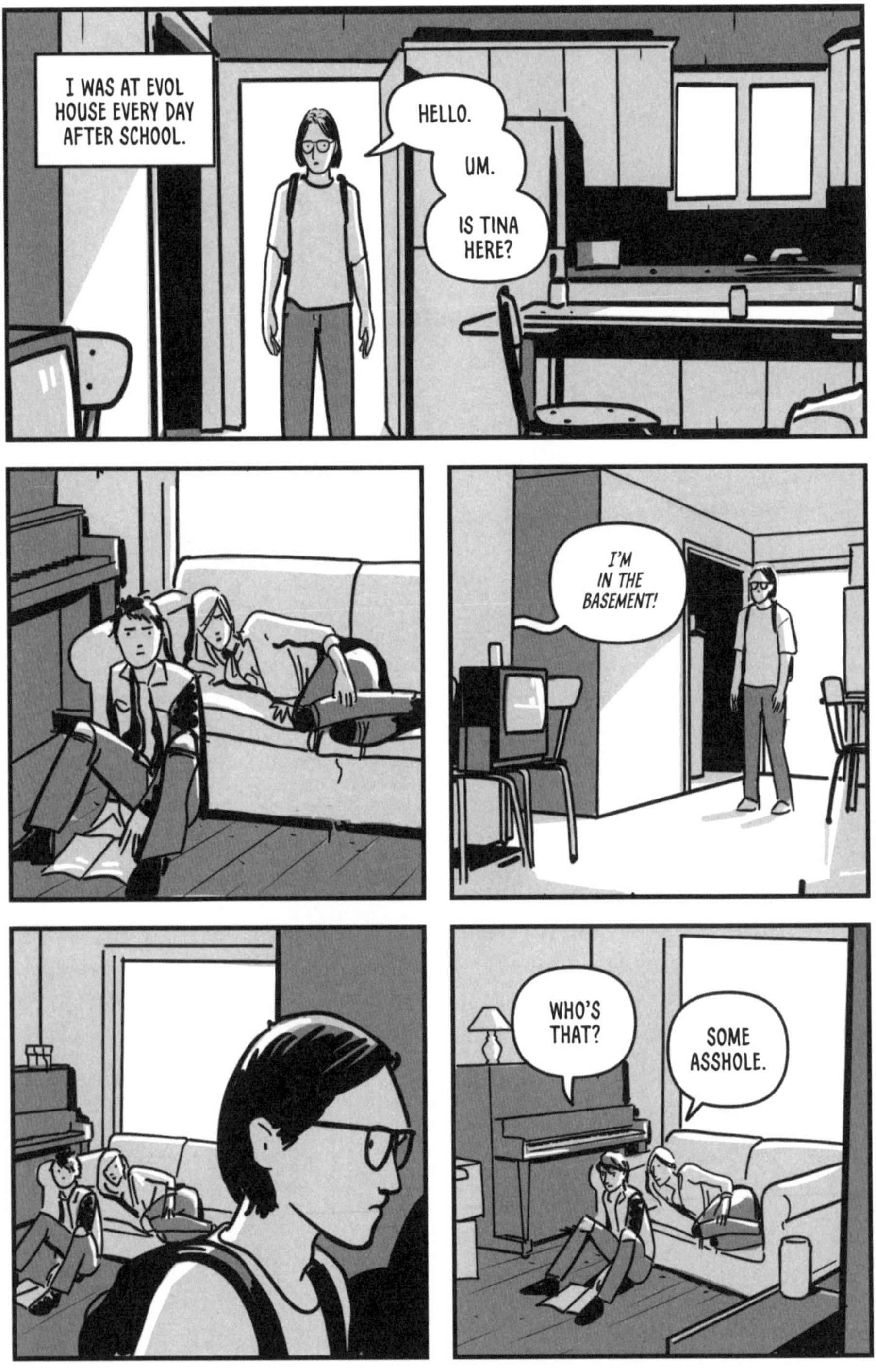
I WAS AT EVOL HOUSE EVERY DAY AFTER SCHOOL.
HELLO.
UM.
IS TINA HERE?
I'M IN THE BASEMENT!
WHO'S THAT?
SOME ASSHOLE.

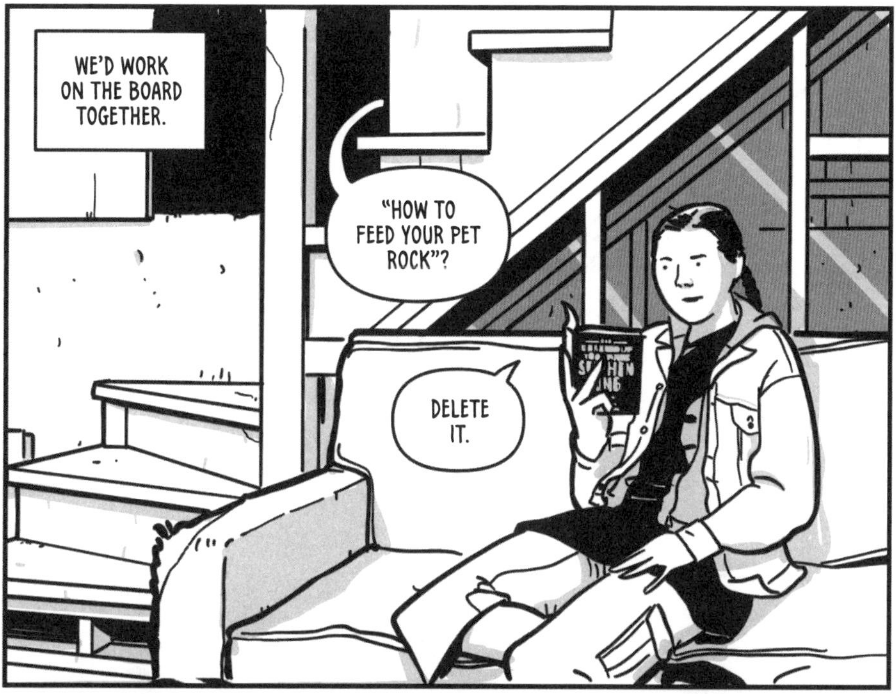
WE'D WORK ON THE BOARD TOGETHER.
"HOW TO FEED YOUR PET ROCK"?
DELETE IT.

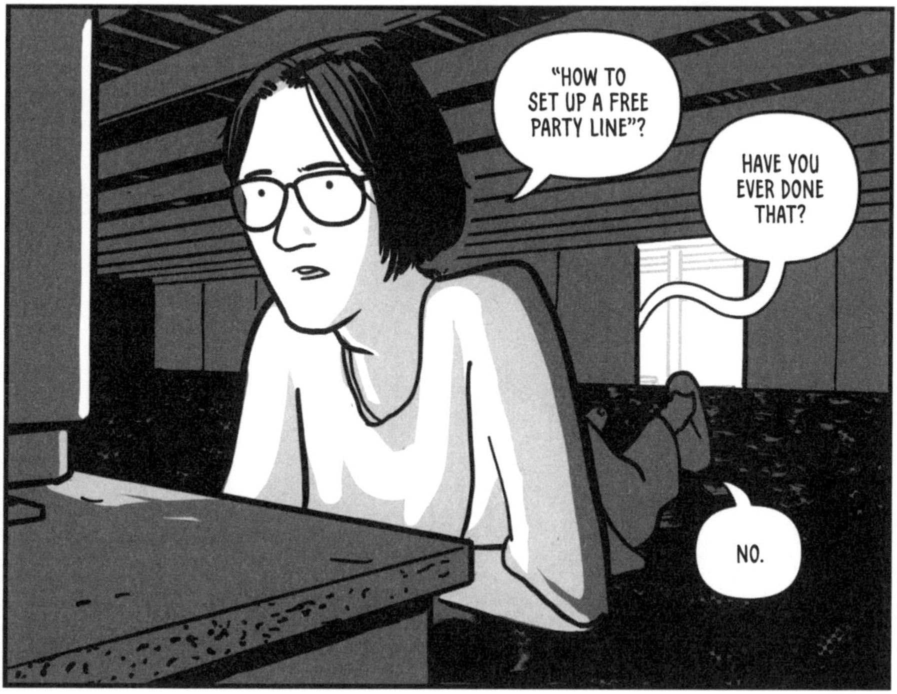
"HOW TO SET UP A FREE PARTY LINE"?
HAVE YOU EVER DONE THAT?
NO.

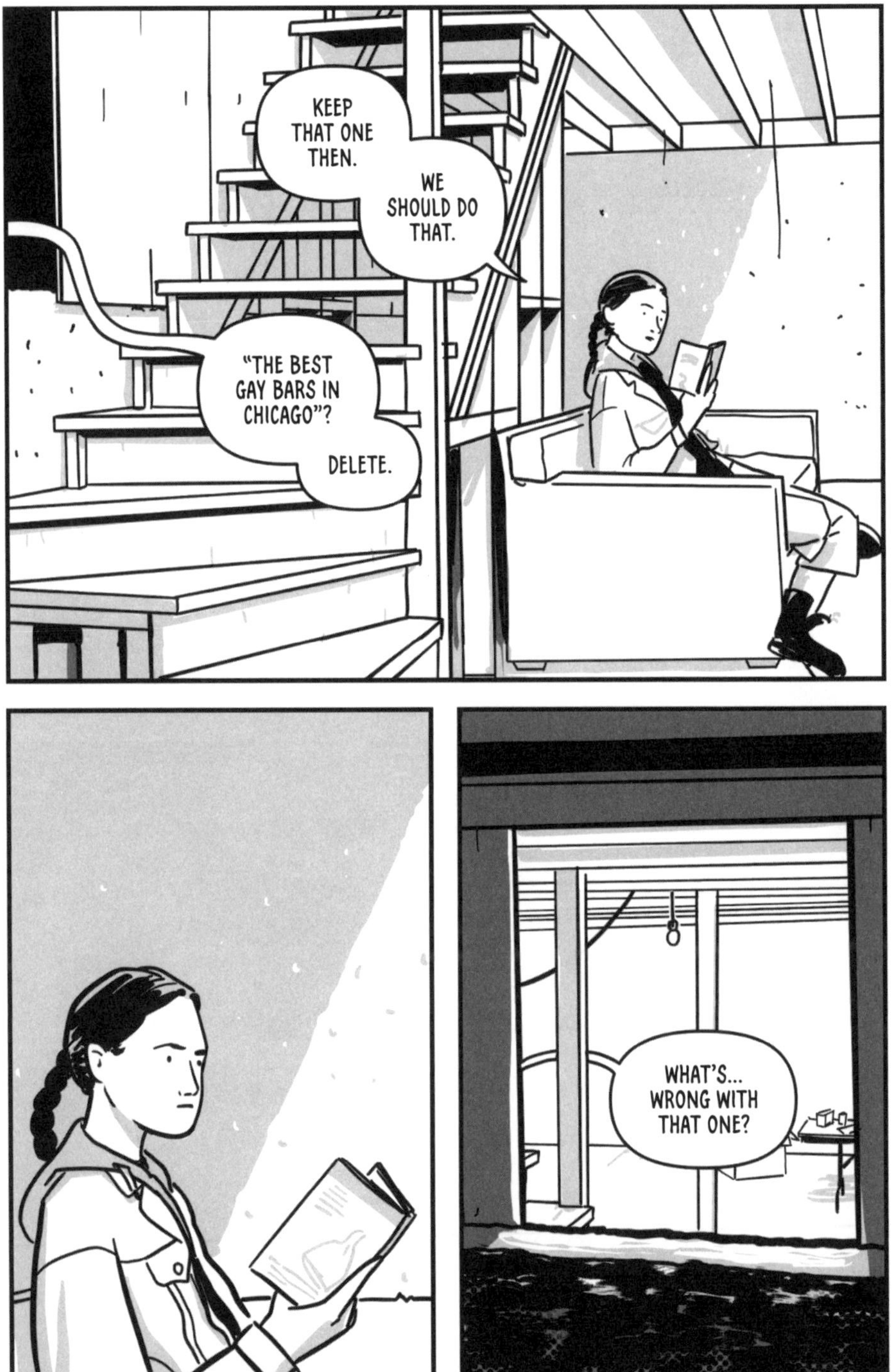
KEEP THAT ONE THEN.
WE SHOULD DO THAT.
"THE BEST GAY BARS IN CHICAGO"?
DELETE.
WHAT'S... WRONG WITH THAT ONE?

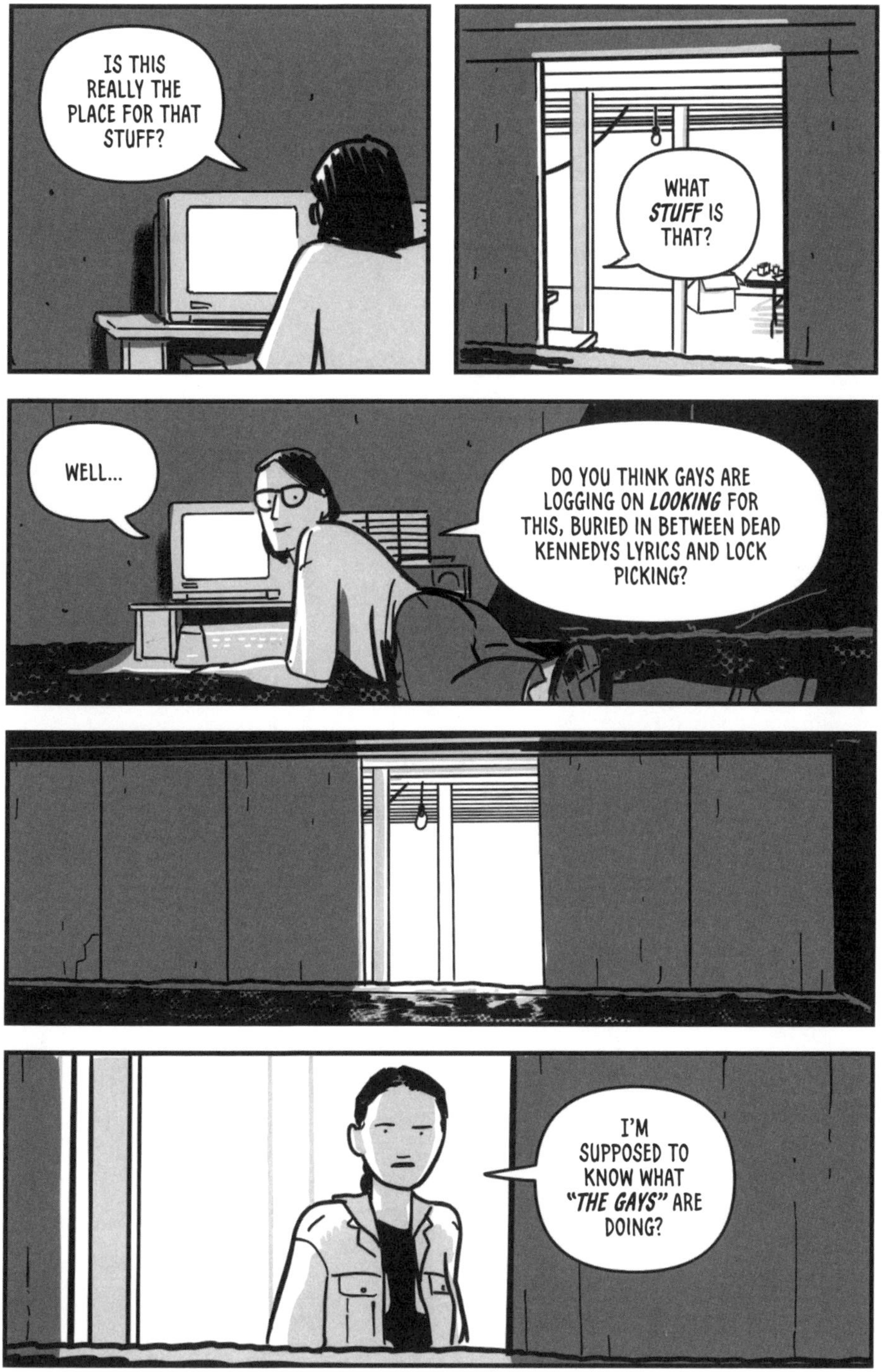
IS THIS REALLY THE PLACE FOR THAT STUFF?
WHAT *STUFF* IS THAT?
WELL...
DO YOU THINK GAYS ARE LOGGING ON *LOOKING* FOR THIS, BURIED IN BETWEEN DEAD KENNEDYS LYRICS AND LOCK PICKING?
I'M SUPPOSED TO KNOW WHAT "*THE GAYS*" ARE DOING?

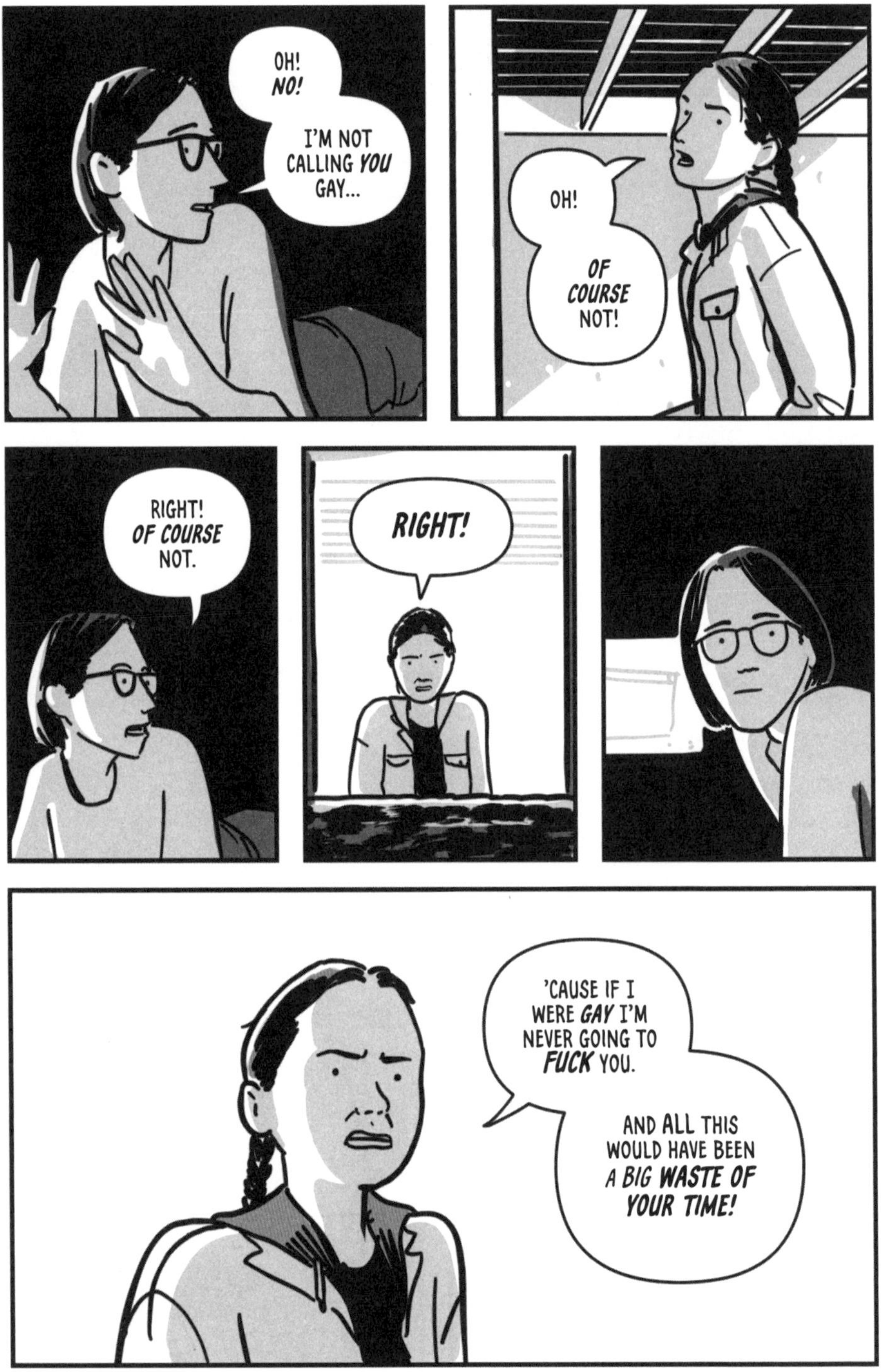
OH! NO!
I'M NOT CALLING YOU GAY...
OH!
OF COURSE NOT!
RIGHT! OF COURSE NOT.
RIGHT!
'CAUSE IF I WERE GAY I'M NEVER GOING TO FUCK YOU.
AND ALL THIS WOULD HAVE BEEN A BIG WASTE OF YOUR TIME!

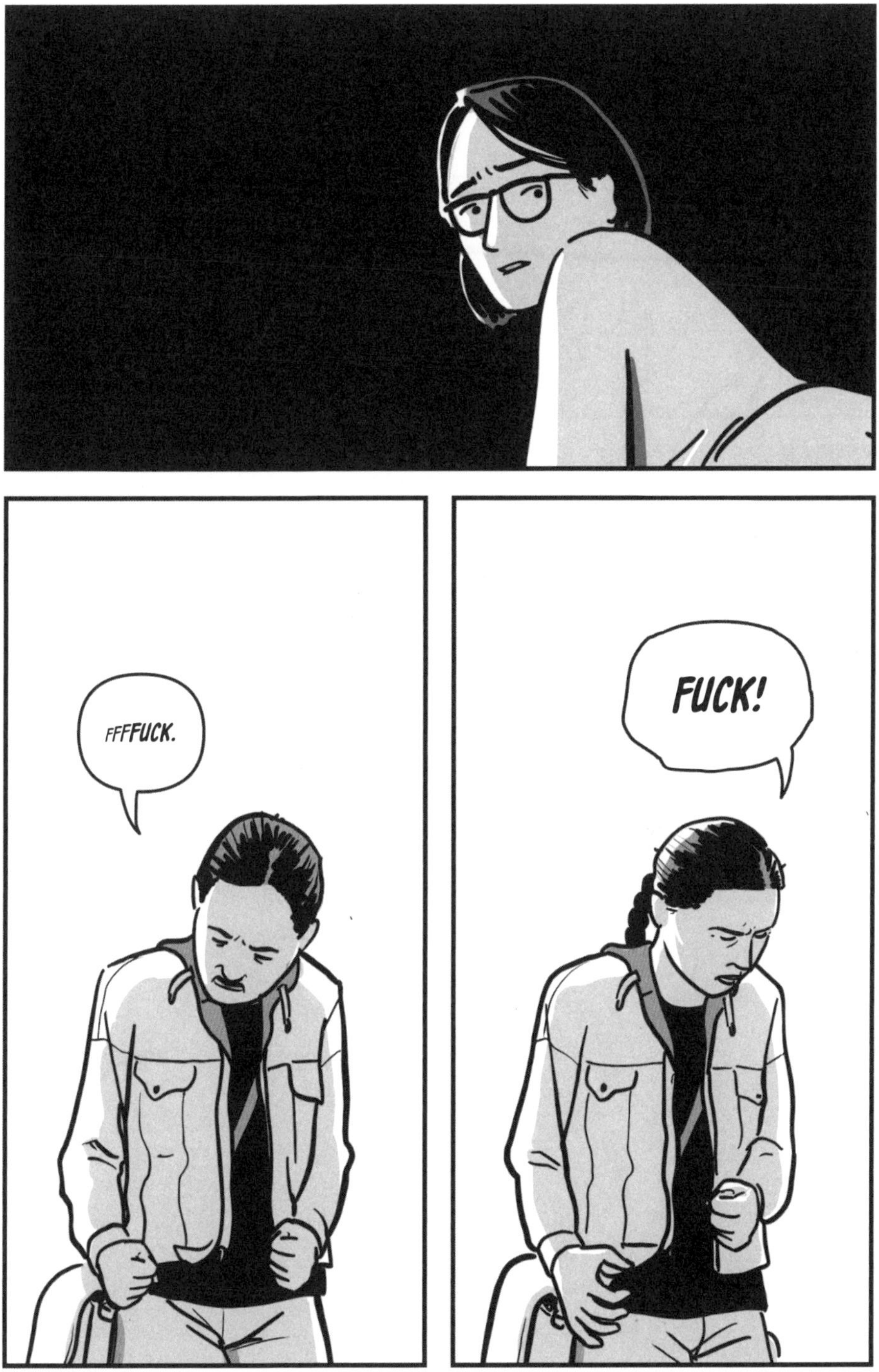
FFFFUCK.
FUCK!

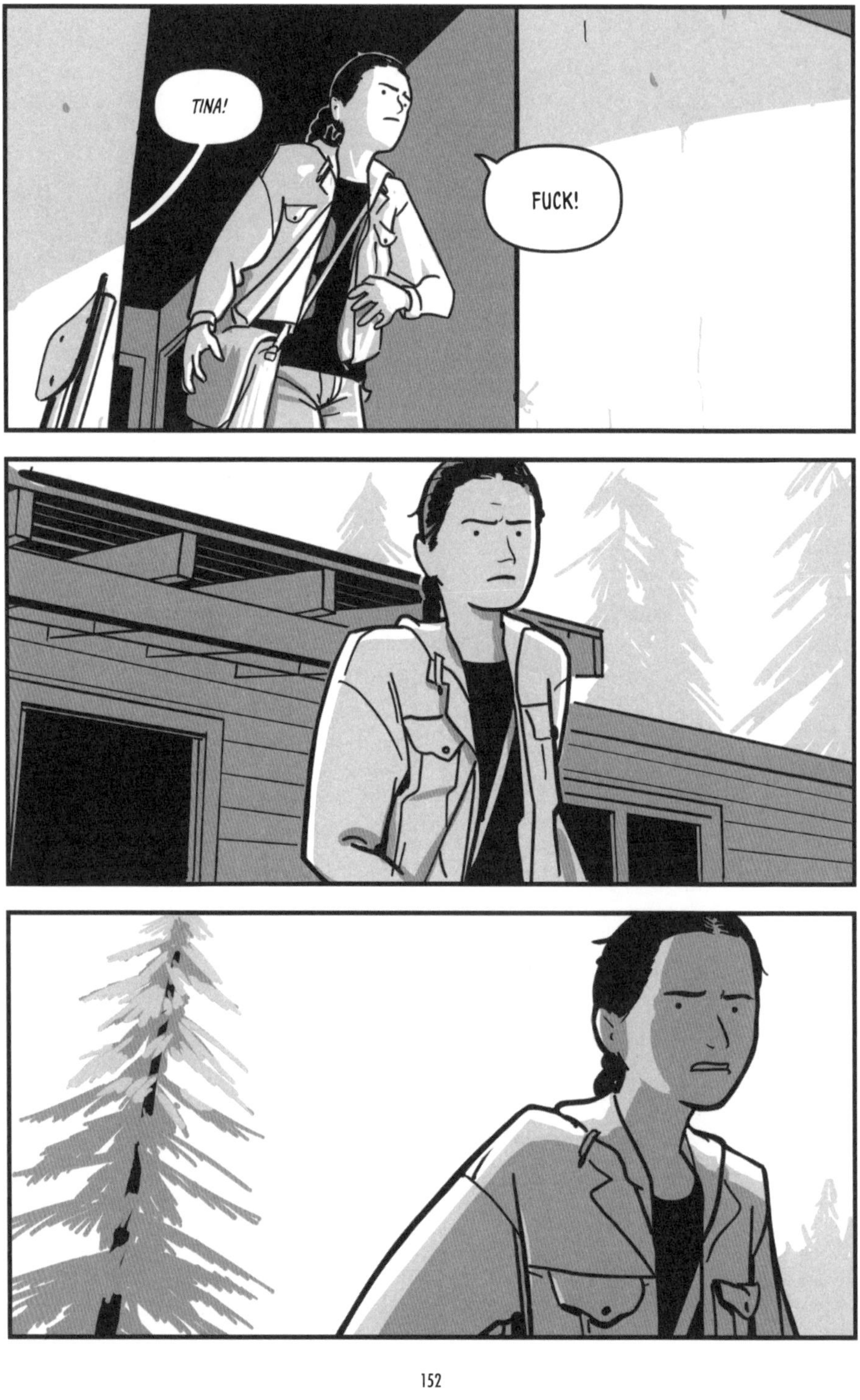
TINA!
FUCK!

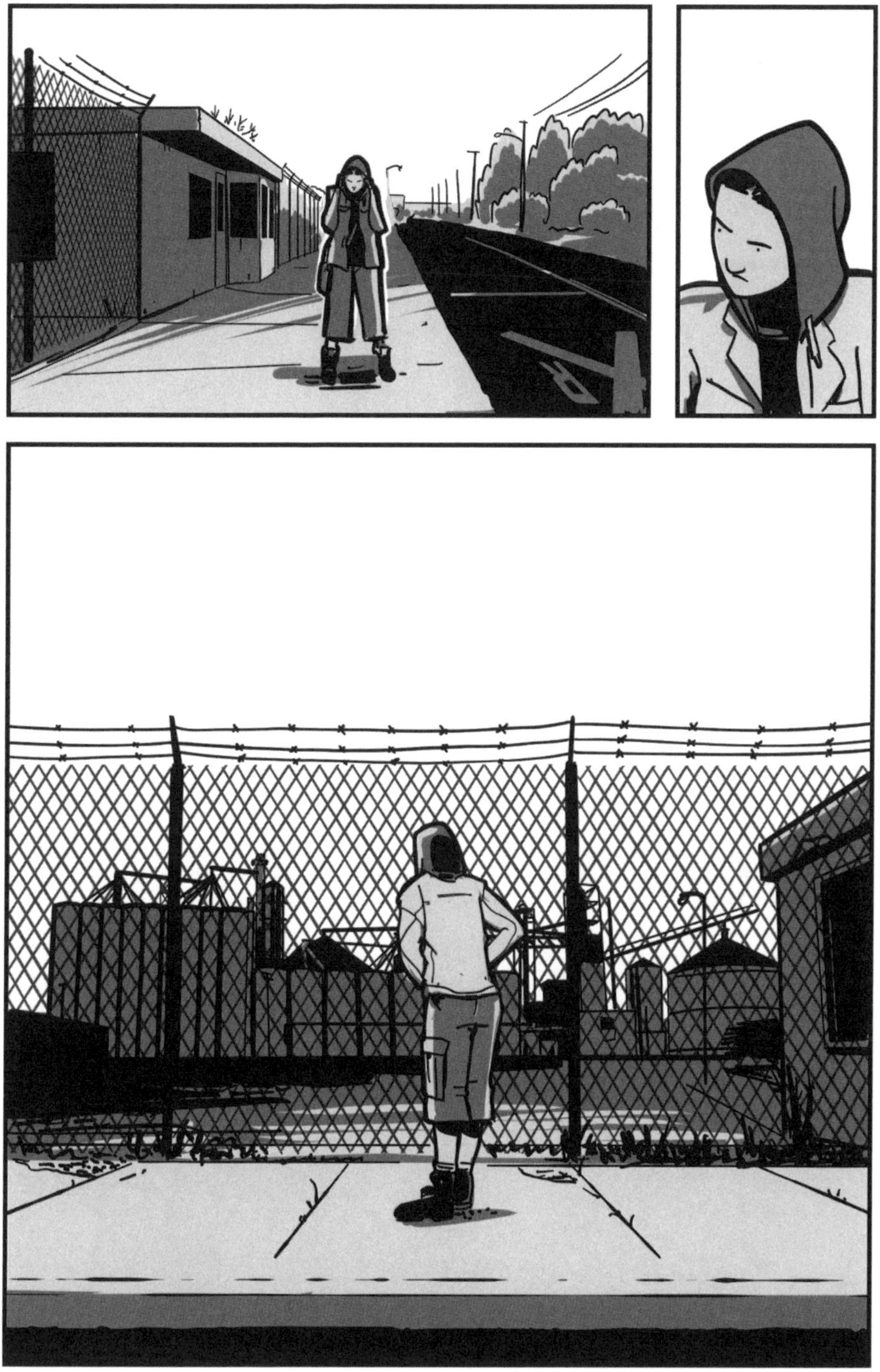

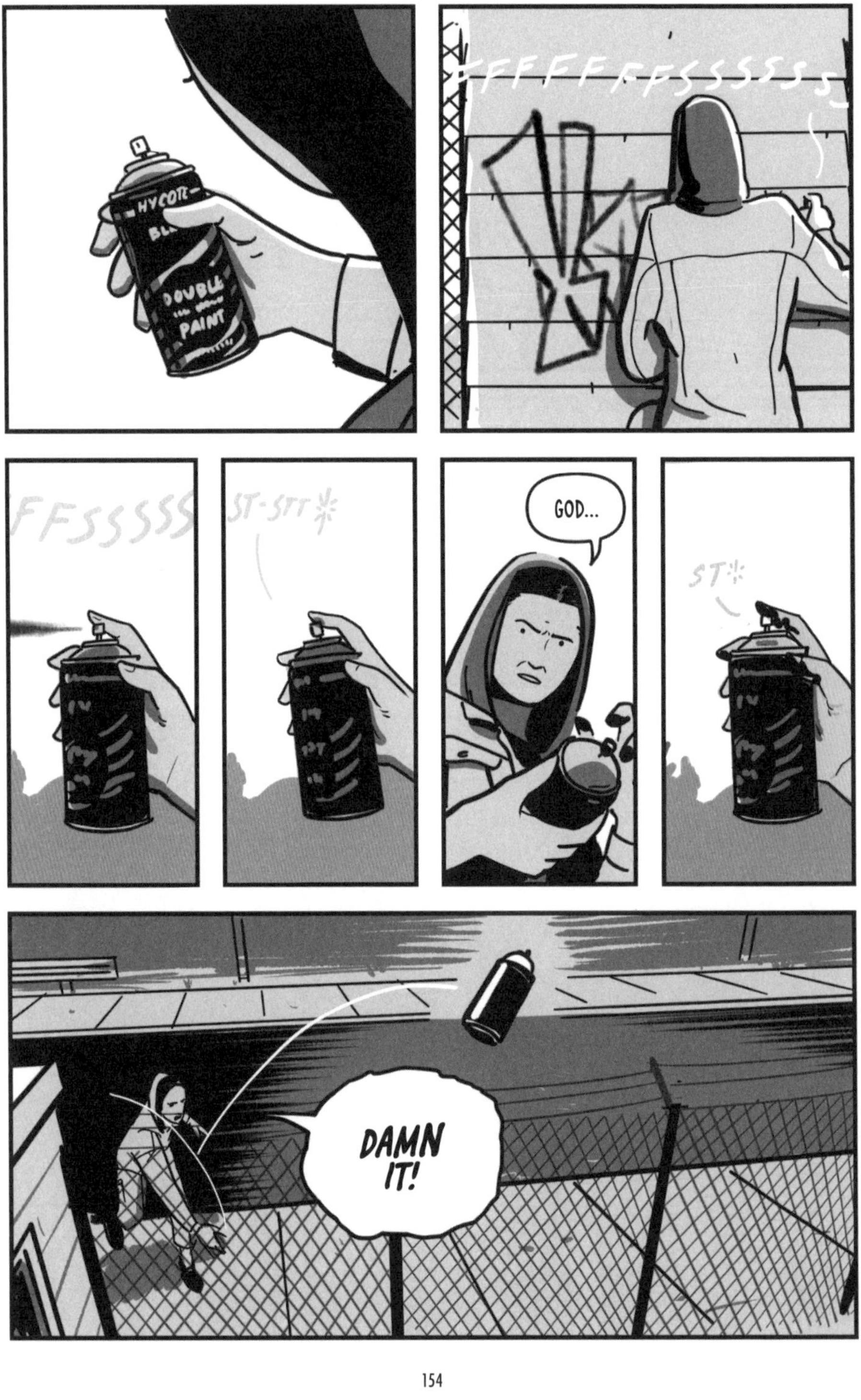
HYCOR
DOUBLE PAINT
FFFFFFFFSSSSSSS
FFSSSSS
ST-STT
GOD...
ST
DAMN IT!

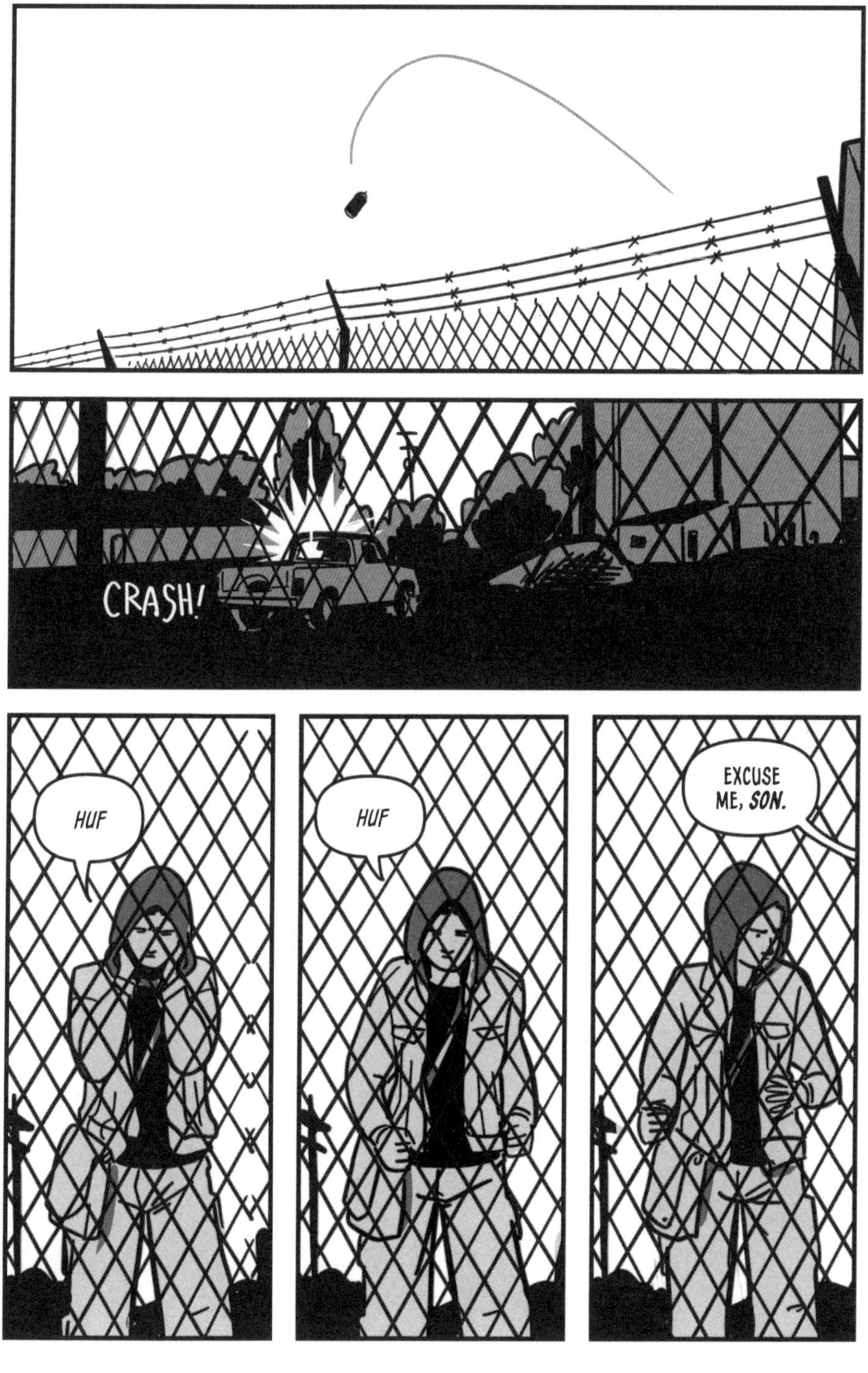
CRASH!
HUF
HUF
EXCUSE ME, SON.

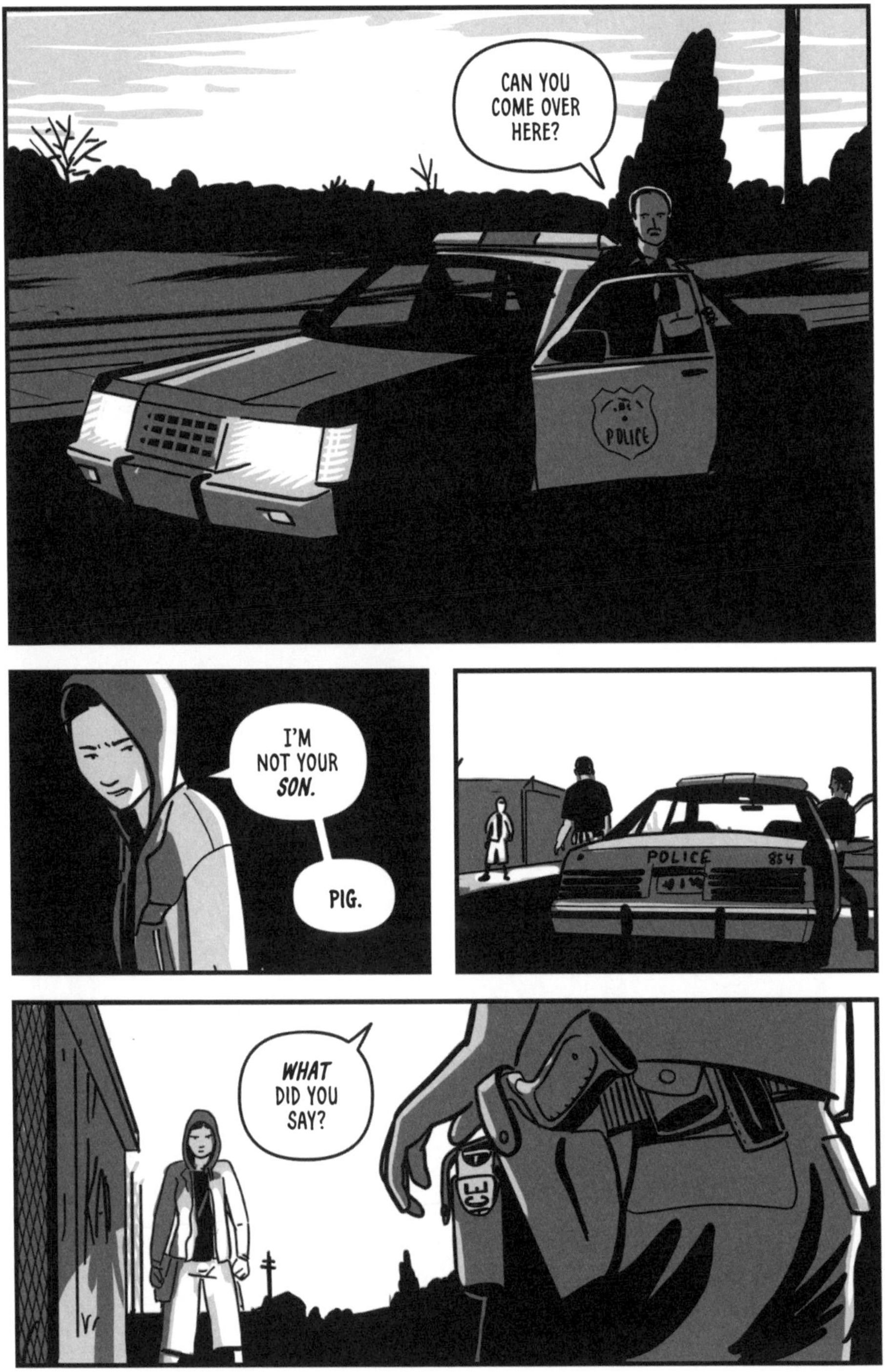
CAN YOU COME OVER HERE?
POLICE
I'M NOT YOUR *SON.*
PIG.
POLICE 854
WHAT DID YOU SAY?

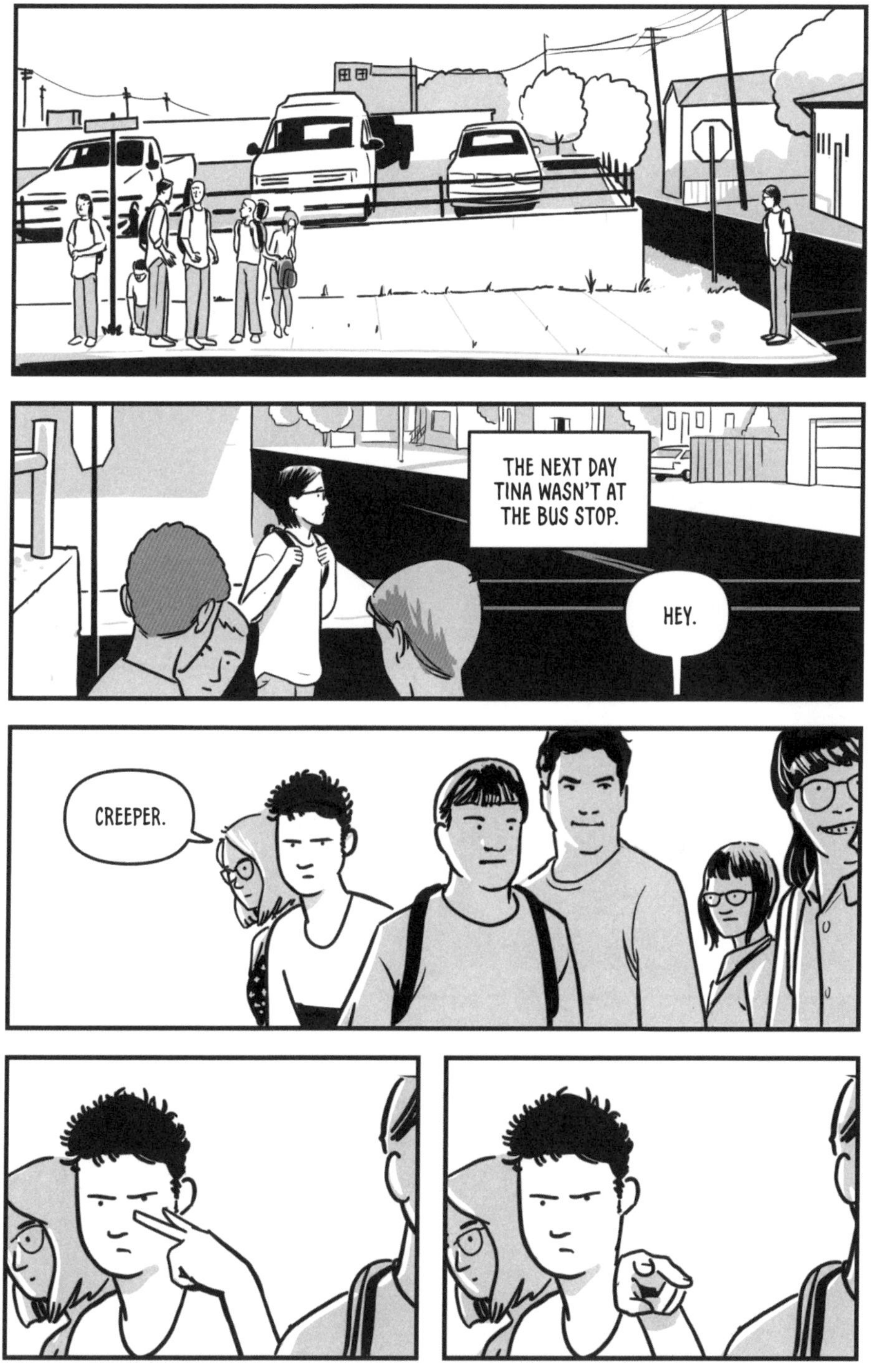
THE NEXT DAY TINA WASN'T AT THE BUS STOP.
HEY.
CREEPER.

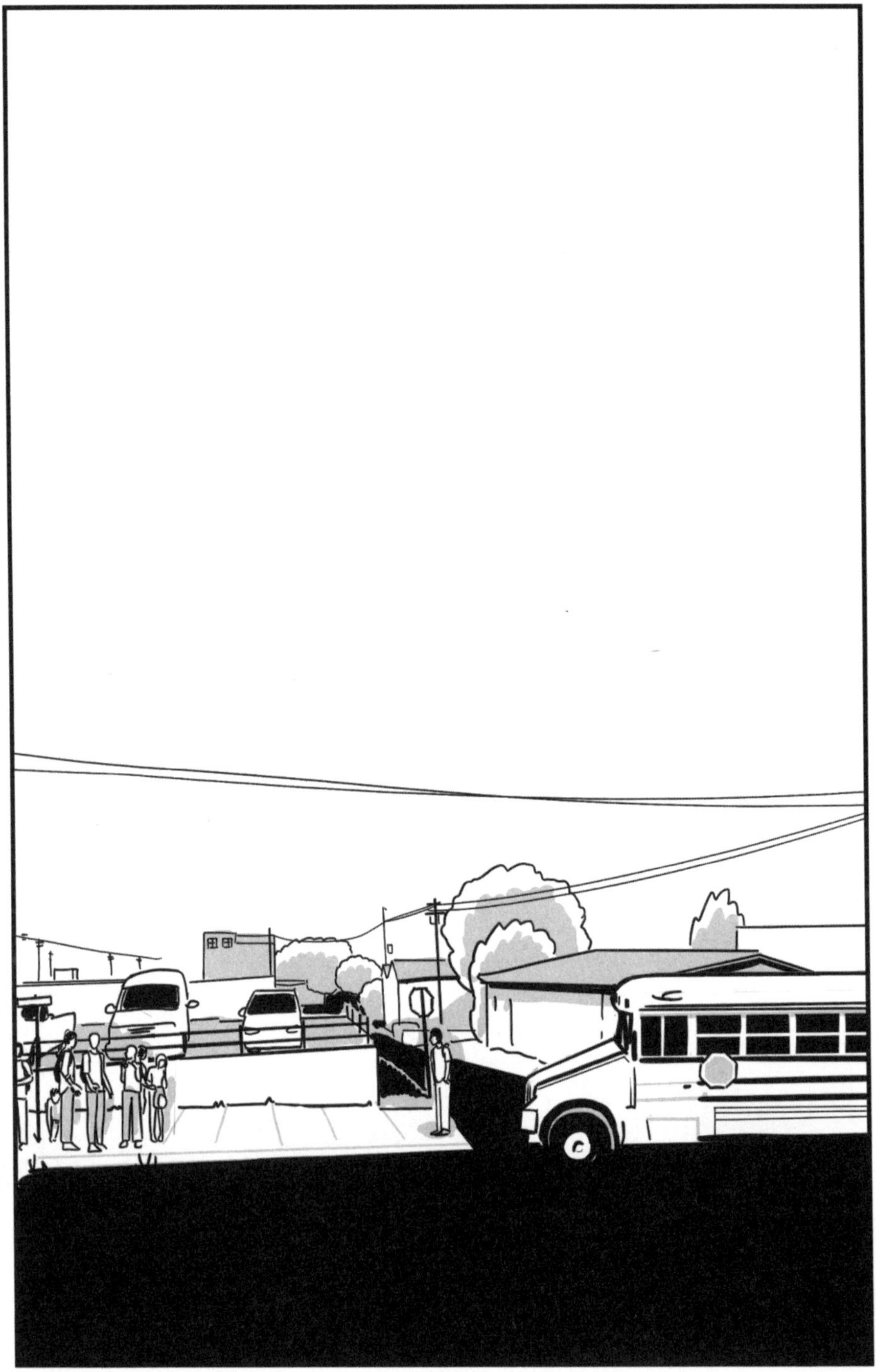

Chapter 5

KAOS

GAT GCS GM GS d -p+ c+++(++++) l++(+++) u+@ e×
m(+) s+/- n--- h× !f(+) g+ w++ t++(+++) r? y?

LET ME TELL YOU ABOUT THE GANG BACK HOME.

THE "FREE BBS BOYS."

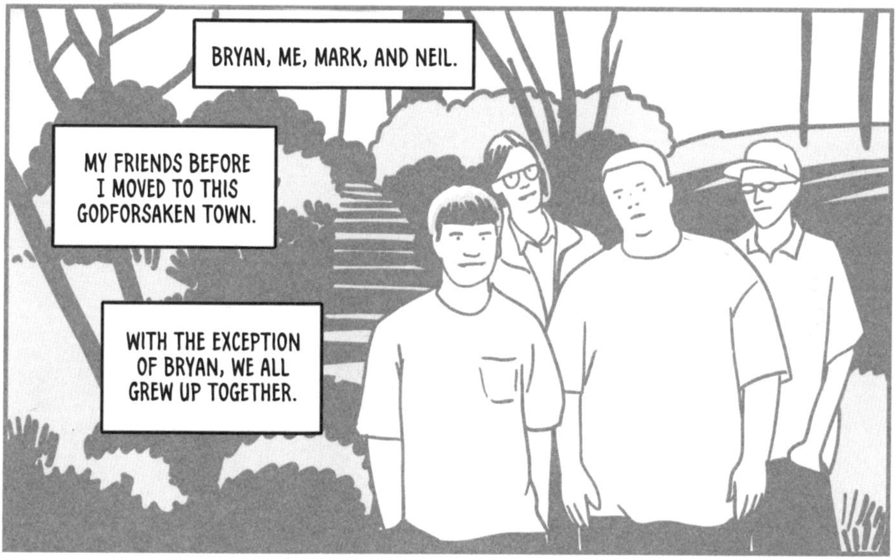
BRYAN, ME, MARK, AND NEIL.
MY FRIENDS BEFORE I MOVED TO THIS GODFORSAKEN TOWN.
WITH THE EXCEPTION OF BRYAN, WE ALL GREW UP TOGETHER.

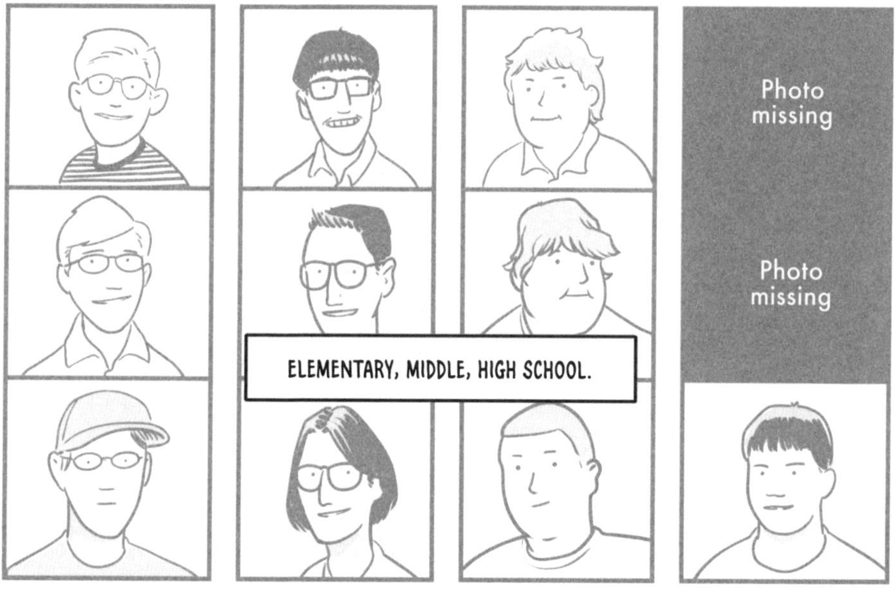
Photo missing
Photo missing
ELEMENTARY, MIDDLE, HIGH SCHOOL.

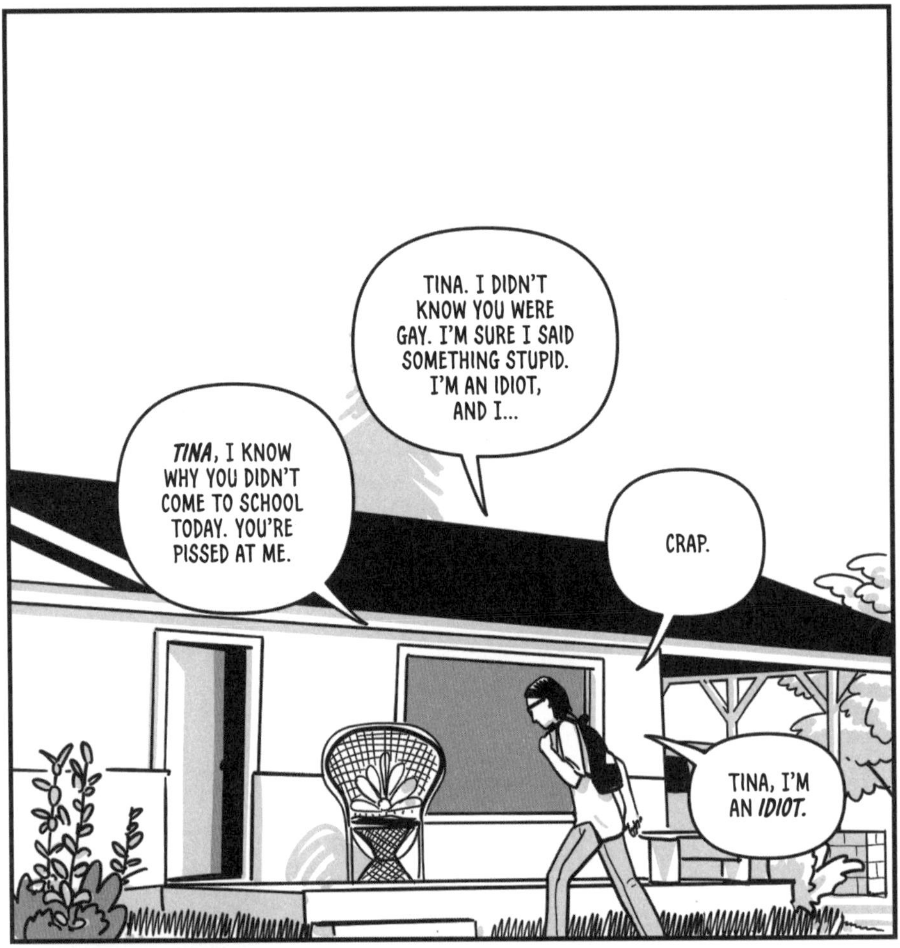
TINA, I KNOW WHY YOU DIDN'T COME TO SCHOOL TODAY. YOU'RE PISSED AT ME.
TINA. I DIDN'T KNOW YOU WERE GAY. I'M SURE I SAID SOMETHING STUPID. I'M AN IDIOT, AND I...
CRAP.
TINA, I'M AN *IDIOT.*

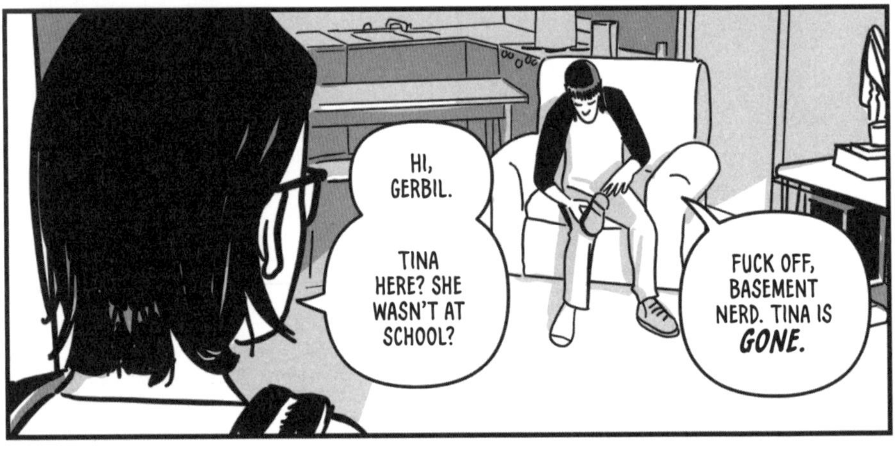
HI, GERBIL.
TINA HERE? SHE WASN'T AT SCHOOL?
FUCK OFF, BASEMENT NERD. TINA IS ***GONE.***

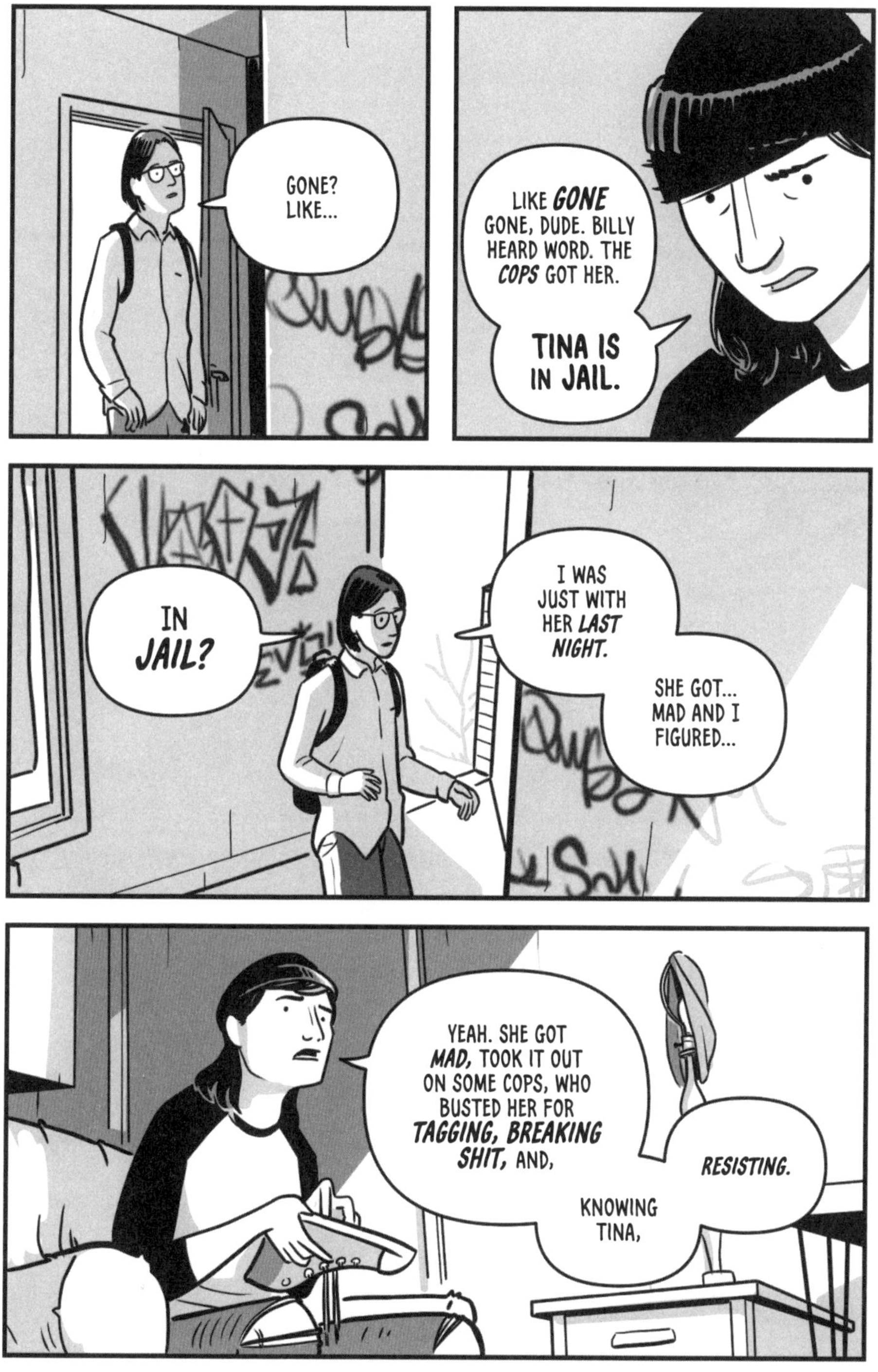
GONE? LIKE...
LIKE *GONE* GONE, DUDE. BILLY HEARD WORD. THE *COPS* GOT HER.
TINA IS IN JAIL.
IN *JAIL?*
I WAS JUST WITH HER *LAST NIGHT.*
SHE GOT... MAD AND I FIGURED...
YEAH. SHE GOT *MAD,* TOOK IT OUT ON SOME COPS, WHO BUSTED HER FOR *TAGGING, BREAKING SHIT,* AND,
KNOWING TINA,
RESISTING.

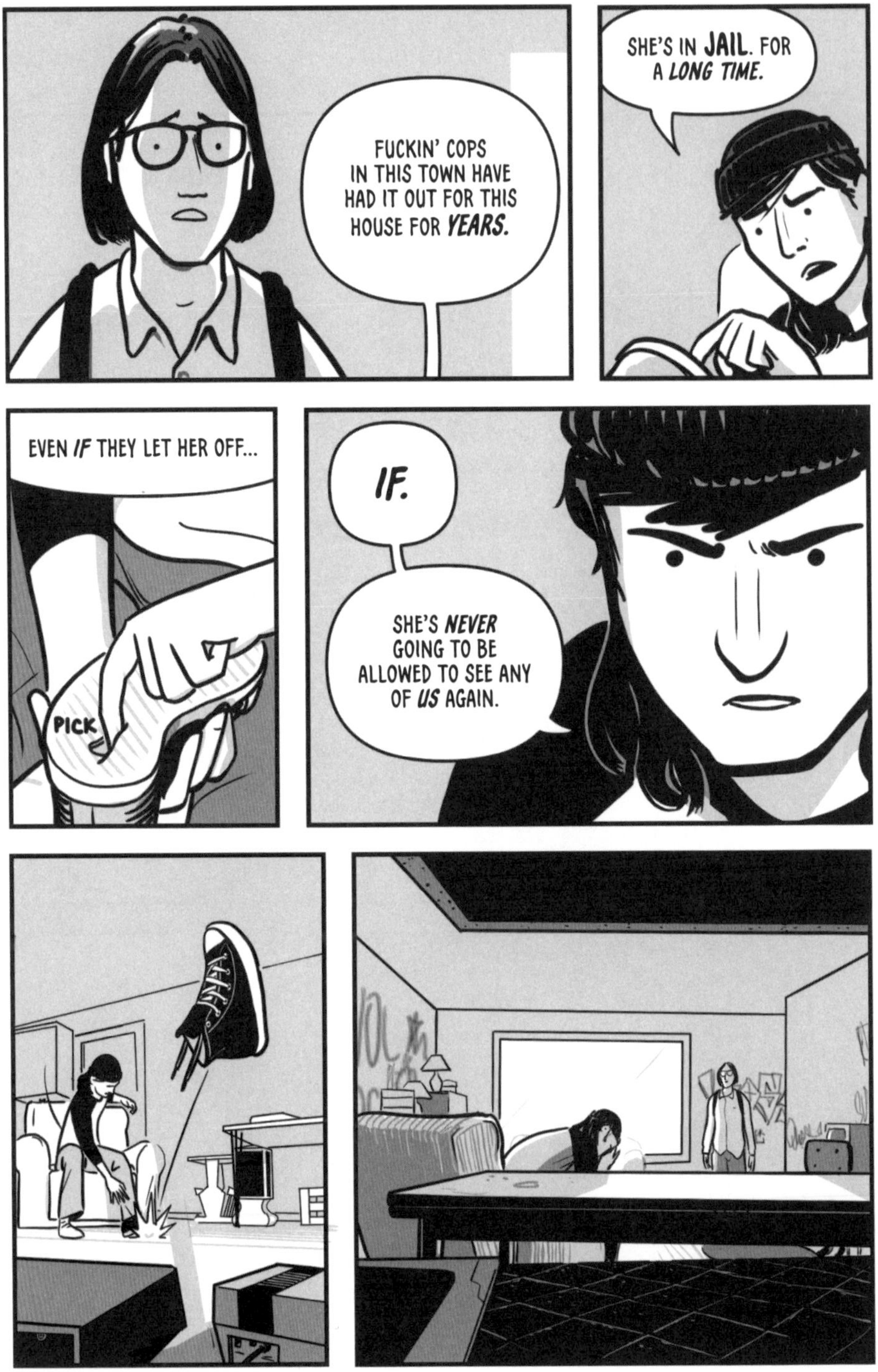

FUCKIN' COPS IN THIS TOWN HAVE HAD IT OUT FOR THIS HOUSE FOR *YEARS.*
SHE'S IN **JAIL**. FOR A *LONG TIME.*
EVEN *IF* THEY LET HER OFF...
PICK
IF.
SHE'S *NEVER* GOING TO BE ALLOWED TO SEE ANY OF *US* AGAIN.

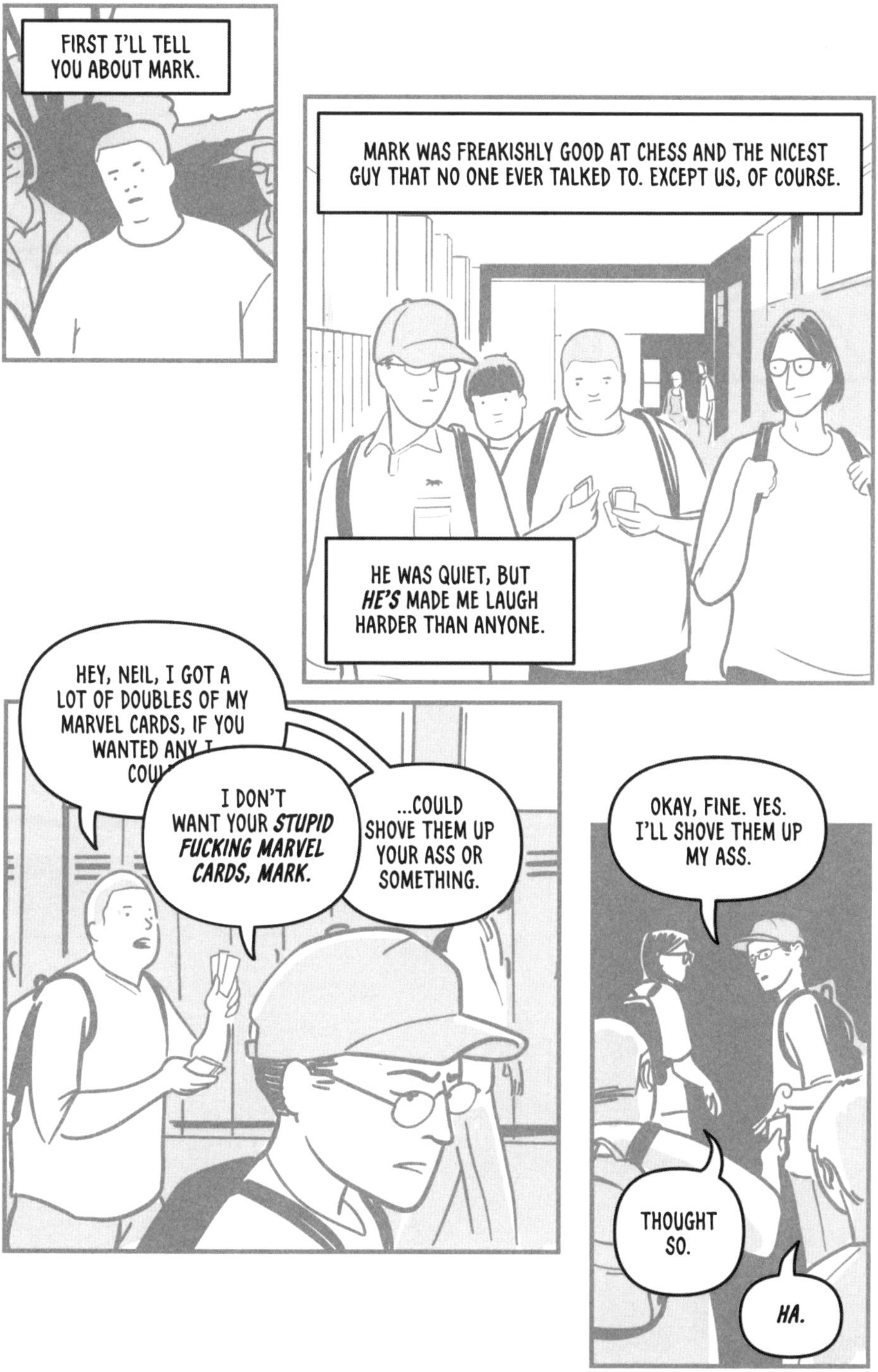
FIRST I'LL TELL YOU ABOUT MARK.
MARK WAS FREAKISHLY GOOD AT CHESS AND THE NICEST GUY THAT NO ONE EVER TALKED TO. EXCEPT US, OF COURSE.
HE WAS QUIET, BUT *HE'S* MADE ME LAUGH HARDER THAN ANYONE.
HEY, NEIL, I GOT A LOT OF DOUBLES OF MY MARVEL CARDS, IF YOU WANTED AN
I DON'T WANT YOUR ***STUPID FUCKING MARVEL CARDS, MARK.***
...COULD SHOVE THEM UP YOUR ASS OR SOMETHING.
OKAY, FINE. YES. I'LL SHOVE THEM UP MY ASS.
THOUGHT SO.
HA.

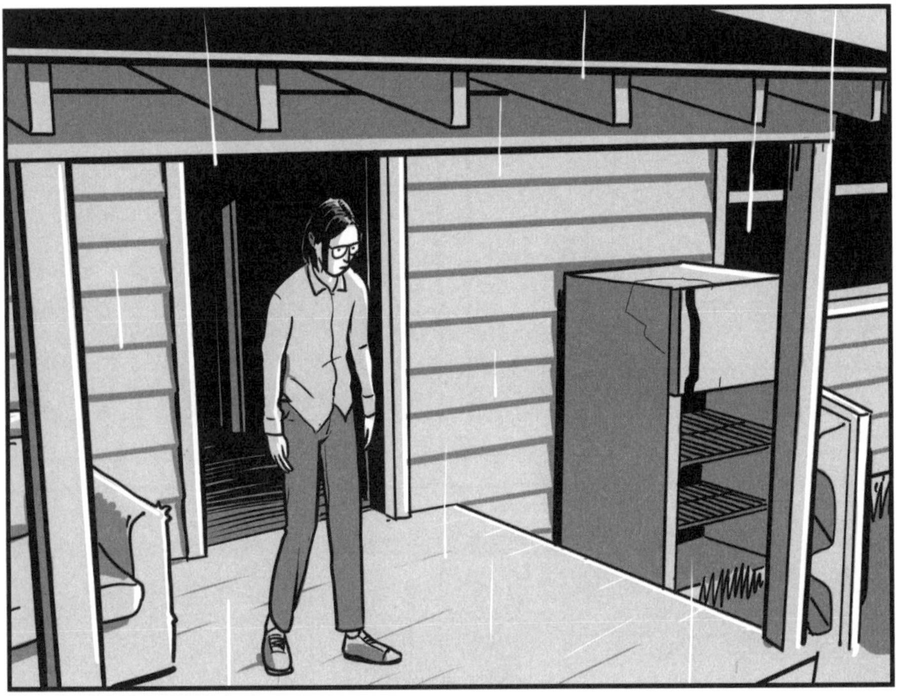

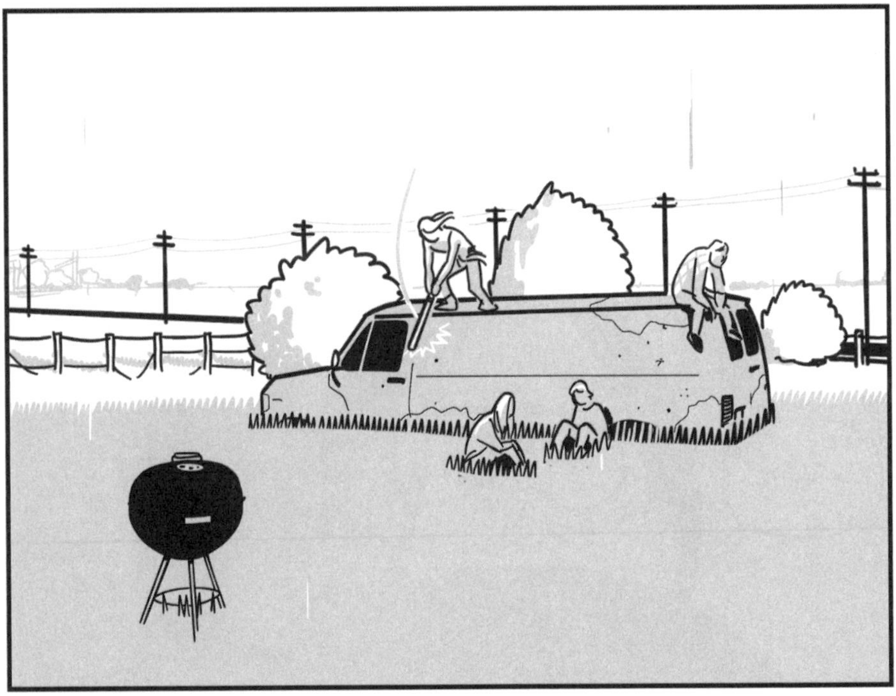

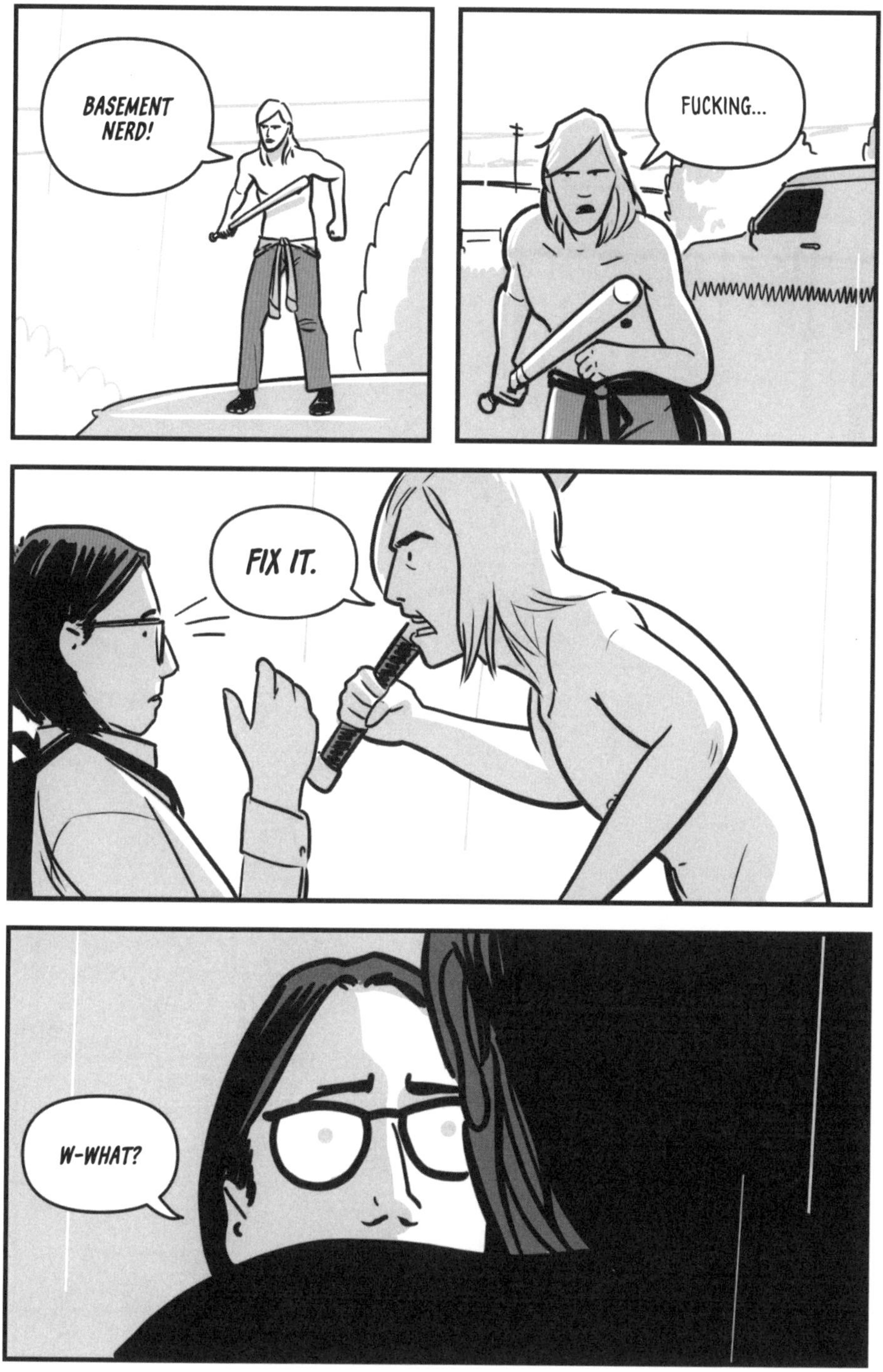
BASEMENT NERD!
FUCKING...
FIX IT.
W-WHAT?

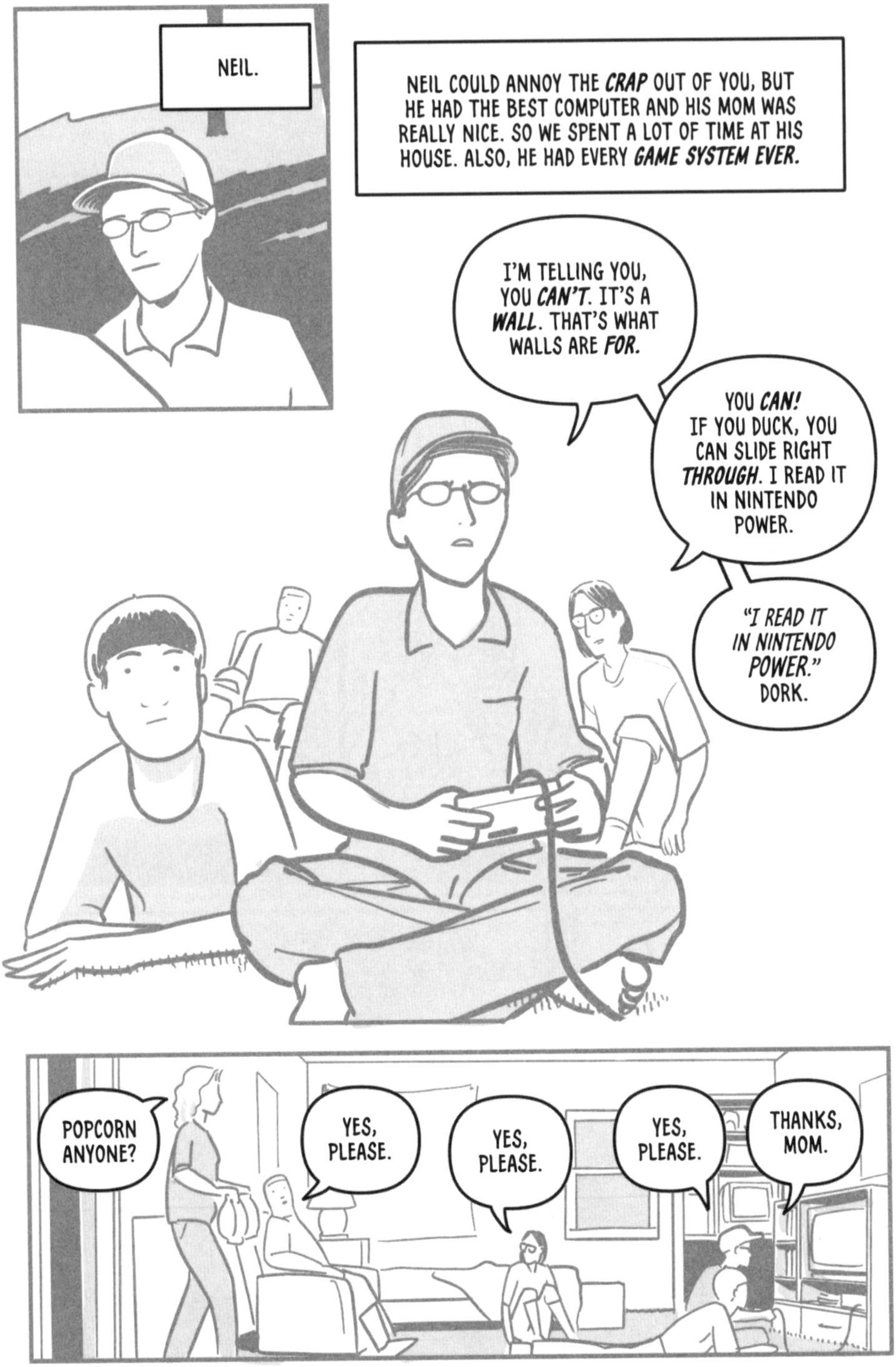
NEIL.
NEIL COULD ANNOY THE *CRAP* OUT OF YOU, BUT HE HAD THE BEST COMPUTER AND HIS MOM WAS REALLY NICE. SO WE SPENT A LOT OF TIME AT HIS HOUSE. ALSO, HE HAD EVERY *GAME SYSTEM EVER.*
I'M TELLING YOU, YOU *CAN'T*. IT'S A *WALL*. THAT'S WHAT WALLS ARE *FOR*.
YOU *CAN!* IF YOU DUCK, YOU CAN SLIDE RIGHT *THROUGH*. I READ IT IN NINTENDO POWER.
"I READ IT IN NINTENDO POWER." DORK.
POPCORN ANYONE?
YES, PLEASE.
YES, PLEASE.
YES, PLEASE.
THANKS, MOM.

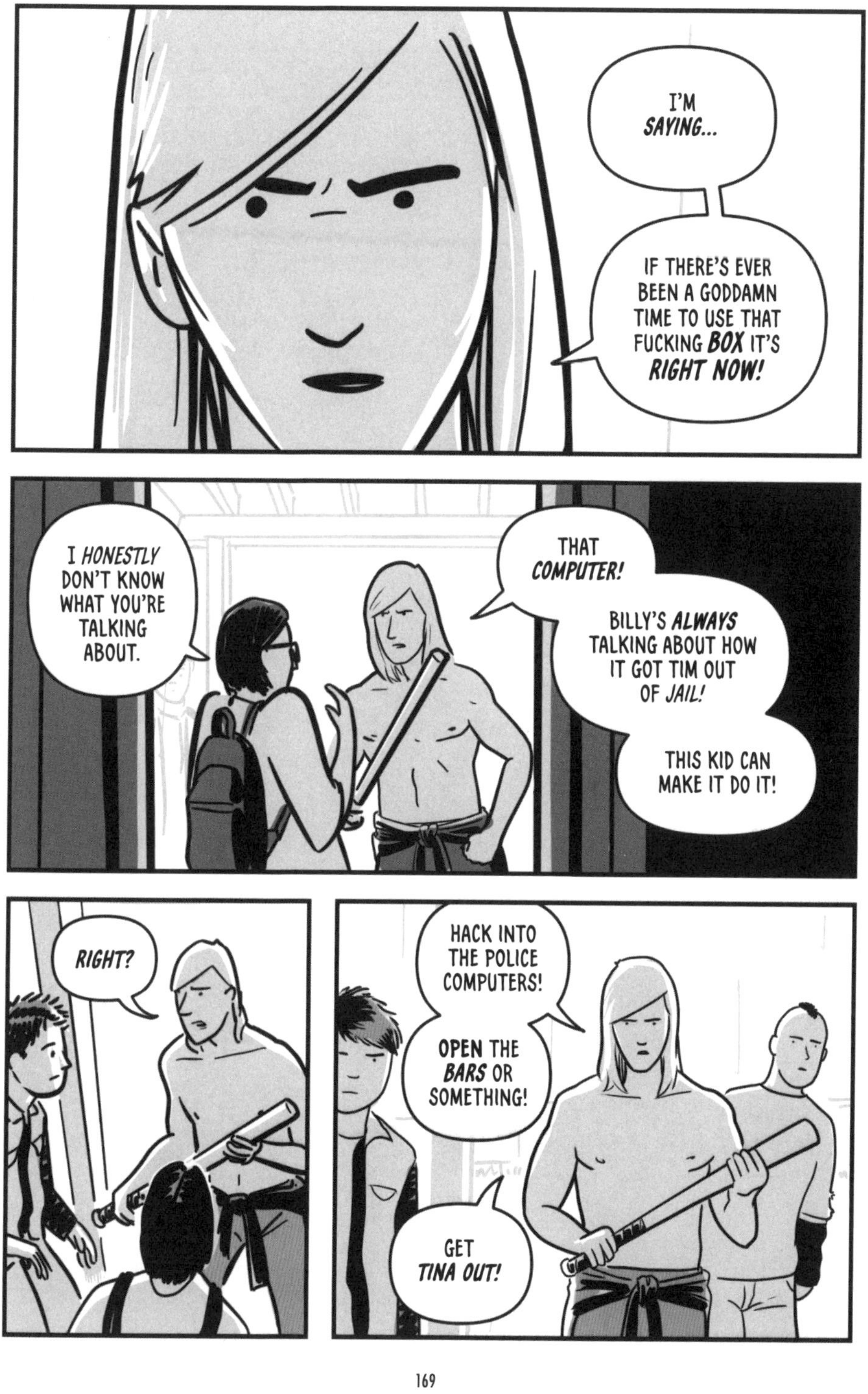

I'M SAYING...
IF THERE'S EVER BEEN A GODDAMN TIME TO USE THAT FUCKING BOX IT'S RIGHT NOW!
I HONESTLY DON'T KNOW WHAT YOU'RE TALKING ABOUT.
THAT COMPUTER!
BILLY'S ALWAYS TALKING ABOUT HOW IT GOT TIM OUT OF JAIL!
THIS KID CAN MAKE IT DO IT!
RIGHT?
HACK INTO THE POLICE COMPUTERS!
OPEN THE BARS OR SOMETHING!
GET TINA OUT!

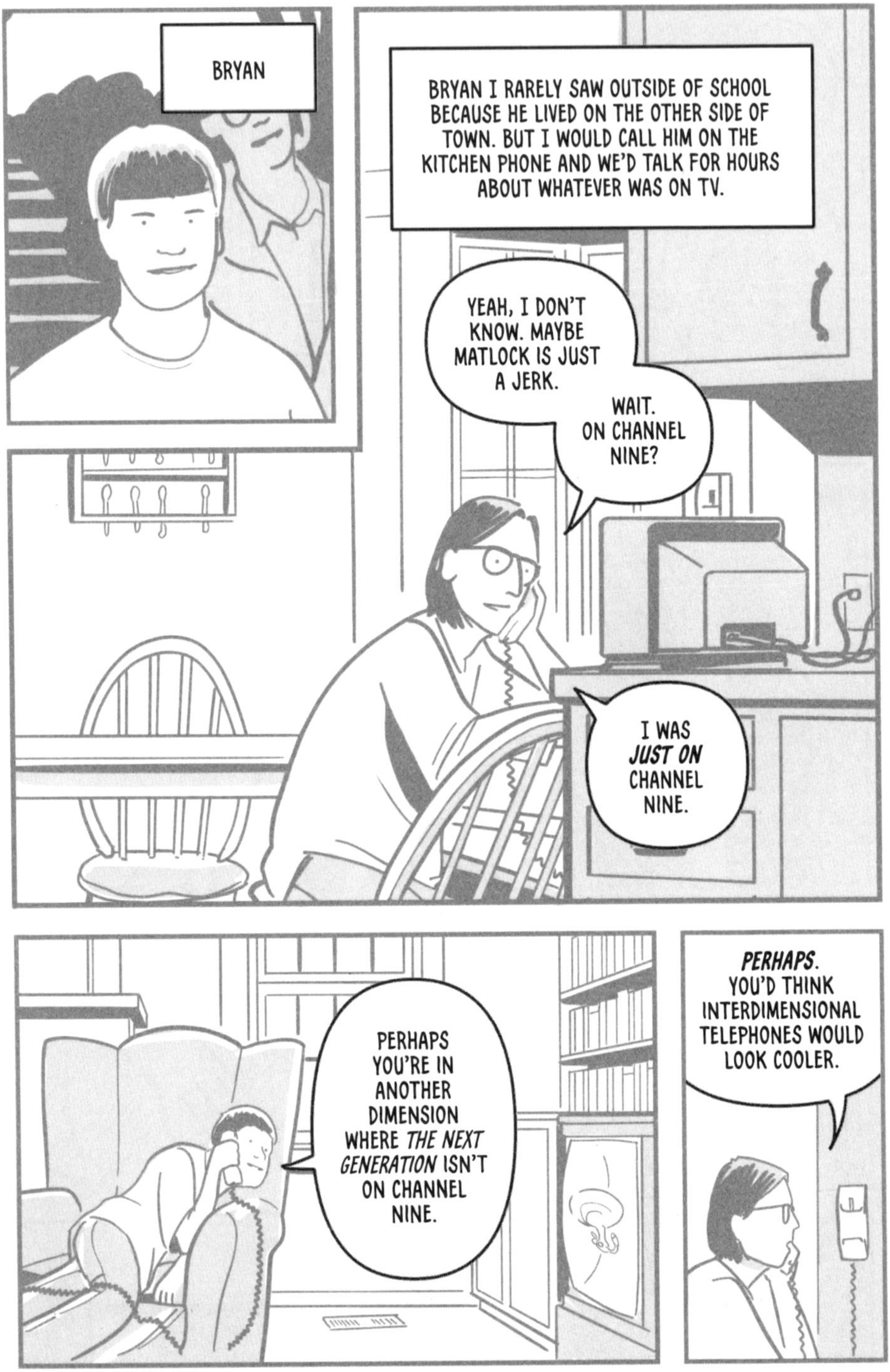
BRYAN
BRYAN I RARELY SAW OUTSIDE OF SCHOOL BECAUSE HE LIVED ON THE OTHER SIDE OF TOWN. BUT I WOULD CALL HIM ON THE KITCHEN PHONE AND WE'D TALK FOR HOURS ABOUT WHATEVER WAS ON TV.
YEAH, I DON'T KNOW. MAYBE MATLOCK IS JUST A JERK.
WAIT. ON CHANNEL NINE?
I WAS *JUST ON* CHANNEL NINE.
PERHAPS YOU'RE IN ANOTHER DIMENSION WHERE *THE NEXT GENERATION* ISN'T ON CHANNEL NINE.
PERHAPS. YOU'D THINK INTERDIMENSIONAL TELEPHONES WOULD LOOK COOLER.

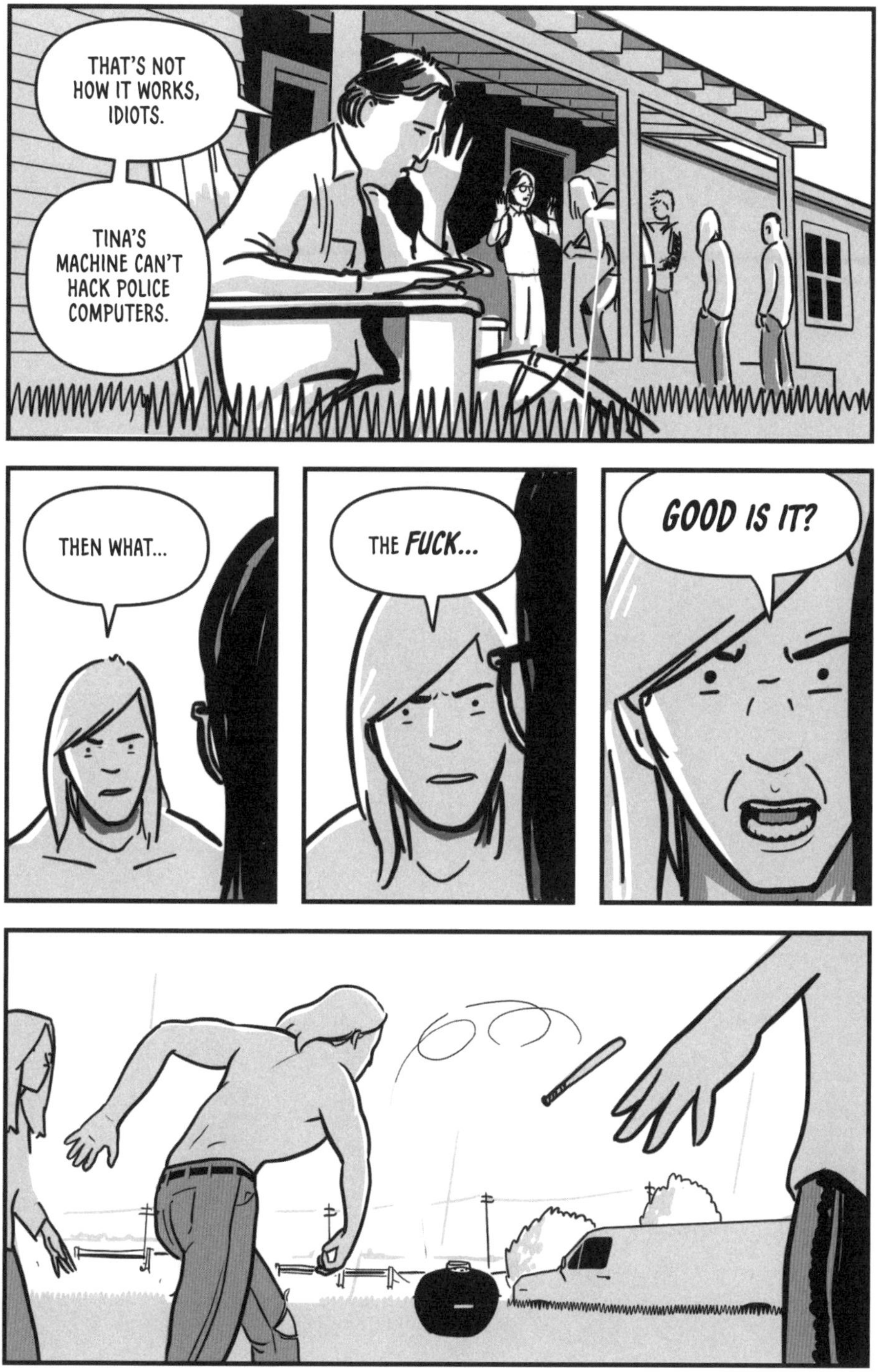
THAT'S NOT HOW IT WORKS, IDIOTS.
TINA'S MACHINE CAN'T HACK POLICE COMPUTERS.
THEN WHAT...
THE FUCK...
GOOD IS IT?

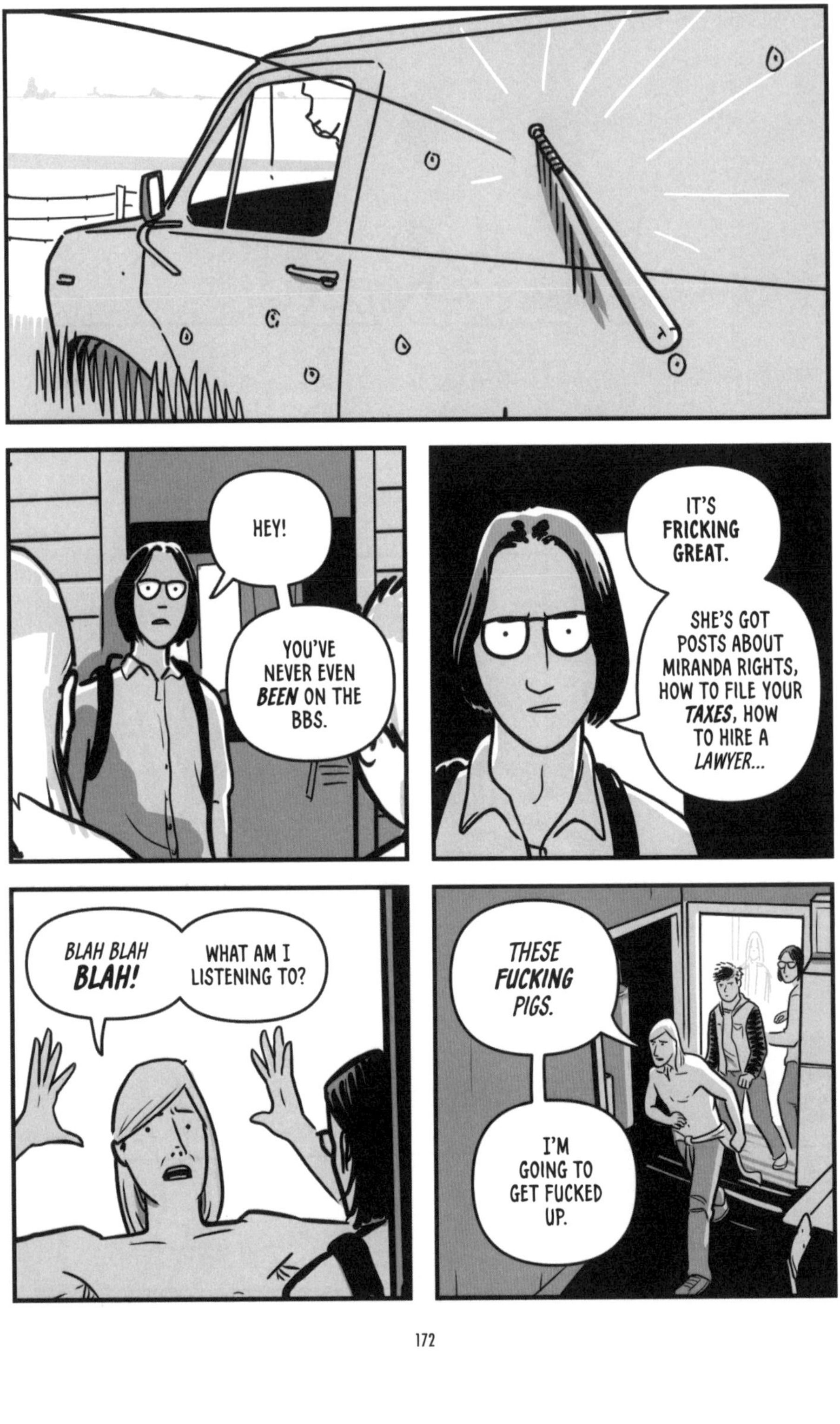
HEY!
YOU'VE NEVER EVEN *BEEN* ON THE BBS.
IT'S FRICKING GREAT.
SHE'S GOT POSTS ABOUT MIRANDA RIGHTS, HOW TO FILE YOUR *TAXES*, HOW TO HIRE A *LAWYER*...
*BLAH BLAH **BLAH!***
WHAT AM I LISTENING TO?
*THESE **FUCKING** PIGS.*
I'M GOING TO GET FUCKED UP.

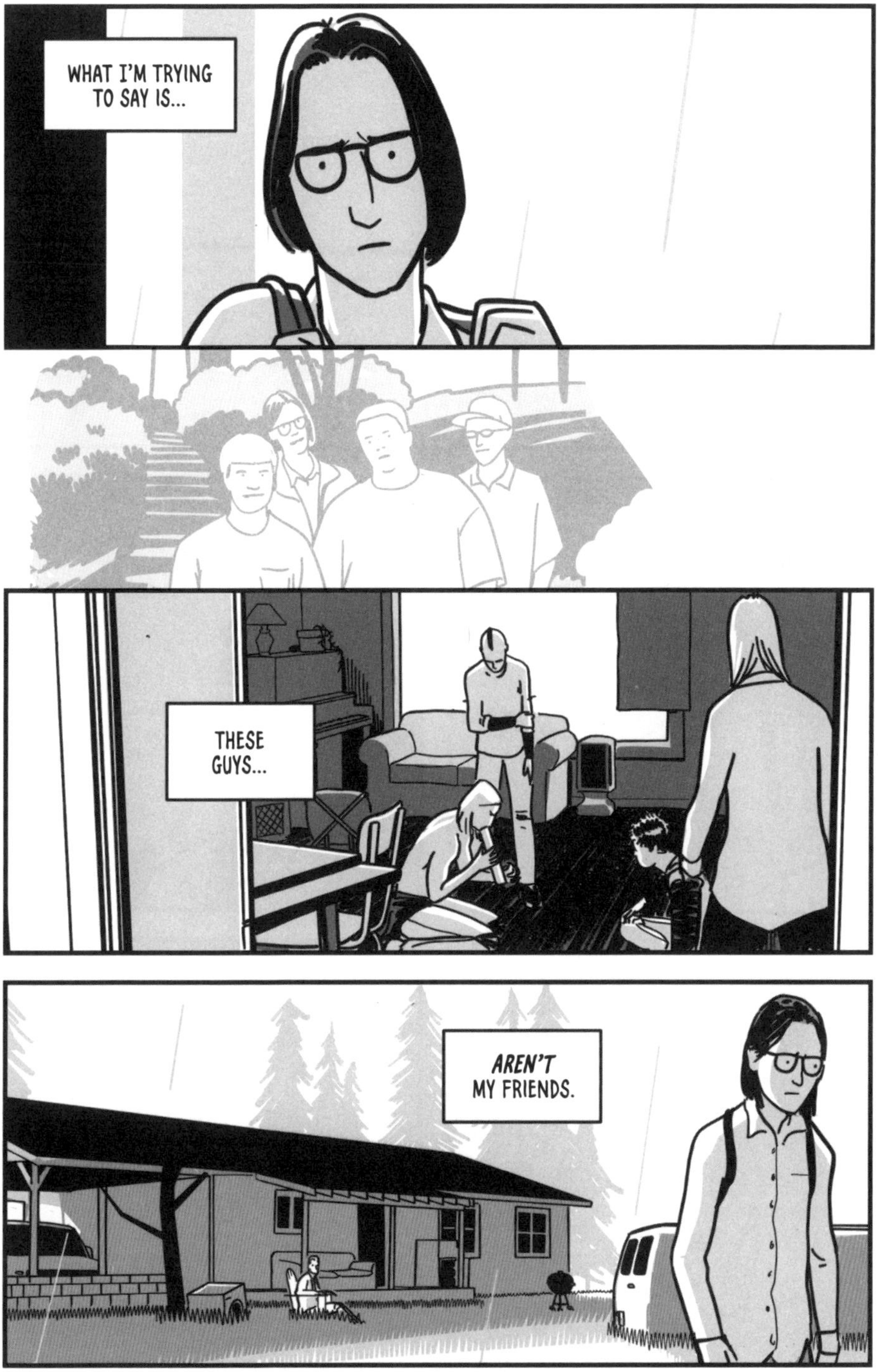
WHAT I'M TRYING
TO SAY IS...
THESE
GUYS...
AREN'T
MY FRIENDS.

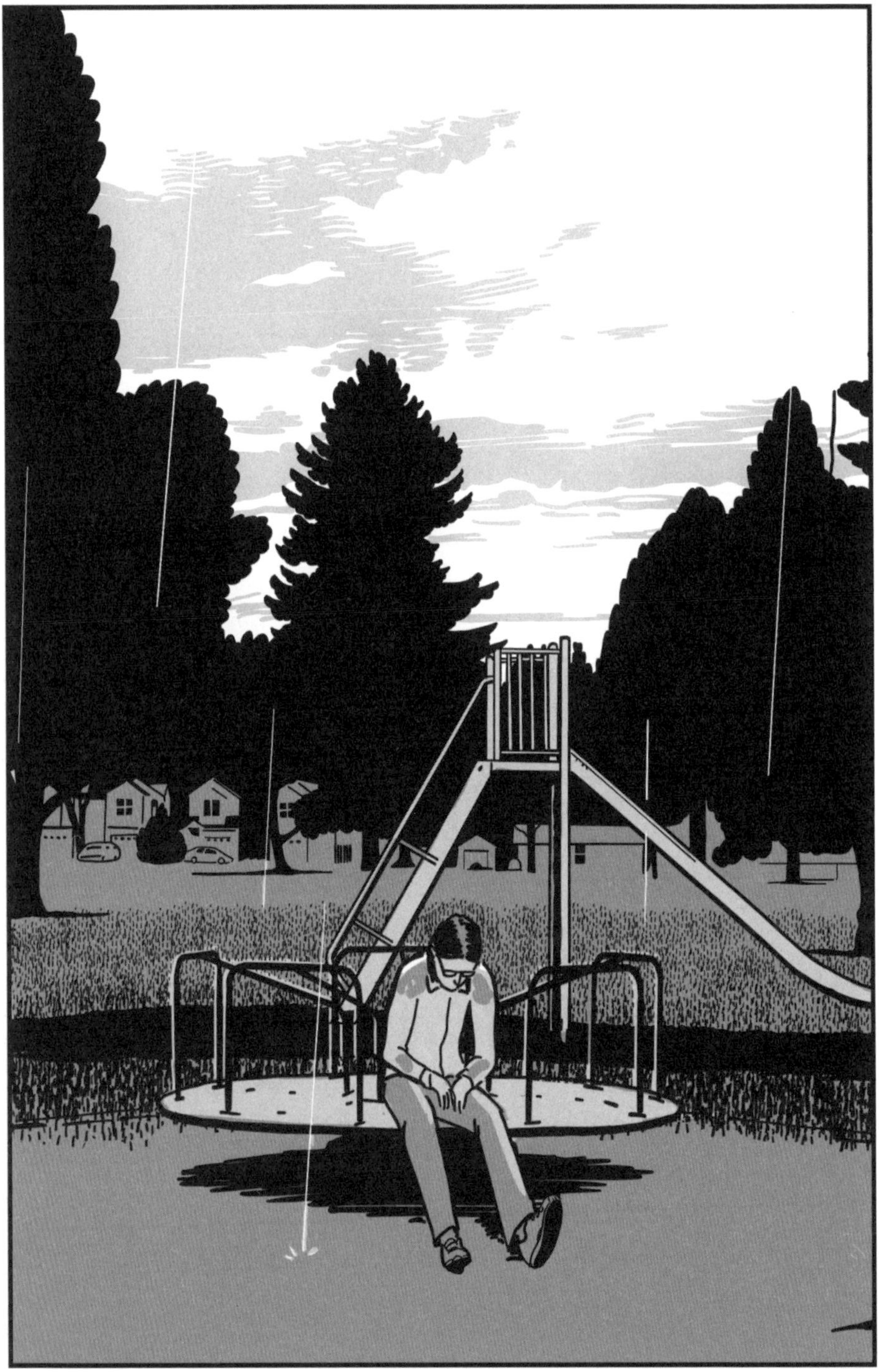

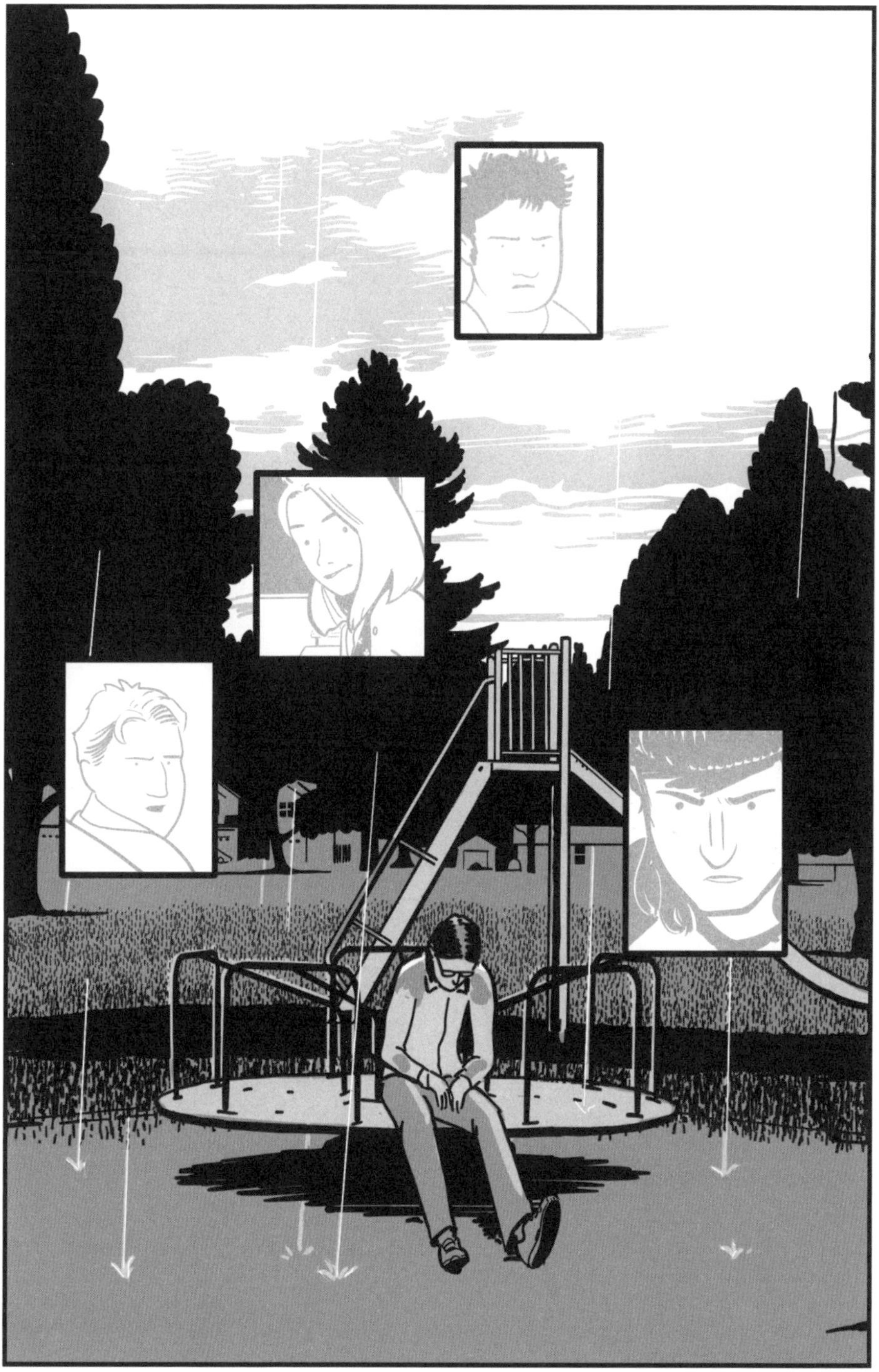

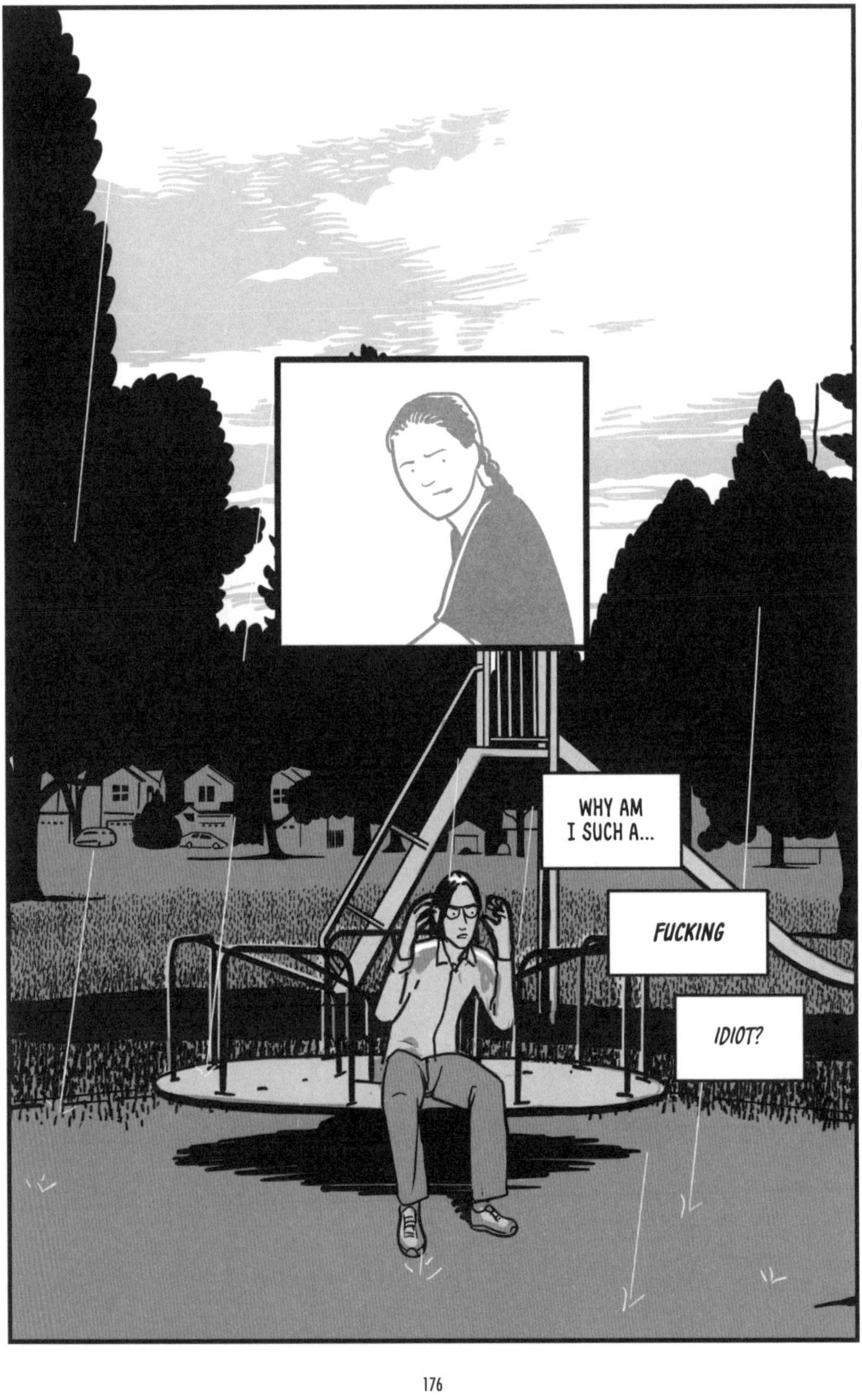
WHY AM I SUCH A...
FUCKING
IDIOT?

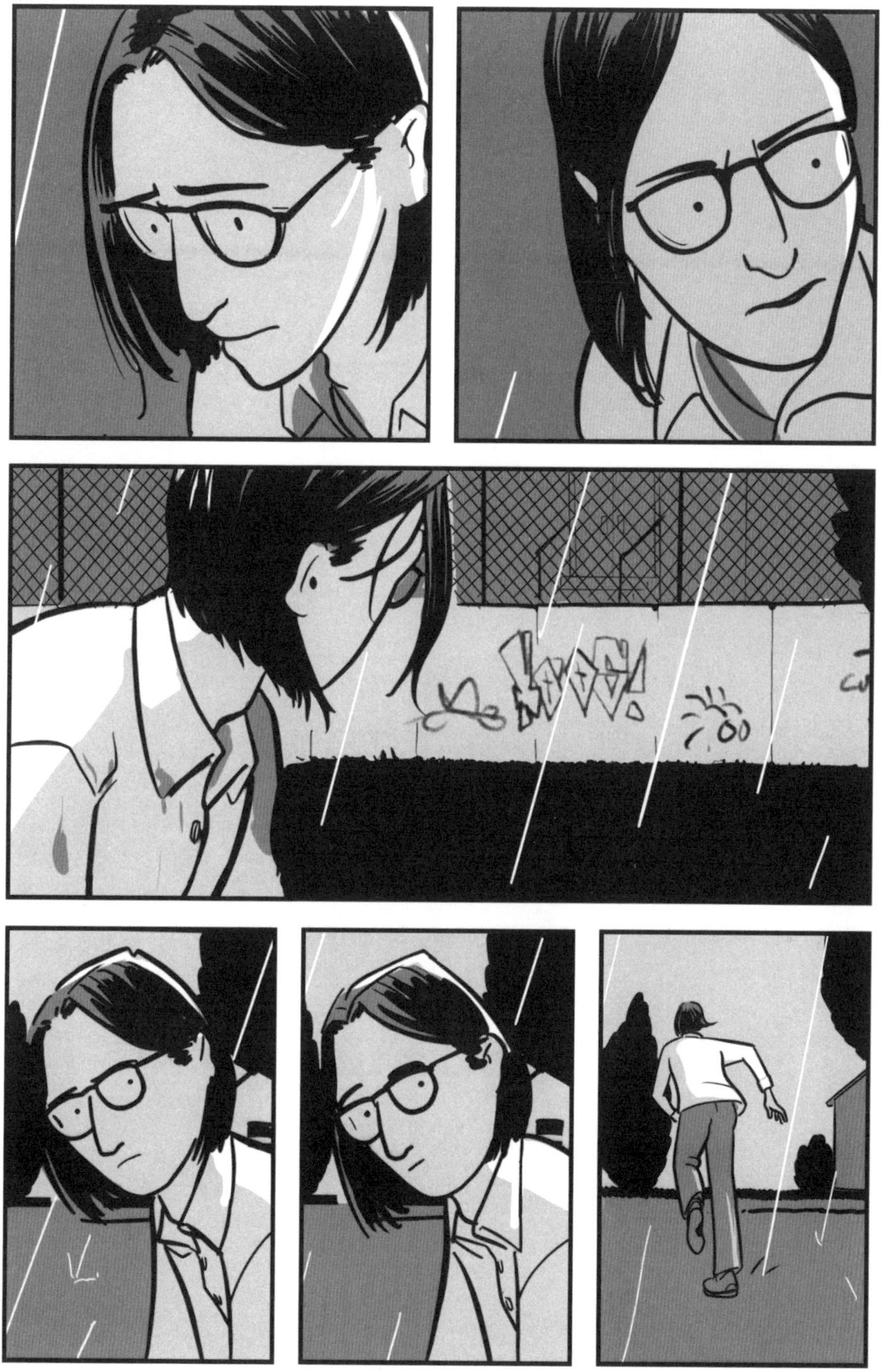

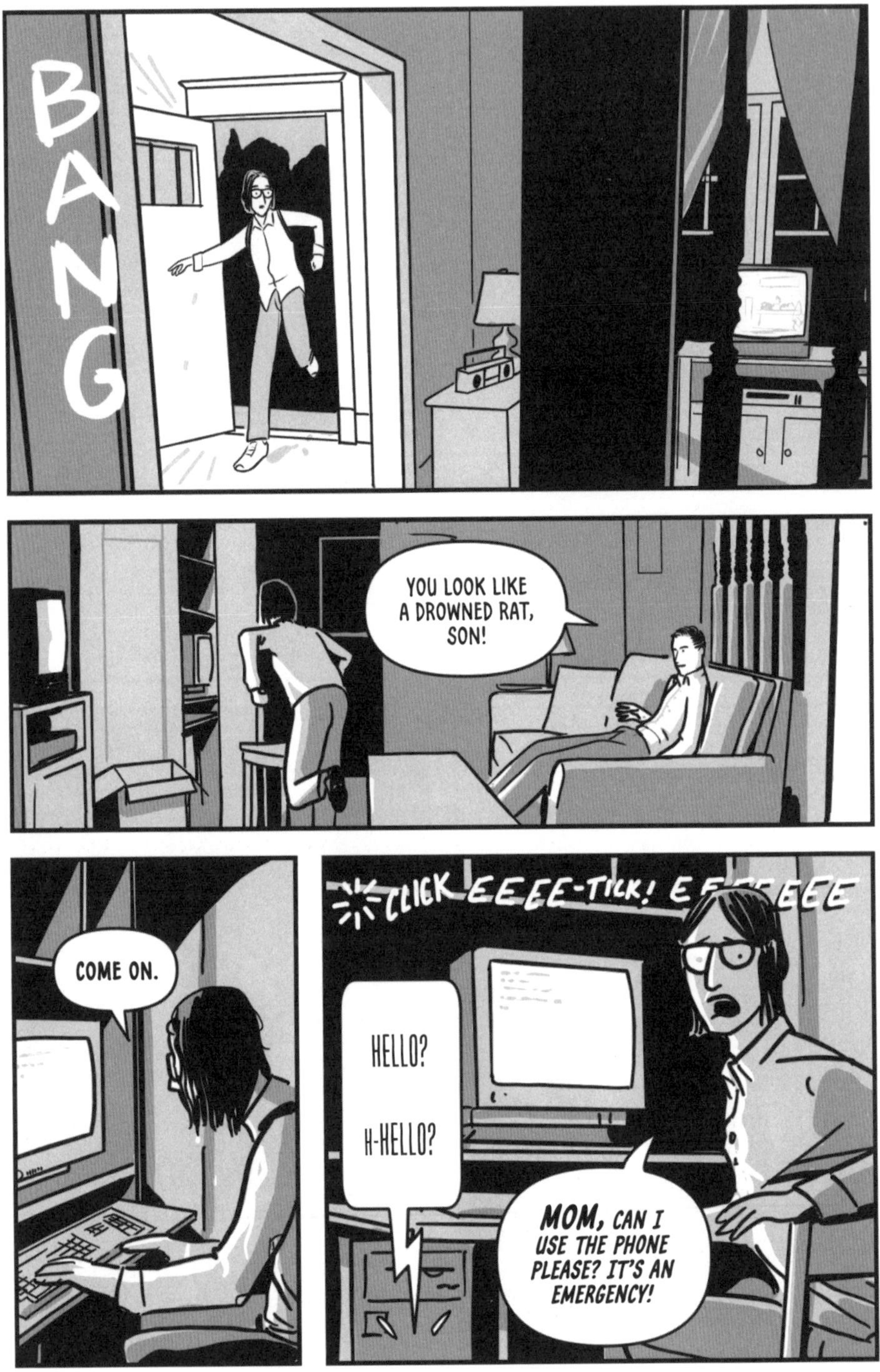
BANG
YOU LOOK LIKE A DROWNED RAT, SON!
COME ON.
CLICK EEEE-TICK!
HELLO?
H-HELLO?
MOM, CAN I USE THE PHONE PLEASE? IT'S AN EMERGENCY!

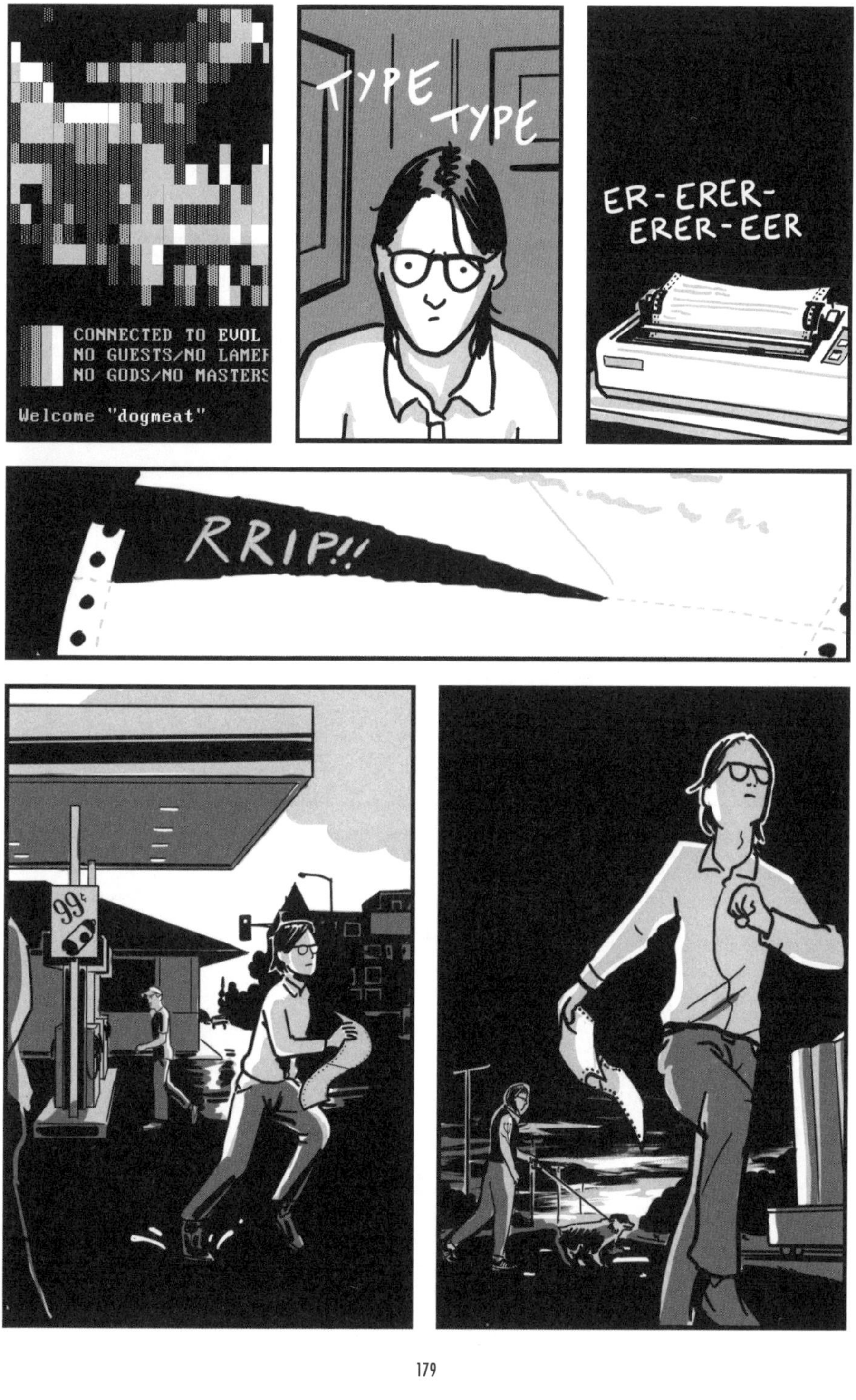
CONNECTED TO EVOL
NO GUESTS/NO LAMER
NO GODS/NO MASTERS
Welcome "dogmeat"
TYPE TYPE
ER-ERER-ERER-EER
RRIP!!
99¢

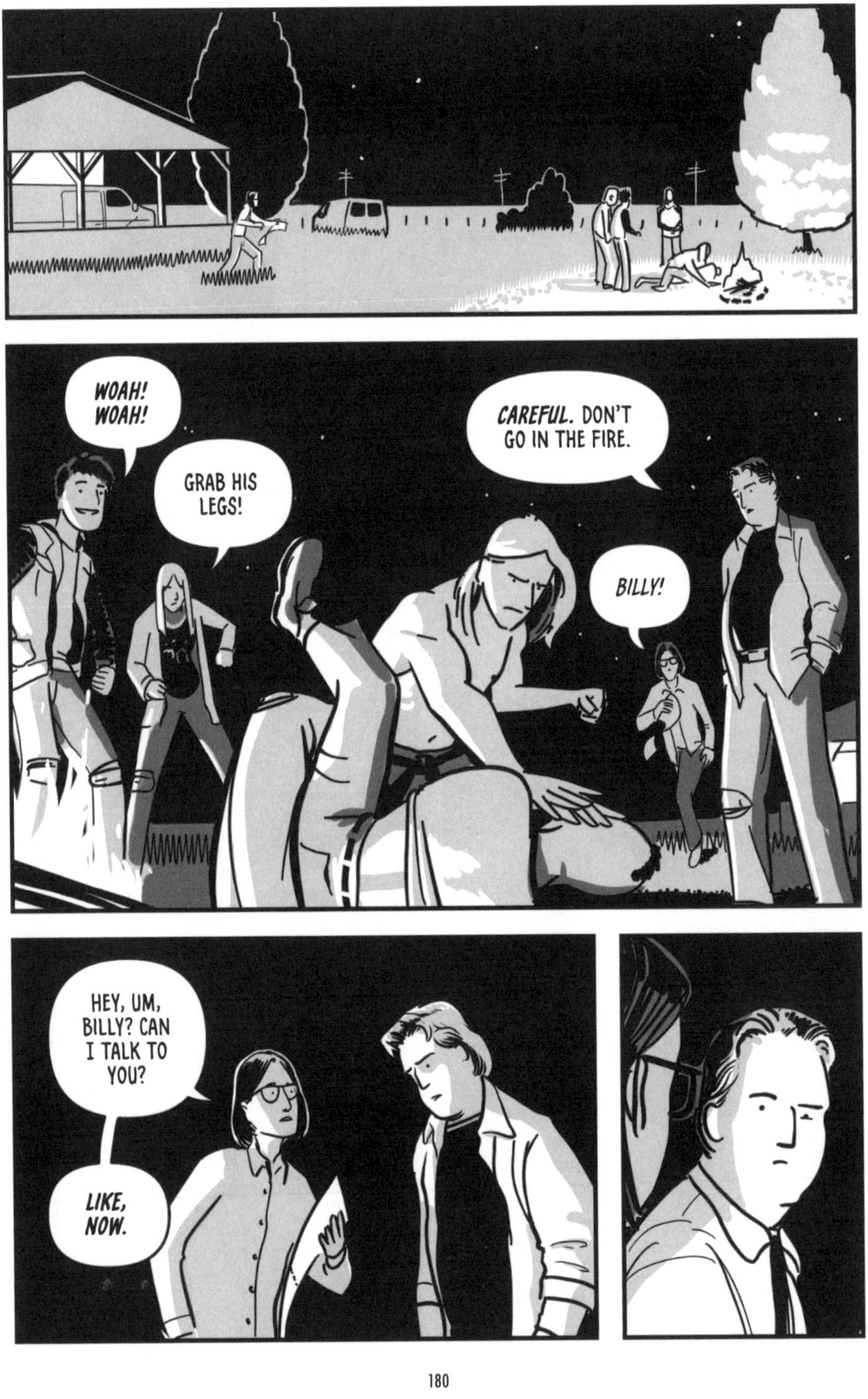
WOAH! WOAH!
GRAB HIS LEGS!
CAREFUL. DON'T GO IN THE FIRE.
BILLY!
HEY, UM, BILLY? CAN I TALK TO YOU?
LIKE, NOW.

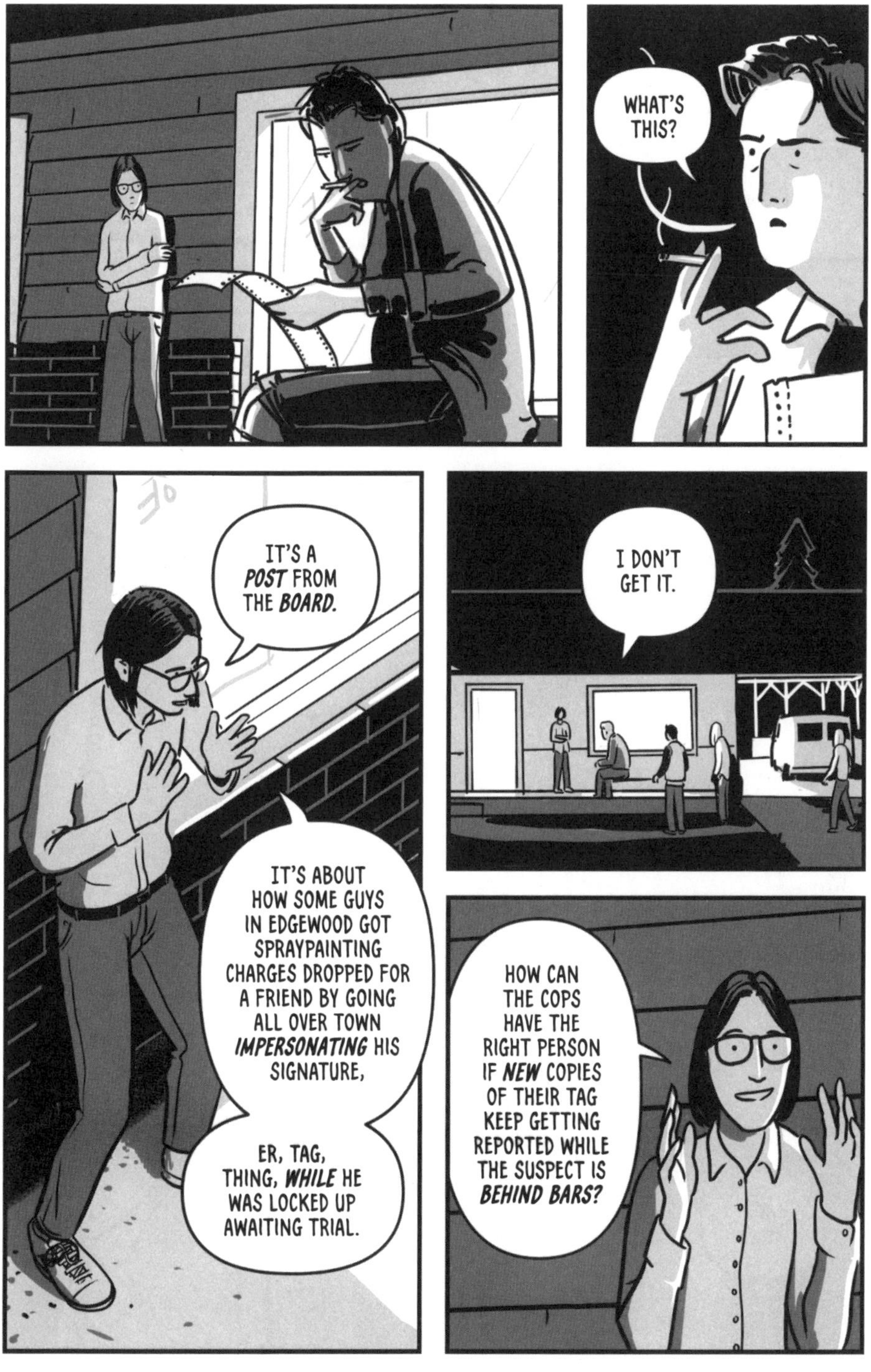
WHAT'S THIS?
IT'S A *POST* FROM THE *BOARD.*
I DON'T GET IT.
IT'S ABOUT HOW SOME GUYS IN EDGEWOOD GOT SPRAYPAINTING CHARGES DROPPED FOR A FRIEND BY GOING ALL OVER TOWN *IMPERSONATING* HIS SIGNATURE,
ER, TAG, THING, *WHILE* HE WAS LOCKED UP AWAITING TRIAL.
HOW CAN THE COPS HAVE THE RIGHT PERSON IF *NEW* COPIES OF THEIR TAG KEEP GETTING REPORTED WHILE THE SUSPECT IS *BEHIND BARS?*

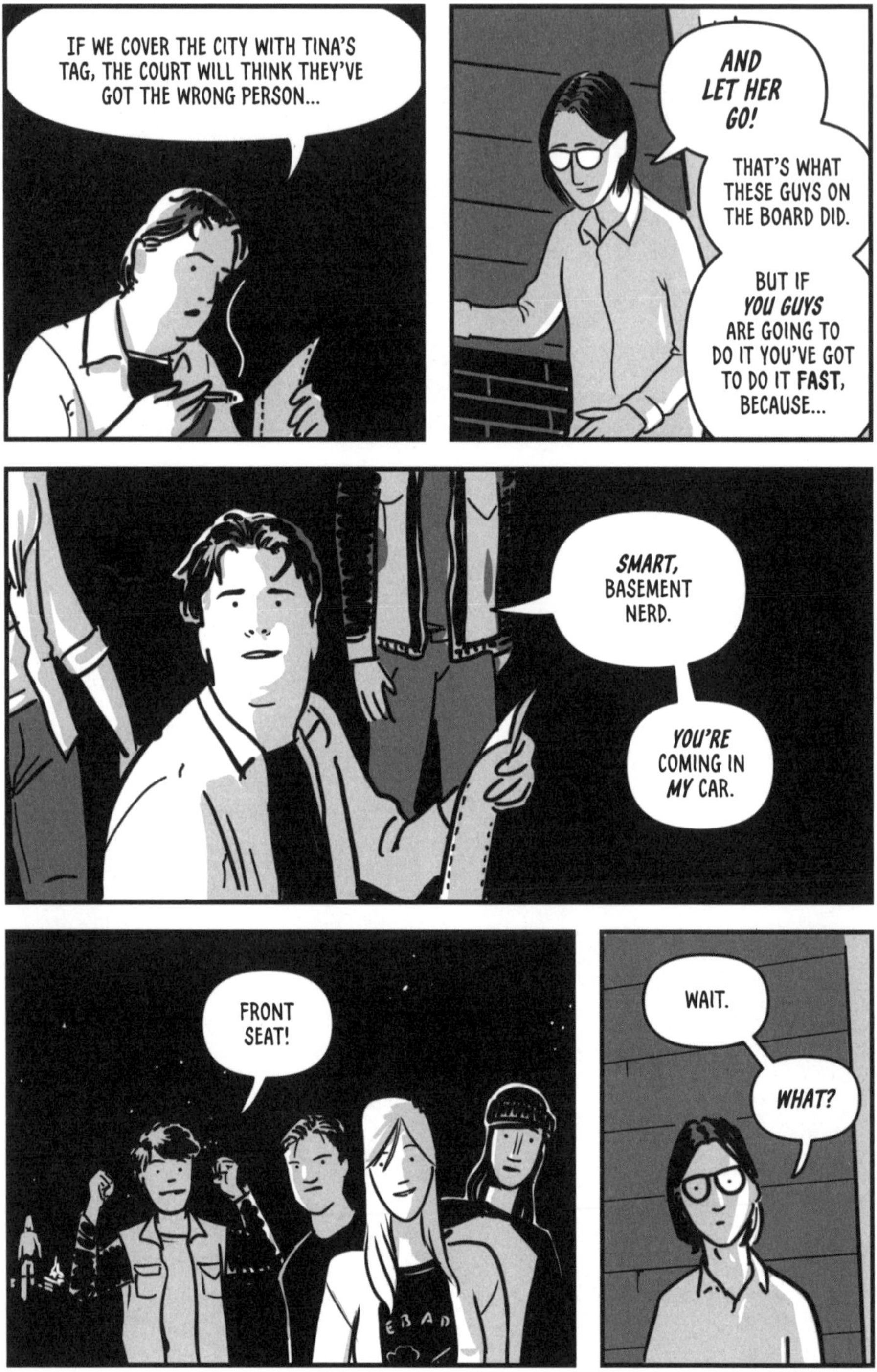
IF WE COVER THE CITY WITH TINA'S TAG, THE COURT WILL THINK THEY'VE GOT THE WRONG PERSON...
AND LET HER GO!
THAT'S WHAT THESE GUYS ON THE BOARD DID.
BUT IF YOU GUYS ARE GOING TO DO IT YOU'VE GOT TO DO IT FAST, BECAUSE...
SMART, BASEMENT NERD.
YOU'RE COMING IN MY CAR.
FRONT SEAT!
WAIT.
WHAT?

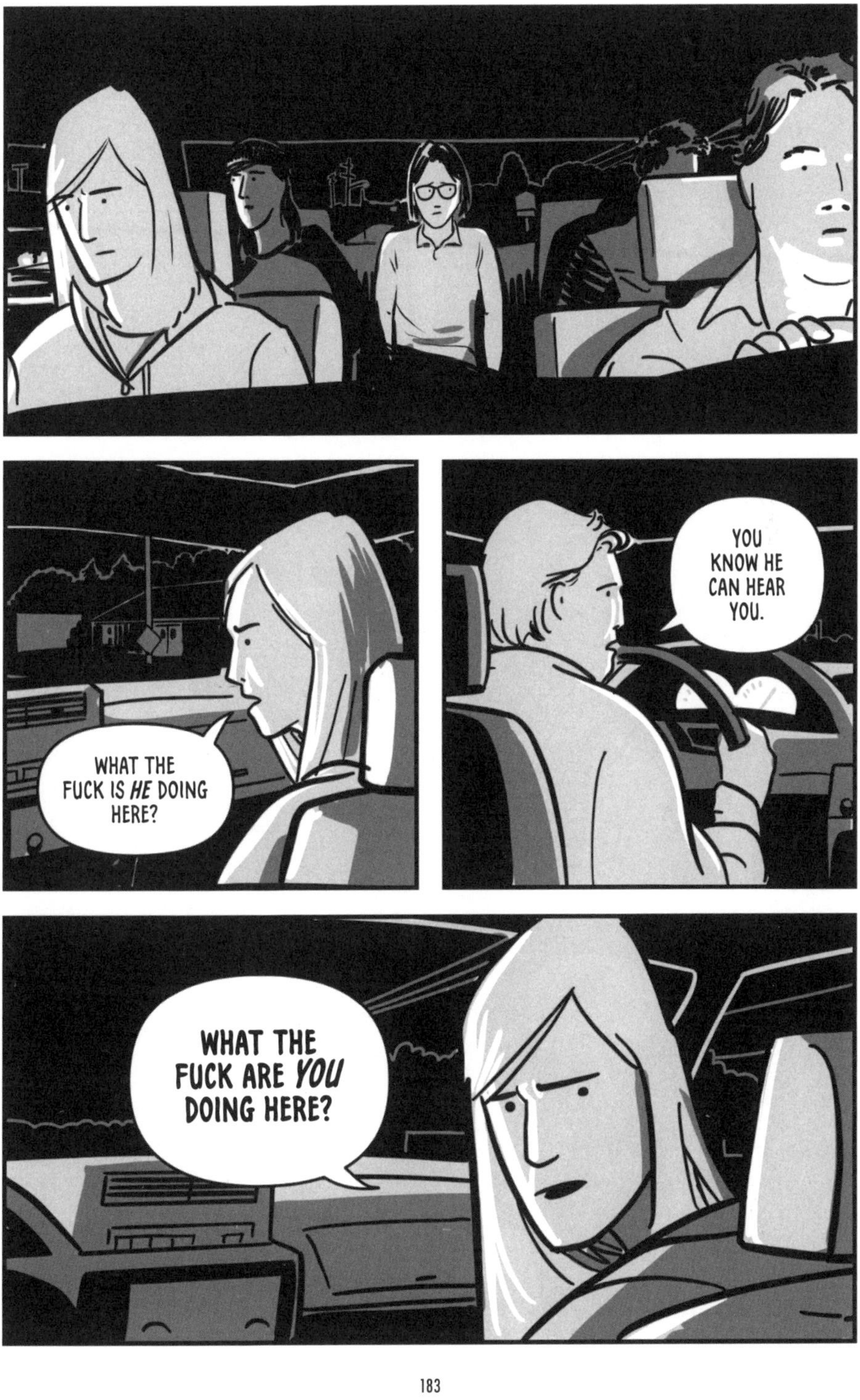
WHAT THE FUCK IS *HE* DOING HERE?
YOU KNOW HE CAN HEAR YOU.
WHAT THE FUCK ARE *YOU* DOING HERE?

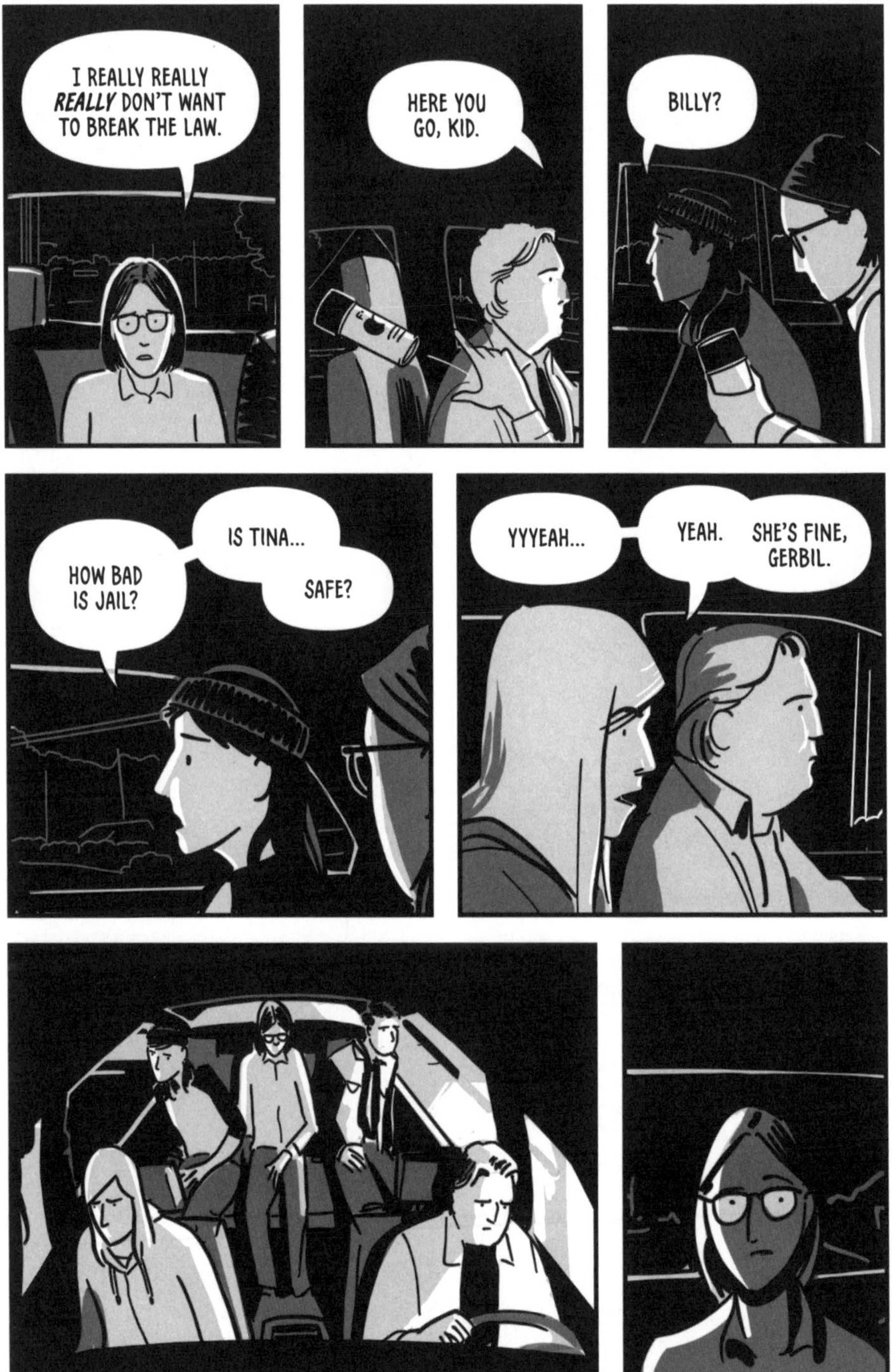
I REALLY REALLY *REALLY* DON'T WANT TO BREAK THE LAW.
HERE YOU GO, KID.
BILLY?
IS TINA...
HOW BAD IS JAIL?
SAFE?
YYYEAH...
YEAH.
SHE'S FINE, GERBIL.

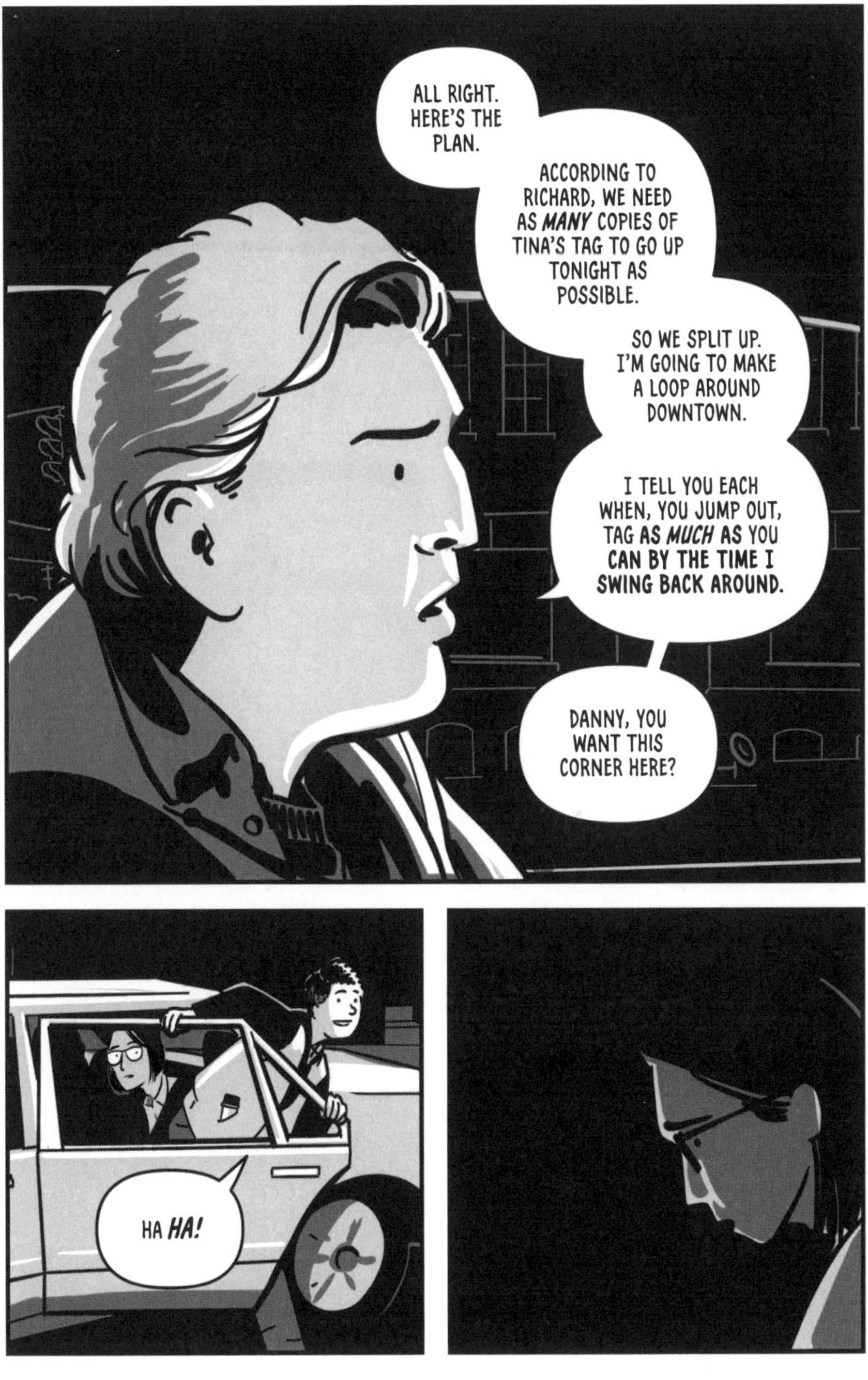
ALL RIGHT. HERE'S THE PLAN.
ACCORDING TO RICHARD, WE NEED AS *MANY* COPIES OF TINA'S TAG TO GO UP TONIGHT AS POSSIBLE.
SO WE SPLIT UP. I'M GOING TO MAKE A LOOP AROUND DOWNTOWN.
I TELL YOU EACH WHEN, YOU JUMP OUT, TAG AS *MUCH* AS YOU CAN BY THE TIME I SWING BACK AROUND.
DANNY, YOU WANT THIS CORNER HERE?
HA *HA!*

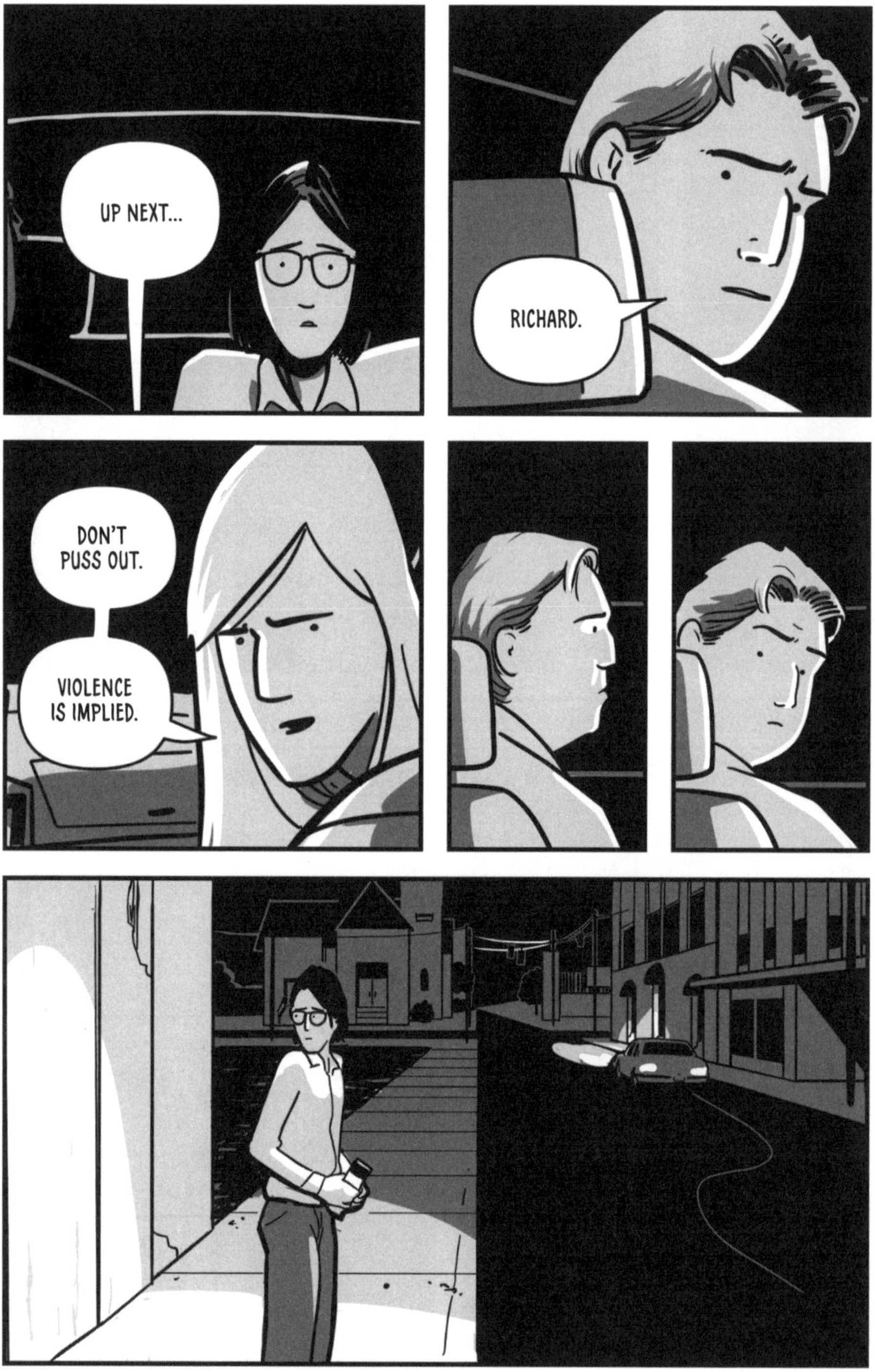
UP NEXT...
RICHARD.
DON'T PUSS OUT.
VIOLENCE IS IMPLIED.

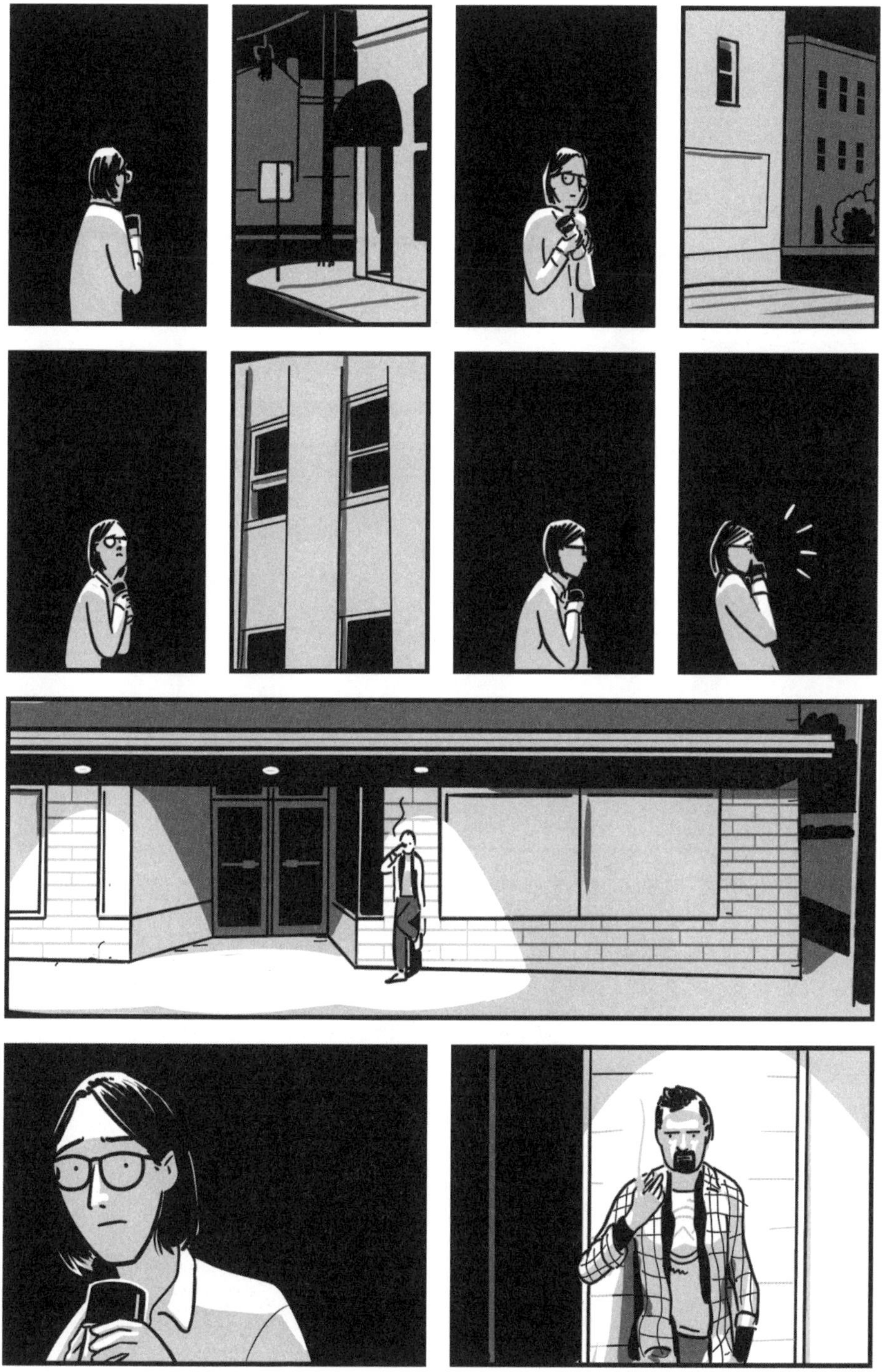

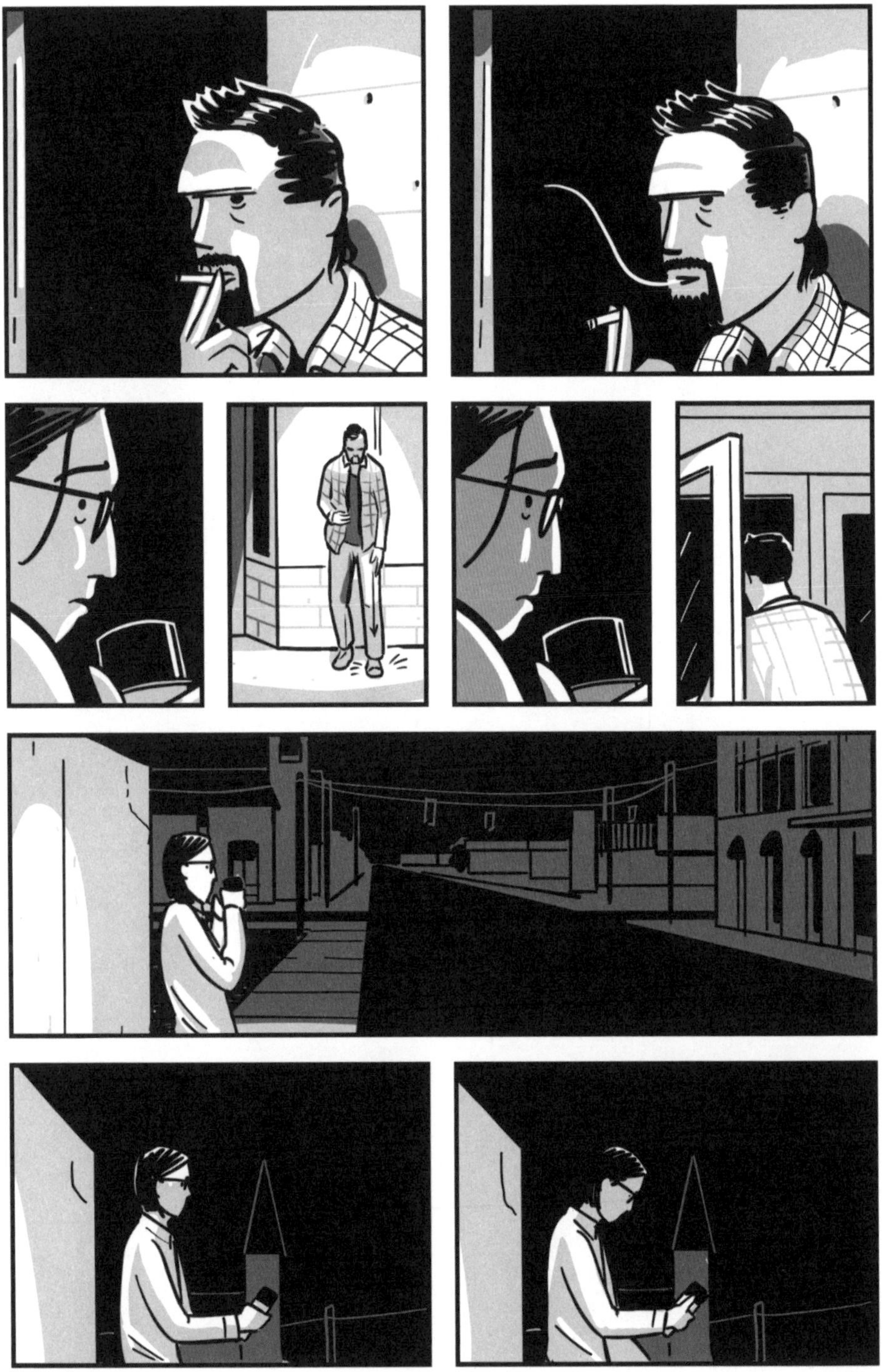

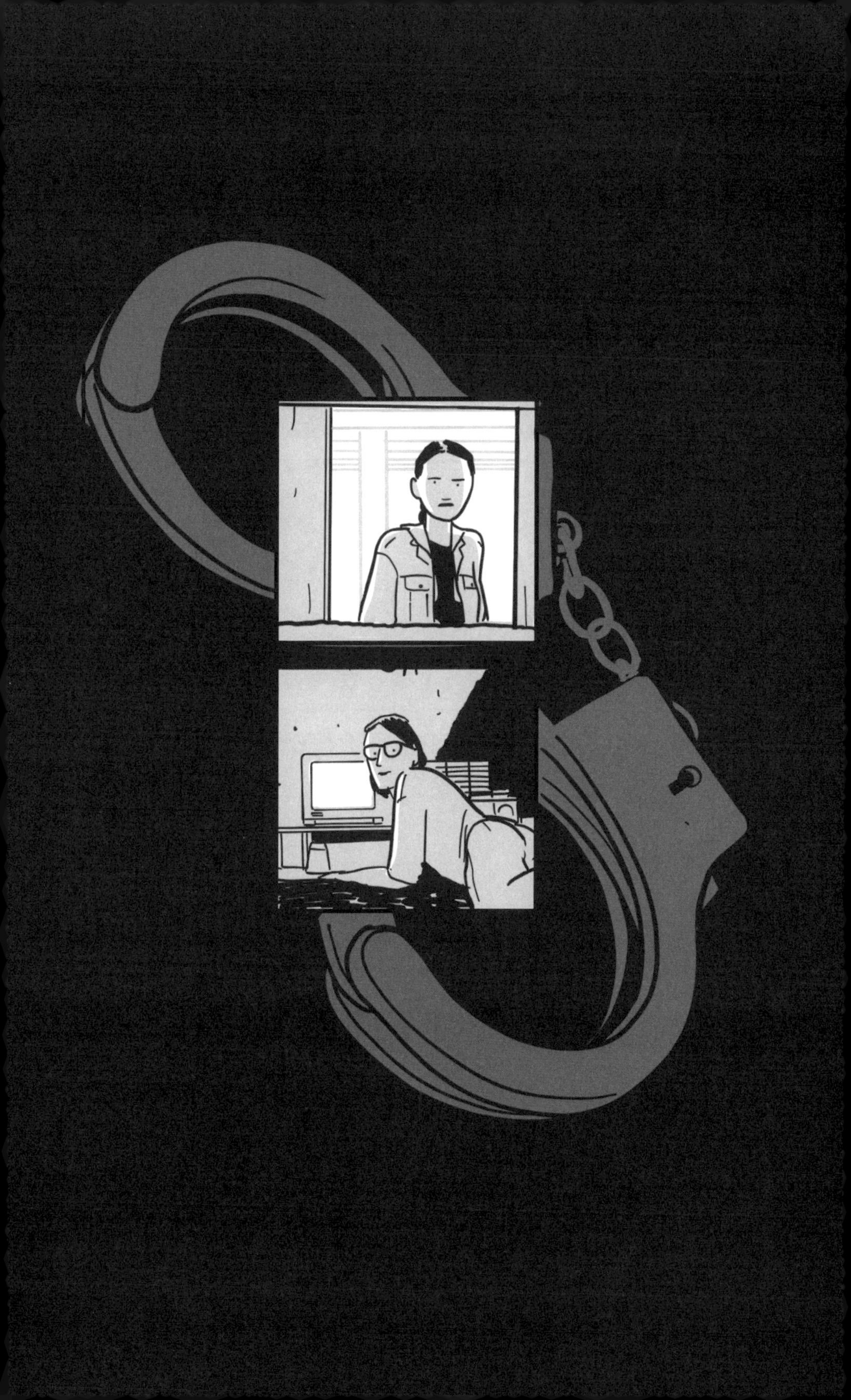

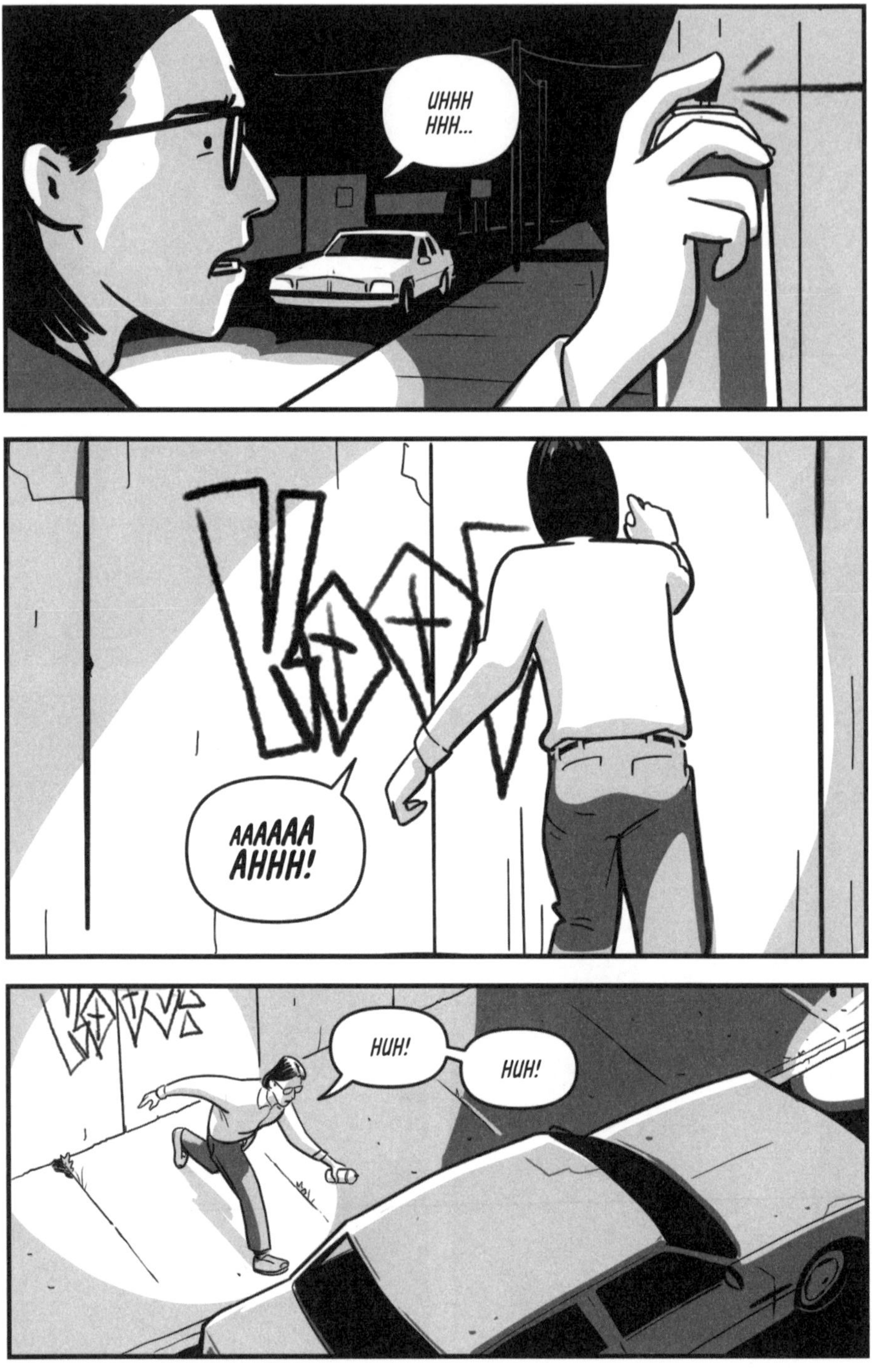
UHHH
HHH...
AAAAAA
AHHH!
HUH!
HUH!

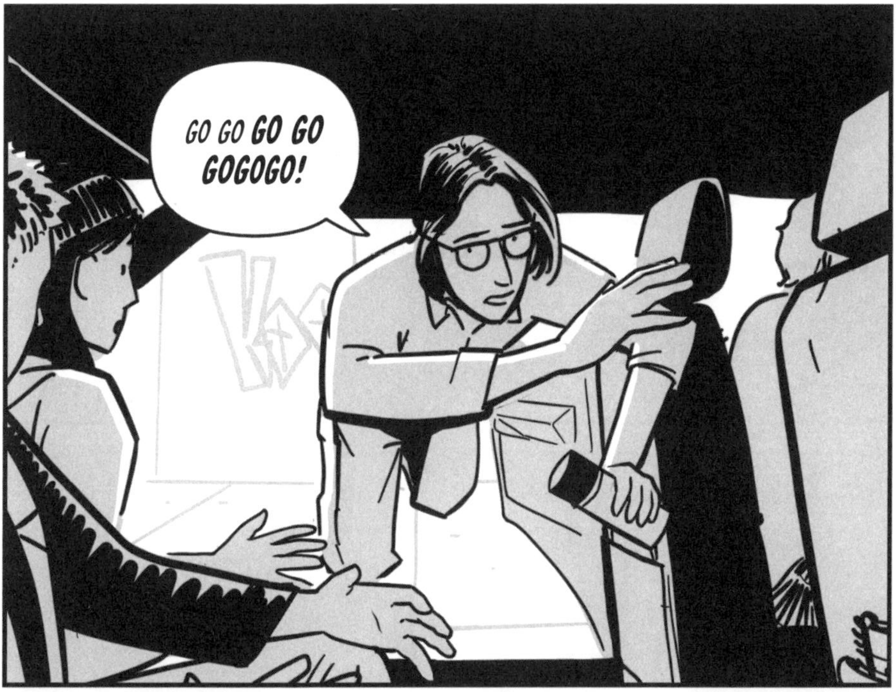
GO GO GO GO
GOGOGO!

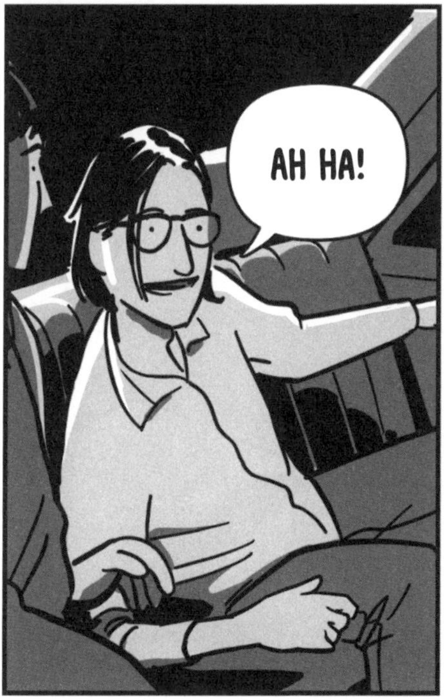
AH HA!

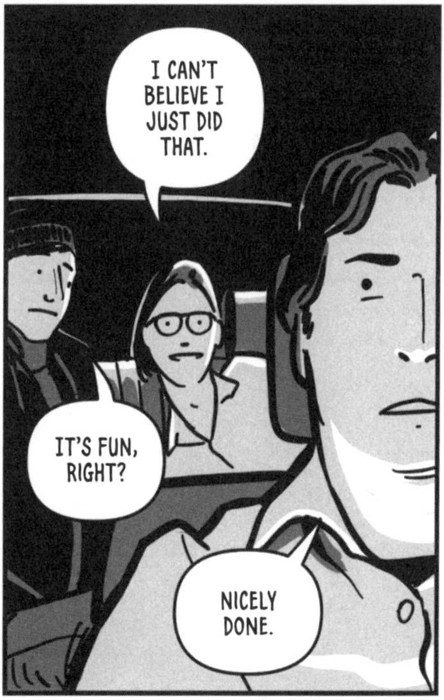
I CAN'T BELIEVE I JUST DID THAT.
IT'S FUN, RIGHT?
NICELY DONE.

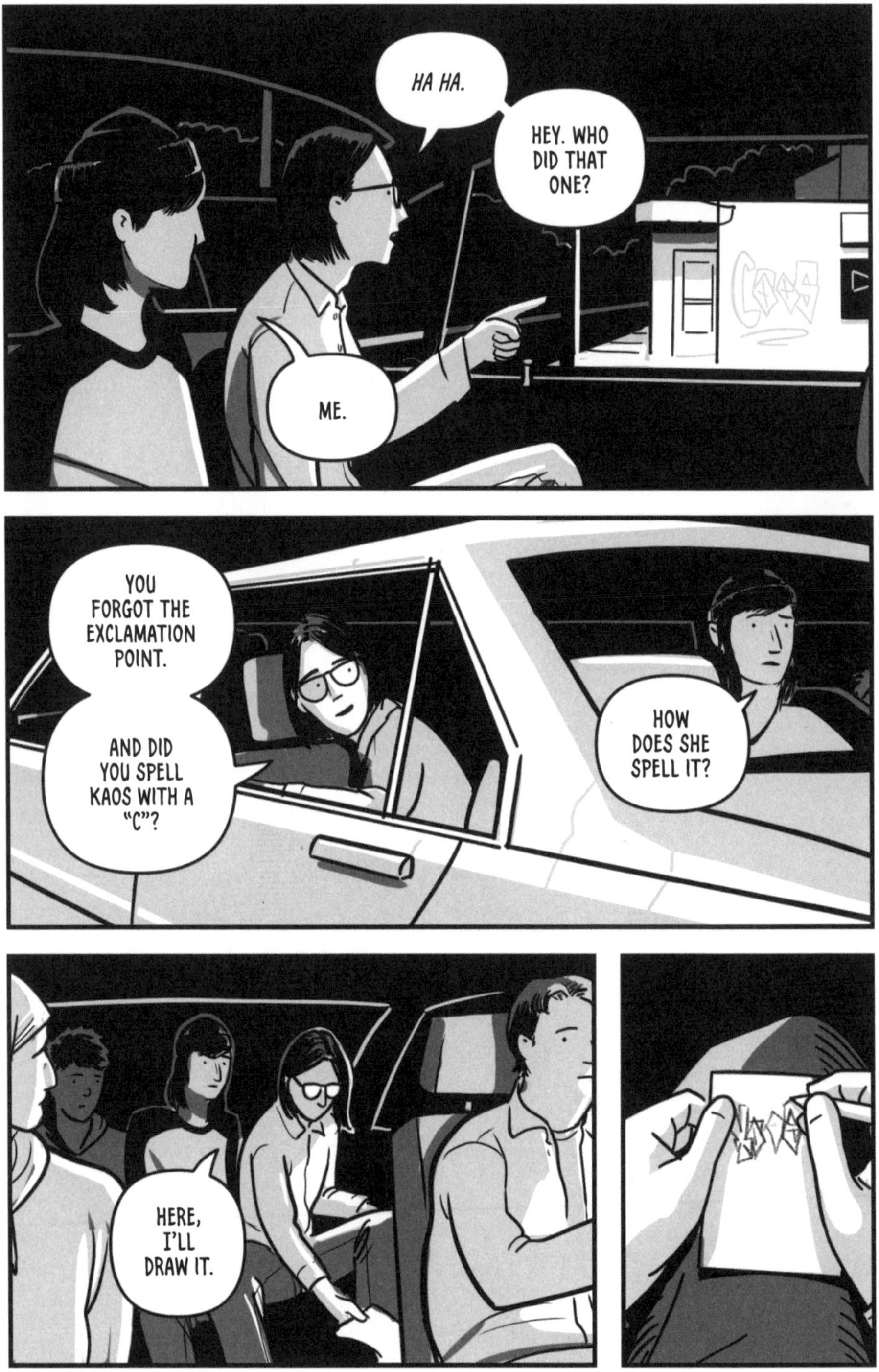
HA HA.
HEY. WHO DID THAT ONE?
ME.
YOU FORGOT THE EXCLAMATION POINT.
AND DID YOU SPELL KAOS WITH A "C"?
HOW DOES SHE SPELL IT?
HERE, I'LL DRAW IT.

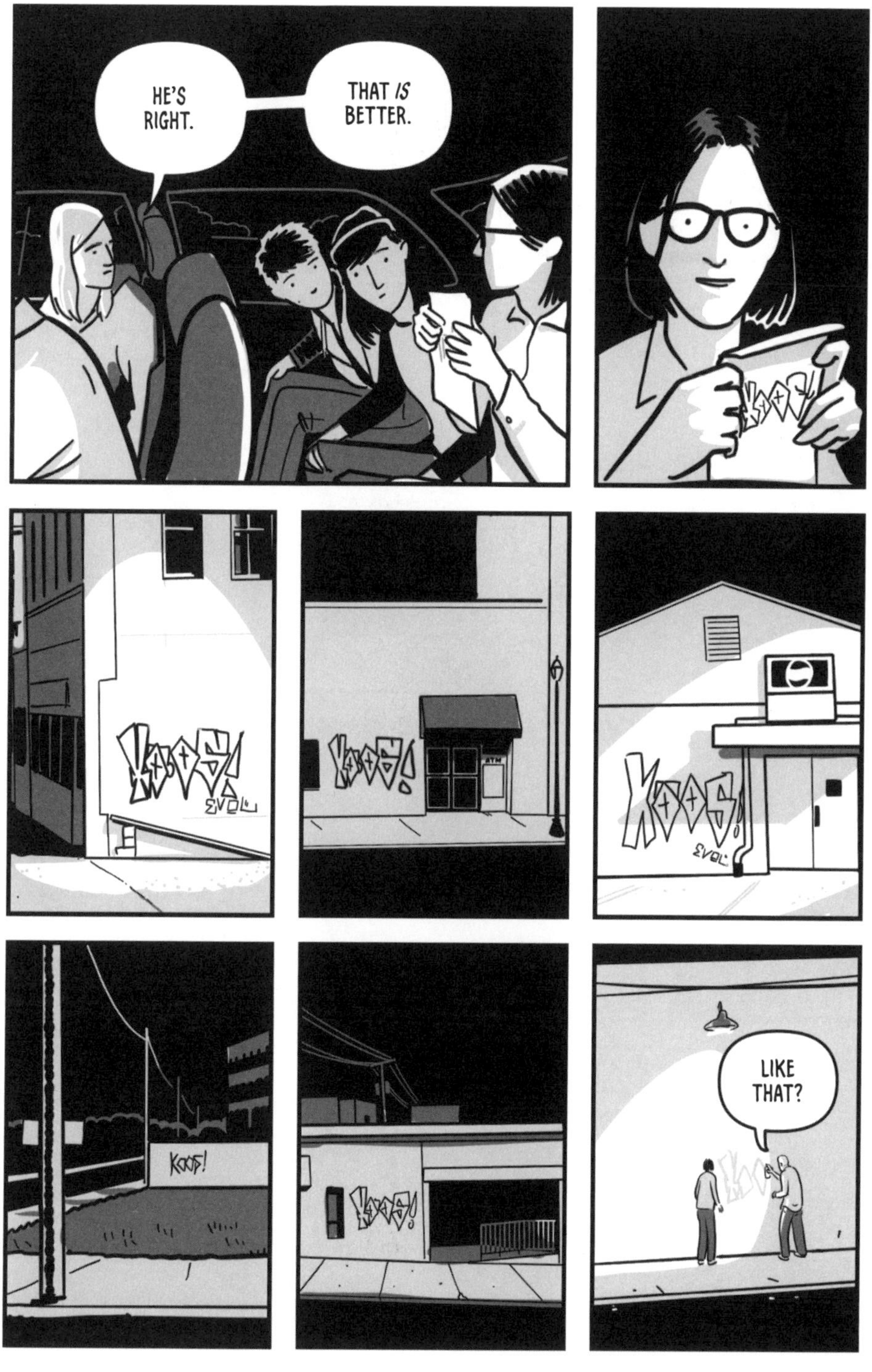
HE'S RIGHT.
THAT *IS* BETTER.
LIKE THAT?

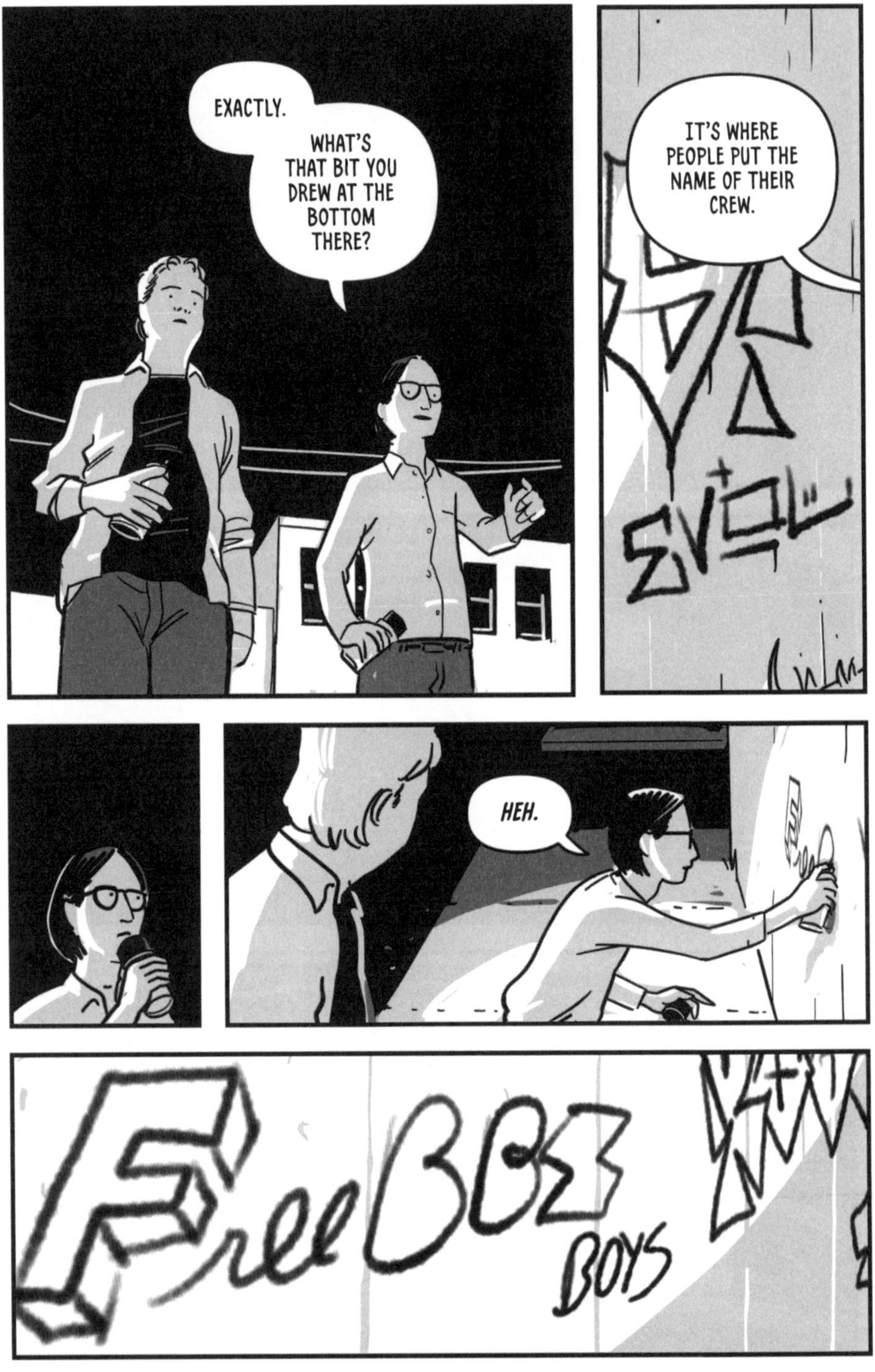
EXACTLY.
WHAT'S THAT BIT YOU DREW AT THE BOTTOM THERE?
IT'S WHERE PEOPLE PUT THE NAME OF THEIR CREW.
HEH.
FreeBOE BOYS

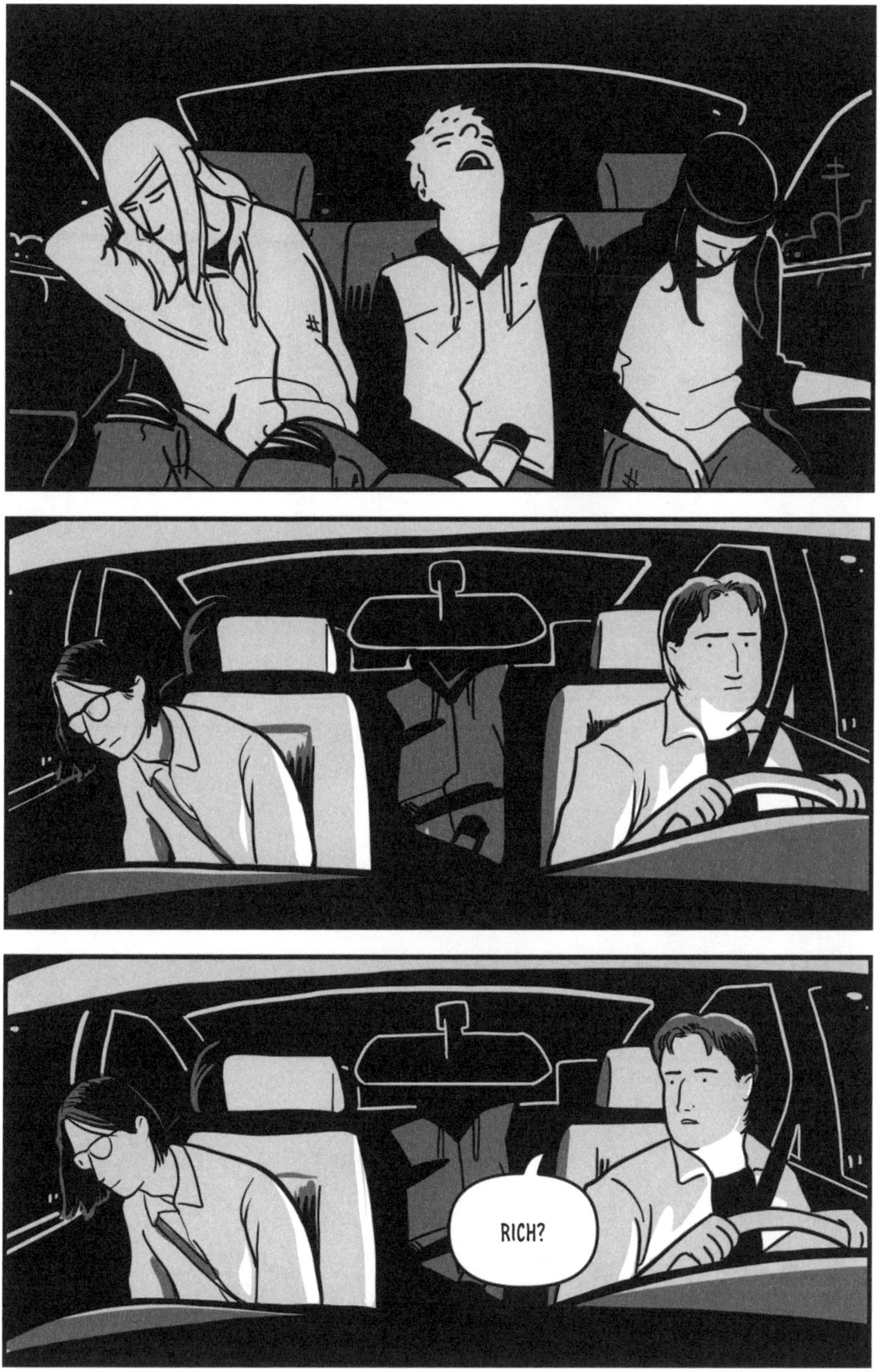
RICH?

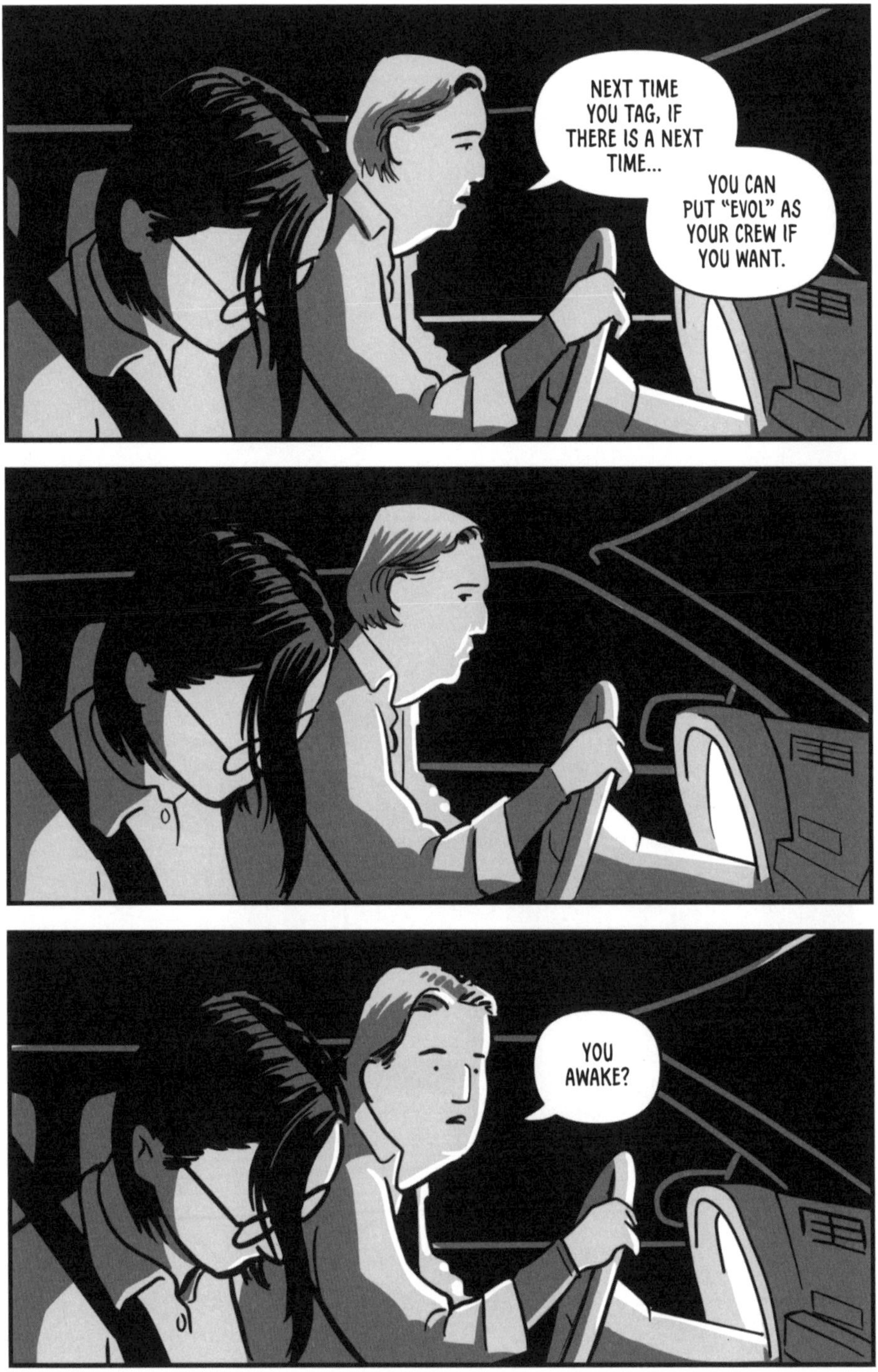
NEXT TIME YOU TAG, IF THERE IS A NEXT TIME...
YOU CAN PUT "EVOL" AS YOUR CREW IF YOU WANT.
YOU AWAKE?

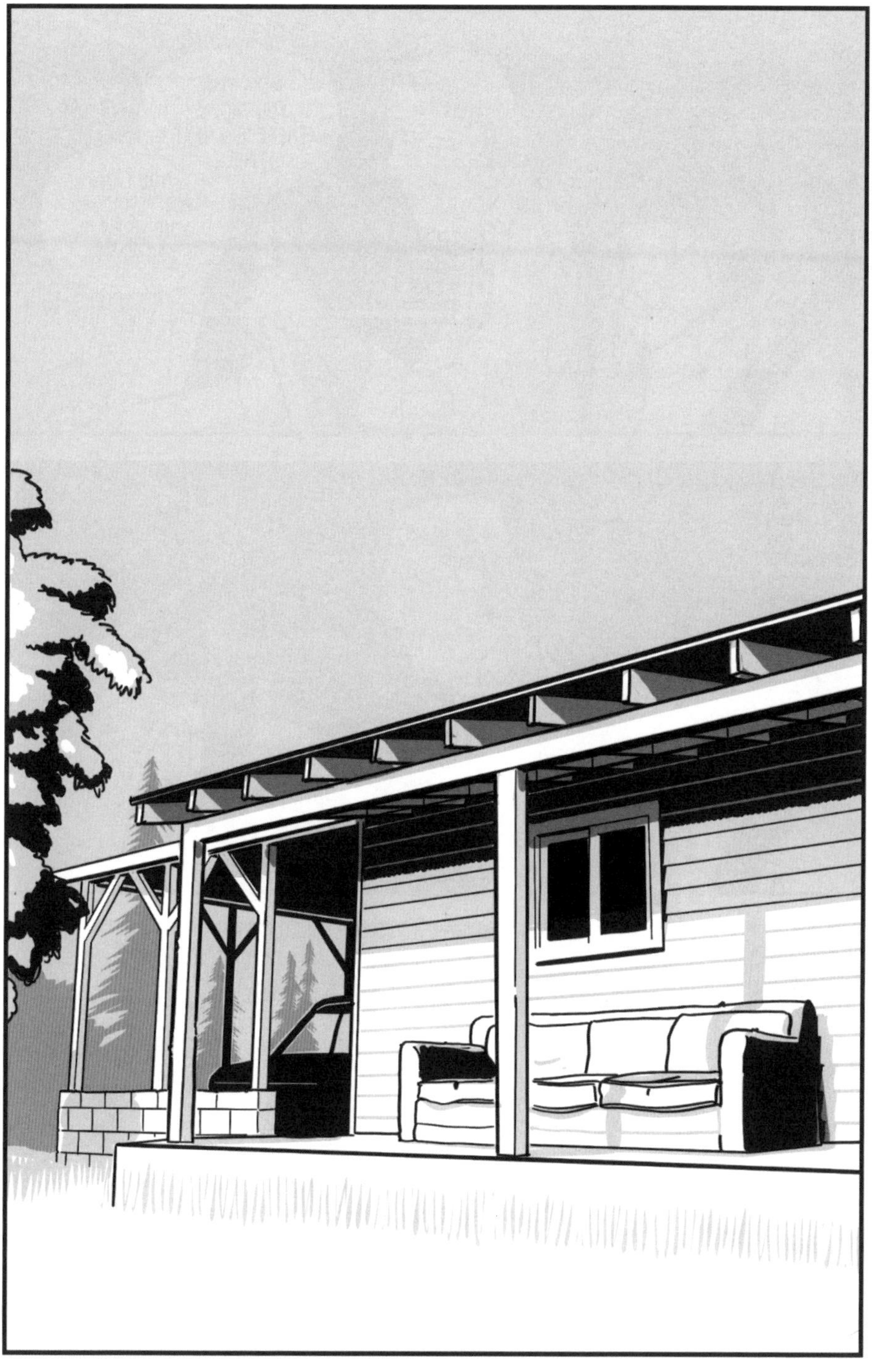

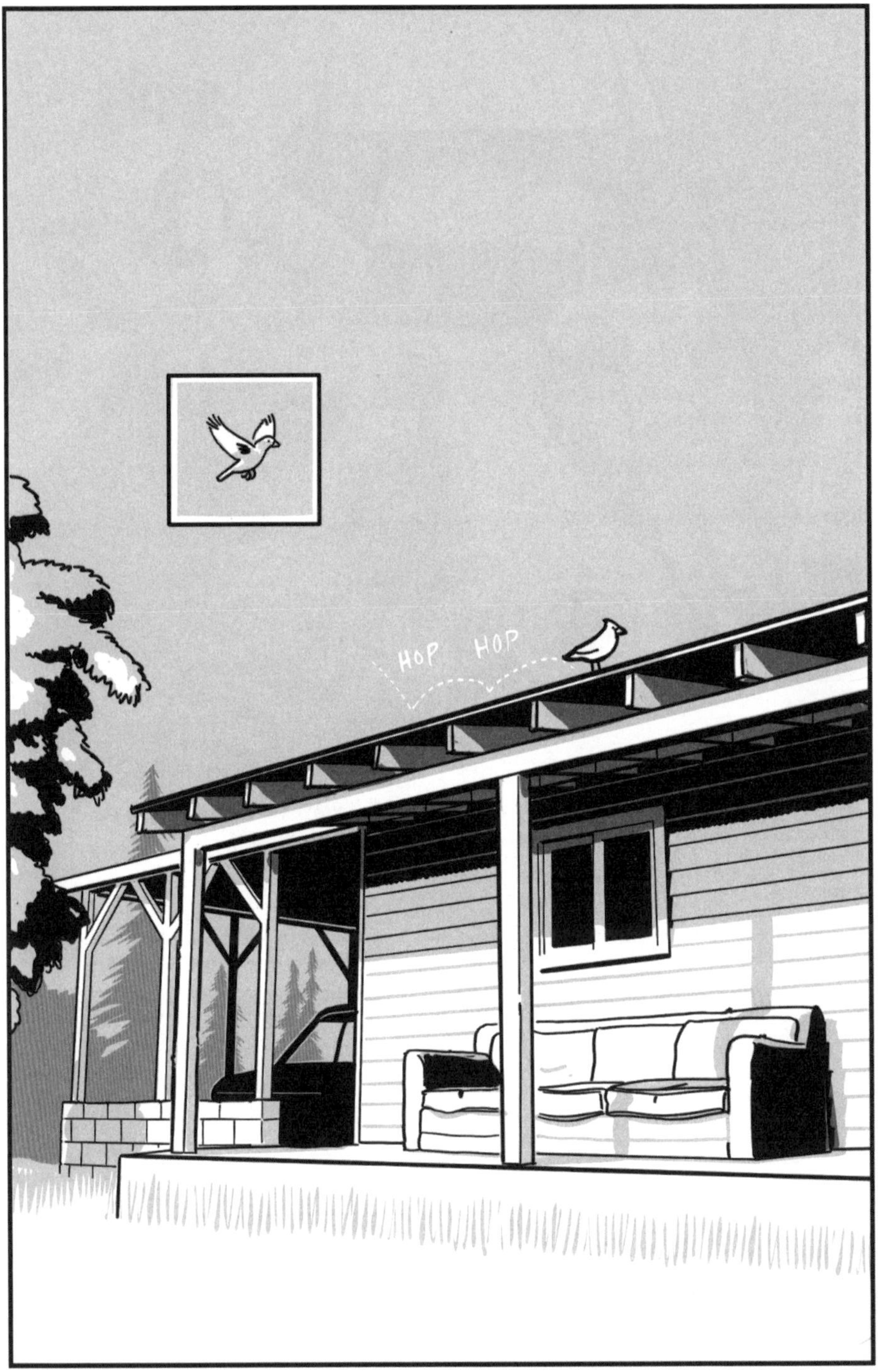
HOP HOP

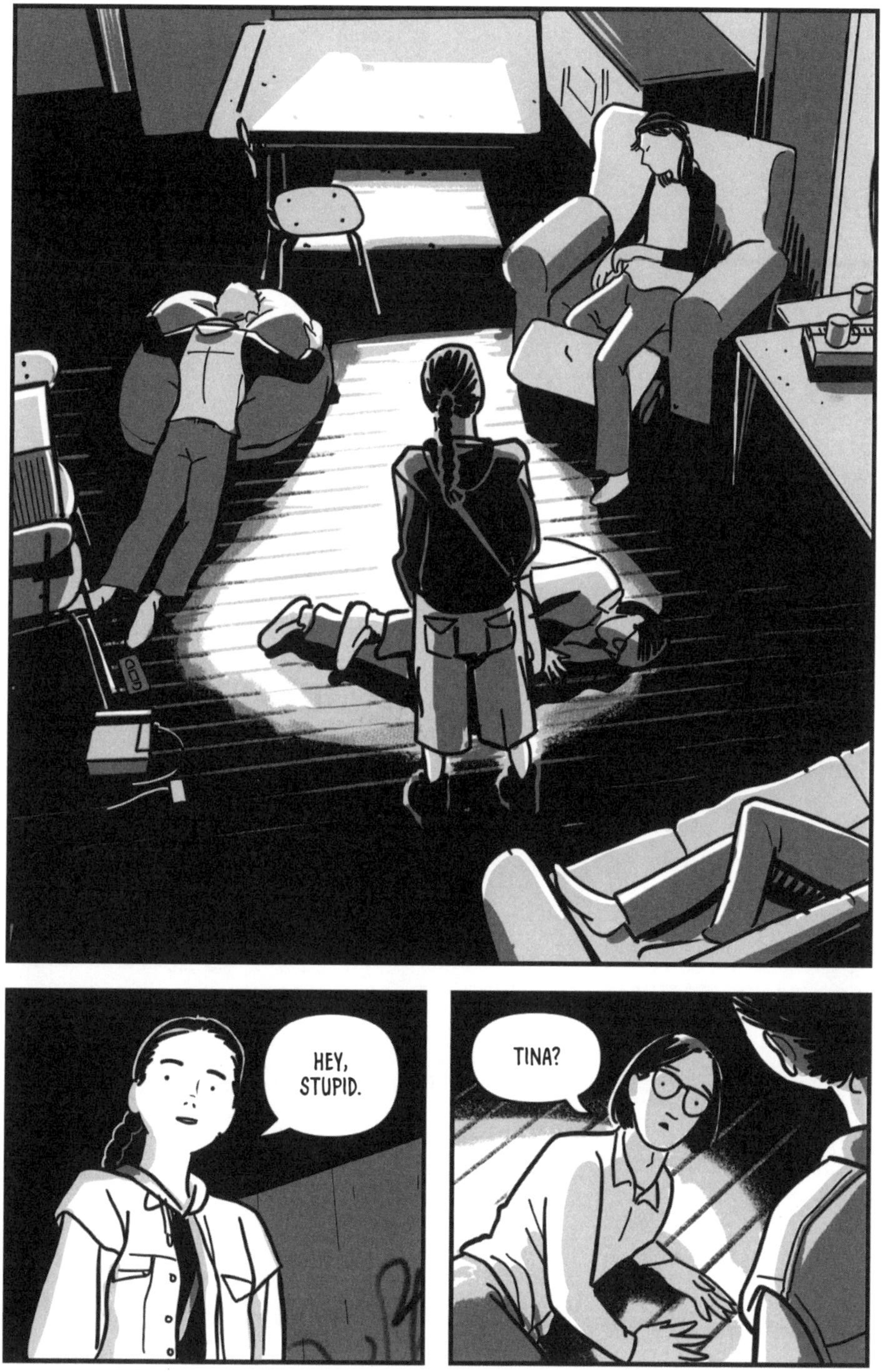
HEY,
STUPID.
TINA?

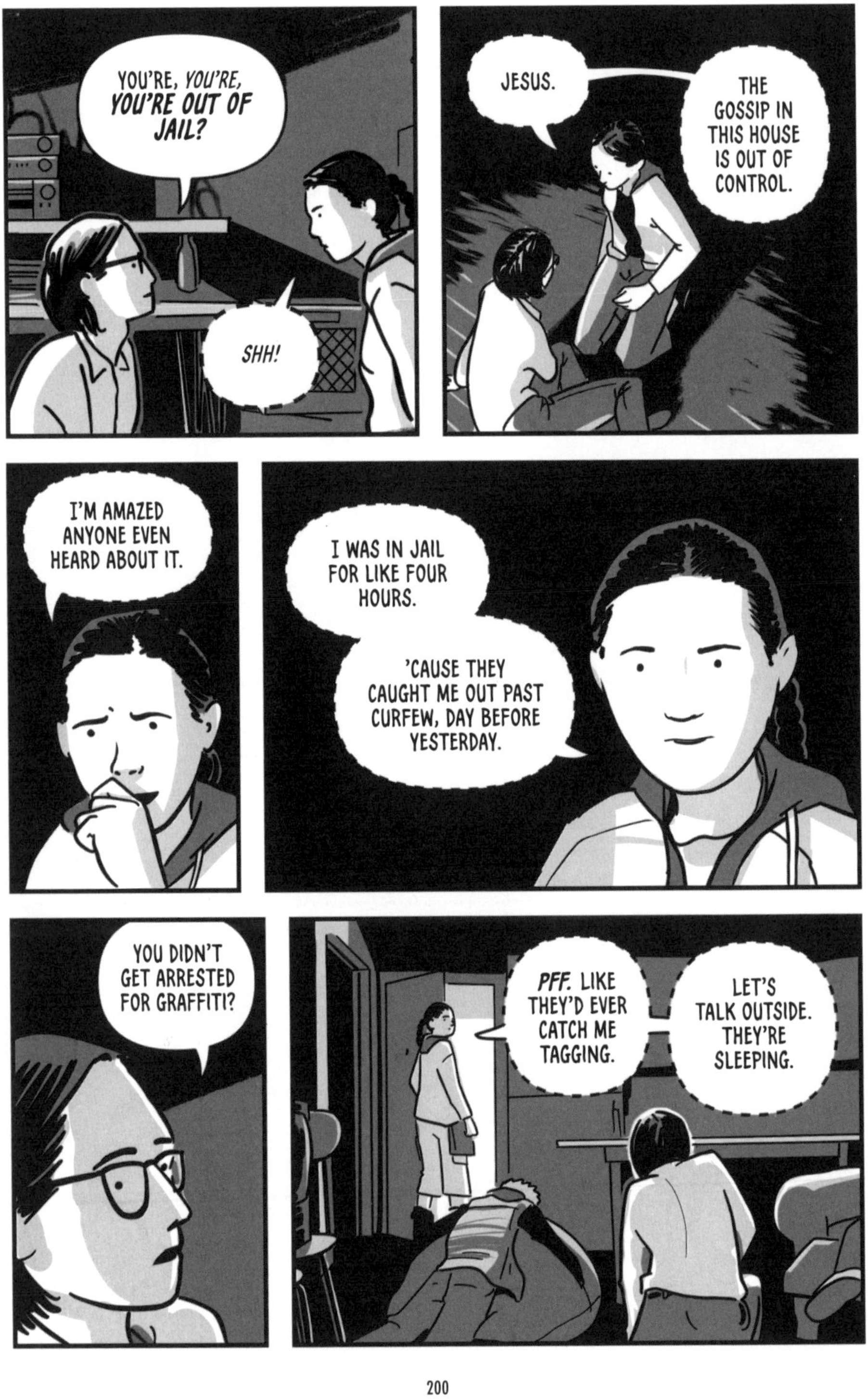
YOU'RE, *YOU'RE*, **YOU'RE OUT OF JAIL?**
SHH!
JESUS.
THE GOSSIP IN THIS HOUSE IS OUT OF CONTROL.
I'M AMAZED ANYONE EVEN HEARD ABOUT IT.
I WAS IN JAIL FOR LIKE FOUR HOURS.
'CAUSE THEY CAUGHT ME OUT PAST CURFEW, DAY BEFORE YESTERDAY.
YOU DIDN'T GET ARRESTED FOR GRAFFITI?
PFF. LIKE THEY'D EVER CATCH ME TAGGING.
LET'S TALK OUTSIDE. THEY'RE SLEEPING.

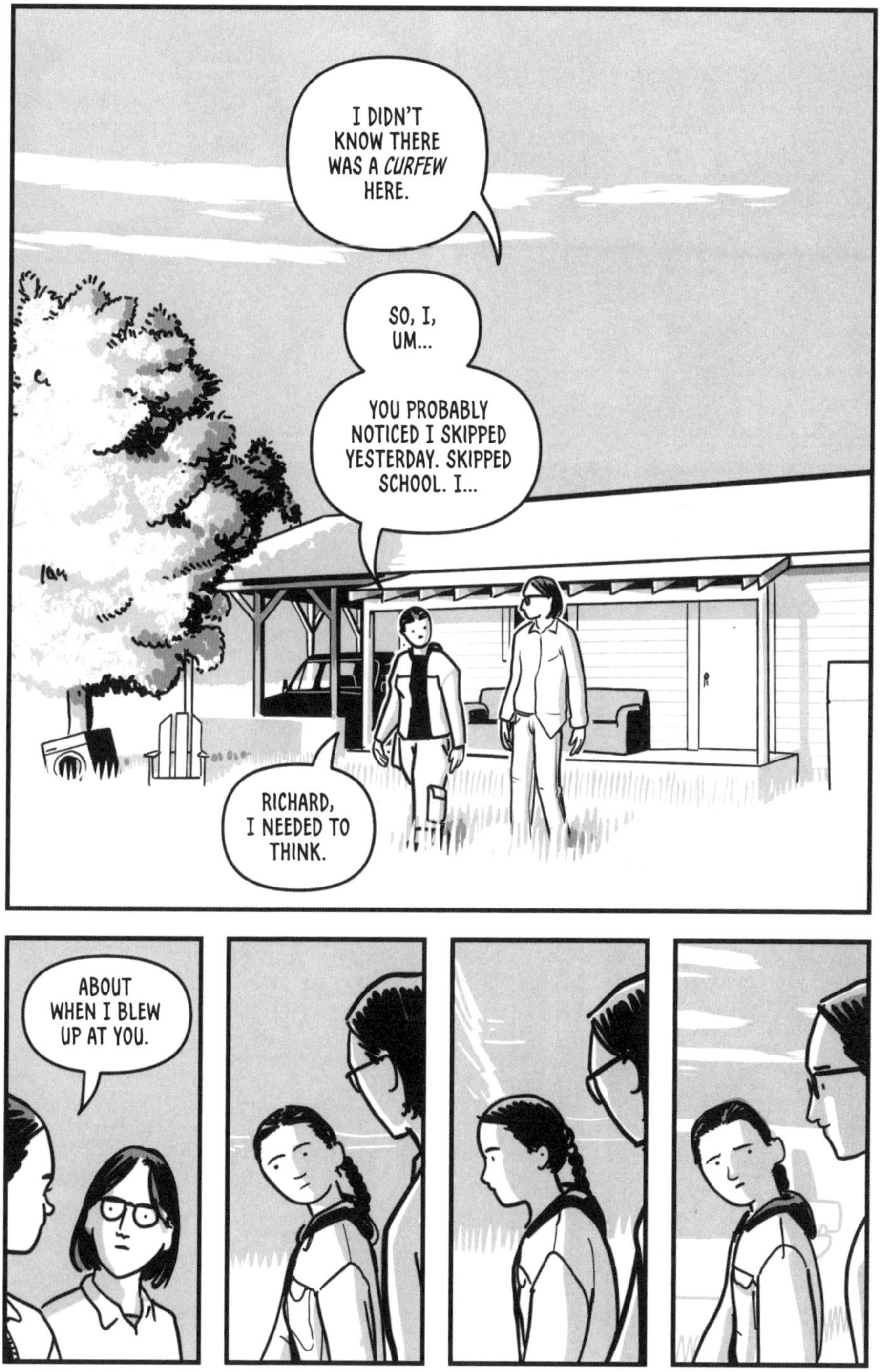

I DIDN'T KNOW THERE WAS A *CURFEW* HERE.
SO, I, UM...
YOU PROBABLY NOTICED I SKIPPED YESTERDAY. SKIPPED SCHOOL. I...
RICHARD, I NEEDED TO THINK.
ABOUT WHEN I BLEW UP AT YOU.

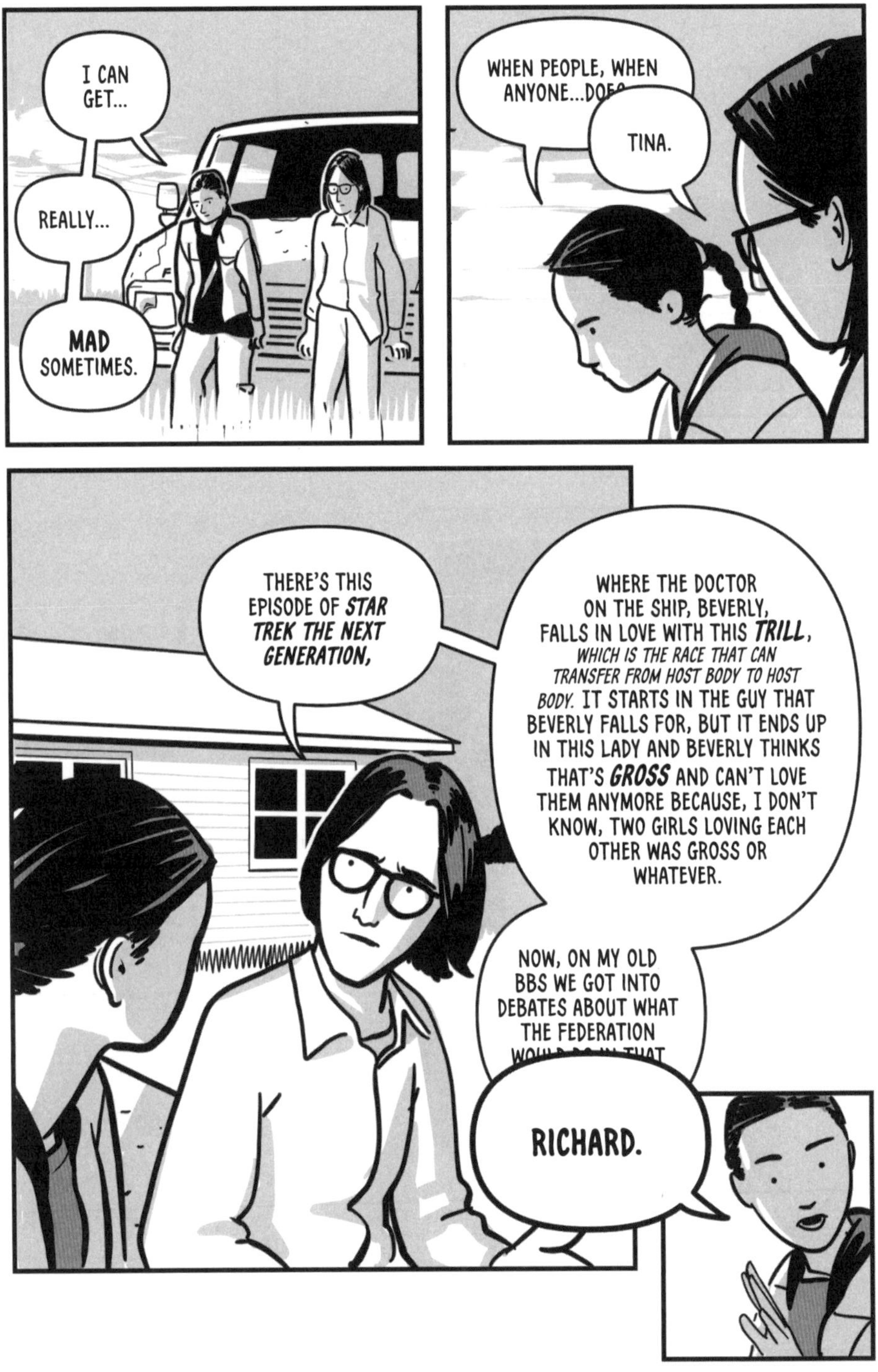
I CAN GET...
REALLY...
MAD SOMETIMES.
WHEN PEOPLE, WHEN ANYONE...DOES
TINA.
THERE'S THIS EPISODE OF STAR TREK THE NEXT GENERATION,
WHERE THE DOCTOR ON THE SHIP, BEVERLY, FALLS IN LOVE WITH THIS TRILL, WHICH IS THE RACE THAT CAN TRANSFER FROM HOST BODY TO HOST BODY. IT STARTS IN THE GUY THAT BEVERLY FALLS FOR, BUT IT ENDS UP IN THIS LADY AND BEVERLY THINKS THAT'S GROSS AND CAN'T LOVE THEM ANYMORE BECAUSE, I DON'T KNOW, TWO GIRLS LOVING EACH OTHER WAS GROSS OR WHATEVER.
NOW, ON MY OLD BBS WE GOT INTO DEBATES ABOUT WHAT THE FEDERATION
RICHARD.

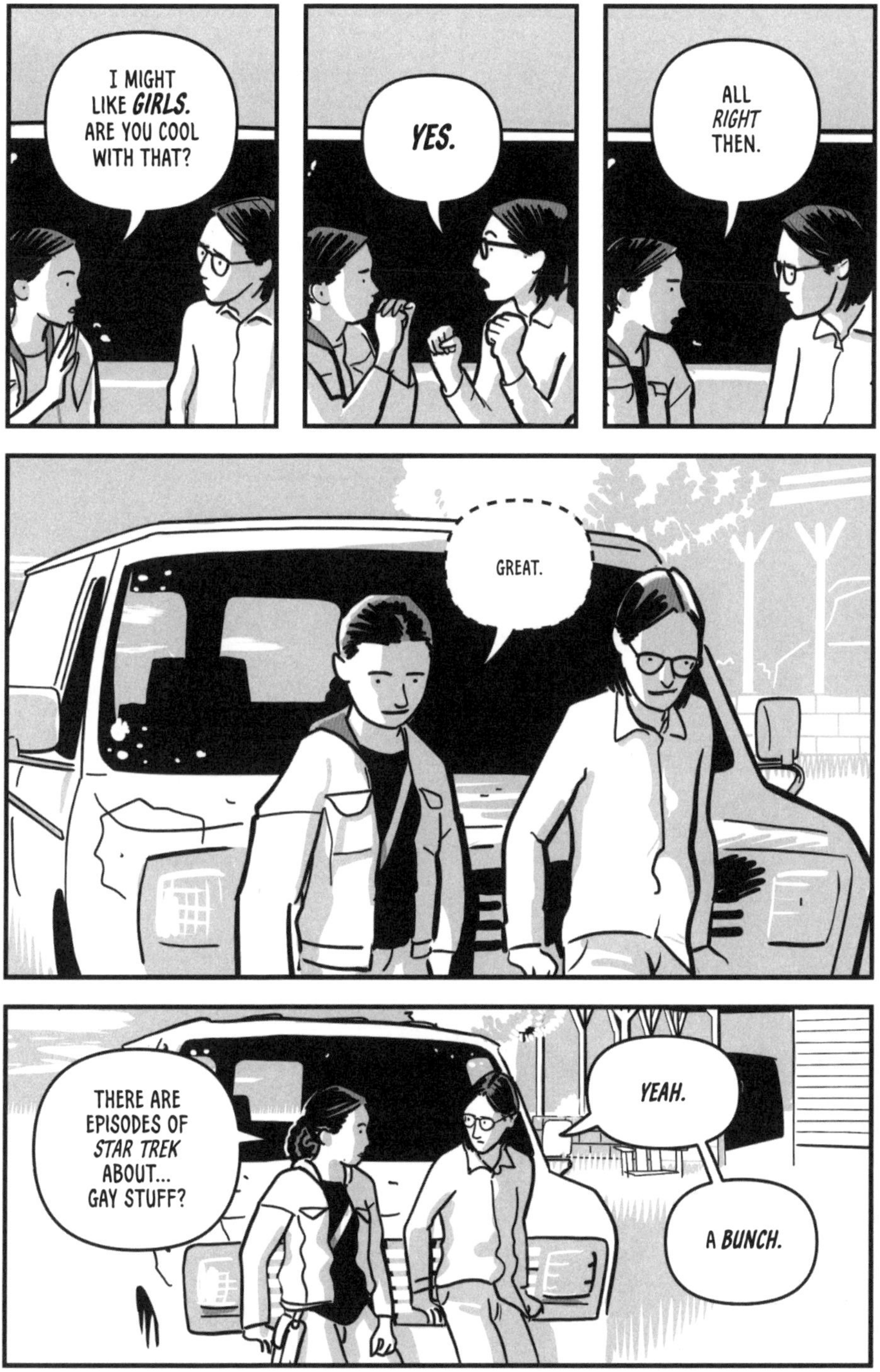
I MIGHT LIKE *GIRLS.* ARE YOU COOL WITH THAT?
YES.
ALL *RIGHT* THEN.
GREAT.
THERE ARE EPISODES OF *STAR TREK* ABOUT... GAY STUFF?
YEAH.
A *BUNCH.*

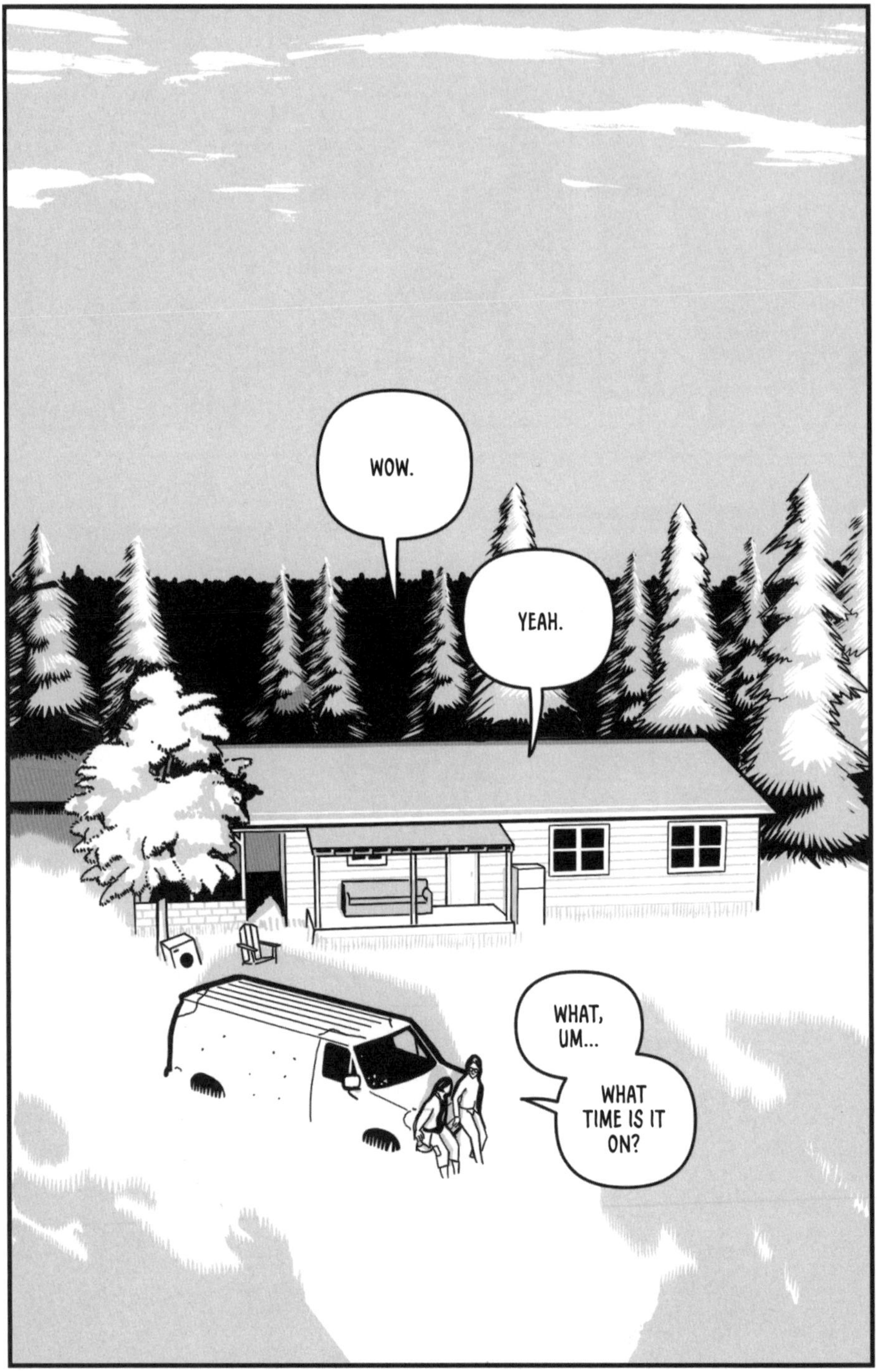
WOW.
YEAH.
WHAT, UM...
WHAT TIME IS IT ON?

Chapter 6

RETENTION OF VISION VANISH

GU D-- -P+ C+L? U E M+ S-/+ N--- H-- F--(+) !G W++ T R? X?

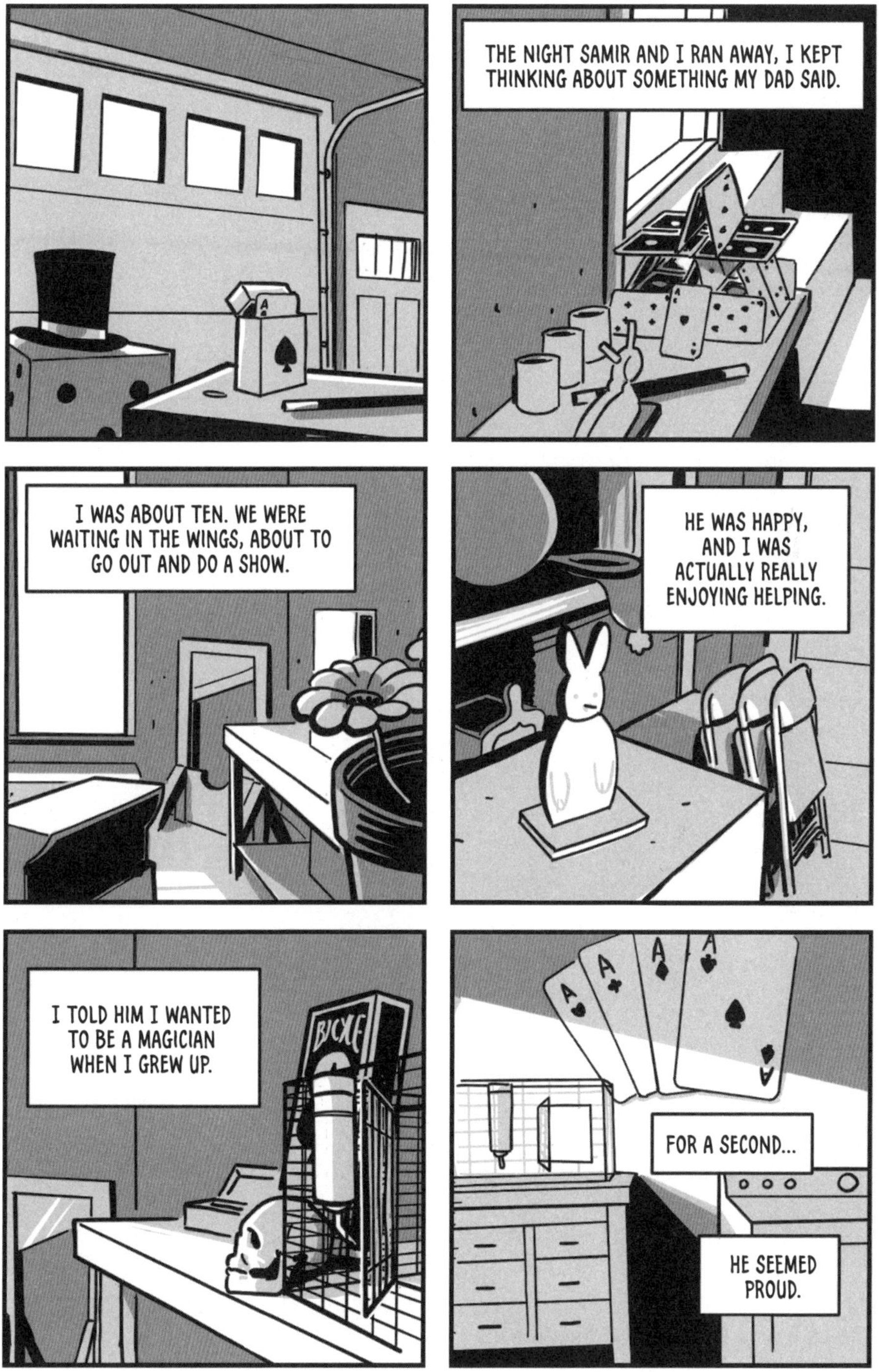
THE NIGHT SAMIR AND I RAN AWAY, I KEPT THINKING ABOUT SOMETHING MY DAD SAID.
I WAS ABOUT TEN. WE WERE WAITING IN THE WINGS, ABOUT TO GO OUT AND DO A SHOW.
HE WAS HAPPY, AND I WAS ACTUALLY REALLY ENJOYING HELPING.
I TOLD HIM I WANTED TO BE A MAGICIAN WHEN I GREW UP.
FOR A SECOND...
HE SEEMED PROUD.

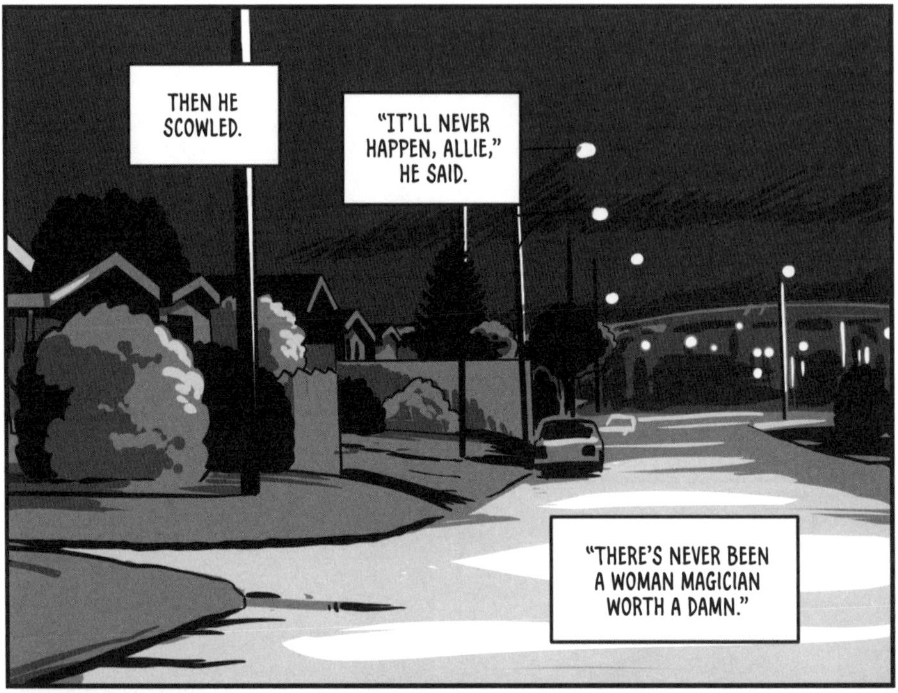
THEN HE SCOWLED.
"IT'LL NEVER HAPPEN, ALLIE," HE SAID.
"THERE'S NEVER BEEN A WOMAN MAGICIAN WORTH A DAMN."

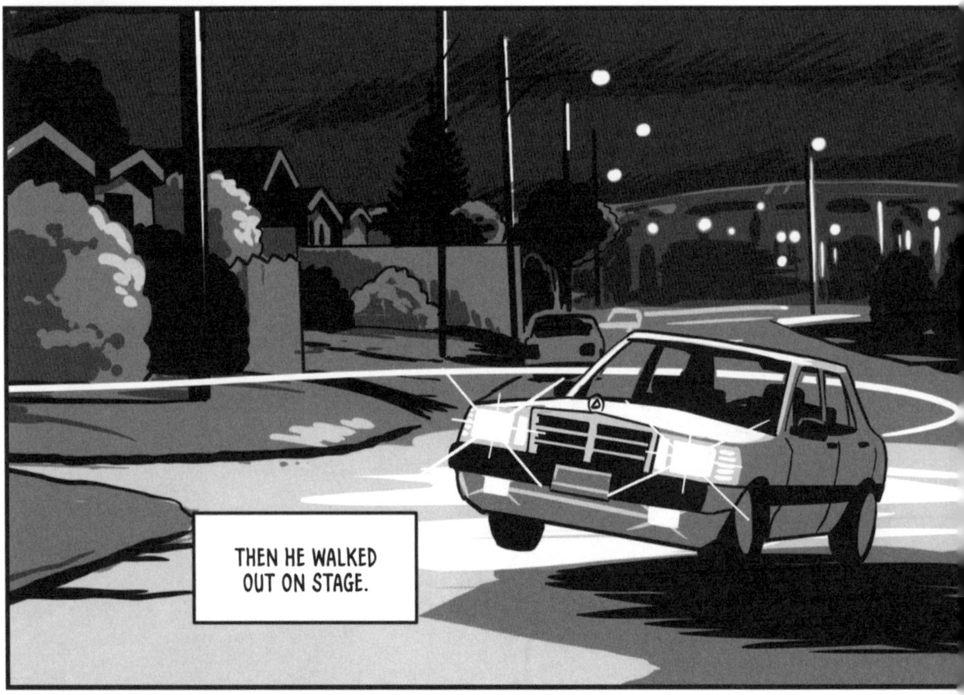
THEN HE WALKED OUT ON STAGE.

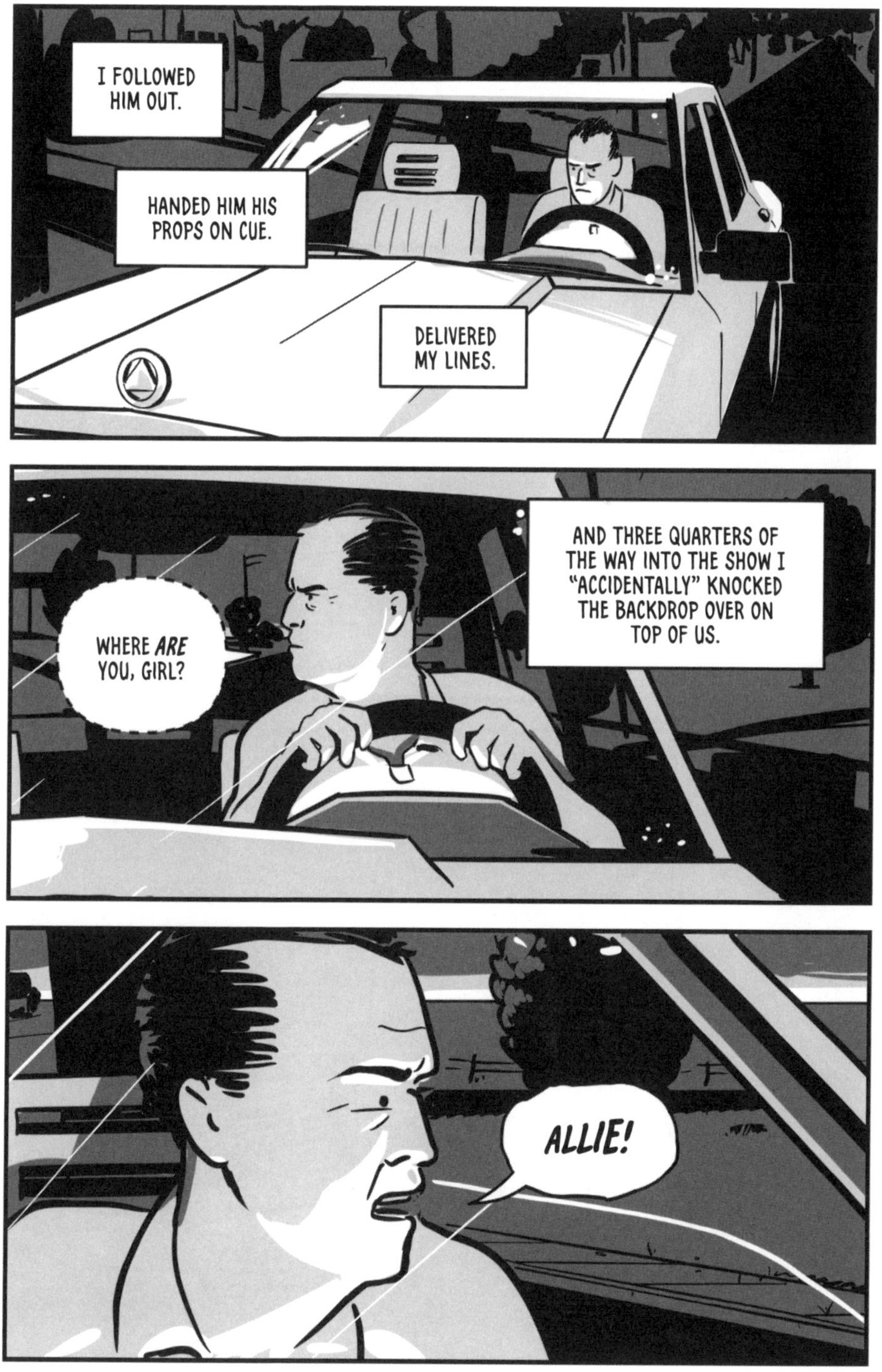
I FOLLOWED HIM OUT.
HANDED HIM HIS PROPS ON CUE.
DELIVERED MY LINES.
AND THREE QUARTERS OF THE WAY INTO THE SHOW I "ACCIDENTALLY" KNOCKED THE BACKDROP OVER ON TOP OF US.
WHERE *ARE* YOU, GIRL?
ALLIE!

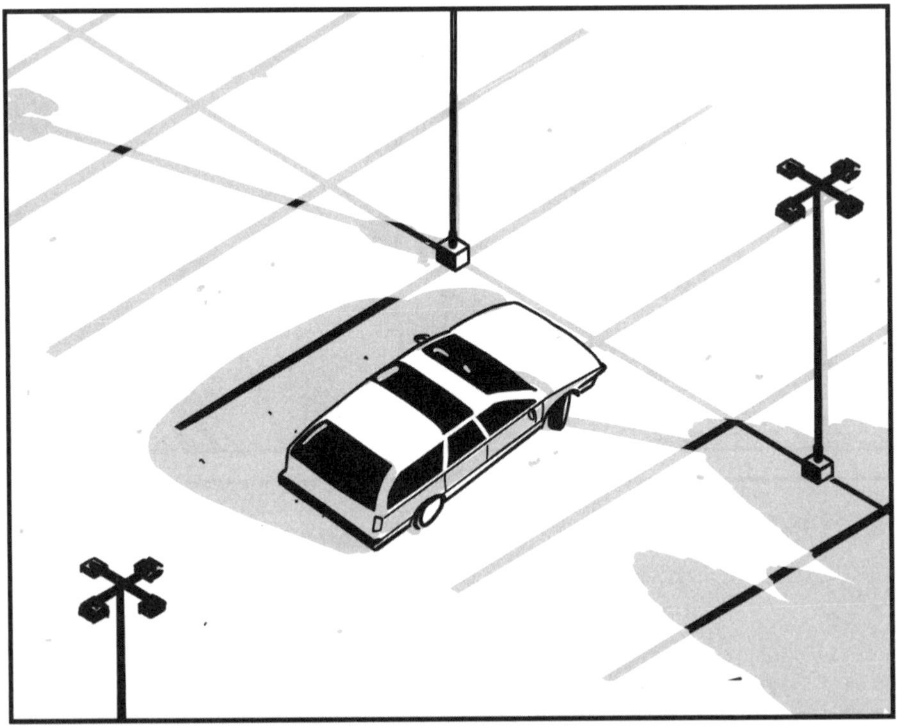

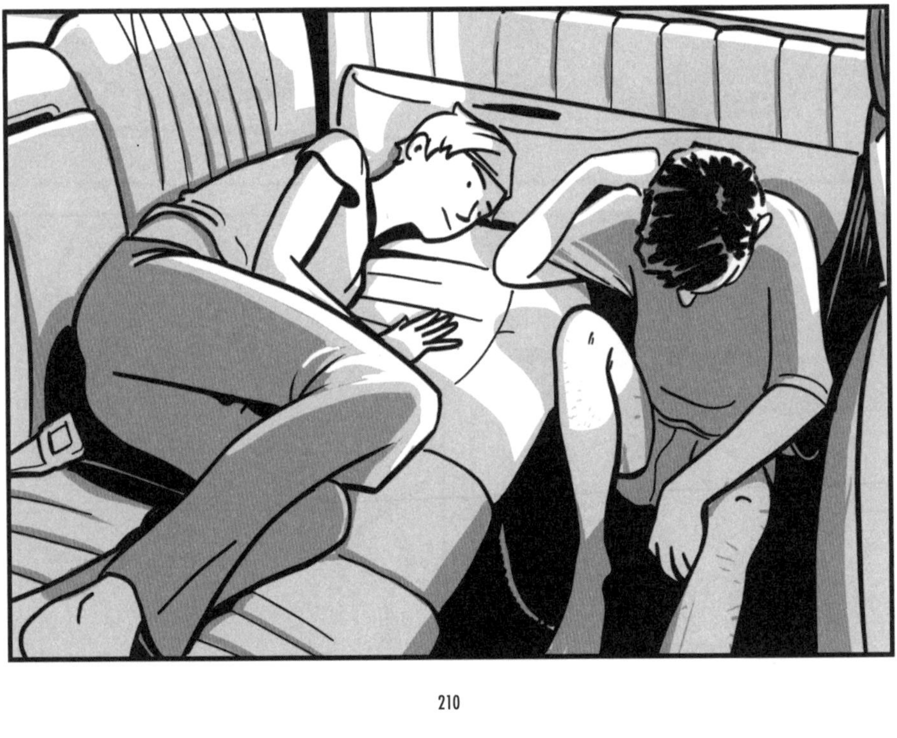

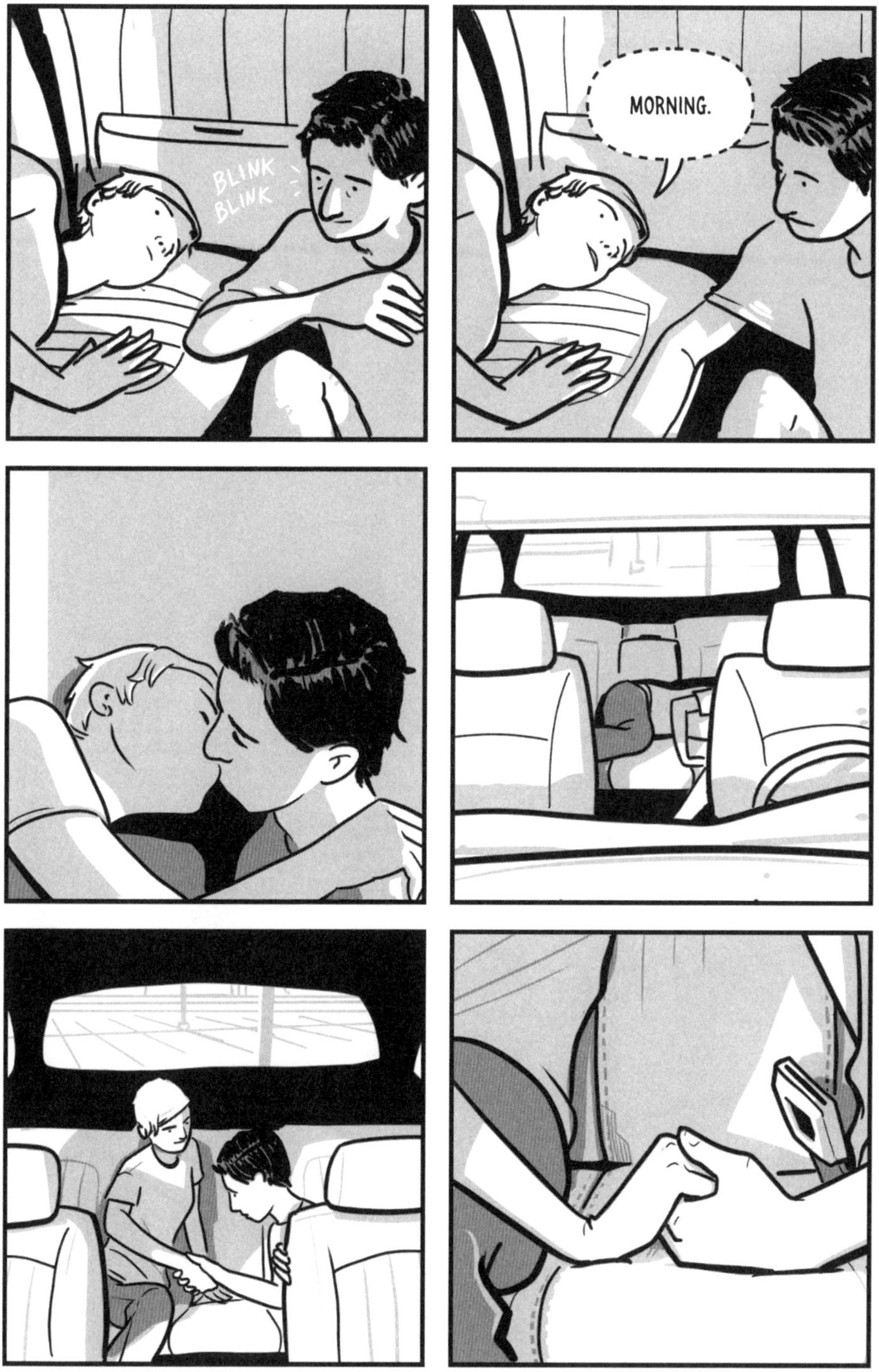
BLINK BLINK
MORNING.

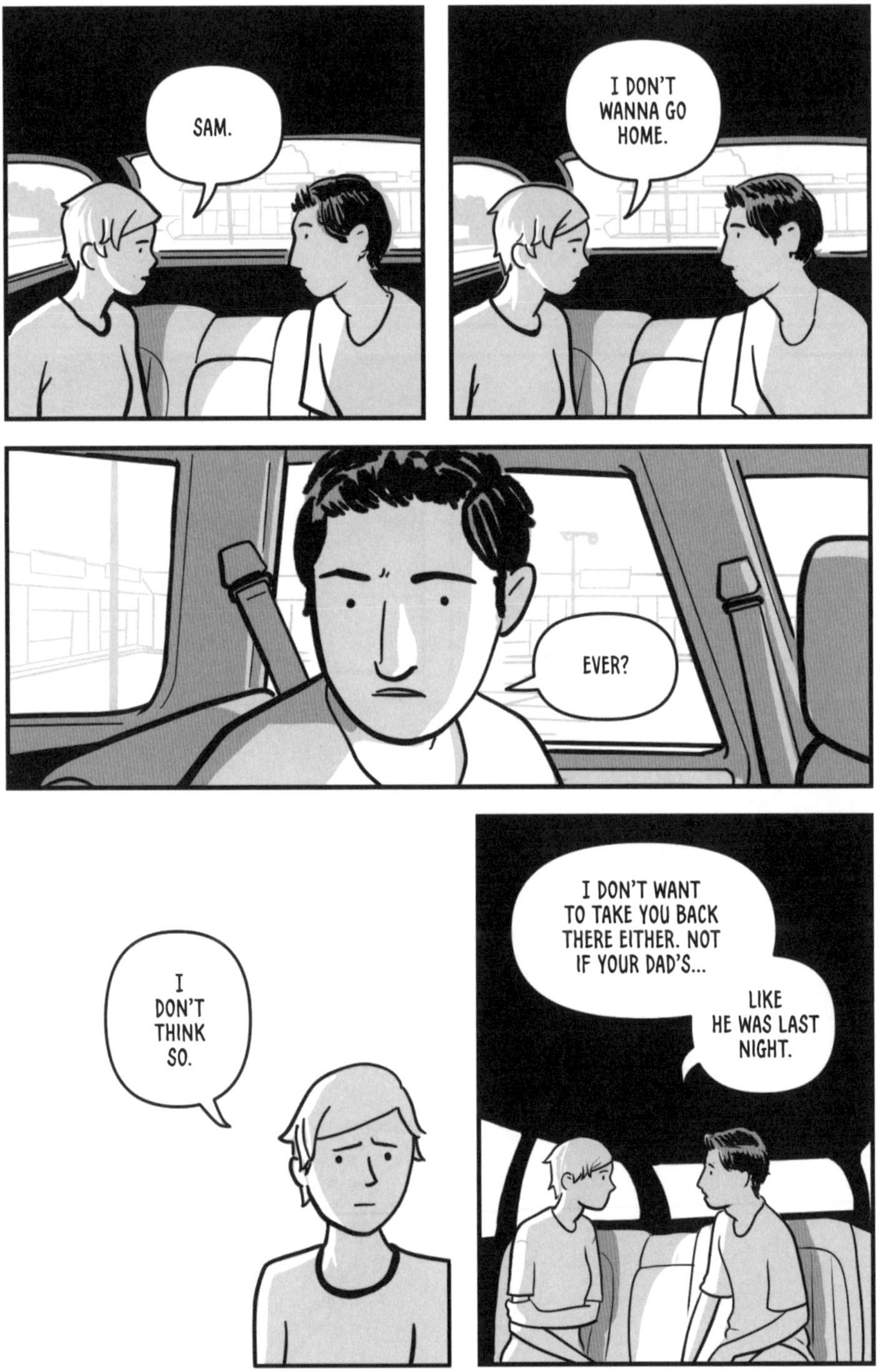
SAM.
I DON'T WANNA GO HOME.
EVER?
I DON'T THINK SO.
I DON'T WANT TO TAKE YOU BACK THERE EITHER. NOT IF YOUR DAD'S...
LIKE HE WAS LAST NIGHT.

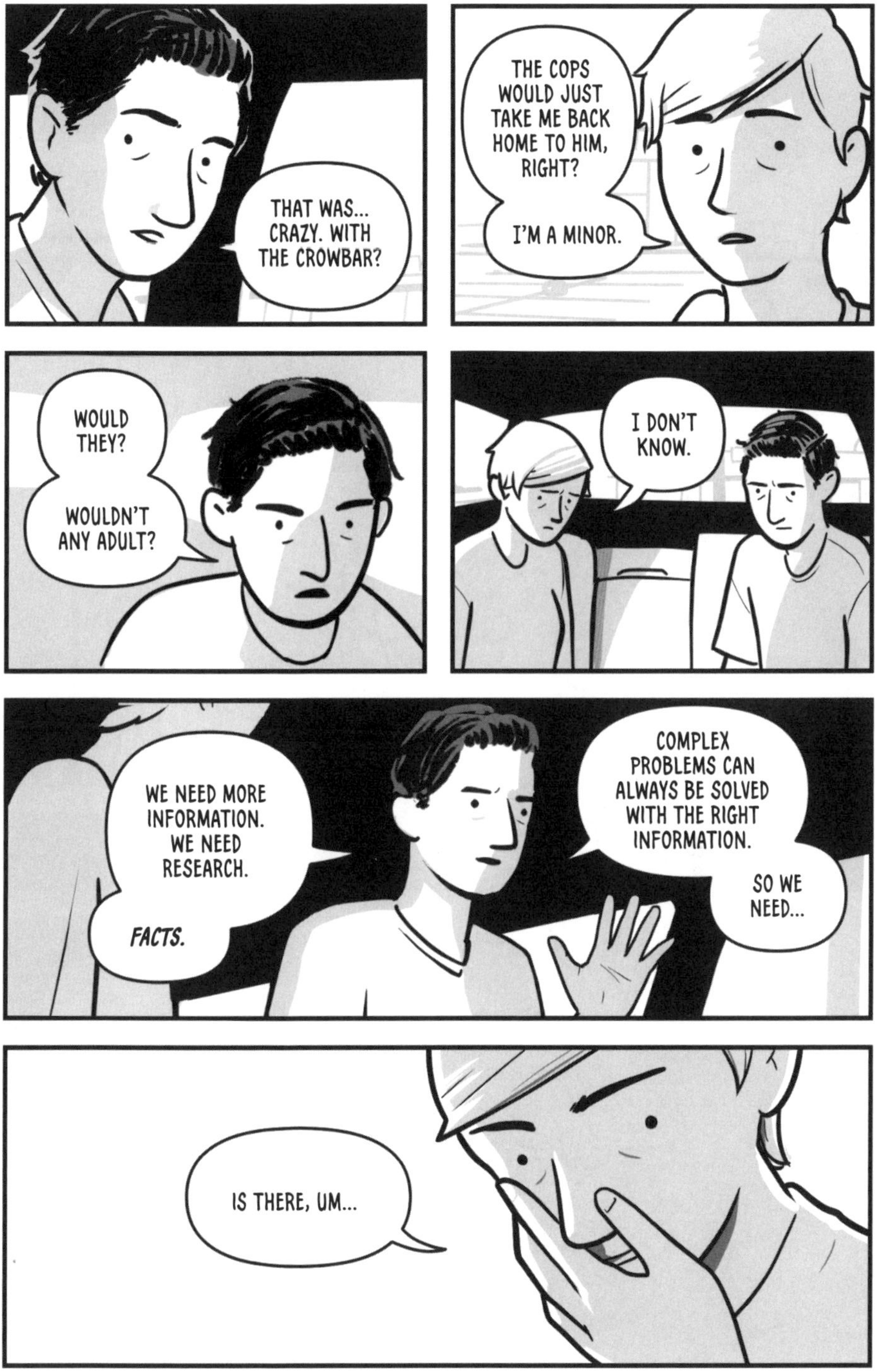
THAT WAS... CRAZY. WITH THE CROWBAR?
THE COPS WOULD JUST TAKE ME BACK HOME TO HIM, RIGHT?
I'M A MINOR.
WOULD THEY?
WOULDN'T ANY ADULT?
I DON'T KNOW.
WE NEED MORE INFORMATION. WE NEED RESEARCH.
FACTS.
COMPLEX PROBLEMS CAN ALWAYS BE SOLVED WITH THE RIGHT INFORMATION.
SO WE NEED...
IS THERE, UM...

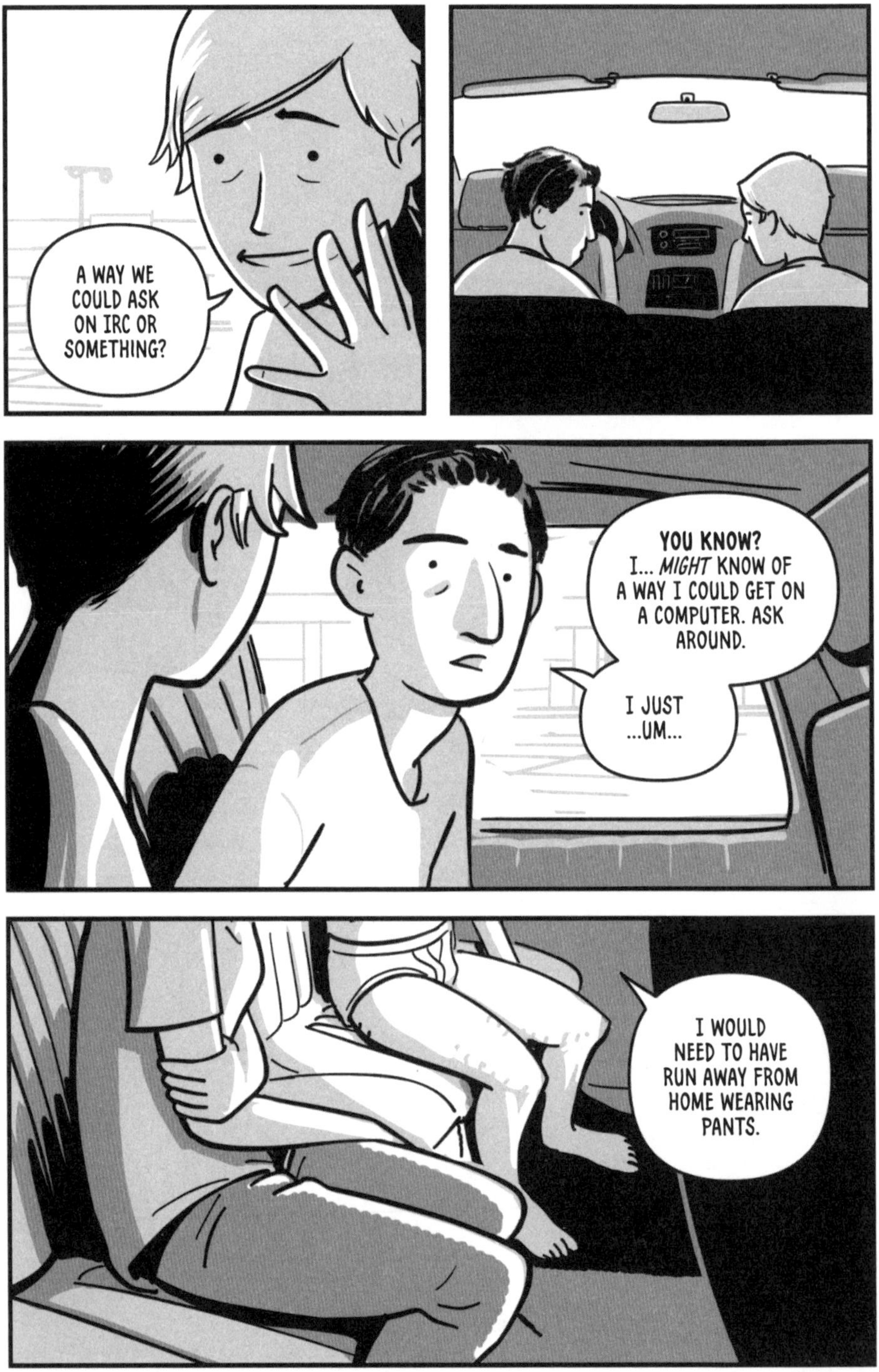
A WAY WE COULD ASK ON IRC OR SOMETHING?
YOU KNOW? I... *MIGHT* KNOW OF A WAY I COULD GET ON A COMPUTER. ASK AROUND.
I JUST ...UM...
I WOULD NEED TO HAVE RUN AWAY FROM HOME WEARING PANTS.

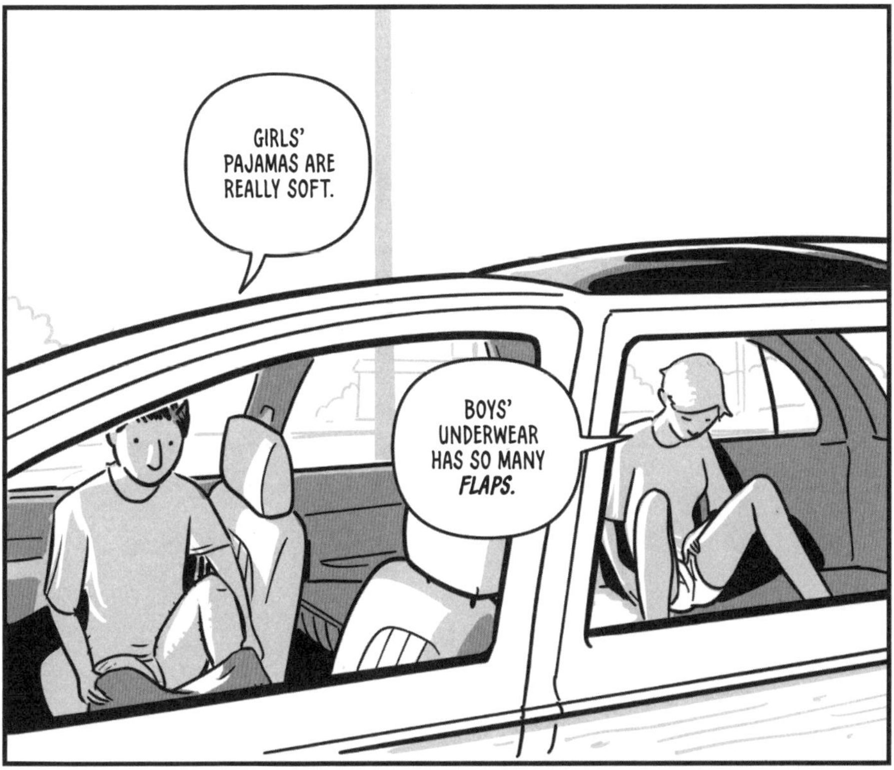
GIRLS' PAJAMAS ARE REALLY SOFT.
BOYS' UNDERWEAR HAS SO MANY *FLAPS.*

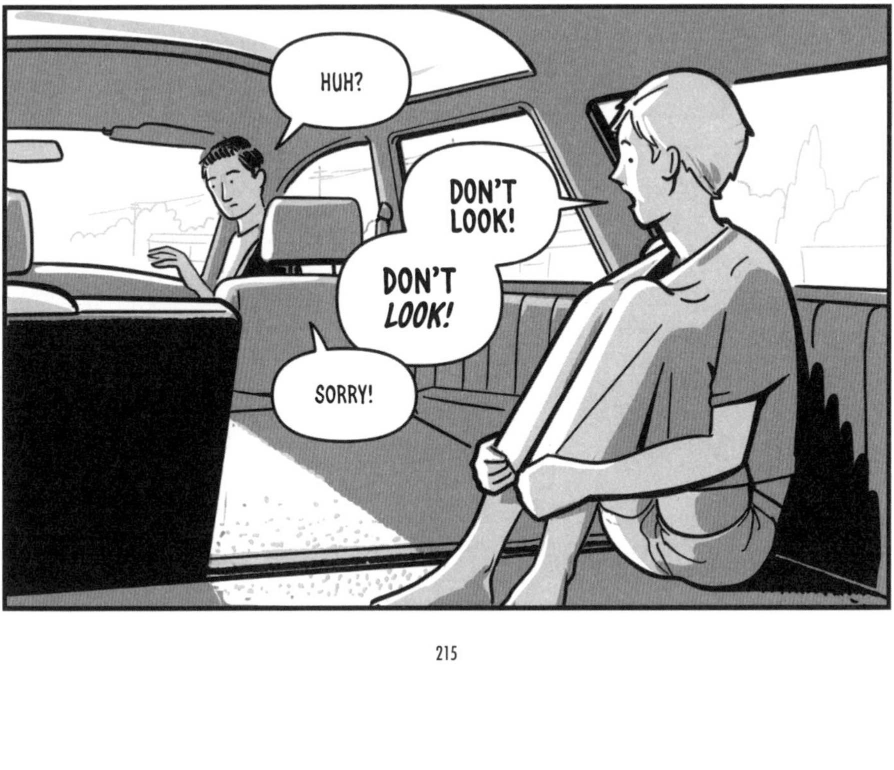
HUH?
DON'T LOOK!
DON'T *LOOK!*
SORRY!

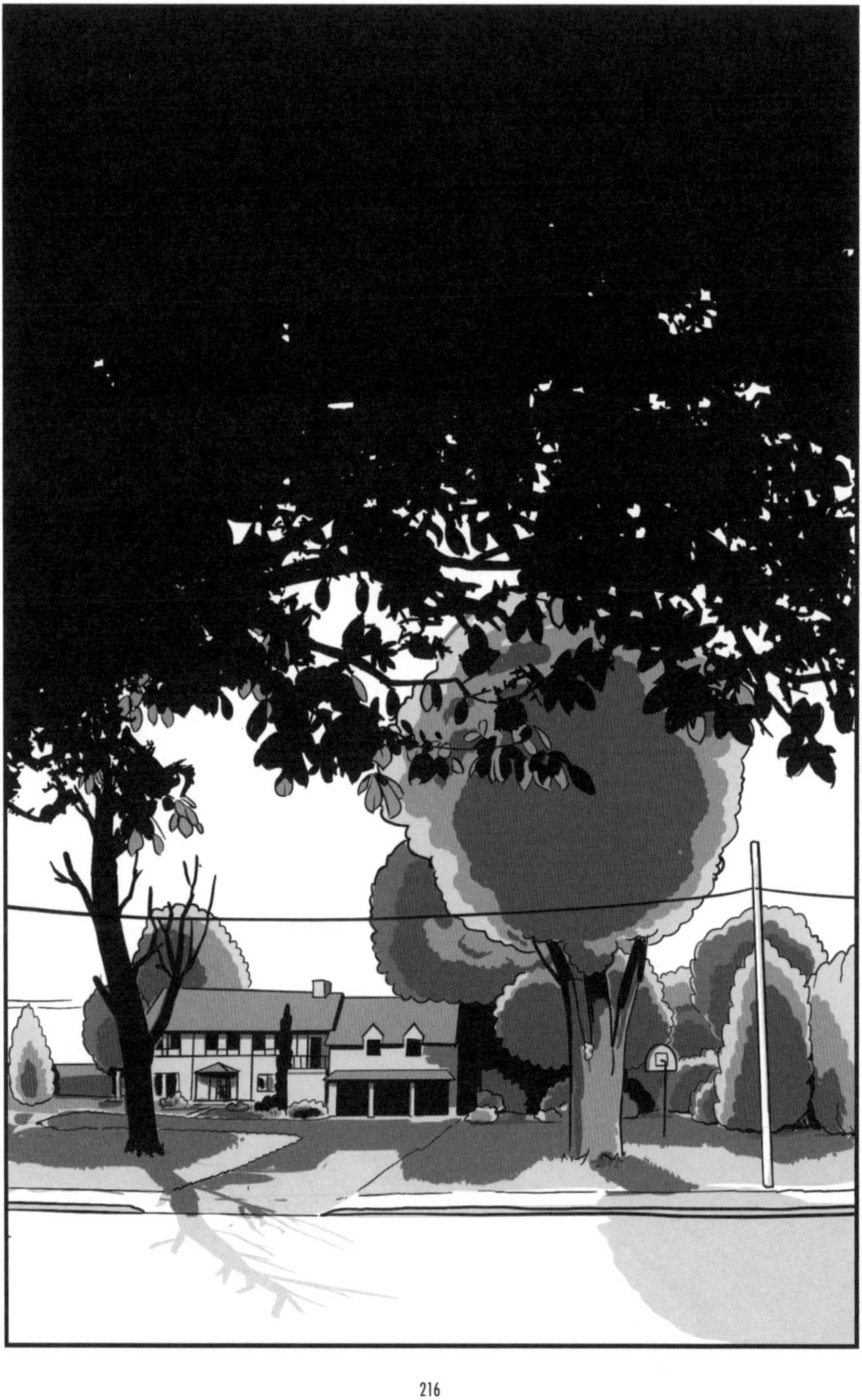

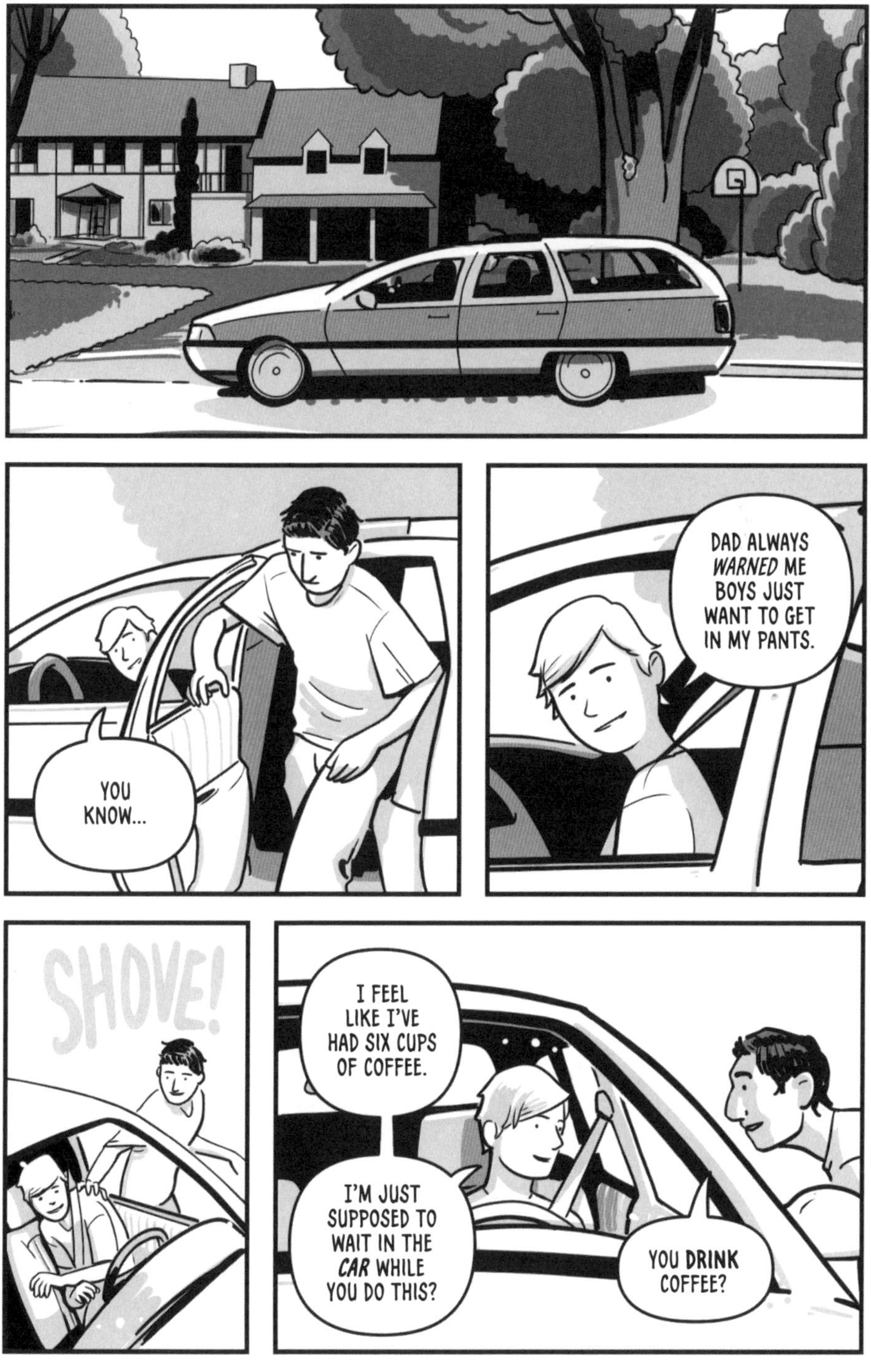
YOU KNOW...
DAD ALWAYS WARNED ME BOYS JUST WANT TO GET IN MY PANTS.
SHOVE!
I FEEL LIKE I'VE HAD SIX CUPS OF COFFEE.
I'M JUST SUPPOSED TO WAIT IN THE CAR WHILE YOU DO THIS?
YOU DRINK COFFEE?

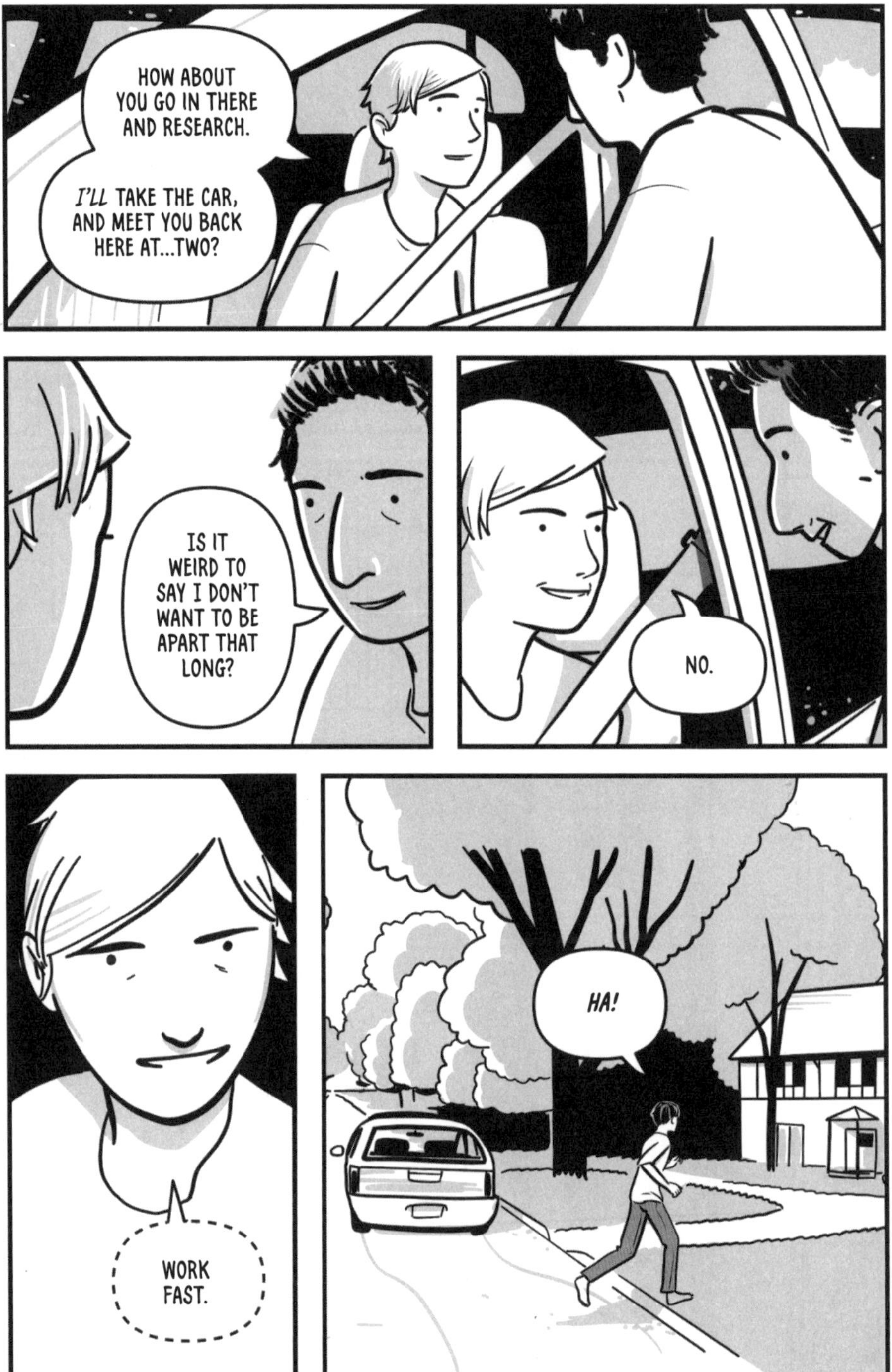
HOW ABOUT YOU GO IN THERE AND RESEARCH.
I'LL TAKE THE CAR, AND MEET YOU BACK HERE AT...TWO?
IS IT WEIRD TO SAY I DON'T WANT TO BE APART THAT LONG?
NO.
WORK FAST.
HA!

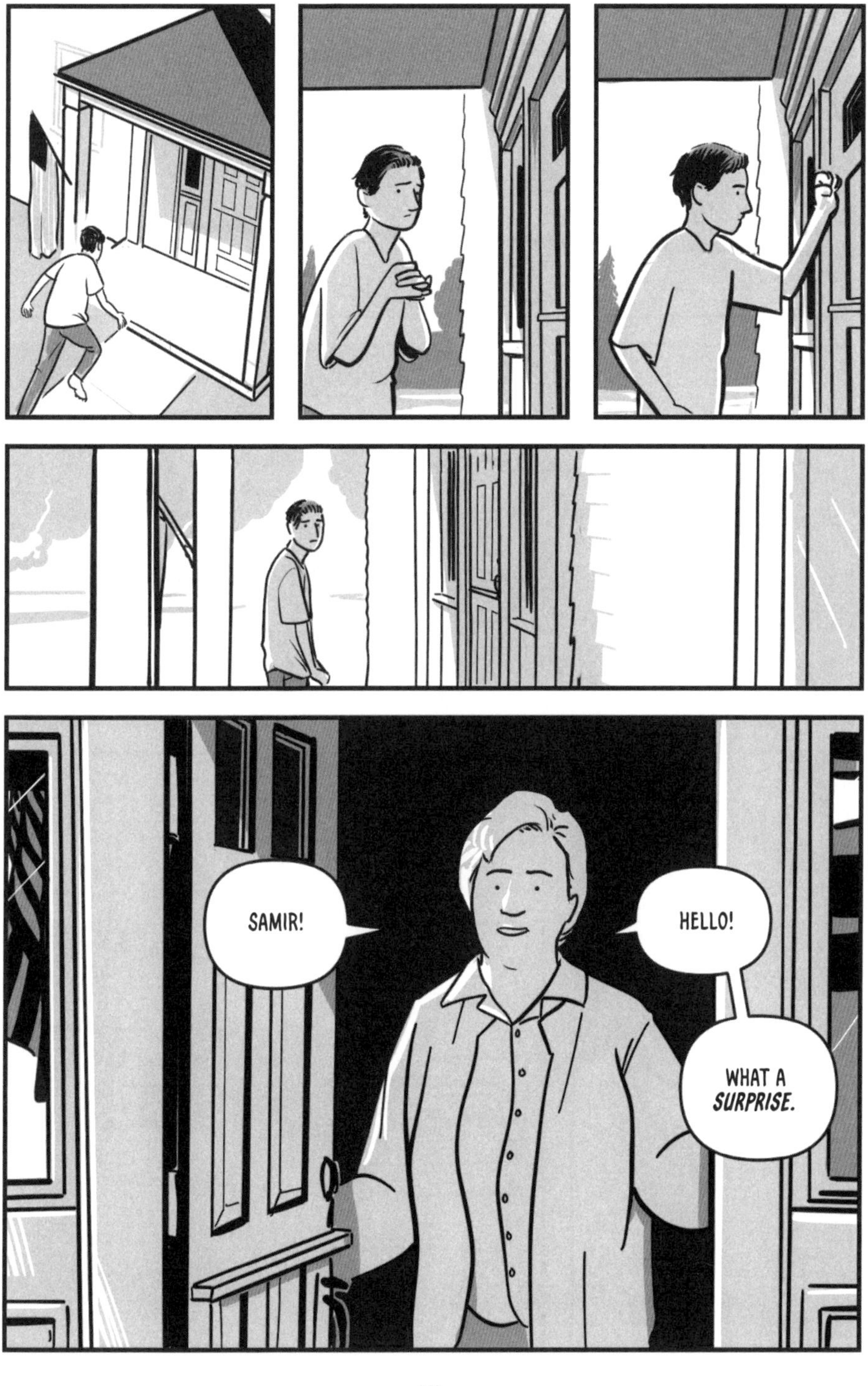
SAMIR!
HELLO!
WHAT A SURPRISE.

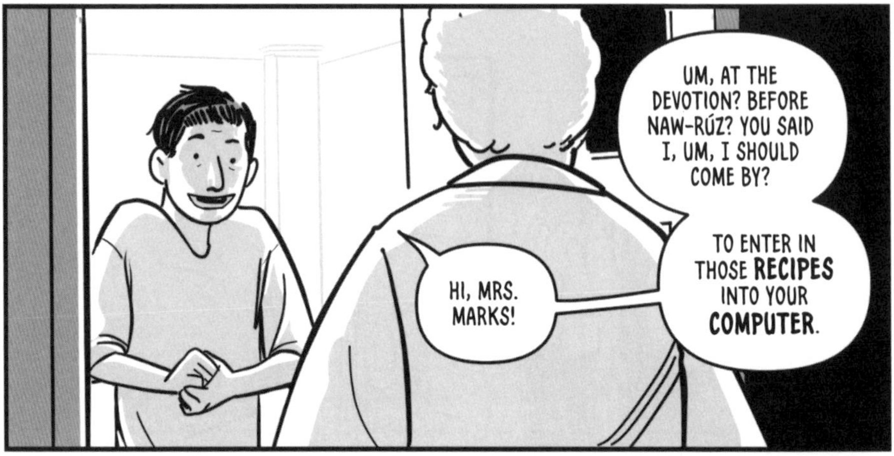

UM, AT THE DEVOTION? BEFORE NAW-RÚZ? YOU SAID I, UM, I SHOULD COME BY?
TO ENTER IN THOSE **RECIPES** INTO YOUR **COMPUTER**.
HI, MRS. MARKS!

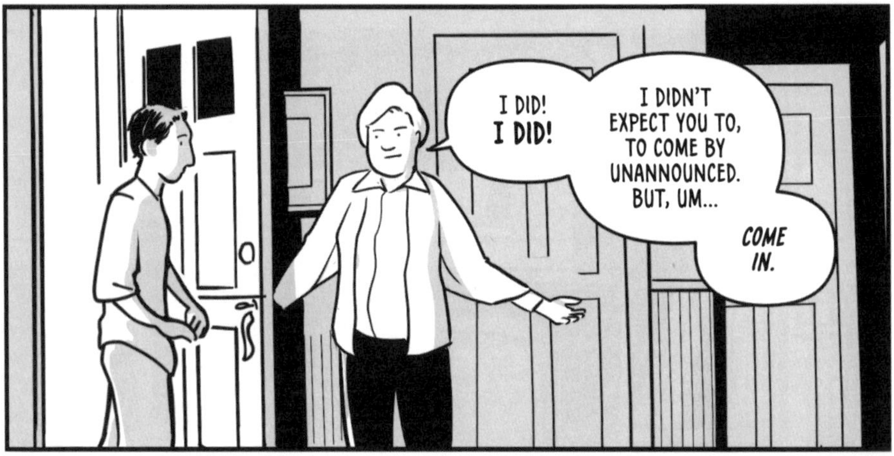

I DID! **I DID!**
I DIDN'T EXPECT YOU TO, TO COME BY UNANNOUNCED. BUT, UM...
COME IN.

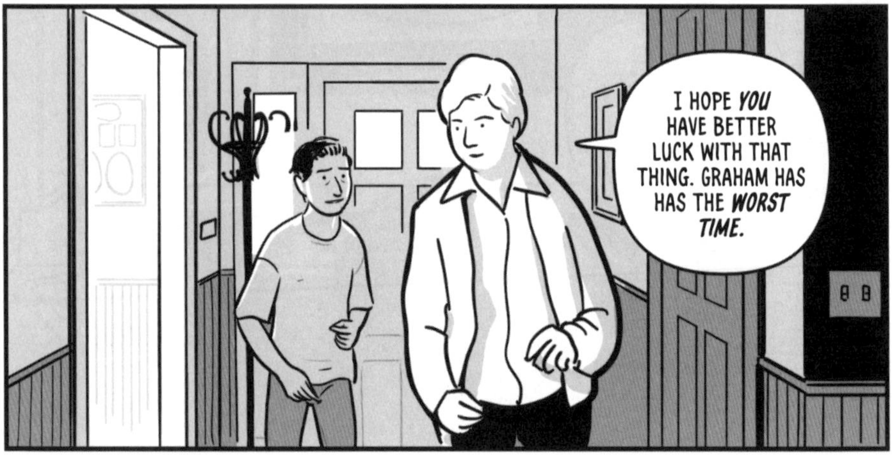

I HOPE *YOU* HAVE BETTER LUCK WITH THAT THING. GRAHAM HAS HAS THE *WORST TIME.*

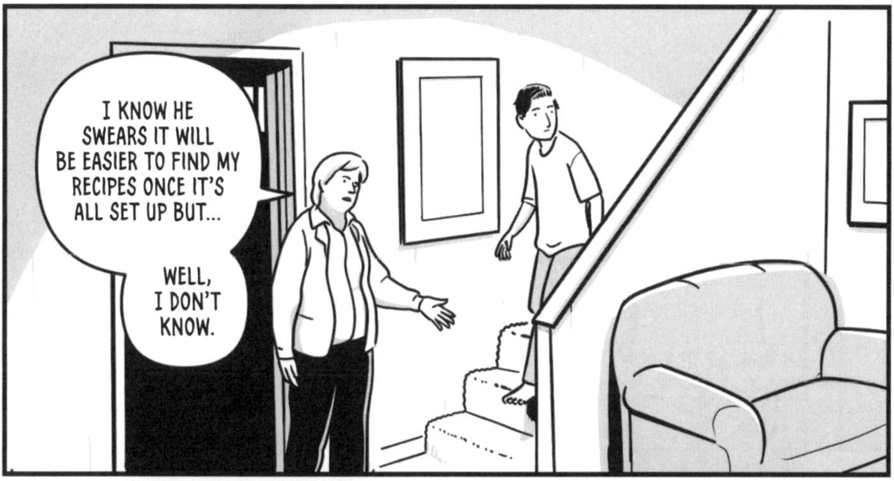
I KNOW HE SWEARS IT WILL BE EASIER TO FIND MY RECIPES ONCE IT'S ALL SET UP BUT...
WELL, I DON'T KNOW.

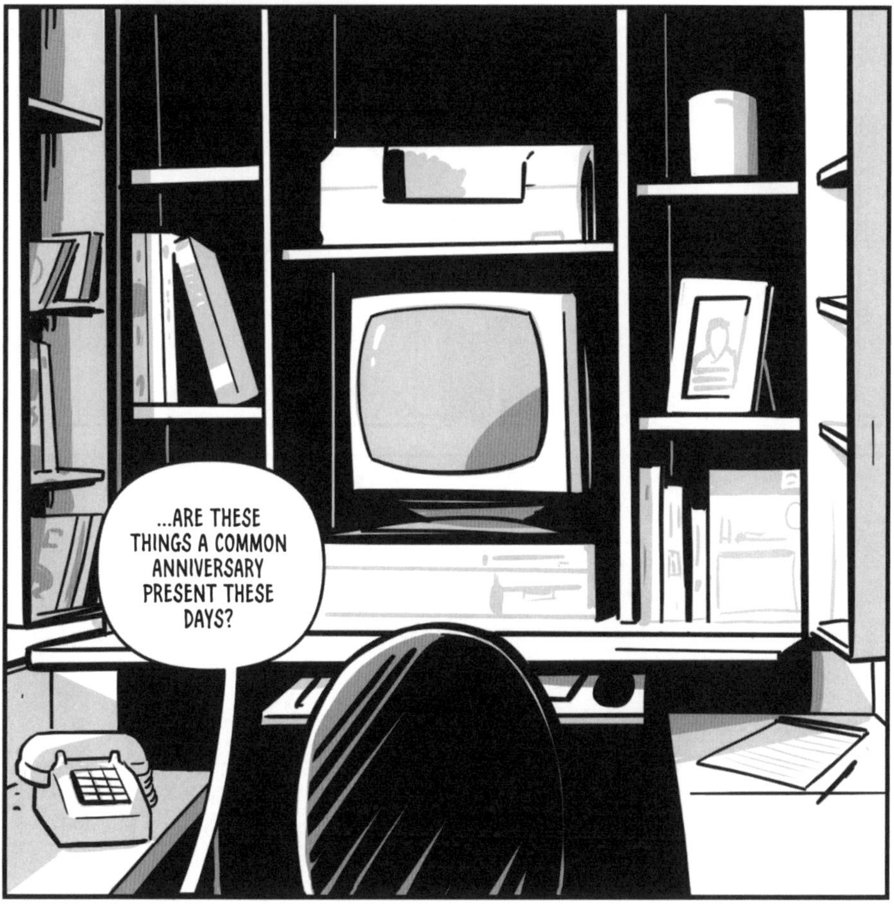
...ARE THESE THINGS A COMMON ANNIVERSARY PRESENT THESE DAYS?

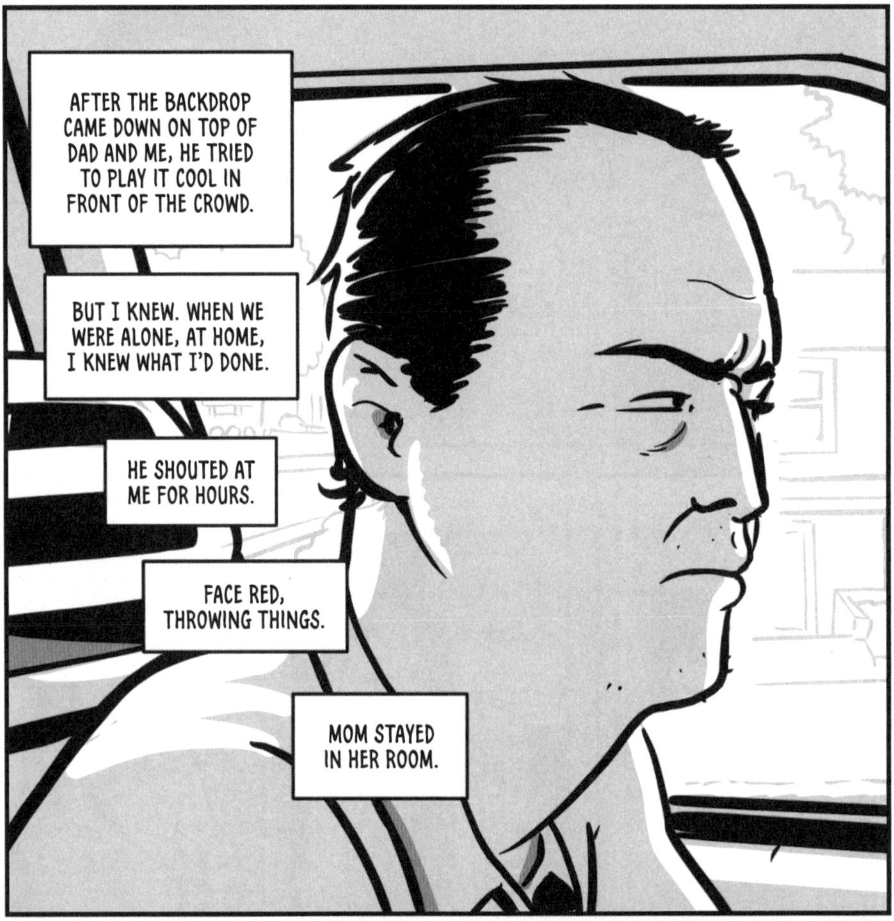
AFTER THE BACKDROP CAME DOWN ON TOP OF DAD AND ME, HE TRIED TO PLAY IT COOL IN FRONT OF THE CROWD.
BUT I KNEW. WHEN WE WERE ALONE, AT HOME, I KNEW WHAT I'D DONE.
HE SHOUTED AT ME FOR HOURS.
FACE RED, THROWING THINGS.
MOM STAYED IN HER ROOM.

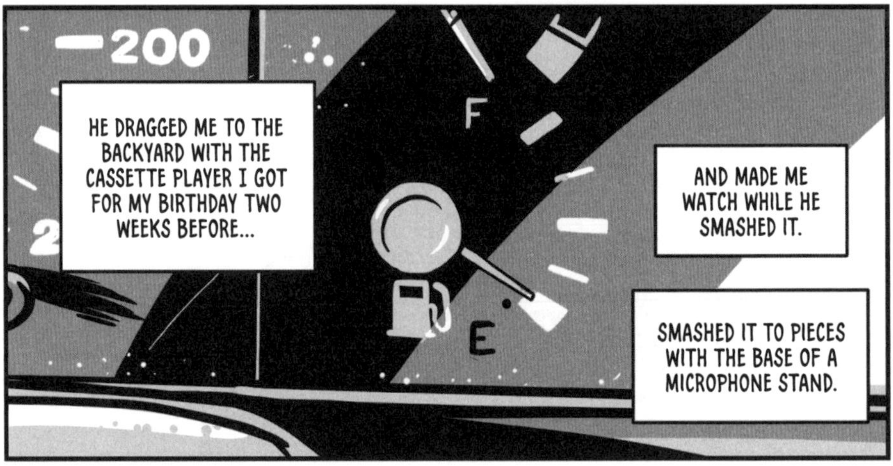
200
F
E
HE DRAGGED ME TO THE BACKYARD WITH THE CASSETTE PLAYER I GOT FOR MY BIRTHDAY TWO WEEKS BEFORE...
AND MADE ME WATCH WHILE HE SMASHED IT.
SMASHED IT TO PIECES WITH THE BASE OF A MICROPHONE STAND.

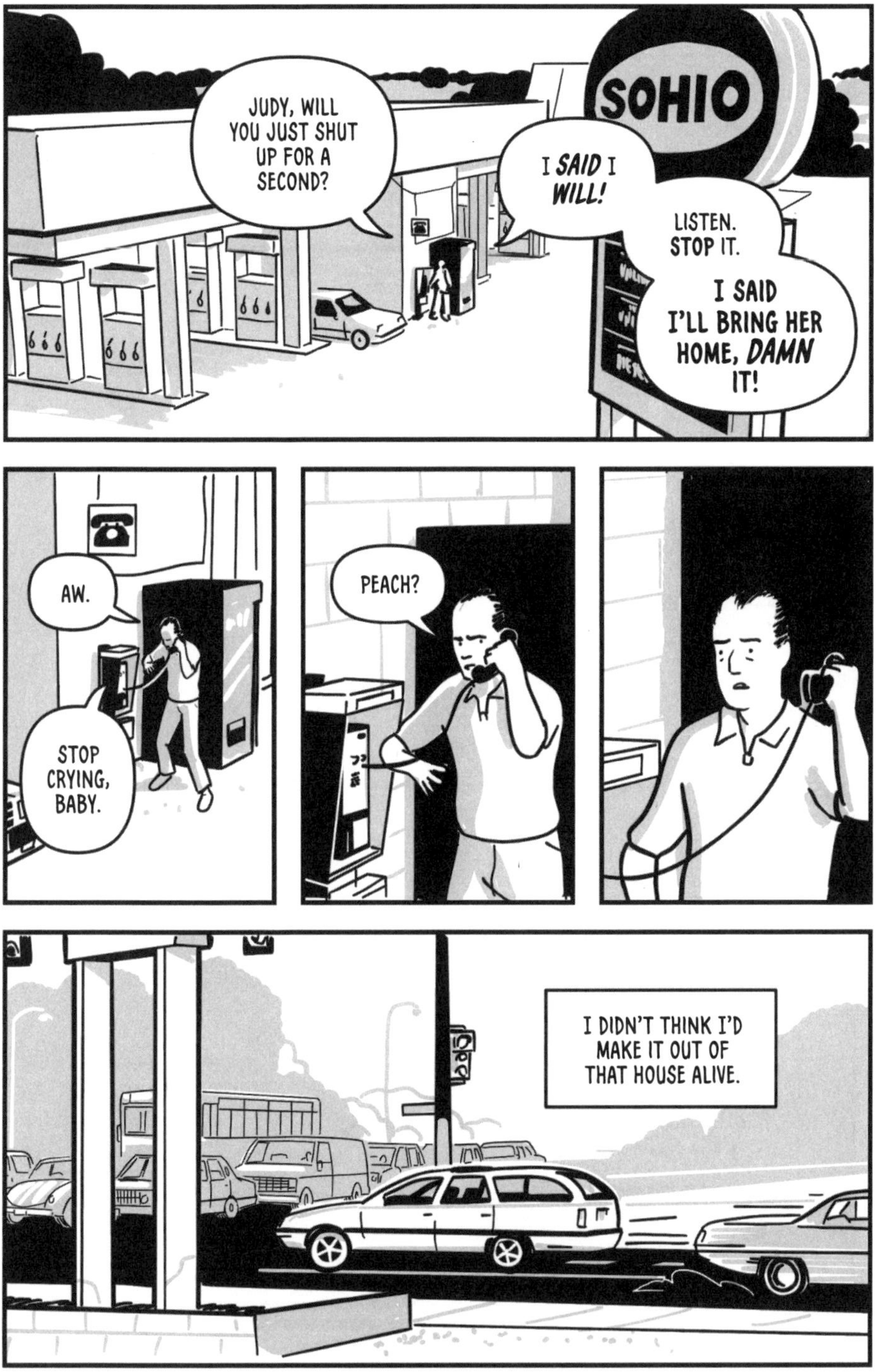
JUDY, WILL YOU JUST SHUT UP FOR A SECOND?
SOHIO
I SAID I WILL!
LISTEN. STOP IT.
I SAID I'LL BRING HER HOME, DAMN IT!
AW.
STOP CRYING, BABY.
PEACH?
I DIDN'T THINK I'D MAKE IT OUT OF THAT HOUSE ALIVE.

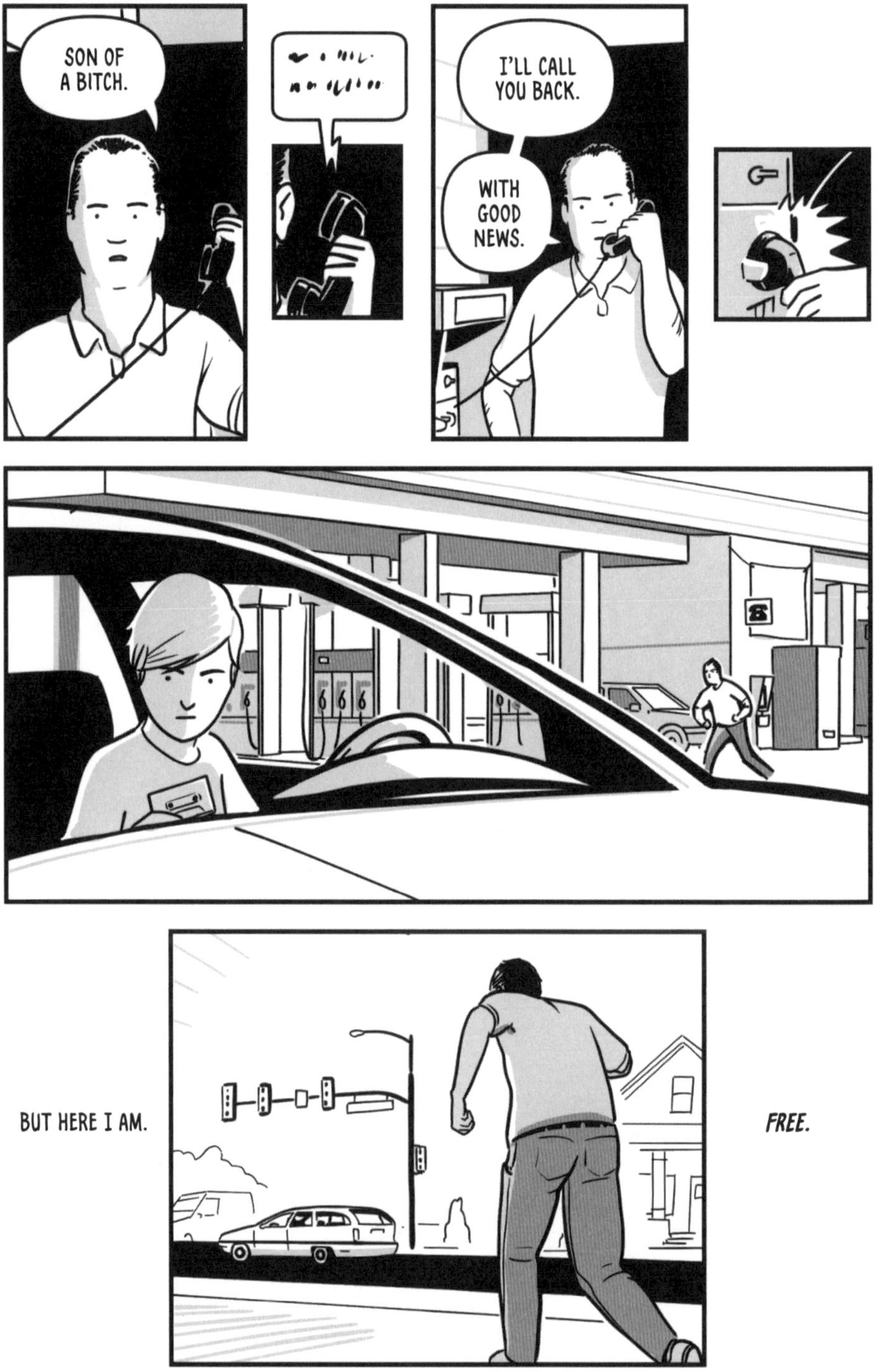
SON OF A BITCH.
I'LL CALL YOU BACK.
WITH GOOD NEWS.
BUT HERE I AM.
FREE.

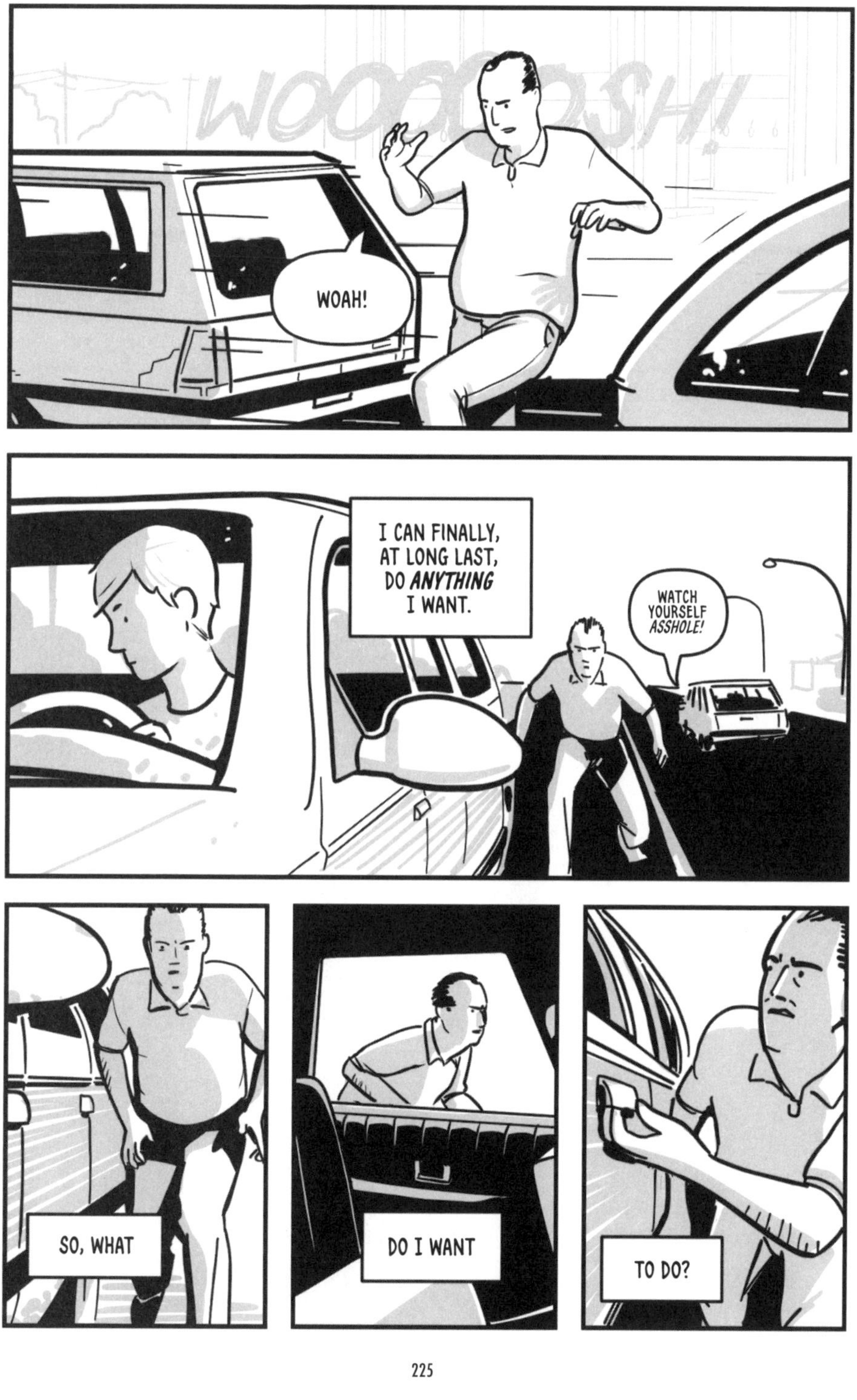
WOOOOOSH!!
WOAH!
I CAN FINALLY, AT LONG LAST, DO *ANYTHING* I WANT.
WATCH YOURSELF *ASSHOLE!*
SO, WHAT
DO I WANT
TO DO?

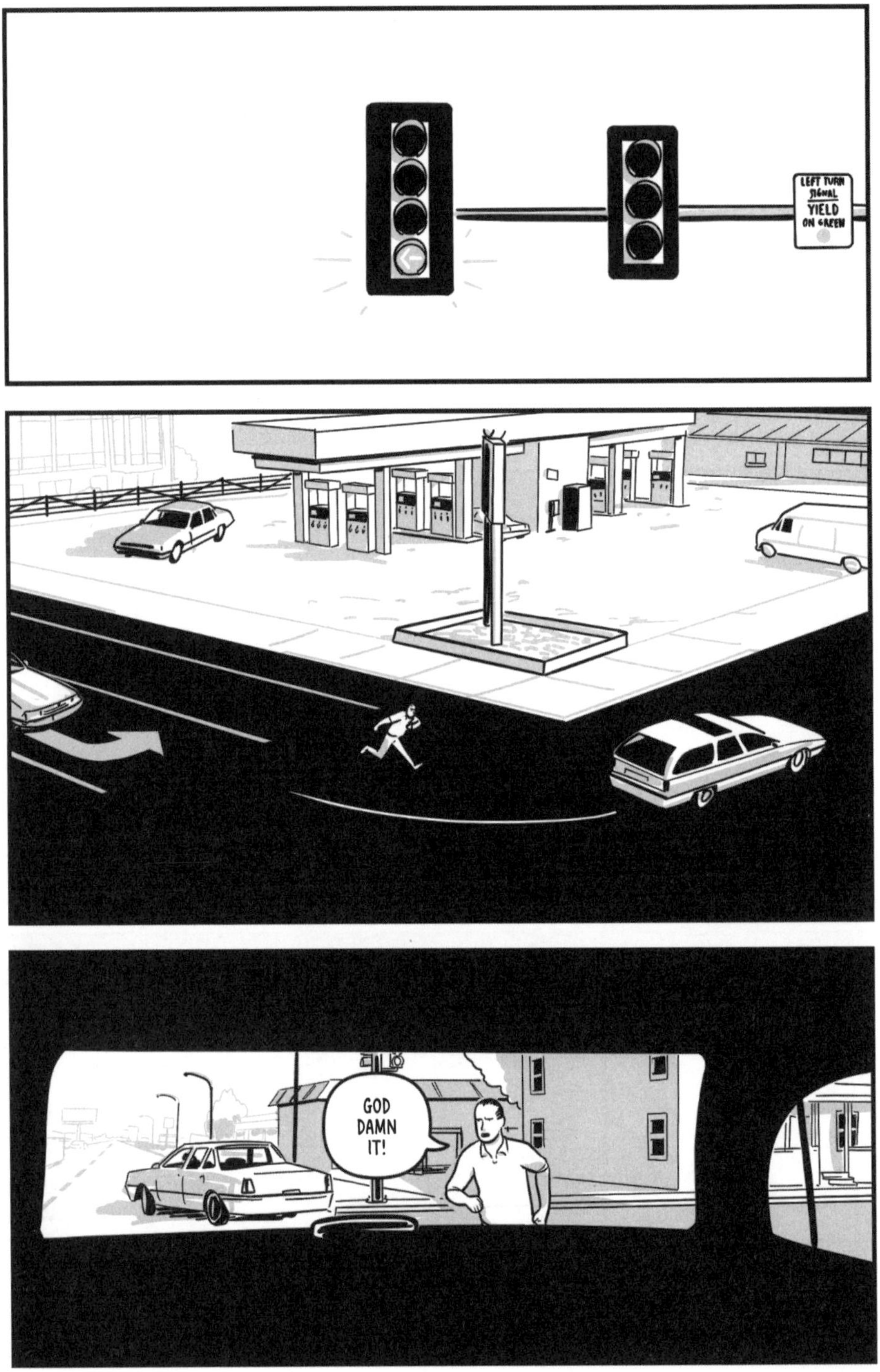
LEFT TURN SIGNAL
YIELD ON GREEN
GOD DAMN IT!

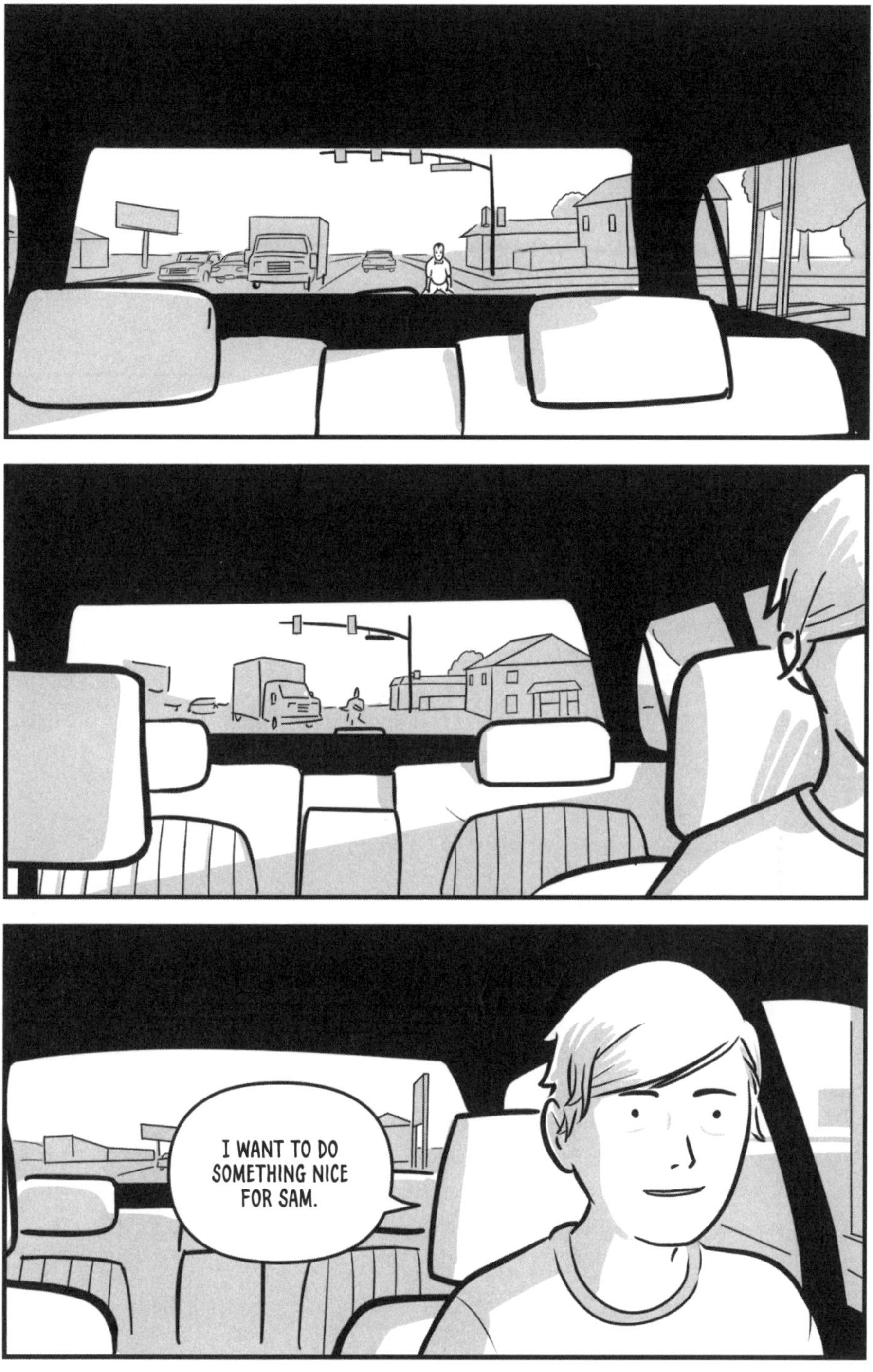
I WANT TO DO SOMETHING NICE FOR SAM.

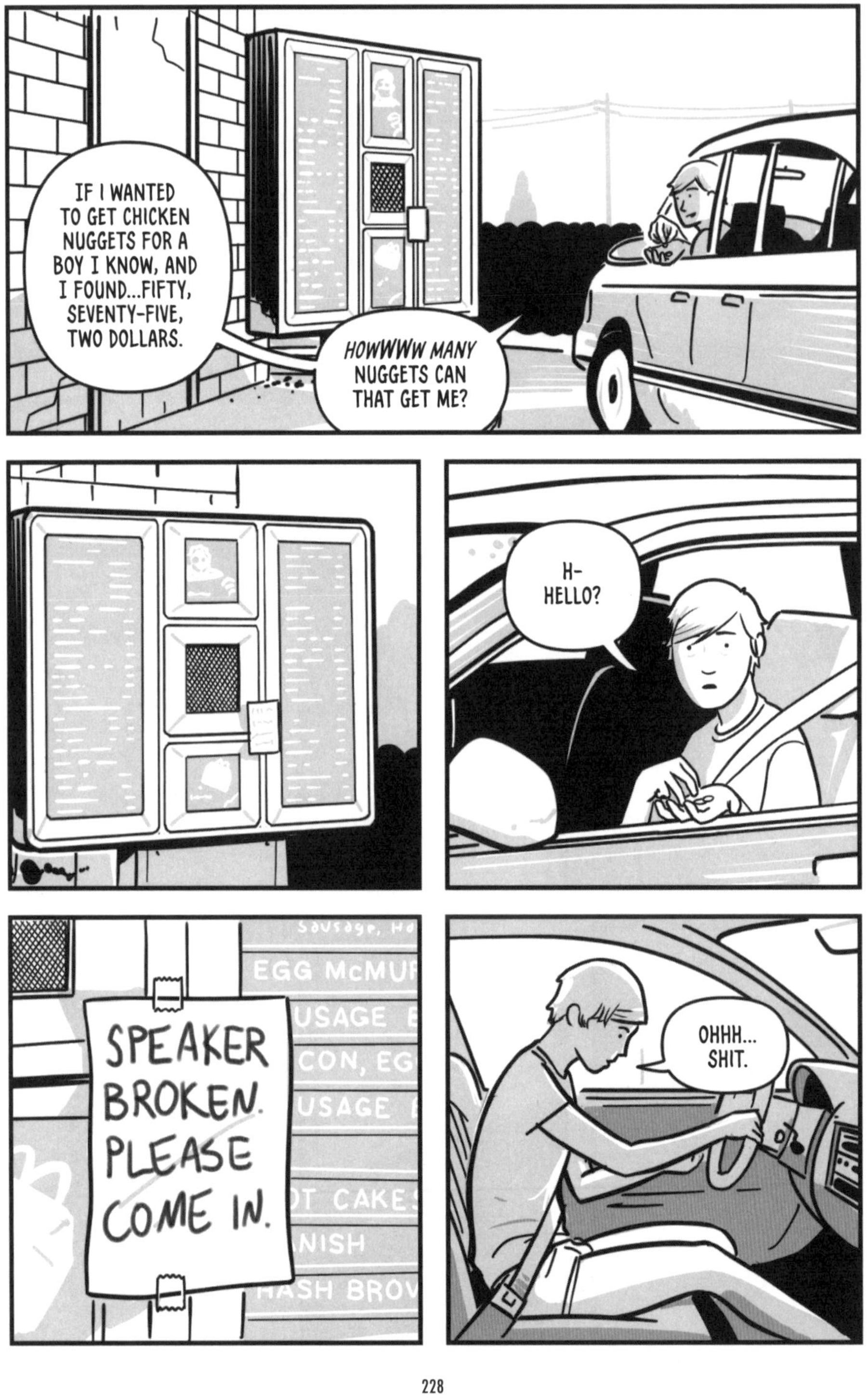
IF I WANTED TO GET CHICKEN NUGGETS FOR A BOY I KNOW, AND I FOUND...FIFTY, SEVENTY-FIVE, TWO DOLLARS.
HOWWWW MANY NUGGETS CAN THAT GET ME?
H- HELLO?
SPEAKER BROKEN. PLEASE COME IN.
OHHH... SHIT.

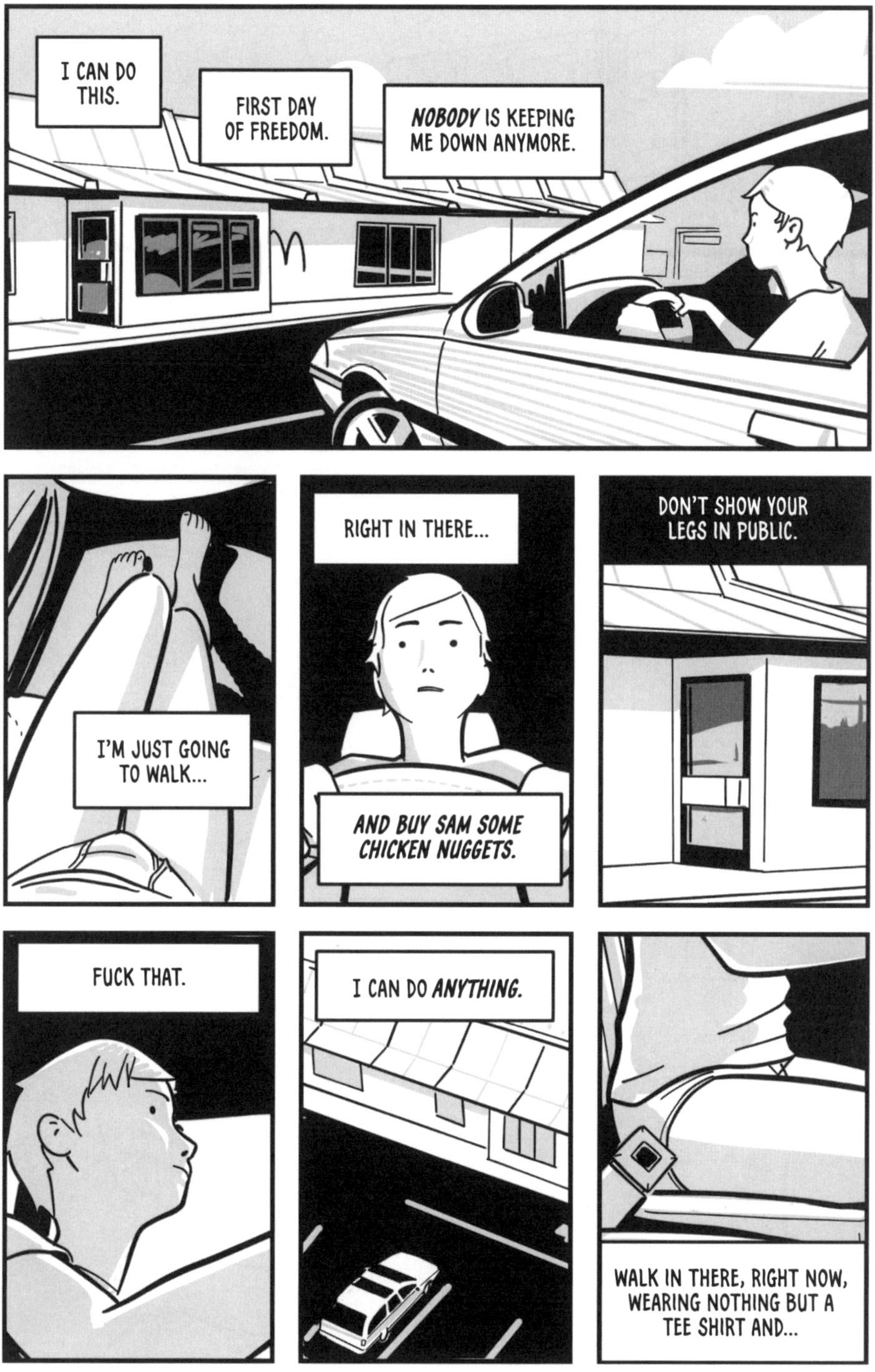
I CAN DO THIS.
FIRST DAY OF FREEDOM.
NOBODY IS KEEPING ME DOWN ANYMORE.
I'M JUST GOING TO WALK...
RIGHT IN THERE...
AND BUY SAM SOME CHICKEN NUGGETS.
DON'T SHOW YOUR LEGS IN PUBLIC.
FUCK THAT.
I CAN DO *ANYTHING.*
WALK IN THERE, RIGHT NOW, WEARING NOTHING BUT A TEE SHIRT AND...

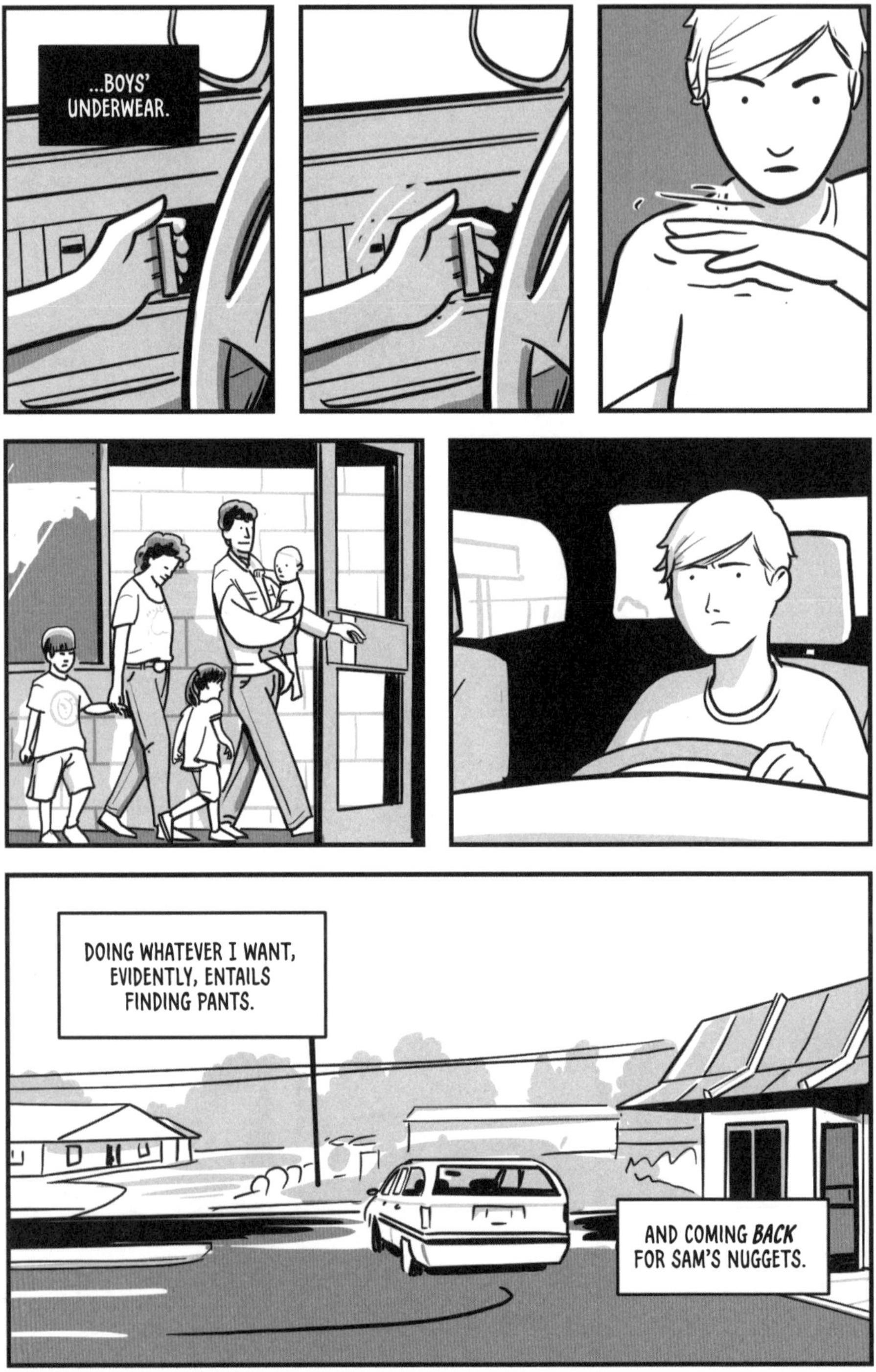
...BOYS' UNDERWEAR.
DOING WHATEVER I WANT, EVIDENTLY, ENTAILS FINDING PANTS.
AND COMING *BACK* FOR SAM'S NUGGETS.

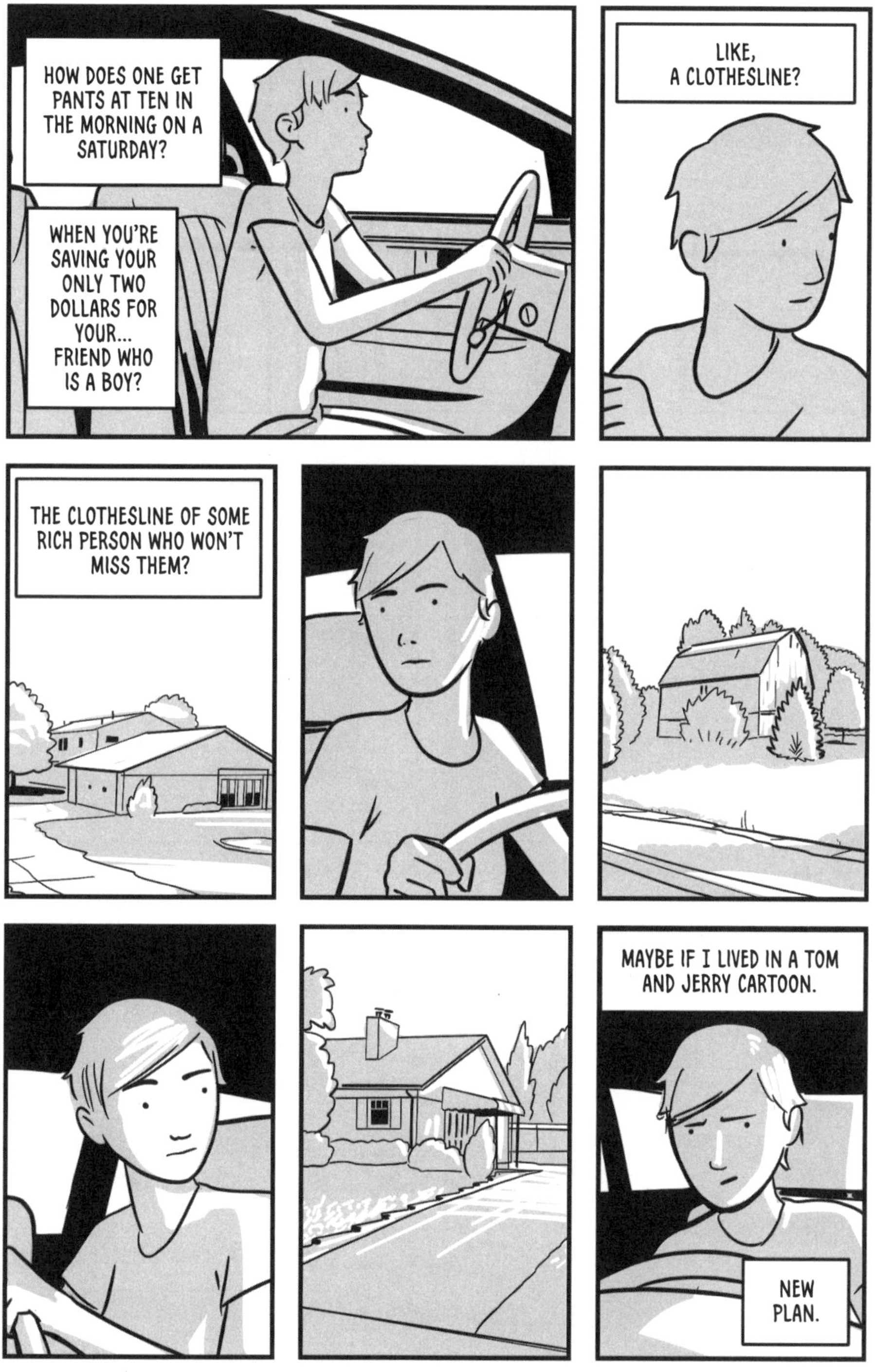
HOW DOES ONE GET PANTS AT TEN IN THE MORNING ON A SATURDAY?
WHEN YOU'RE SAVING YOUR ONLY TWO DOLLARS FOR YOUR... FRIEND WHO IS A BOY?
LIKE, A CLOTHESLINE?
THE CLOTHESLINE OF SOME RICH PERSON WHO WON'T MISS THEM?
MAYBE IF I LIVED IN A TOM AND JERRY CARTOON.
NEW PLAN.

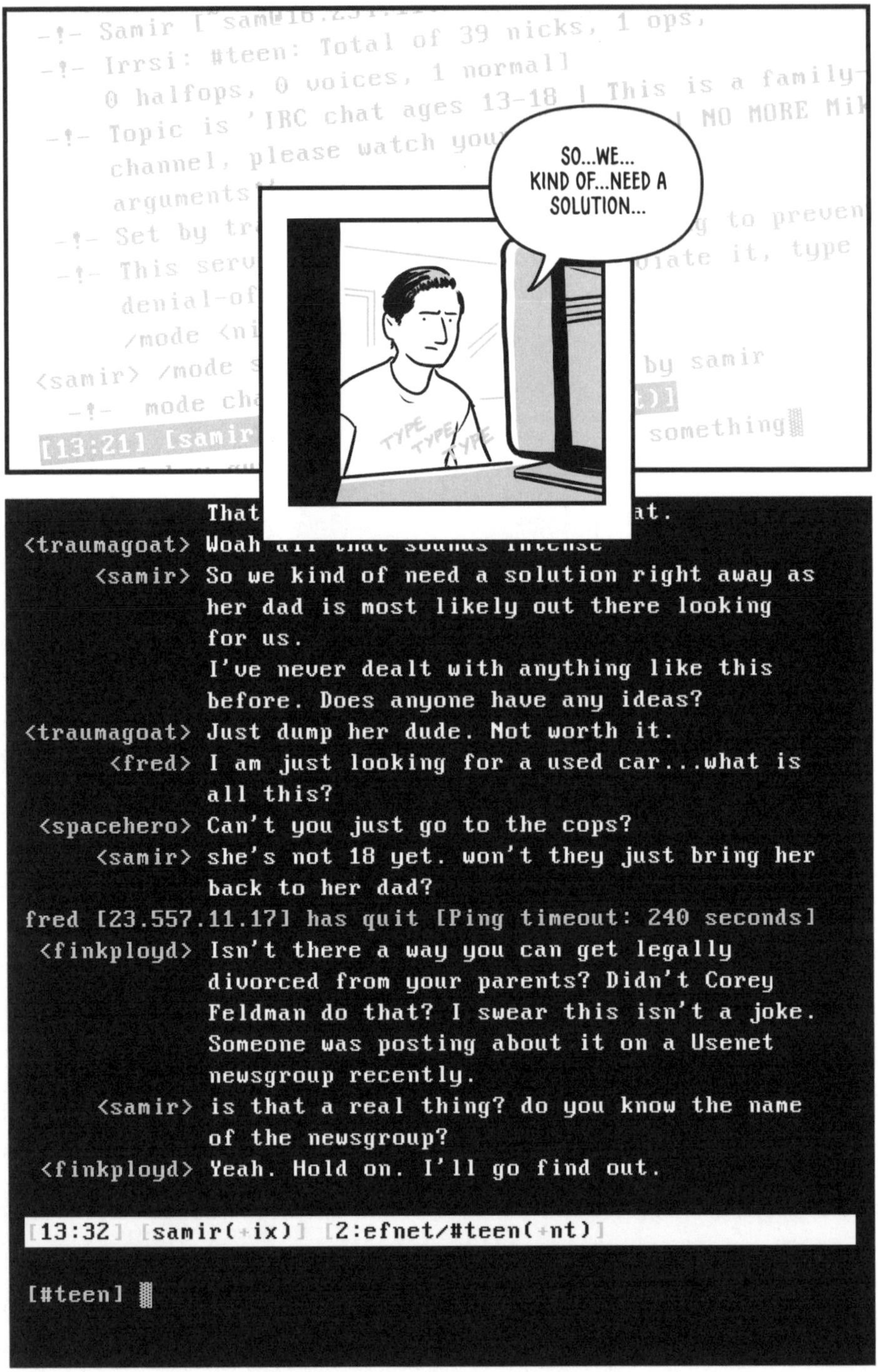
-!- Samir
-!- Irrsi: #teen: Total of 39 nicks, 1 ops,
0 halfops, 0 voices, 1 normal]
-!- Topic is 'IRC chat ages 13-18 | This is a family-
channel, please watch you
NO MORE Mik
arguments
-!- Set by
to preven
-!- This serv
viate it, type
denial-of
/mode
<samir> /mode
by samir
-!- mode ch
[13:21] [samir
something
SO...WE... KIND OF...NEED A SOLUTION...
TYPE TYPE TYPE
That
at.
<traumagoat> Woah
<samir> So we kind of need a solution right away as her dad is most likely out there looking for us.
I've never dealt with anything like this before. Does anyone have any ideas?
<traumagoat> Just dump her dude. Not worth it.
<fred> I am just looking for a used car...what is all this?
<spacehero> Can't you just go to the cops?
<samir> she's not 18 yet. won't they just bring her back to her dad?
fred [23.557.11.17] has quit [Ping timeout: 240 seconds]
<finkployd> Isn't there a way you can get legally divorced from your parents? Didn't Corey Feldman do that? I swear this isn't a joke. Someone was posting about it on a Usenet newsgroup recently.
<samir> is that a real thing? do you know the name of the newsgroup?
<finkployd> Yeah. Hold on. I'll go find out.
[13:32] [samir(+ix)] [2:efnet/#teen(+nt)]
[#teen]

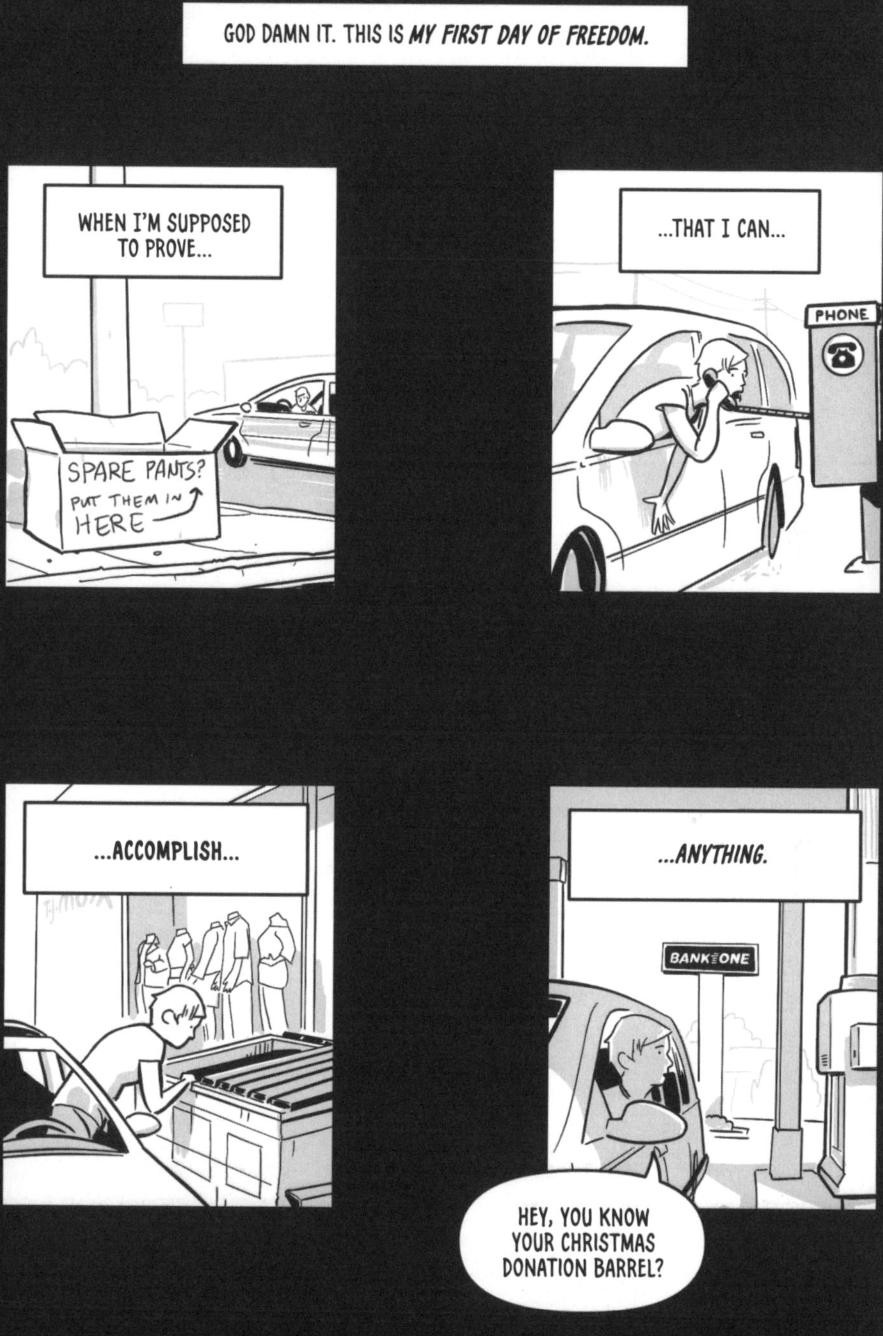
GOD DAMN IT. THIS IS *MY FIRST DAY OF FREEDOM.*
WHEN I'M SUPPOSED TO PROVE...
SPARE PANTS? PUT THEM IN HERE
...THAT I CAN...
PHONE
...ACCOMPLISH...
...*ANYTHING.*
BANK ONE
HEY, YOU KNOW YOUR CHRISTMAS DONATION BARREL?

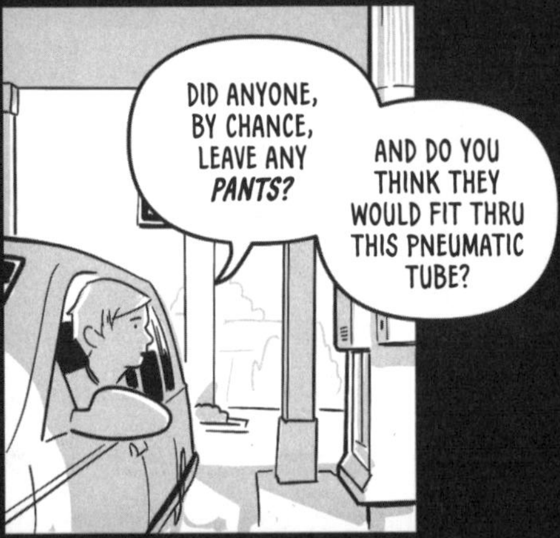
DID ANYONE, BY CHANCE, LEAVE ANY *PANTS?*
AND DO YOU THINK THEY WOULD FIT THRU THIS PNEUMATIC TUBE?

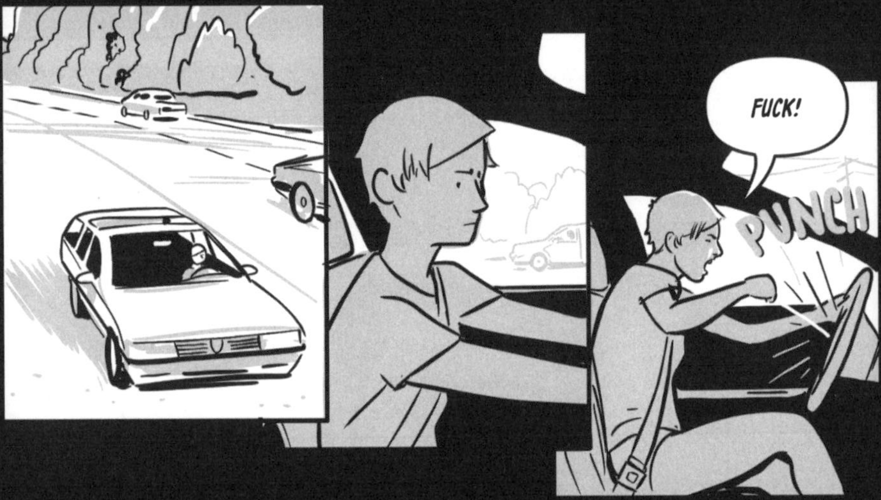
FUCK!
PUNCH

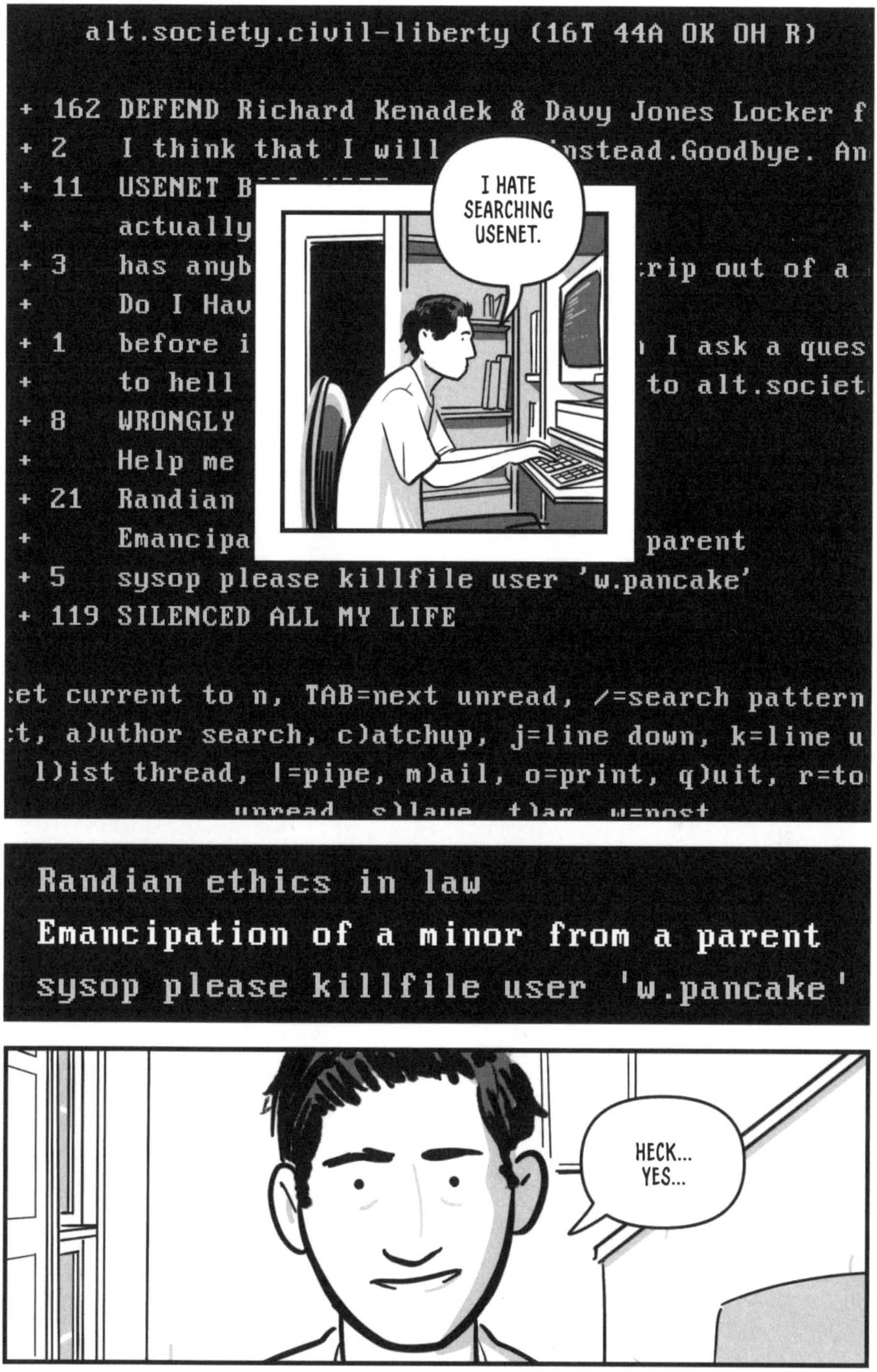

alt.society.civil-liberty (16T 44A 0K 0H R)
+ 162 DEFEND Richard Kenadek & Davy Jones Locker f
+ 2 I think that I will
instead.Goodbye. An
+ 11 USENET B
+ actually
+ 3 has anyb
rip out of a
+ Do I Hav
+ 1 before i
I ask a ques
+ to hell
to alt.societ
+ 8 WRONGLY
+ Help me
+ 21 Randian
+ Emancipa
parent
+ 5 sysop please killfile user 'w.pancake'
+ 119 SILENCED ALL MY LIFE
et current to n, TAB=next unread, /=search pattern
t, a)uthor search, c)atchup, j=line down, k=line u
l)ist thread, |=pipe, m)ail, o=print, q)uit, r=to
I HATE SEARCHING USENET.
Randian ethics in law
Emancipation of a minor from a parent
sysop please killfile user 'w.pancake'
HECK... YES...

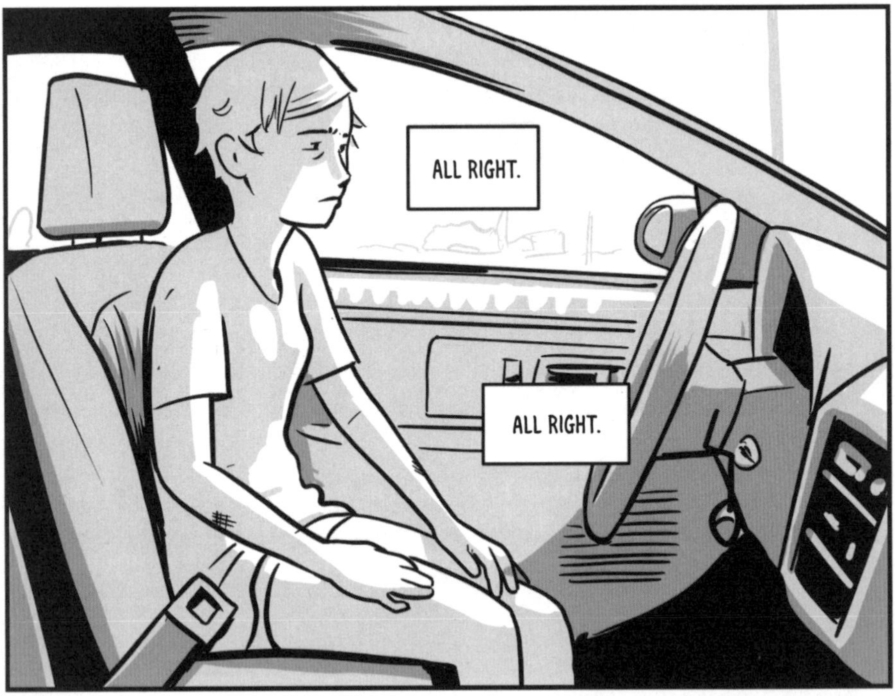
ALL RIGHT.
ALL RIGHT.

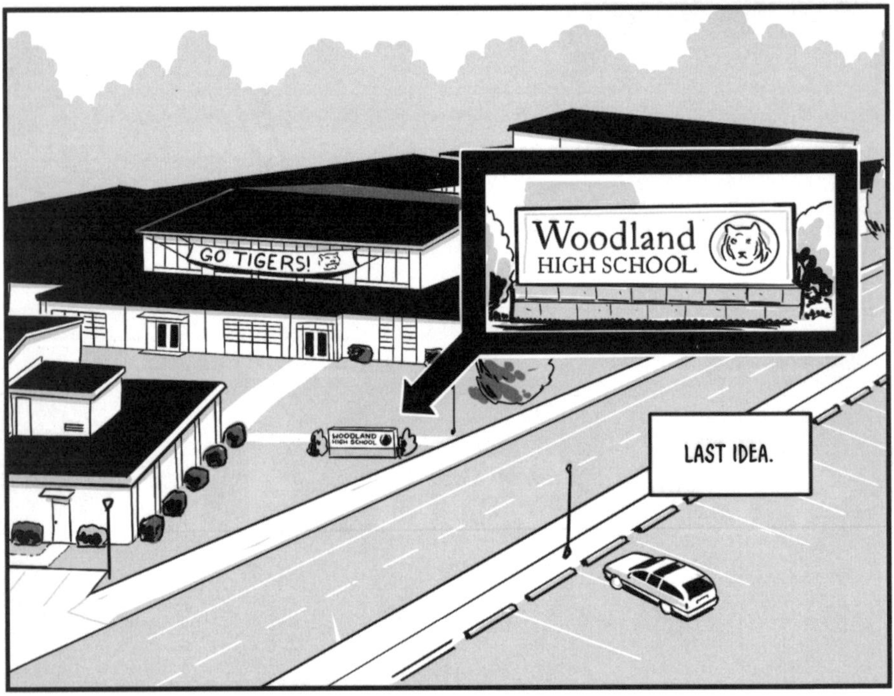
GO TIGERS!
Woodland
HIGH SCHOOL
LAST IDEA.

From: kaosie@info.coolhouse.net
Newsgroups: alt.society.civil-liberty
In-Reply-To: <u31.111$UI2.11089@news.bellsouth.net>
Subject: Re: Emancipation of a Minor from a Parent

In response to cwpitts earlier, it's totally
possible for a court to decide to separate you from
your parents if it's in your or their best interest.
You mentioned a family friend who's a lawyer? I'd
contact them. Or drop me a line. There are other
options.

-=X=- -=X=- -=X=-

"With the first link, the chain is forged. The first
speech censured... the first thought forbidden...
the first freedom denied, chains us all, irrevocably."
419-958-4143

FRICKING...

PERFECT!

419-958-4143

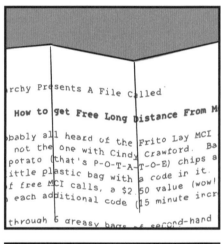

...rchy Presents A File Called

How to get Free Long Distance From M...

...bably all heard of the Frito Lay MCI
...not the one with Cindy Crawford. Ba...
...potato (that's P-O-T-A-T-O-E) chips a...
...ittle plastic bag with a code in it.
...f free MCI calls, a $2.50 value (wow!
... each additional code (15 minute incr...

...through 6 greasy bags of second-hand...

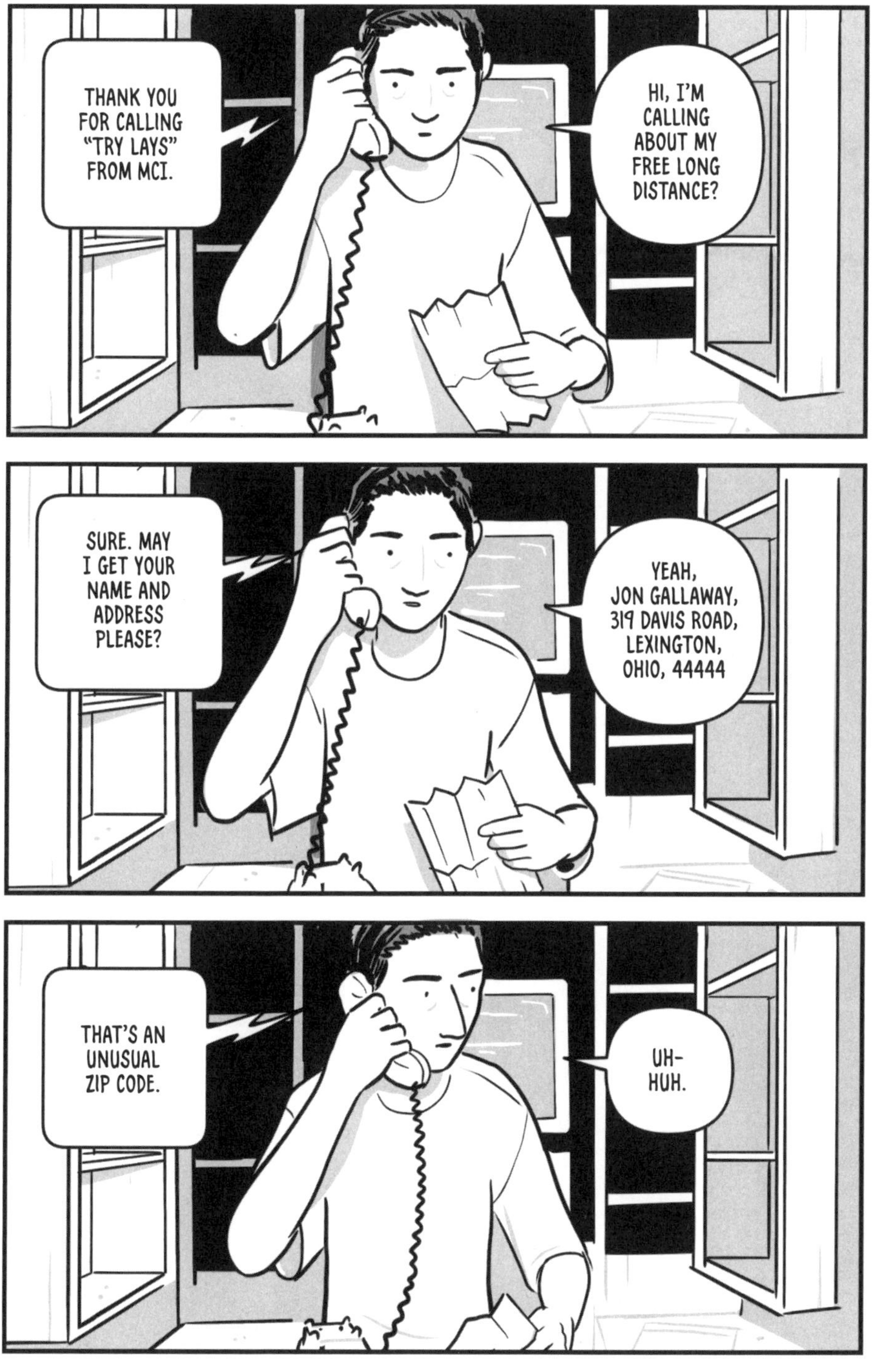
THANK YOU FOR CALLING "TRY LAYS" FROM MCI.
HI, I'M CALLING ABOUT MY FREE LONG DISTANCE?
SURE. MAY I GET YOUR NAME AND ADDRESS PLEASE?
YEAH, JON GALLAWAY, 319 DAVIS ROAD, LEXINGTON, OHIO, 44444
THAT'S AN UNUSUAL ZIP CODE.
UH-HUH.

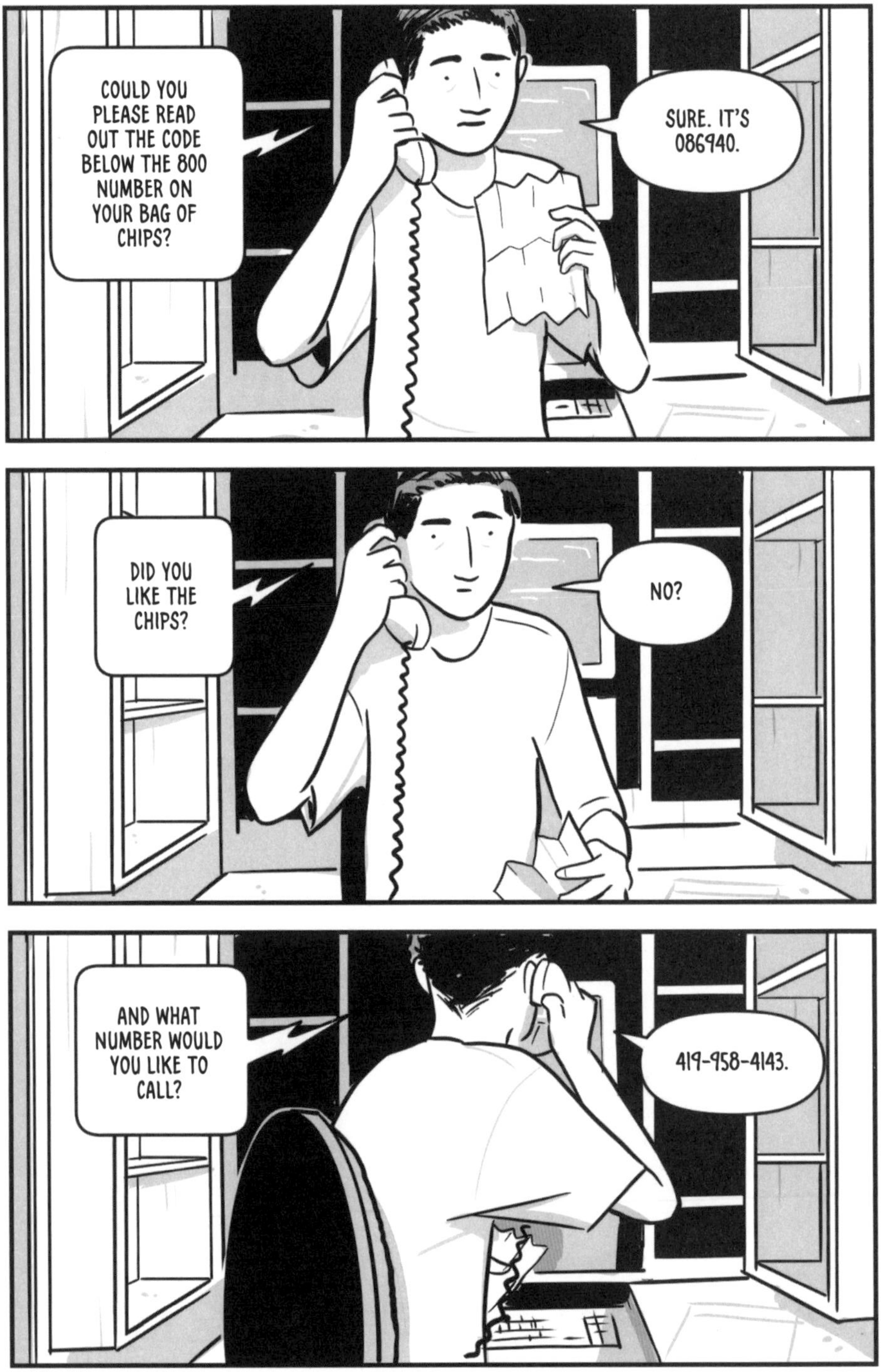
COULD YOU PLEASE READ OUT THE CODE BELOW THE 800 NUMBER ON YOUR BAG OF CHIPS?
SURE. IT'S 086940.
DID YOU LIKE THE CHIPS?
NO?
AND WHAT NUMBER WOULD YOU LIKE TO CALL?
419-958-4143.

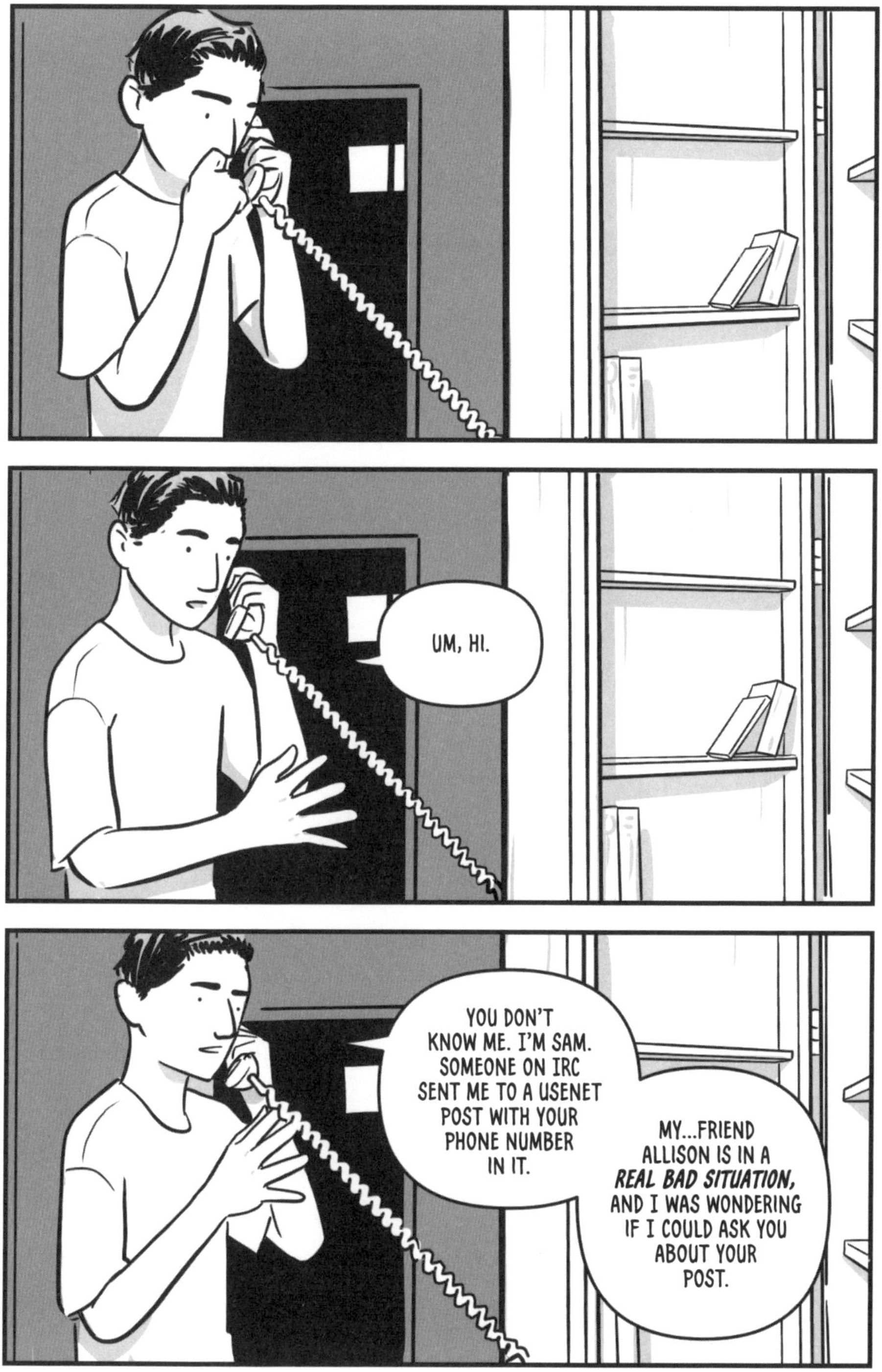
UM, HI.
YOU DON'T KNOW ME. I'M SAM. SOMEONE ON IRC SENT ME TO A USENET POST WITH YOUR PHONE NUMBER IN IT.
MY...FRIEND ALLISON IS IN A *REAL BAD SITUATION,* AND I WAS WONDERING IF I COULD ASK YOU ABOUT YOUR POST.

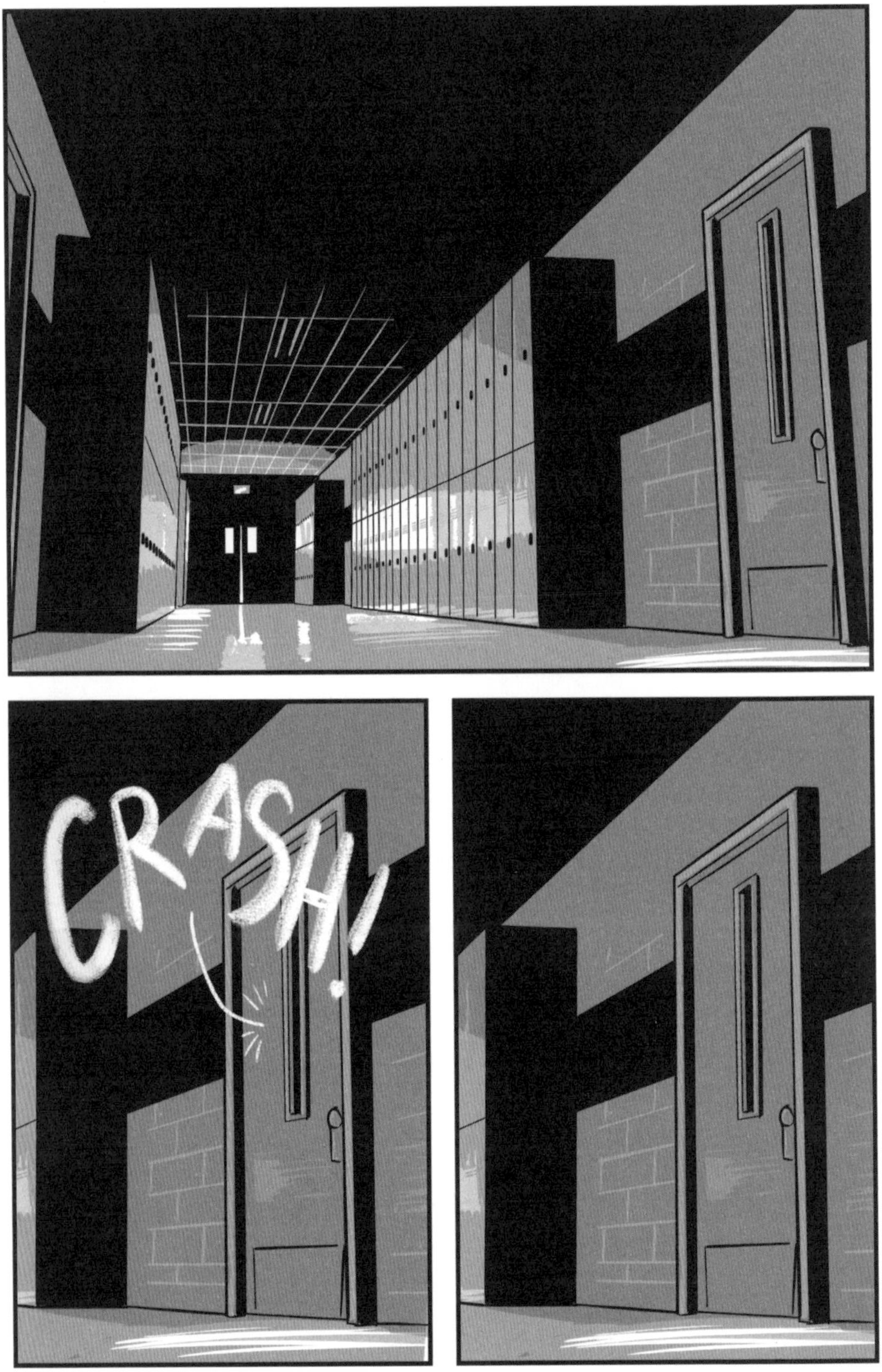
CRASH!

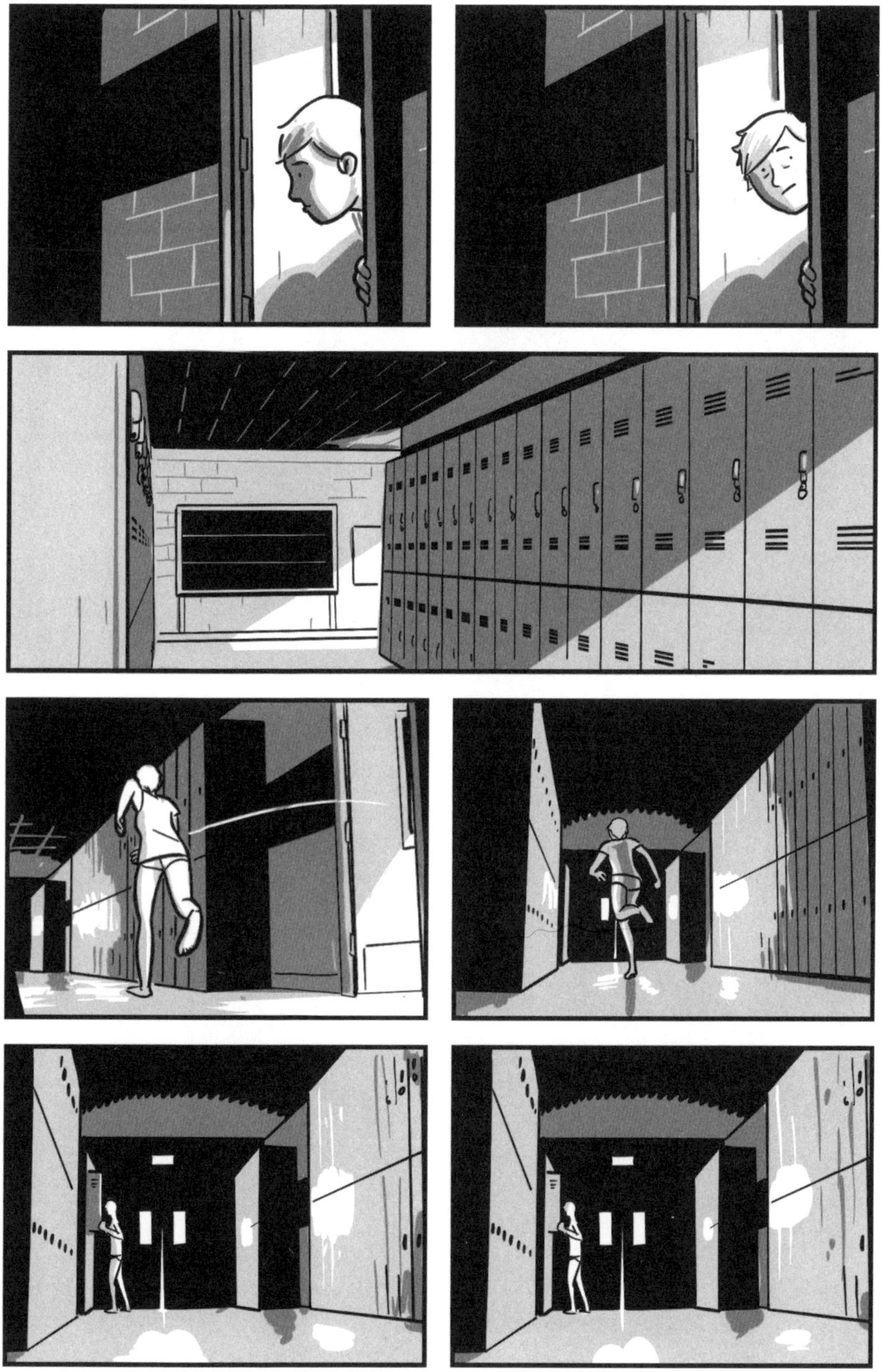

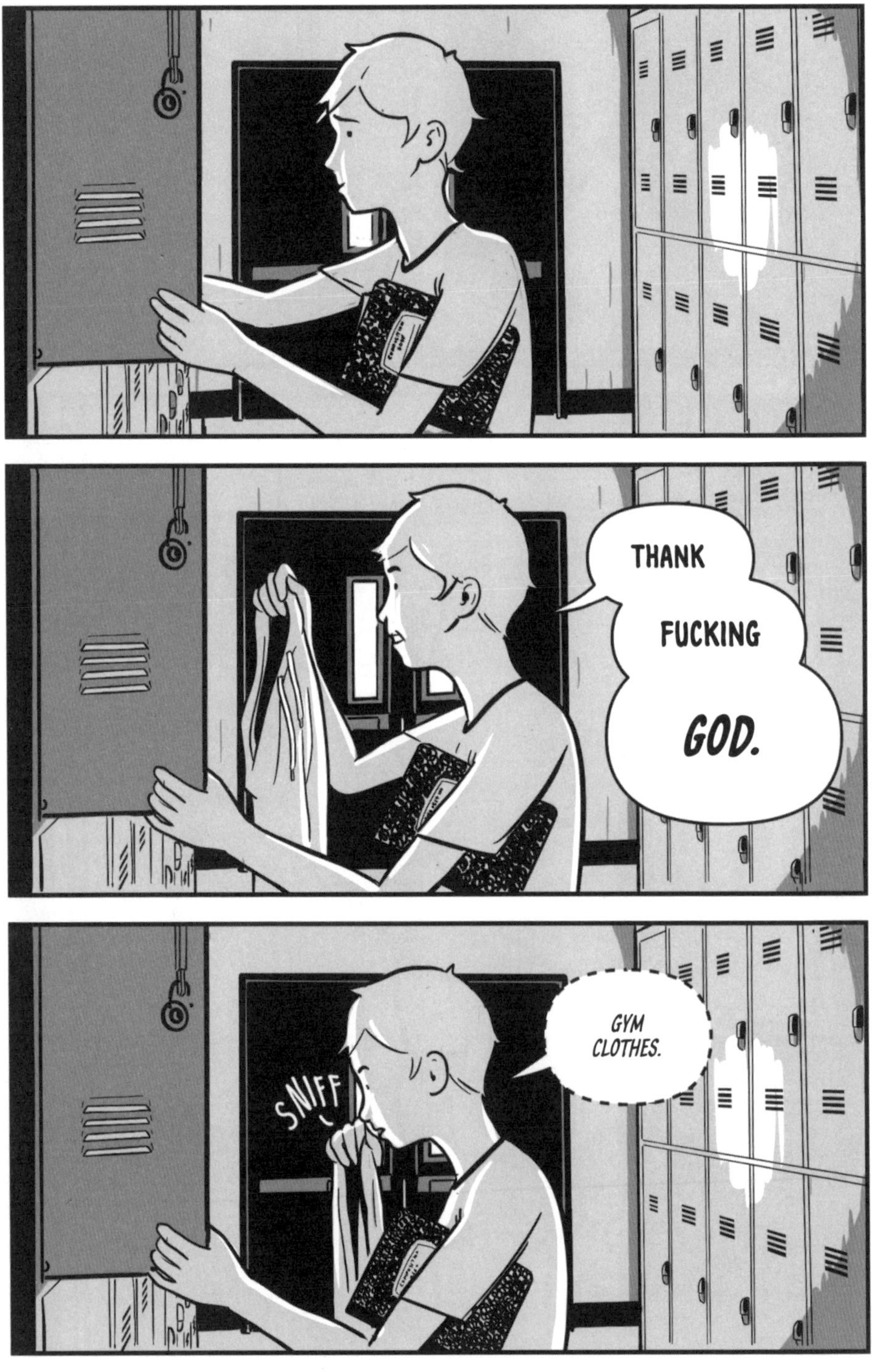
THANK FUCKING GOD.
GYM CLOTHES.
SNIFF

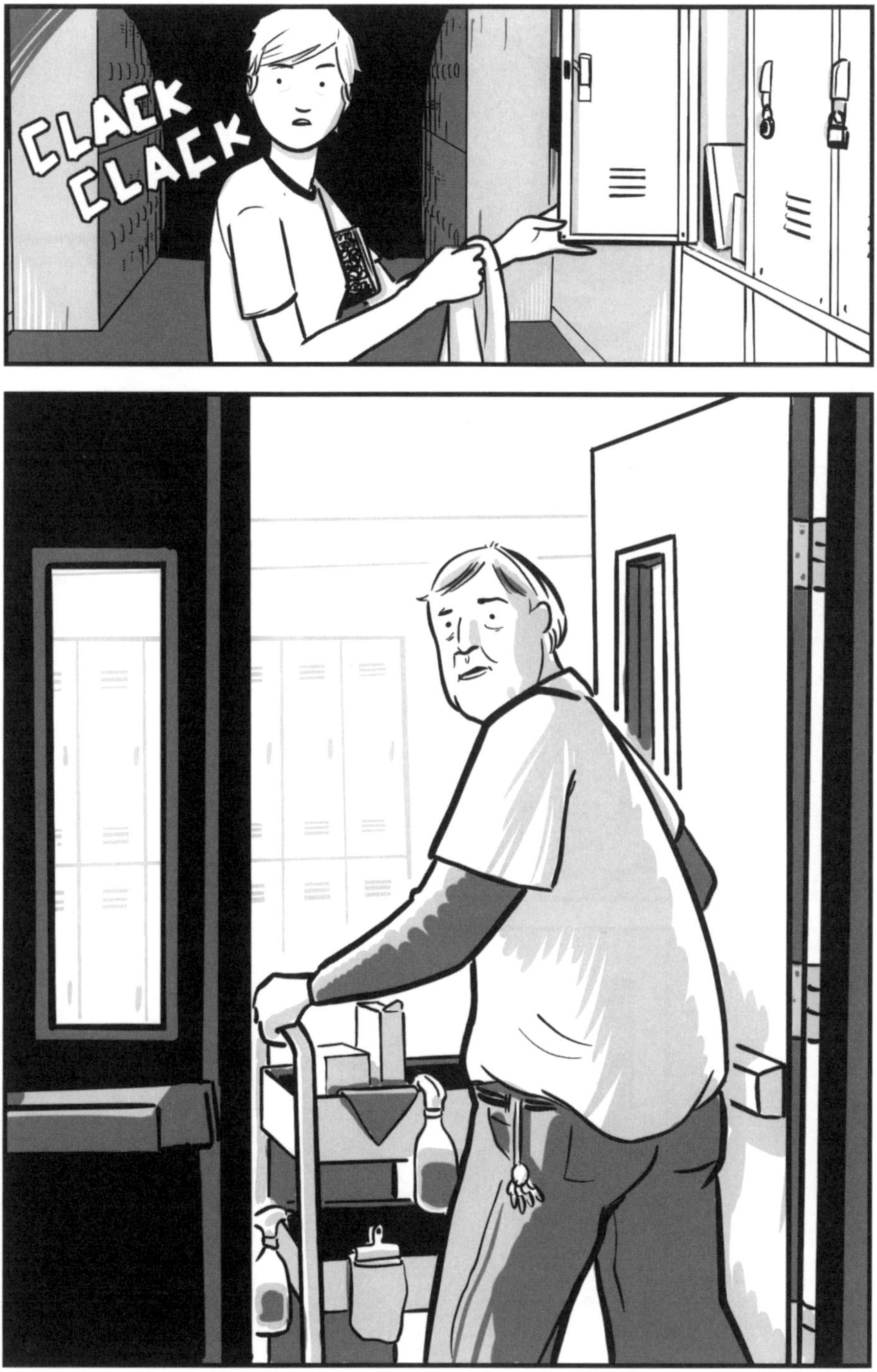
CLACK
CLACK

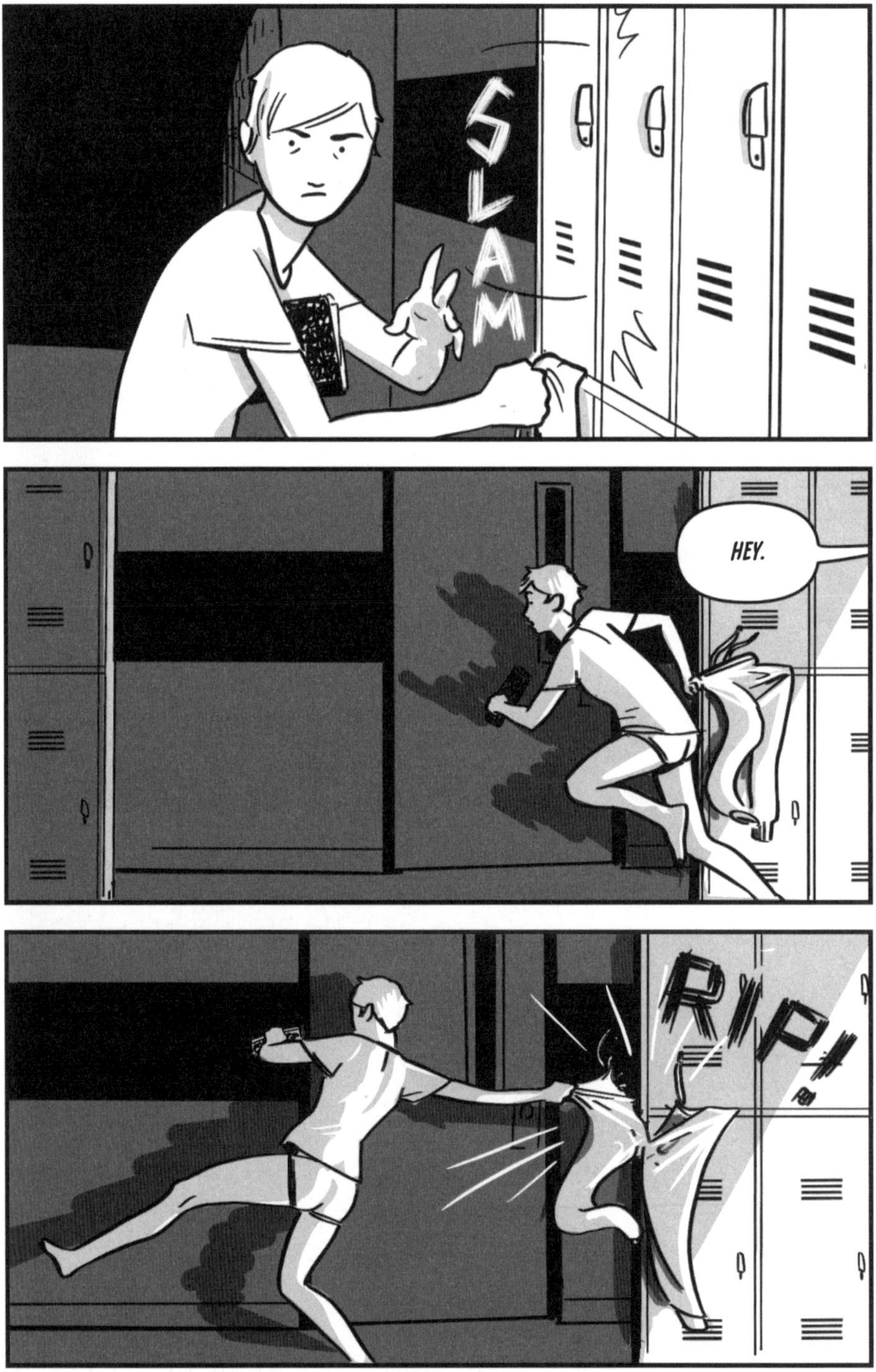
SLAM
HEY.
RIP!

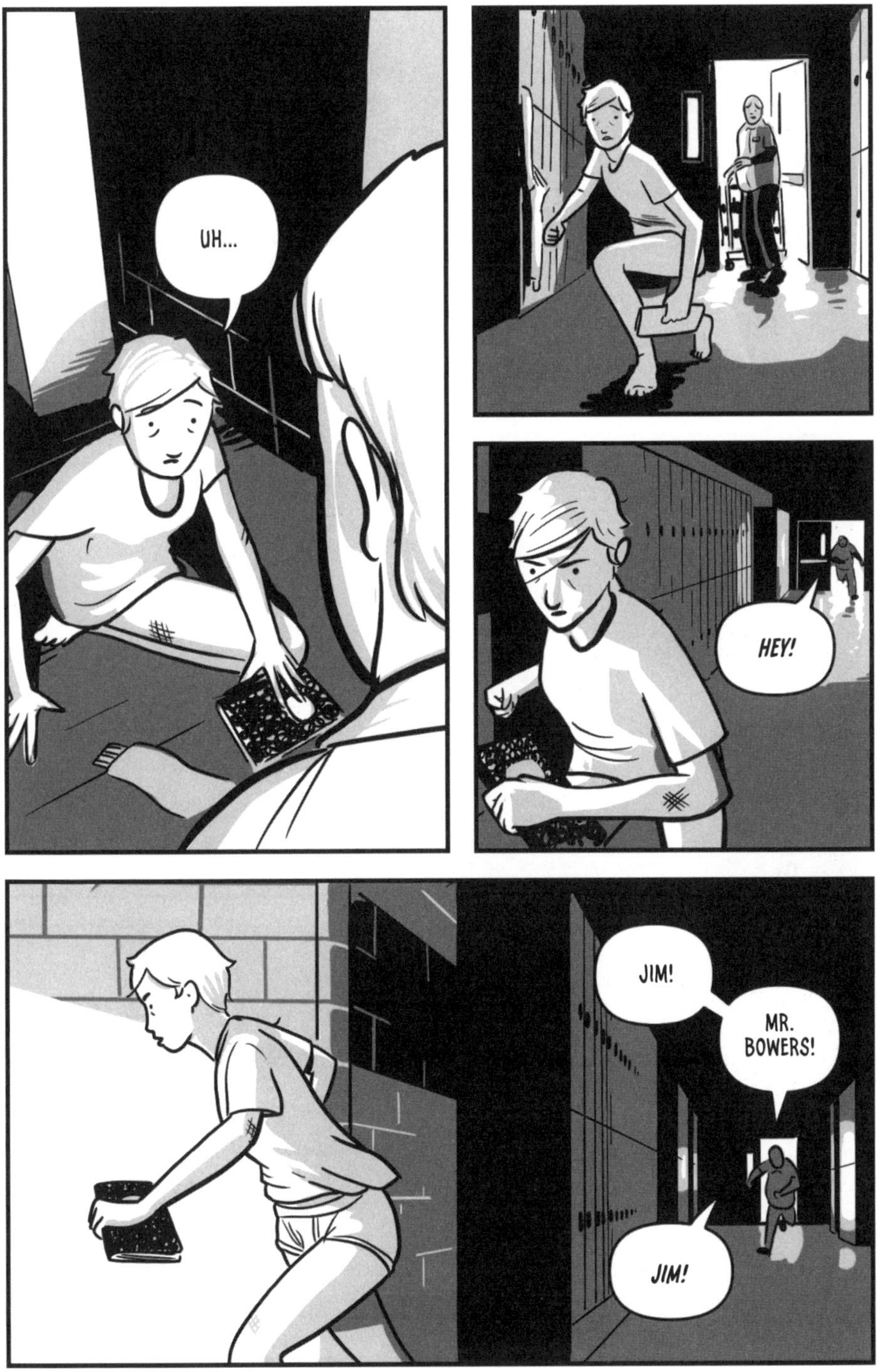
UH...
HEY!
JIM!
MR. BOWERS!
JIM!

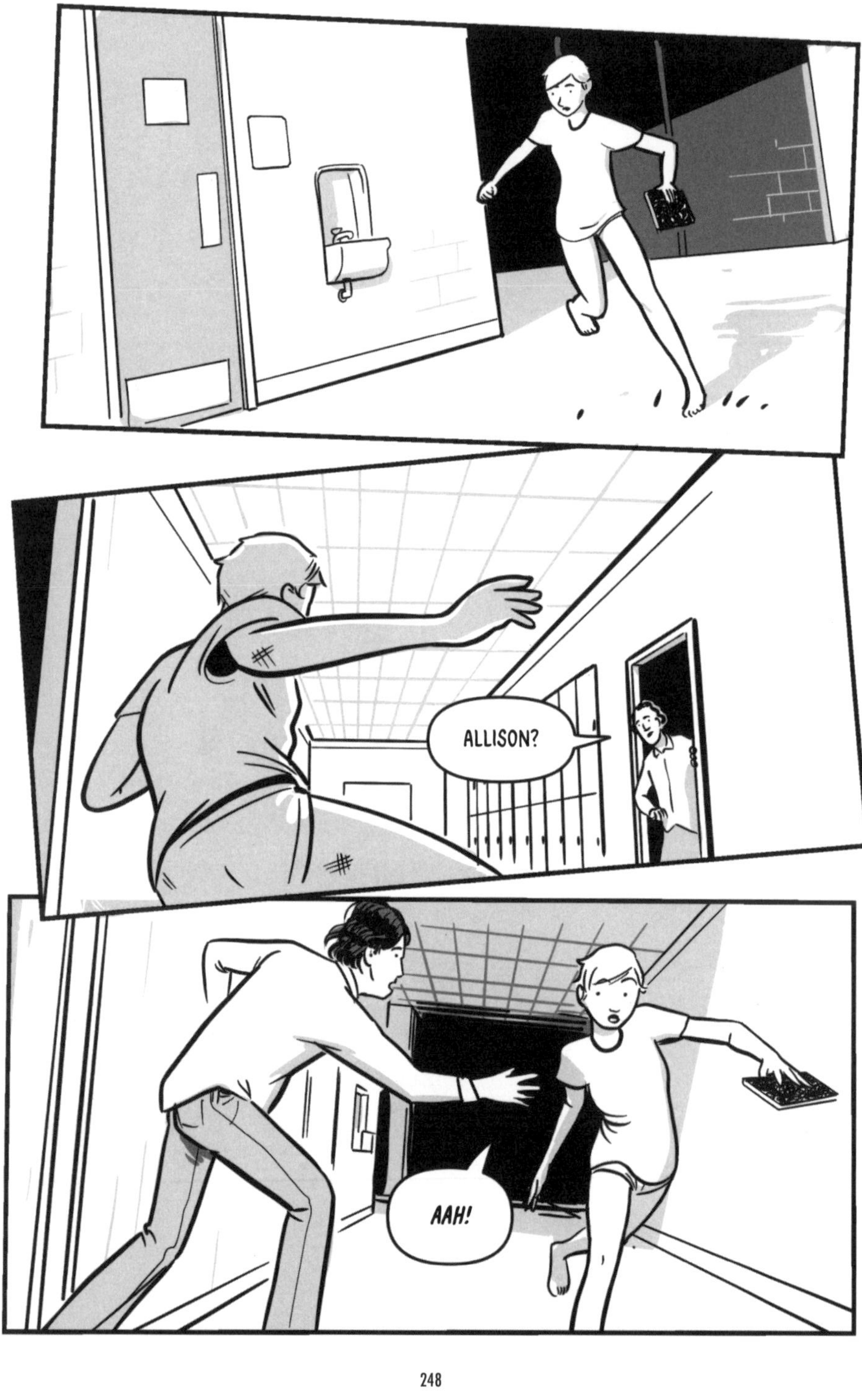
ALLISON?
AAH!

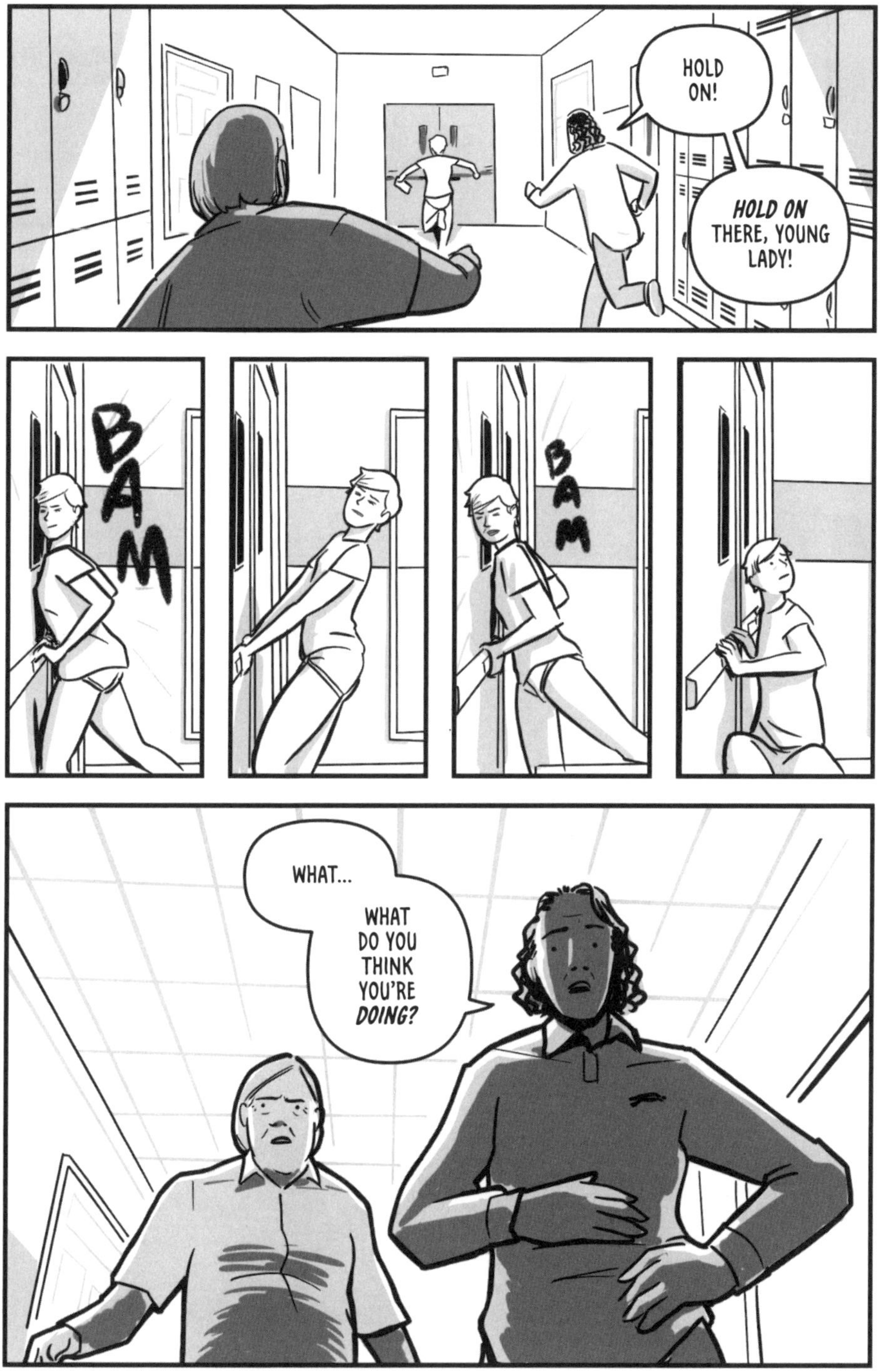
HOLD ON!
HOLD ON THERE, YOUNG LADY!
BAM
BAM
WHAT...
WHAT DO YOU THINK YOU'RE *DOING?*

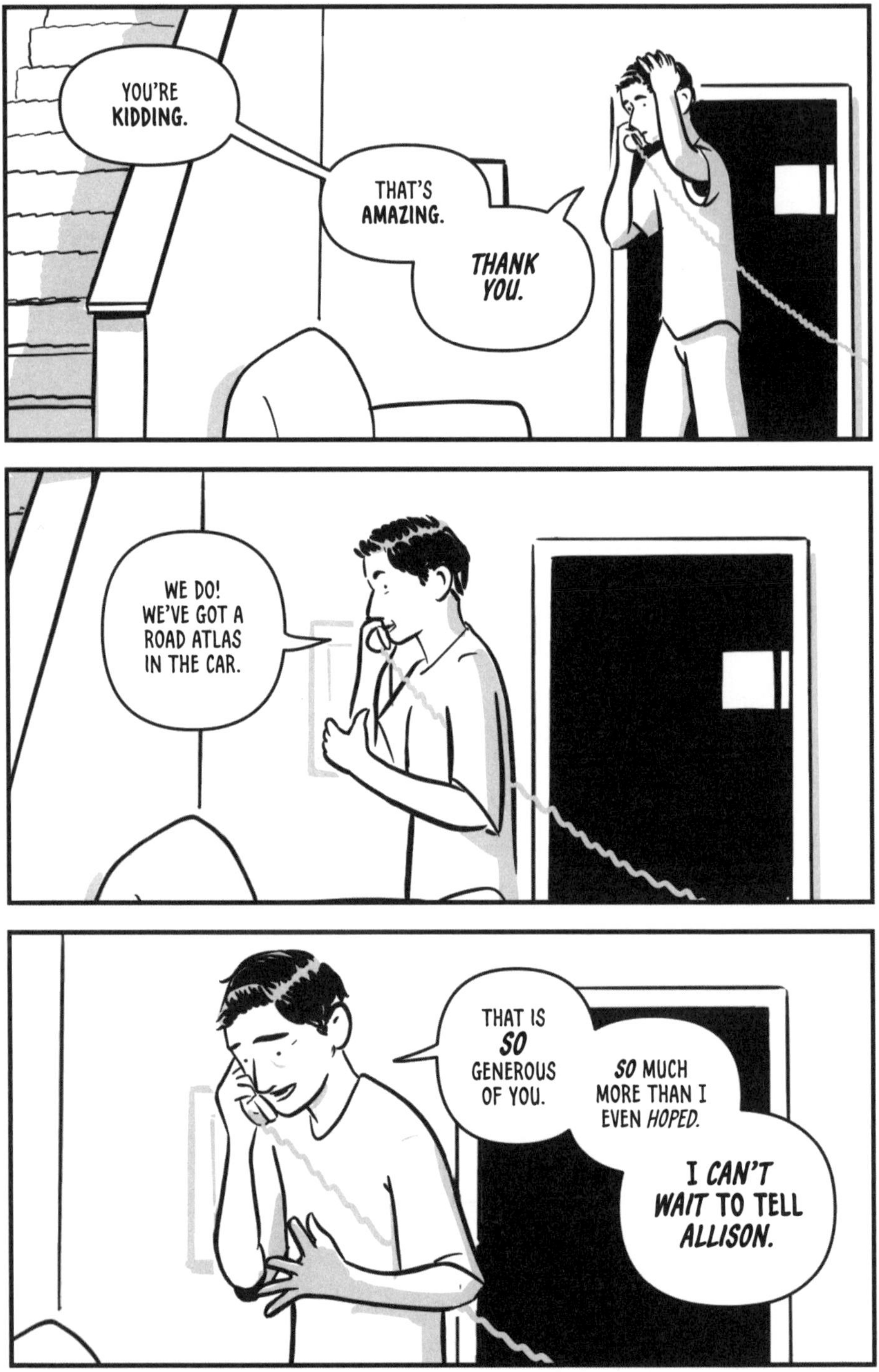
YOU'RE KIDDING.
THAT'S AMAZING.
THANK YOU.
WE DO! WE'VE GOT A ROAD ATLAS IN THE CAR.
THAT IS SO GENEROUS OF YOU.
SO MUCH MORE THAN I EVEN HOPED.
I CAN'T WAIT TO TELL ALLISON.

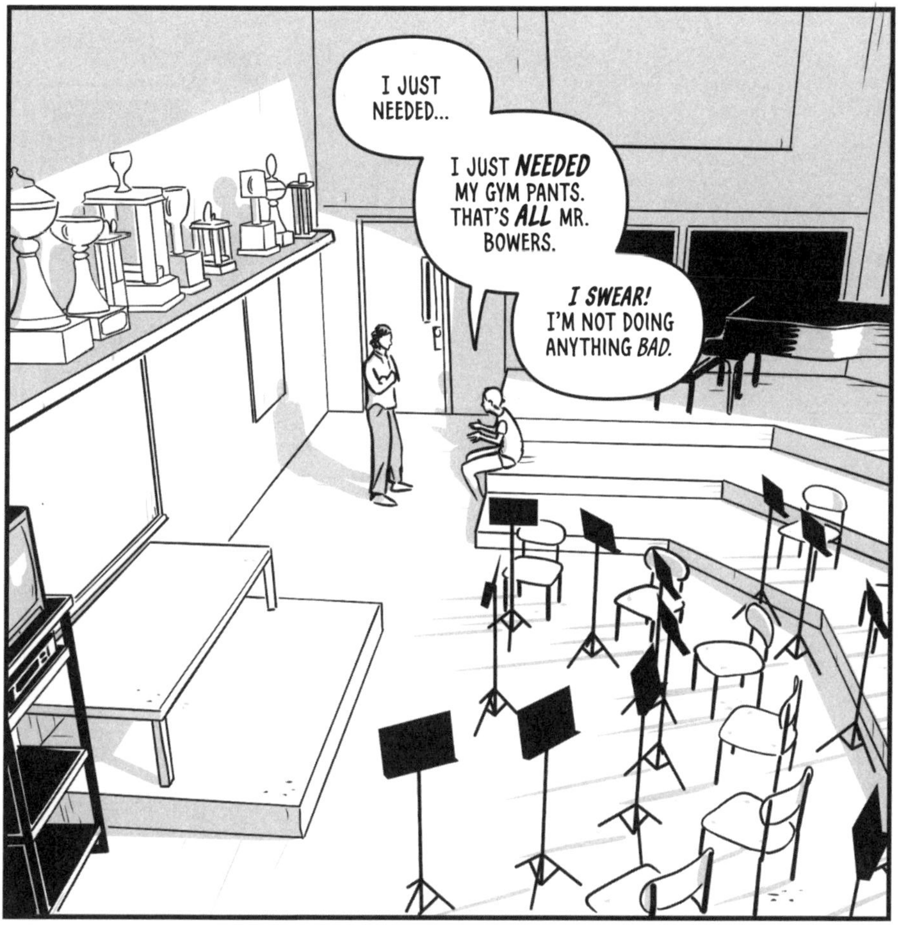
I JUST NEEDED...
I JUST NEEDED MY GYM PANTS. THAT'S ALL MR. BOWERS.
I SWEAR! I'M NOT DOING ANYTHING BAD.

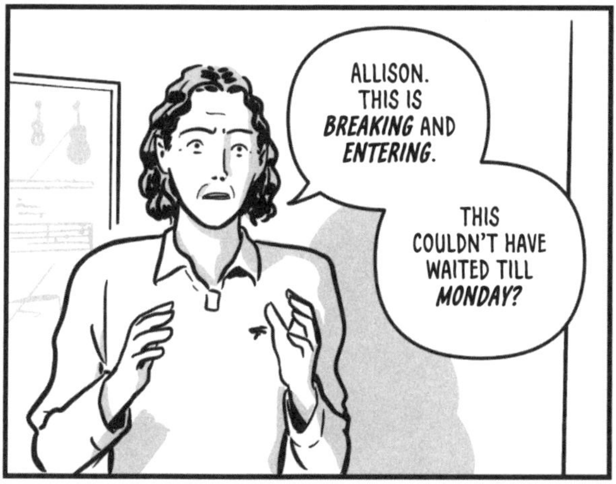
ALLISON. THIS IS BREAKING AND ENTERING.
THIS COULDN'T HAVE WAITED TILL MONDAY?

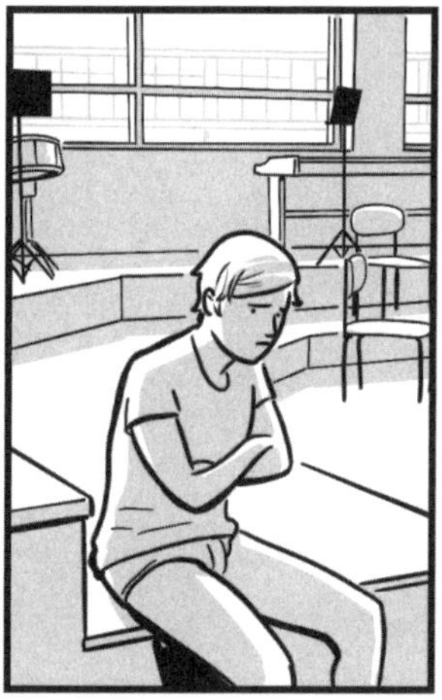

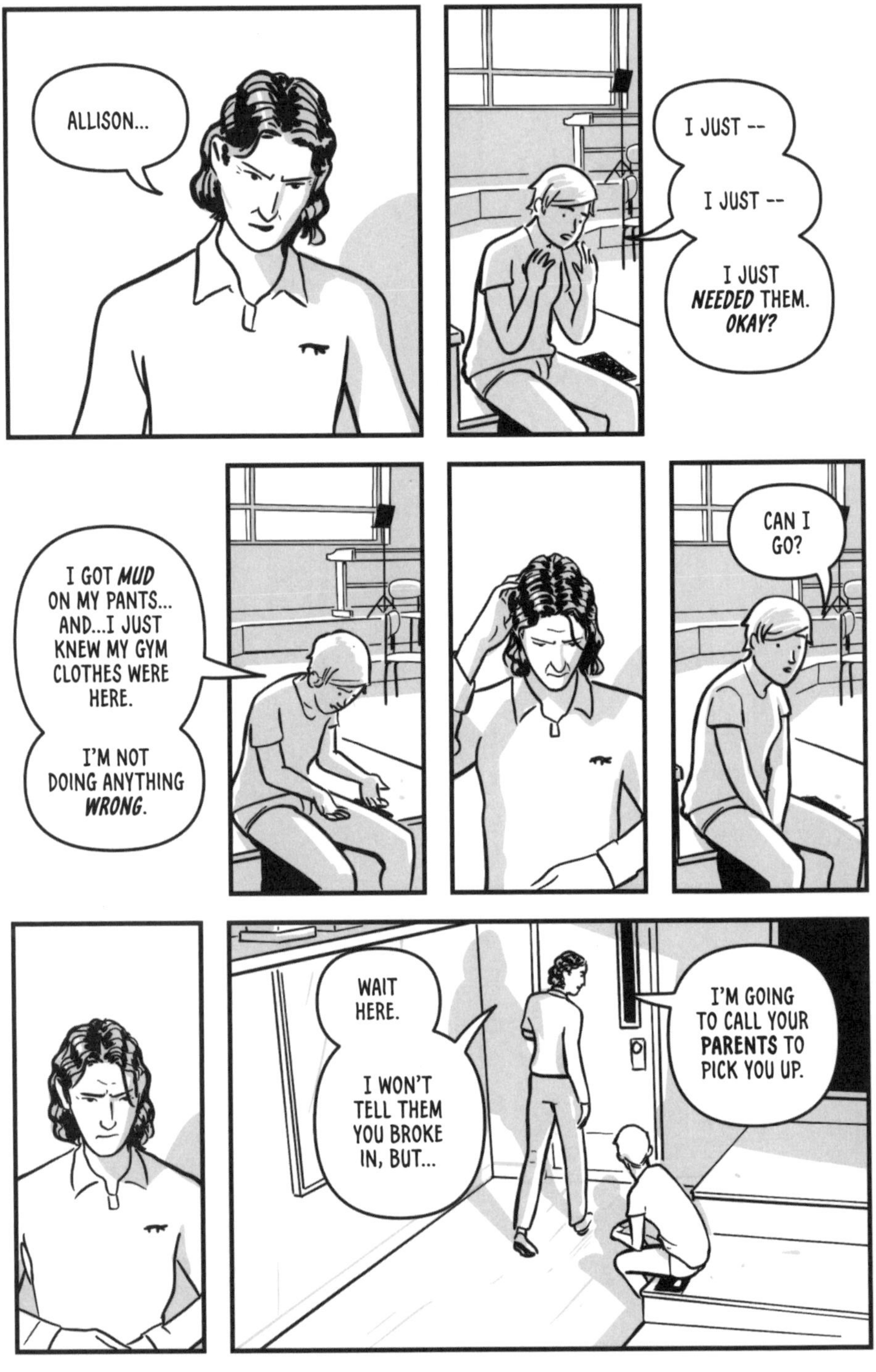
ALLISON...
I JUST --
I JUST --
I JUST *NEEDED* THEM. *OKAY?*
I GOT *MUD* ON MY PANTS... AND...I JUST KNEW MY GYM CLOTHES WERE HERE.
I'M NOT DOING ANYTHING *WRONG*.
CAN I GO?
WAIT HERE.
I WON'T TELL THEM YOU BROKE IN, BUT...
I'M GOING TO CALL YOUR **PARENTS** TO PICK YOU UP.

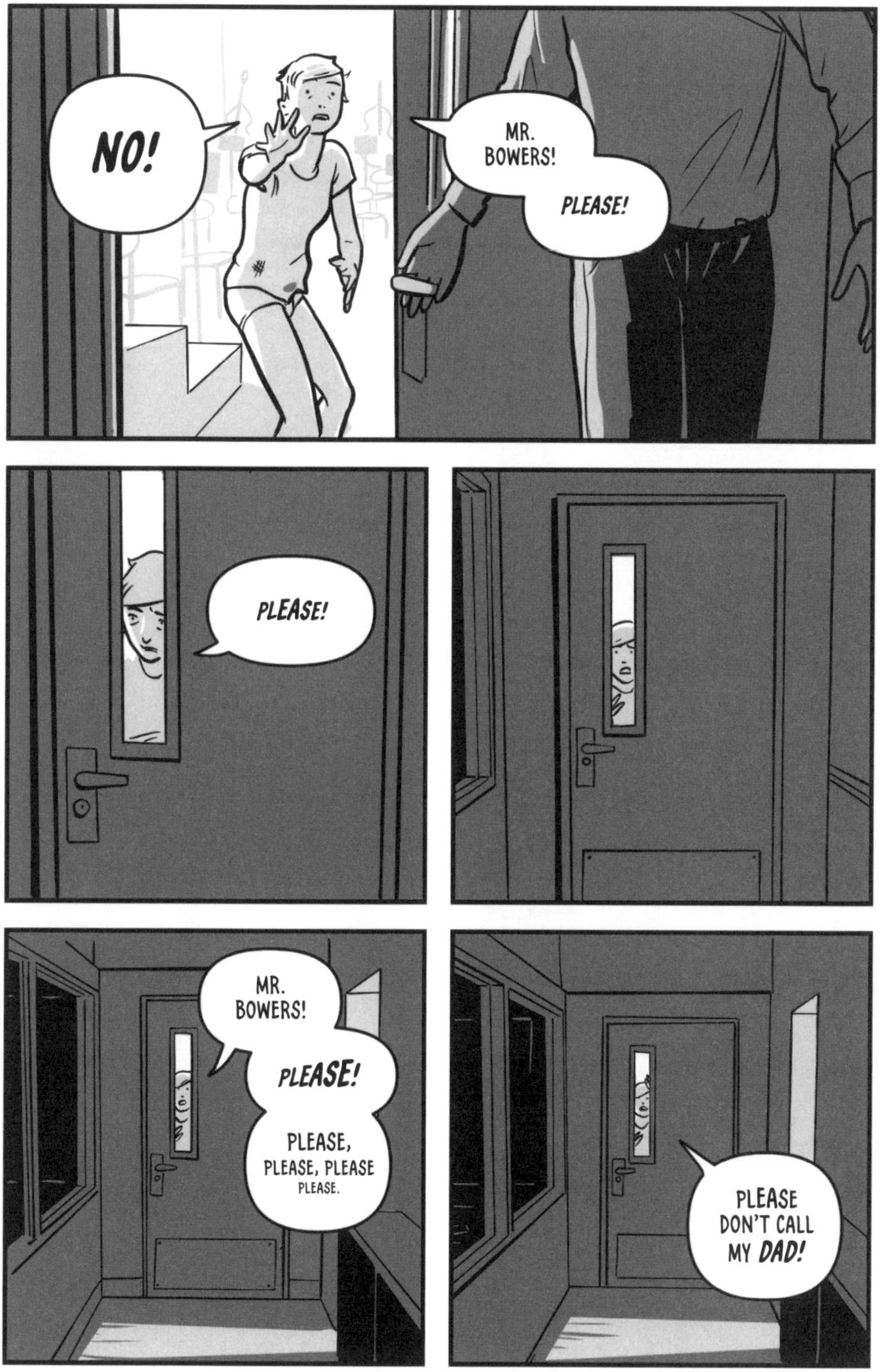
NO!
MR. BOWERS!
PLEASE!
PLEASE!
MR. BOWERS!
PLEASE!
PLEASE, PLEASE, PLEASE PLEASE.
PLEASE DON'T CALL MY DAD!

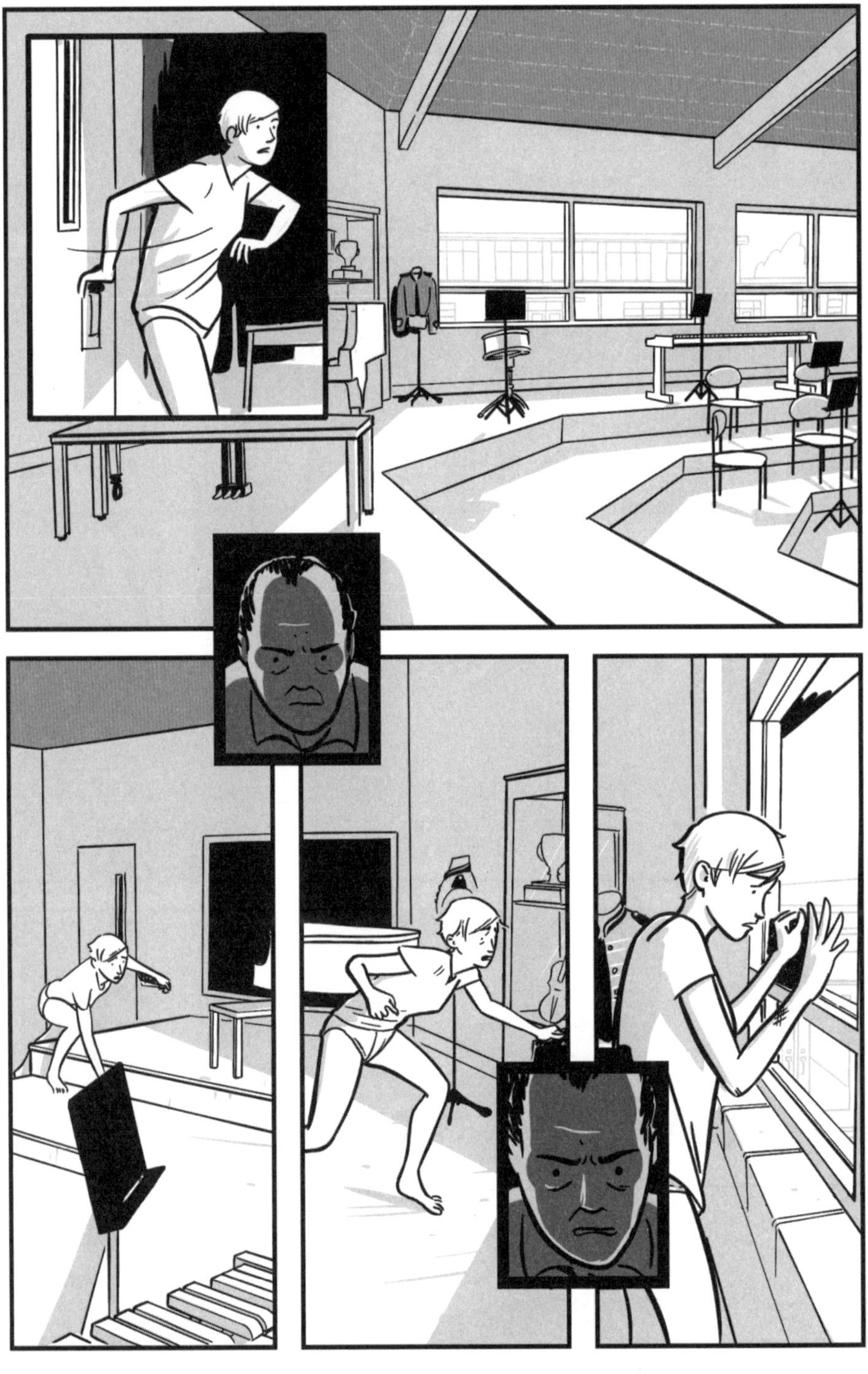

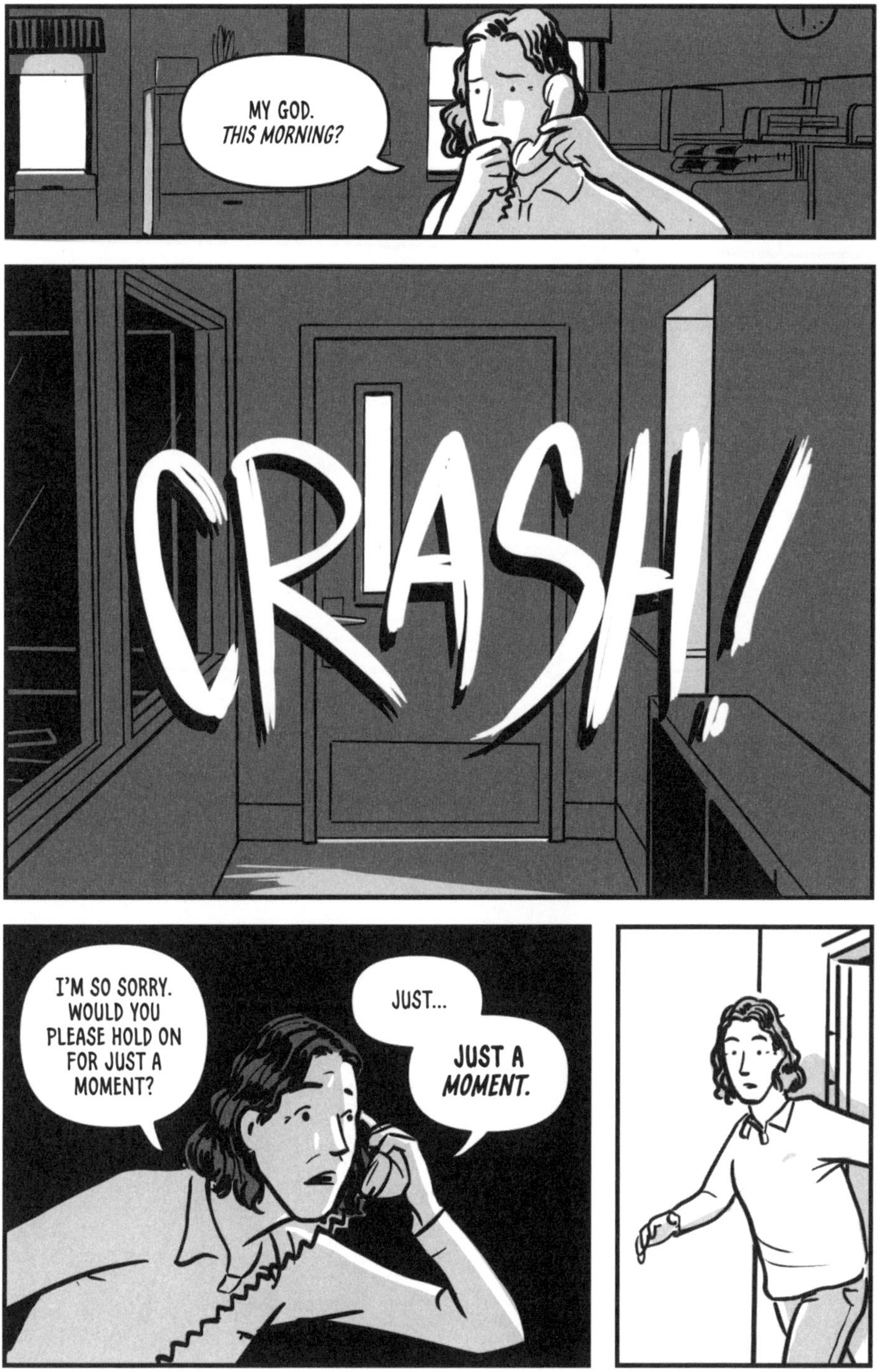
MY GOD. *THIS MORNING?*
CRASH!
I'M SO SORRY. WOULD YOU PLEASE HOLD ON FOR JUST A MOMENT?
JUST...
JUST A *MOMENT.*

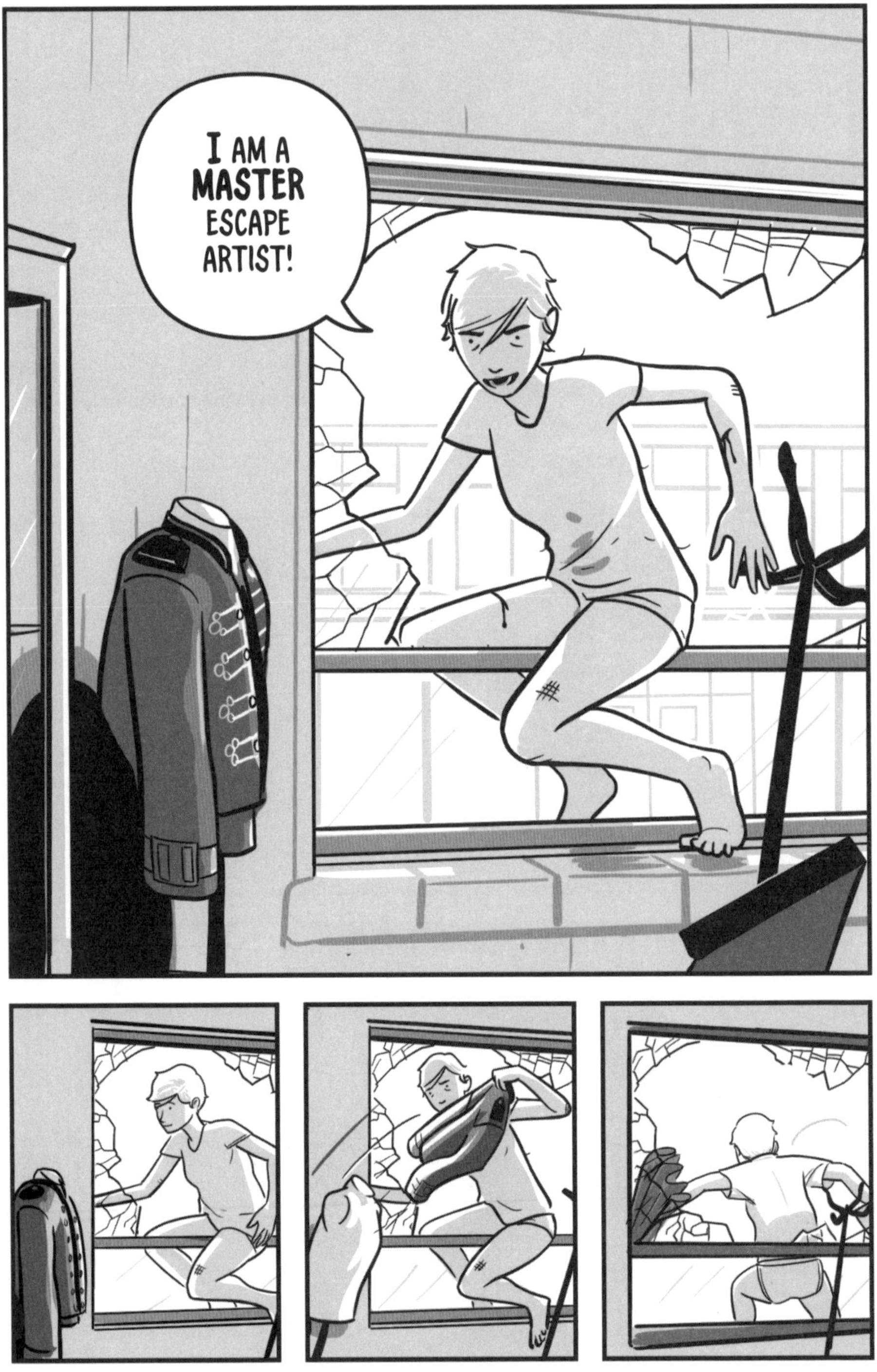
I AM A MASTER ESCAPE ARTIST!

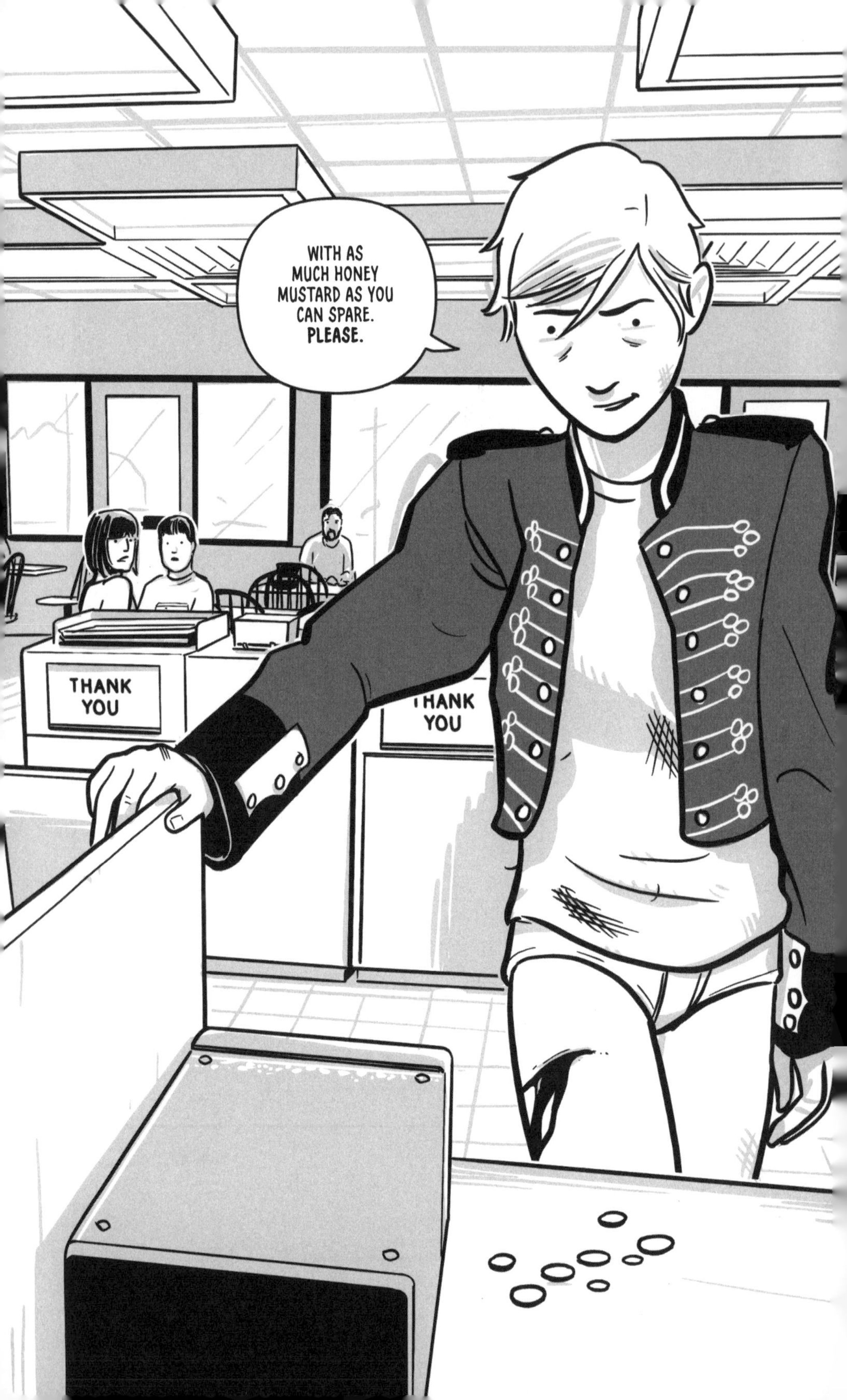
WITH AS MUCH HONEY MUSTARD AS YOU CAN SPARE. PLEASE.
THANK YOU
THANK YOU

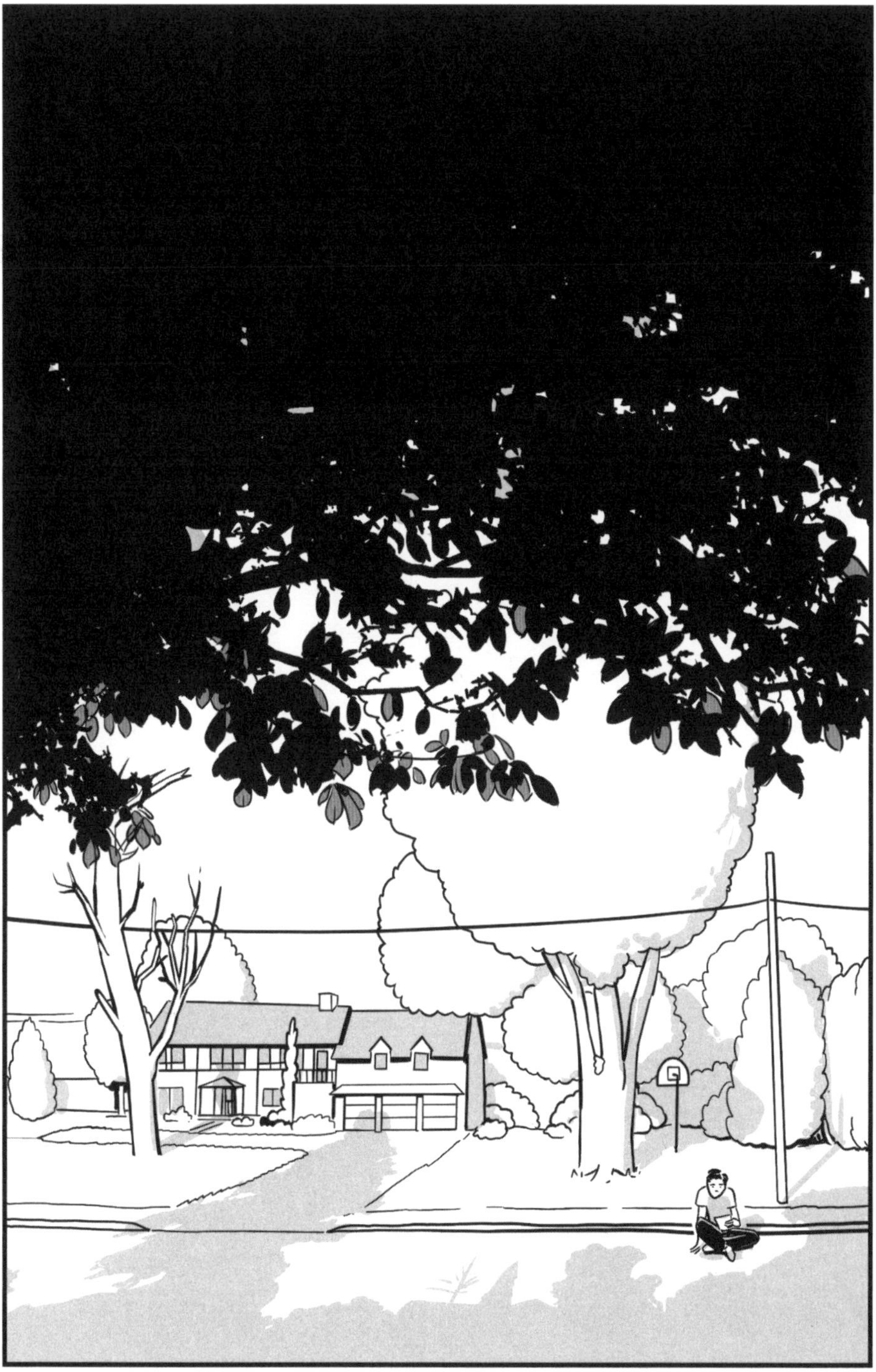

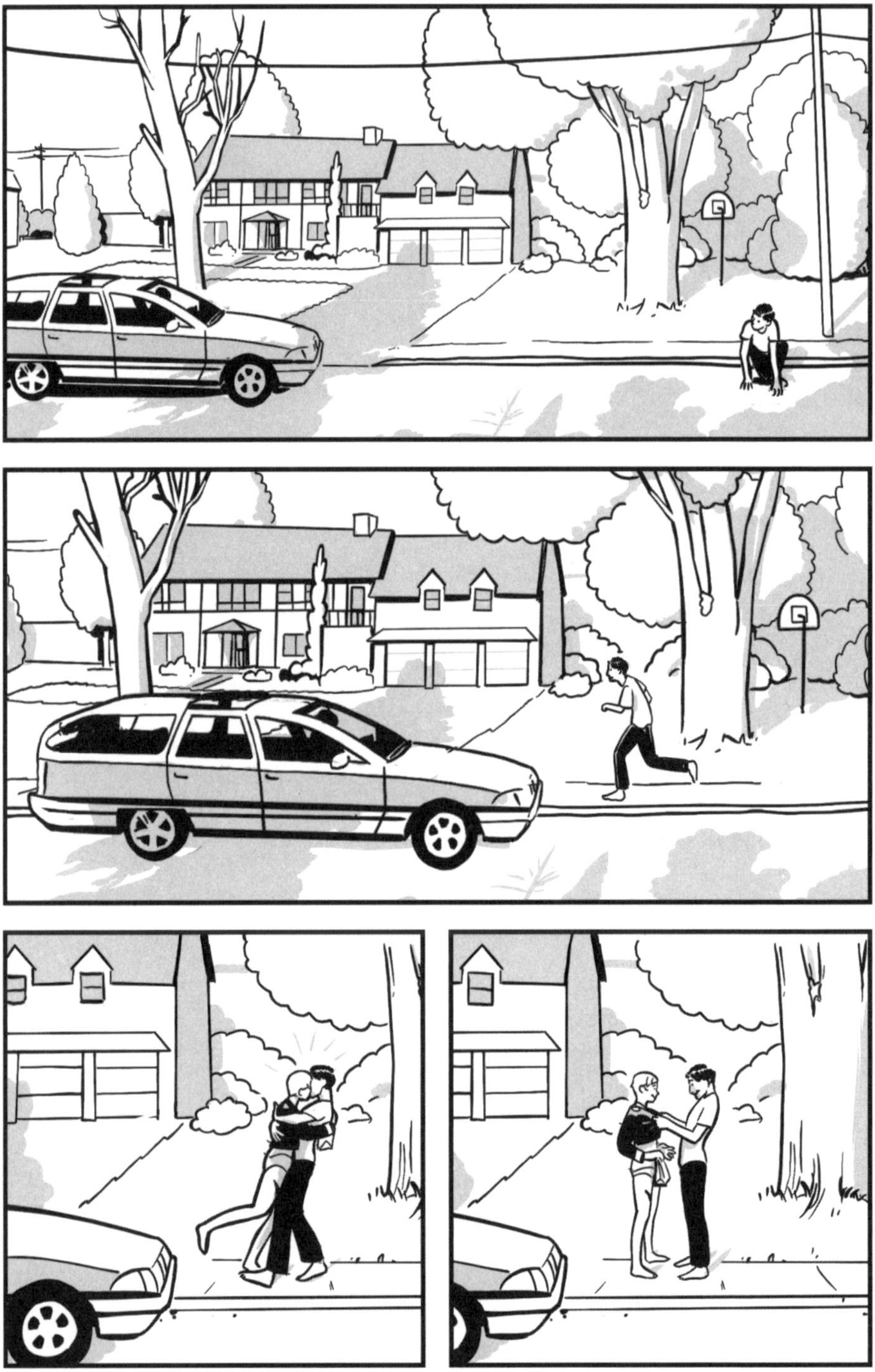

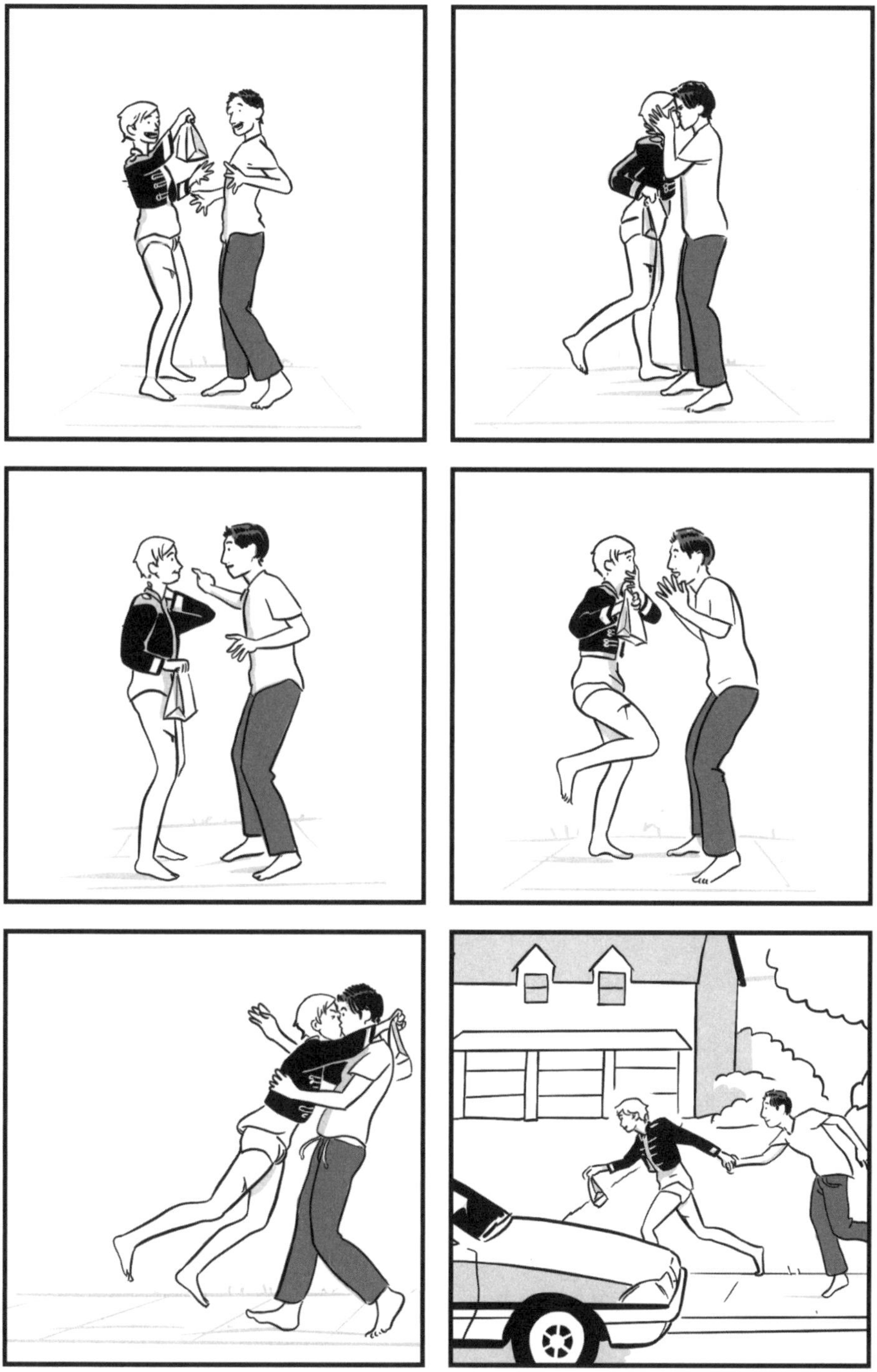

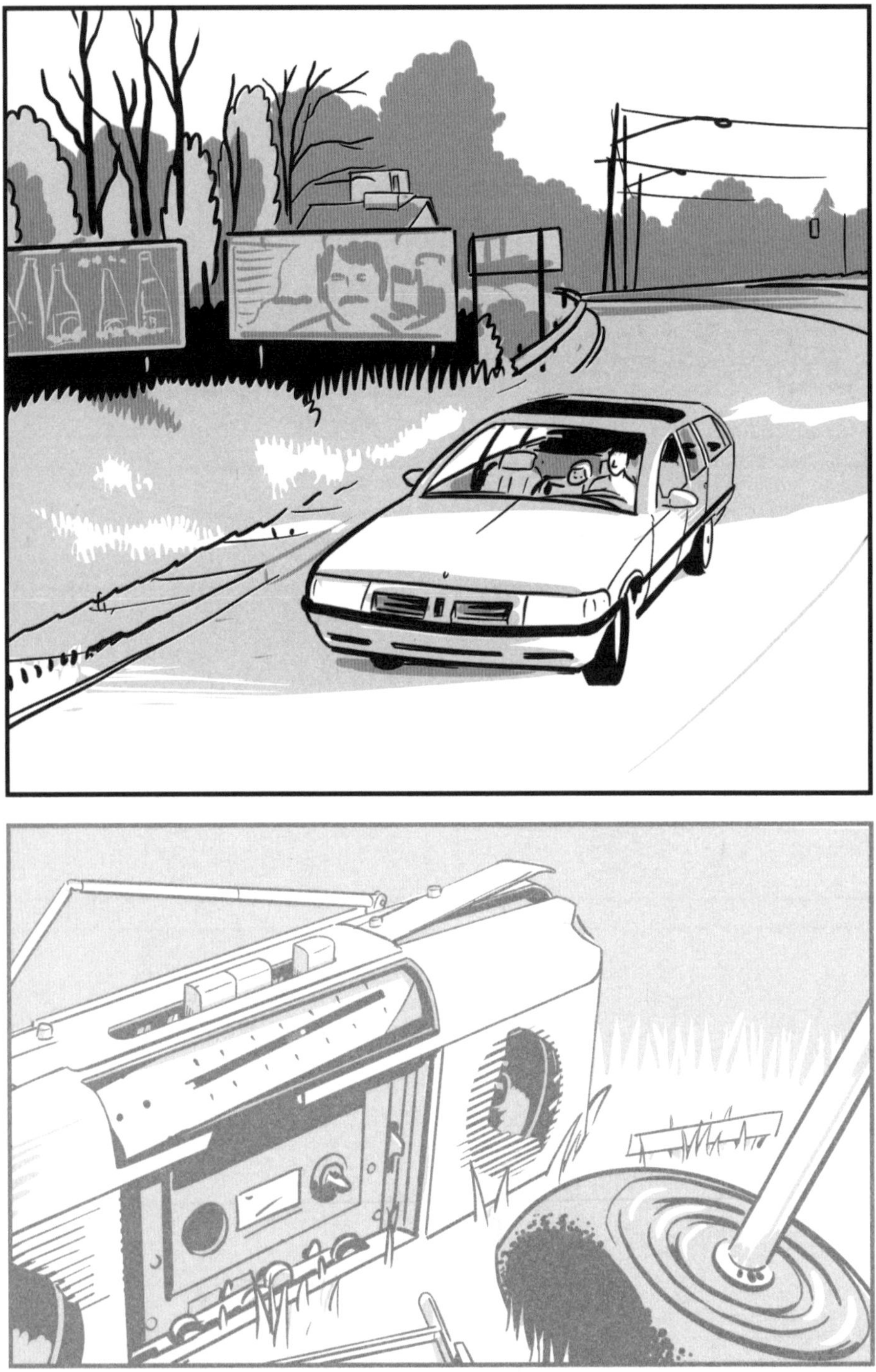

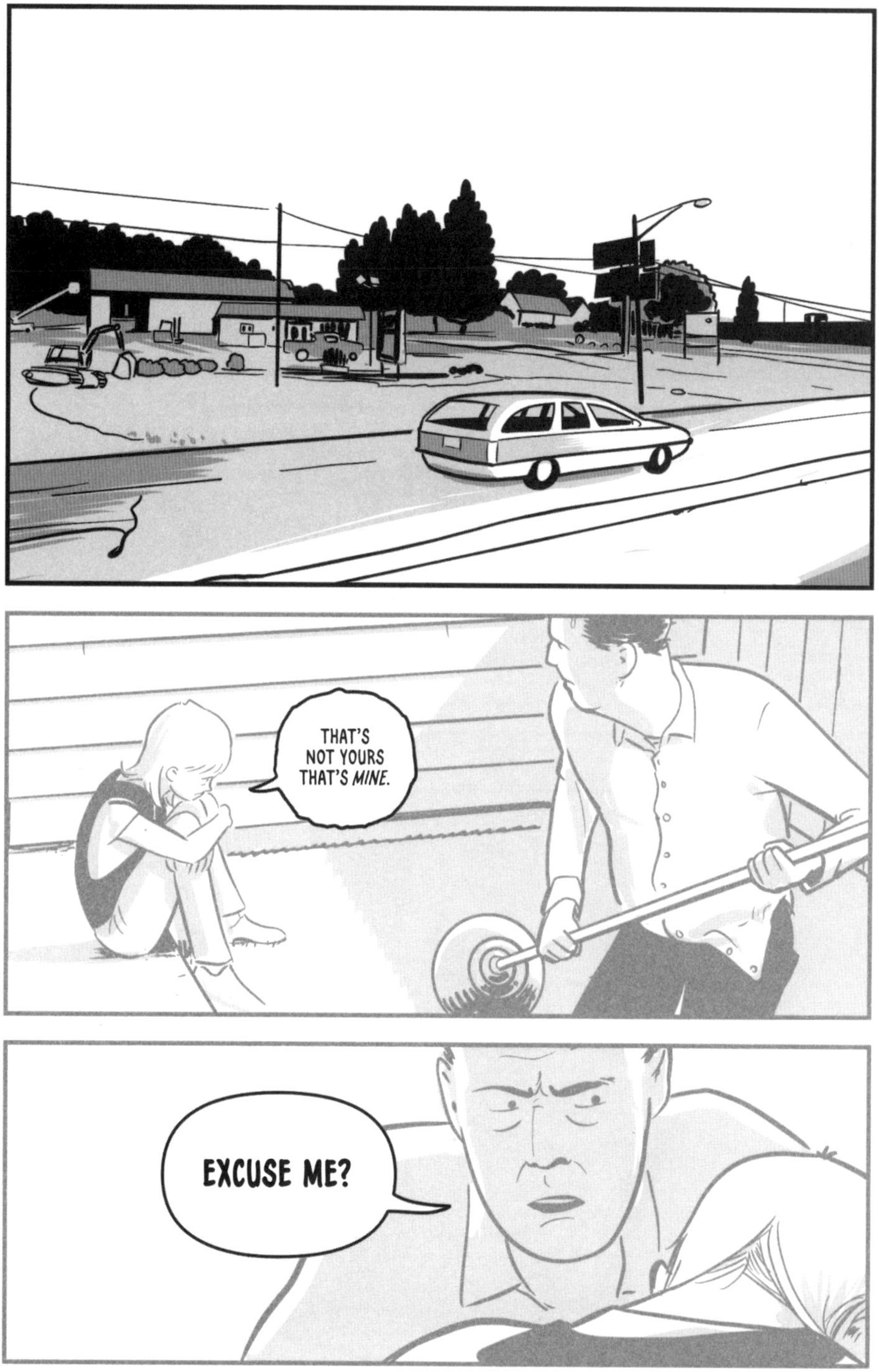
THAT'S NOT YOURS THAT'S *MINE*.
EXCUSE ME?

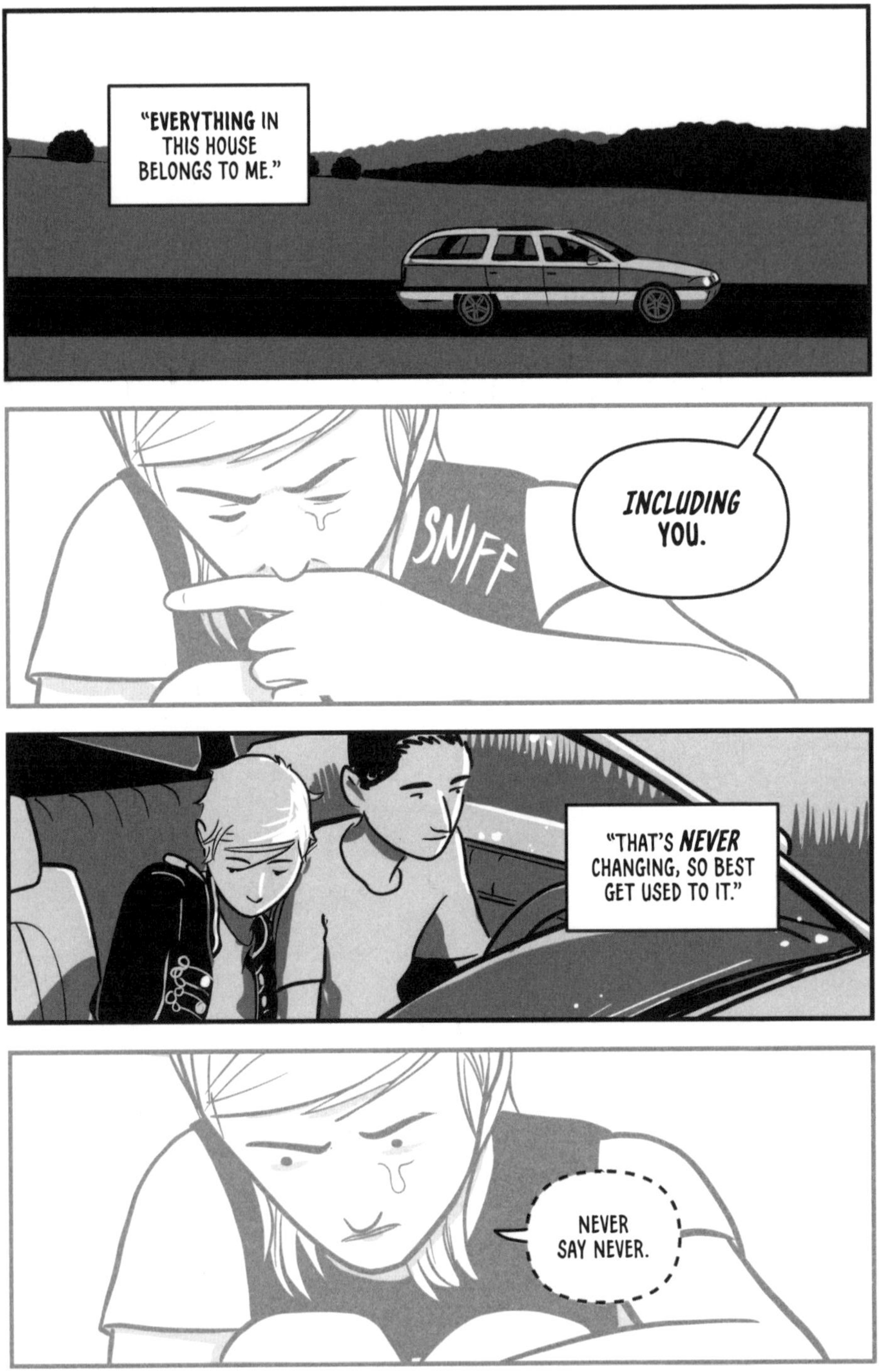
"EVERYTHING IN THIS HOUSE BELONGS TO ME."
SNIFF
INCLUDING YOU.
"THAT'S NEVER CHANGING, SO BEST GET USED TO IT."
NEVER SAY NEVER.

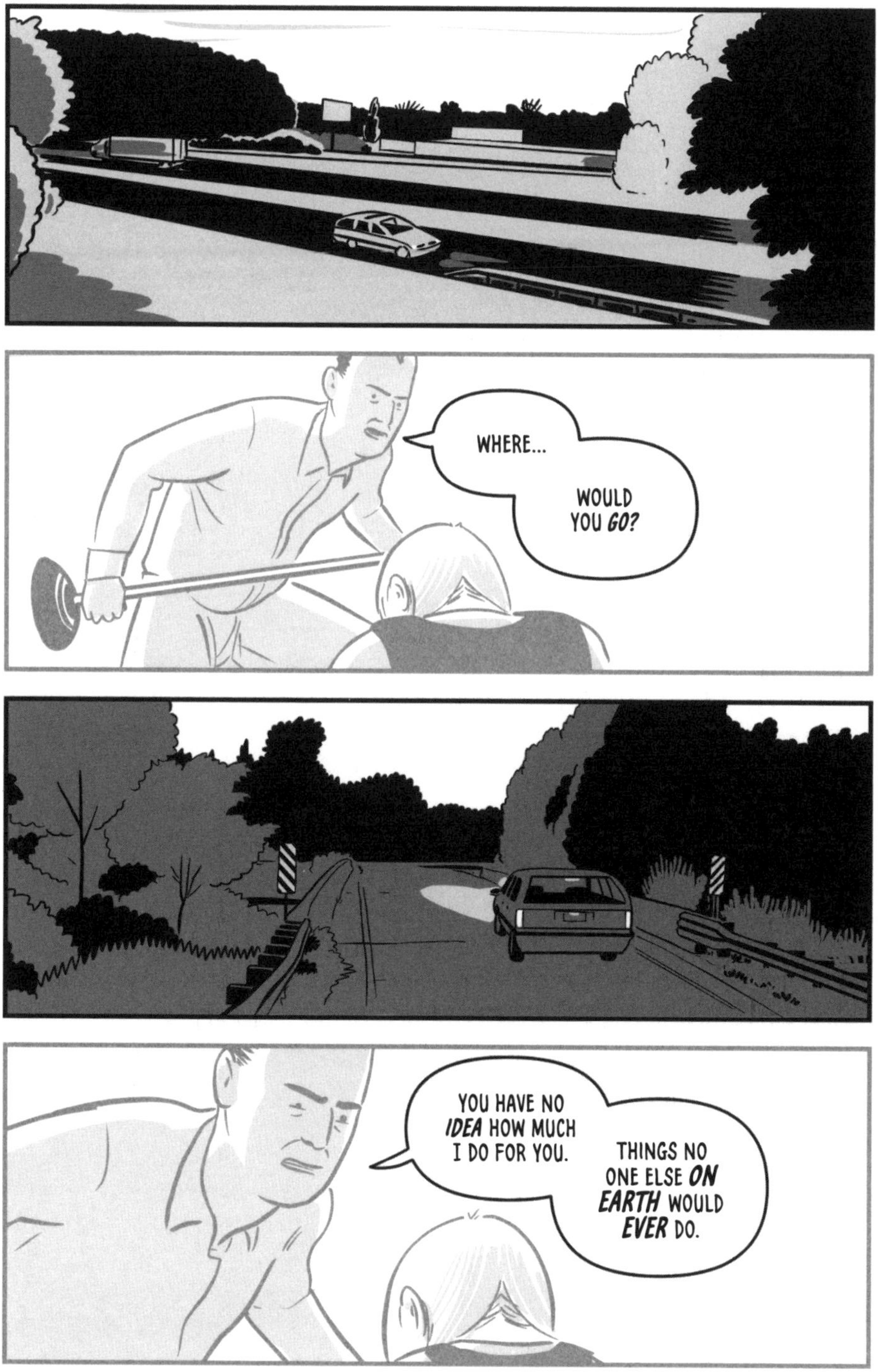
WHERE...
WOULD YOU *GO?*
YOU HAVE NO *IDEA* HOW MUCH I DO FOR YOU.
THINGS NO ONE ELSE *ON EARTH* WOULD *EVER* DO.

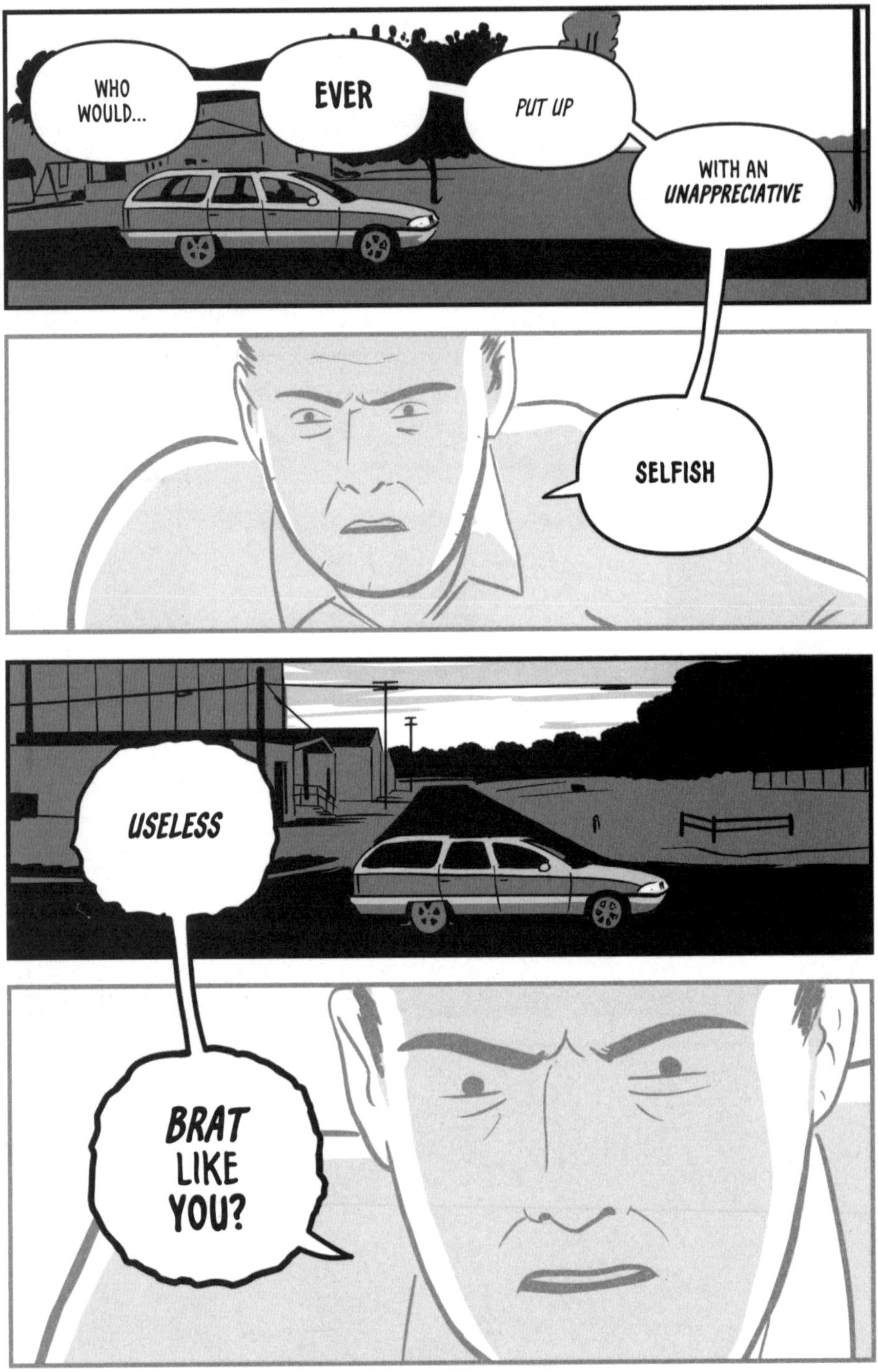
WHO WOULD...
EVER
PUT UP
WITH AN UNAPPRECIATIVE
SELFISH
USELESS
BRAT LIKE YOU?

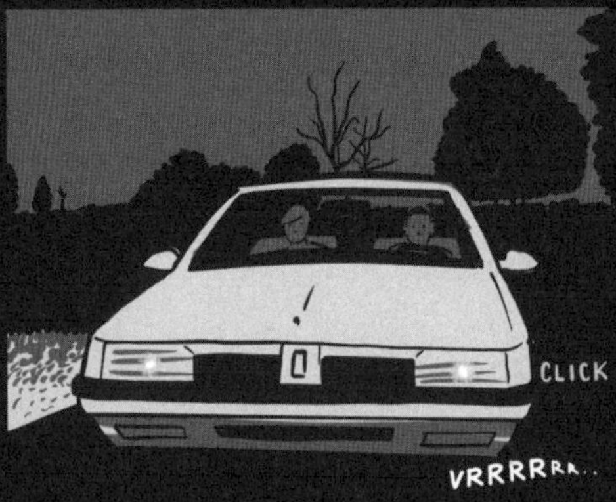
CLICK
VRRRRrr..

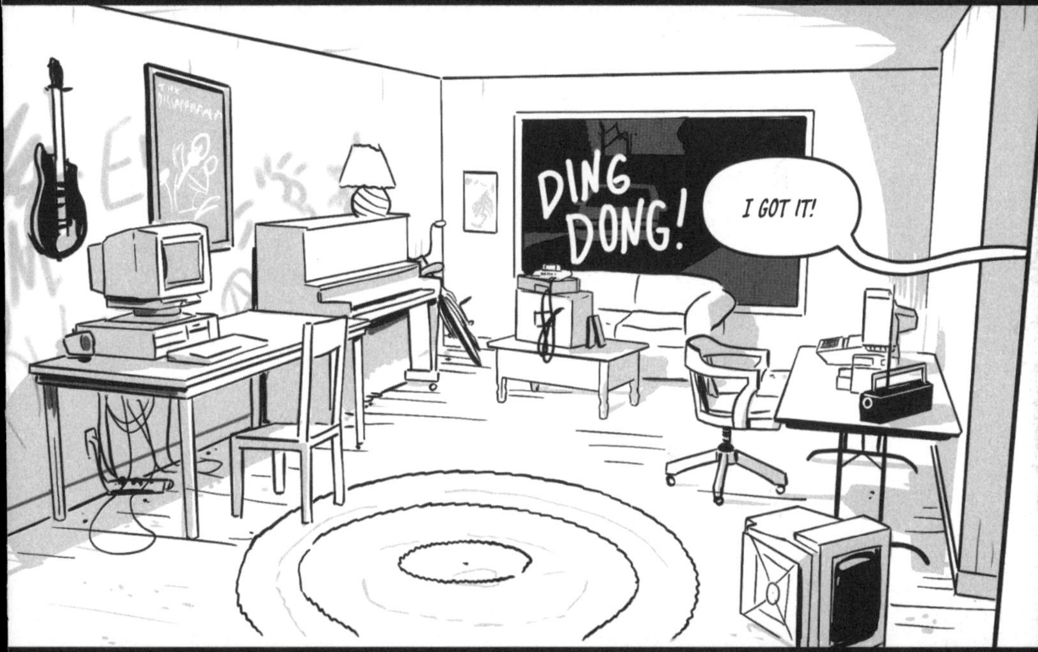
DING DONG!
I GOT IT!

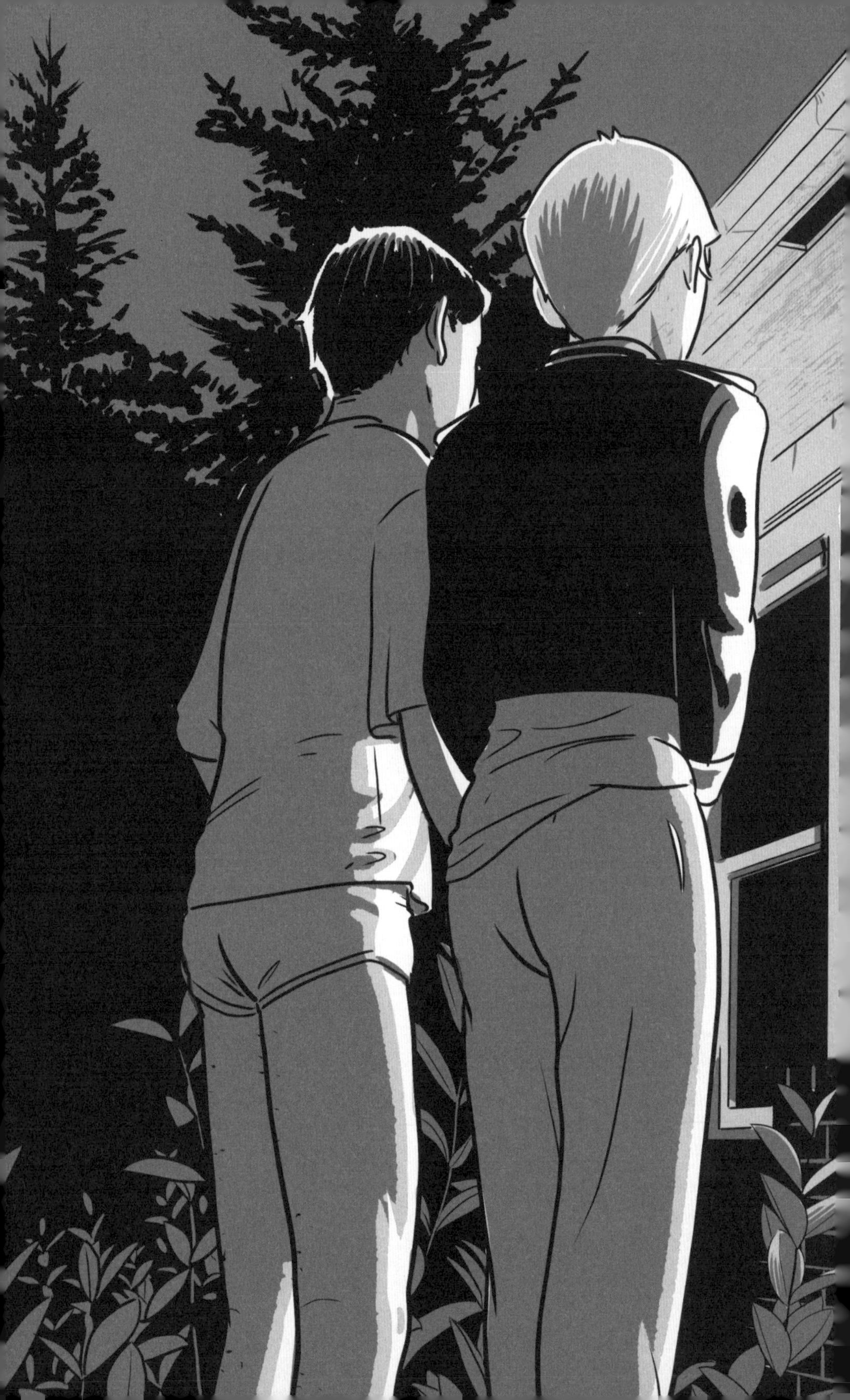

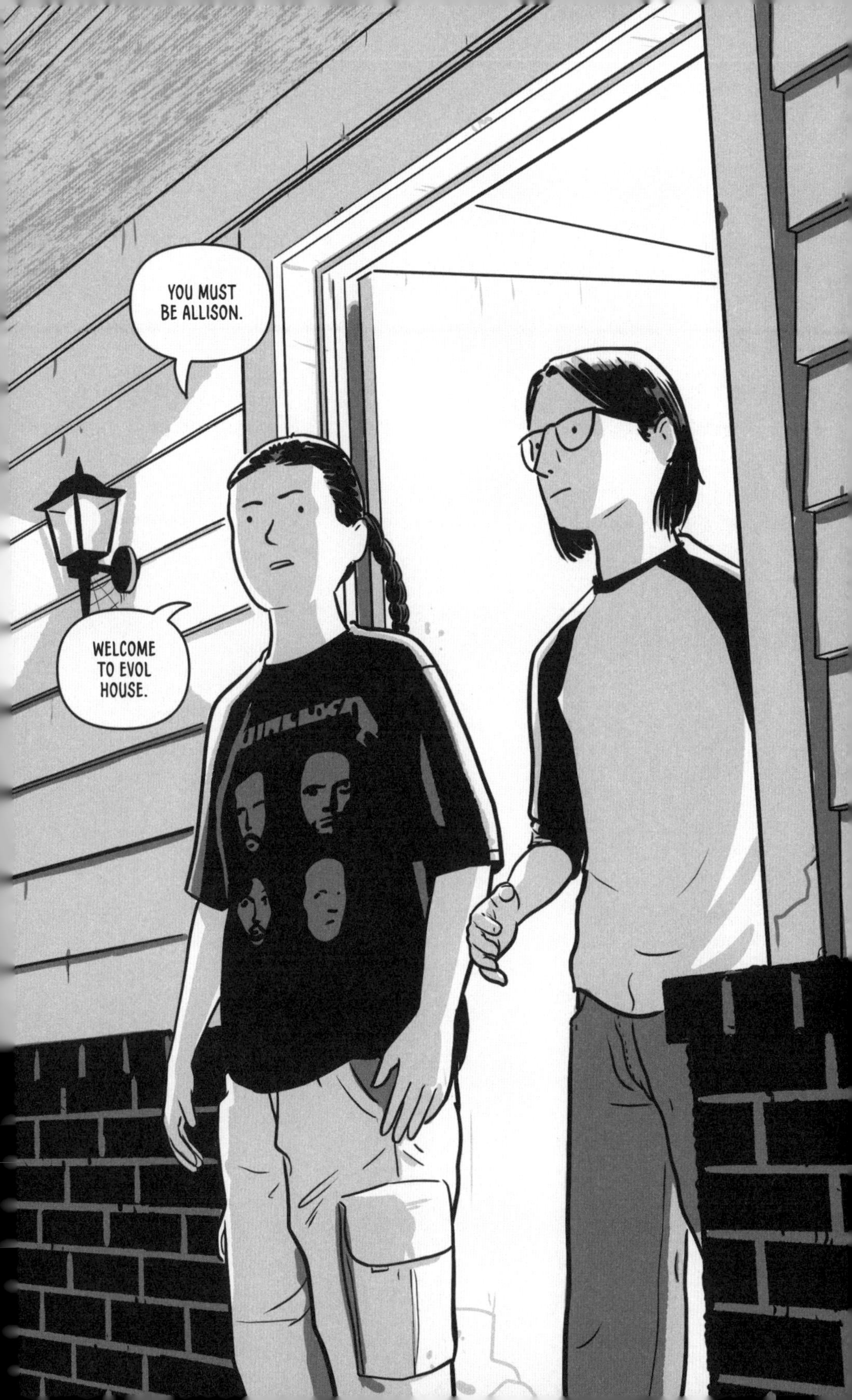
YOU MUST BE ALLISON.
WELCOME TO EVOL HOUSE.

THANK YOU

Andrew Arnold
Andy Baio
Andy McMillan
Angela Piller
Anis Mojgani
Barb Fitzsimmons
Barry Deutsch
Brooke Shelly
Bryan Williams
Carson Mischel
Charlie Douma
Charlie Olsen
Cheri Kessner
Chris A'Lurede
Chris Higgins
Cory Doctorow
Dan Wineman
David Gordon Green
David Pedroni
Debbie Deuble Hill
Dylan Meconis
Eberhardt Press
Fergus
Fozzy
Helioscope Studio
J. Holden
Jack Lee
Jason Scott
Jello Biafra
Joe Besch
Josh Millard
Julian Lawitschka
Katie Lane
Kelly Thompson
Kevin Simmons

Kirby Ferguson
Lucy Bellwood
Martha Maynard
Michael Kurt
Nora Ryan
Pat Castaldo
Pete Kyrou
Rich Thomas
Rose Pleuler
Sarah Mirk
Ted Dahmke
The Enthusiasm Collective
The Independent Publishing
    Resource Center
Wesley Mueller
Will Nevin
XOXO Outpost
Yori Kvitchko

System:~ id$ who -HTu

USER	S	COMMENT
Andrew Arnold	-	Editorial Director
Barb Fitzsimmons	-	Creative Director
Martha Maynard	-	Design Assistant
Rose Pleuler	-	Associate Editor
Rich Thomas	-	Publishing Director

HarperAlley is an imprint of HarperCollins Publishers.

System:~ id$ getfacl ~/incredible_doom.*

www.harperalley.com
www.incredibledoom.com
www.matthewbogart.net
www.jesseholden.com

System:~ id$ stat -cf ~/incredible_doom.*

ISBN 978-0-06-306494-2 (trade bdg.)
ISBN 978-0-06-306493-5 (pbk.)

Typography by Matthew Bogart
21 22 23 24 25 EP 10 9 8 7 6 5 4 3 2 1
❖
First Edition

System:~ id$ more ~/.plan

Incredible Doom vol 2 coming 2022
.plan (END)